Elizabeth Missing Sewell

Cleve hall

Elizabeth Missing Sewell

Cleve hall

ISBN/EAN: 9783337414153

Printed in Europe, USA, Canada, Australia, Japan

Cover: Foto ©Andreas Hilbeck / pixelio.de

More available books at **www.hansebooks.com**

BY

ELIZABETH M. SEWELL.

Tho' justice be thy plea, consider this,—
That in the course of justice none of us
Should see salvation.
THE MERCHANT OF VENICE

NEW EDITION

LONDON
LONGMANS, GREEN, AND CO.
1886

CLEVE HALL.

CHAPTER I.

IT was an old gable-ended farm-house, standing back from the road, with a smooth piece of turf in front, neatly kept, and divided down the centre by a broad strip of pavement.

Five or six large elm trees shaded it on the left ; on the right, behind some broad meadows, rose a steep bank, forming the further extremity of a rocky ravine, through which ran a by-road from the highway, probably leading to some sequestered hamlet. The whole surface of the country was hilly, almost claiming the appellation of mountainous. A long range of steep downs stretched for a considerable distance beyond the ravine towards the north-east ; whilst in front of the farm, at about the distance of a mile, the horizon was bounded by a hill, clothed with thick plantations, amongst which the sighing of the soft evening wind was heard mingling with the heavy swell of the ocean.

The view was very lovely, seen in the mellow evening light ; the meadows rich with the golden flowers of early summer, and the fresh green on the trees and hedges, sparkling as their trembling leaves caught the glancing rays of the sinking sun. Yet it was solitary. No building was in sight except the quaint, gray farm-house, with its ivy-covered chimneys, and broad, open porch ; and though there were sounds about the farm,—the carter-boy's whistle,—the clatter of the milk-pails, as the dairymaids crossed the yard,—and occasionally the neighing of a horse, or the lowing of a cow ; yet they were all hushed,—softened by that indescribable atmosphere of quietness, which prepares the gentle evening for the deeper solemnity of night.

A

A woman, who might have been about fifty years old—the mistress of the farm apparently—was leaning over the low garden-wall. She was rather peculiar in appearance ; her dress scrupulously neat, but decidedly old-fashioned ; the cotton gown scanty and rather short ; a checked handkerchief folded over her shoulders, and a cap white as snow, and quilled in perfect order, fitting close around a pale, worn face. Her attitude told that she was listening, and the breeze brought to the ear the distant trampling of a horse, departing however, not approaching. It was followed with fixed attention, till the last echo had died away, and then a sigh was heaved, and slowly and thoughtfully the woman walked towards the house.

'Mrs Robinson ! Nurse ! Granny, dear ! won't you speak to me ?' said a quick, merry voice, and a child of about thirteen years of age, though in height and size very much younger, threw open the heavy wicket-gate, and ran up to her. The woman turned suddenly, a smile passed over her face, a mixture of pleasure and respect, yet her tone had something in it of reproach.

'Out alone, Miss Rachel ! what does your papa say to that ?'

'Oh ! papa is gone in to see John Strong, and I ran on before him. I shall be at home now before he is. He is coming to see you, Granny.'

'He said he would,' was the reply.

'And you think he always keeps his word, don't you ? Give me a kiss and let me go ; I must be at home and have a talk with Miss Campbell and Ella before papa returns ; so keep him as long as you can.' She threw her arm round her friend's neck. 'Granny, you aren't happy to-night,' she whispered.

'Happy as I can be, Miss Rachel, when there's so much in the world to make one otherwise. But you don't know anything of that, so run home and be thankful.'

Rachel stood for a moment in thought. The change in her face was very marked. It was a countenance formed for happiness, brilliant with intelligence, radiant in health, and singularly lovely in its outline. But the small, laughing mouth, and the merry, hazel eyes, and open forehead, shaded by curls of bright chestnut hair, might have been termed infantine till thought came ;—then the whole being seemed to alter, and the gay child became in one instant the self-collected, deeply-inquiring woman.

'1 don't know anything about it, I suppose, Granny,' she said,

in reply to Mrs Robinson's remark, 'though I think I do sometimes. Shall I ever know it as you do?'

'That's for days to come, Miss Rachel. Who can tell?'

'You can,' said Rachel, quickly; then, correcting herself, she
added, reverently, 'I don't mean you can tell what is to happen,
but you can say whether I shall be likely to have the same
things to bear that you have.'

'God forbid you should ever have to trouble for the same
things that trouble me, Miss Rachel. Things must be bad
indeed if they are not mended by that time.'

'And the General won't live for ever,' said Rachel, quickly;
but a glance at her friend's face made her retract her words. 'I
don't want him to die, you know, Granny; but it is always something about him which makes papa, and you, and every one
unhappy; so I can't like him, and I couldn't be sorry if he were
gone away anywhere.'

'There's many a worse man than General Vivian goes for a
saint in this world, Miss Rachel,' replied Mrs Robinson, 'as you
may some day know to your cost. Poor old man! If he makes
others sad he is sad enough himself.'

'He doesn't look sad,' said Rachel. 'He doesn't seem as if
he felt anything.'

'That's what folks say of me, sometimes, Miss Rachel;' and
a smile, which, however, gave only a wintry brightness to the
grave face, accompanied the words. Rachel once more caressed
her fondly.

'Granny, Granny, that's naughty. Papa says if you had a
colder heart you would have a merrier face. But it's merry
enough for me. There's not a face in all the village, away from
home, that I love so well, except'——

'Except whose? Don't be afraid, Miss Rachel; you know I
am not given to being jealous!'

'Well! one that's more to you than I am, though I love you
dearly. So we can't be jealous when we both love the same.'

'Miss Mildred!' exclaimed Mrs Robinson; 'but I always put
her aside. I thought it might be some of the newer friends that
you have taken to.'

'Miss Campbell, and Ella, and Clement,' replied Rachel,
gaily. 'No; I love them all, you know I must, they are so
kind: but they are not like your dear old face, Granny; they are
not parts of the very old times.'

'Thirteen years ago! eh, Miss Rachel? What an age to be

sure ! But you do grow, I will say that for you ; you will be a woman after all, if you live long enough.'

'Thank you, Granny, dear ! I hope I shall. Now please gather me a whole heap of the climbing roses for Mrs Campbell. She always likes to have flowers brought her, though she doesn't keep them long.'

Rachel's hands were filled with the best roses which grew against the house, and the best lavender from the farm garden, under the promise, however, that she was not to give all away, but to retain some for herself for a remembrance. Her ringing laugh, as the injunction was given, made the old walls echo again.

' Why, Granny, as if I needed it ! Don't I think of you every morning, and don't I talk to papa about you every night?—what should I need a remembrance for? Do you know,' and her tone changed, as she placed one finger against her heart, ' it's written in here ; I can feel it, though I don't see it—your name, I mean ; and there are others, too—and I know I shall never want keepsakes like some people, for I can't forget ; no, if I wished it, I couldn't.'

A kiss was the answer, lingering and fond, like that of a parent, and a murmur, ' Heaven's blessing on you, child !' and Rachel tossed the wicket-gate open, and ran quickly up the road which passed through the ravine.

CHAPTER II.

IT was about an hour later the same evening; lights were glimmering in the cottages dotted by the side of the narrow road, and perched, as it seemed, upon almost inaccessible rocks, which formed the picturesque village of Encombe; and although here and there, might be seen a labourer returning from some distant work, or a woman wearily toiling up a height after an errand to the nearest town, the cottagers were, for the most part, collecting around their own hearths, and even the voices of the children were gradually being hushed in sleep. At the lower end of a steep strip of garden, reached by a flight of steps from the road, two persons, a man and a boy, were, however, conversing together, as they stood looking up the village, nearly the whole length of which was visible from the point they had chosen. The occupation of the man was evident at the first sight; he was a weather-beaten, hardy fisherman—probably a smuggler—for there was an expression of cunning in his keen, black eyes, and a sneer upon his lip, which accorded little with the free, frank tone and manner natural to an ordinary seafaring life. His glance, moreover, showed the quickness of one accustomed to watch and be watched; and his tone, when he spoke, had in it an accent of command. The boy also wore a sailor's hat, and his coat was rough, and his striped, blue, linen shirt made of coarse material. Yet even a cursory inspection would certainly have suggested a doubt whether the two were equals in rank. The age of the lad might have been eighteen; his face was bronzed by exposure to storms, and his manner betrayed a mind impatient of control, and caring little for the refinements of civilised life; but his features were totally free from the look of cunning which was so marked in those of his companion. His blue eye, indeed, was peculiarly clear and open in its expression, though flashing with all the keenness of a passionate spirit; his forehead was thoughtful; his mouth told of pride and great wilfulness, and yet its haughty curl seemed occasionally about to melt into a smile of sad, almost feminine sweetness; and his voice, even when he spoke shortly and contemptuously, had a refined intonation, belonging to a very different class from that of his companion. He might have been formed for high and noble purposes, yet he lingered now in the society of his rough comrade, apparently with no thought but that of idly passing away time which he had neither inclination nor energy to employ.

Full twenty minutes elapsed, and still he leaned upon the garden-gate, sometimes speaking to the fisherman, but more often gazing with a fixed eye before him. Occasionally, however, he stooped to pick up a stone, and tossed it down the steep bank, and watched it as it tumbled from point to point, till touching a sharp point of rock, it perhaps fell with a quick impetus into the foaming brook, that rushed down the centre of the ravine.

He had just cast another stone; it did not follow its predecessors; the twisted root of a tree stopped it, and it sank quietly into its place upon the bank.

'They don't all go,' murmured the boy to himself.

'What don't go?' asked the man, with a surly smile.

'Nothing that you know of,' was the reply; 'is he coming yet?'

'Can't say; don't see him. Suppose now, you were to make the best use of your legs, and be off to the flagstaff to see. It's not much of a stretch.'

'More than I choose to take,' answered the boy; and he flung himself upon the ground. 'I am not made for that at least,' he muttered to himself.

The fisherman evinced no surprise at the refusal, but opening the gate, descended the steps, and sauntered a few paces up the road. A merry shout, a few moments afterwards, caught the boy's ear, and he started up.

'Well! he's come; it can't be helped.' He flung the gate open, and at one spring bounded into the road.

The fisherman stood on the projecting point of a rock closing in the angle of the road, and beckoned to him. The boy still paused. Once he even turned directly away, and went a few paces in the opposite direction, and waited for an instant, as if undecided whether to return; but another shout of 'Ronald! Ronald!' startled him; and flinging his hat into the air, he gave a wild answering cry, and ran forwards to the rock, where his companion awaited him.

They were not alone together then; a third individual had joined them; a boy probably about two years younger than Ronald, and bearing in every look and feature the stamp of gentle birth and careful education. He was tall and slight; his face very intelligent; his voice sweet and refined; and when he joined in the fisherman's coarse laugh, and addressed him in terms of equality, it was evident there could be no real congeniality.

'Why, Goff, you are a harder master than Mr Lester!' he exclaimed, as the fisherman, in rather an uncivil manner, held before him a huge old-fashioned watch, and pointed to the hour. ''Tis but five minutes.'

'May be you'll learn the value of five minutes to your cost, one of these days, Master Clement!' replied Goff. 'Ronald has been here, waiting to see you, the last half hour.'

'Ronald is not like me,' replied Clement; 'he is his own master. See if I won't be mine, before long, Goff, eh?'

'Them that will can always find the way,' replied the fisherman. 'Are you come to tell us you'll be here to-morrow for the sail, Master Clement?'

Clement looked up hastily, and his eye encountered Ronald's. The boy was standing at a little distance watching him narrowly, a strange mixture of feelings expressed in his handsome face. A bitter pride, perhaps, was written there most clearly ; yet a glance of compassion, blended it might have been with self-reproach, fell upon Clement.

'You 'll be ready, Ronald, as you promised ?' said Clement, appealing to him.

' I made no promise,' was his reply.

'But you are going ?'

'Ay, going ; wind and waves, and heaven and earth forbidding !' exclaimed Ronald, impetuously. Spurning from him a stone against which his foot had been resting, he added, ' My doings are no law for yours.'

Clement regarded him wonderingly, whilst a sarcastic smile curled the fisherman's lips.

'Don't mind him, Master Clement,' he said ; 'it's his way. Six o'clock, to-morrow evening, at the West Point. We 'll have a short run, with a fair wind, as it 's like to be, and be back in time for the old lady's tea.'

'What do you say, Ronald ? It 's to be done, isn't it ?' inquired Clement.

'Ask Goff !' and the look of pride passed away from Ronald's face, and seating himself on a stone, he rested his arms upon his knees. At that moment the loud barking of a dog was heard in the distance.

'Ah! the Captain !' exclaimed Goff. 'He's as good as his word, at least. Come, Ronald, my lad, there's work for you now.'

Ronald did not move, even when Goff touched him roughly with his foot. Clement stooped down, and put his arm round him caressingly.

'Ronald, it was your notion ; why won't you go ?'

' I am going ;' but Ronald's head was not raised.

'Then why shouldn't I go ?'

Ronald started from his bending posture, as a large Newfoundland dog rushed upon him, and tried to place his two fore-paws upon his shoulders. 'Down, Rollo! down !'—he patted the dog's head, and caught it between both his hands, looking at it as if reading a human countenance, then seizing Clement's arm, he dragged him to the edge of the ravine, and pointing to a broken, tangled path, rushed down it. Clement followed. The dog waited and watched them, irresolute ; but the next moment he was coursing at full speed along the road by which a man, dressed in a shaggy greatcoat, and a low-crowned glazed hat, with a heavy stick in his hand, was seen approaching.

'To-morrow, at West Point, at six,' called out the fisherman, as the boys disappeared from sight.

'To-morrow, at six, yes!' was heard in Clement's clear, refined tones.

'To-morrow, at six—no!' added another voice, deep, rich, and full; and the fisherman burst into an angry laugh, and shouted after them, 'that he would be made a fool by no one.'

'My hopeful boy you are calling after, eh! Master Goff?' was the observation by which the attention of the fisherman was drawn to the person who had now joined him.

'Hopeful, indeed, Captain. Why, he's taken to turn lately like a weathercock. If it goes on, I wish you joy of anything you'll ever do with him.' A scowl rested on the stranger's face, which was not needed to render it unprepossessing, for it was rarely that a countenance could be seen on which so many evil passions were to be traced. There was a strong likeness to Ronald; it might have been told at once that they were father and son; but whilst the pride of the boy's face was softened by thought, and his reckless bearing was checked by some eager, though it might be transient feelings of the necessity of self-command, the father's countenance showed little but a dogged resolution, the result of habitual selfishness and indulgence in habits which had nearly obliterated every sign of higher education or feeling.

'He is coming with us to-night,' he remarked; not replying directly to the fisherman's observation.

'That's as he will, Captain; as you know quite as well as I. He is off now with the young springald, and who's to catch him?'

The stranger uttered a profane ejaculation, and walked to the edge of the ravine, looked down it, and then returned again. 'He'll be back, he's not a fellow to miss the fun. How go matters at the point?'

'All ready, only waiting for Captain Vivian,' said Goff, with something of a contemptuous laugh.

'And Captain Vivian's son; the boy has a mind to drive me frantic. But there is no need to wait.'

'No need and no power,' said Goff. 'Time and tide wait for no man; so, by your leave, Captain, we'll let the two youngsters be off.'

'You wouldn't have taken the other boy,' exclaimed Captain Vivian, quickly.

'Not quite such a fool as that; no,—he's a mere land sawney: nothing's to be made of him—as dainty as a girl. What a fine fellow will be spoiled if Ronald takes after him !'

The frown on Captain Vivian's face became terrific; and Goff softened his words. 'No fear of that though, Captain. See Ronald in a gale of wind ! that's the time when he's a man. Come, are you ready?'

He received no answer. A crowd of angry feelings seemed working in Captain Vivian's mind, and throwing his stick backwards and forwards, he strode on silently; Goff accompanying him, and occasionally stealing aside to the edge of the ravine to discover whether any glimpse could be obtained of Ronald.

CHAPTER III.

'EIGHT o'clock ! Where is Clement?' The question was asked, in a querulous tone, by a lady seemingly infirm, rather from indolence and illness than from age, as, ordering the door to be shut, and wrapping a shawl around her, she drew near the tea-table, spread in a small, neat, but poorly-furnished drawing-room. It was answered in a girlish voice, but the accent was scarcely more amiable.

'Indeed, grandmamma, I can't say; he has been out ever since six.' The speaker was a young girl of about sixteen, tall, graceful, and rather foreign-looking, from the darkness of her complexion, and the dreamy, yet very intellectual expression of her splendid dark eyes, the only feature in the face which could lay claim to real beauty. She was stationed by the urn, and her attention was given more to the teacups than to the person who addressed her.

'You might as well learn, Ella, to be civil when you are spoken to. Why can't you look at me ?'

'I am pouring out the tea, grandmamma. Oh dear, what a slop ! Louisa, do run into the pantry and bring me a cloth.'

'Louisa not gone to bed ! how is that ? Louisa, why don't you go to bed ?'

'Because I am reading, grandmamma.'

'But you ought to be in bed; it's a great deal too late. Where's your aunt? why doesn't she make you go to bed?'

'Aunt Bertha went down the village, and isn't come in,' replied Louisa, without attempting to rise from the low stool on which she had placed herself to be out of the reach of observation, and able at her leisure to study a volume of fairy tales.

'Very wrong, very forgetful,' was murmured, and Mrs Campbell sank back again in her chair, without repeating the order for Louisa to go.

Ella just glanced at her sister, and, forgetting the slop, handed a cup of tea to her grandmamma; and pouring out one for herself, and helping herself to some toast, gave her whole attention to a book, which she kept by her half hidden by the tea-tray. The room was very silent again for some minutes. Then Mrs Campbell took up her cup, and complained that the tea was cold, and Ella said the water didn't boil, and the bell was rung; but it was not answered.

'Very wrong of Bertha, indeed,' repeated Mrs Campbell to herself; 'and why don't they answer the bell? but there's only Betsy and the girl. Oh dear!'

Ella sighed, oh dear! too, but she took no other notice.

The door opened. Mrs Campbell began in a fretful tone: 'It is too bad, the water doesn't boil in the least;' but she stopped on finding that she was not addressing a servant, but a young lady. 'Bertha,' and she leaned forward, and spoke with something approaching to energy, 'why don't you tell us when you are going out? We have been waiting this half-hour, and the tea is quite cold, and no one answers the bell. I can't think what possesses you all. Where have you been?'

'I was called out to see Hannah Dobbs, ma'am; she is worse; and then I had to go up to the Rectory, and other things besides.' The last words were uttered in an undertone, but they were in no way hasty or confused. 'Louisa, you ought to be in bed;' and Louisa in an instant jumped up from her seat, closed her book, said quickly, 'Good night, grandmamma; good night, Ella; good night, Aunt Bertha,' and was gone.

Bertha walked up to the tea-table: 'The water is not cold, Ella. You must have poured out grandmamma's tea before she was ready for it. Just put away your book, and attend to what you are doing.' Ella's book was taken from her, and placed on a side-table. No remonstrance was made, but Ella leaned back in her chair, and allowed her aunt to fetch Mrs Campbell's cup, pour away the cold tea, and replenish it with something which, if it was not strong, at least had the merit of warmth.

'Clement is not come in, is he?' said Bertha, in a low voice to Ella, as she bent over the tea-table.

'No, I have not heard him.'

Bertha's face became very grave, but it was a gravity which suited her, for it softened and rendered her features expressive. It was that which they wanted to give them the beauty to which they ought to have laid claim from regularity. Bertha Campbell was a striking-looking person, very tall, and slight, and refined in figure and manner ; not exactly graceful—she was too stiff in her movements for that,—and not exactly interesting—she was too rigid and self-controlled—too much like an automaton for interest; but the stamp of a lady was upon her every action. As she moved about the room now, putting a chair in its proper place, brightening the lamp, handing her mother the milk and sugar, and placing a footstool for her, an indescribable spirit of order and repose seemed to follow her. The room assumed quite a different aspect under her auspices, and yet what she did was almost too trifling to be noticed.

Mrs Campbell spoke again more gently and cheerfully. 'Did you see Mr Lester at the Rectory, Bertha?'

'No, ma'am. Rachel was expecting him; she left him at the farm. I gave my message to her. Can I do anything more for you, before I take off my bonnet?'

'No, child, nothing; but make haste down ; the tea won't be fit to drink if you don't.'

Bertha glanced again round the room, told Ella she was sitting in a very awkward attitude, and disappeared ; and she was no sooner gone than Ella, having poured out a cup of tea for her aunt, stole quietly to the table on which her book had been placed, and returned to her studies.

Bertha came down again, took the tea which Ella had prepared, without making any remark upon it, helped herself to some very cold toast, and completed her repast with a piece of dry bread ; and then, placing the empty cups and plates upon the tray, rang the bell.

The summons was answered by a very young girl.

'Jane, that weak arm of yours won't do to lift this heavy tray ; you had better let me carry it for you.'

'O Aunt Bertha!' escaped from Ella's lips.

'Why not, Ella? what harm can it do me?' and Bertha lifted

the tray and carried it out of the room, whilst the little servant girl wiped away the crumbs from the cloth, and placed a few books on the table.

Bertha did not immediately return ; and at the sound of a heavy opening door Mrs Campbell, who had seemed inclined to sleep, roused herself, and inquired whether that was Clement come in.

' I don't think so, grandmamma ; I fancy it must be Aunt Bertha gone out.'

' Gone out again, it can't be ; go and see.' Ella obeyed reluctantly.

' It was Aunt Bertha, grandmamma,' and there was a tone of triumph in Ella's voice. ' She was standing under the veran-dah ; she is there now.'

' Tell her to come in instantly ; she will catch her death of cold.' The message was given in audible, authoritative accents, such accents as might well have roused a storm of angry feelings in Bertha's breast ; but she came back into the room with Ella, with her quiet, gliding step, and merely said, ' I went out to see what kind of night it was likely to be, ma'am. Shall I read to you ?' She took up a book, and, seating herself by her mother's arm-chair, began to read aloud. Ella took no notice of this, but resting both her elbows on the table, riveted her eyes upon the page before her.

Bertha's voice was rather monotonous ; her reading had the same absence of expression as her face ; perhaps she was not giving her full attention to the book, for she paused sometimes in wrong places, as if listening, and looked up,—quietly and slowly, though—for she was never hurried—at the least sound. ' There is Clement,' she said, at last. No one else seemed to have heard anything, but that was not strange ; a very loud clock in the hall had just struck ten, and the sound was likely to drown all others.

' It is very wrong of him,' said Mrs Campbell, hastily.

' Yes, very wrong,' repeated Bertha, thoughtfully.

' It is a beautiful moonlight evening ; I dare say he has been wandering on the shore,' said Ella, not raising her eyes from her book.

Bertha went to meet him. They were heard talking to-gether in the little entrance hall, but the words were indis-tinct.

' Where have you been, Clement ?' asked Mrs Campbell, as

they entered the room. The boy's eye sparkled with a flash of irritation, but he answered gaily—

'Been! grandmamma, oh, to a hundred places—along the cliff, down on the shore, watching the stars; it's a wonderful night. Ella, I wish you had been with me.'

'Ella knows better than to wish anything of the kind,' said Mrs Campbell. 'It is a great deal too late for you. Whom had you with you?'

'Part of the time I was alone,' was Clement's evasive reply, and Mrs Campbell seemed satisfied; but Ella looked up at her brother and laughed.

Bertha was very cold and stiff. She asked Clement if he was hungry, and when he said, 'yes, ravenous,' told him he must wait till after prayers, and then he might have some cold meat, and at the same moment she rang the bell.

Bertha read prayers,—reverently and simply; but the tone might have suited a sermon; and Ella fidgeted, and Clement was once heard to yawn.

'Don't let Clement be late, Bertha,' said Mrs Campbell, as she took a night candle in her hand, and, going up to her daughter, gave her a cold kiss.

'No, ma'am, he will have his supper directly.'

'And don't be late yourself, Bertha. I hear you moving about in your room, and it disturbs me.'

'No, ma'am!' Bertha opened the door for her mother.

'Good night, grandmamma,' said Ella; and Clement drew near also, though his step was a little doubtful.

'Good night, loves. Clement, you stamp dreadfully over my head at night.'

'Do I, grandmamma? I can't help it; it is my heavy boots.'

'You may wear slippers,' said Bertha, shortly; but Mrs Campbell did not appear to need the apology. She kissed him affectionately, and went up-stairs, Ella following her. Bertha and Clement stood lingering over the fire. Clement raked up the ashes, and tried to make a blaze, and Bertha remarked that it was no good; he must make haste and eat his supper, and go to bed.

'I wish supper would come,' said Clement, pettishly. 'What is that woman, Betsy, doing with herself?'

'She has more to attend to than she ought to have,' was the reply. 'She can't be expected to have supper ready at all hours of the night.'

'If she is so busy, why doesn't she have more help?' asked Clement.

'Because we can't afford it, Clement.' The boy kicked away a stool which was in his way, and started up from the chair into which he had flung himself.

'The answer for everything, Aunt Bertha; are we never to be able to afford it?'

'Time will show for us,' replied Bertha; 'for you, Clement, it is in your own power.'

'If I were rich, you would all be rich too,' he exclaimed. 'But, Aunt Bertha, who can soften stone walls? Not I.'

'It is no question of softening stone walls, Clement; that is neither your business nor mine. The work is in your own power.'

'Yes, plod, plod, night and day; work one's brain till it hasn't an idea left in it, and then get a crust of bread to live upon; and that is the life of a gentleman!'

'The life of a good many gentlemen,' replied Bertha. 'But here is your supper, Clement; make haste and eat it, for we mustn't really be late.'

Clement sat down to the table. Some slices of cold mutton were put in a plate for him, with a piece of bread. He asked for some pickle.

'You can't have any to-night,' said Bertha; 'it is locked up.'

'And no salad?—nothing?'

'It is a very good supper if you are hungry; and if you are not, you don't want anything,' answered Bertha.

'Who keeps the keys? Grandmamma?' and before Bertha could stop him he was at the top of the stairs, knocking loudly at Mrs Campbell's door. He returned holding up the keys triumphantly.

'Now, Aunt Bertha!' but Bertha took no notice. 'Which cupboard is it, Aunt Bertha?' No answer.

He only laughed and ran away to the kitchen. Betsy, the cook, followed him as he came back, and put down on the table a jar of pickles and the remains of a cold tart. 'So, Aunt Bertha, I have not been foraging for nothing; come, you will have some with me.' But he failed to extract a smile from Bertha, who stood looking on whilst he ate his supper, with an appetite which, as he himself had described it, was ravenous.

Bertha broke the silence. 'Clement, what time did Ronald leave you?'

'Oh! about half-past nine, more or less; I had no watch.'

'And you walked on the shore all that time?'

'Yes, there and on the cliffs. He was in one of his moods; I couldn't leave him.'

'He ought not to have been with you,' said Bertha.

'He said that, and told me to go; but we had made the engagement to meet. And where was the harm?'

'Where is at any time the harm of disobedience, Clement?'

'Now, Aunt Bertha, I don't understand you,' and Clement hastily finished his tumbler of beer, and rose and stood by the fire. 'Who tells me not to be with Ronald?'

'I tell you, and that ought to be sufficient.' Her tone was very authoritative, and the angry flush rose in Clement's cheek, and he bit his lip.

'You know, Clement, that there is disobedience to the spirit of a law as well as to the letter. What matters it that you have never been absolutely commanded by my mother not to be with Ronald? You are as well aware as I am that both she and Mr Lester disapprove of it.'

'Without a reason!' exclaimed Clement. 'I will never listen to any one who doesn't give me a reason.'

'Then you will be a slave to yourself, Clement, and a miserable man.'

'As you will,' he replied, carelessly. 'I will run my chance of misery, but I never will leave a noble-hearted fellow, like Ronald, merely because there happens to be a prejudice against him. And you, Aunt Bertha, to try to persuade me not!—you who are always looking after him, and turning and twisting him at your will.'

'Not at my will, Clement,' replied Bertha. 'He would not be what he is if he were turned at my will,' she added, in an undertone.

'He might not be the better for being different,' exclaimed Clement, 'or if he were, I shouldn't like him as well.'

'No, and there is the danger, Clement; but we won't argue the point : Mr Lester wishes you not to be with him; my mother wishes it also. You have no right to require more.'

'But I must and I do require more,' exclaimed Clement, impatiently, yet without any real ill-humour; 'and I ask of you, Aunt Bertha, whether there isn't a prejudice against Ronald which would prevent grandmamma and Mr Lester from liking him if he were an angel. And I will ask, too,' he continued, interrupting Bertha as she was about to reply, 'whether the prejudice is not fostered by my grandfather, and whether it is not because of him that every pleasure I have in life is thwarted.'

'Clement, that is speaking very disrespectfully. I can't answer such questions. Your grandfather has strong reasons, fearful reasons, for dreading an intimacy with Ronald.'

'With a cousin! not very near perhaps, but still my relation, and the only fellow in the neighbourhood who suits me! Am I then to live the life of a hermit, Aunt Bertha?'

'You are required to lead a studious, steady life, to prepare yourself for the University, if you ever wish to have a place in your grandfather's favour.'

'Then I will go without the place; I will give it up. The favour of a rich old general! there will be many candidates for it.'

'And you will break my mother's heart, grieve Mr Lester, disappoint all our hopes, merely because you won't bring yourself to relinquish a companionship which, after all, cannot be congenial.'

'I will stand by Ronald at all risks, Aunt Bertha; I will never sacrifice my friendship to the will of a'——

'Take care, Clement,' and Bertha held up her finger warningly; 'you are speaking of your grandfather.'

'Yet he has never shown me kindness,' exclaimed Clement; 'he never asks me to his house—he scarcely pays me the common civilities of a stranger. And, Aunt Bertha, let him be my grandfather a hundred times over, yet he is my father's enemy.'

'Your father, Clement, was his own enemy.'

'And therefore every one turns against him.'

'Yes, every one, even his only son,' replied Bertha. Her tone was so sad that Clement was startled.

'I don't understand you, Aunt Bertha,' he said.

'And therefore you will not act upon faith,' answered Bertha. 'O Clement! it is a fatal principle to go upon; it will be your ruin. I have told you before, and I repeat it; disobey and thwart your grandfather, and untold misery will be the consequence.'

'What misery? What consequence? Why will you always speak so mysteriously, Aunt Bertha?'

'Because I am not at liberty to speak in any other way,' said Bertha. 'But, Clement, all this is but idle talking. If I could convince you beyond the possibility of doubt, that your intimacy with Ronald would lead you into mischief, it would not in the most remote degree add to the duty of obedience to the known will of all the persons whom you are most bound to obey.'

Clement was silent. Bertha took up a candlestick and gave it to him. He did not wish her good night, but stood thinking.

' Aunt Bertha,' and he suddenly raised his eyes from the floor, ' you knew Ronald many years ago.'

' Yes, many, Clement ; before you can remember.'

' And you were always kind to him.'

' Yes, I hope so. I wish to be kind to every one.'

' But you were specially kind to him, and you are so now ; and you have influence over him.'

' I don't know as to the influence. If I have, it is not from any power of my own.'

' You were his mother's friend,' said Clement ; 'he told me that to-night.'

' Yes,' was Bertha's cold reply : but she sat down for an instant, and her hand trembled as she laid her candlestick on the table. Clement did not see or comprehend the signs of inward feeling ; he went on :

' Ronald says you were very fond of her.'

' Yes, I was. Good night, Clement ; remember, if you sit up late, you will disturb grandmamma.' She took his hand—it was as impassive as her own—and she let it fall again quietly. Clement moved towards the door, but paused to say impatiently, in answer to the injunction, again repeated, to go to bed at once—

' I shall go presently. I have an exercise to prepare for Mr Lester.'

Bertha waited till she had heard him enter his room and lock the door, and then she made a tour of inspection of the rooms, saw that every shutter was fastened and every bolt drawn, and retired to rest herself.

CHAPTER IV.

MRS CAMPBELL'S cottage closely adjoined the Rectory, only a steep, reedy bank, and a little rivulet divided them, and a rough bridge over the stream formed an easy mode of communication. The Rectory stood high, on a smooth, sloping lawn, a little way up the ascent of the range of the Encombe hills, which entirely sheltered it from the north. The library windows fronting the south-east commanded a view over a small bay, shut in by rugged cliffs of red sandstone rising at the western extremity into a bold headland. Beyond, towards the north-west, the landscape was more bounded ; the rough ground at the top of the ravine, in which the village was hidden, and the thick plantation of what appeared to be a gentleman's park, closing in the horizon.

Rachel Lester was sitting in the library with her father ; he was writing, she was busy with a slate and a Latin exercise. Rachel was receiving rather a learned education ; an only child, with no mother, and a very classically-inclined father, that was natural. Mr Lester looked very old to be the father of such a child as Rachel. He was nearly sixty in appearance, though not quite so much in reality. His hair was gray, and his countenance worn. It was a very intellectual, studious face, softened by the expression of extreme benevolence ; but there was great firmness in the lines of his mouth ; there could be no doubt that he could, when he chose, be severe. His attention was entirely given now to his occupation. He was engaged with a letter, interlined and corrected, often causing him to pause and consider, and sometimes to throw himself back in his chair, and pass his hand across his eyes, as if in painful recollection.

His feelings may be traced in the words which flowed from his pen :—

' I need not say that you are continually in my thoughts, and always with the longing to meet your wishes. I desire heartily to find an opening, and can only entreat you to trust us if we seem to delay. Remember that if we seize the wrong moment, everything will fail. Mildred lives upon the hope of success, but even she does not yet perceive the way to it. My dear Vivian, you must be patient ; you must pray to be so ; remembering the offence, and bearing the punishment. In the meantime, your children are well, and doing well—in the way, at least, to do so, though there are many faults to be corrected. Their education is not in all ways what I like ; but there is no direct evil in it, and the defect cannot be remedied. Here, again, we must be patient. Clement may be all that we could wish to see him. He is generous-hearted and refined in taste, but easily led into things which at first sight one would be apt to fancy foreign to his nature. I think this arises from vanity. He loves admiration, and does not much care from whom it comes. You will not like to hear this ; but you wished to know the truth and the worst, and I give it you. He has no vicious habits, but if he were born to luxury I should feel he might become a sentimentalist. His favourite virtues are of the heroic cast ; so are his favourite heroes. He has great notions of self-sacrifice, but very little idea of self-restraint.

'There is a singular likeness between him and Ella in character as well as in countenance. They are twins both in mind and body, except that Clement will never be what Ella is in point of talent. She really has wonderful powers, but with the singular inconsistency of genius she is as variable as the winds, and as indolent as—I can form no comparison for her indolence— there is nothing in nature like it. I should very much like to remove Clement from her influence. It is all-powerful with him, partly, I suppose, from the twin-feeling which is always so strong, but chiefly from his exceeding admiration of her powers of mind. He will not see her defects, and it is very painful to be obliged to point them out.

'The little ones have great promise of good if they are properly managed. Louisa is quick, determined, and wilful ; but capable of ripening into an extremely sensible, useful woman. Fanny is too pretty for her own advantage, or at least she has heard too much of her beauty for simplicity; but she is exceedingly affectionate, and very true, and the truth gives me great hope of her.

'If the home were but different ! You will understand all I mean by that—you, who have known Bertha Campbell so well, and have reaped the benefit of her virtues, and felt the consequences of her defects. But we must take her, my dear Vivian, as she is ; and be grateful that at least the children will never have a low, or insincere example set before them. She is not to be altered ; and really I, who know her in her most pleasing form, often think that there is scarcely anything in her I should wish to alter. But I can see all that you complain of, and, what is more, all the consequences. The evil, I suspect, lies very far back. When I am inclined to be severe, I wish that I could open Mrs Campbell's eyes to the lasting evils of that system of perpetual check which has absolutely paralysed Bertha's powers. To see what she has done would be a sufficient punishment.

'You would like me to tell you that your children's home at

the Lodge is very cheerful and good for them, and that their
prospects at the Park are brightening. Now this, you see, I
cannot do quite ; but I have given you something to comfort
you, only, as I said before, patience must be your motto.

‘ Mildred writes to you so often, that I need not say anything
about her. She is looking better than usual. I think that the
neighbourhood of the children has done much for her, and you
know what she is in natural cheerfulness and wonderful submission. But I am afraid it may be hope deferred, for as yet the
General has allowed no advances. I do not mean that he
entirely neglects the children ; he notices them if they meet,
and the other day he sent Clement a fishing-rod, which the boy,
stupidly enough, was on the point of returning, thinking it
rather an insult than a kindness, because some one—I guess
who—had put it into his head, that unless his grandfather
would fully forgive and receive both you and them, it was
lowering to accept any favour from him. No one but John
Vivian would have suggested the idea, knowing what deadly
enmity it might cause. If it were not for the watch we may keep
over him, it would be one of the greatest trials of my faith that
such a fellow as your cousin should be here just at this moment.
The thorn he is in our path no one can tell ; and there is his
boy—a fallen angel, if one may say so without profaneness—
coming in contact with Clement continually, and exciting in
him, what he does in every one, an interest which at last becomes fascination. All actual authority over Clement must lie
with Mrs Campbell, who is jealous of my interference ; so I
cannot entirely forbid any intercourse with Ronald, and I am
not sure that I should do so if I could. The boys must meet ;
they are near neighbours and cousins, and too strict discipline
might lead the way to deceit, when the temptation to be together
occasionally is so great. One of the most unfortunate points in
the acquaintance is, that it serves to keep up the General’s
suspicion. Your cousin, Captain Vivian, as he is called now,
owing, I suppose, to his connection with a trading vessel commonly said to be used for smuggling purposes, is becoming
daily more low in his tastes, and finds congenial society in the
place—poachers, smugglers, &c. My heart sickens when I
think of his influence for evil ; I trace it continually. The
people have a kind of traditional respect for him ; he is a Vivian,
and therefore they never can look upon him quite as a mere
mortal. They see what he is, but they regard his offences very

much as we used to regard the crimes of the heathen gods, and, in consequence, are not ashamed to follow him.

'I feel I am giving you a great deal of pain in writing all this, raking up in a way the ashes of the past. But, my dear Vivian, there must be truth between us. Your cousin's name should be buried from this moment, if it could promote your real welfare ; but I should only deceive you, and in the end increase the bitterness of your trial, if I allowed you to think that he is not now, as he has been ever, your evil genius. I still hold the opinions I mentioned in my last letter as to his past deeds, and am anxiously seeking for an opportunity to unravel the mystery. Your sister-in-law and I discuss plans continually, but hitherto we have failed to arrive at a satisfactory conclusion. If we could soften the General, we might reach the truth ; but how is that to be done ?

'One thing you must remember for your comfort as regards the children, that there are counter-influences for good. John Vivian, himself, is to Clement merely an object of wondering disgust. The boy's natural refinement keeps him out of the reach of the chief temptations which such a man could offer. And Ronald is open to influences which may—God grant it prove so—turn the balance in favour of all we could most desire. He has his mother's face and in a measure her disposition, so at least I am told by your sister-in-law, who sees him often and talks to him a good deal. I was very much surprised to find when Mrs Campbell came here, that Bertha and Ronald were old acquaintances. Bertha is so reserved that I can get nothing from her as to how they first knew each other, except that one day she told me his mother had been a friend of hers. Certainly since she has been at Encombe there has been a marked change in him. It is strange, is it not? that she should have power over a wild, untamed spirit like his, and yet do so little in her own family. But it is her own family—that, I suppose, is the secret; and when she has to work in it, she cannot be free.

'Your father, I sometimes fancy, keeps a little aloof from me, and I don't wonder at it. He must know the wish that is nearest to my heart. His walking powers are not quite what they were, but he rides a great deal and looks uncommonly well. Mildred, as I said, hopes, and lives upon hope—that is her nature ; and yet with such constant suffering it really is marvellous. My little Rachel is with her often, but not quite as frequently as she used

to be, for she is working diligently under Miss Campbell's super-
intendence. She began doing lessons with Ella, but soon gave
that up. As to keeping pace with Ella, I really don't know who
could do so. I sometimes indulge a dream of finding a way to
the General's heart by Ella's means. He could not help appre-
ciating her wonderful talents; and then he might become proud of
her. Mildred would know how to bring her out, but the children
are so very little with her! She does not dare show herself too
eager for their society; and if ever they do go to the Hall, they
are kept out of the General's way as much as possible. You may
imagine how this chafes Clement's proud temper, and he comes
back to me, and raves of insult and subjection, and talks about
Ronald and a seafaring life which they might lead together; but
it will all come to nothing. He has not enough of the spirit of
endurance in him to make a sailor; and he is too old for the navy,
and would not choose to enter the merchant service. Ronald
might do for it very well; in fact, I am at this moment negotiat-
ing something of the kind for him at his own request. You will
understand that I have a double motive for his good and Clement's; the separation is so very much to be desired.

'One word about myself, and then good-bye. You ask me
how I am, and what I do, and what my hopes and pleasures are.
I am very well, I never was better, and I work contentedly in my
parish, and my earthly hopes and pleasures are centred in Rachel.

'That answer will not satisfy you, I know. It tells too little of
my inner self. My dear Vivian, that must be a sealed book. If
I were to attempt to describe the struggles of a heart which has
yet to learn submission to the Divine Will, I should make myself
a woman in weakness. Suffice it that I have one treasure left to
render my home bright. Yet you must not fancy I am miserable
or even unhappy; only sobered. Mildred and I sometimes
venture to compare notes upon these subjects; but I don't think
it is wise in us, except that to see her is the deepest lesson one
could receive in humility. An old woman said to me the other
day: " Miss Mildred seems to be always a smiling and a praying
—and sure that was what the saints used to do." Certainly the
poor have especial reason to think her a saint; for, in spite of
her infirmities, she manages, principally through Mrs Robinson,
to make herself at home with all their affairs, and is considered
quite their best domestic adviser.'

The letter was concluded, sealed, and directed to 'E. B.
Vivian, Esq., Kingston, Jamaica.'

Then Rachel spoke: 'Dear papa, may I take your letter to the post ? I am going out.'

Mr Lester did not at first appear to hear her. He was gazing at the words he had just written, probably following them in his mind on their distant mission. He answered, however, after a short pause, 'No, dear child, thank you ;' but he spoke in an absent tone. Presently he said, 'How old are you, Rachel ?'

'Thirteen, papa ! I shall be fourteen my next birthday.'

'A very great age for such a very little woman,' said Mr Lester, smiling ; and, as Rachel seated herself on his knee, and put her arm round his neck, he added : 'When do you ever mean to be anything but a baby ?'

'Never to you, papa ; but Nurse Robinson told me last evening that I really was grown.'

'She sees what she wishes,' replied Mr Lester ; 'she has set her heart upon your being a fine young lady.'

Rachel clapped her hands together, and her merry laugh made Mr Lester's grave face also relax into something more than a smile.

'Well, Rachel, shouldn't you like to be a fine young lady ! '

'Should you like me to be one, papa ?' said Rachel, archly.

'Perhaps not ; you wouldn't be so convenient to nurse. You are such a doll now, that you may very well pass for ten. But, Rachel,' and his voice became very serious, 'I should like to think you were old enough to share some of my cares.'

The deep look of thought came over Rachel's face, as her eye rested for a moment on a picture over the mantelpiece, the likeness of her mother, and of two sisters and a brother, all older than herself, and all now lying side by side in the churchyard of Encombe. She had never known the comfort of their love, but they were the dearest treasures of her young heart ; and, whenever tempted to thoughtlessness by her natural gaiety of heart, a glance at the picture was sufficient to remind her that she was to live to be her father's consolation.

Mr Lester's eye followed hers. 'You may help me so much, Rachel, if you will,' he continued.

'Papa,' and she leaned her face on his shoulder, and her voice was low and tremulous, 'will you pray to God to teach me how?'

He kissed her fondly and repeatedly. 'I do pray for you, my child, daily and hourly, and God hears my prayers. He has made you my chief solace hitherto, and He will make you so still more; I do not doubt it.'

'Are you unhappy, papa, now?'

'I can scarcely say unhappy, Rachel, but very anxious; not for myself,' he added, hastily, seeing her look alarmed.

'For Clement?' asked Rachel, doubtfully.

Mr Lester half-smiled, whilst he hesitated to answer. 'Yes, for Clement, partly; what made you think of him?'

'Because you are often grave, papa, after he has been here; and because he seems to make every one anxious. Miss Campbell is always troubling about him for one reason or another.'

'Miss Campbell never talks to you about him, does she?' inquired Mr Lester, quickly.

'Not exactly, but she lets out little things; and Ella talks a great deal, only she thinks Clement perfect.'

'And what do you think?'

'Oh, I think him dreadfully naughty,' exclaimed Rachel. 'I like Ronald Vivian, though he is so rough, twenty times as well as I do Clement.'

'You don't see much of either of them to be able to judge,' observed Mr Lester.

'No; only we meet them sometimes, when we are out walking, and Miss Campbell always speaks to Ronald, and he attends to her, but Clement never does.'

'That is one of his great defects,' said Mr Lester; 'you and Ella should try to cure him of it.'

'Ella upholds him,' replied Rachel.

'Then you must try and persuade her out of it.'

'Ella is not to be persuaded,' replied Rachel; 'and she talks of Clement as if he were such a great person. I tell her sometimes that I think he must be a prince in disguise.'

'She thinks he will inherit his grandfather's fortune, and live at the Hall,' said Mr Lester.

'And he will, won't he, papa?'

'We don't know, my dear; there is no good in dwelling upon such things. Clement must learn to do his duty without thinking of the consequences.'

'And Ella must learn to teach him,' said Rachel, thoughtfully.

'Yes, that is the great duty for her; and Rachel, my darling, you have had more advantages than she has, and I think you may help to give her strength. This was what I wanted especially to say to you. You have little to do with Clement; but you

have a great deal to do with Ella, and you must turn your opportunities to the best account.'

'But, papa, she is so clever, I can't keep up with her ; and
she is older.'

'Very true ; but, Rachel, it is not talent which really influences the world, but high, steady principle. You are not very
clever, but you may be very good, and if you are, you may help
to make Ella good too ; and if she is good she will lead Clement
right ; and if Clement is led right'——

' What, papa ?'

Mr Lester paused : 'It would make me very happy, Rachel.'
He seemed tempted to say more to her, but after a short consideration he merely added, 'You don't wish for any other
motive, do you ?'

' Oh no, papa! only—Clement is no relation.'

' He is the son of one whom I once loved, and whom I still
love as if he were my younger brother,' said Mr Lester ; 'and
his father is away, and there is no one else to guide him. Is not
that a sufficient reason to be anxious for him ?'

'Yes,' replied Rachel, as her father stood up and began to put
aside his writing materials. The ' yes ' was doubtful.

' Are you not satisfied, my child ?'

'Not quite, papa,' was Rachel's honest answer. 'There is
always a mystery about Clement.'

'And you must be contented, my darling, to bear with mystery. It is a very necessary lesson to learn ; but so far I will
tell you. General Vivian has had cause to be displeased with
his son, and therefore he looks with suspicion upon Clement ;
and everything which Clement does that is careless and wrong
increases his grandfather's doubts of his character. Now, you
can see why I, as his father's friend, am especially anxious as to
his conduct ; and so I hope you will see also how important
it is for every one who has influence of any kind over either
Ella or Clement, to try and lead them in the right way. I can't
answer any more questions, Rachel ; and remember you must
never talk upon the subject to any one but me.'

Rachel was a little awed by her father's manner. Her countenance showed it. Yet the feeling vanished in a moment as he
stooped to kiss her, and she said, ' I am going to see Aunt
Mildred to-day ; you don't mind ?'

' No, my child ; how should I ? I shall be going to the Hall
myself, probably, and if you are there we will walk home together.'

' Then I may stay a long time, if she asks me ? '

' Yes ; but who is to go with you ? '

' Miss Campbell and Ella to the Lodge gate, and if I don't stay they will wait for me, but they are not going in.' Rachel could have wondered and asked the reason why, but she checked herself.

' One more kiss, papa.' And she ran gaily out of the room, and her joyous voice was heard as she went singing up the stairs to prepare for her walk.

CHAPTER V.

CLEVE HALL was a long, low, irregular, red-brick house, part of which dated as far back as the time of Henry VII. The history of the Vivians was written in its gables, and clustering chimneys, and turrets, and oriel windows of all shapes and sizes,—for by far the greater number of its possessors had thought it necessary to add to or alter it ; almost the only thing which had descended unchanged being the huge griffin, the family crest, standing erect above the entrance porch.

A quiet, solemn-looking place it was, resting under the guardianship of the Encombe Hills, and shut in by plantations on every side except towards the sea ; a place to which childish memories might cling, with vivid recollections of long summer days, spent under the shade of the old oaks whilst listening to the soft murmurs of the sea, or of winter evenings in the great library, or rainy days in the billiard-room, or long twilights passed in recounting the tales belonging to the grim old family pictures. Many such places there are in England—few perhaps more interesting than Cleve Hall in its stately, sobering quietness.

It was in a handsome though narrow room, in the oldest part of the house, that Rachel Lester was sitting on that evening as it drew towards sunset. She had drawn a stool into the depth of the oriel window, and was endeavouring to read by the fading light. Twilight is not, as every one knows, a cheerful hour, and Miss Vivian's morning-room, as the apartment was usually called, was low, and the windows were small and deep. Yet it was not gloomy, there were books, pictures, flowers, cabinets of shells, a piano, and a table with a work-basket and drawing materials,—all giving notions of constant, cheerful employment, and of the comfort and elegancies of life ; and though the shadows were deepening, yet the rich sunset hues were pouring in through the windows, and lighting up the lower end of the apartment with a flood of crimson.

The sun was setting over the sea, which could be seen through an opening in the shrubbery, with the jagged edge of the cliff forming its boundary. It brought indications of a change of weather ; the clouds were gathering angrily in the west, some heaped together in huge masses touched at their edges by streaks of gold, others rushing across the sky in long, feathery flakes, becoming brilliantly red when they came within reach of the departing rays, and melting away in hues scarcely perceptible as they stretched themselves far into the grayish-blue vault above them.

The wind moaned ominously amongst the Cleve woods, the leaves moved restlessly to and fro, and flights of birds were winging their way rapidly from the cliffs, whilst even from that distance the foam of the white breakers might be seen as they tossed their chafed waters upon the beach. It was clear that a storm was rising, and that rapidly.

'O Aunt Mildred ! can you see that boat ? how it goes up and down, and all its sails up ! How beautiful it looks !' Rachel had put down her book, and was pointing with one hand to the window, whilst the other rested upon the arm of a couch, on which lay a lady whose age it would have been difficult to tell. Seen in the twilight she looked still young, but her complexion was worn and sallow, probably from the illness of years. Her face was painfully thin, and her fingers were very long and slender ; yet the impression she gave was not that of suffering, and scarcely of resignation, at least when she spoke. Some persons are said to have tears in their voices. Mildred Vivian certainly had a smile in hers. 'What boat, darling ?' she said, in answer to Rachel's observation. 'Oh, I see it now. Please move a very little. How fast it goes ! the wind must be in its favour.'

'Should you like to be in it, Aunt Mildred ?'

'Like it ? O Rachel ! yes ; should I not ? It is fifteen years since I was in a boat.'

'Where is it going, I wonder,' said Rachel. 'Where would you go, Aunt Mildred, if you were in it ?'

Mildred paused. Rachel could not see her face clearly, for the shadows were deepening every instant. 'I should go far away from England, dear child.' The very lightest sound of a sigh could be heard, following the words.

'You should take me with you wherever you went, dear Aunt Mildred.'

'What, away from papa?'

'Oh! no, no; but he must go with us. We could not live away from each other, could we?'

'I can't say that, Rachel. We did live some years without knowing each other,' replied Mildred.

'Yes; but I always wanted something.'

'And did not know that it was a mock aunt,' observed Mildred, in a tone of amusement.

'I don't like your saying mock, dear Aunt Mildred,' exclaimed Rachel. 'You are more real than a great many real aunts, I am sure.'

'More real in love, dear child; that I am quite sure of.'

'But you could do without me,' said Rachel, thoughtfully.

'I shouldn't like to do without you; I mustn't say I could not.'

'Aunt Mildred,' and Rachel spoke anxiously, 'I know I couldn't do without papa.'

'Ah, Rachel! you don't know.'

'But must I try? Am I very wicked to feel that I couldn't?'

'Not at all wicked; only, Rachel, we can do without whatever God may please to take from us.'

'But we should die,' said Rachel.

'No, dear Rachel, we should only be made more fit to die.'

'And He has taken so much from you!' exclaimed Rachel, flinging her arm round Mildred's neck. 'Was it all needed to make you fit to die?'

'All, Rachel! every pang, every sorrow; there was not one too many. And He has left such mercies! Perhaps some day He will add the greatest of all—the thankfulness which one ought to have.'

Rachel stood up again, nearer to the window. The boat was fast becoming indistinct in the dull light and the far distance.

'Can you see it still?' said Mildred, sitting more upright.

'Just. How the wind is rising! I shouldn't like to be in the boat; I should be afraid.'

Mildred did not reply, and Rachel, too, was silent for some

time. The last gleams of the sunset were melting away, and the room was becoming very dark. 'Mr Lester will be here soon,' said Mildred; 'or will he wait till the moon has risen?'

It was strange that there was no answer. Rachel's face was pressed against the window-pane. She seemed straining her eyes to obtain the least glimpse of the boat. A sudden gust of wind howled through the trees, and, as it died away, Rachel turned from the window, and kneeling by Mildred's couch, exclaimed, as she burst into tears, 'Perhaps Clement will be out to-night.' There was no exclamation of surprise or terror. Mildred's hand was placed lovingly on the child's head, and she said quietly, 'Are you sure?'

'Not sure; I think so,—and—Aunt Mildred, it may be my fault.'

'Yours, my love, how?'

'Because if I would have done all they wished me to do, he would not have gone.'

'Whom do you mean by they, Rachel? You must be more clear.' Mildred rather raised herself on her couch, and a tone of anxiety might have been observed in the first words she uttered; but even at the close of the sentence it was checked.

'Ella and Clement are they,' replied Rachel, speaking hurriedly, and not very intelligibly. 'I went there before I came away, and Clement was talking to Ella.'

'And did they tell you what they were talking about?'

'I heard a little as I went in, and then they were obliged to tell me more. Clement did not say, though, that he was going in the boat, only that he had an engagement; but I am sure he was, and I saw him with Goff in the village afterwards; and '——

'Go on,' said Mildred.

Rachel drew a long breath. 'I could have stopped him, Aunt Mildred, if I had chosen it. He said if I would go to the shore with him and Ella, and read poetry—something of Lord Byron's which he wanted Ella to hear,—then he would stay at home. But papa doesn't like me to read the book, and so I said no; and now perhaps Clement is gone, and the storm will come, and he will be drowned. O Aunt Mildred! was it very wrong? Was it very wrong?' she repeated in a trembling voice, as Mildred delayed answering.

'No, dear Rachel; how could it be? but '——

'Hark! there is some one,' interrupted Rachel, listening. 'Papa will be come for me, and what will he say?'

'Not that it was your fault, Rachel, whatever happens. But we must trust.'

'And he may not have gone,' said Rachel, in a calmer tone.

'No, he may not.—That must be Mr Lester's voice.'

Rachel ran out to meet him. Mr Lester entered hurriedly. The storm, he said, was rising like a hurricane, and he was anxious to be at home. He shook hands with Mildred, and sat down by her, and asked after General Vivian ; but his manner was reserved and abstracted. Mildred looked at him, as if she would read it ; but she was puzzled.

'Rachel, you had better go for your bonnet,' she said ; and Rachel drew near and whispered, 'Will you tell papa when I am gone ?'

'Yes, dear love ; don't come back till I send for you.' Rachel ran away. 'Rachel is anxious for Clement,' said Mildred, as soon as the door was closed.

'She need not be to-night ; he is safe ; Goff did not take him ;' but Mr Lester's tone was less calm than his words.

'Thank God for that,' said Mildred, with a sigh of gratitude. 'It may be a fearful night.'

Mr Lester looked out into the dim twilight, and stood as if in a reverie. Presently he said, 'It is not from Clement's obedience that he is safe. It was Ronald who interfered. Mark Wood told me he thought he was going, and I believed he was, till I met Ronald. These are things which make me feel that he must have a father's hand over him soon, if possible.'

'Have you any plan ; anything to propose ?' inquired Mildred, anxiously.

'No ; but I have been writing. My letter ought to have gone to-day, only I kept it open till I had seen you. Can you give me any hope ?'

'Dear Mr Lester ! how can you ask ?' and Mildred's lip quivered. 'Should I keep it from you a moment if I had ?'

'Yet I could not be contented without asking,' said Mr Lester. 'He will think my letter miserably cold, for I had no comfort to give him but words, and I was obliged to tell him that Clement doesn't satisfy me.'

'I have not yet sounded the matter,' said Mildred, speaking in a tone which indicated great self-restraint. 'Incautiousness would do immense mischief. If I take my father at the wrong moment, he may forbid the subject ever being mentioned again ; and I feel as if we should be more certain of our end if we could gain admittance to his heart first in some other way. I have thought of asking him to let Ella stay with me.'

' It is a strong measure,' said Mr Lester. ' I should be afraid Ella would not win him. He will see her faults, and exaggerate them.'

' Perhaps so.' Mildred considered for a moment, and then said, as if speaking to herself, ' Is it not unaccountable ; so good, and honourable, and kind-hearted as my dear father is to all others,—so clear-sighted too, especially in discovering injustice or prejudice ? '

' Not unaccountable ; it is human nature. "A brother offended is harder to be won than a strong city." '

' And the Campbells to have settled in the neighbourhood ! ' said Mildred ; ' it widens the breach infinitely. He cannot en-dure even their names.'

' No,' replied Mr Lester ; ' and the very fact of seeing the children, I often think, reminds him of the connection.'

' And Edward then must linger in a distant land, away from his children, working without hope.'

' Better that than to return and be rejected. If the experiment were to fail, we should have nothing else to fall back upon. We must wait for time and softening influences. Through God's mercy they may open a way. Oh ! if any words could but teach those children what may depend on their present conduct ! ' The exclamation came from the very bottom of his heart.

' Does Miss Campbell complain as she did ? ' inquired Mildred.

' Yes, and for the most part justly.'

' But she is not merciful,' said Mildred.

' That is not to be expected from her education. She is antagonistic to them always.'

' She is the person to be reached,' continued Mildred.

' She is reached continually in a way. I tell her her faults, and she hears them all patiently, for she is very humble-minded ; but I see no results.'

' Yet, so good as you say she is, her character must tell.'

' One would think so ; yet one infirmity will neutralise a dozen virtues. How one trembles to hear people talk so lightly as they do of what they call failings ! '

Mildred sighed. ' Yes,' she said, after a moment's silence, ' it would be a curious and fearful history to write,—the history of failings.'

'It will be written one day,' said Mr Lester, solemnly ; 'and then may God have mercy upon us !'

A pause followed. It was interrupted by a heavy, booming sound, heard distinctly amidst the roar of the rising storm. Mildred started up.

'A ship in distress !' said Mr Lester.

Mildred sank back, and covered her eyes. Mr Lester took up his hat.

'You will leave Rachel with me,' said Mildred, quietly.

'Yes, indeed, if you will keep her. I wish she could always be as safe. God bless you.' He pressed her hand affectionately.

'And you will take every one with you whom you think may be useful,' said Mildred ; 'and remember,'—her voice changed,— 'there is room at the Hall for all who may need shelter.'

'Yes, I am sure of that always. Good-bye.'

Mildred's face was perfectly colourless ; and when another boom of the signal gun was heard, she clasped her hands together, and prayed fervently to Him at 'whose command the winds blow and lift up the waves of the sea, and who stilleth the rage thereof.'

CHAPTER VI.

PEOPLE were hurrying to the shore, making their way thither by the nearest paths, and guided by the uncertain light of the moon, as it escaped from behind the racking clouds which were rushing over the heavens. Mr Lester's road was narrow, and tangled by brushwood and briars. It led directly through the woods to an open heath terminated by the cliffs. A rough road, sometimes traversed by carts, crossed the heath, and when Mr Lester emerged from the copse, he found the road already reached by stragglers from the lone cottages between Encombe and the neighbouring town of Cleve. Women and children, as well as men, were amongst them. There was a strange, fascinating horror in the thought of a scene of danger ; and some, it was to be feared, had in view a prospect of personal advantage, to be gained at the expense of the unfortunate owners of the distressed vessel. Mr Lester mingled amongst

them at first unperceived. The greater number were unknown
to him, as not belonging to his own parish, and the light was
too indistinct to allow of his being recognised by them.

D'ye see her?' asked a rough, farmer-looking man, of a boy
who had been to the edge of the cliff.

'See her? yes, as well as a body can in such a blinking light.
She's off Dark Head Point, on the rocks, I'm thinking; and
sore work 'twill be to get safe in.'

'Many folks down on the beach?' inquired the farmer.

'Aye, a crowd. I heard the Captain's voice amongst the
loudest.'

'No doubt of that,' was the reply. 'Where's there ever a
skirl without him?'

'Aye, where? He was in Cleve this afternoon, blustering;
and I heard it said, if he went on so he'd some day be taken up
to the old General. That is a sight I'd give one of my eyes to
see. But he's a brave fellow after all, is the Captain.'

'Brave, is he? That's as folks think. Stay!'——

There was a momentary pause, as if with one consent, as a
shrill cry of horror was brought to the ear in a sudden lull of the
tempest, and then, with an instantaneous impulse, a rush was
made to the beach. Mr Lester was amongst the first to reach it.
It was a scene of darkness and confusion. The moonbeams
touched the white foam of the curling waves, whilst they rose
majestically in the form of lowering arches, and broke against
the rocks with a crashing sound, which seemed as if it must
shake the firm cliffs to their centre. Beyond, the spray of the
troubled sea, and the misty clouds, caused an obscurity every
moment increasing, as the last faint light of sunset faded in the
far west. The crowds on the shore were, for the most part,
crossing and recrossing each other, bringing contradictory
reports, arguing, exclaiming, asseverating; but in one spot a
few men had collected, and were discussing in loud and angry
tones the possibility of rendering assistance to the distressed
vessel, which could be seen lying directly in a line with the
angle of the steep cliff usually known by the name of Dark
Head Point.

'We must throw a rope from the cliff; no boat will live in
such a sea,' said a coarse voice, which would have been known
at once as Captain Vivian's even without the profaneness that
was the constant accompaniment of his words. .

'Too far,' replied Goff, who was standing by his side, exa-

C

mining the scene with a cool, practised eye, and not even shrinking when a second cry of agonising distress fell upon the ear.
' They must even go, if 'tis Heaven's will they should.'

Captain Vivian moved away to obtain a view from a higher
position, and at the same moment Mr Lester drew near.

' Too far, Goff? and will no one try the boat ? '

Goff touched his hat, but his manner was surly : ' Your reverence may try. It 's just tossing away your life, but you can try.'

Mr Lester considered. It was madness, utter madness, for
him at least. He looked round for another opinion.

' A quarter of an hour hence the tide will have turned,' said
a fisherman who was standing near.

' And a quarter of an hour hence,' exclaimed Goff, ' they will
be in '——

Mr Lester stopped him. ' On earth, we trust, Goff. Fifty
pounds reward,' he shouted loudly, ' to any one who will undertake to man the boat and be off to the ship !' but his voice was
lost in the roar of the elements, and the deep call of another gun
of distress. Once more he looked round, hopeless and despairing. Ronald Vivian was close to him.

' Mr Lester, one word with you.' He drew him aside : ' If I
never return, say to Miss Campbell that I obeyed her.' He
caught hold of the boat to push it from the beach.

Mr Lester held him back. ' Ronald ! this is actual frenzy !
Your father and Goff are the only persons fit to go.'

' Their lives are precious,' said the boy, scornfully. ' Mine ! '
—he seized Mr Lester's hand—' I am but a stumbling-block in
the path. Clement will be safe when I am gone.' Again he
laid hold of the boat.

At that moment a shout arose from the cliff. ' They are off !
brave fellows ! they are off !' followed by a deep, muttered prayer,
' God help them !' and like one body, the crowd hurried to the
spot from whence they could best watch the fate of the little boat,
which in desperation had at length been committed to the waves.
It was manned by three experienced sailors, and bravely and resolutely it made its way, followed by a breathless silence, as one
moment it was borne upon the crest of the waves, and the next
sank into the deep abyss of the angry water as if never to rise
again.

Ronald had thrown himself upon the beach, and his head was
buried in his hands. Mr Lester spoke to him gently: ' It is best,
Ronald, as it is ; we must pray for them.'

Ronald made no answer. 'They are gone! they are gone!' was the cry heard amidst the tempest, and he started to his feet. But the black speck, though scarcely discernible, was still to be seen breasting the waves; it was nearing the ship. Ronald rushed to the edge of the water, and stood there with his arms folded moodily upon his breast. Mr Lester followed him near, yet not so near as to be observed. The moonlight fell upon the boy's tall firmly-built figure and noble features. The expression of his countenance was very painful ;—cold and proud, and when he heard his father's coarse voice shouting from the cliffs, recklessly desperate. 'Ronald,' said Mr Lester, approaching to him, 'you would have done a brave deed, and God accepts the will.'

'Perhaps so,' was the answer. 'It is all that is allowed to me ;' and he moved away.

The boat was not to be seen ; whether sunk, or passed beyond the power of sight, none could say. The moon was hidden by a thick cloud. The howling of the wind, the rush of the waters, silenced every other sound ; and only a light raised in the unfortunate vessel showed that human life was at stake. The darkness continued for several minutes, — minutes which seemed hours. A voice from the crowd uttered a loud, shrill call. Some said it was answered, but it might have been only the scream of the stormy blast. 'Try again!' and a second time the sharp yell seemed to rush over the wide waste of waters, seeking for a response. It came ; yes, it was a human voice ; a cheer, a cry of exultation, and the moon for a moment appearing showed the little boat crowded with people, tossed upon the crest of a mountainous wave. It will be swamped ; it must be ; a huge mass of waters is about to fall upon it; but no, it has risen again, the awful power conquered by human skill : still it seems to make no progress, and now it is lost to sight; the moon has sunk back again into darkness. Oh! for one minute of peace on the restless ocean to make certain the door of escape.

Ronald never moved nor spoke. His eyes were riveted, as by a basilisk fascination, on the spot where the boat was likely to appear. And it did appear, nearing the shore, guided by a hand which knew well how to break the force of every wave, and direct it amidst the rough breakers. It was all but in ; all but within safe reach of the shore. A cheer rose, loud, prolonged ; ending—surely it was a scream of terror! A wave had passed over the boat, and it was upset.

Fearful, awful, was the scene that followed ; struggles for life, —ineffectual attempts at assistance,—the engulphing of last hopes in the foaming ocean. A man's head was seen rising above the waters, his hand was clasping the shaggy weeds depending from a rock ; they seemed firm, but the power of death was in the grasp, and they were giving way ; in another moment he would be gone. Ronald flung aside his coat, and cast himself into the sea ; few saw him, none cheered him, he was doomed.

They had sunk both together ; but they rose again, the stranger clinging to Ronald as he struggled with the water. A mighty wave is near, it must cover them ; but no, they have risen upon its crest ; and now, as if in angry disappointment, it has cast them from it ;—they are safe !

Mr Lester was at some distance. Seven men had with great difficulty been rescued, and he was giving directions for their restoration. Another boat was being manned for the purpose of going back again to the ship ; all was excitement and confusion. None noticed Ronald, or thought of him. He knelt by the side of the man whom he had saved, chafing his hands, covering him with the coat which he had himself thrown aside, and at length, with the assistance of another boy of about his own age, though much inferior to himself in power, carried him to the shelter of a boat-house.

The senses, which had been paralysed as much by horror as by the actual risk that had been run, soon returned, and by that time other assistance was at hand, and arrangements were made for conveying the man to the farm. Ronald's manner was indifferent and cold ; he answered the few questions put to him shortly and uncourteously ; and, when he found his charge in safe hands, took advantage of the suggestions made that he should look after himself, to walk away alone towards his own home.

CHAPTER VII.

THE morning after the storm rose bright, clear, and comparatively calm, though deep shadows from flying clouds were still crossing the sea, and the white breakers tossed their diminished heads with an anger not yet exhausted.

Bertha Campbell, Ella, and Clement were together on a little hillock from which a wide view of the sea was to be obtained. Dark Head Point was visible, and the wreck of the shattered vessel, stranded amongst the rocks upon which it had drifted during the night.

'Three lives lost!' said Ella; 'how terrible!' and she shuddered.

'And seven saved!' said Bertha. 'That one ought to be thankful for.'

'Eight,' observed Clement, quickly; 'Ronald saved one.'

'Yes, I heard it,' said Bertha. There was a glistening in her eye, but it was a strangely imperturbable manner.

'Clement would have done the same if he had been there,' said Ella.

'Yes, he might.'

'Might! O Aunt Bertha! it is certain.'

'He has not been tried, Ella.'

'And therefore you doubt me, Aunt Bertha,' said Clement, haughtily. 'Thank you for your opinion of me.'

'I only judge from what I see, Clement. If you are not equal to ordinary duties, I don't know why I am to expect you to perform extraordinary ones.'

'Ronald does not do ordinary duties that I can ever see,' continued Clement.

'Ronald is no guide for you,' replied Bertha. 'At this moment you are neglecting your work.'

'Who can be expected to work such a morning as this?' exclaimed Clement. 'Mr Lester himself is gone down to the village and to the shore.'

'It is his business, Clement; it is not yours.'

'And it is his pleasure!' exclaimed Clement. 'He is gone to the farm to see Ronald's friend.'

Bertha merely repeated her observation, that Mr Lester attended to his business, and therefore Clement ought to attend to his, and then suggested to Ella that it was time for the children's lessons to begin. Ella said, 'Is it?' but she did not move from the grass upon which she was seated, leaning against the stone that supported the flag-staff, and gazing dreamily upon the sea.

'You will take cold, Ella,' said Bertha; 'it is a great deal too damp to sit upon the grass.'

'Oh no, I shan't, Aunt Bertha. The grass is quite dry.'

Bertha stooped down to feel it, and showed the drops glisten-ing on her hand.

'I never take cold by sitting on the grass,' said Ella; 'I never take cold at all, indeed, except when I sit in a draught.'

'Every one takes cold, Ella, who sits upon wet grass.'

'Every one except me,' repeated Ella. 'Aunt Bertha, if you are going in, will you just tell the little ones to get their lessons ready. I suppose one must move,' she added, rising lazily.

Bertha went into the house, and Ella turned to her brother, and said, 'She is put out.'

'Of course she is,' replied Clement; 'she is always put out. And isn't it aggravating, Ella, the way in which she never will give me credit for a single thing that is brave or noble? One would think I was a mere automaton.'

'I don't mind her,' said Ella; 'she hasn't a spark of poetry or enthusiasm in her composition. If she had been on the shore, I venture to say she would have stayed to calculate exactly the claims of her own life before she would have ventured to risk it for another.'

'It won't do for me that sort of thing,' said Clement, pursuing the bent of his own thoughts. 'If they want me to listen to them they mustn't try to keep me in leading-strings in that fashion. Why, there are many boys who have been half over the world and are their own masters at my age.'

'It will come to an end,' said Ella, reseating herself on a stone; 'all things come to an end if one waits long enough.'

'Very well for a girl!' he exclaimed, impetuously; 'but what is to be done with the years that go by whilst one is waiting?'

'Make them a preparation for those which are to come, Cle-ment,' said a grave voice.

Clement started, for it was Mr Lester's. He was looking very pale, very haggard,—a year might have passed over him since the last evening. His manner too was different from its usual quiet, almost stern rigidity; its restlessness showed how much he must have gone through. Ella was very fond of him, and all her better feelings were called forth when she saw him suffering. She begged him now to go into the house, and let her fetch him a glass of wine. She was sure he was over-tired, and if he didn't take care he would be ill. But he would not go in; 'He would rather,' he said, 'remain with them where they were; the fresh air would do him good;' and he sat down by Ella at the foot of the flag-staff.

'Those tiresome lessons!' murmured Ella to her brother.

'Oh, nonsense, you can't go now,' was his reply, in an undertone.

'A few minutes can't signify,' added Ella, rather speaking to
herself than to Clement. 'Dear Mr Lester, do let me go in and
bring you something out here.' She spoke now with animation
and eagerness: her heart was in her words.

'Thank you, dear child, no. One can't forget last night,
Ella.'

'No,' replied Ella, awed by his manner.

'And Clement might have been exposed to danger too,' he
continued.

'Goff would never take me, sir, if there was danger,' said
Clement, a little moodily.

'He ought not to take you at all, Clement.' Mr Lester's
voice trembled.

'You are too tired to talk, sir,' said Ella, looking at him
anxiously. 'Shall we leave you?'

'Yes; and yet,'—he placed his hand on her head,—'Ella, one
thought was in my mind, haunting it all last night,—that
Clement might have been where others then were. I wonder
whether either of you thought of it too.'

'I believe it was wrong in me to propose going out on the
water, sir,' said Clement, candidly; 'but when I had made an
engagement, I didn't like to break it.'

'An after engagement cannot cancel a former one,' said Mr
Lester. 'Our first engagement in all cases is to God.'

'He was never absolutely told not to go,' said Ella.

Clement refused to accept the excuse: 'He knew,' he said,
'that it was not quite right, but it seemed such a little thing, he
couldn't really believe it signified; certainly he should have gone
but for some blunder of Ronald's which made them all late.' And
then he muttered something about seafaring life, and that he
must prepare if he ever intended to go to sea.

Mr Lester was silent. Clement knew that he had said what
was very painful; and, anxious to turn the conversation, he
asked whether Ronald's friend was recovered.

'Yes, tolerably; he has gone to Cleve: his name is Bruce;
the vessel was an American.'

The answers were given shortly, and Clement was afraid to
pursue the subject.

'I had better go in to the lessons now,' said Ella. She did

not know what else to say or do, and the claim of the forgotten duty reasserted itself.

'I am going home,' said Mr Lester: 'tell your aunt I shall not see her probably to-day; I must be alone as much as possible.' The last words were spoken in an undertone. He stood up to go. 'Clement, are you ready for me?'

'Yes, sir; that is, I shall be. I will follow you.'

'I would rather you should go with me;' and Mr Lester paused, and his eyes wandered over the sea.

'Here is Rachel!' said Ella, as she turned towards the parsonage garden. Mr Lester's face brightened in an instant.

'How she runs!' continued Ella: 'I never could move so fast.'

It seemed but one bound, and Rachel was at her father's side. 'Nurse Robinson is waiting for you, papa. She says you expected her. And, Ella, dear,' and Rachel produced a folded paper, 'I have copied the lines, and thank you so much; they are beautiful.'

'May I see them?' said Mr Lester, taking them from her hand.

'Longfellow's "Excelsior,"' said Ella, looking over his shoulder. 'Rachel, and Clement, and I mean to make a Latin translation of them.'

'Papa, you admire them, don't you?' asked Rachel, noticing the peculiar expression of his face.

'Of course I do, my love; who could help it?'

'And you think them very true and right in their meaning?'

'Yes, entirely so.'

'And you like us to like them?'

Mr Lester paused. Ella looked up at him quickly. Her dark, expressive eyes seemed in a moment to read the meaning of his silence, and as the colour rushed to her cheeks, she said, 'Mr Lester wishes us to follow them, not merely to like them.' She did not wait to hear his answer, but walked slowly into the house without wishing any one good-bye.

Bertha was in the little room which opened from the drawing-room, and was used as a schoolroom. It had no carpet, and its chief furniture consisted of tables, stools, and book-cases. There was only one piano in the house, and that was in the drawing-room. Everything in the apartment was neat, it could not be otherwise when Bertha Campbell superintended, but the room had the same air of poverty as the rest of the house; a poverty contrasting remarkably with the appearance of the persons who inhabited it.

Bertha was energetic and simple in all she did, and would have dusted a room as willingly as she would have studied a foreign language; but no one, on looking at her, would have supposed that she was born to such work; whilst Ella with her indolent, graceful movements, and little Fanny with her slight figure and delicate features, seemed only fitted for the luxury of an eastern climate. Louisa, indeed, was different, but even she moved and spoke with an air of command which would have needed a dozen servants to be in attendance instead of the tidy little girl who did duty as both housemaid and parlour-maid.

When Ella returned from the garden, she found Bertha engaged in hearing Louisa's lessons, and superintending Fanny's copy. She did not appear to perceive that her aunt had been taking her duties for her. It was so common a circumstance as not, in Ella's eyes, to need ' Thank you,' and Bertha, on her part, made no remark upon Ella's absence; but Louisa was reproved rather sharply for a blunder she had just made, and Fanny was told that if she did not hold her pen better she would be sent up-stairs. Ella threw herself into a low seat, and, leaning back, exclaimed that it was tremendously hot, and she was dying with sleep: she wished it was the fashion in England to take siestas.

' You can have one, if you like it,' said Bertha, a little satirically.

' Very well for you to say, Aunt Bertha, who can manage your time as you like. Oh dear! these tiresome lessons! Fanny, are you ready with your French translation?'

' Not quite,' said Fanny.

' Then, why aren't you?'

' I hadn't time to do it last evening.'

'You know you would insist upon going such a distance in your walk, Ella,' observed Bertha. 'The children came in a great deal too late to finish what they had to do.'

' I can't hear it, if it is not ready,' said Ella. ' What can you do, Fanny?'

' I can say my dates, and vocabulary, and dialogue, I think.'

' Well, come then.'

' Had you not better go up-stairs, and put your shawl away, Ella?' said Bertha, 'and then you will come down quite fresh again.'

'No, thank you. It is a great deal too hot to move,' and Ella tossed her shawl into the farthest corner of the room. Bertha put down the lesson-book, took up the shawl, and sent Louisa up-stairs with it.

'Now, Fanny,' said Ella.

Fanny began, and repeated a tolerably correct lesson, or, at least, such as seemed to be so; for it was one of Ella's theories that it was useless to make children say things exactly as they were in the book.

'It can't have taken Fanny much time to learn that, Ella,' observed Bertha; 'she can't have read it over more than twice or three times.'

'She knows the sense very well,' said Ella; 'and that is all one wants.'

'All one wants for to-day, but not for to-morrow. The sense is the spirit, the words are the body; how can you retain the spirit if you give up the body?'

'It is too hot to argue,' said Ella. 'But if spirit has to act upon spirit, what need is there of a body?'

'Spirit alone never does act upon spirit in this world,' said Bertha.

Ella yawned, and closed her eyes. A tingling, irritable bell was just then rung. Bertha gave Louisa her book, told her she had made three mistakes, and hurried out of the room, almost before Ella had time to unclose her eyes, and ask what was the matter.

Ella certainly exerted herself more when left to herself. It seemed as if a perverse feeling made her determined upon show-ing herself more indolent in proportion as Bertha was energetic. She drew her chair closer to the table, finished hearing Fanny's lesson, then made her go back to her copy, and bade Louisa bring her French History. That lesson was pleasant enough. Ella liked being read to, and she was very fond of history, and had a marvellous memory for dates.

'I have finished the ten pages,' said Louisa, as she came to the conclusion of a chapter.

'Never mind, go on; you must hear about Henri Quatre.'

Louisa glanced at the clock. 'It is a quarter to one, Ella, and it is my music-lesson day.'

Ella's sigh might have been that of a martyr.

'I shall give you your lesson in the evening, go on now.'

'And shall I say the questions in the evening?'

'We will see, go on.'

Louisa was not fond of history, and cared but little for Henri Quatre; and she was provoked at having all her time occupied and so much added to her lesson hours. She read very badly, and Ella was impatient, and, striking the table in irritation, shook Fanny's hand, and made her blot an exercise which she had begun; the copy having long since been brought to an end, and put aside with scarcely a glance or an observation. Fanny burst into tears. She was a very untidy writer, and her exercise books were proverbially slovenly, and Bertha had lately endeavoured to stimulate her to carefulness by the promise of a reward whenever six exercises should be written without a blot.

'You shouldn't cry, Fanny,' said Louisa; 'you will make your eyes red, and then you won't be fit to be seen.'

And it is so silly, too,' said Ella; 'crying about nothing! what does it signify? Take it up with your blotting paper, and it will all be right.'

She returned again to Henri Quatre, and left Fanny to mourn in lonely sorrow over the loss of her anticipated present; for Aunt Bertha had no mercy upon excuses. The blot was there, that was enough. There would be no question of how it came.

The clock struck one. 'I should have just time for my music lesson,' said Louisa, imploringly.

'What? yes!' Ella was still dreaming over the history.

'Louisa, hasn't Aunt Bertha got the Henriade? Just go and fetch it, there's a good child.'

'The what, Ella?'

'The Henriade, Voltaire's Henriade; don't you know?'

Louisa walked slowly out of the room, and came back with a message that Aunt Bertha was engaged, and couldn't attend to anything of the kind at present. Ella did not seem quite to hear. Louisa went to the piano, opened it, and put up her music-book.

'Louisa, it won't take you a minute; just run across the garden up to the Rectory. Mr Lester has the Henriade. I am nearly sure I saw it in his study the other day. He will let me have it.'

Louisa looked excessively discomposed, and did not move.

'Go, child, go,' said Ella.

'Shall I go?' asked Fanny. She was very tired of lessons, and much enjoyed the thought of a run across the turf.

'Yes; only you don't understand. There, give me a piece of

paper and a pencil ; not that one, that is slate-pencil. Where is the one you were drawing with last night ?'

'I don't know ; I left it on the table. Louisa, it was your turn to put away the things.'

'O Fanny! indeed, if you remember, I took two days to-gether, because you had a headache.'

'That was a week ago,' said Fanny, fretfully ; 'it was your turn, I am sure.'

'Never mind whose turn it was,' exclaimed Ella ; 'only fetch me a pencil.'

'I don't know where to find one,' said Fanny.

'Not know where to find a pencil ? Why, there are hundreds in the house. Louisa, give me one of your drawing-pencils.'

'Aunt Bertha said I was not to lend them,' said Louisa.

Ella's colour rose. 'I can't trouble myself about that. I must have one.'

Louisa had evidently no intention of obeying. She sat playing with the leaves of the music-book, her face resolutely directed away. Ella took up a pen, and began to write with it instead.

'There, Fanny,' and she tossed the note to the child, who ran off with it. Ella was too much annoyed with Louisa to take any notice of her ; and the practising was begun and continued whilst Ella sat at the table drawing mathematical figures on a sheet of note paper.

'That is the first dinner-bell,' said Louisa, and she jumped down from her seat, and shut up the piano.

No answer.

'Fanny will be late,' she continued, 'she won't hear the bell.'

'She has plenty of time,' replied Ella, coldly.

'Grandmamma will be angry,' persisted Louisa.

'You had better go and get ready yourself, Louisa,' said Ella.

'I must put the room tidy first,' was the answer ; and Louisa, with the most determined spirit of neatness and provokingness, not only moved away everything which belonged to herself and to Fanny, but also divers little articles of property appertaining to Ella. 'Fanny will be late,' she repeated, as she hastened out of the room, leaving Ella nothing to distract her eye from the contemplation of the tables and chairs, except the sheet of note paper on which she was scribbling.

The second dinner-bell rang, and Ella was not ready, and Fanny was still at the Rectory. Mrs Campbell was exceedingly annoyed, for punctuality was her darling virtue, and Louisa triumphantly told the history of how and why it all happened, and was informed by her grandmamma that she was the only person in the house tó be depended upon; whilst Bertha reminded Ella that if she had come in in proper time, the lessons would have been all finished by one o'clock.

Fanny appeared when dinner was half over ; and being received by harsh words and severe glances, burst into another fit of crying, and was again warned by Mrs Campbell, as the most conclusive and natural argument for self-restraint, that she would quite spoil her face, and make herself such a figure she would not be fit to be seen.

That had been a very instructive morning to the children. They had had lessons in unpunctuality, ingratitude, self-indulgence, procrastination, absence of sympathy, impatience, disobedience to orders, ill-nature, self-conceit, and vanity, and all through the medium of French exercises and the life of Henri Quatre.

CHAPTER VIII.

ELLA had a fit of the Henriade that afternoon, and could not go out; so she said. She wanted to compare the great epic poems of different countries, and she had a notion of writing an essay upon them. She had read Dante often, and knew Milton by heart, Homer was familiar to her, and she had a vague idea of the merits of the Lusiad, which, no doubt, was more than half the world could boast of. Not that Ella thought much about the world. With all her wonderful talent, she was free from conceit, and had scarcely any wish for admiration. When she talked of writing an essay upon epic poets, it was solely for her own amusement. She had no grand visions of fame and flattery; and if, now and then, a stray word of astonishment as to her mental powers reached her ears, it was always received with surprise. That which was so easy to her, could not, she supposed, be difficult to other people.

And then Ella never, or very rarely, finished anything. She always worked from impulse, and her natural temperament was extremely indolent. Clement could sometimes persuade her to conclude what she had begun, but no one else. And he was very like herself, and seldom fancied to-day what he had delighted in yesterday. They were two very interesting, clever, agreeable companions, when they chose to be ; but the clouds on a windy day were not more changeable, and they always required the stimulus of success to make them pursue any subject. Ella's portfolio was filled with notes from history, unfinished poems, imitations of various authors, problems from Euclid, observations on botany, hints upon geology, copies of Hebrew and Arabic letters, interpersed with grotesque caricatures, clever pencil sketches, or grand designs in some new style of water-colours. The marvel was, that in attempting to know so much, she should succeed in knowing anything. A person with less natural powers would have been utterly crushed by the mountain of mental dust accumulated by these broken ideas ; but Ella's memory was so retentive, and her powers of perception were so keen, that, give her any fragments of knowledge, however broken, and she could put them together, when occasion required, so as to present a very fair semblance of real information.

'Ella knows everything,' was Mrs Campbell's proud remark, when some chance observation brought out from the stores of her granddaughter's memory a forgotten or obsolete fact.

'Ella does nothing,' was Bertha's mournful observation to Mr Lester, when conversing upon the children's future prospects.

There are different powers of mind required for knowing and doing. People often cultivate the former whilst they neglect the latter. They do not see that we may know without doing, but we can scarcely continue long in doing without knowing.

But to give Ella all the excuse possible, she had had very little teaching or training in either the one or the other. After an infancy passed in the enervating climate of the West Indies, she had been sent to England, and placed under the care of persons who did not understand her, and who, if they had understood her, would not have known how to guide her. Mrs Campbell was in her younger days, the most rigid of disciplinarians. She had tutored, and checked, and warned, and fretted her own daughters, until one in despair rushed into a hasty and unfortunate marriage, and the other became a pattern of obedience and self-denial, but with all her warm, natural impulses chilled, her powers of enjoyment deadened, and her notions of goodness, either moral or religious, absorbed in the one stern idea of duty—duty both for herself and others, but without mercy and without love.

And Ella had no natural love of duty. Perhaps it may be said that we none of us have. Yet, surely, this is not so. There is an innate taste for duty, which goes with the love of order and regularity, and the spirit of perseverance. Some persons like to continue any habits they have commenced; they like to keep to rules; they are very particular about punctuality and neatness; all these things are the germs of duty. When softened by unselfishness and warm feelings they will form a very superior character. But Ella's mind, and Ella's theories—and she very early began to form theories—were all based upon two principles, inclination and affection. If they happened to correspond with duty, it was so much the better; if they did not—she really could not do what she felt no interest in doing, she could not work for people who were indifferent to her.

Mrs Campbell, with the singular weakness which makes the most rigid of parents spoil their grandchildren, had early given way to this argument. Ella did so much when work was her choice, that she was allowed to do little or nothing when it was not; whilst Bertha, following the severe reasoning in which she had herself been trained, looked with nearly equal regret upon Ella's doings or not doings, because she said that work performed merely from choice was as little valuable in a moral point of view as idleness.

Ella's had been a trying, fretting, uncongenial life, and she thought herself a martyr. She was by nature intensely proud, and the moment any accusation was brought against herself, she tried that ready weapon of self-defence, retaliation. If Bertha complained of Ella's being indolent and unpractical, Ella complained of Bertha's being cold and harsh. If the one forgot from indolence, the other forgot from over-occupation. If the one was unpunctual because she would not make an effort to be the reverse, the other was so because she was at every one's call for some act of self-denying kindness, and therefore could not reckon her time her own.

There is nothing so blinding as this spirit of retaliation, this pride which makes us always take the offensive when called to stand upon the defensive. It was the greatest possible effort for Ella to confess herself in the wrong. If she ever did, it was not at the moment of accusation, when acknowledgment would have been gracious and humble; but on some after occasion, when other circumstances had softened her feelings, and made it a matter of certainty that the affair would be passed over lightly.

And so Ella Vivian knew nothing of herself, and very little of others, and lived in a world of self-indulgence and self-reliance, all the more dangerous, because her talents made it easy to her to be agreeable, and her freedom from many of the more open and grave faults of her age made it almost impossible to convince her that she was not as good or even better than others.

Mrs Campbell had been at Encombe three months: before that time they had lived at a small country town in the north. No exact reason was given for the change, except that the country was beautiful, and the sea air invigorating, and the village in the neighbourhood of Cleve Hall. To be near their grandfather seemed to Ella quite a sufficient cause for the migration, and she had conjured up many visions of grandeur and enjoyment both for herself and Clement, which were all, however, dispersed on their arrival. Cleve Hall was less open to them than any other house in the village. General Vivian was less known to them than any other person. Even Aunt Mildred, the gentle, cheerful, loving Aunt Mildred, whose smile was fascination, and her voice like the echo of the softest music, was as a person *tabooed*. They rarely saw her; when they did, their visits were short and unsatisfactory. She evidently wished to keep them with her, but she never did. She wished to make them at home with her, but the mystery which enveloped everything at Cleve mutually repelled them. They spoke of their father, and the subject was diverted. They expressed a desire to see something in a distant part of the house, and an excuse was at hand. They asked to run in the garden, and the timepiece was consulted to know whether it would be the hour for Grandpapa to be there also. And if, by any chance, they met the General, the first impulse of every grown-up person who accompanied them seemed to be to avoid him.

Of course Ella asked the meaning of all this. At sixteen, with a most determined will, and a keen curiosity, who would not have done so? And very unsatisfactory were the answers which she received. Mrs Campbell generally began at once to remark upon General Vivian's unbending character; whilst Bertha, dreading to give confidence where she felt none, used generally to stop her by the observation, 'You will know all about it, my dear, in time.'

But Ella felt that she did not know all about it, and that she was not likely to do so. Her father ought to be the heir of Cleve; and Clement was his only son. She had heard of some disagreement with her grandfather, and she knew that her father had lived for many years in the West Indies in consequence; but it seemed very hard that the punishment should also fall upon the children. Bertha told her that her father was a poor man, and certainly, from some cause or other, Ella saw they were all poor. But General Vivian had houses, and lands, and carriages, and servants, and all the luxuries of life at command. A very small sacrifice on his part would have made them comparatively affluent. Why was it not asked for? Ella chafed under her privations. She felt there must be injustice somewhere, and she could not resign herself to it, and when tormented by her own ill-regulated mind, she shared her anger with her twin brother Clement.

And Clement was a willing recipient of all her complaints. Proud and self-indulgent, like Ella, he could not endure to remain in a position which he believed beneath him. But for the influence of his cousin, Ronald Vivian, he might, like her, have spent his time in day-dreams of grandeur; but Ronald was fiery and impetuous, and full of the spirit of adventure; and Clement, feeling the power of his strong will, and admiring the noble points of his character, followed him whenever and wherever he was able, and fancied that in partaking his pursuits he was escaping from boyhood to manhood, and therefore at liberty to be his own master.

Such was the state of affairs at Encombe Lodge; most unfortunate for all, most especially trying to Bertha Campbell.

Ella was only sixteen, whilst Bertha was two-and-thirty. Respect, therefore, was due from the one to the other, if it were only from difference of age. Yet Bertha had great difficulty in exacting it; partly owing to the fact that when the children first came to live with them, Mrs Campbell took the sole charge upon herself, and spoiled them by over-indulgence, whilst she was always blaming Bertha; and partly owing to Bertha's own defect of manner and Ella's superiority of intellect, which made her at sixteen almost a woman. Now, whenever there was a difference between them, Mrs Campbell was appealed to, and invariably took Ella's part; and thus the breach was widened. The ill-feeling extended itself to Clement, who always approved Ella's decisions, and never could bear Aunt Bertha's cold way of reminding him of what he had to do. It was better with the little ones. Louisa liked Aunt Bertha because she was always the same. She suffered so much from Ella's moods,

D

that it was a perfect luxury to turn to some one who was certain to give her a patient hearing, and never found fault unless there was really a cause. She did not love her. Aunt Bertha was not attractive to children ; she was so slow and methodical, and so little understood how to enter into their amusements ; but Louisa respected and obeyed her, and made Fanny do the same. It would have been a great comfort to the children if they had been allowed always to do their lessons with Bertha ; but it was one of Ella's few dreams of usefulness, consequent upon rather a long fit of illness, that she would educate her younger sisters ; and in the days of convalescence she wrote two chapters of a work on education, and formed a plan for a new grammar, which was to make German as easy to learn as French or Italian ; and when pronounced to be quite well, how could she think herself otherwise than competent to undertake any educational task, however important !

Ella had imbibed too many high principles not to have great notions of goodness, and she was too clever not to put them into some tangible form ; but she never liked trying virtues upon herself ; she preferred rather seeing how they suited others. Her theories for Louisa and Fanny were perfectly admirable ; she talked of nothing but education for a whole month, especially to her grandmamma, who was entirely convinced by her, and believed that she was fully as competent to the work as Bertha, if not more so. The plan had been tried now for three months,—ever since they came to Encombe. Bertha resigned herself to it, for the simple reason that there was nothing else to be done ; and when she found that Ella's want of steadiness and perseverance was a stumbling-block in the way of the children's improvement, she quietly undertook all that was left undone, and so, without intending it, increased Ella's self-deception.

Certainly, if there was a martyr in the family it was Bertha. The trials which she had endured in her comparatively short life might have crushed a less brave and enduring spirit to the dust. Little, indeed, did Ella think when she laughed at, and teased, and disobeyed her quiet, cold-mannered, impassive aunt, that thought for her, care for her interests, anxiety for her future prospects, had robbed Bertha's cheek of its bloom, and caused the dark lines of anxiety to shade her forehead. Perhaps it might have been better for her if she had known it ; better if the veil which was cast over the history of her family had been thrown aside, and she had seen herself the helpless, poverty-striken child of a disinherited man, indebted for every comfort which she enjoyed to the self-denying exertions of one whose daily life was rendered miserable by her thoughtless negligence.

CHAPTER IX.

' AUNT BERTHA, we may put on our old things and go to the shore, mayn't we?' Louisa's voice was heard from the top of the stairs. She had been trying to persuade Fanny that it would be better to wear an old bonnet ; and Fanny was not inclined to agree, because she looked much prettier in a new one.

· 'Yes, to the shore ; I shall be ready in five minutes ;' and Louisa retired triumphant. Louisa was in time herself, and contrived that Fanny should be the same ; a circumstance to which she did not fail to draw Bertha's attention, and received as an answer, that punctuality was a good thing, but humility was a better. They set off across the garden to the Rectory, as they were to call for Rachel on their way.

' I dare say Clement will be on the shore,' said Fanny ; 'he said he should go there after he had done with Mr Lester.'

Bertha looked grave.

' Is there any reason why Clement should not go ?' asked the quick-eyed Louisa.

' None, if he does what he ought to do,' was the cautious reply.

' Old Mrs Clarke, the sexton's mother, says he gets about amongst all kinds of people,' said Fanny, ' when he goes to the shore.'

' When did old Mrs Clarke talk to you upon such subjects ?' inquired Bertha.

' Oh ! the other day,' replied Louisa, 'when we went to see her with Ella. She says,' she added, drawing up her head, ' that it is not fit for the heir of such a place as Cleve Hall to be spending his time amongst smugglers and low people.'

' It is not fit for any one who wishes to be a gentleman,' said Bertha, rather sternly ; 'but remember, children, you are not to talk to Mrs Clarke or to any one in that way.'

'We can't help it,' said Fanny; 'she talks to us.'

Bertha's conscience a little reproached her. Perhaps, after all, she was wrong in not giving Ella more confidence. She might learn to be discreet if she were trusted. But Bertha had never received confidence, and it was not easy to learn to give it. She walked on very silently and thoughtfully; and the children, finding she did not enter into what they said, ran along the path together.

They came in front of the Rectory, and passed the library window. Louisa, of course, looked in; her curiosity was insatiable. 'Aunt Bertha,'—and she drew near her aunt,—'there was a stranger with Mr Lester, I am sure.'

'Perhaps so, my dear;' and Bertha only moved on the faster.

'But who could it be?' continued Louisa.

'It must be one of the shipwrecked people,' said Fanny; 'perhaps it was the captain of the vessel.'

'He looked rather like a sailor,' observed Louisa; 'do you think it was the captain, Aunt Bertha?'

'My love, how can I tell? and what does it signify?'

'But if it was the captain, I should like to hear all he has to say, and how it all happened,' said Fanny; 'I dare say he would tell us; and we might make a story out of it. Do you know, Aunt Bertha, we began making out a story yesterday, only Ella said it was nonsense.'

'I'll tell you who it was,' said Louisa, with the air of one who has deeply considered a subject; 'it's that Mr Bruce whom Ronald saved.'

'What do you know about Mr Bruce?' inquired Bertha.

'Oh! the dairy-woman from the farm told Betsy about him, and she told me. He is not very well, and perhaps he may stay at the farm, and perhaps he may be at the Inn at Cleve.'

'Then it is not likely he should be here,' said Bertha.

'He may be going to Cleve by and by,' said Louisa; 'I am sure it is Mr Bruce.' She nodded her head with an air which admitted no open dissent from her opinion.

'Well; we need not trouble ourselves about it; we are not likely to see him,' said Bertha; 'and here is Rachel.'

'And Mrs Robinson with her,' whispered Fanny; whilst Louisa pronounced decidedly, 'I don't like Mrs Robinson.'

Rachel ran up to them. Mrs Robinson came slowly behind. She was a very different person under different circumstances, and to different people. Now she was not so much reserved as very stiff. She made a respectful curtsey to Bertha, and would have passed on, but Rachel would not let her go. 'Granny, dear, you must wait, and tell Miss Campbell and the others all about it; they will like to hear so much. Wouldn't you like to hear all about the shipwrecked people who were taken in at the farm?' she added, addressing Bertha.

'We wont trouble Mrs Robinson if she is in a hurry,' replied Bertha, civilly, but rather formally : 'you must tell us yourself, Rachel.'

'But I can't. Granny tells stories so much better than I do, and I can't remember it all. There were five Americans, and a Frenchman, and a German, weren't there? And they slept—where did they sleep? O Granny! you must tell all about it.'

'Not now, Miss Rachel; another time, my dear.'

'But tell her just about Ronald. Miss Campbell likes to hear about him always.'

'The young gentleman was off to the ship by daylight,' said Mrs Robinson, speaking very slowly, 'helping to get the goods on shore ; for there are some left on board, though the ship is likely, they say, to go to pieces. But that's like him, ma'am, as you know.'

'And Mr Bruce wanted to see him and thank him,' added Rachel; 'but Ronald is so strange he won't go near him.'

'And it's Mr Bruce who is in the library with your papa, Rachel ; isn't it ?' inquired Louisa.

Mrs Robinson answered for her rather quickly, 'Yes, Miss Louisa, it is Mr Bruce. He is going into Cleve this afternoon, to look about him. I think, ma'am, if you are thinking of the shore you had best make haste, if you will excuse my saying so ; the tide will be on the turn soon.' She moved away.

'There now,' and Louisa clapped her hands ; 'didn't I say it was Mr Bruce ? I am always right. What is he like, Rachel ?'

'Oh! I don't know. I only saw him for a moment. He came into the room with papa, and said how d'ye do; but of course I didn't stare at him.'

'I should have stared, though,' whispered Louisa. 'I think he looks very like a sailor.'

'I wish I could have asked him how he felt when he believed he was going to be drowned,' said Rachel, very thoughtfully. 'Papa told me once, that some people, when they have been nearly drowned, have had all their lives come back to them,—all they have done.'

She stopped suddenly, as if trying to realise the idea. Bertha lingered also.

'Do you think it is so? Do you think it is possible?' said Rachel.

'Quite possible, dear Rachel.'

'But do you think it is so?'

'Yes, if people say it.'

'And do they look like other people, and come back and live amongst them, as they did before?'

'They look like others,—one may hope they don't live quite like them.'

'Then, Miss Campbell,' and Rachel clung closely to Bertha's side, and her voice was full of awe, 'I wish that God would let me be nearly drowned.'

Bertha half-started.

'It isn't wicked, is it?' continued Rachel, anxiously, as she watched the expression of Bertha's countenance. 'But I would bear anything, yes, anything in all the world, to be very, wonderfully good. Wouldn't you?' In her enthusiasm she caught Bertha's hand, and held it as they walked on together.

'Yes indeed, Rachel;' and Bertha's cold, calm eyes sparkled with a lightning flash of animation.

'Wonderfully good,' continued Rachel; 'not a little good, but, oh!' and she drew a long breath, 'so very, very,—beyond all thought. Will God make us so, if we wish it?'

Bertha hesitated. 'We may hope He will, if we can bear the means.'

There was a pause; and then Bertha heard, almost in a whisper, the words, 'I would try.'

Rachel seemed considering something deeply; and after a few seconds, resuming her natural tone, said: 'Is there any harm in thinking about it a great deal, and liking it, in a way?'

'What do you mean, Rachel?'

'I can't exactly explain; but don't you know how Ella likes to read about knights, and tournaments, and persons being brave and generous,—what one reads in Froissart, and those books?'

'Yes; well:' and Bertha turned to her with an air of mingled wonder and interest.

'Then, when Ella reads about such things, and gets into a way about them, I never feel as she does; but I do feel it when I read about martyrs, and people who have been so good; and it makes my heart beat fast, and my head seems almost dizzy, as if I could do anything to be like them. Is it wrong?'

'Of course not, dear Rachel; you can't help it.'

'But do you ever feel it?'

The answer was low and doubtful : 'I hope I do.'

'I don't think all people do,' continued Rachel; 'and it puzzles me, and sometimes I think that, perhaps, it is being proud and presumptuous to long to be first in anything.'

'We can only be first by being last in those things,' said Bertha.

'No; and perhaps I am not willing to be last : and yet it seems '—— she hesitated, and added : 'Aunt Mildred says she should not wish for the glory, if she might only have the love.'

Bertha's eyes glistened.

'Aunt Mildred would be so glad if she could have you to talk to as I have,' continued Rachel, eagerly.

'Aunt Mildred doesn't know anything about me,' replied Bertha ; whilst her manner became in a moment constrained.

'I talk to her about you,' said Rachel, 'and she very often says she should like to see you. Will you go with me to the Hall some day?'

'Aunt Mildred is very kind, and talks about things which interests you, Rachel,' replied Bertha ; 'but I don't believe she would really like to see me.'

'Not if she says it?' exclaimed Rachael. 'O Miss Campbell! then she would say what was not true.'

'She would like to see me, for your sake,' replied Bertha, in the same tone of cold reserve ; 'she would not wish it for her own.'

The conversation dropped. When Bertha assumed this peculiar manner she was impenetrable.

Rachel was chilled, yet she was very fond of Bertha Campbell ; she had an intuitive appreciation of her excellence,—a conviction that upon the points nearest her own heart she might obtain sympathy from her. Might! for it was never certain. Bertha was unable to bring out her own feelings ; perhaps even she was uncertain that she had them, and often she expressed wonder when Rachel expected sympathy. Yet Rachel's simple, true devotion, and her open-hearted warmth of affection, often touched a chord in Bertha's heart which seemed to unlock a new source of untold pleasure. Love in religion was very new to her. She had been educated with a dread of expressing strong feeling of any kind ; and had known fatal results from the indulgence of what she had been taught to call enthusiasm ; and so she always suspected that evil must lurk under it.

Yet she could not warn Rachel, still less in any way reprove her. Even when unable to comprehend her, she could see that Rachel possessed something which was wanting in herself, and which would make her life much happier. Perhaps the charm was all the greater because it seemed beyond her reach. She felt as though Rachel belonged to a different race, and as if by being with her a vent was opened for the latent poetry of feeling which, unknown to herself, was unquestionably a part of her own character.

They reached the shore ; the wind had gone down rapidly since the morning, and now the sea was as calm as if the wrathful tempest had never passed over it. The hulk of the dismantled vessel, however, bore witness to its fatal work, and the shore was covered with persons groping about in the hope of picking up something that might be worth carrying away. Bertha had forgotten this possibility, and when she saw the numbers assembled, her first impulse was to go back. Louisa strongly opposed the idea, and Fanny nearly cried with disappointment.

'You know, Aunt Bertha,' said Louisa, 'that if we go back we shall have had no walk at all to speak of, and grandmamma wishes'——

'I am the best judge of grandmamma's wishes, Louisa : there are too many people here, a great deal. I can't possibly let you go amongst them.'

Rachel gazed wistfully on the vessel. 'The tide is so far out that we could have gone quite close to it,' she said. 'How unfortunate !'

'And it will be all to pieces in a day or two,' observed Louisa. 'Goff says there isn't a chance for it.'

'Goff, my dear Louisa ! how do you know anything of what he thinks ?'

'Oh ! because a man came to the back door when Fanny and I were in the garden this morning, and we heard him talking to Betsy, and telling what the people in the village said.'

'Always listening,' was Bertha's comment : to which Louisa replied, with a blush, that she could not help hearing what was said quite close to her ; adding, however, directly afterwards,

'That is, I think I might have got out of the way if I had wished it.'

'I should like Ronald to be here to tell us where the rock was that Mr Bruce was clinging to,' said Rachel, as they stood upon the summit of the cliff and looked down.

Bertha had appeared uninterested before, but she woke up at the observation. 'It was the farthest of those great rocks you see out towards the point,' she said.

'Oh! the Lion, and the Bear, and the Fox, we always call them,' exclaimed Fanny. 'It must have been the Lion, for that has the most sea-weed growing upon it.'

'Yes, the Lion's mane, as Ella calls it,' observed Louisa. 'She said one day she meant to write some verses about it. I dare say she will, now there has been such an adventure.'

'And Ronald will be the hero!' exclaimed Fanny, clapping her hands. 'Won't it be fun, Rachel?'

Rachel did not answer directly.

'Shouldn't you like Ella to write something about it?' again inquired Fanny.

'I don't quite know; I don't think I should like Ronald to be written about, at least not in that way.'

'Rachel, how absurd!' exclaimed Louisa. 'Why not?'

Bertha listened attentively to the reply.

'I can't exactly say; it is something I feel, but Miss Campbell will know;' and Rachel turned to Bertha, feeling at once that she was speaking to some one who would understand without words. 'If Ella could write just what Ronald felt, I shouldn't care,' she continued. 'But then how could she?'

'She might imagine it,' said Louisa.

'But if it were imagination, it wouldn't be true.'

'And it must be some one different from Ella to understand Ronald truly,' said Bertha, in a low voice.

'Thank you, thank you; that was just what I meant, only I couldn't explain.'

Louisa and Fanny moved away, not caring for the explanation. Rachel held Bertha's hand, and drew her nearer to the edge of the cliff. Her eyes were riveted on the rock, and a long time elapsed before she spoke. At last, without any preface, she said, 'Miss Campbell, is Ronald good?'

Silence was her answer; and when she looked round a tear was rolling down Bertha's cheek. Rachel asked no more questions, but followed Louisa and Fanny; and Bertha was left alone.

The children seated themselves on a bench placed on the top of the cliff. Louisa and Fanny were sufficiently amused by watching what was going on below; and even Rachel, though she occasionally glanced at the spot where Bertha was standing, soon entered into their interest, and laughed more merrily than either.

'A beautiful evening, young ladies,' said a voice behind them. Rachel started, and involuntarily stood up to move away when she saw Captain Vivian.

'Come down to see the fun, I suppose?' he continued.

'Yes, thank you, I think,—Louisa, had we not better go to your aunt?'

'Oh! never mind me; don't let me interrupt you. How d'ye do, Miss Campbell?' and Captain Vivian held out his hand to Bertha, who at that moment came up. Bertha greeted him formally, and a sign to the children told them they were to go on; and with an instinctive terror of Captain Vivian, they ran till they were quite beyond the reach of his voice.

'It's a long time since we met to talk, Miss Campbell. I've been away a good deal till lately. But you are looking as if the sea air agreed with you.'

He evidently meant to be courteous; and though Bertha was so pale as to belie the compliment which had been paid her, she showed no wish to shun the interview.

'I scarcely expected to find you at Encombe, when we came here, Captain Vivian,' she said.

'You thought I should keep farther from the General's quarters. Well, perhaps it might be just as well if I did; but there's something in the sight of old ocean after all which tempts a man, when he's been used to it; and the Grange was empty, and so Ronald and I have e'en taken up our quarters there.'

'Ronald is as fond of the sea as yourself,' remarked Bertha.

'Perhaps he may be, but he's a strange fellow is Ronald; one never knows what he will be at.'

'His taste for the sea was a taste from infancy,' said Bertha. 'I remember'——

He interrupted her quickly; 'Yes, yes. You are right; he always had a taste for it; but he's too old.'

'For the naval service? yes,' replied Bertha, timidly.

'For any service, unless I choose it;' and in an instant an angry flush overspread Captain Vivian's face, whilst he muttered to himself, 'Am I never to be left alone?'

Bertha stood her ground. 'We have not met for so long, Captain Vivian,' she said, 'that you must forgive me if I touch upon unwelcome subjects.'

'I don't know what long acquaintance it requires to learn that interference must always be unwelcome,' he replied. 'But you are one of Mr Lester's apt scholars, Miss Bertha.'

'My interference, if you can call it such,' replied Bertha, 'dates long before my acquaintance with Mr Lester.'

'Then it is the old story,' he exclaimed. 'I should have thought that years might have taught you wisdom.'

'I trust they have in some measure,' replied Bertha; 'but they have not taught me that there is either wisdom or goodness in looking with indifference upon the child of'——

He interrupted her, and his manner changed into patronising indifference.

'We won't quarrel, Miss Bertha; we have had enough of that in our day. Since we are neighbours, we may as well be friendly when we meet.'

'Quite as well,' said Bertha; 'if we are to meet at all.'

He seemed a little piqued, and answered hastily, 'Oh! then you had thought of cutting me, had you? The way of the world; off with old friends, and on with new.'

'I could not have supposed that you would look upon me as a friend,' replied Bertha. 'It was scarcely the light in which I was regarded in former times.'

He bit his lip. 'I didn't mean,—of course, I never supposed you would bear malice.'

'I have nothing to bear malice for, Captain Vivian,' replied Bertha. 'I was not the person to suffer.' And there was a stress upon the pronoun which made the coarse, rough man whom she addressed, shrink as with the touch of some sudden pain.

'I don't know why you are so fond of going back to these old times,' he said. 'Why can't we meet, and forget them?'

'Because,' replied Bertha, boldly, 'they are the only grounds upon which our acquaintance can possibly rest. You must be fully aware, Captain Vivian, that if we were now, for the first time, living in the same village, we could never be anything to each other but strangers.'

'Too proud!' he exclaimed, in a tone which yet had very little pride in it. 'Aiming at the Hall, I suppose.'

'Aiming at nothing, I hope,' replied Bertha, as she fixed her eyes upon him, till his sank beneath their gaze; 'but the man who has brought exile, and disgrace, and poverty into a family, can little expect to be received as a friend.'

His face became deadly pale ; twice he tried to speak, and twice the words seemed kept back by some violent inward agitation.

'I know more than I once did, you see,' continued Bertha.

'Aye ! from that meddling, false-hearted'—— he was going to add a string of violent epithets to Mr Lester's name, but Bertha prevented him. Her cold, quiet, womanly dignity seemed to have a strange power over him.

'Mr Lester is my friend,' she said. 'If he can be mentioned in terms of respect, well ; if not, this is the first and last time, Captain Vivian, that I will hear his name from your lips.'

'And what has he been telling you, then ?'

The question was put anxiously, and with a certain tone of deference.

'It must be only painful, and quite unnecessary for me to repeat what you already know so well,' replied Bertha. 'It is sufficient, that after having assisted to ruin the prospects of the father, you yet have it in your power to show repentance by your conduct to the son. Edward Vivian's fate would have been very different from what it is but for your influence. Clement may be restored to all that his father has lost, if only you will not stand in his way.'

'I stand in his way !' and the laugh which accompanied the words made Bertha shrink. 'Why, one would think I was the old General's ally, likely to come over him with smooth words. How can I stand in the boy's way ?'

'You are the General's enemy,' replied Bertha.

'And if I am, what 's that to any one but myself.'

'It may be very much to Clement, if his grandfather thinks that he is your friend,' replied Bertha.

'Tut, tut !' he exclaimed, impatiently ; 'this is all idle talking, Miss Bertha. The boy 's a fine fellow enough, and likes free air and sea breezes ; and Ronald has taken to him—and where 's the harm ?'

'Merely,' replied Bertha, coldly, 'that Ronald's friendship is a sin in General Vivian's eyes.'

'But if it is no sin in reality, since you will harp upon the old question of conscience.'

'It must be sin to Clement,' replied Bertha, 'when it is against the wishes of all his friends.'

'What is that to me?—let his friends take care of him.'

'His friends have very little power, as I suspect you know full well by this time, Captain Vivian,' replied Bertha. 'My mother is too infirm, and has indulged him too much for years. Mr Lester is most kind, but he has only authority over his lessons. Clement is left, most unhappily, to himself; and his whole success in life depends upon the favour of his grandfather. Is it a very hard thing to ask that you should not interfere to mar his prospects?'

'I have told you before,' he exclaimed, 'that there is no interference on my part. It is Ronald's doings, if there is anything of the kind; but I don't see it: they are together every now and then.'

'And not alone,' continued Bertha; 'Ronald's companions become Clement's also—Goff, for instance.'

'Pshaw! if you are as squeamish as that, you must needs shut your boy up in a glass case. But I'll say one thing to you, Miss Bertha; you have shown me a bit of your mind, you must needs let me show you a bit of mine. Fair play's a jewel. Don't you interfere with my game, if you want me not to interfere with yours. Remember my boy is not to be preached over into a milksop, and his head filled with fancies of merchant service, and all that nonsense. Ronald will be what I choose to make him; and I give you warning, that if there's any attempt to turn him another way, I'll be your match.'

Bertha changed colour, but the determined lines of her mouth became more marked as she said, 'Captain Vivian, you may threaten but you will not frighten me; the promise which I made to Marian on her death-bed will be kept, God helping me, before all others.'

A storm of fearful passion was visible in Captain Vivian's dark countenance, but Bertha regarded him with perfect calmness; and as again her searching gaze rested on him, the exclamation which was about to escape his lips was checked, and muttering between his teeth, 'Do your will and take the consequences,' he turned from her without another word.

CHAPTER X.

THREE days had passed since the storm. The weather had become very warm ; it would have been oppressive but for the soft air, just sufficient to stir the foliage of the trees before the windows of Mildred Vivian's apartment. The flower-beds, disordered by the rush of the tempest, were again restored to their usual appearance of trim neatness ; the lawn was newly mown, and Mildred, lying on her sofa by the open window, appeared to be thoroughly enjoying the luxurious repose of the morning.

Yes, thoroughly enjoying it ; no one could have doubted that, notwithstanding the thin, drawn look of her features, their habitual expression of bodily pain. She was reading, or perhaps, more strictly speaking, intending to read : for although a book lay open before her, her eyes wandered chiefly amongst the flowers or pursued the course of the buzzing insects and fluttering birds, following them as they rose in the air, and resting with an expression of longing thankfulness upon the depths of the blue heavens. Such extreme quietness as there was in that secluded garden at Cleve Hall might have been very trying to many, even on a brilliant summer's day ; but it was part of Mildred's home, associated with all that she had ever loved ; and where others would have dwelt mournfully on past joys, she had taught herself to be happy, and to seize on present blessings.

A little door, leading into the more public part of the grounds, opened, and a tall, gray-haired man, who had certainly reached, and probably passed, the age of seventy, entered the garden. He walked proudly, and with tolerable firmness, and the stick which he carried was no support to him ; his head was raised, his chin slightly elevated—perhaps that added to the self-possessed, self-dependent look, which was the first impression conveyed by his handsome features. For he was strikingly handsome—the forehead high, the nose just sufficiently aquiline for dignity, the dark blue eyes quick and piercing, the mouth—the real character was inscribed there ; but we will leave it for words to tell.

He sat down by Mildred's sofa, slowly—he had been suffering from rheumatism—and he bit his lips as if in pain ; but Mildred did not ask him how he was, but waited for him to break the silence.

'I have been round the park, Mildred; the storm has done a good deal of mischief.'

'Has it indeed, sir? I thought there were no trees blown down.'

'Who told you that?' he asked quickly.

'I forget, sir, who; but I understood it.'

'Then they deceived you, Mildred; purposely perhaps,' he added in an undertone. 'The Great Black Oak, of five hundred years' standing, is down, child. But what does it matter?' He tried to laugh. 'It only follows the family fortunes.'

'I hoped it was to be the type of their remaining firm,' said Mildred, assuming a lighter tone; 'but it is best not to think about such things.'

'Do you never think about them, then?' he continued, regarding her with an expression of tenderness which was at variance with the accent of his voice.

'Sometimes I do, dear sir; but I don't think it is wise.'

'No, child; no, it is not at all wise; but I thought I would tell you myself, lest you should fret.'

'It was very kind,' replied Mildred, in an absent tone; then breaking suddenly into another subject, she asked, 'Did you go beyond the park, sir?'

'No, I meant to go; but my back was stiff, so I turned back; —Prince was troublesome too.'

'Prince has not exercise enough, sir; I wish you would let Groves take him out regularly.'

'And throw him down; that won't do, Mildred. No, if Prince grows too strong for his master, he must seek another.'

'I hope not, sir; you wouldn't bear to part with him.'

'Would I not?' A smile of resolution almost forbidding crossed his face; 'then, Mildred, you know nothing about me.'

'I don't mean that you would not do anything, or part with anything, that you considered right, sir,' began Mildred.

He caught up her words—'Considered right, that is what you always say; is right—it ought to be.'

Mildred was silent.

'Is right,' he continued, speaking his own thoughts rather than addressing her; 'I set off in life with that motto, and I have followed it. Who can have done so more? who can have sacrificed more—eh! Mildred?'

'Certainly, sir; no one can doubt your principle,' replied Mildred, keeping her eyes upon the work which she had taken up since her father entered.

'Only it is a principle you don't agree with. What woman ever did?'

'Woman's feelings carry them away, so it is said,' replied Mildred, with a smile. 'But, my dear father, why should we go over the old ground?'

'Well, as you say, why should we?' and he sighed deeply.

Mildred laid her thin, white hand upon the scanty gray hairs which covered his head, and as she fondly smoothed them, said, 'If I could make you listen to my principle instead of to your own, I should ask such a great favour.' He would not turn to look at her, but he suffered her to kiss his forehead; and she added, in a tone so low that it was almost a whisper, 'Would it vex you very much if Ella were to come and see me?'

Very striking it was, the change which passed over his face. Its expression had been gentle and sad the moment before, gentle notwithstanding the unyielding determination which was described by the lines of his mouth, and which broke forth in the tones of his voice; but even as Mildred spoke, it was gone, conquered, as it would have seemed, by some sudden mental suffering which he could not control, yet against which he struggled with all the intensity of an ungovernable will.

Mildred must have known the effect her words would have, yet she seemed neither to watch nor wait, nor be anxious for his reply. She took up her work, and tried to thread her needle, but her hand was unsteady; the cotton rolled upon the floor, ·and she bent over the side of the sofa to pick it up. He saw her movement, and stooped too, but it was an effort; and as he raised himself again, he said bitterly, 'Your father is an old man, Mildred. Wait but a little while, and you may do as you wish without asking.'

'It will be too late to have any wish then, sir,' said Mildred, quietly.

He leaned back in the arm-chair, resting his hand upon the stick which he laid across it. His tone was still constrained as he said, 'How long have you had this new fancy?'

'It is a very old one, dear sir,' replied ·Mildred: 'I can never see the children by going to them.'

'And their grandmother knew that, crafty old woman that she is!'

'But the children, sir,' said Mildred, humbly; 'must they suffer?'

'I'll tell you what, Mildred'—General Vivian rose from his

chair with an energy which for the moment conquered the infirmities of age—'there is no more cunning, designing old fox in
England than that woman ; but I 'll outwit her.'

'We don't like her, certainly, sir, either of us,' said Mildred ;
'but then so much the more reason, perhaps, for taking the children from her : don't you think so ?'

'And so give her cause to triumph over us ! What made her
bring them here but the determination to thrust them upon me ?
No, Mildred, let them alone—Campbells and Vivians—Campbells and Vivians,' he repeated, muttering the words ; 'it can't
be ! it wasn't meant to be.'

'But the children are Vivians, dear sir,' said Mildred. She
was afraid then, for she looked up at him stealthily. 'Yes,' he
said, pondering upon the words ; and Mildred heard him add, as
he turned away from her, 'And so are others.'

'Clement is very young,' observed Mildred, replying to his
thoughts, rather than his words.

'And therefore the more sure a victim,' he exclaimed, impetuously ; the volcano, which had been working secretly, bursting forth. 'Am I blind, Mildred ? Can I not see the boy's
course as plainly as if it were written in letters of fire before
me ? And is all to be sacrificed ? all for which I have striven in
life—the inheritance of my ancestors ; the good of my people ;
the honourable name, to attain which I have practised the self-
denial of years ? But let it go,' he continued, moodily ; 'since
even you, Mildred, cannot value it.' He moved to the window,
and stood there, listening, it might have seemed, to the note of
the wood-pigeon, and the plashing of the fountain in the garden.

Mildred's hands were clasped together, possibly in suffering,
but more probably in prayer. Hers was not a face to betray much
internal agitation —perhaps she had been too much accustomed
to these scenes to be startled or deeply pained by them—but
something of the hopeful expression passed from her face as, after
the lapse of a few seconds, she said, very slowly, 'I can see the
risk, dear sir ; but I can see the duty to the children also.'

'I will do my duty by them,' he replied, quickly. 'I will
help the boy. Let him go to college ; I will support him there.
Let him show that there is yet something left in the Vivian
blood which I need not blush to own, and I may even do more.
And the girls shall not want, Campbells though they are—
Campbells in every look and motion—they shall have aid too,
as and when I see fit. But it shall not be extorted from me,

E

Mildred : it shall be at my own time. They shall see that nothing has been gained, rather that everything has been lost, by thrusting them upon me.'

'It was a great mistake of Mrs Campbell, almost wrong indeed,' said Mildred ; 'but we only give her a just cause for complaint, so at least it seems to me, by neglecting our own share of duty to the children.'

'I don't acknowledge the duty,' he replied, sternly.

Mildred hesitated. 'Then, dear sir, if not from duty to them, at least from kindness to me. It would be such a great'—satisfaction she was going to say, but the word was changed into 'pleasure.' She looked at him pleadingly, but his head was turned away ; he did not or would not hear.

'There is too much draught for you here,' he said, abruptly ; 'they must move your sofa back.' He put his hand out to touch the bell. Mildred stopped him: 'Only one moment, dear sir ; indeed it won't hurt me.'

He looked impatient, and his eye wandered to the door, which was open. A light breeze rushed through the room, and partially blew aside a green silk curtain which hung at the lower end. The edge of the curtain was caught by the point of an old oak chair, and the picture which it covered was displayed to view. It represented three figures : one was Mildred, kneeling against a garden seat, her arm thrown around the neck of a young girl, who was seated with a book in her lap, which both seemed to be studying. They were very unlike—Mildred's face so thoughtful even in its youthful happiness ; her sister's—for it was evident they were sisters,—so brilliant, intelligent, inquisitive, joyous, and with something in it of her father's commanding spirit, to which Mildred, as she clung to her, seemed only too willing to submit. Behind them stood a boy, apparently some years older, tall, erect, noble-looking ; with the open forehead, the slightly aquiline nose, and piercing eye which marked him for the son of General Vivian ; but also with the full lip and self-indulgent yielding outline of the small mouth, which showed that in some points, and those perhaps the most essential for success and honour in life, the father and the child could never be one.

It was scarcely a glance which General Vivian cast at the picture ; but it made Mildred's cheek almost livid, whilst she watched him, as he walked to the end of the room, and deliberately replaced the curtain, and removed the oak chair, so that the same thing might not happen a second time, and then returned to seat himself once more by her side, his countenance, perhaps a shade more stern that it was before. Mildred did not wait for an observation from him. She spoke hurriedly, apparently saying what she scarcely intended or wished to say.

'Ella should be very little in your way, dear sir.'

A pause, and silence—this time not wilful: the old man's eyes were bent upon the ground, his thoughts perhaps wandering back into far distant years. He did not catch her words. A dog's bark was heard.

'It must be Clement,' said Mildred, in a timid voice.

General Vivian started.

'Do as you will, child;' and he stood up to leave her, just as Clement, rushing through the garden, entered by the window.

'Clement, don't you see your grandfather?' Mildred spoke reprovingly, for the boy's first impulse was to rush up to her sofa; and a smile of displeasure curled General Vivian's lips as he observed the hasty self-recollection, mingled with fear, which made the blood rise in Clement's cheek, whilst shyly approaching he muttered an apology. The excuse was received coldly, and Clement's colour deepened, and he looked at the window, wishing evidently to make his escape.

'Reverence to elders is not one of the lessons taught in modern education,' said General Vivian, addressing Mildred, 'so we must not, I suppose, expect too much.'

Mildred smiled. 'Clement is not generally so forgetful, my dear father; but you did not think of finding any one here except me, Clement, did you?'

'I thought Mr Lester might be here,' replied Clement, a little sulkily; 'and I was going to ask him to order me some fishing-flies in Cleve.'

'He is going over there, is he?' asked Mildred, in a tone of interest.

'Yes, so he said, to see Mr Bruce.'

'Is that the gentleman who was saved in the storm?'

'Yes, the man whom Ronald saved,' said Clement.

There was a quick flash in General Vivian's eye, and he sat down. Mildred went on—

'And so you want some fishing-flies, do you, Clement?'

'Yes, like some that Goff got for Ronald; he means to show me how to use them.'

'Who! Goff?' inquired Mildred, quickly.

'Oh ! no, not he ; Ronald.   There used to be famous sport at
the last place he was at, so he's quite up in it.   Goff laughs at
that sober kind of work, and says there's no fun like that of
catching fish at night, with lights on a river, which is never
done here.'

'That is poachers' work very often,' said Mildred.

'I don't know where the right is of preserving fish for one
man more than another,' replied Clement.   'Goff says'——

Mildred interrupted him.   'Why, Clement, one would think
that Goff was your tutor.'

Clement laughed.   'Well, he is a kind of tutor in some things ;
he and Captain Vivian are such knowing fellows ; up to so many
things.'

'They are up to teaching you slang,' said Mildred.   'I wish
they may do nothing worse.   What does Mr Lester say to their
instruction ?'

'Oh ! he hasn't much to do with it so long as I am in for
hours.'

Mildred looked at her father, who was leaning back in the arm
chair, with his eye fixed upon the carpet.

'Hardman, the gamekeeper, fishes too,' she said, timidly, addressing General Vivian ; 'he might be a better master than
Ronald.   Don't you think so, sir ? '

'Clement chooses his own friends,' was the reply.

'Not quite, I think,' replied Mildred ; 'he would not wish to
have any friends whom you might disapprove.'

'I don't want to make friends,' said Clement ; 'I only want
some one to go fishing with, and put me in the way of it.'

'And if Hardman could teach you as well as Ronald, you
would be as well contented to have him,' observed Mildred.

Clement looked annoyed, and muttered something about
Hardman being a bore.

'Of course,' observed General Vivian, coldly, 'it is Ronald's
society which is the point.   I have told you so before,' he added,
speaking to Mildred.

'Grandpapa doesn't wish you to make friends with Ronald,'
said Mildred.

'I have no one else to be friends with,' replied Clement,
quickly.   He did not intend to be impertinent, but he was irritated, and his tone was certainly wanting in respect.

Mildred looked very pained.   'O Clement !' and Clement in
a moment recovered himself.

'I beg your pardon, sir, I didn't mean any harm ; only it's dull going out alone, and not much better with Hardman.'

'And so you choose Mr Ronald Vivian for a companion. I warn you once for all, my boy '—and General Vivian leaned forward, and fixed his eager eye upon his grandson with an expression of authority beneath which Clement actually quailed : 'There are two roads before you,—one leads to Heaven, the other—I leave you to guess where ;—if you want to travel that way, follow Ronald Vivian.'

'It's not true,' exclaimed Clement, impetuously ; but he was stopped by Mildred.

'Clement, Clement, remember he is your grandfather; remember. Dear sir ! he doesn't mean it.'

'Don't be afraid, Mildred, I understand him quite. He has had my warning, let him attend to it.'

General Vivian left the room ; Clement knelt on one knee by Mildred's sofa.

'Aunt Mildred, why does he speak so ? Why does he hurt me so ? What makes him say such cruel things of Ronald ?'

Mildred put her hand before his mouth ; 'Clement, you are talking of your grandfather.'

He drew back and stood up proudly ; 'If he were twenty times my grandfather, what he says of Ronald is false.'

Mildred did not speak ; a pink spot, the flush of mental agitation, burnt upon her cheeks.

Clement's tone softened ; 'Aunt Mildred, you know that it is false.'

'No, Clement'—Mildred's voice was low, and her breath came with difficulty ; 'it is true,—for you wilfully to follow Ronald Vivian would lead you to destruction, for it would be disobedience.'

'But when grandpapa is unjust, unfair—when he doesn't know Ronald—when he doesn't even speak to him ! Why Mr Lester allows that there is the spirit of a hero in Ronald, if it could but be brought out.'

'But you cannot be the person to do it, Clement,' said Mildred, gently.

'I don't see that; I am more of a gentleman. I can tell him a good many things which he never knew of, and he often asks my opinion ;' a gleam of self-gratulation passed over Clement's face as he spoke.

Mildred laid her hand upon his : 'Dear Clement, at your age, you have enough to do to keep yourself straight ; it is better not to think of others.'

'But Ronald is not what they say !' exclaimed Clement, shrinking from the implied censure ; 'if he were'——

'That is nothing to the point ; at your age there is only one course open to you—to obey;' and as Clement's expressive mouth showed how his spirit rebelled against the word, Mildred added, 'I know it seems very hard to do so without comprehending why.'

'Yes, it is very hard, Aunt Mildred ; and no one will talk to me about things plainly, and I hate mysteries. Won't you tell me what it all means ?'

Mildred hesitated for a moment, and then said : 'I think you must know it all. Captain Vivian and your father were friends once ; but it would have been better for them if they had not been. Captain Vivian led your father to do things which your grandfather disapproved, and he was very angry, and'——

'Disinherited him,' said Clement.

'Yes.' The word was uttered very abruptly, and Mildred continued : 'Your grandfather is afraid now that Ronald may have the same influence over you.'

'And so he is unjust to him !' exclaimed Clement.

Mildred smiled, and pointed to a seat. 'Clement, may I give you a lecture ?'

Clement sat down half moodily.

'That was just as your father used to look in the old days,' she continued, with a mixture of sadness and playfulness. 'I used to lecture him sometimes, Clement, though he was much older than I was.'

There was something indescribably winning in her tone, and Clement's face relaxed. 'I hate lectures, Aunt Mildred,' he said, 'and I have such a number.'

'From Mr Lester?'

'Oh, I don't mind his ; but Aunt Bertha is at me from morning till night, and I can't stand it. It makes me say sharp things when I don't wish it.'

'And then she is vexed, and lectures a little more ?' asked Mildred.

'Yes, and then I reply, and then she won't speak, and so we are at daggers drawn. O Aunt Mildred, I wish I had men to deal with. I can't abide women.'

Mildred laughed.

' I can't bear them in that way—that lecturing way,' continued Clement ; 'they do say such a great deal.'

' And the young gentlemen do so many things to deserve the great deal,' replied Mildred. 'But I can really understand, Clement, that it is trying to be kept under a woman's control ; only—you see I am not going to acquit you quite—I think it is the old question of obedience, any how.'

' I could obey as well as any one, if they would only be rational,' observed Clement.

' That is to say, rational according to your notions,' replied Mildred. 'I don't exactly see how you would be obeying any one but yourself then.'

Clement coloured a little, and said, quickly, 'Well, but that's what every one must do; you wouldn't have one a slave, without any judgment of one's own ?'

' Sixteen is rather young to have a judgment,' said Mildred, quietly. ' But,' she added, observing that Clement looked blank, ' at any rate, having a judgment, and acting upon it, are different things.'

' That is slavery completely !' exclaimed Clement, 'to give up when one knows people are wrong.'

' What would the world be like if it were not done?' inquired Mildred. 'How would there be any law or order ? '

' Perhaps in public matters it may be necessary,' said Clement.

'What is good in public matters must be good in private,' continued Mildred. 'If what is ordered is not contrary to the law of God, we are bound to submit to lawful authority.'

' And so I am to be kept under grandmamma's thumb all my life !' exclaimed Clement, impatiently.

' I don't see why we are to trouble about all your life,' replied Mildred. 'It is easy enough, I think, to see what your duty is for the present.'

' And what is it ?' he asked, rather sulkily.

> 'Come when you are called ; do as you are bid ;
> Shut the door after you, and you'll never be chid,'

said Mildred, lightly.

' And be a baby in leading-strings !' exclaimed Clement.

' And be what God wishes and intends you to be,' said Mildred, very gravely ; 'that is the real point. If God puts persons in authority over us, He expects us to obey them.'

' But, according to that, no one would be at liberty to go

against the wishes of parents, and such kind of people,' said Clement ; 'not if they were ever so old.'

'There may be different claims for grown-up people,' replied Mildred ; 'and they are competent to judge about them. No law of a parent can take the place of God's law, in the Bible, or even of the laws of your country.'

'Then if people abuse Ronald, and say false things of him, and tell me to cut him, I may refuse to do it,' exclaimed Clement ; 'because they are untrue and unjust, and are going against the Bible.'

Mildred smiled rather sadly. ' O Clement ! 'what a quibble !'

' It's no quibble ; it is truth ;' he replied, triumphantly, looking up with a most self-satisfied air.

' I can't argue with you, Clement, in that mood,' said Mildred ; and she took up her work.

'What mood, Aunt Mildred ?'

'A mood in which you are trusting to yourself, and thinking how clever you are.'

The colour rushed to his face, angrily, and he muttered, ' But you can't refute what I said.'

'You are not required to cut Ronald, only not to be much with him,' said Mildred. ' If you were, there is no moral law against it.'

'Charity, I should have thought,' observed Clement, quickly.

'Charity against the fifth commandment,' replied Mildred ; and changing her manner, she added more lightly, ' but you are only arguing for the sake of argument,—you agree with me I know, really.'

Clement's anger was as quickly gone really, as Mildred's vexation was apparently ; he laughed in reply to her words, and owned that he did dearly love an argument.

Mildred shook her head. 'We shall never agree there, Clement ; I can't endure arguing.'

' Then you are just exactly unlike Aunt Bertha. She would argue from morning till night.'

' And you try to provoke her into it.'

' There's no occasion to provoke her ; she comes into it of her own accord, and Ella stands by and listens.'

' And takes your part ?'

' Of course, she is bound to do that. In fact, Aunt Mildred, it is the only thing to be done at the Lodge, to make any fun. It is awfully dull work there sometimes.'

Clement yawned audibly.

'You should find your way to the Hall oftener,' said Mildred; 'only I am afraid it would not be much better than "awfully dull" here, unless you were to take it into your head to read to me.'

His face brightened. 'Read to you? Should you like it? I read to Ella a great deal, when we can get alone, but when Aunt Bertha is there I don't, because she lectures so about the books.'

'Byron and Moore, I suppose?' said Mildred.

'How do you know that?' he exclaimed.

'Merely because they are just what all boys of your age like. But, Clement, Aunt Bertha is quite right about Ella.'

'Perhaps so,' he answered, carelessly; 'but Aunt Bertha preaches up Hallam's "Middle Ages," and that I vow I won't read.'

'You might find something between, perhaps,' said Mildred, laughing. 'Walter Scott, for instance.'

'Oh, Ella knows Walter Scott by heart, and Byron too, for that matter. In fact, she knows everything, it's my belief. I never saw such a girl. I can't say what she has not learnt by heart; all Childe Harold, and the Corsair, and the Giaour, and Darkness'——

'She should come and say them to me,' said Mildred.

'She would be afraid; she would think you thought them wicked.'

'Perhaps I don't think them very good,' said Mildred; 'but still I should like to hear her say them.'

'That is another thing just precisely different from Aunt Bertha,' said Clement. 'She purses up her mouth just so'— and he made an absurd face—'if Ella only quotes a few lines.'

'I shall purse up my mouth,' said Mildred, 'if Ella won't make me a few promises about her reading. You know, Clement, you wouldn't bear to see her grow up anything but a nice, refined person, and she won't be refined if she is not particular about her reading; that is really what makes Aunt Bertha afraid, and what I should be afraid of too.'

'Ella is so clever,' said Clement. 'Clever people don't want to be preached to like dunces.'

'Perhaps I think they want to be preached to more; but any how, Clement, you wouldn't like Ella not to be quite a lady.'

'Oh no, of course not ; but she can't help herself ; she is born one.'

'Yes, she would look like a lady always ; but she need not be so in mind. And one especial mode in which people grow to be unladylike and unrefined is by reading everything which happens to come before them. Young men, and boys, even, may do a good deal for their sisters in that way, by keeping things from them ; there is a little sermon for you, Clement.'

'Ella never attends to me,' said Clement ; 'she looks down upon me. She is quite beyond me in Latin and Greek, too, for that matter.'

'I don't think Latin and Greek have much to do with persons looking down upon one,' said Mildred ; 'Ella doesn't look down upon Rachel Lester.'

'Aunt Mildred ! how can you tell that ?'

'Merely from little things she has said. It is inconsistency which makes people look down upon one.'

'And I am very inconsistent,' said Clement. He sighed ; yet at the very moment he was glancing at Mildred, to see if she would not contradict his words. 'You think me so, Aunt Mildred ?' he continued.

She looked up playfully. 'I don't see that I am called upon to answer. I have only known you a short time.'

'I am not so changeable as Ella,' said Clement ; 'she is never alike for two hours together.'

'You are twins,' replied Mildred.

'I always keep to the same likings,' continued Clement;—'in books, that is ; and I have been trying to fish every day for a fortnight ; and I have dinned into Mr Lester's ears ever since we came here that I hate College, and want to go to sea, and a heap more things besides. I am sure I don't change half as much as Ella. Now, do I, Aunt Mildred ?'

'I can't say.'

'But am I inconsistent ? Do you think I am ?'

'You told me just now that you were, very,' said Mildred, quietly.

He blushed a little, and laughed awkwardly. ' Well, yes ; but do you think me so ?'

There was a little satire in Mildred's tone, as she said, 'Do you really wish to know ?'

The hesitation in his manner was scarcely perceptible, yet he did hesitate, and the 'Yes,' when it passed his lips, was by no means hearty.

'We will wait till another day,' said Mildred.

He was piqued. 'I would rather hear now, if you please; I don't at all care about knowing what any one thinks of me.'

'Because you have such a good opinion of yourself,' replied Mildred, in a tone between jest and earnest.

'I don't know that, Aunt Mildred. I don't quite see why you should say it. Mr Lester never told me I had a good opinion of myself.'

His tone was pettish, and Mildred became grave.

'We will talk about the inconsistency and conceit another time, dear Clement. By and by, perhaps, you will find out more of yourself than I can tell you; only just now I am afraid I must send you away, because I am a little tired; but you must come again soon and bring Ella, and tell me what success you have had in your fishing.'

Still he stood thinking, rather moodily.

'Aunt Mildred, what must I do to give you a good opinion of me?'

'I have a good opinion of you, my dear boy, in many ways.'

'Yes, but in all ways. How can I make you respect me?'

'A question requiring a long answer, Clement; but one thing I should respect you for at once, if you would put aside your own will, and follow your grandpapa's, about Ronald.'

'Oh, that! but respect has nothing to do with that.'

'More, perhaps, than you think.'

'But I can't be kept under, like a baby in long clothes.'

'Good-bye, dear Clement, you must go;' and Mildred held out her hand to him.

He saw she looked pained. 'Well, Aunt Mildred, perhaps, to oblige you, I might.'

'Thank you, dear boy; give me a kiss before you go.' The bright expression was gone from her face, but that was unnoticed by him; his thoughts were given to his fishing-rod.

'You would find Hardman, the keeper, at home, if you were to call for him now, I suspect,' said Mildred.

'Yes, thank you; good-bye!' and he rushed across the garden, as hastily as he had entered it.

Alas! for Mildred. Was it not the same character again which she had in bygone years so anxiously watched?—the spirit of self-conceit, self-justification, rebellion against the least shadow of censure, the weak pride which could not obey? And all with so fair an exterior! The look, and tone, and manner of a gentleman;

the refined taste, the appreciation of excellence, the poetical heroism of day-dreams !

She unfastened a hair bracelet, and looked at a miniature in the clasp, covered by a gold lid, and tears dimmed her eyes, and fell down her cheeks as she murmured, ' Father, teach me how to aid him ! '

CHAPTER XI.

CLEMENT pursued his way to the keeper's lodge, humming snatches of songs, as he hurried on swinging a stick in his hand, and knocking down nettles and brambles. He was not disconcerted by anything which Mildred had said ; perhaps it would have been well for him if he had been. Vanity, mingled with self-conceit and self-will, was the strongest characteristic ; and now, even when putting aside his own wishes, he soothed himself with the thought that he was yielding rather as a conde- scension than on a principle of obedience. His grandfather was old and fidgety ; and Mildred was a woman, and had a woman's weakness ; and so, if they really did fuss about his going out fishing with Ronald, it might be as well to give in. And Clement went on whistling merrily, and looking forward as was his wont to pleasure in one way, if he could not have it in an- other. There was no strength of resolution, no inward principle in this ; it was simply giving in for the moment, because he did not like to be openly rebellious.

Hardman was not at home ; he was gone to Cleve, so his wife said : and to Cleve Clement determined to follow him,—or if not able to go quite so far, as he was to return for an evening lesson with Mr Lester at a certain hour, he would go part of the way. His mind was bent upon this new fancy of fishing, and he could not bear any obstacle or delay, and fancied he was doing some- thing to attain his object when he was walking in the same direction as Hardman.

' Good day to you, Master Clement ! ' called out a rough voice from behind a hedge, as Clement strolled on leisurely through the fields.

' Good day to you, old fellow ! What are you doing up here ?'

' What are you doing, Master Clement ? is the question.' And

Goff, slowly unfastening a gate which separated them, joined Clement on the other side of the hedge.

'I thought you were never off your post out there,' said Clement, pointing in the direction of the headland near which the shipwreck had happened.

'That's according to circumstances, young gentleman. I may have my business inland as well as other folks. I say, you can tell where your master's gone, can't you?'

'I have not got a master that I know of,' said Clement, haughtily.

'You needn't flush up like that, young gentleman. Master or no master, he keeps you pretty strict.'

'He keeps me as I choose to be kept;' said Clement. 'He hasn't a grain of power over me.'

'Well! did I ever know such a milksop, then?' And Goff laughed, contemptuously.

Clement's eyes flashed with anger, but Goff only laughed the more. 'Why, what a pity to throw away such a spirit! The boy's got something in him, after all. I say, my young sir, what made you fail me, the other night, in that fashion? I've had it on my mind ever since to call you to account.'

'What other night? I don't know what you are talking about,' replied Clement, hastily. 'You failed me, if that's what you mean, the night of the storm; and a good thing too, as it turned out.'

'Good or not, that's nothing to do with the matter. If a youngster makes a promise to me I expect it's to be kept; and if it isn't, why I know how to trust him another time.'

'You told me to be down at the boat-house by six,' said Clement, his tone rising with irritation, 'and I was there strict to a moment; and there were you, off.'

'And you only too glad to find me so,' exclaimed Goff. 'What a white face we should have seen if you'd been nearing the point, as Ronald and I were, when the squall came on. That young fellow is desperate in a storm: he'd have had us stand out and brave it, if I hadn't been fixed against it. And well enough I was! We shouldn't have been left with two shreds together ten minutes after we got back.'

'It's time enough to talk of white faces when you have seen them,' exclaimed Clement, proudly. 'But that is not what I was thinking of. You were off, you say, yourself; so where's the fault to find with me?'

'That 'twas your message which sent me off,' said Goff, coolly,
'Mine !—my message?'
'Whose else could it be ? Ronald brought it.'
'Ronald? It was false—it was a lie!' and Clement's face
became crimson, whilst, pacing up and down the rough road
before the gate, he went on muttering to himself, 'False fellow !
A lie ! Won't I make him eat his words? False fellow !'
'Not so false, neither, Master Clement. He only said what
he knew was true ; that 'twas likely to be a rough evening, and
so we'd best be off without you.'
'And he said that I said it !' exclaimed Clement, stopping
suddenly.
'Well ! there's no need to take it so much to heart,' replied
Goff, evading a direct answer. ''Tis but to show that you've
got more pluck in you than he gives you credit for ; and that's
soon done. There's more to be done in that way, in this part
of the world, than idle folks wot of.'
His familiar wink accompanying the words was very repulsive
to Clement's fastidiousness ; and as Goff drew nearer, and even
touched him on the shoulder, patronisingly, he drew back.
'Oh ! if that's your line, keep to it,' said Goff; and he took
up the small telescope, his constant companion, which he had
laid upon the ground during his conversation with Clement.
'Of course, I'm not going to thrust fun on them that haven't
spirit for it. There's enough work for me without that; and for
Ronald, too.'
The mention of Ronald's name again touched Clement's angry
feeling.
'I'll trouble you not to speak of that youngster again,' he exclaimed, haughtily. 'I have an account to settle with him ; and
I mean to see to it.'
Goff eyed him with a glance of sarcastic superiority. 'I wish
you joy of getting your match ! Why, Ronald—Ronald Vivian !
—he'd make three such as you, my boy !'
'If he could make fifty such, he should answer for his words!'
exclaimed Clement, in a tone which showed that his vanity was
stung to the quick. 'So mean !—so cowardly !—to make it
appear that I was afraid !—that I wouldn't risk what he did !'
And again he began to pace up and down the road.
Goff made no comment upon his words, but, resting his glass
upon the gatepost, looked long and attentively in the direction
where the headland, suddenly terminating, gave a long line of

the sea to view. A little vessel was making its way rapidly from the shore, the wind being favourable.

'She's a jolly little craft,' muttered Goff to himself; 'how she does cut along !'

The observation attracted Clement, but he tried not to show it.

Goff continued :—'A jolly little craft, if there ever was one ! If it had been her, now, the other night, and Ronald in her— instead of that old hulk, with the Frenchman at the helm—she'd have ridden out the gale like a queen !'

'Ronald couldn't manage a vessel,' exclaimed Clement, quickly.

'Couldn't he, now? Why, just you try—that's all !'

'I wouldn't trust myself with him,' said Clement.

'Why, no, to be sure; you wouldn't trust yourself in anything but a Lord Mayor's barge, in a river three feet deep !'

'I'd trust myself in anything that Ronald trusts himself in,' exclaimed Clement, not seeing his own inconsistency, 'let it be a cockle-shell, or a man-of-war.'

'Or a neat little trimmer, like her yonder?' said Goff.

'That, or anything,' replied Clement.

'Take you at your word, then,' said Goff, quickly. 'Will you go, now, for a lark, some day, and try her?'

Clement hesitated; he felt that he should be wrong in agreeing to the proposal; but his vanity—his mortified vanity—how could he resist it ?

'Good-bye! and joy be with you, for a land-lubber!' exclaimed Goff. 'You'll never learn to manage a craft !'

Clement caught at the word. 'Manage?—Yes, 1 would go directly, if 1 might be taught to manage it. It would help me, if I go to sea,' he continued, in an undertone to his conscience.

'Folks can't manage all at once ; they must learn their trade first,' was Goff's discouraging reply. 'So good-bye to ye !' He walked away a few paces, but very slowly; and then he turned round, and looked again at Clement, and nodded.

Clement was intensely irritated. 'I say, old fellow ! I'll be with you, some night, down at the point, when you don't expect me; and see if I don't find out as much of your affairs as Ronald knows. He manage a vessel, indeed !' and Clement laughed loudly and contemptuously.

'You'll please to wait to be asked before you give your company where you aren't needed, Master Clement,' said Goff, stopping, and looking at him surlily. 'Meddle with what doesn't concern you, and I'd as soon cudgel your head as I would—this thistle,' and he knocked off the top of one which stood in his way.

Clement's laugh was neither as loud nor as contemptuous as before. He muttered something about finding Ronald, and making him answer for his words ; and, looking at his watch, turned sharply round, and walked back to Encombe.

CHAPTER XII.

M R LESTER was not returned when Clement reached home ; that was an excuse for idleness, though there was sufficient work prepared for him to attend to by himself. Ella persuaded him that there were difficulties not to be mastered alone, and accordingly he lounged away his time in an arm-chair, threaten-ing Ronald, and making the excuse that his walk had tired him. So the whole afternoon was wasted ; for, as it happened, Mr Lester did not come back from Cleve till very late. He had been detained, he sent word, by business ; and Louisa contrived to discover, before the evening was over, that he had been seen in Cleve, walking with Mr Bruce, and had afterwards returned with him to the farm. This latter piece of information she extracted from Rachel, who appeared at the Lodge in the even-ing with some flowers for Mrs Campbell, which had been sent her by Mrs Robinson. Why Mr Bruce should have gone to the farm, Rachel did not profess to know, but Louisa settled the question without any difficulty. Cleve was an odious place, and the farm was very quiet and comfortable, and much nearer the shore ; and Louisa had some indistinct idea that Mr Bruce was detained at Encombe by some secret business connected with the wreck. What—she had not fully decided ; having failed, as yet, in determining to her own satisfaction whether he was partly the owner of the vessel, and so interested in its fate merely as a matter of business, or some hero of romance, whose story by and by was to astonish them all. The former idea suited the report brought by Rachel, who had just left him at the Parsonage, where he was to drink tea. 'There was nothing in him very wonderful to look at,' she said; 'he was as yellow as a bit of parchment; and somebody had said he had come to England for his health. He spoke like a gentleman,—that was one thing; but he seemed to dislike talking, and she had not once seen him smile;' an observation which drew from Ella the remark that, for that reason, he would be so much the better fitted to live with Mrs Robinson, who was known to have cried so much the day she was born, that she had never got over it.

This information of Rachel's was but the beginning of speculation and curiosity for Louisa; though there was in reality but little to give rise to either. Mr Bruce certainly settled himself at the farm, but he was a quiet individual, very much out of health, and suffering especially from the cold and shock he had endured the night of the wreck. Moreover, he was always upon the point of departure for London; so that he could not be looked upon as a resident subject for gossip, and no one probably but Louisa would have thought it worth while to make any remarks upon his comings and goings. She, however, always knew when he drank tea at the Rectory, and when Mr Lester went to visit him at the farm; and she learned from Rachel a good many details as to the furniture of his apartment, and the curious things he had 'put about the room,' as she expressed it, in order to make it look comfortable,—strange, foreign, Indian-looking things,—boxes, and figures, and a few books,—not a great many,—for Rachel doubted if he were fond of reading.

Once, however, Louisa came home herself in great triumph, having seen Mr Bruce at the door of the farm garden, and even spoken to him,—that is, as she acknowledged afterwards, he only said, 'How d'ye do?' and she said, 'Very well, I thank you;' but then he looked at her very earnestly, and that was particularly flattering from a person whom no one knew anything about.

Had Louisa been in Rachel's place, Mr Bruce's affairs would have had no chance of remaining private, for Rachel was at the farm constantly. Perhaps Mrs Robinson urged her coming to cheer her lonely guest,—perhaps Mr Bruce himself liked the society of the simple, earnest-minded, affectionate child. Rachel seldom told who asked her; and in reply to the questions as to how she amused herself when there, replied, that she read, and talked, and looked at curiosities; a very natural and rational answer, but not particularly informing to Louisa's inquisitive-

ness.   A few attempts were made to induce Aunt Bertha to
intrude upon Mrs Robinson's privacy, but there was an antipathy felt, though not expressed, which kept Bertha and Mrs
Robinson apart.   Mrs Robinson evidently did not 'take kindly'
to the Lodge.   Even though the children were Rachel's friends,
she could not bring herself to ask them to come within the gate ;
at least when Bertha was with them.   If she met them alone
it was different ; yet even then there was a restraint ; it was
as if she always had a double feeling about them, and was inclined to give them a kiss on one cheek and a slap on the other ;
and Bertha's chilling manner never helped to surmount the
difficulty.

Since Mr Bruce had been at the farm, the coolness was still
more evident.   Mrs Robinson could not well be rude, but she
was as nearly so as it was in her nature to be, and almost told
them sometimes that she had rather they would walk in any
other direction.   She said so one evening especially, when
Rachel, Fanny, and Louisa, were walking together, and Louisa
was rather eager to be allowed to see the garden.   Bertha was
some little way behind ; if she had been near, Louisa would
scarcely have ventured to insist, as she did, upon being allowed
to come in just for five minutes.

'It's too late, Miss Louisa ; another time, if you please,' was
Mrs Robinson's discouraging reply to the proposal.

'But we won't be five minutes ; no, not three,' persisted
Louisa ; 'we will just run round once, and then be back ; we
shall have done it before ·Aunt Bertha comes up.'

'May be your aunt wouldn't like it, Miss Louisa,' replied
Mrs Robinson, decidedly.

'May be she would,' retorted Louisa, perversely, and rather
rudely.

Mrs Robinson froze into a statue.   'Young ladies should learn
to behave themselves, and not take liberties,' she answered.
'Good evening, Miss Rachel, my dear.   It's my advice to you
all to get home.'

She walked away without any softening word ; but Rachel
followed her.   'Granny, dear, you shouldn't mind Louisa ; it's
her nature.'

'So much the worse, my dear ; it's hard to put off nature.
But I'm not troubling about that.'

'Well, what are you troubling yourself about ; it's always
something.   Isn't Mr Bruce's room large enough for him ?'

Mrs Robinson smiled. 'Why, you know, Miss Rachel, he's got the old back room looking out upon the elms, and it would hold a regiment.'

'Then he is fidgety about his tea, and bread and butter.'

'He doesn't take tea; he always drinks coffee.' Mrs Robinson's face relaxed a little more, as it always did when she was talking to Rachel.

'Then it's something I am not to know, so I won't tease you, Granny; only I wish you would tell me.'

They were standing by a low door which opened into the garden. Mrs Robinson pushed it open.

'He's in there, you may go and speak a word to him if you will.'

Rachel seemed doubtful. 'Louisa won't like it; and Miss Campbell too;—no, perhaps I had better not;' yet she evidently wished to go.

'He has been teaching the parrot to say your name,' said Mrs Robinson.

That was a very great temptation, and Rachel ran back to her companions. Bertha had joined them now, and was hurrying them away. She did not like them, she said, to be staring over the wall in that way; it looked so curious.

'Mrs Robinson wants me to go in one minute. Mr Bruce has a parrot for me; might I go, do you think?'

'Oh yes, to be sure,' exclaimed Louisa; 'and we will walk up and down the road till you come out.'

'Louisa, you forget yourself. Does Mr Bruce want to see you, Rachel?' inquired Bertha.

'I don't know that he wants to see me exactly; but he has a parrot for me.'

'Mr Lester will be coming by and by, ma'am,' observed Mrs Robinson, drawing near the gate. 'Miss Rachel may go back with him, if you please to leave her.'

Bertha's sense of duty was touched: Rachel was under her especial charge. 'I don't know,' she replied; 'I can't say that I have permission to leave her.'

'I see Mr Bruce very often; papa lets me,' whispered Rachel, pleadingly.

Bertha still hesitated; her back was to the garden gate; she could not see Louisa's glance at Fanny, and the finger which was pointed in that direction.

'I see him; don't you?' whispered Fanny.

Louisa moved a few steps aside. 'Yes, close to the door; 1 do believe he's coming.'

Mr Bruce appeared in the doorway. Mrs Robinson saw his shadow, she could not have seen himself.

'Never mind, Miss Rachel, then, to-night,' she said. 'Good evening, ma'am, and she dropped a respectful curtsey to Bertha, which yet plainly said, 'the sooner you go the better.'

Rachel acquiesced, but with an air of disappointment which brightened into sunshine as she glanced at the garden doorway; and, hastily appealing to Bertha for permission, she threw open the wicket-gate of the entrance court, and rushing up to her new friend, exclaimed, 'I mustn't stay, but I may just thank you; it was so kind. I am so very much obliged about the parrot.'

'And I am very glad you are glad, my child.' Only the tone reached the place where the rest were standing; the words were unintelligible.

'You don't look at all well, ma'am,' said Mrs Robinson to Bertha; 'hadn't you better come in and rest?'

Bertha was very pale; her eye had a wandering, almost vacant, look. 'Thank you, no. I had better go home. Rachel! I wish she would come.' She moved, apparently intending to enter within the wicket, but Mrs Robinson placed herself so as to prevent her. 'I will call her, ma'am,' and Bertha drew back.

Mr Bruce has taken Rachel to see the parrot,' said Fanny. 'I wish he would let me go too.'

'I can see him, and I can see Rachel too,' said Louisa, stretching her neck, 'just round the walk; there they are. Now I think they are going in-doors. Mr Bruce's room opens into the garden; that is—it doesn't open exactly, it is up-stairs,—the large room. Aunt Bertha, you have been in Mr Bruce's room, haven't you?'

Bertha did not hear; she was resting against the low wall, not seemingly impatient, only very worn and wearied. They were kept but a few moments; Rachel came running back, Mrs Robinson slowly following, with the parrot in his cage.

'Miss Rachel would have you see it, ma'am,' she said, apologetically, to Bertha.

'It will talk, it will say my name!' exclaimed Rachel, in delight. 'Pretty Poll! do speak, Polly!'

Of course the parrot did not speak: what bird ever did when it was told to do so?

'He will if Mr Bruce tells him,' said Rachel. She glanced wistfully at the doorway.

'Miss Campbell wants to go home. You mustn't keep her any more to-night with the bird,' observed Mrs Robinson, hurriedly.

The parrot uttered a loud scream, and a short, sharp word; it was not Rachel, though Fanny persisted it was.

'He said it quite plainly just now,' said Rachel, in a vexed tone; 'but never mind. There, Granny dear, take it away; never mind. I didn't mean to be troublesome and keep you, dear Miss Campbell,' she added in her most winning manner.

'I should like to hear it speak again,' said Bertha, and she withdrew her hand, which Rachel had taken hold of. She had no intention of being ungracious, but she was not thinking of Rachel at the moment.

Rachel thought she was angry, and went up to Mrs Robinson, who was standing apart. 'I am so sorry, Granny; I know it was naughty of me.'

'Never mind, my darling; it is her way.' But even Mrs Robinson was a little quick in her manner, and poor Rachel's sensitive feelings were touched, and tears stood in her eyes. She did not go near the parrot.

'It said, " How d'ye do," Aunt Bertha, that was all,' exclaimed Louisa, impatiently. 'Parrots always say, " How d'ye do." '

'And a good deal besides, sometimes, Louisa,' replied Bertha, gravely and stiffly.

Fanny tapped the cage,—the scream followed again, and the word, which Louisa now asserted to be a name—Flora, she thought it was like—at which Fanny laughed heartily, declaring, with vehemence, that it was much more like Charlie, or hungry, or fetch me. Bertha said nothing; and as Louisa's proposition of summoning Mr Bruce to be the interpreter was unseconded, the bird was consigned to Mrs Robinson's care, and the little party moved homewards.

CHAPTER XIII.

THEY were at home early; Bertha had insisted upon it; she had business in the village, she said; and so, when the children had set themselves to their evening lessons, and Ella was reading to her grandmamma, Bertha stole quietly out at the back-gate, and walked leisurely down the lane. She still looked pale, but it was not so much from the wear of bodily as of mental fatigue. That, indeed, was the expression of her features generally; probably from the consciousness of having the comfort of others depending upon her, and having so many causes for anxiety; but this evening there was not only gravity in her face, but doubt and perplexity.

' She walked with her eyes bent on the ground, thinking, and then occasionally looked up as though expecting to see something which might startle her, but the village was very quiet; the men were still at their work in the fields, the women preparing for their return, and the children, just let out of school, were busy in the play-ground, and only interrupted the quietness of the hour by distant shouts of laughter.

Bertha pursued her way by the lane which led from the parsonage to the village, and after passing a few of the principal cottages, ascended a steep path, terminating in a long flight of steps, which was the short way from the village to the church. Encombe Church was at some little distance from the village; it stood by itself, on the summit of a square hill, which on three sides rose abruptly from the plain, and on the other leaned as it were against the range of lofty downs encircling the village. The ground must once have formed part of an open heath, for gorse, and heather, and fern still covered it in luxuriance, and the wild downs rose immediately above it, and rough land, only in part enclosed, stretched away to the east and west. It was a marvel what the little church should do there alone, looking over the wooded plain to the blue horizon of the ocean. Except at the times of service, it seemed to have no lesson to preach to the poor, nor any word of warning to offer to the rich ; for the busy stir of life had deserted it, and the white grave-stones told their tales to the happy birds and the glad insects, but had no daily and hourly voice for the reckless or the thoughtless of mankind.

Yet it was very solemn to worship there : hopeful with the hope of Heaven in the brilliant summer mornings, when dew-drops, sparkling with living light, hung upon the grass, and sunshine, flickering and quivering, lay in broad masses of burnished silver upon the sea ; and calming as with the repose of the last, long sleep, in the still evenings, when the rush of the waves came like a requiem for the dead, moaning over the sandy beach ; and awful, subduing, crushing to all human vanity and folly, when the harsh roar of the wintry elements thundered around the strong old walls, and told of that Almighty Power which shall one day ' break in pieces the foundations of the earth,' and summon the world to judgment.

Bertha reached the summit of the hill, and then paused to rest. A stone bench in the porch was her seat, and for a few moments she remained gazing, apparently without interest, upon the lovely view, set as in a picture-frame, in the rough Norman archway. But a shadow, the long shadow of a human figure, fell upon the graves, and she rose up suddenly, and stepped forth into the open air. Ronald Vivian was there to meet her.

'I hoped you would be punctual,' she said, and her voice was slightly tremulous.

'It was hard work to be so,' said the boy, abruptly. But he held out his hand as he spoke, and grasped Bertha's with a heartiness which seemed as if it must at once break down her chilling shyness. 'My father was off with Goff early, and I am to meet him two hours hence,' he continued ; 'if it was not for that, I couldn't have come. But you have been walking, you must be tired.' He brushed away the sand and dust which had collected on the bench, and took off a light upper coat, and laid it for Bertha to sit upon.

'Thank you, Ronald ; I am glad you came ;' but Bertha's manner was so nervous as to be almost cold.

He waited, however, for her to begin the conversation, standing at a little distance, and leaning against the archway in an attitude of attention and deference. He looked upon her evidently as a superior being.

'You did what I wished the other night,' began Bertha, 'in keeping Clement from going with Goff, and I wanted to thank you.'

'I did what I could; but I got into disgrace : never mind that, though.'

'Disgrace with your father?'

'No, not with him ; he knew nothing about it; but Goff abused Clement, and Clement abuses me. Yet I said nothing but the truth. It was Goff's misrepresentation ; I couldn't tell a falsehood.'

'Clement does not think you did.'

Ronald laughed shortly. 'He says he does; and he threatens a good deal ; but that won't matter. I shan't notice it.'

' No, indeed, I trust not,' exclaimed Bertha ; 'it would be worse than anything if you were to quarrel.'

' He would keep aloof from me in that case,' said Ronald, rather proudly ; 'and so you would be satisfied.'

' The old feeling, Ronald,' observed Bertha, quietly, but very gravely.

' It would be what you wish, and what Mr Lester wishes,' replied Ronald.

' Perhaps so ; but we would have you keep apart from the knowledge that it is best —not because you are too proud to be with him.'

' I know I am not fit company for him,' he replied, moodily, ' nor for any one,' was added, in an undertone.

' We will not talk of that, Ronald ; my wishes and Mr Lester's have nothing to do with the question of fitness.'

' But you have said as much,' he continued.

' I said it when I thought it,—but opinions change ; you have set him a noble example lately.'

The boy bit his lip, and turned away abruptly.

' When Clement shall risk his life to save that of another, it will be time enough to consider whether you are a fit companion,' continued Bertha. ' Mr Lester thanks you, Ronald ; so do I.'

' There was no danger ; we could both swim,' he said, gruffly, and still without looking at her.

' Perhaps so,' was Bertha's only answer.   She understood him thoroughly, and changed the subject.

' And you will still keep your promise, Ronald !'

' As long as it is required ; but Mr Lester says I may be gone shortly.'

' Two months, it may be, or three,—and we have to gain your father's consent.'

' Yet he will never ask mine for anything,—he will force me, drag me with him at his will, down, down, down,' and Ronald's voice sank till it was lost in a whisper of awe.

' Not against your own will, dear Ronald,' replied Bertha, her tone changing from its usual chilling monotony into the tender interest of an elder sister.   ' No one, not even the spirit of evil himself, can harm us against our will.'

' It is easy for those to talk,' he replied, 'who are never tempted.'

' I am not tempted as you are, it is true.   Yet I am in a different way ; and when I fall, Ronald, it is my own will which makes me do so.'

'You!' he exclaimed, impetuously. 'Miss Campbell, you can never will to do wrong.'

'Perhaps not often,—I hope not; but I may not will strongly to do right, and the end is the same.'

Ronald was thoughtful; he repeated the word 'strongly' to himself.

'Yes,' continued Bertha, answering what she believed to be in his mind. 'A weak will must, unless strengthened, end like a sinful will. But you have not naturally a weak will, Ronald. You have great faults, but they are strong faults; and the same strength which has hitherto so frequently carried you away into sin, may, through God's mercy, lead you far on the road to goodness.'

He looked up suddenly, and the gleaming of the sinking sun flashed across his face, and brightened into intensity the glance of his eye. But it was for a moment only, and again his eyes were cast down, and the cloud gathered upon his brow.

'And you may have much to keep you upright, a noble object for which to live,' continued Bertha.

'When I am pointed at as the son of a drunkard, the comrade of smugglers!' he muttered, scornfully.

'Rather,' replied Bertha, 'when you shall be known as the child of one who lived the life of a saint upon earth, and left to you the task to retrieve the name she bore from dishonour. Ronald, have you forgotten your mother?'

He made no reply—but throwing himself upon the rough bench, hid his face against the worn stones of the porch; and a sound, as of a sob, escaped him, but it was stifled; and Bertha, without noticing it, continued—

'It is the anniversary of your mother's death, Ronald; eight years ago, on this night, she died.'

A shudder passed over his frame, as he murmured, 'And left me to ruin.'

'And left you a work which, in her woman's weakness, she could probably never have performed. She did not then know its full extent; but now, if it be permitted to the dead to watch what passes upon earth, she would surely long that you may be able to accomplish it. Ronald, your father did a grievous injury; you may retrieve it.'

'It would take the labour of twenty lives to retrieve his injuries,' said Ronald, in the moody tone which was natural to him whenever his father was mentioned.

Bertha was silenced for a moment ; she seemed pained, dis-heartened. 'And you do not wish to know what you may have it in your power to do ?' she asked, somewhat reproachfully.

He rose up, and there was an accent of haughtiness in his reply. ' I do know it ; to keep away from Clement, that his grandfather may not think him disgraced by having me for a companion.'

' Something more than that, Ronald,' said Bertha, sadly. ' Would you listen if I were to tell it you ?'

The intonation of her voice strangely touched him. Perhaps it bore him back to other and innocent days, when, seated by his little bed, in the home where his best and happiest hours had been spent, Bertha Campbell had soothed him to sleep with the soft monotony of her voice, whilst repeating the hymns which suited his tender age. He placed himself opposite to her ; but his head was still turned aside. It might have been thought that he was watching the course of a vessel dimly seen in the far horizon,—but that it passed on, and still his eye remained fixed upon the same point, where the golden clouds were gather-ing into fantastic masses around the sinking sun.

There was a silence of some seconds. Much that was to be told would be painful both to relate and to hear, and past events seemed crowded together inextricably in Bertha's mind. ' I must go back,' she said, at length, ' to my early days,—the days when I first lived at Encombe. Perhaps you do not know that it is my native place, the home of my family for many generations. We lived in the old farm ; it was a manor house then ; but we were poor, my father was extravagant, and we could not keep it up in anything like a fitting style. General Vivian was our nearest neighbour, but we were not friends : family feuds, dating almost a century back, had been handed down to us, and General Vivian was not a person to let them sleep ! neither, perhaps, was my father. General Vivian was a careful, cautious, strict man ; he had but one grand object in life—to redeem the family property which his father's extravagance had well nigh wasted : he devoted all his energies,—and he has great energies, marvellous ones,— to this purpose. It would be wrong to judge, but it seems that he made it his idol, and, because it was a noble object, could not see that there might be danger in it. But let that be as it may, General Vivian saved his inheritance,—my father for-feited his. You may imagine from this how unlike they were, and how little they could understand each other. So, too, Mrs

Vivian and my mother, the Miss Vivians and my sister and I,
had no mutual interests ; and distaste became dislike, and we
grew up—I don't know how—it was very wrong—but the feeling became at last utter aversion in all, except '—— Bertha's
voice trembled, and the concluding words of the sentence were
inaudible.

She went on nervously,—' My sister Flora was very pretty
and attractive. She was older than myself, and every one was
accustomed to defer to her ; perhaps that made her wilful ; my
father especially would not check her in anything. General
Vivian, as you must know, had one son, a very engaging person,
generous and open-hearted, but utterly thoughtless. Notwithstanding the family differences, we met him occasionally in
walks and rides ; he was, in fact, almost the only gentleman we
ever saw, and perhaps it was natural enough that he and Flora
should become attached to each other. But there was nothing
understood or acknowledged, except between themselves : the
General would have been fearfully angry if the notion had been
suggested to him ; his wife, the only person who might have
influenced him, was just dead ; and my father and mother were
too much occupied with the pecuniary difficulties which were
daily increasing, to take heed to any lesser matter. I saw
what was going on, but I was too young to interfere. Flora
was full of hope, and her affections were very strong, whilst
Mr Vivian never allowed his thoughts to dwell upon anything
but the gratification of the moment ; and, at length, totally
putting aside the possibility of his father's disapprobation, he
persuaded Flora to engage herself to him without asking the
consent of her own parents or of his. They kept the fact
entirely to themselves, and all that I saw was that they took
every opportunity of being together, and that when separated
Flora's spirits entirely sank. This made me very anxious, and
I was secretly glad, for her sake, when at length it was determined that she should leave the Manor House for a time, and
go abroad, in the hope of enabling my father to retrieve his
affairs. We left Encombe. I thought I was only going for a
time ; I fancied that the Manor House was still to be my home.
It was a great mercy that I was not able to see the future. Yet
I had some presentiment of evil ; I could scarcely help it ; Flora
was so dreadfully miserable at the thought of the long absence.
Mr Vivian saw her the last evening, and I believe the promise
between them was renewed ; Flora was then, in a degree com-

forted, and we set out on our journey in tolerable spirits. Our first rest, for any length of time, was at a German watering-place, small, but just growing into fashion, and filled most unhappily, not only with hotels and boarding-houses, but gambling-houses. My father's early habits had accustomed him to think lightly of gambling, and it soon became his chief amusement. He would never play high, and so managed to go on without bringing himself into any great difficulties ; but our home became the resort of his associates at the gaming-table, and amongst others, of—Captain Vivian.'

Ronald started.

'Yes,' continued Bertha, 'it was there, Ronald, that my first acquaintance with your father may be said to have begun. He was not then what he is now ;'—her voice sank as she said this, and Ronald turned away his face ; he could not bear its change to be seen. 'He was young, handsome, agreeable,'—— she hesitated, and repeated, 'in a certain way he was agreeable ; he had seen a great deal of the world, and was very clever ; he could tell amusing anecdotes ; gentlemen especially liked him ; they did not care for things which distressed Flora and me. Dear Ronald ! you must forgive me if I speak too freely.'

'Say what you will,' he replied, with a bitter laugh, 'you cannot tell what I can.'

'And yet in some way, Ronald, I may be a better, a more charitable judge. I have never suffered as you have ; at least in daily life. In other ways ;—but you must let me go on regularly. I had seen Captain Vivian before, but never to know him ; in fact, I was too much of a child to be brought in contact with him. He claimed acquaintance with us as having a connection with our old home ; his father and General Vivian were first cousins. I did not know then that all social intercourse between the two branches of the family had ceased for some years.'

'For thirty years the General has been too proud to acknowledge us !' exclaimed Ronald, indignantly.

'Think of him gently and justly, Ronald, if you can. He may have feared the acquaintance for his son. If he did, events have proved that he had cause to do so.'

'My father might not have been what he is, if his relations had not cast him off,' replied Ronald.

'Perhaps not ; one cannot say ;' and Bertha's thoughts reverted to Clement, and her anxiety lest he should in like manner be discarded. 'At that time, when we met in Germany, I fear his habits were too deeply rooted to be altered. We saw a great deal of him. Like every one else, he admired Flora, and to my dismay, I perceived that my father was inclined to encourage him. Captain Vivian had the reputation then of being rich, and probably my father thought that, considering the state of our family affairs, it would be a desirable marriage. At all events, he threw them constantly together, and when, on one occasion, I expressed my dislike to the society which the acquaintance involved, I was reproved and told that I should bring myself into mischief if I interfered with matters which did not concern me. Things went on in this way for some time. Flora said very little. I was sure she disliked Captain Vivian, but she had not courage openly to thwart my father's wishes. When alone she was very miserable ; when in company she exerted herself so as to be the life of the party. No one really knew anything about her feelings. I was too young to have her confidence, and she was afraid of my mother. Your father was very fond of her ; and when I saw that, I pitied him, for I felt that his affection could never be returned. But I did not know then with how fixed and stern a resolution he can pursue an object when once his will is given to it. He was resolved to marry Flora, and if, instead of common coldness, he had been met with open detestation, I believe it would not have made him swerve a hair's breadth from his determination. It was just at this time, after the separation of a year, that Mr Vivian arrived in Germany, on his way to Italy, for a summer tour. What communication had been kept up between him and Flora in that interval I do not know. Some there certainly must have been, for he was the last person in the world to bear silence and suspense. I suspect he came prepared for the state of affairs which I have described, and determined to put an end to it. But it was by no means an easy task. My father's feeling against General Vivian was as inveterate as the General's against him, and Mr Vivian could with difficulty gain admittance to the house. When there, he could in no way compete with his cousin. There were strong prejudices against him, and although he was the heir of Cleve, the property was entirely at the General's disposal ; and he could not offer anything like the fortune at that time possessed by Captain Vivian. Yet I imagine that even from the first moment of their meeting, your father felt that Flora's choice was made. She was, indeed, too much afraid of her parents, openly to express her preference ; but even when she strove to conceal it, it showed itself in innumerable everyday trifles. A man of less resolute purpose might have drawn back, but Captain Vivian persisted in his attentions, and'—— Bertha hesitated, and her words came with difficulty.

Ronald spoke impatiently,—'Go on, I can bear all.'

'I don't wish to give you pain unnecessarily,' she replied.

'No pain is like concealment, Miss Campbell.'

'And perhaps in some ways, what I have said may be an excuse for Captain Vivian,' continued Bertha. 'He had great provocation,—some, at least; but it was hard to take advantage of a character so open and trusting as that of Edward Vivian. Your father gambled, Ronald; he made Edward do the same; he led him on step by step, till his debts became very heavy. I don't like to think it was done purposely, but it appeared like it. Certainly he made use of Mr Vivian's weakness. They were friends all this time outwardly. I think Mr Vivian was sorry for the disappointment of your father's affections; and having no fear of him as a rival, he gave him his confidence, and consulted him in his difficulties. Immediately afterwards, by some means, no one knew how, tidings of Mr Vivian's gambling debts reached the General. He was fearfully angry. I saw some of the letters which passed; Mr Vivian showed them to Flora. He was full of repentance; but habit and evil companionship were too strong for him, and after a short interval he returned to his former practices. Everything was made known to the General through some secret channel, and when still more indignant reproaches and threats of disinheritance reached Mr Vivian, they were in the same way communicated to my father. Poor Edward found himself without friends, without support; it was very much his own doing; he was sadly, sadly weak, but all turned against him :—even the persons who had first led him into evil,—who were still encouraging him in it;—for I know that at this very time it was Captain Vivian who enticed him again and again to the gaming-table, and laughed at him when he would have drawn back.'

A suppressed groan escaped from Ronald. Bertha went on rapidly—

'Perhaps you can guess the end of all this. Mr Vivian did not venture to propose openly for my sister, knowing the feeling that was excited against him, and fearing that if he said anything, my father would forbid him the house. Flora, too, was very unhappy, from various causes. She had to bear with great absence of sympathy in her own family, and constant fits of temper. All her affectionate feelings were crushed and repelled ; and at length, in a moment of desperation, she was persuaded to marry Edward Vivian, without the knowledge or consent of her parents. It was a fatal step, Ronald, and most bitterly punished. I need not repeat all that took place in consequence ; it would not be important to you, and it is only miserable for me. My father, in his anger, refused to hold any communication with them, and would not advance them a penny. They were exiled from our house, and left to depend upon such resources as might be obtained from General Vivian. What his feelings would be, it remained to be shown. Mr Vivian wrote himself, acknowledging his offence, entreating to be forgiven, but he received no answer: he wrote again, and still there was delay. At length, after the lapse of several weeks, the stern decision came, in a few short, cutting sentences from the General, without even a softening word from Edward's sisters, and only one heart-broken, re-proachful line from his old nurse, Mrs Robinson ;—he was dis-inherited.'

' But my father ? ' exclaimed Ronald ; 'he had nothing to do with it ? '

' He left Germany instantly,' replied Bertha, 'when the fact of my sister's marriage was known. He travelled night and day; and it was by him that the intelligence was made known to General Vivian. Goff, who had been in Edward's service, but had been dismissed for dishonesty, and had afterwards been en-gaged by Captain Vivian, accompanied him, and was called to be a witness to the truth of some of his statements. All this I first knew a few weeks since, in conversation with Mr Lester. At the time everything was a mystery, and there was no one to clear it up. My own family were too proud and too angry to make any effort for reconciliation ; and Edward Vivian had no friend in whom he could confide, except Mr Lester, who had formerly been his tutor, but who, unfortunately, was at that time travelling in the East. No one was surprised at the General's conduct; it was only in keeping with the severity, and what he called strict justice, which had marked him through life. But what did in a measure astonish both Edward and our own family, when the letters were sent to us, was the style of the accusations brought forward. The General spoke of deadly ingratitude, dishonour, disgrace in the eyes of the world, and a false use of that to which Edward had no claim, except at his father's pleasure., Some one

the little prospect he has of providing for his children would be gone if he were to do so. And they have grown up without knowing him ; I don't think even Ella and Clement can recollect him ; and so there is the want of a father's authority. It is all very sad. But it might be altered ;—I think so at least. Ronald,'—and Bertha spoke hurriedly yet earnestly,—'you might do much.'

He stood up proudly ; the marks of a stern self-control were visible in the slight frown upon his forehead, and the compression of his lips, which scarcely parted as he said coldly, 'What duty does Miss Campbell require of a son against his father ? '

'Not against your father: God forbid ! ' exclaimed Bertha. ' But, O Ronald ! if injustice has been done'——

'It shall be undone,' he replied, firmly, 'at any sacrifice.'

Bertha continued :—' My words must seem harsh, Ronald ; yet I would serve your father rather than injure him. The time indeed is so long past that it might be very difficult to prove what we suspect ; but if the attempt were made, it must be followed up, and that publicly—in a court of justice. It might be madness in us, but it would be eternal disgrace for him. Mr Lester and I have talked over the matter repeatedly. For the General's sake, we dread to bring forward a case which we could not prove. It would recall past griefs, and probably cause some fatal catastrophe. Yet we cannot let the matter rest ; for not to speak is Edward Vivian's ruin. One idea we have had has been that he should himself return to England to sift the matter ; but there are many objections to this. His presence might irritate the General, and I should dread a meeting between him and Captain Vivian ; whilst even to enter upon the subject with the General, in order to obtain information, seems next to impossible, though we have thought of it. The past is a sealed book : not even to his own daughters would he relate the particulars of all that transpired in that one unhappy interview with your father, although something there was which weighed so heavily upon him that it did the work of years upon his frame. Ronald, your father's own words can alone throw light upon the mystery.'

Bertha paused, but Ronald stood silent as though some secret power had paralysed him.

'I do not see the way to obtain them,' she added, 'yet the time may come, conscience may one day waken ; and Ronald, if you should be near him in that hour, I conjure you, by all that you hold most sacred, remember your promise.'

He sank upon the bench, and sobbed like a child.

Bertha drew near and spoke anxiously—' It is not against your father that I would for worlds wish you to act ; but you may lead him, urge him, to acknowledge if he has in any way done Edward Vivian wrong by false words. His own confession would never be turned against him, except so far as it might restore Edward to General Vivian's favour. And you may stand in the way between your father and Clement. He hates Clement. He is the child of the woman who rejected him. Save the poor boy from his temptations, and God may in mercy bless your work, and withdraw the curse which must now rest upon the man who laboured for another's ruin.'

A convulsive shudder passed over Ronald's frame, and then he became motionless.

' Ronald,' said Bertha, as she bent over him, ' it is all but your mother's voice which bids you take courage and be comforted.'

The words were powerless. She heard him murmur to himself,—' The curse ; the curse.' And again he groaned in anguish.

' To be redeemed by you, as it would have been by her,' continued Bertha.

' She was an angel,' he exclaimed, starting up, with a vehemence which might have caused a less firm heart than Bertha's to tremble at the storm of feeling she was awakening ; ' and I '——

' You may be one, Ronald,—even more '——

His bitter laugh rang sharply, hopelessly, on the ear.

' Go,' he exclaimed ; ' talk to others, preach, labour ; there are hundreds to listen ; your words are wasted on me,—the outcast ! '

' An outcast ? so young, so misled ! O Ronald ! never, never ! '

' You know not to whom you speak,' he continued, his voice assuming a tone of fierce sarcasm, more terrible than the outburst of passion. ' Have you lived the life which I have lived ? seen what I have seen ? known what I have known ? Go ! let me be what I am doomed to be.'

' Ronald, I do not know, God forbid that I ever should know, the secrets of such scenes as you have been accustomed to ; but this I know, that were they the blackest and deadliest which the

human heart could conceive, there must be hope and the certain prospect of escape, whilst the feeling of horror at them
remains.'

He covered his face with his hands.

'It is from God,' continued Bertha, soothingly, 'from His
Spirit; it is the call to repentance,—the answer to your mother's
prayers.'

'And to my father's deeds, in which I have joined,' he said, in
a tone like the underswell of the sea. Then, uncovering his face,
he gazed upon her, calmly and steadily, and added—'Miss
Campbell, you need not fear. Whatever may be my own course,
justice shall one day be done.' He stood, intending to leave her.
Bertha detained him.

'Ronald, you must not and shall not go. I have a claim that
you should listen to me, for I was your mother's friend, her only
one. It was to me she made her last request,—that, as God
should grant me the power, I would watch over her boy. In her
name I require you now to hearken to me.'

He sat down, not sullenly, but as if in a stupor.

'I know your purpose,' continued Bertha, her tone becoming
severe in its deep earnestness; 'you will from this night bend all
the energies of your mind to discover and counteract the evil
which your father has caused; most earnestly, most entirely, I
thank and trust you. But there are two ways open before you;
—in the one you may accomplish your work and be yourself
saved; in the other you may perform it and be lost. And
Ronald, intensely though I long for the reconciliation and restoration of Edward Vivian and his family,—though it is the one
object for which it seems now that I have to live,—I would rather
see them struggle on in poverty and sorrow for years, and suffer
myself with them, than I would know that any word of mine, or
any efforts for them, had led you even one step on the way which
must tend to destruction. Ronald, you may labour in proud
despair, or in humble hope. If you are proud, you are lost.'

'Proud!' he repeated, bitterly and doubtfully.

'Yes, little though you may think it, pride is your snare. You
will work for others; you will not work for yourself.'

'I may save others, I cannot save myself,' he replied, in a
softened tone.

'You cannot save others except by saving yourself. You wish
to aid Clement; you can have no right influence, you can give
nothing but an inconsistent example, unless your actions are

grounded upon right motives; the most deceitful of all motives is pride, and its end is despair.'

'Then I have reached the end,' he said, sternly.

' No, Ronald, impossible. Let the past be what it may, even in old age it is retrievable,—how much more so in youth !'

' I have known no youth,' he replied ; 'the sins of my childhood have been the sins of a man, and my punishment must be the punishment of a man.'

' And your strength will be the strength of a man,' answered Bertha ; 'the firm resolution, the unshaken will'——

' Which is pride,' he said quickly. .

' Pride when we rest upon it as our own ; faith, when we seek it from God. Ronald, do you ever pray ?'

He answered abruptly, and yet not angrily,—' In storms, on the ocean, in the face of death, yes, I have prayed then.'

'But in quietness and solitude ? In your own chamber ? calmly, thoughtfully, regularly ?'

He smiled as in scorn at the question.

' Your mother prayed, Ronald ; will not you.'

' She prayed because she was fit to pray.'

' And you will pray because you would become fit,—because there are dangers surrounding you, only to be conquered by self·restraint, watchfulness, earnestness, purity, faith ; and you are reckless, proud, full of sinful memories, bowed down by a burden of past offences. You will pray because you long for pardon, for the knowledge that the love of a Heavenly Father will be with you, to guard you from the influence of an earthly one. You will pray, because without prayer life must be misery, and death despair. O Ronald ! will you not do as your mother did ?'

He made no reply : he even moved away, and Bertha was left for a few moments alone. She knelt in the old church porch, and a prayer rose up to heaven in the stillness of that summer evening—a prayer for one amongst the lost sheep, the erring and the straying, who had left undone those things which they ought to have done, and had done those things which they ought not to have done, and in whom there was no health ; and even as it was uttered, Ronald stood at a distance, too self-distrustful to own his feelings, too shy to express them in action, yet praying also, with uncovered head, and closed eyes, humbly and earnestly, for grace that might enable him hereafter to live a godly, righteous, and sober life, to the glory of God's holy Name.

They stood together again in the entrance of the porch. Twilight was gathering around, though the light yet glowed brilliantly in the far west.

Ronald broke the silence—'Miss Campbell, you must pray for me, and your prayers will be heard.'

'All earnest prayers are heard, Ronald; especially those of the sorrowful and penitent. But you will act too?'

'I don't know how; it is all chaos.'

'But the first steps are plain : no sinful words, restraint over your temper, a refusal to join in intemperance '——

'Yes, plain ;'—he seemed pondering the word doubtfully.

'And practicable. What ought to be can be,—only pray.' She smiled, and held out her hand, and he raised it respectfully to his lips.

He did not see the tear which glistened in her eye as she left him under the old church porch, the faint gleams of the setting sun gilding his tall figure.

CHAPTER XIV.

'A NOTE for you, Ella ;' and Rachel Lester ran into the schoolroom at the Lodge, holding a little twisted paper between her fingers. 'But I beg pardon; I forgot, I mustn't interrupt. How busy you all are this morning !'

'Ella has been strict all the week,' said Fanny, looking up from her writing ; 'and it's dreadful work, Rachel.'

'Oh no, Fanny,' exclaimed Rachel ; and she went round and stood behind the child's chair, and offered to mend her pen. 'I know you don't like lessons half as well when they are not regular ; I am sure I don't.'

'But it won't last,' said Louisa, with a knowing nod, which almost upset the gravity of Rachel's face.

'I don't know why you are to say that, Louisa,' said Ella ; 'you know we are always regular when there are no interruptions.'

'Somehow interruptions come every day,' persisted Louisa.

'I have brought them to-day, I am afraid,' said Rachel. 'This note is from your Aunt Mildred, I think, Ella.'

Ella read her note with an air of importance, and stood gazing upon it afterwards, as if there was some weighty matter to be determined.

Louisa held up her exercise book, and said,—'Just look it over, please, Rachel. Ella won't now, she's busy ;' and Rachel went to the other side of the table.

'I will attend to the exercise, thank you, Rachel,' said Ella, looking round quickly. She was very jealous of her own authority; probably because she felt that it rested on an insecure foundation. Rachel sat down, and began to read ; and Louisa and Fanny glanced at each other, and made a sign intended to show that a storm was impending.

'I must go to grandmamma,' said Ella, in a tone of dignified self-consciousness. She moved to the door with her usual languid pace.

'When am I to see you again, Ella?' asked Rachel.

'And what are we to do about our lessons? we have just finished our exercises,' inquired Fanny, fretfully.

'My dear, I can't attend to you ;' and Ella walked out of the room, without answering Rachel's question.

Rachel could not help feeling annoyed. She had some special messages to give from her papa, and she was not to go back without having them answered ; and this delay would be very inconvenient, for she had several things to prepare for Bertha, who gave her German lessons three times a week.

The children were provoked, too. They liked regularity, even when they complained of it ; and although they seized upon the excuse to go on with some new story books, they were by no means comfortable.

Ella went to her grandmamma's room. Bertha was there, and she drew back.

'Come in, Ella ; what do you want?' How chilling the tone of voice was ! How utterly unlike the sympathising tenderness which had touched Ronald's better feelings !

'I want to speak to grandmamma, said Ella.

'Do you, my darling? Oh, then, Bertha, these things can wait ;' and Mrs Campbell pointed to a pile of account books.

'Betsey is going to Cleve, and she ought to pay the books,' replied Bertha.

'Not to-day ; she must wait. There will be another opportunity, I dare say, to-morrow.'

'Couldn't you leave what you have to say, Ella, till the children's lessons are finished ?' asked Bertha.

'It won't take two minutes,' said Ella. 'Grandmamma, I have had a note from Aunt Mildred.'

'We know all about that, Ella,' observed Bertha ; 'grandmamma heard from your aunt yesterday herself.'

'Then, grandmamma, when am I to go?'

'There is no hurry about settling the time now, Ella. The accounts must be finished first.'

'But I must know, because of getting my things ready ; and Aunt Mildred begs me to write and tell her.'

'We will talk about it, Ella, my dear ; we will see about it,' said Mrs Campbell, nervously.

'But by and by will do just as well,' remarked Bertha. 'It is not a matter of consequence whether you go one day or another, Ella.'

'If I don't go this week the fine weather may be gone ; and Aunt Mildred wouldn't like me to be there when it is wet,' said Ella.

'But an hour can't make any difference,' continued Bertha ; 'and Betsey must go to Cleve this morning.'

'Mr Lester's cook will be going to-morrow, Louisa says,' replied Ella ; 'she would pay the books.'

Bertha's temper was irritated to the utmost extent of forbearance. She gathered the account books together, without trusting herself with another word.

'You can tell Betsey to wait, and come back to me yourself, presently, Bertha,' said Mrs Campbell, making a compromise with her conscience, as Bertha was going away.

The door closed, not quite gently, and Ella sat down by her grandmamma, and muttered, 'Aunt Bertha is so dreadfully soon put out.'

Perhaps it was not quite wise in Bertha to do as she did,—go to the schoolroom—it might have been better for Ella's misdeeds to bear their own fruit,—but regularity was her mania, and she felt that the children were becoming irregular. Rachel ran up to her as she entered the room ; 'Dear Miss Campbell ! I wanted to see you so much ; I have a message from papa.'

Bertha had felt lonely and dispirited just before, but that bright face, and the musical voice, and loving accent, had an influence which she could not withstand. Yet she was cold still ; she would have appeared so at least to those who did not comprehend her. 'Wait one moment, dear Rachel. Children, what are you about?'

'Reading till Ella comes back,' said Louisa.

'Put away your books, and tell me what you have to do.'

'I have an hour's music to practise,' said Fanny, mournfully.

'Well, then, set about it at once. And Louisa?'

'Oh! a great many things,' said Louisa, carelessly. 'French dictation, and geography, and lessons for to-morrow, and reading history, and sums. I shan't have done till I don't know what o'clock.'

. 'Then begin something directly. Where is your slate? Show me what sum you are doing.'

'Ella was explaining to me about decimal fractions, last time,' said Louisa.

'Decimal fractions! nonsense! where did you leave off with me? The rule of three;—there, take that sum, No. 19, and work it while I am here. Not a word to be spoken, remember. Now, Rachel;' and Bertha opened the window, and stepped out upon the little lawn, followed by Rachel.

'I won't keep you a minute, at least not many, dear Miss Campbell,' began Rachel.

'Never mind, I have time to spare; Ella won't be back again for the next half-hour;' and Bertha sighed.

'I wish I could help you, and I wish'—Rachel hesitated— 'I wish Ella didn't trouble you.'

'We won't talk about her,' said Bertha, shortly.

Rachel was thrown back, and ventured upon no more expressions of sympathy. 'Papa says, dear Miss Campbell, that he wants you to come up and see him this evening; he wanted to know if perhaps you would come and drink tea with me; but he mayn't be at home till late himself. He has several poor people to see, and he may be kept.'

'Yes, I will come, certainly.' Quite different Bertha's accent was then; there was even a tone of excitement in it.

Rachel's quick ear caught the change.

'Dear Miss Campbell, may I say one thing more to you? Perhaps it is not exactly the right time, but if you could spare me a few moments.'

'As many as you like.'

'And you won't be offended?'

'I don't think I could be offended at anything you would say, Rachel.'

'Because you are so kind, and make allowances for me; but I am half afraid of this.' Her colour went and came very quickly,

and she stopped for some seconds, and at last said,—O Miss Campbell ! I do so wish every one was comfortable.'

'A universal wish, at least, Rachel.'

'Oh no !' exclaimed Rachel ; 'it can't be ; at least—I don't mean to be rude—but if every one wished it, every one would be.'

'Not quite,' replied Bertha ; 'God sends afflictions.'

'But those would not make one uncomfortable, would they ? but unhappy. And, do you know, I think it is much worse to be uncomfortable than unhappy.'

Bertha could not help laughing. 'Well perhaps it may be,—though it is not the general view of the case. But you have nothing to make you uncomfortable, Rachel ?'

'Not at home, and I never used to have anywhere.'

'Till we came here,' said Bertha.

Rachel hesitated a little. 'I suppose, where there are so many people, things must be more uncomfortable ; but I am very sorry about it, and I should like so—it came into my head that perhaps you could tell me something to do to help to make them less so. You know that I am going to be confirmed in October.'

'Are you ? I didn't know it ; but what has that to do with your being confirmed ?'

'Nothing exactly ; only thinking about that put the other into my head. Papa says it is a great starting-point in life, and that I am to think over all my duties, and see how I can perform them better than I have done. And he told me to think about what I did and said with my companions, and to consider whether I could make things better in any way. That was what reminded me of being uncomfortable,—for I don't think Ella is comfortable, and I don't think I am when I am with her.'

'Ella is a very difficult person to live with,' said Bertha.

'She is never two days alike,' continued Rachel. 'That puzzles me ; because when I think I know how to get on with her, she turns round and is quite different.'

'She is a genius,' said Bertha, rather bitterly ; 'and so she has been spoiled.'

Rachel was thoughtful. 'I used to think,' she said, 'that it would be very delightful to be exceedingly clever, but I don't think I do now.'

'Cleverness is all very well,' said Bertha ; 'but it is good for nothing if people can't govern themselves.'

'But clever people always do so much in the world,' said Rachel.

'I am not so sure of that, Rachel. The hard work of the world is done by straightforward goodness, not by talent. Ella will never do anything.'

'You always say that,' said Rachel : 'and it makes me unhappy.'

'I say it, because I think it,' replied Bertha. 'Louisa is twice as useful as Ella now.'

'And you don't know any way in which I could help Ella to be more useful?' asked Rachel, the colour rushing to her temples, as she added,—' It sounds conceited, but papa told me I was to try.'

'You will be cleverer than I am, if you can find out,' replied Bertha.

'Aunt Mildred says,' continued Rachel, 'that if we want tó lead people any particular way, we must begin by going two steps with them, and then we may be able to persuade them to go one step with us.'

Bertha shook her head ; it sounded like a dangerous maxim ; at any rate she was not accustomed to it.

'I don't mean two wrong steps, of course,' pursued Rachel, reading the doubtful expression of Bertha's countenance ; 'and Aunt Mildred, when she said it, told me I was not to trouble my head about it now, because I have enough to do to lead myself ; but that it might be useful to remember when I grew up. I could not help thinking about it, though, a little, when papa talked to me about being useful, and setting a good example ; and at last I made up my mind that I would ask you if you could tell me anything in which I went against Ella. I am very nearly sure I do sometimes, without meaning it.'

'She goes against herself,' replied Bertha. 'There is nothing to be done with persons who do that.'

'And you don't think it is my fault ?'

'No, dear Rachel, what could make you think it was ?'

'Because, do you know, Miss Campbell, I can't help looking up to Ella ; and so, when things go wrong, I can't help fancying the fault must be mine.'

'As to cleverness,' said Bertha, 'every one must look up to her.'

'And she has such grand notions,' continued Rachel. 'I think sometimes she would have been such a great person if she had been a man ; and that perhaps the misfortune is her being a woman. Would she have been better as a man, do you think ?'

'Really, dear Rachel, I never troubled myself to think. I believe we are all best as God has made us.'

'But such a great mind seems shut up in a woman's body,' said Rachel, laughing.

'It is not a great mind, Rachel. Great minds do great things.'

'Ella begins a great many,' said Rachel.

'But she does not finish them. A thing is not done till it is finished.' A smile crossed Bertha's face as she said this, and she added—'That is a truism ; at least it sounds like one ; but I am sure half the world forget it. And then people go shares with others in their duties, and so deceive themselves. Ella goes shares with you, Rachel.'

'How ? I don't understand ?'

'She has grand notions of what is right, and, when the fit is upon her, she forms beautiful plans of duty, and begins them ; but she grows tired of them and leaves you or the children to finish them. Then she has a vague idea that because they are done by some one, it is the same as if they were done by her. All this is terrible self-deception. It will be her ruin if it is allowed to go on.'

'And I can't do anything, then ?' said Rachel, sadly.

'I suppose we all do something when we attend to our own duties,' replied Bertha. 'Ella would be much worse if it were not for you.'

'But, about going two steps with her ?' said Rachel, thoughtfully. 'Can't you tell me what Aunt Mildred means by that ?'

'I don't understand how we are to go two steps with any one who is going the wrong way,' said Bertha, rather shortly. 'I think, Rachel, you had better leave Ella to herself.'

Rachel's was a very warm heart, and there was an innate truthfulness in her character, which was her bond of sympathy with Bertha. It kept her now from being utterly repelled ; but it was very trying to give confidence, and seek it, and find nothing in return. She walked on, silent and disappointed. Bertha's heart smote her ; and something whispered to her that she did not care to talk about Ella, or try to improve her, and that she ought to do so.

'Don't go, Rachel, dear,' she said, as Rachel turned into the path to the Rectory. 'Have you nothing more to say ?'

'Nothing thank you. But you will come and drink tea this evening ?'

'Yes, and shall Ella come too ?' It was a great effort for Bertha to propose this. She did not wish it at all, but it was an amends to her conscience. A few moments before Rachel would have said that it would be pleasanter to have a quiet hour alone with Miss Campbell, but she did not feel that now. She only thought herself very stupid in having mentioned Ella's name.

'Yes, if you please,' she replied , 'you know we drink tea at half-past six, so you will be back in time to read to Mrs Campbell. Papa has altered the hour, because of having to go across the hills, nearly every day, to see poor little Barney Wood. Do you know, Miss Campbell,'—and Rachel became animated in the consciousness that she was going to say something agreeable, —' Ronald Vivian has been so kind to Barney ; he has cut him out a little ship, and he goes to read to him sometimes. Isn't it good of him ?'

Bertha kissed Rachel ;—that was her answer ; and Rachel ran away, feeling that she had, in some unknown way, made her peace.

CHAPTER XV.

ELLA deceived herself, but so also did Bertha Campbell. Was that possible ?—so strict as Bertha was in her self-examination, so very rigid both in the theory and the practice of duty, and above all, so very true both by nature and long habit ?

'The heart is deceitful above all things.'

This is, of course, peculiarly true of the affections, especially when the feeling nursed is the one gentle point in a character otherwise unyielding. But the expression must include also the whole bent and disposition of the mind. The one object which we love, or for the success of which we labour, be it ever so pure, ever so disinterested,—human friendship,—a work of benevolence,—the carrying out of some noble principle,—that is our temptation. If we do not watch, and strive, and continually balance it by other claims, it will one day be the cause of our fall.

This seems to be the secret of much of that inconsistency

which is a stumbling-block to the young in the characters of those whom they are taught to reverence. Good men devote themselves to the support of a theory, or to the advancement of some definite object, and, unconsciously to themselves, it too often takes the place of God. The range of their sympathies, and consequently of the virtues they practise, is narrowed, and others see with surprise, and often consternation, that whilst professing the very highest principles, and devoting themselves to the very noblest purposes, they can yet utterly overlook the simplest and most obvious duties.

Thus it was, at least in a degree, with Bertha Campbell. Naturally warm-hearted, yet painfully reserved, she had early in life been brought in contact with a person who had excited her keenest interest, and, by giving confidence, had in time been able to exact it. This was the beginning of her affection for Ronald Vivian's mother. Reserved people are grateful to those who teach them unreserve. Bertha was grateful to Mrs Vivian. Gratitude, deepened by compassion, became love,—that romantic feeling which is so continually the day-dream of a young girl's life, and which may not be the less dangerous because the world sees in it nothing to condemn.

And so Bertha's dormant sympathies flowed into this one channel, which she had dug for herself, and found no vent in those which had been formed for her by God. Mrs Campbell, doubt-less, had much cause to blame herself for this, but Bertha could not be said to be innocent. Because she liked to be with Mrs Vivian, and knew that her society was appreciated, and her presence felt as a comfort by one otherwise lonely and desolate, she made excuses to her conscience for the neglect of little home duties, and attributed her mother's reproaches to harshness of temper and want of sympathy with her pleasures. Mrs Camp-bell was in consequence estranged from her, and bestowed her affections upon the children. Bertha was hurt at this. She was not exactly jealous; it was not in her disposition; but her pride was wounded, and Ella's talents causing her to be brought for-ward far beyond her years, they were continually jarring. So the coldness spread. Bertha knew her faults, and kept a strict watch over them ; but she knew them by their effects, not their cause. She was always doctoring herself for symptoms, whilst she had never reached the root of the disease. And now, un-known to herself, under the guise of the most sacred of all feel-ings,—a desire to save from ruin the child of the friend whom she had dearly loved,—the same seed of evil was again being nurtured in her heart. To Ronald she could give sympathy, tenderness, and the most untiring interest : he was, in another form, the romance of her early life ; to Ella and Clement she could offer nothing but rules of duty and cold advice. Was this selfishness ?

By the strictest inquiry as to her faults, Bertha could not have discovered it. The friends who knew her most intimately, and watched her most narrowly, could not have accused her of it.

Only in one way could she have perceived it : by examining whether the scales of duty were equally balanced,—whether in throwing the weight of her energy into one, she had not, from a secret bias, lightened the other.

And this kind of self-examination Bertha had not learned to practice. She inquired rather into the quality than the extent of her duties, and as long as those which she had set herself were attended to thoroughly and honestly, she saw no need to ask whether there might not be others neglected.

Yet Rachel's conversation left an unpleasant impression on her mind ; it touched her conscience, though she was not quite aware of the fact, and, in consequence, made her feel more irritated with Ella than before. And certainly, there was much to complain of that morning ; Ella stayed nearly half an hour with her grandmamma, persuading her that it was quite necessary she should go to the Hall the next day ; and when at length, she had obtained the desired consent, ran up-stairs to consult Betsey about a box for packing her things, taking up the servant's time, so that the bedrooms were not finished till twelve o'clock. The children's lessons might have been scattered to the winds, but for Bertha. As it was, they went on most energetically and satisfactorily ; but it was at the expense of poor Bertha's time, and in a certain way, of her health, for she was obliged in consequence to give up a walk before dinner, which had been specially recommended her, in order to write the letters that ought properly to have been finished whilst Ella was with the children.

Very little trouble and labour this would have been to Bertha, if Ella had been at all considerate or grateful ; but she was so in the habit of letting her duties fall quietly upon Bertha's shoulders, that she really was not aware at last who was bearing the burden, and therefore scarcely ever thought of saying, 'Thank you.' What was still more provoking, it never seemed to cross her mind that it was her duty to provide, in some way, for the children's instruction during her absence. She was one of those easy-tempered persons who never seem to imagine that they give trouble, because they have never been in the habit of taking it. 'Things will go on somehow,' was a very favourite saying of hers ; the somehow, meaning *anyhow,* so long as her own plans were not interfered with.

It is a grievous pity that we do not all learn to call our faults by their right names. Ella acknowledged herself to be indolent, —that she did not object to ; it was rather a refined fault. She would have been deeply mortified if it had been suggested to her that she was selfish, for she was always dreaming of heroism, and heroines are never selfish.

And on that day particularly Ella was a heroine in her own eyes, for she was indulging a long-cherished romance. She thought it was about her Aunt Mildred, but it was really, as is the case with most persons who give themselves to romance, about herself. Ella believed herself to be, as she expressed it, 'bewitched with Aunt Mildred.' They had not met above five or six times ; but Mildred's sweet face, her quiet grace, and earnest thoughtfulness, were most attractive to Ella's excitable imagination. And then the solemn grandeur of the old Hall, the seclusion of Mildred's room, opening into the private garden, her grandfather's dignity, the deference of the servants, and, above all, the mystery which had so long been connected with the home of her father's childhood ;—it was not wonderful that these things should work upon Ella with an influence amounting to fascination. It had been her dream for the last two months that she should go and stay at Cleve, and a very innocent dream it seemed ; 'but, unfortunately, though Aunt Mildred appeared in the foreground in Ella's imaginary pictures, she herself was always peeping over her shoulder ; and if the dream had been examined when carried on to its termination, it would have been found that, at last, Ella was to reign triumphant at Cleve, her grandfather's idol, Aunt Mildred's pet,—safe from grandmamma's nervous anxieties and Aunt Bertha's lectures,— the centre of interest to the whole family.

With what an instinctive stateliness of manner did Ella leave the house that afternoon, arm-in-arm with Clement, to ramble over the hills ! Bertha had taken the children ; Mrs Campbell was inclined to be left alone, probably to sleep. Clement was yawning, and complaining of dullness ; and what better could be

devised under such trying circumstances than a long walk? Ella
was not fond of mounting the hills : she liked much better to go
to the sea-shore, and read poetry ; but she had been taking a
mental stimulant, and for once said ' Yes,' when Clement proposed that they should try and reach the Beacon, a pile of stones,
raised as a kind of landmark, on the top of the highest hill, which
rose a little to the north-west of Encombe.

They set off vigorously over the rough stones of a long lane ;
mounted a high gate, made their way across a field of stubble,
and emerged upon the fine turf of the hills. Clement stopped to
take breath and rest, for the ascent, even as far as they had gone,
was tiring. Ella dragged him on : 'For shame ! false-hearted !
to want rest just at the beginning ; how will you hold out to the
end ?'

'As well as you do, I will answer for that. The hare and the
tortoise, remember.'

' I always admired the hare the most, though I respected the
tortoise,' exclaimed Ella, hastening on ; and then stopping for a
moment, quite breathless, and laughing at Clement's plodding
steps ; ' you see, Clement,' she said, as he drew near, the good
of doing things at a start is, that you gain time by it, to find a
little amusement with your neighbours. The world would be a
very dull world if every one went through it only minding his
own concerns, as you do now.'

' There is something in that,' said Clement, throwing himself
upon the grass ; ' but what are you to do, Ella, when there is no
amusement to find ?'

' Oh, make it. I should always make it,' replied Ella. ' If it
was not in life, I would get it from books ; and if it was not to
be had in books, I would invent it.'

' Very well for you who have brains ; but for a poor fellow who
has none !'

' Nonsense, Clement ; I won't have you say that. Now for
another start !' And almost before the words were spoken, Ella
had made a rush, and was several yards in advance.

Clement followed at a distance. A call from Ella hastened
his steps.

' Mr Lester and Rachel going towards the foot of the Beacon ;
shall we catch up with them ?' She did not wait for an answer
but hurried forward.

Clement stood still for an instant, and perceiving a short cut
up a steep bank, which Ella could scarcely have ascended, was

H

about to hasten after her, when, happening to look round, he perceived Ronald Vivian coming up the hill, with the firm tread and
athletic gait of a mountaineer; not hurrying like Ella, not
leisurely and indolently moving on with unsteady pace like himself, but at every stride making a marked progress, which
promised in a few seconds to bring them to the same level. The
two boys caught sight of each other at the same moment. Clement stopped.

They were only half friends, for Clement had not forgiven
Ronald for his interference on the night of the storm, and was all
the more irritable because he had found that there was really no
ground for offence. Ronald had indeed urged Goff to go without
him, but he had never pretended to give a message which he had
not received. The attraction which drew them together was like
that of the rattlesnake ; and it was with an assumption of superiority that Clement exclaimed; ' Halloo ! what errand are you
upon now, Ronald ? '

' Nothing of consequence,' was the reply, shouted forth in
Ronald's loudest tones ; and, without pausing, he went on in an
opposite direction from that which Clement was taking.

His indifference piqued Clement, and he called again, ' I say,
Ronald, stop, can't you ? What on earth does he go on at that
pace for ? ' he muttered to himself, as Ronald, either naturally or
wilfully deaf, strode forward.

Another loud, shrill call, so loud that Ronald could not but
hear, and stop in answer to it ; and Clement, irritated and proud,
walked up to him leisurely, taking rather a delight in observing
one or two impatient gestures.

A scowl was on Ronald's face. His temper was by nature
very quickly aroused, and had been, till lately, at times, quite
ungovernable.

' I 'll tell you what, young sir,' he begun, as Clement came up to
him, 'you must learn that I have something else to do than to stand
kicking my heels together for you. Why don't you make haste ? '

' Why didn't you stop ? ' inquired Clement.

' Why should I ? We have nothing to say to each other.'

' We shall have a great deal, if you can't be civil, Master Ronald,' said Clement. ' But there is no need to fret yourself. I
only want a plain answer to a plain question. Where are you
going ? '

' Where you are not required to follow,' replied Ronald.
' Your course is up the hills, I take it.'

'And yours along them. I am not so ignorant, you see, as you may fancy.'

Ronald's colour rose; but some inward thought checked his anger. 'I was impatient just now,' he said, 'and I am sorry.' He held out his hand.

The words came out so naturally, that Clement scarcely understood that an apology had been offered. Yet he took the hand extended to him, saying, 'You needn't be so close ; I don't want to tell upon you.'

'There is nothing to be told,' replied Ronald ; 'but our ways don't go together.'

'Why not? Ella and I are only taking an afternoon's walk. Why shouldn't we go with you?'

'Because I shall be better without you,' said Ronald, bluntly ; 'the road is a rough one.'

'Oh, nonsense for that ! Ella doesn't care for rough roads ; and as for me,' and Clement laughed satirically, 'as if I couldn't do what you do !'

'That may be. But, Clement, you are not coming with me,' and tossing his stick into the air, Ronald strode onward.

'I am not, eh?' exclaimed Clement ; 'we'll see that, young gentleman !' He flung down a few wild-flowers which he had been carrying for Ella, and pressed forward, keeping Ronald in sight, yet not attempting to join him.

He had forgotten Ella; he generally did forget everything but the impulse of the moment; and he had an impression that Ella was going along the foot of the hills in a direction parallel with his own, and would be sure to join Mr Lester. He did not exactly say it to himself, but it was a kind of vague conviction, enough to satisfy him ; so he went on.

The path was winding, occasionally almost dangerous, for it was nothing more than a sheep-track, and the hills were in some parts very nearly precipitous. But Clement had a firm tread and a steady eye ; he kept Ronald in view, except when at intervals a projecting point hid him for a moment from sight, and felt something of the eagerness of a chase, as from time to time he ascended a high mound or a steep bank, to obtain a more general view of the course he was taking.

Then he did once or twice look for Ella, and at first he saw her hurrying on after two figures, whom he supposed to be Mr Lester and Rachel, and afterwards he observed her stop to rest, and shouted after her to show her where he was, but he did not wait to listen whether she answered him. When he looked the third time, she was not in sight, but, of course, he supposed, she had heard him, and, seeing him at a distance, had joined Mr Lester.

CHAPTER XVI.

THE direction which Ronald took, and which Clement followed, led at length into another of those deep gorges with which the Encombe Hills abounded, formed, in all probability, by the constant fretting of some mountain stream, wearing away the rocks.

Greystone Gorge, as it was called, was much narrower than the ravine in which the village of Encombe had been built. The stream, to which it must have owed its origin, had long been dried up, and it was now, for the most part, quite barren and stony, except where some few patches of rank grass had sprung up among the rocks. At the upper extremity, however, a solitary ash-tree, the relic probably of the woods which had formerly clothed the hills, had taken root, and with the cliff behind, formed a shelter for a good-sized cottage, a small cow-shed, and a pigsty. Under the shade of the tree, a party of children were at play, collected around a little hand-carriage, in which a sickly boy, of about five years of age, was lying; but Ronald's figure was no sooner seen descending the height, than a scream of mingled fear and delight burst forth, and in a moment they were scattered in all directions, hiding themselves in the house, or behind the cow-shed, and one of the more adventurous climbing up the face of the almost perpendicular cliff.

Ronald called to them with a rough but good-natured reproof: 'Why, you silly imps! what are you after? here Johnnie,—Martha; here I say. One would think that I was the Black Rider.' They came up to him, and he unslung a basket which he had been carrying on a pole over his shoulder, and, placing it on the ground, told them to take it between them into the cottage.

'I thought 'tweren't no one but you, Master Ronald,' exclaimed Johnnie, seizing the basket by one handle, and nearly upsetting it; 'but Martha declared as how there was two of you, and then I said you always come alone, so it couldn't be you.'

'What has Martha been doing to see double?' exclaimed Ronald. 'I shan't trust her if she does that.'

'There was another, and that's he,' exclaimed Martha, and pointing to the top of the rocks, she added : 'He's a skulking down, but I can see him.'

'He shall skulk to some purpose,' exclaimed Ronald, springing up the rocks again with the agility of a wild goat, and in his eagerness not hearing the cries of the sickly boy under the ash-tree, who called after him in a voice of agony, 'that he would break his neck, and then he shouldn't see him any more.' From point to point he swung himself with rapidity which it was pain to follow ; his feet seeming scarcely to touch the rock, his eye giving quick glances around.

'He's got him; there they be!' exclaimed Johnnie ; and draw-ing his little sister towards him, he showed her where, on an overhanging platform, Ronald and Clement stood confronting each other.

'Spy !' burst from Ronald's lips.

Clement laughed. 'I was not to come, wasn't I? I have shown you now that I will come, when and where I choose.'

'Not without my consent,' replied Ronald, coolly. 'You will go back.'

'Not at your order, Master Ronald ; or we will try which is the strongest.'

'Ay, try!' and Ronald shrugged his shoulders contemptu-ously. 'I should be sorry, young sir, to have to pitch you over the rocks.' He folded his arms, and nodding his head as he looked up at the cliffs, added : 'If you take my advice, you'll be off.'

'I take no advice except from my superiors,' exclaimed Clement.

Ronald's eyes flashed, he lifted up his hand, and touched Clement's shoulder.

His grasp was shaken off indignantly, and Clement clenched his fist, and drew nearer to the edge of the rock.

'Ronald ! Ronald !' screamed a voice from below. The sick boy was raising himself in his little carriage, and stretching out his hands.

Ronald's hand, which had been raised to ward off the antici-pated blow, fell by his side. 'As you will,' he said, quite calmly ;

'we are fools to quarrel;' and he turned suddenly round, and sprang down the cliffs. The next moment he was at the side of the child's carriage.

'Barney, what made you call? What frightens you?'

'I don't know. You'd have tumbled over,' said the child, 'and I wanted you.'

'I was coming to you; you mustn't be impatient.'

'He looked as if he would have thrown you down,' continued the boy.

'Perhaps he would, but I should have picked myself up.'

'But you couldn't; God wouldn't have let you; you'd have been killed;' and tears of nervous fright chased themselves down the little fellow's cheeks.

'No matter perhaps for that, if I had been,' muttered Ronald.

Barney caught the words. 'It must matter,' he said. 'Father says it don't, but the clergyman says it does; he taught me a hymn about it. I can say it;' and without waiting for permission, he began, and went through the verse till just at the end of the last line, when he stopped, and, looking up at Ronald, said with a keenly intelligent smile, 'He's a listening; he's no business to listen.'

Clement was close at hand.

'Go on,' said Ronald; and the second verse of the hymn was begun and finished, and then Barney stretched out his wasted hands to Ronald, and said, 'Won't you carry me?' And Ronald lifted him in his strong arms, and bore him a few paces up the rock to a stone seat, and resting the child in his lap, he bade him look down the gorge, and see if any one was coming up.

'Father's coming, I think; no, 'tisn't he, 'tis the black cow. Father won't be home yet. Shan't you have time to stay?'

'I don't know; if I can't, I will come again. But you must wait here a minute, whilst I go and talk with the young gentleman. You'll be comfortable if I put my coat down for you.'

He took off his coat, and, folding it together, stretched it over the stone, and laid the child upon it. 'There, Barney, just for two minutes. You can look at me all the time; you won't care, will you?'

Barney's face betokened tears; but Ronald stopped them. 'You told me yesterday you meant to try and be good, and not cry any more.'

'I wouldn't if you didn't go away.'

'But if I do, you mustn't; that's what would be right; and when I come back we will open the basket.'

'Have you brought them?' exclaimed the child, his eyes sparkling, and the colour rising to his pale cheeks.

'Yes, two flags, beautiful flags for the little ship, and some tiny men, and a cake besides, and a picture book. You shall see them presently, but you must let me go now;' and he gently loosened the tight hold with which Barney grasped his sleeve, and, nodding to him, hurried down the bank.

Clement had not moved from the ash-tree; he was standing there, moodily, watching Ronald and the child. When Ronald drew near he glanced around, as though he would fain have made his escape.

Ronald went up to him at once. 'You have seen all there is to see; now, Clement, will you go?'

'I don't see why you should make such secrets about nothing,' replied Clement, taking up the offensive. 'Why couldn't you tell me at once you were coming to see the child? I shouldn't have troubled myself then.'

'Because I didn't choose to answer impertinent questions;' and, seeing Clement's colour rise, Ronald added, 'I am not going to be angry, Clement, but once for all I tell you that now you must go.'

'I don't see that,' was Clement's reply.

'Then you must learn to see it. Mr Lester and Miss Campbell would wish it; you know that as well as I do.'

'I am not going to submit to a woman,' exclaimed Clement, 'and Mr Lester has no authority.'

'Perhaps not. It makes no difference to me.'

'And you will be a turn-coat, after all,' exclaimed Clement; 'tied to a woman's apron-string! Well, then!' and his lips curled into a sneer; 'perhaps you are right; we had better part.'

Ronald's hand grasped the knotted head of the stick which he held in his hand, till every muscle seemed strained to suffering.

'And when I thought we were to be friends!' pursued Clement, his tone softening. 'You told me we should be.'

'Yes, when I thought there was no obstacle.'

'Obstacle! When persons choose to be friends, what is to prevent it?'

'It can't be,' was Ronald's reply.

'But it can, and shall be, if I wish it. We are not always to be kept under lock and key : the world will one day be free to us.'

Ronald laid his rough hand upon Clement's arm : 'Good-bye, old fellow ! It won't do.' The faltering of his voice belied the indifference of his words. ' You 'll thank me for it some day,' he added.

'Thank you for making me know how to trust in a friend,' exclaimed Clement, the scornful accent again marking his words.

'Our paths lie apart,' continued Ronald. 'You don't see it now, Clement, but you will.'

'And time enough then to change,' replied Clement.

'Too late then,' replied Ronald. He moved a few steps aside, perhaps not to betray his inward feelings, and mounting upon a pile of stones, looked down the gorge. In another minute he returned to Clement, and his voice was altered from stern earnestness to eagerness which bordered upon excitement : ' I can't have you stay. There is a short way up the cliff, by the brushwood. Come, we must go—both.' He sprang forward, and Clement, almost frightened by his wild manner, followed him.

They reached the top of the gorge and paused.

'There is my father,' said Ronald, coldly.

A man was seen coming up the gorge.

' I must go to him ;' yet he lingered.

' Ronald,' said Clement, ' you are so strange ! '

' Am I ? Yes, I know I am. O Clement !' and he sank upon the ground, and buried his face in his hands.

' Ronald, you won't let me help you, or I would.'

' Help me by leaving me. Go, go—it is sin to be together. Sin,' he repeated, in an undertone, and then a faint, mocking laugh followed the words : 'why should I care for sin ? '

' We must all care,' said Clement, timidly.

'Ay ! all—while there is time—while there is hope.' He started up suddenly, and grasped Clement's arm : ' There is time and hope for you : keep from me, or there will be none—none.'

A child's cry fell faintly but clearly on the ear.

Ronald leaned back against the rock, and his lip quivered : ' Clement, I have been passionate, wicked : forgive me.' He hurried down the cliff, Clement not daring to follow him.

CHAPTER XVII.

RO..ALD stood again by the side of the sick boy, and spoke soothingly, and caressed him as before; but the child noticed the change.

'You went away and left me,' he said, fretfully ; 'you told me you wouldn't, and you did.'

'I couldn't help it, Barney; I didn't mean to go. Shall I carry you in-doors now? and we will unpack the basket.' His heart was not in his words, for his eye was at every instant glancing down the ravine.

'I don't want to see the basket; I want you to stay, and you are going away.'

'By and by, not yet. You will like to see the new flags.'

'Yes, out here ; if you'd sit down and take me up. It's so hard !' and the poor child twisted himself uneasily on his stony couch.

'In-doors, on the cushion,' said Ronald, 'it might be better than my knee. Won't you go and try?'

No, I don't like the cushion ; I want to be taken up. Oh, it hurts !' and the poor little fellow tried to move so as to ease his back, and finding it useless, began to cry.

Ronald put his arm round him and gently raised him : 'Now, Barney; there's a good boy, don't cry. You must learn to be a man. You won't be, if you cry. Now, isn't that better?'

'But you won't take me; if you'd let me sit up. I don't want to go in-doors; I want to sit up.'

'O Barney, Barney ! you've been spoiled; you have had your own way till you are naughty.'

The fretful, wizen face was calmed directly. 'I don't want to be naughty. Mr Lester says I shan't go to heaven if I am.'

Ronald lifted him up fondly, and set him on his knee; but Barney was not satisfied.

'No, I'll go in, and I'll see the flags. That's not spoiled, is it?' he added, gazing wistfully into Ronald's face.

Ronald only replied by kissing the little thin cheek; and lifting the child in his arms, held him with the firmness of a man, whilst his touch was gentle as a woman's, and carried him towards the cottage.

The building hid from them the length of the ravine, but a

sudden angle in the path brought them in front of it. Barney's head was resting upon Ronald's arm, and he feebly turned it, for his ear had caught another footstep: 'It's Captain John ; ain't it Captain John ?   He won't be coming to take me : you won't let him ?' and he clung closely and tremblingly to Ronald.

'Foolish child ! what's there to be afraid of ?' but Ronald's own voice was not as indifferent as his words.

'He said he'd carry me off one day,' whispered Barney; 'and grandfather said, if he were father, he'd give me up.'

'Because you were good for nothing, I suppose,' said Ronald, good-naturedly.   'But, never mind; he won't want to do it now; and grandfather's not with him.'

'Are you sure ?   But Captain John will want to have me.'

'He wants me, if he wants any one,' said Ronald, gravely.

'Tell him he mustn't ; I can't bear you to go.'

Ronald smiled grimly.   'There's no must for him,' he muttered to himself.

'I thought every one must sometimes,' persisted the child.

'Sometimes, perhaps.'   Ronald hurried forward so as to reach the door of the cottage before his father, who was walking leisurely up the gorge, could see and stop him. .

The little room which he entered was neater than the external appearance of the house would have indicated.   Fishing tackle, indeed, hung on the whitewashed walls, and the floor was only of stone sanded over, and the ceiling was formed of rafters black-ened by smoke from the large, open hearth, in which wood was the accustomed fuel ; but there was an evident attempt at some-thing even of refinement in the arrangement of a few cottage prints, and the flowers placed in the window-seat ; and Barney's little couch was covered with a bright chintz, whilst a curtain of the same material had been put up to shut out the draught from the window.   Evidently a woman's hand had been at work ; but there was no woman to be seen, and Ronald himself laid his little charge gently on the couch and placed the pillows com-fortably for him, and said, ' Now, Barney, that will do, won't it? and I will take out the flags and the picture-book, and you can show them to Martha and Johnnie.'

'There's Captain John coming, and he wants you,' said the child, in a changed voice.   His gaze, as he caught hold of Ronald, was anxious, almost terrified.

Captain Vivian stood in the doorway : 'Absent without leave, Ronald !   You'll please to answer for yourself.'

There was a momentary pause, as it seemed of self-distrust, for Ronald's words came slowly : ' No need for that, father ; you see where I have been without asking.'

' Fooling away your time ; but we must teach you better than that. I say, child, where 's your father ? '

' Gone out with grandfather,' replied the boy, quietly and timidly. ' Grandfather came and fetched him.'

' Umph ! How long ago ? '

' A good bit, I think it was ; ' and the child looked up at Ronald for protection from the rough voice.

' And you, sir ! ' Captain Vivian turned to Ronald—' Let me hear what you are after here.'

' Keeping my word,' replied Ronald. ' I promised to come and see the child, and I came.'

' Promises ! Perchance, since you are in the humour for them, I may remind you of others. Where 's the boy Clement Vivian ? '

' He is not in my charge,' replied Ronald.

' And he has not been here ? You have not seen him ? '

' He has been here, and I have seen him,' replied Ronald ; ' but he is gone.'

' And you let him go. You dared to disobey my orders.' Captain Vivian's voice was fiercely threatening.

' You gave me none,' was the reply.

' A quibble ! I pointed him out upon the hill, and told you that to meet him and keep him would be doing good service ? '

' You said it,' replied Ronald ; ' but I judged that he would not be profited by the meeting.'

A torrent of fearful words burst from the lips of the enraged father.

' Don't be afraid, Barney—don't cry ; ' and Ronald stooped down and stroked the child's head, and pressed his little hand, which was trembling with nervousness. ' Father,' he continued, hurriedly, ' I have not disobeyed you in the letter—in the spirit I have and will. Nay, hear me to the end,' as Captain Vivian would have interrupted him ; ' I will, because I must. It shall never be said that by my aid Clement Vivian has become what I am.'

' Foolish boy ! ' Captain Vivian's tone changed into a soft sneer, more painful even than his violence. ' Who says that Clement Vivian is to become what you are ? and if he were, what need to be ashamed of being like a brave boy, who can lord it over the boldest at his pleasure.'

'But cannot lord it over himself,' murmured Ronald; and then, in a louder tone, he continued, 'Father, I will speak to you plainly. Whilst Clement was my friend only, like any other friend, and you encouraged our being together for that purpose only, it was well: when you urge me to seek his society for a different reason, you enter upon a course where I will not follow you.'

'Well learned from the lips of Miss Campbell and Mr Lester, —perfectly learned; but it shan't last. Listen, Ronald, my boy; it's time we should begin to understand each other. Obedience! —that's the word. Mr Lester himself can't preach it better than I can. What's more,' and Captain Vivian struck his stick upon the ground, 'he can't enforce it better. Talk to me of shame and sorrow, and all they call religion! There'll be more shame and more sorrow for you in one hour of your father's anger than in all the threats they hold out from yonder pulpit at Encombe.'

'I am ready to endure it,' was the calm reply.

'Then try it; take your own will, and '——

Ronald's countenance changed to an expression of agony: 'Stop! father, in mercy; require of me what you will, do with me as you will, only do not ask me to lead Clement to ruin.'

'Him? and why not him? Why is he to be cared for more than others? I warn you, boy, that he is a serpent in your path, and one day you will wish that you had crushed him.'

Instead of replying, Ronald moved again towards the door.

'Ay, go!' exclaimed Captain Vivian, whilst at the same time he stretched out his arm to stop him; 'wander where you will; seek your own friends, you will soon have need of them; for remember, Ronald,' and his voice became sullenly fierce, 'refuse to do my bidding, and your father's doors will be closed against you for ever.'

As he spoke, Ronald pushed aside his arm, hurried from the cottage, and mounted the gorge by the same path which he had ascended with Clement.

He hurried on wildly over rocks and bushes, clambering up heights which, in calmer moments, even he might have thought inaccessible. The self-control he had exerted had strained his mind almost to frenzy, and even his better feelings seemed urging him on to despair. His father! was such a man worthy of the name of parent? could he claim his obedience? Was it really the act of a merciful Providence which could subject him to such a fiend-like power? and if it were not——a hurricane of thoughts rushed over his mind. Why should he struggle?—evil was powerful, not good. Evil had been present to him from his childhood—it was his portion, his doom; and scenes of riot and guilt rose up before him, with their horrible excitement; and it seemed as if a strong hand were forcing him back, to forget his misery in recklessness, and yield himself, body and soul, to the tempter whom he had been striving to resist.

Weak Ronald was at the very moment of victory—for he did not know that he had conquered. So fierce had been the struggle of that inward self-restraint to a spirit long unaccustomed to the slightest check, that it seemed as if the effort had only succeeded in breaking up the strong powers of his mind, and rendering it a chaos of bewildering wretchedness. He sat himself down upon the grass, and hid his face between his knees, feeling, though unconsciously, that the clearness of the unclouded sky, and the brilliancy of the glorious sun, added tenfold to his sense of misery; and faintly from afar came the tinkling of the sheep-bell, and the lowing of the cattle in the valley, mingling with the chirping of the grasshopper, and the whirring of the insects floating in the air; but all hushed to Ronald's ear, which caught nothing but the booming of the ocean, murmuring in its ceaseless tones : ' The wicked are like the troubled sea when it cannot rest, whose waters cast up mire and dirt. There is no peace, saith my God, to the wicked.'

So he sat for minutes, and thought them hours; and so he might have sat even till night, conscious of nothing but the sense of hopeless weakness and desolation, when a gentle hand touched him, and a childish but most musical voice said, in a low and frightened tone, ' Ronald, is it you? Are you ill?'

It was Rachel Lester. He started up, and his haggard face confirmed the suspicion she had expressed.

' I thought it was you, but I was afraid. You are ill; I will run and fetch papa : he is just coming.'

' No, no ;' Ronald stopped her, as she would have hastened away; 'not Mr Lester; I can't see him; and I am not ill, not at all, only tired; I must go.'

Rachel looked doubtful. ' You are very pale, Ronald; papa would rather see you, I am sure.'

' He can do me no good—good-bye.'

She looked wistfully in his face, and tears gathered in her

eyes : ' Ronald, you are so very unhappy ; I wish I could do anything for you.' Most touching and earnest was the tone ; and Ronald paused as he was about to leave her, and said, ' Thank you, Rachel ; that is more than many would say.'

'Papa would do a great deal for you,' she replied, ' if you would tell him what is the matter. May I say it to him ?'

' Say what ?—that I am ill ? '

' Yes, if you are ill ! but if it is only that things vex you, he would like to help you if you would let him.'

' And if he could,' said Ronald, bitterly.

' But he can help every one ; at least, he can't, but God can, through him.'

' Mr Lester can do a great deal, I know that, Rachel,' said Ronald, his moody tone changing into the gentle accent in which he had spoken to the child at the cottage; 'but there may be some things beyond his cure. Don't fret, though,' he added, seeing that Rachel's face expressed her commiseration for feel-ings which yet she was unable to understand ; ' my troubles won't come in your way.'

' They will, though,' said Rachel ; ' I can't bear to see you so, Ronald.'

Ronald's smile passed over his face, as a gleam of sad sunshine at the close of a day of storms.

' God made us all to be happy,' continued Rachel ; ' so papa · says.'

' He made you to be happy, Rachel,' exclaimed Ronald, earnestly.

' And you too, Ronald.'

He shook his head.

' But we must be happy if we make others happy,' continued Rachel.

' Perhaps so, if we do.'

' But you do. You make little Barney happy.' She paused, expecting his assent, but he did not give it, and she went on. ' He was crying for you the other day, when papa and I went to see him.'

' He cries for a great many things,' said Ronald, with some impatience of tone.

' Please don't say so ; he loves you very much, and he would not at all know what to do without you.'

' He will be taken soon,' replied Ronald, mournfully, yet not despondingly.

'And then he will be like an angel, and God will give you some one else to take care of. O Ronald! can any one be unhappy who can work for God?'

Silence followed for a few seconds, whilst Ronald gazed intently upon the expanse of the sea, with its high horizon blending with the sky; then a sigh escaped him as if some load had passed from his heart. He turned round abruptly; 'Good-bye, Rachel; you are good, if no one else is.'

'Good-bye, Ronald; we are going to see Barney.'

Ronald walked a few steps slowly away, and then returned to say; 'Barney wants another little cushion for his head, Rachel, if you could let him have it.'

'Yes, I will be sure and remember.'

He walked on again, his step blither and firmer; and again he came back; 'I left him in a hurry just now, and could not show him the picture-book I brought. Perhaps you will for me, —and will you say I will try and see him again to-morrow?'

'Thank you; he will be so glad. Are you going up the hills?'

'I don't know, perhaps so;' but the tone, sad and indifferent though it was, had lost its accent of despair. Something had changed the current of Ronald's moody thoughts, and led him out of himself. Perhaps he was treasuring in his heart the words, comforting and hopeful as the sweet little face which had just been gazing upon him—'Can any one be unhappy who can work for God?'

Rachel watched him as he walked away, with that sense of interest and surprise, mingled with awe, which children always feel when brought in contact with the suffering of persons older than themselves; and at length waking up suddenly to the consciousness that she was alone upon the hills, and that her father ought by this time to have joined her, she was about to run back to the place where she had left him, when a faint yet sharp cry of distress broke upon the stillness, followed by another, and another; and the next instant Ronald repassed her, though at some little distance, making his way in the direction of the rugged cliff of rock and shingle, which formed the highest point of the beacon.

CHAPTER XVIII.

'ARE you going far, sir, this afternoon?' Mrs Robinson stopped Mr Bruce, as his hand was upon the fastening of the little gate in the courtyard.

'To the church ; I may go further, but I have not much heart to go anywhere.'

Perhaps it was illness which made Mr Bruce speak so despondingly. He did appear very much out of health ; his complexion had the yellow parchment look common to persons who have lived long in a hot climate.

'You haven't been into the church yet, sir.'

'Not yet. Mr Lester forbids the week days, and sent me last Sunday to Cleve.'

'Yes, sir, yes ; I remember. Perhaps it might be as well if I went, too, for the keys. Jacob Clarke is an odd man.'

'There is no reason. I have met Jacob at the Parsonage.'

'He's very blind,' said Mrs Robinson, in a meditative tone ; 'and deaf, too, sometimes.'

'I shall do very well ; don't trouble yourself. I shall go to the Parsonage to drink tea.'

His manner was that of a man whose mind is quite preoccupied ; and it might have appeared unkind to persons who only knew him slightly. But Mrs Robinson did not take it to heart much, certainly not as much as Mr Bruce himself, when a momentary self-recollection reminded him of his tone, which had been sharper than his words. He looked back at her, and nodded ; 'Good-bye, Granny !'—he must have learned to call her that from Rachel Lester—don't expect me till you see me ; but don't worry about me.'

The sober, melancholy-visaged woman shook her head : 'Thoughtless—always the same ! But 'tis to be expected !' and with a resigned air she repaired to the farm-kitchen, to superintend some arrangements for her guest's comfort.

Half an hour afterwards she was at the gate again, for she had heard it open, and thought he must be returned. It had been opened, but by Goff, the fisherman, not by Mr Bruce. He came up to her with a swaggering air.

'Your friend at home, eh?'

'Not at home,' was the short answer.

'Gone up the hills, I suppose?'

' Perhaps so.'

' But you can't say for certain, if your life depended on it !'

' Mr Bruce doesn't trouble himself to tell me for certain where he's going.'

' And you don't trouble yourself to ask, of course ! And you don't know, either, I suppose, how long he means to be staying in these parts ?'

' He doesn't tell me.'

' Nor where he comes from, nor where he is going to ! nor nothing about him ! Before I'd trust such a man !'——

' You aren't asked to trust him,' was the quiet reply.

' He'd find it mighty different if I was ! I suppose, now, he gives a load of trouble ?'

' As much and as little as most people.'

' A sort of chap who's made to melt in your fingers, I should say !' continued Goff.

' He's a gentleman who does not trouble himself about other people, at all events !' said Mrs Robinson, indignantly.

' Ay! a gentleman ! I should have said, now, he was that ; though 'tisn't all gentlefolks that's to be trusted. But he's true blood, is he ? I learned to know the difference, in the old days, when you and I lived up at the Hall together.'

' I don't remember when you and I ever lived at any place together, Mr Goff,' said Mrs Robinson, haughtily. ' I recollect when you were a farm-youth upon the estate ; and perhaps it might have been as well for you if you had kept to your calling.'

' That's as folks think. Every one to his liking. Your friend, now, I should say, would never have had a sea fancy, like mine ?'

' I never asked him.'

' Oh ! but you can find out fast enough, from what a man talks of and goes after. Why, there's the Captain ! you couldn't be with him five minutes, before you'd know he was a sailor.'

' If all sailors are like Captain Vivian,' replied Mrs Robinson, ' the fewer the better !'

' Then your friend's not a sailor. I thought as much as that the night of the wreck. He'd never have let himself be cap-sized, if he'd had an ounce of old ocean in him. He's from foreign parts, though ?'

' The vessel came from America, as you know.'

' Yes, sure, I do know. Who should better ? for I've had more to do with her than most folks. But I should say it might have

I

touched at other places—Jamaica, now ; I 'm downright certain somebody said it had touched at Jamaica.'

' Perhaps it might. Have you anything more to say, particular, Mr Goff? I must go in-doors.'

' Only that I 've got a nephew living in Jamaica ; and I should just like to know whether this gentleman knows anything about him.'

' Not likely, I should think.'

' I don't know. 'Tisn't such a large place. I 've had a good many thoughts about my nephew lately. Possibly you 'd do a good deed, and ask about him ? '

' I can't trouble Mr Bruce about anybody's nephew !' exclaimed Mrs Robinson. ' He has enough to do to take care of himself.'

' Umph !—and his children, I suppose. You wouldn't have him not take a care for them ? '

' Not if he has any. But I can't stand here any longer. If you want to see Mr Bruce, you 'll please to leave a message.'

' No, I can't say I wished particularly to see him ; only I thought that, being, as I supposed, fresh from Jamaica, he might be able to give me a word or two about my nephew. Or perchance, when he writes, he 'd make an inquiry for me. When will he be in ? '

' I can't say.'

' Somewhere before eight, I suppose ? '

' I don't know ; he is likely to be out all the evening.'

' Ay ! gone up to Parson Lester's ; I could have guessed so much.'

' I didn't say he was gone there.'

' Only if he 's to be out all the evening, he 's not likely to be gone anywhere else. There's a way, you see, of putting two and two together. But never mind, I 'm not going to trouble him nor you neither ; so good afternoon to you.'

He went out at the wicket-gate. Mrs Robinson's countena ce wa3 wonderfully imperturbable ; but certainly, after that interview, a shade of restless anxiety might have been traced in it.

And Mr Bruce pursued his way to the cottage of Jacob Clarke, the sexton. It stood alone, at the end of the lane leading to the church hill ; and some might have thought it a desolate home for the sickly man who inhabited it ; but Jacob would not have exchanged it for the most spacious dwelling-house in the village. It was a palace to him, for it was in full view of the church ; and

in the church, since its restoration by General Vivian and Mr
Lester, all the pride of the sexton's hurt seemed to have concentrated itself.

He was working in his garden when Mr Bruce came up ; but
the moment he saw him the spade was laid aside, and he was
feeling in his pocket for the heavy keys, which were his inseparable companions.

'You'll be for going up, I suppose, sir' he said, almost before
Mr Bruce came within hearing.

'I was thinking of it, Jacob ; but I won't trouble you, if you'll
just let me take the keys. You are busy I see. How are your
eyes this afternoon?'

'Baddish ; this left one, special. They say I shan't get any
better till I get worse, and then I can have something done to
them ; but I rub on with hoping.'

'Happy for you that you can. Just let me have the keys, and
I will bring them back quite safely. You can trust me.'

'I trust your voice more than your look' replied Jacob, with a
grim smile. 'I've learned a good deal to know people of late by
their voices ; and there's a sound in your that somehow comes
home to me natural.'

Mr Bruce stretched out his hand for the keys.

Jacob hesitated. 'I'm thinking,—I'll tell ye what, I'll e'en
go up with ye ; the digging will do well eough to-morrow, and
I should just like to know what you'll say o the old place. 'Tis
a beautiful one outside now, ain't it ?'

'Yes, very beautiful. The old walls, I see.'

'Ay ! sure ; we should all have broke ur hearts if the old
walls had been down. It's the windows that's new chiefly—
outside, that is ; inside, you'll see it's wonerful.'

'And all done by Mr Lester?'

'No, no ; Mr Lester helped, as a good man would ; but 'twas
the General, chief. He'd been thinking f it, they say, for a
long time, and 'twas the first thing that seemed to cheer him up
after all his troubles.'

They were ascending the steps together as Jacob said this.
Mr Bruce stopped.

'You're out of breath, sir.'

'No, scarcely ; but I am not very strong How long ago did
you say it was since the restoration of the curch?'

'Some twelve years now, sir, since it was nished ; but it took
a long time about. I declare now I was srry, in a way, when

it came to an end ; and so, I suspect, was the General ; he was up here most every day, watching how it went on.'

'He began it after his troubles ; he has had a good many, I suppose?'

'You may say that; a hard life, poor old gentleman ! And now between seventy and eighty, and no one near him but Miss Mildred ; and all the old feuds as bitter as ever ! Somehow it's strange when a man's travelling to his grave. But there! it's the way of the world.'

'There have been family disputes, then?'

'Not so much disputes ; but the General's uppish,—bent on his own ways. It's been the fashion of the Vivians from father to son.'

'And the General is very determined?'

'Firm as an old oak. He'd break, but he'd never bend. I can't help thinking sometimes, on looking back, that 'twould have been better for him if he could. But now, sir, just take your seat here, and look round. You won't get a finer sight than that all over the country.' Jacob pointed to a wooden bench placed at the top of the steps for the accommodation of the old people. 'You'll not be sorry to rest, I dare say, after this pull up the steps ; and you'll get a notion of the country which may help you. There's not a bit of the village, as you see, to be seen; only the hills. But on to the right there are the woods—the Cleve woods. That is the beginning of General Vivian's property.'

'How far does it extend?' inquired Mr Bruce.

'Extend ! Why, he's got the whole of Encombe, not a cottage in the place but belongs to him. Only one farm—the Grange they call it—which is not his; and sorrow's the day that Captain John ever went to live in it.'

'Captain Vivian, I suppose you mean. I have heard some of the poor people speak of him as Captain John.'

'They call him that, I can't say exactly why. He's not a regular captain, though he's had a good deal to do with the sea, they say, of late years. He likes sailor fashions, and so he goes by the name : but he's not fit to be a Vivian.' Jacob lowered his voice, as if communicating this fact confidentially.

Mr Bruce turned away his head—the sexton's face seemed peering into his. Jacob continued in the same undertone : 'The long and the short of the matter is, he's a disgrace to the family, and the ruin and the curse of every one that joins with him.

And he's been so for years, and his fathers before him; and no
wonder the General can't abide him, when he's been working
against him and his set from a boy.'

'From a boy? I thought the great quarrel had been of late
years, about—about—General Vivian's son.'

'Oh! you've heard of all that, have you?' said Jacob, with
some disappointment in his tone. Sure enough, there was a
great quarrel about Master Edward; but 'twasn't that was the
beginning, as who should know better than I?'

'Because you lived in the family, I suppose,' said Mr Bruce,
rising from his seat.

'You'd best rest a minute or two longer, sir; your voice is
quite shaky now; and there's no hurry. What were you saying?
Oh! about my having lived in the family. Well, I did live
there, or, at least my father did, which was much the same thing.
He was the butler, and I worked in the garden, and about in
different ways, making myself useful; and so of course I came
to know a good deal of the goings on; and sad enough they were
at times.'

'But General Vivian always lived a very steady life,' said Mr
Bruce, quietly.

'Oh! steady as old time, for that; too steady perhaps; at least,
somehow it didn't seem to turn out well. But you see, his father,
and his grandfather before him, had been just acting different;
—spending here, and throwing away there, till at last, when the
General came into his property, I've been told, there wasn't fifty
acres of it strictly his own, 'twas all so hampered with debts;
and Captain John's friends having a pretty large share of the
claims. Theirs was the younger branch of the family; and they
lived in the neighbourhood, and were always quarrelling, and
bringing lawsuits, and these and the extravagance had just
ruined the property.

'Well! the General, as I said, was a firm man, not a bit like
those that had gone before him. Where he got his character
nobody could think; but 'tis said that his mother was something
of the same kind. If she was, she hadn't power to keep her husband from ruin or next to it. Perhaps she may have tried most
with the children; for certain it is, that when the General came
into his property—and that was when he was very young, only
twenty-five, after his elder brother's death—he set his mind to
one thought, and only one, how to get matters straight. My
father was in his service then, and for old love's sake—for he'd

known him from a boy—helped him right and left. But 'twas
hard work; and there isn't many that would have borne to live
as they did in those days—the General still keeping to be a
soldier, and scrimping and pinching: and no servants scarce at
the Hall; no company when he was at home; no carriages—
scarce, indeed, butter to your bread. But it answered: what,
indeed, wouldn't answer which the General set his mind to?
First one thing was paid off, and then another; and the rumour
got abroad that Cleve Hall was looking up in the world again;
and, sure enough, 'twas true. No thanks, though, to any of the
other Vivians, who did all they could to stop matters, and nearly
sent the General frantic; for with all his close ways for himself,
he wasn't a bit so with others; and when claims were made, if
there was but a shadow of honesty in them, he was ever for
paying them; being honourable, he called it. As my father
used to say, he was always riding his virtues to death; and 'tis
my belief, the other Vivians would have been much more honourable, if they hadn't known that what they set up for they
were sure to have.'

'And they were living in Encombe, then?' inquired Mr
Bruce.

'Near it, sir. I hope I ain't tiring you. I thought you
seemed to have a care to know about them. They had a house
the other side of Cleve, and a good bit of property in the neighbourhood. The General would have given anything they asked
for the land, but they never would part with it. 'Twas their
pleasure to be close to him, to spite him. I don't think, though,
he took it much to heart then; he didn't see the trouble it was
like to bring upon him.'

'But he married at last,—'twas after a good many years.
His lady was very young, and wonderfully pretty: not a bit like
what you'd have thought he'd choose. I don't mean as to being
pretty, but as to lightheartedness, and not thinking. As for him,
he'd never been young, care had come upon him so early, and his
stiff ways and set notions weren't to be broken. And so when
they came to live at the Hall—that was directly he married—for
'twas one of his notions never to marry till he could bring his
wife to her settled home—things were not so very much changed
from what they had been before; I mean as to servants and
housekeeping. I know even in my own father 'twas to be seen.
He'd been so taught to be particular, that he couldn't for
the life of him abide a penny's being spent where there wasn't

strict occasion. And very good of course it was, only now and then it struck me that he didn't see where there was occasion. The lady, as I said, was different. She liked to have things handsome about her, and to see her friends, and to be gay; and the General was desperately fond of her, and indulged her in her fancies as much as 'twas in his nature. But 'twasn't done with a hearty good-will; and specially it used to fret him—so I've heard—to see Master Edward turning after his mother's fashions rather than after his own. Are you in a hurry, sir?' for Mr Bruce moved impatiently.

'No, no ; go on. Master Edward, you say, turned after his mother?'

'Yes, sir, in a way ; but I don't think he ever had her thought —for Mrs Vivian, with all her merry ways, had a care for every one about her. But perhaps it wasn't to be expected of Master Edward. He was young, and an only son, and the property was all to be his ; and so he looked upon it as his own too early, it's my belief. Anyhow, from time to time there was black looks at the Hall, and 'twas well seen things weren't going on smoothly. Captain John was at the bottom of a good deal then, as he has been since. He was much about Master Edward's age, and spite of all the General could say, they made friends together. Not so strange that, as you may think,' continued Jacob, observing that Mr Bruce gave a start, as he supposed, of surprise. ' I remember Captain John myself in those days ; and there was a good deal that a man might like, particularly a young man, not very knowing of the world, like Master Edward. He was very free-spoken and hearty ; and that took with Master Edward all the more because his father thwarted him, and his life up at the Hall was too set up and stiff for a young man's mind.'

'Mr Vivian had sisters, though,' observed Mr Bruce, with something of reproach in his tone.

'Well, he had ; and a prettier, nicer pair of young ladies there wasn't to be found in all the country round. But, you know, sir, we see it every day ; women can't make up all to men, any more than men can make up all to women. There's a need of their own kind ; and so, when Master Edward came from school and from college, he must needs take to Captain John, just because he hadn't any one else to go to. And this made the General desperate. His mother and the young ladies, I believe, tried a good deal to stop it. I know my father said, that many's the time he has come into the room and heard them begging

Master Edward, for dear life, just to keep away from what the General didn't approve. But he was strange, Master Edward was ;—somehow strong and not strong—strong for his own will, and not strong for anything else ; and so he'd promise for a time, and then, when Captain John came in his way, it was all the same as before. And you see, sir,' and Jacob lowered his tone as if knowing that he was approaching a dangerous topic, ' he was afraid of his father ; so, in fact, they all were. It was at the bottom of a deal of mischief. If a thing was wrong, 'twas always to be kept from the General, because he'd no mercy.'

' But I thought the General was gentle to women,' said Mr Bruce ; ' you said he was so to his wife.'

' Gentle in his own way, but 'twas a lion's gentleness. Cross him in his fancies once, and you'd never do it a second time. Not that he went off in a passion—'twas all cold and stony ; but knocking at his heart, when he was offended, was like knocking at a wall. He was wonderfully proud, though, of his daughters, specially of Miss Edith, the eldest. Folks said that 'twas be-cause she was so like her mother. And certain she was very like her ; not quite so pretty, perhaps, and yet with a face that did one's heart good to look upon : and always a pleasant smile and a merry word—and such a laugh ! Ah, sir, the Hall's a different place now from what it was when she was living ! She lies now'——

Mr Bruce rose suddenly. ' We will go into the church ; give me the keys.' He held out his hand for them, but without staying to receive them, hurried along the little paved path leading to the porch.

Jacob followed him with a wondering gaze. ' Poor gentle-man ! Then what they say of him is true, and he's daft, sure !' With a slow step he plodded along the strip of worn pavement, murmuring as he went, ' He'd have heard to the end for certain if he wasn't daft.'

But Mr. Bruce was standing composedly in the porch now ; and conscious, probably, of his own impatience, he addressed the sexton with something of an apology for his abruptness : ' I was feeling the cold ; it is cold in the wind. Let me have the keys, and, thank you, I won't keep you.'

' By your leave, sir'—Jacob's self-love was a little wounded, for he had been wasting his words—' the keys are my chief charge, as you may say, and I'd best look after them ; so I'll

Just open the door and wait, for it seems you 'll not be wanting
to have much told you.'

His tone of annoyance was evident, and Mr Bruce's manner
softened into consideration.

'You shall tell me more, Jacob, only not now—not now,' he
repeated to himself, and he took the man's hand and wrung it
heartily. 'Thank you, you loved them all ; yes, I know you
did.'

'Daft!' was again Jacob's comment to himself; but he
changed his intention, and instead of resting himself in the
porch, followed Mr Bruce into the church.

It was of moderate size, and consisted of two aisles. The east
end of the south aisle was a kind of chapel for the Vivian family,
divided from the chancel by an oak screen, but open to the rest
of the church. Three large, exquisitely-worked monuments, of
the date of the fourteenth century, the carving of which had been
cleaned, and in part coloured and gilded according to the original
design, filled up the centre. The deeply-cut letters engraven
upon them, told that the recumbent figures, so meekly lifting up
their hands to heaven, were the effigies of William and Everard
Vivian, and of Walter and Eleanor his wife, the first of the name
who were the possessors of the manor of Cleve.

The stranger did not pause to examine any part of the church
in detail. He stayed not to mark the beauty of the decorated
chancel-screen, nor to marvel at the exceeding richness of the
stone reredos, nor the gorgeousness of the east window. He
passed without notice the long flickering lines of fairy light
streaming across the marble tombs ; but his eye wandered over
the walls, and the pavement, marked with quaint figures of the
honoured of olden time, and more modern yet already half-
defaced inscriptions, till it rested upon a small plate, let into the
floor of the Vivian chapel, and inscribed with the name of Edith
Vivian.

'Yes, that 's where she lies, sir.'

It was a ghastly face which met the sexton's gaze, but he
could not see its change; and the voice which answered him
was unaltered, save perhaps that the tone was lowered, to suit
the sacredness of the building.

'I see—I know it is the Vivian chapel.'

'The place where they all rest, sir, from father to son, from
generation to generation. But there 'll be none to follow now.'

The stranger gazed upon that small brass plate with a fixedness which seemed fascination. 'Seventeen years ago,' he murmured to himself.

'Just seventeen, come Michaelmas — the year after the troubles ; they broke her heart.'

The words were heard, for a tremulous shudder passed over the stranger's frame ; and seizing Jacob's arm, and holding it by a grasp which it was impossible to resist, he led him again into the porch. There, standing before him, quietly, yet with a sternness, the result of strong self-control rather than of anger, he repeated ; 'They broke her heart, did you say ?'

'Why, yes, yes, sir,' Jacob looked around him in alarm.

'You were telling me about it before,—let me hear.'

The tone was too decided to be disobeyed ; yet Jacob's voice shook as he began, and his words were uttered unequally, whilst stealthily he raised his dim eyes to catch, if possible, the impression which he was making upon the moody, sullen, withered-looking man, whose excitable feelings he had evidently, but unexpectedly, from some unknown cause, aroused.

'They said it was caused by the troubles,' he began, 'and I never heard there was reason to doubt it. Sure enough, before they came, she was blithe as a bird ; and the day she heard of them she fell sick,—and the same day twelvemonth they laid her in her grave. Would you wish to hear more, sir ?'

There was neither assent nor dissent. It seemed that the stranger could not trust himself with words.

Jacob went on : 'You know about Master Edward, sir ; perhaps there's no need to go over the story ; and who can tell the rights of it ?'

'Ay ! who ?' exclaimed the stranger, impetuously.

'It's my belief there's more to be known about that matter than people think for,' continued the sexton, more heartily, feeling encouraged by even a word of sympathy ; 'my father always said so, and he was like to know the truth, seeing he lived so long in the family ; but the General was never one to be dealt with like other folks. You know, sir, Master Edward went abroad.'

'I have heard so.'

'That was after he left college, and after his mother's death. Poor lady ! if she had lived, no doubt things would have been different. As it was, he only got into mischief when he was at home ; and the General, 'twas said, thought that a new country might give him new notions. To say the truth of him, he had

not got any that were what you may say bad, only quite different
from his father's; the General being set upon keeping up dignity,
as he called it, and getting back more and more of the estate, and
setting off his family upon a new footing ; and Master Edward
not thinking a whit about it, but only mindful to take things
easy himself, and let every one else do the same.   I 've heard tell,
too, that one of the causes why the General was so bent upon
getting his son out of the country just then, was because of the
young lady, one of the Campbells,—they lived at the Manor
Farm; you 'll know Mrs Campbell of the Lodge now, sir ?   She's
the mother.'

'Yes, yes;' the quick tone was not impatience, but agony.

'The truth of that, sir, is what I can't vouch for.   If there was
anything going on, they managed to keep it wonderfully close ;
but the General might have found it out ; and if he did, he was
sure to make the most of it, I 'll warrant you.   He hated the
Campbells like mad.   They had always sided with the other
Vivians ; and there was some old, family difference from I can't
tell how many years back; and of late the Campbells had gone
down in the world, and there had been some bad marriages, which
had brought them still lower.   Old Mrs Campbell—she that 's at
the Lodge now—was the daughter of some man quite nothing
compared with the General, and so there were relations and con-
nections whom he didn't choose to have anything to do with ; in
fact, I 've heard my father say that it was quite a cat-and-dog life
the two families lived ; and you may well think, sir, how troubled
the General would be when he thought his only son was likely to
mix himself up with them.   Anyhow, Master Edward went abroad.
And glad enough he was to go, 'tis my belief, except for the
thought of parting with his sisters, 'specially Miss Edith.   She
was, in a way, his favourite.   I saw them as they stood together
before the door, just as the carriage was coming up to take Master
Edward away.   She was like an angel, so loving and pretty, and
putting her arm round his neck, and kissing him, and telling him
that 'twouldn't be home till he came back ; and he smiling, and
trying to comfort her, and saying how he was going to enjoy
himself; and then, looking up at Miss Mildred, who was lying
on her sofa by the window—for 'twas just then she began to get
ill—and nodding to her, and promising to bring her all kinds of
fine things from abroad.   Ay ! they were mainly set upon one
another, these two sisters and Master Edward.'

'And the General ?'

' He looked on upon them, stern-like, with his arms crossed in his fashion, saying the young ladies were silly, and would make any one a fool, with their care ; yet pleased too, for he patted Miss Edith on the cheek, and called her Sunbeam, which was the name some of the villagers gave her ; and then he shook Master Edward's hand heartily, and said, " God bless you, my boy ;" and it's my belief there was a tear in his eye. If there was, it's the first tear that ever mortal saw there. Miss Edith had the last word. Master Edward put his head out of the carriage-window and said,—the words stayed in my mind for days after,—" Edith, darling ! keep up ; you'll soon learn to live without me." 'Twas a man's mistake, sir. She tried to live without him, and she died.'

The sexton paused, for his voice had grown tremulous and husky ; and Mr Bruce, too, passed his hand over his eyes, and sat down, his hands firmly clenching the stick on which he rested.

Jacob continued—' Soon after Master Edward's departure, the Campbells went, and then Encombe and Cleve were quiet enough, with no gentry about, but the General and the two young ladies. That is the time I can remember best myself. I had work in the garden : and my father having, as I told you, been butler for so many years, I was pretty often in the house, and got a tolerable glimmering of how things went on.'

' And Edith ?'—the words escaped hurriedly, and were immediately corrected,—' Miss Vivian ? was she well then and happy ?'

' She took on sadly at first,' replied the sexton ; ' but 'twasn't a heart to live upon trouble ; and when news came that Master Edward was well and happy, and likely to return before long, she cheered up mainly, and for the first part of that year she was the life of the house. 'Twould have been rather a dull one but for her. Miss Mildred was very cheerful, but quiet-like ; and the General never seemed so proud of her as he was of Miss Edith. He would go to her when there was business to be done, for she was more clear-headed, and ready to do everything for everybody, and a kind word for all ; but she wasn't blythe, like Miss Edith, who was always singing and dancing about the house. And then Miss Mildred was sickly ; and somehow the General was one who didn't take to sickly folks ; he didn't understand them, and was always thinking they could get up and do just the same as others. The two young ladies, though, were marvellous fond of each other; 'twas quite a sight to see them together, they were so one-like; and so, upon the whole, it was a very happy home.'

'Till the storm came.'—It was a voice like the rising of a storm which spoke. Jacob stopped for an instant, startled by it.

'Ay, sir, as you say, till the storm came; and that was soon enough. Master Edward had been away some months when it began to brew; how I don't quite know, but when the letters came of a morning, I used to hear my father say, he'd rather face a cannon-ball than carry them up to the General; he was so put out by the news he had. Some rumour was afloat that Master Edward had been spending a deal of money; and that seemed likely enough, seeing that 'twas always his way; but no one knew for certain. At last one morning, I'd been in the garden, weeding the flower-beds, and then I was sent into the park to give some help about a fence that was to be moved; and as I was hard at work, not thinking of anything, one of the boys working with me looked up, and, says he, "Jacob, who's that coming across here?" 'Twas a tall, swaggering-looking fellow, walking quite as if he was some-body, and was to be obeyed; and behind, a short, bluff man, a kind of servant. The first I knew directly, for I'd seen Captain Vivian often enough, and had a full remembrance of him, and his doings. The other I've learned to know better since; you may have seen him yourself, sir, whilst you've been here,— a rough-looking fellow, a fisherman he is now, or a smuggler, as most people say, he's always out upon the Point.'

'Goff! yes, I know him well, very well;' and there was a marked emphasis upon the words.

'He had work about the place out-of-doors, as a boy; and then he was taken into the house, and made a servant for Master Edward, and he had carried him abroad; but it seems somehow they hadn't suited, and he had been turned over to the Captain. So it was they were together that day. I learned all that, though afterwards.'

'Yes, well! But that day?'

'Ay, that day, sir; you needn't think I'm likely to forget it. I saw the Captain and the other fellow go straight up to the house, and, said I to myself, there's mischief coming with that man, as sure as summer comes with swallows. I didn't exactly think what kind of mischief, for I hadn't heard much about where he'd been lately; else my thoughts would surely have turned to Master

Edward. But something led me to go into the house, and wait to hear what was going on. I followed them up to the door, and the Captain, he gave a tremendous pull at the bell, and such a peal there was sounding through the house ! And when the door was opened, it was a kind of king's voice that said he must see General Vivian directly. My father happened to be in the library at the time, where the young ladies were sitting. It was close to the front steps, and you could hear quite plainly what any one said. He told me afterwards that Miss Mildred turned very pale when she heard the Captain's voice, and, said she, " Edith, you go to my father and tell him who's here." She couldn't go herself and she wouldn't trust anybody else with the message, knowing how the General would hate it. Miss Edith went up to her chair and kissed her, and said " Never mind, Mildred, we'll hope on," or some words of that kind ; but she was cast down herself seemingly, for she walked quite slowly out of the room.

'Captain John was shown into the little drawing-room, and a good long time he was kept waiting ; and my father heard him storming away because of it with Goff ;—for he would make him go with him ; he wouldn't have him sent into the servants' hall, as was the custom. At last the General rang his study bell, and my father answered it, as he always did. Miss Edith was behind the General's chair, smoothing his hair, and fondling him ; and, to look at them, I dare say you might have called them brother and sister instead of father and child ; for he was a wonderfully fine-looking man in those days, was the General, and bore his years bravely, " Captain Vivian's waiting to see me, Clarke, I hear," said the General ; " he may come up. Edith, you must go." His voice was as firm as mine is now, and you wouldn't have known that he thought or cared for the man a straw; only that he had a trick of crossing his legs and moving his left foot up and down when he was sorely pressed, and the less he said the faster his foot went ; 'twas his way of venting his passion. The foot went like a see-saw that morning ; and Miss Edith said to my father when she left the room, " Clarke, don't you let the General be tired out." That was as much as to say, you be on your watch for what's going on ; for my father was a trusty and knowing man, and many a time when the young ladies had been troubled with persons coming to worry the General, they had got him to go in and interrupt them. So my father showed Captain Vivian into the study, and he saw the General stand up and bow, which was all the greeting he gave ; and any one but Captain John might

have been cowed by his manner. But not a bit he; before my
father was out of the room he began, saying that he had come
from a long distance, and he thought it hard he should be kept
waiting, and all in such a rough way that the General was put
askew almost before a word had been spoken.

'My father went back to his work. Not a word did he tell
me or any one, then; such a cautious man he was about everything which concerned the General's interest. But I was mainly
curious; and, as I could get nothing out of him, I made friends
with the housekeeper, as was my custom sometimes, and got a
permission from her that I might come into the house and dine.
I was standing in the servants' hall, waiting about a little, and
doing just what few things there was to be done, when my father
came in, and says he to the footman, "Here's a stranger come to
dine with you, Charles;" and with that he brought in Goff.
Twasn't a pleasant hearing, exactly, for in former days no one
had ever taken much to the man; but he had come from foreign
parts, and he'd seen Master Edward lately; and so there was a
good deal to say and to hear, and we all got round him and
began asking him questions. I've often thought since how
queer he was on that day,—not a bit like what he's turned out
since,—no blustering and storming, but a sort of creep-mouse
look, which somehow turned quite against me; and every now
and then stopping to hear if there was a bell, or a sound. But
he wasn't likely to hear that with the clatter which was going
on in the hall, and after a while he seemed to give up listening,
and began to talk very fast, telling heaps of odd stories, and
hinting things now and then about Master Edward which nearly
made my hair stand on end. Yet he never spoke out; and
when my father taxed him once with what he had been saying,
and asked him to explain, he caught himself up quite short, and
looked for all the world as if he knew he was telling what wasn't
true. Certainly, I fancied him less than ever, specially when I
saw what a friend he was to the ale flagon. Why he drank it
as if 'twas water!

'There was dinner in the housekeeper's room for my father,
but not a bit did he seem to trouble himself to eat. I had a
notion that he couldn't make up his mind to let Goff out of his
sight, for he was in and out of the hall continually; and, said he
once to Goff, "Your Master's holding a long story up-stairs."
"There's plenty to say, when folks have been so long parted,"
said Goff; and with that he gave a kind of inside chuckle, and

laid down his knife just as he was cutting a bit of cheese, and
set himself again to listen. Sure enough at that moment there
was a bell, a quick, ringing one, from the General's room. I
chanced to be looking at the man at the moment. His face—
you wouldn't scarce believe it, for he's all over hard and brown
now, as if he was made of mahogany—but he hadn't seen such
rough times in those days, and, as I sat opposite to him, I noticed
that it turned of a sudden, not white, but a sort of grayish
colour, just for all the world as if he was going off into a fit.
'Twas only for a moment, though. He seized hold of the ale
jug, and such a drink as he took! it seemed all to go at a gulp;
and then down went the cup on the table, and he stood up, and
it crossed my mind that he'd had enough to make him unsteady. But not a whit that! It had only brought back the
right colour to his cheek; and says he, quickly, "That's for
me." My father caught him up with, "How do you know it's
for you?" He was taken aback, and his eyes quite flashed out,
but he only laughed and said, oh! he supposed it was, and he
must be ready; and, strange enough, when my father went up-
stairs he brought down word that Goff was to go up directly. I
didn't dare ask if anything was the matter, so many being about;
but I was certain that something was wrong, for my father had
a look on him which I'd seen often enough to understand.
But dinner went on, and was finished, and every one went to
his work; and I was to have gone to mine, only my father had
something for me to do in his pantry. It wasn't so far from the
hall but that I could hear people go in and out, and up and
down-stairs; and, after a while—two hours I'm sure it was
from the time I first saw the Captain come—he and Goff took
their departure,—not blustering and noisy, as they had come,
but stealing out and walking off to the village, without a word
of good-bye to any one.

'There was no sound in the house for near half an hour afterwards. The young ladies had had their lunch; and where they
were, or what they were doing, I couldn't say, only I missed Miss
Edith's voice, for she used to go singing about like a bird. It
came over me, I remember, as something awful that, with so
many near, there shouldn't be one to be heard; but before long
a heavy door slammed to, and then came the General's step
along the open gallery over the hall. He was going the way to
the young ladies' sitting-room.

'My father called me then, and I stood talking with him in

the hall, about some errand he wished me to do for him in Cleve. It might have been three minutes, or not so much, we were there. I was just asking him where I should find the man he wanted to see; and I remember he bade me attend, and laid his hand on my shoulder, in his kind way, when a scream—sharp and piteous, scarce like a human scream—rang through the old house. 'Twas Miss Edith's voice; and my father and I glanced at each other in horror, and rushed up-stairs.'

'She was dead!' escaped from Mr Bruce's lips; and he covered his face with his hands, and sank, shuddering, upon the bench.

'No, sir. She had had her death-stroke; but she was not to die then. She was lying on the floor insensible, Miss Mildred kneeling by her; quiet—you wouldn't have known there was aught strange, save that her face seemed all of a sudden changed into stone. And the General was there too; standing up before them, stern as on a battle-field, but his eyes fixed with a horrible stare straight before him. They did not let me stay more than a moment. Mrs Robinson was called, and I was sent off to Cleve for a doctor. I came back in less than an hour. The General had shut himself up in his room; Miss Mildred was with her sister. No one could tell anything that had happened for certain; only that Captain John and Goff had gone off from Encombe like a shot, and somehow—the news was about, that Master Edward and Miss Campbell were married.'

'And that was all?' exclaimed Mr Bruce, standing up, and grasping the sexton's arm.

'Bad enough 'twould have been, sir, if it had been all,' replied the sexton, hastily; 'but worse there must have been, far worse than that. 'Tisn't for me to say, when no one knows for sure; but a part of the truth was abroad quick enough. Master Edward had done something very dreadful, and was disinherited. What his sins were, it had been left for Captain Vivian and that fellow Goff to tell.'

A groan was the only reply.

'My story will soon enough be ended now, sir,' continued the sexton. 'The beginning of troubles was the end of the family history. They laid Miss Edith on her bed, and for weeks she never rose up from it. And day after day the word came that she was growing weaker and weaker, and that her brain was wandering; and doctors came from London, and nurses; and they talked, and ordered, and watched, and at last they got her round

K

in a way; and she came down-stairs, and moved about, and went into the garden. But it was her ghost only, not' herself. She could never be kept still, but was always dragging herself up and down the shrubbery walk by the great road, listening for a carriage, if it might draw up; or, when she was in-doors, standing before a picture of Master Edward, that's now in Miss Mildred's room, or pacing the gallery over the hall. But she never mentioned his name; no, not even to Miss Mildred. And at last, all of a sudden, the cloud came over her again, and she gave way, as it were, in a moment; and once more they took her to her bed, and never moved her from it till they carried her to her grave.'

The sexton paused, to dash away a tear. 'There was peace for her,' he added, in a tone of deep reverence. 'She had lived an angel's life, and she was ready for death. The sorrow was for him that had killed her.'

He was silent for a moment and then continued—

''Tis a heavy word to say of a father against his child, and he loving her as he did. But 'twas the General's way; there was no mercy. He'd have given his son to be shot, if it had come in the way of duty, and been the first to pull the trigger; and so, when he thought himself called on to give him up, he cast him off in a moment, and fancied that others could do the same. But they who said the General was a hard man, spoke of things they didn't understand. The day that Captain John brought the ill news, the General was hale and strong as the strongest man of his age in England. When he came out of his room three days afterwards to go to church, his hair was silvery gray, and he had the look and gait of a man of seventy. There, sir, I've done now; and I've tired you, no doubt; and my digging will be waiting for me. Will it please you to go into the church again?'

No answer came. The question was repeated, and Mr Bruce spoke as in a dream.

'The church, did you say? But the mystery—has it never been cleared up?'

'The mystery, sir? Oh! Master Edward's; yes, I understand. Cleared up, I can't say it has been, for no one can say for certain what passed between the General and Captain Vivian; but, of course, the marriage and the notion of Master Edward's gambling, was at the bottom of it; and cause enough for his being disinherited, according to the General's principles. He who'd been all his life striving to redeem the property, and making it the one thing he worked for—it was natural enough, perhaps, that he should take fright at the notion of its falling into hands which would scatter it. But what he really thought and felt, it isn't for such as I to guess at; and indeed I don't fancy there's any one that can tell, except, may be, Mr Lester. He came to live at Encombe just afterwards ; and he'd been Master Edward's tutor, and often staying at the Hall, and had worked hard, I've heard, to make the General and his son understand each other. I believe the General did open his mind to him at first, but when Mr Lester didn't quite agree, he closed up again, and lived for all the world as if shut up in a shell. That is to say, on that subject he's shut up, not on others. He gave himself much more to the poor people about that time, and set to work at the church, and grew more thoughtful for Miss Mildred, and took to petting and making much of her. Somehow, it seems to me, when I'm thinking over it all awhiles, that he's been for years like a man who knows he's very wrong in one way, but won't for the life of him give up, and so tries to keep his conscience clear by being good in all others. Mayn't it be so, sir?'

The sexton looked up at his companion inquiringly.

His answer was a half-crown, thrust into his hand ; and without a word, Mr Bruce turned away, and in a few seconds was seen striding up the pathway to the hills, with the speed of a maniac.

CHAPTER XIX.

ELLA had left Clement behind, without a thought. Mr Lester and Rachel, she imagined, were before her, and her inclination was to hasten after them. They were, however, at a considerable distance; and she went on, with her usual impetuosity, when interested, gaining ground upon them, but heeding little the direction she was taking, and without considering how she was to return. Once she heard Clement's call and answered it; but her voice was weak, and the sound did not reach him. So she must have proceeded half-walking and half-running, for more than a mile, but she was drawing nearer and nearer her object, and her efforts would soon end. The two figures sat down for a moment to rest, and a most uncomfortable misgiving crossed Ella's mind. The man was taller than Mr Lester, he looked unlike a gentleman, now that she could see him more distinctly, and the girl was dressed differently from Rachel. Ella could not recognise them at all; they were not even Encombe people : probably they belonged to Cleve, and were going thither by the short way, over the hills. That was quite out of the direction of the Beacon, and Clement would miss her. She looked round for him, and called. There was no answer; but the man who was sitting down heard her, and approached.

Ella was not frightened, but perplexed. The hills were very lonely, the paths in some parts confusing. One thing, however, was clear,—at least she thought it so,—that Clement would follow her in the direction of the Beacon; and when the stranger came up, Ella answered his question as to what she wanted, by begging to be told the nearest road to it.

'A good way off from the Beacon it is,' replied the man; 'a mile at the least. You aren't thinking of going up there by yourself, Miss?'

'I was going: I want to meet my brother,' was Ella's reply.

'Oh, your brother! that's different. Well, you must keep along under the hollow now, till you get to the pile of stones yonder, and then take the path to the right, and that will bring you into Crossdell; and from thence you may scramble up till you get to the foot of the Beacon. But, dear me !'—and he looked at Ella's slight figure with a kind of patronising compassion; 'you'll never get up, anyhow ; and if you do, you'll never find your way down again; or you'll get upon the Croome; and there'll be a business !'   .

'The Croome !' repeated Ella ; 'that is where the cliff falls away so, isn't it ?'

'Yes, the steep side of the Beacon, away to the east,' was the answer. 'Folks that don't know much about it are apt to set foot upon the Croome, taking it all for firm ground ; and then, ten to one, if they don't go down and down, till they'd give half they're worth to stop. However, I dare say your brother knows all about that, and he won't take you the dangerous side.'

A little fear there was in Ella's mind, but with it a good deal of excitement. Yet she could not at once decide whether to advance or go back. She asked how far it was from the point she had now reached to Encombe: about a mile and a half. That really seemed nothing ; and to have had a tiresome walk all by herself, for nothing—it would be too absurd! And then she should certainly miss Clement, and he would find his way to the Beacon, and she should be outdone. In Ella's chivalrous moments, when she was mistress over her natural indolence, there was nothing she disliked more than being beaten in anything, even in a walk ; and moreover she had an innate love of adventure, nearly allied to her poetical tastes, all of which urged her to the side of boldness. Without acknowledging to her new acquaintance the fact of having lost Clement, lest he should dissuade her from her intention, she thanked him, wished him good-bye, and proceeded on her upward way with a springing step and an eager spirit, and had reached the other extremity of the hollow before he had disappeared along the downward path which led to the town of Cleve.

Her heart did sink a little when she looked up and saw the height still above her, the summit of the Beacon being even then not visible. But it required only an effort ; she was strong, and there was quite sufficient time, and Clement might miss her if she turned back; and Ella, who would have lounged for hours in an easy chair, dreaming over poetry, and thinking the smallest exertion too great, now, once roused, was willing to risk any amount of fatigue, or even danger, rather than fail in her purpose.

She began the ascent ; at first an easy one, for the sheep-track was her guide, and offered a sure footing; but after some distance it ceased, and she was obliged to make her way as she could over the slippery turf. The Beacon point was before her, however, then, and this gave her confidence and energy. Yet she did not trust herself to look round, lest she should turn giddy ; for the hill was becoming more and more precipitous, and from not knowing the right direction to take, Ella had chosen the steepest site that was accessible. At last, however, having reached a little hollow, where she could find a firm footing, she turned, and sat down to rest. The view beneath her was most lovely, commanding the slope of the hills, and the Encombe ravine, with the Cleve woods and the town of Cleve in the distance; and beyond a wide expanse of the sea, changing at every instant, now glittering with islands of light, now dark with deep purple shadows, as the sun escaped from, or was hidden beneath, the heavy clouds which were crossing the sky. Perfectly enjoyable it would have been, if only she had been sitting on the summit of the Beacon, with Clement by her side. As it was, the exquisite beauty, added to the comfort of rest, induced her to linger minute after minute; and it was not till a sensation of cold and dampness stole over her, that she thought of proceeding.

A slight mist rested on the summit; that was provoking, it would prevent her seeing the view to perfection. But it might pass away; at any rate, she felt it would be wise to hasten, lest it should increase. Once more she was ascending, rather more cautiously, for she was no longer stepping upon turf, but upon loose shingles and rough stones, which hurt her feet. It crossed her mind whether she should go back, for the mist was thickening very rapidly. But to be so near the top, and not to reach it! It was out of the question; it would be ignoble; and, after all, what harm could happen to her? She had but to step carefully; and, once at the top, her descent would be rapid and easy, and she should soon escape from the mist, which was always thicker on the hills than in the valleys. Enterprising Ella was, certainly; hers might have been the spirit of a crusader, could it always have felt the same stimulus. A steep, high bank, almost a cliff, was before her; the damp, heavy mist was gathering around her; she was weary and breathless; sharp flints had torn her boots, and one had wounded her foot so as to make it painful for her to walk; but she would not yield. One more great effort. Scrambling, slipping back, clinging to a stone which gave way, seizing upon the stem of a juniper-bush, and finding a footing for a moment, and then grasping the edge of the bank, and dragging herself up almost in despair, and Ella had achieved her object, and stood upon the narrow platform of the highest hill, and touched the pile of stones which formed the Beacon.

She was very triumphant—very excited. The toil was a hundred-fold repaid by success; so she felt, for the first minute. The second, a chill came over her, mental as well as physical; but the latter was predominant. A cold blast was sweeping over the hills; and sadly and ominously it moaned through the hollows below her. View there was none; the mist covered the country like a garment, and, gathering around Ella, crept, as it seemed, into her frame, numbing her fingers, and bringing that indescribable sense of blind dreariness which makes one fancy, for the moment, that warmth and light have disappeared from the earth for ever.

Of course there was but one thought in Ella's mind—descent as quick as possible. She again called Clement, though with little expectation of being heard ; and, receiving no answer, set herself to her task. The cliff was her first difficulty ; she could not trust it in going down, as she had in ascending, so she felt her way cautiously along the edge of the platform, till she reached a less precipitous bank, and, sliding down without difficulty, found herself standing on what seemed a beaten track. This must, of course, she thought, be the right path, which she had missed through ignorance ; and she went on boldly and cheerfully, congratulating herself on her success. Yet it was rather bewildering, to be wandering on in this way, without being able to see more than a few yards before her ; and once it crossed Ella's mind that the track was leading her rather away from the direction she had taken in ascending. Very far away, however, it could not be, for she was quite sure that she was going towards Encombe ; and every now and then she stopped and called Clement, again hoping that he might be near, and join her.

The path which Ella had entered upon was broad at first, sloping along the side of the hill; then it grew narrower and steeper, and occasionally it ceased altogether for a few paces ; but a path there certainly was, so that she did not feel any misgivings. At length, however, it became very perplexing ; there seemed to be two tracks—one to the right, broad, but exceedingly precipitous, almost indeed perpendicular, leading, as she supposed, towards Cleve ; the other very narrow, but more easy, carried round the hill, and therefore leading away from Encombe. Either seemed an evil, and Ella paused to consider, and for the first time felt sufficiently uncomfortable heartily to repent her expedition. To descend by any means was still the only thing to be done, for there was no time to be lost. It was growing late, and the mist was thickening into rain ; and after a moment's consideration she chose the narrow path, as leading, she believed, more directly to Encombe.

It was tolerably level, and therefore easy at first ; and Ella congratulated herself upon this, and went on hopefully, yet not very quickly. It was not quite as firm as that which she had left ; the soil was loose, and the stones rolled away under her feet. This did not signify, as long as the slope was gradual ; but it became steeper,—the path was scarcely to be called one. Ella was obliged to throw herself, in a manner, from one projection to another : yet it was still descent, and descent was her object. She was forced to move on ; the stones gave way as she touched

them; and there were no large ones to grasp. It became not
walking, or jumping from point to point, but one perpetual slide,
slide; above, below, around her—all was sliding; and when she
tried to stop, the very effort to sustain herself gave an impetus to
the stones on which she rested; and down they went, rolling on
and on, and making all they touched roll with them, till the rush
was as the crash of pebbles on a beach; and at length—was it
the splash of water which reached Ella's ear?

The black tarn was beneath her. She was clinging to the side
of the Croome.

The cry which echoed through the hills reached the ears of
Mr Bruce as he wandered beneath the Beacon, and was heard
by Rachel Lester as she stood at the head of Greystone Gorge,
and startled Ronald in his lonely wretchedness;—it was the cry
of extremity of peril. To go back was impossible; the very effort
to grasp the cliff would but precipitate Ella into the lake. To go
forward was equally impossible; the end might approach more
slowly, but it would not be the less certain. To stand motionless
upon the spot where for the moment she had found her footing,
was the only safety; and this security was but the verge of despair; for even the sound of Ella's voice, as in her agony she called
Clement, Clement, seemed to precipitate the rush of the restless,
shivering cliff, and increase the perpetual quick plash, the knell
of the dark waters, as they closed over the stones which sank into
their depth.

Years were gathered into those moments,—the years of Ella's
life; the tale of her wilfulness, her folly, her pride, her indolence
—not passing before her in detail, but all concentrated into one
feeling of despair.

Again, one last effort! But Ella's voice was feeble with horror,
and it was but the wailing wind which took up the lingering notes
and prolonged the ineffectual cry. Yet a change came. A gleam
of sunshine was struggling amidst the vapour that floated over
the tarn. A few moments more, and the mist rolled away; whilst
heavy wreaths gathered together upon the summit of the hill,
leaving clear below a narrow sheet of water, unruffled save by
the falling stones, dark with almost unfathomable depth, and
coldly throwing back the lines of light which crossed its bosom,
as if too conscious of the dread secrets which it hid to permit
them to penetrate its surface.

It was but a little distance across from the spot where Ella
stood. She could see a small hovel on the opposite bank, some-

times used for shelter by shepherds, and distinguish the rocks scattered along the margin of the tarn, and the sheep grazing upon the scanty foliage. She could even look beyond, and trace the path which would lead her to the village ; and very far away she fancied that she could perceive the tower of Encombe Church, though it was very indistinct. Life, safety, happiness, were within her sight, almost within her grasp ; but so also were the crumbling rocks, and the waters of the dark tarn, and the valley of the shadow of death.

There was a sound on the lake ; not the falling of stones ; it was a steadier, softer, more even plash. It was behind her, and she dared not look round ; the pressure of her foot might be death. She called again, and a voice sounded from below, and a little boat with a man in it glided into sight. Ella stretched out one hand ; her impulse was to throw herself into the water. A hasty gesture warned her to pause.

' Be still : if you value your life, neither move nor speak. There is a rope in the boat ; I will throw it to you,' shouted Mr Bruce from below ; and the boat glided away again out of sight, and she was left to loneliness, and the ceaseless plash of the falling stones.

Minutes passed away ; her strength was failing ; the position in which she stood was becoming unbearable ; and there were no signs of the promised help. She could not have been left ; it was madness to think so ; yet Ella's mind was in that state in which reason has lost its power ; and the dreams of a maniac are.not more wild than the suggestions and misgivings which flashed across her, checked only by the strong instinct of self-preservation.

But a voice came at last from above, a man's voice. ' Are you there ?' was shouted ; and Ella's answering scream was sharper than the cry of a dying animal. A pause followed ; two persons seemed to be holding a consultation. Ella could hear their murmurs. The delay was agony ; in another minute her power of endurance would be gone. They called again, for they could not see her, and could only be directed by the voice to the spot which she had reached. Then she heard in louder tones, a debate which seemed almost angry in its eagerness. ' Throw the rope.' ' No ; it will not reach her, and she will go down.' ' If we could but see her !' Another shout and another answer. ' Fasten the rope round me first.' It was Mr Bruce who spoke. The suggestion seemed to be approved, for there was a momentary silence. Then came the noise of the stones disturbed from their resting-place, and rushing faster, faster, falling behind and around Ella. But Mr Bruce was drawing near; she could see him; he was moving very cautiously, and, as it appeared, with some instinct or fore-knowledge, which taught him where to place his foot on the firmest spot. The rope also held by his companion secured him; but even with that aid he dared not approach very close. The movement of the stones might loosen those on which Ella was standing. 'Now, catch it.' He flung the end of the rope towards her. She moved,—caught it for an instant,—lost it again,—felt herself sliding,—once more caught it, and clung to it, and was dragged upwards.

'Fasten it round your waist,' shouted Ronald, from above.

Impossible! Ella's strength was giving way. The rope was large; she could not twist it. She felt her hold lessening, yet despair was life. One instant more, and she was within reach of Mr Bruce's arm, supported by him with one hand, whilst he threw the rope around her with the other; and at that moment she fainted away.

It must have been almost a superhuman strength which upheld her; but Ronald Vivian stood above, with his giant power, his indomitable resolution; and another—weak indeed, comparatively, in body, but urged by the overwhelming impulse of a father's love—was straining every nerve for her preservation; and when at length she was laid on the firm ground, Edward Vivian bent over his daughter, and forgetting every necessity for concealment, exclaimed, 'My Ella, my precious child! Thank God, she is safe!'

CHAPTER XX.

THAT night Mr Vivian sat in a large, low, old-fashioned room at the Manor Farm, his chair drawn in front of the fire, which Mrs Robinson had insisted upon lighting when he returned, cold, damp, and far from well, after an expedition over the hills, which had been longer, he said, than he had intended. With him sat Mr Lester, his grave countenance wearing a look of disquieting thought, as, leaning his elbow upon the table, he gazed fixedly before him. Tea was just over; it had been but a scanty meal; though Mrs Robinson, in her hospitality and affection, had provided largely for the weary wanderer, and urged upon Mr Lester the duty of making him take care of himself. Mr Vivian was not to be persuaded; his cup of tea had been swallowed hastily, and scarcely anything else on the table was touched; a question was pending, which was food sufficient for the mind, and, for the moment, for the body also—What is to be done next?

'I can trust Ronald implicitly,' was Mr Lester's observation.

'Yet you were vexed when I told you I had betrayed myself.'

'Vexed for your own want of caution. Are you never to learn prudence, Vivian?'

'When my child had just been saved from death!' he exclaimed. 'Lester, you will one day drive me to hate you.'

'A man who puts himself in a position where self-restraint is necessary, ought first to be certain that he can practise it,' replied Mr Lester. 'But it is useless to waste time in lectures which will not be listened to.'

'Spare me at least till you have had experience,' was the answer. 'Live for eighteen years in a foreign land, separated from your children, bound to work which you hate, your constitution worn by a horrible climate, and then talk to me of prudence, if you can.'

'Most true, my dear Vivian; none can feel it more strongly, than myself. But a few months more delay;—and the claims of the children, your sister's influence, my own inquiries as to the past, might have opened a door for your return honourably and openly.'

'Never, never; in that opinion at least we cannot be agreed; and remember that my knowledge of my father is more intimate than yours.'

'I am not saying there would be hope if you took him by surprise. All I contend for is, that, with patience and prudence, we might at least have worked upon him.'

Mr Vivian shook his head doubtfully, and his tone was irritable, as he said;—'It is no good to discuss what might have been. I am here;—I am known to be here. Now for the next step.'

'To leave the neighbourhood before your secret has spread further, would be my advice,' replied Mr Lester.

'And live the same life that I have been living for so many years,—lonely, hopeless, and with the aggravation of being within reach of my children, and yet unable to approach them.'

'So it must be till we have discovered the full extent of your
cousin's villany.'

'Pshaw! Forgive me, Lester; you rest upon that point as if
it would at once change the whole tone of my father's mind.
Let John Vivian be what he may, let him have injured and
calumniated me as he may, I tell you there are sins enough at
my own door, for which I alone am answerable, which, in my
reasonable moments, must, I feel, shut up every avenue to
reconciliation.'

Mr Lester looked very pained.

'I know what you would say,' continued Mr Vivian. 'Why,
if I had no hope, should I have returned to England? That is
the question of a man reasoning upon feelings which he is too
fortunate to understand. Say, I had no hope,—it is true; yet
can you not imagine it possible to act without it, when the
object is restoration to a father's affection? Let him do with
my inheritance as he will; if he will see and bless me, I shall
die happy.' Mr Vivian's voice faltered, but he recovered himself, and added—'Besides, if I have no hope for myself, I have
for my children.'

'And so had I,' replied Mr Lester.

'Yes; and your hope was fed by everyday events, by intercourse with Mildred; and it was not the hope of one whose all
lay trembling in the balance; whilst mine—Lester, death would
have been preferable to the life I was leading; and if the step I
have taken should bring me to it, I could scarcely repent that I
had yielded.'

'Who is to say that it will not bring you to it?' replied Mr
Lester, earnestly. 'You have to deal with a desperate man.'

'We have been pitted against each other before this,' was the
reply. 'Let him do his worst; I don't fear him.'

'There would be comparatively little cause to fear, if everything were open,' replied Mr Lester. 'If you had appeared at
Encombe in your own character, John Vivian would have been
powerless, for all eyes would have been upon him. Now, on the
contrary, no one notices either him or you, and he can carry on
his machinations unperceived.'

'You speak as if it was my own choice which brought me to
Encombe,' replied Mr Vivian. 'But for the wreck, I should
never have ventured to visit the place without your sanction.'

'We will waive the point of your returning to England at all,'
replied Mr Lester; 'it is only a vexatious one. But when you

were here, you must acknowledge that you insisted upon remaining. You disbelieved me when I said that it was impossible to keep your secret.'

'Yet you declare I am safe, and that Ronald Vivian is to be
trusted.'

'As surely as I am to be trusted myself; but you forget, my
dear Vivian, the possibility of exciting suspicion in your cousin
or his wretched ally, Goff.'

'I trust to Mrs Robinson for that; she knows everything that
goes on, and has ears and eyes in all parts of the village. And
as to being known, remember that even she did not recognise
me. Eighteen years in a West Indian climate, with two attacks
of yellow fever to boot—there can be no safer disguise than such
a change; even if I had not been most careful as to concealment
in other ways.'

'Still look at the possibility; it must always be wise to fear
the worst.'

'Well, then; my hopeful cousin knows me, and publishes the
news, and what is to follow?'

'That is the point; he will not publish it.'

'But, for the sake of argument, suppose he does? My father
will hear of it; and how will he take it?'

'So as to ruin every prospect, both for you and for the children,' exclaimed Mr Lester. 'Eighteen years have done their
work upon him, as they must upon all, in sharpening and har-
dening the edges of character. The principle upon which he
first acted was what he believed to be a right one; but he
carried it out without check or balance from other principles,
and now it has become prejudice. If at this moment you
were to appear before him, he would turn from you as from a
stranger.'

Mr Vivian shuddered, and his voice sounded faint and hollow,
as he said: 'My father! is it possible?'

'Quite possible. There is nothing in this world so stern as a
petrified affection.'

'Yet you would have given me hope if I had remained in
Jamaica?'

'Yes, hope in your father's justice; he is still open to that,
and if we weaken him upon one point, we weaken him upon all.
If we could place before him the proofs of your cousin's treachery,
for treacherous I have not the smallest doubt he was; if we could
show him that you were not guilty to the extent which he believes,

'his strong sense of honour would be touched, and he would feel himself bound to redeem the injury he has done you. But there has, as yet, been no time for this. The letter which you wrote in answer to my first communication of our suspicions, has only just reached us ; and we must deal with your father cautiously, even, for the sake of his age. Once, however, as I said, touch his sense of justice, and I should have hope. Mildred and I would place your character in its true light. We would make him feel how nobly you have borne your exile ; how devotedly you have laboured for your children.'

Mr Vivian interrupted him impatiently :—' I tell you, Lester, as I have told you before, you are mistaken. The amount of my offence is not the question. When I lost five pounds at the gaming-table, I sinned in my father's eyes as if I had lost five thousand. When I married without his consent, I grieved him as if I had chosen my wife from the very dregs of the people.'

' True, in a certain sense ; but there is one thing which you forget. When a man sins against the virtue which he holds most dear, his repentance is keen in proportion to the estimation with which he regards it. Justice has been your father's idol. If we can show him that he has been unjust, I can scarcely doubt that, in his eagerness to atone for the wrong he has done, he may be induced to overlook what, under other circumstances, he would have considered unpardonable.'

Mr Vivian considered for a few moments—then he said— ' Perhaps you are right. I have known him so influenced in former days. But how to obtain the proofs of injustice ? '

' There, of course, lies the difficulty. The lapse of time is one very great obstacle. If I had known, years ago, what I know now, I should have had every hope of bringing the matter to a speedy conclusion ; but, as you are aware, it was not till I became acquainted with your sister-in-law, and learned from her the particulars of what took place at the time of your marriage, that I had any idea of the falsity of your cousin's statements. Unquestionably he swindled your father out of a large sum on that occasion. General Vivian once told me that he paid him more than five thousand pounds, on a solemn condition that he was never to be applied to for a similar sacrifice again. That was the result of his feelings of honour, added to his hasty pride. If he had but condescended to make inquiry of you, instead of receiving John Vivian's statements, he would have known that the utmost extent of your debts was not' ——

'One thousand ;—a much larger sum, I confess, than I had any right to risk ; or as you will say, and as I say now, I had no right to risk a penny. But on what pretence John Vivian could have extracted five thousand from my father, is utterly beyond my comprehension.'

' Then, as to the letters,' continued Mr Lester, ' none reached Cleve, though you say you wrote constantly. He must have stopped them for his own foul purposes. There is no want of charity, I trust, in thinking so.'

' Whatever may have been my offence against him, he has had his revenge,' said Mr Vivian ; and a heavy sigh escaped him.

' No, Vivian, he has not had his revenge, whilst a chance remains of seeing either you or your boy restored to the inheritance you have lost. The injury he has already done has quickened and goaded his revenge, because it has placed himself in danger. The man is twice your enemy whose hatred has led him to degradation.'

' Twice my enemy, indeed !' repeated Mr Vivian ; ' first to myself ; but, O Lester ! far more terribly, it may be, to my boy !'

Mr Lester's face showed some painful thought ; perhaps it crossed his mind that the sins of parents are punished in the faults of their children. But he shook off the feeling, whatever it was, and answered, ' Our trust for Clement must be in a Higher Power than our own.'

' And you don't think it would influence him for good to know that I was at hand.'

' It might do so, if the secret could be made known without risk. But we come back always to the same point ; not so much what we are to do, as when. It is the Gordian knot of many difficulties in life besides ours.'

' Then cut it !' exclaimed Mr Vivian, impetuously.

' That is the principle upon which you have acted through life, my dear Vivian ; and what has been the result ?'

The look of self-reproaching anguish which followed the question, almost made Mr Lester repent that he had put it. Yet it had done its work.

' Yes, you are right ; impatience has been my ruin !' and Edward Vivian's head was bowed upon his hands, as if, even to his truest friend, he dared not show the extent of his remorse.

Mr Lester spoke more gently. ' There is no ruin, Vivian,

while there is hope ; and no one but yourself need destroy your
hope. You have made, I fear, a false step ; but it is not irretrievable. Leave this place ; hide yourself in London, and suffer
your sister, Bertha Campbell, and myself, to work out our own
plans. You may safely trust us to use our utmost efforts ; and
from time to time you will hear of our proceedings, whilst you
will have the comfort of feeling yourself within reach of your
children. Content yourself with this life for a while. You say
that you can remain in England for a year. We will not look
forward beyond ; before it is over, I trust — nay more, I
sincerely believe—that we shall once more see you restored to
Cleve.'

' And go from Encombe without seeing Mildred?' exclaimed
Mr Vivian.

' It may be necessary. I will not, at this moment, absolutely
say that it is. But if John Vivian's suspicions are aroused, you
have not a day to lose : either he will quit the place himself,
and so we shall lose all chance of substantiating our charges
against him; or——you will laugh at my fears; but a desperate
man will do desperate deeds.'

Mr Vivian considered for a few seconds : ' I cannot see the
necessity. Let me be brave, Lester ; let me go at once to my
father : severe, prejudiced though he is, I am still his son. Let
me say to him that John Vivian deceived him : you yourself own
that there would be hope then in his justice.'

' But the proofs of the deceit, where are they ? '

' My own word ! ' exclaimed Mr Vivian, haughtily.

' The word of one man against another,' was Mr Lester's quiet
reply.

' John Vivian's word against mine !—Lester, you dare not say
that my father would take it.'

' I say that he would pride himself upon weighing both equally
in the balance ; and the stronger was the leaning towards you, the
more hope there would be for your enemy. Yet I own it may
come to this—it may be our last and only resource ; and if it were
so, I would run the risk, and trust to God for the issue. But
before I attempted it, I would use every effort to put the matter
in so clear a light that the strongest prejudice—even General
Vivian's—must own itself conquered. Remember, you will come
before your father, not as the son whom he has always loved, but
as the spendthrift gambler—I am using harsh words, but I know
full well your father's feeling—who wounded him in the tenderest

point, and brought sorrow, and what he considers disgrace, upon his house.'

A silence of some moments followed. The words had indeed been severe, and Mr Vivian's proud spirit could little brook them.

Mr Lester spoke again : 'My dear Vivian, if I did not know the exaggeration of your father's mind, and if I were not certain that years of true repentance had followed upon the offences of youth, I could not speak as I do; but it is the very consciousness of the prejudice against which you have to struggle which makes me fearful lest you should begin the combat at a disadvantage. If you were what your father thinks you, I could not raise a finger to help you. Being what I know you are, I would sacrifice fortune and happiness, and even life, for your sake.'

'Yes, I know it, my truest, kindest friend. I was wrong ;' and Mr Vivian stretched out one hand in reconciliation, while the other vainly strove to hide the tears which gathered in his eyes.

'But,' continued Mr Lester, more lightly, 'I must not have to deal with wilfulness and impatience. So far, Vivian, you are unaltered: endurance is the lesson which you have yet to learn.'

'Eighteen years !—latterly years of utter loneliness. It was not possible to endure longer.'

'All things which God gives us to endure are possible,' replied Mr Lester ; 'that is, of course, if we look at them in the right way.'

'And to bear the same life still,' continued Mr Vivian, 'with no fixed hope or limit. Can it be necessary?'

'I think it so ; but the decision must be left to yourself.'

'And if it should be right ! if it should be necessary ! O Lester ! my heart grows sick with the prospect.'

'My principle of endurance might sound too stern for you,' said Mr Lester. 'You would rather hear me speak of hope.'

'I would hear you speak of that which would be your own comfort.'

'My comfort would be in punishment,' replied Mr Lester, 'with love and hope to soften it, yet still unmistakeably and undeniably punishment. I have found it so myself,' he continued, earnestly. 'There are sufferings which come upon us immediately from the hand of God, without, as far as we can discover, any fault of our own. Such, we may believe, are trials of our

L

faith, sent in mercy, to give us the opportunity of victory. But there are others, the consequences of our sins, and which we cannot fail to trace directly to that source. These we too often look upon as the natural effects of our own folly, and so weary ourselves with fruitless regrets, vain longings to undo the past; till at length we grow despairing, and the feelings of God's love, which can alone uphold us in our suffering, is lost in the consciousness of our own wretchedness. From your letters, Vivian, I am sure you understand that state of mind too well.'

'Understand it, yes; it was the spirit of my existence for years.'

'So once for a time was it mine, and I thought it was repentance, and dreaded to discourage it; but repentance is love, and in this feeling there is no love.'

'Not when we think of the love which has borne with us through all our wanderings?'

'That thought will not come when we are writhing under the consequences of our transgressions. We are then thinking only of ourselves. In such a state of mind there is but one thing which I find will calm me—to accept the suffering, whatever it may be, as coming at once from God as a punishment, or perhaps, more truly speaking, a correction; not to try to escape from it, nor even to allow myself to wish that I had not incurred it, but humbly and thankfully to submit to it. There is a sense of dignity and energy in this willing acceptance of our lot, which I believe to be absolutely essential to save us from the loss of self-respect, that must otherwise accompany sufferings resulting from past sin. Our will becomes one with God's will, and love must follow necessarily. My dear Vivian, am I wrong in speaking to you as I have often written?'

'Right, and most kind; but I must think of what you say another time. If I follow your advice, I shall have full leisure.'

'I trust not for long. Miss Campbell has already enlisted a champion in your cause.'

Mr Vivian heaved a deep sigh: 'Poor Bertha, I longed to see and talk to her also. There are some things in which she alone can sympathise. Yet she was little more than a child when we parted.'

'She is a woman now, and a noble one; with faults indeed—who is without them?—but with a spirit of devoted unselfishness, which fits her for any work that may be given her. If it had not been for this afternoon's adventure, I was going to suggest, what perhaps would have startled you, that you should meet her at the Rectory, and make yourself known to her.'.

'Before I see Mildred : is that fair ?'

'We must take circumstances as they come before us. You could not possibly go to the Hall without the greatest risk, and Mildred cannot come to you. Besides, I have an idea that Miss Campbell already suspects the truth. It is one thing which has made me especially uneasy.'

'How ? I have most carefully avoided her.'

'Rachel gave me the hint, though unintentionally. Your present to her excited Miss Campbell's interest and curiosity strangely.'

'My poor bird ! It belonged to the child of a friend in Jamaica, who was named after my dear wife. I thought no one but myself would recognise the name in its uncouth notes.'

'Bertha did; and she has asked many questions about you which Rachel repeated to me. We should do wisely to trust her.'

Mr Vivian's countenance changed : 'You will think me a coward, Lester. One moment I long for the meeting—the next I dread it. The remembrances which the expression of her face, the sound of her voice, will recall, are so intensely painful, I should but make a fool of myself.'

'Nevertheless it is due to her, when she is working for you in every way, with all her heart.'

'And my precious Mildred to be left,' continued Mr Vivian, musingly.

'We will not say that absolutely. I desire almost more than you do to put Mildred in possession of the truth ; but it would be agony to know you were here, and not to see you. And indeed, Vivian, you must not remain even for another day, if you wish to make your secret safe.'

'My own folly again!' exclaimed Mr Vivian. 'Yet how, at such a moment, could I remember the boy was near ?'

'That is your least danger. Honourable as he is, he would die rather than betray you. But Mrs Robinson tells me that Goff has been here asking curious and impertinent questions. If his suspicions are in the most remote degree excited, it would be madness to delay your departure.'

'To-morrow, then,—must it be ?'

'To-morrow I would advise ; but I would not go too sud-denly or secretly. Come to me early at the Rectory. Let Mrs

Robinson give out publicly that you have business in London for a few days. In the middle of the day you can set off, and all will seem to follow in the natural course. It will be supposed you are to return, and we may hope to escape observation.'

Mr Vivian was thoughtful. 'That boy Ronald,' he said, 'to have saved my own life, and the life of my child, and yet to be my deadly foe!'

'Ronald is no one's foe,' replied Mr Lester. 'He has that in him which would make him every one's friend, could the check once be securely placed upon his ungoverned feelings. Throw yourself upon his honour, and you are safe.'

'I was afraid to do so at the time. The words escape me at a moment when he was not, I hoped, near enough to catch them. Nothing in his manner showed that he had done so; and when my presence of mind returned, I felt it might be better to leave them without comment.'

Mr Lester looked a little anxious.

'You don't thoroughly trust him,' continued Mr Vivian.

'I could do so entirely if I cared less. He already knows, I believe, something of the position of affairs, so far as his father is concerned. Miss Campbell is his friend—she was his mother's friend—and she has great influence with him. Last evening she had a long interview with him, and to-night she was to tell me what had passed. It might be wise to return with me to the Rectory. We shall find her there probably; and we could see our way more clearly, if we knew exactly how far Ronald would go with us or against us.'

Mr Vivian hesitated.

'Have you any other plan?'

'A mad one! To go to Mildred, and then throw myself upon my father's mercy. The impulse is almost uncontrollable.'

'So have been all your impulses through life. A false step at this moment, and farewell to hope for ever.

Mr Vivian paced the room in extreme agitation.

'Your hat! Vivian. You will come?' That firm yet gentle voice had controlled him before, in his most excited moments, and now he obeyed it as by an instinct. They went down-stairs together. Mrs Robinson met them.

'Only to the Rectory,' said Mr Lester, smiling as he saw her disturbed face.

'And you won't return home late by yourself. O Master Edward! you will be careful. Sir, you won't let him.'

Mr Vivian took her hand affectionately : 'Dear Granny, you mustn't be afraid for me. These are not days for robbery and murder in the highways.

'But that fellow Goff, Master Edward,—I beg your pardon, —Mr Bruce,' and she drew back respectfully, as one of the farm servants crossed the passage.

'Don't fear, I won't keep you up late;' and Mr Vivian nodded a kindly good-bye. But Mr Lester lingered behind.

'I have hope,' he whispered. 'He will consent to go for the present ; and for the future we must trust all to God.'

'Thank you, sir. Yes, we must all do that, indeed,' and Mrs Robinson dropped a formal yet reverent curtsey, and retired.

CHAPTER XXI.

IT was about nine o'clock, and Bertha and Rachel were together in Mr Lester's study. Bertha was only just come, and she still wore the shawl which she had thrown over her shoulders as she crossed the garden ; she looked fagged but excited.

'And you are quite sure Ella will be pretty well to-morrow ?' said Rachel.

'Yes, I hope,—I think so. But, O Rachel ! such a fearful situation ! If Mr Bruce had not tried to cross the tarn in the tiny boat, when he heard her scream, he would never have discovered her as quickly as he did.'

Bertha sank down trembling in the arm-chair.

Rachel drew a footstool towards her, and sat down at her feet. 'I was afraid to ask to see her,' she said.

'She was better alone,' replied Bertha; 'Mr Hargrave told me that perfect quietness was indispensable. I think the fainting was good for her in some ways. I dread what it will be when she can recall it all more distinctly. Yet one ought to be so thankful!' and Bertha heaved a sigh, which ended in a shudder.

'I don't think Ella can forget it,' said Rachel, thoughtfully.

'It is not meant she should ; but she is very slow in learning her lessons.'

Rachel's faced expressed a little wonder.

'Everything that happens gives us some lesson, if we choose,
said Bertha ; 'but you don't understand that yet, Rachel.'

'Don't I? dear Miss Campbell. Isn't it like what papa says,
"That crosses cease to be crosses when we take them up instead
of looking at them."'

'Yes, something like it ; but, Rachel, it is so odd, I can't think
to-night.' Bertha put her hand to her head, and rising, walked
up and down the room, and then sat down again. 'Would you
fetch me a little sal volatile, Rachel?' and Rachel, rather frightened, left the room. Bertha leant her head back in the chair.
That swimming, faint, weak feeling which made her so ashamed
of herself must surely be hysterical, and she must struggle against
it. She seized a book,—the page was all in motion before her.
She saw no letters,—only a phantom scene of a steep cliff, and
rolling, shivering pebbles ; and Ella sliding—sliding,—and the
dark gulf below. She was upon the verge of giving way, when
Rachel held out to her the glass of sal volatile. Bertha drank it
off : 'Thank you, dear ; now I am better. Oh, that horrible
cliff!' and she shook again from head to foot.

Rachel held her hand, 'Dear Miss Campbell! she is safe.'

'Yes, I know it ; it might not have been : we must thank God.
Rachel dear, would you mind——I think, if you would read to
me, I could try and listen.'

'The Bible?' said Rachel, timidly.

'Yes—St John ; the seventeenth chapter, if you don't
mind.'

Rachel brought a Bible ; but she felt shy. She had never had
to comfort or help any one older than herself before, at least in
that way. And Bertha was so above her—so shut up from her !
She turned over the leaves slowly.

Bertha's eyes were shut ; she looked quite ill. Rachel felt as
if she could not begin. If it had been little Barney Wood who
had asked her, she would have had no hesitation. Her voice was
quite low from nervousness when she spoke the first sentence ;
but as she went on, her own feelings were carried away by the
words, and the rich, musical tones grew deeply earnest, and acting with a soothing charm upon Bertha's over-worked temperament, gradually lulled her into tranquillity.

Rachel's hand was resting on Bertha's lap : Bertha stroked it
fondly as the chapter was ended, and the book closed.

'Thank you, dear Rachel, you have done me good ; you do
me good always.'

'Because you are so kind, you say that, dear Miss Campbell. It is very easy to read.'

'Yes, only I could not bear some people's reading. O Rachel! I wonder who made you what you are?'

'God made me,' said Rachel, quietly.

Bertha smiled. 'God makes us, and we unmake ourselves,' she said. 'But you have had a safe childhood, Rachel.'

'I know persons think so,' said Rachel, thoughtfully.

'And don't you?'

'I can't tell; if I was good, I dare say I should feel it so. But sometimes—it is very wrong, Miss Campbell?—I think it is like Paradise with the serpent in it.'

'Yes, the safest home on earth must be that,' said Bertha. 'But, Rachel, you must be thankful still that yours is not what other homes are.' She spoke with an earnestness which showed that the difference had lately been peculiarly brought before her.

'I try to be thankful,' replied Rachel; 'but you know,'—and she smiled shyly—'when the serpent comes I am not; and that makes me unhappy—very unhappy sometimes.'

'Ah, Rachel! so you fancy; but you can't really know what unhappiness, or, at least, sorrow, means.'

'I did know it once,'—Rachel's colour went and came quickly —'when dear mamma died, and my little sister; I thought then I was never to be happy again.'

'Only papa taught you how,' said Bertha, kindly.

'Yes, he teaches me always; and he lets me tell him my difficulties. Do you know, Miss Campbell,'—and she moved her stool so as to look up in Bertha's face—'I have some great ones.'

Bertha's hand rested affectionately upon Rachel's head, as she replied : 'Yes, dear child, great ones to you, no doubt.'

'Such wonderful, puzzling questions come into my head,' continued Rachel; 'and it seems as if I could do nothing till they were settled. But I must not stop for them, must I? Papa tells me,' she added, her voice sinking, 'that they are the serpent's questions, and if I stay to answer them, they will keep me back; and what I want is to go on and on, never to grow tired, or to fall back; because '—— she hid her face in Bertha's lap. 'O Miss Campbell! papa says, those who strive the most, will stand near, and have a bright, bright crown; and I could not bear to be far off!'

Bertha's eyes were full of tears; she could but kiss Rachel and say: 'Ah! Rachel, if it were possible to make Ella think as you do!'

'Ella will be sure to try more after to-day,' said Rachel.

Bertha was very grave: 'I hope so. She ought to remember the warning. But she has had many. One moment more, and it would have been all over.' The shuddering feelings seemed about to return.

'Don't talk about it, dear Miss Campbell,' said Rachel, anxiously. 'It makes you ill again.'

'I try not, but I feel as if I must. It haunts me so; and when I close my eyes, it all comes before me again.'

'It was very dreadful,' said Rachel, 'when papa came and told me of it; and it must have been much worse for you.'

'I longed so very much for your papa,' continued Bertha. 'I thought at first, when I saw Ronald and Mr Bruce at a distance with Ella, that Mr Bruce was Mr Lester, and my heart sank terribly when I found he was not.'

'Papa says, Mr Bruce did more for her than even Ronald,' observed Rachel; 'did Ella thank him very much?'

'He would not stay to be thanked,' replied Bertha. 'You know they brought her home in Farmer Corbin's little chaise, and Mrs Corbin came with her. She was so dizzy, she scarcely knew what was going on; and when they came to the shrubbery gate, Mr Bruce said, that now she would be in such good hands, he would leave her. He was gone before Ella could know it, and without even waiting to see me. Very strange!' Bertha fell into a reverie.

Rachel also was thoughtful, and once she seemed about to make an observation, but she checked herself. There was a silence of some moments. When they spoke again, the subject was changed.

'How little papa and I thought what was going to happen when we set off for our walk this afternoon!' said Rachel. 'I was so happy. It was such a delicious afternoon; and we went above the hollow, instead of under it, which is just what I like. And then I had to look forward to coming back and drinking tea with Ella and you. And now it is all so different! It seems as if I never could trust to anything again.'

Bertha smiled: 'You will, though, Rachel; in a day or two— a week at the utmost—you will feel just as you did before, or, at least, very nearly so.'

'But that will be wicked,' said Rachel.

'Not exactly. We are so formed by God that we can't help it ; and the world would stand still if it were not so.'

'I don't understand that ; it does seem wrong.'

'Just think,' replied Bertha, 'what the state of the world would be if we did not believe that things were to be to-morrow as they are to-day. No one would form plans, or make engagements, or provide in any way for the future ; all business would be at an end, and universal confusion would follow. It always seems to me one of the most astonishing things in human nature that, with our great experience of change, we yet should have such untiring faith in continuance. Sometimes,'—Bertha paused and glanced at Rachel, doubting whether she might venture to carry out her own thought ; then, as the eager, inquiring eye was bent upon her with evident interest, she added, 'sometimes I think that it must be a relic of the higher nature in which we were first created, and in which there would have been, we may be-lieve, no sudden change, but only a gradual transition from one state of existence to another. If one may say it without irrever-ence, it seems like all our deep instincts—such as the craving for perfection, and the inextinguishable love of life—to belong properly to Him, who, as the Bible says, " is the same yesterday, to-day, and to-morrow." But, Rachel, I don't know why I should talk in that way to you.'

' I like it,' said Rachel, quickly—' it is the way papa talks— and it makes me feel as I do sometimes when I am left all alone, and I stand still and think how wonderful it is to live.'

' Yes,' replied Bertha, ' so wonderful, that if we believe in our own existence, there is nothing else which need surprise us.'

Rachel put her hand to her forehead. ' It makes one dizzy,' she said ; 'and do you know, Miss Campbell, all the thoughts and the feelings come upon me, now and then, in such a strange way, just as if they were the only things worth caring for, and as if I could do nothing but sit in the middle of the world and think.'

' The feeling must be good and useful occasionally,' said Bertha ; 'but, dear Rachel, you must not let yourself become a dreamer.'

' No'—Rachel's face grew sad. ' Papa says it is my tempta-tion, and that I shall never conquer it, except by learning to live out of myself,—living, as he calls it, in the life of others.'

' Being unselfish. I am sure I think you are that ;' and

Bertha bent down and kissed the lovely little face, which was gazing up at her with its marvellous expression of inward thought.

Rachel blushed deeply, whilst a watery mist for the moment dimmed the brightness of her deep blue eyes. 'Dear Miss Campbell, I like you to say that; but I ought not to like it, because I am not unselfish; but I do long to be so, more than I can tell. Something which papa said, has helped me though when I have been inclined to despair because the dreamy fits have come upon me, and I have felt as if I must give way to them.'

'Papa has helped you then, as he has me,' observed Bertha; 'he has given me a number of useful hints.'

'He seems to understand so well,' replied Rachel. 'One day when I was talking about persons' natural dispositions, and how strange it was they were so different, he said to me, that if we look into our own characters, we shall find that God has given us all some quality to counterbalance our natural faults. A passionate person generally has energy, and an indolent person kindheartedness, and a selfish person perseverance. There is always something, which, if we use it properly, will be a great assistance to us. Of course he meant with God's help. And then he said to me that my disposition led me to dream away my time, and to think of puzzling questions, instead of being really good; and that if I gave way to it too much I should grow up to be selfish; but he said that I had something in me which would counteract it, if I tried very hard and prayed very earnestly; he called it benevolence.' Rachel stopped, and a smile passed over her face as she added,—'That seems a grown-up virtue. I never can fancy a benevolent child; it seems so very droll.'

Bertha smiled too, as she exclaimed, 'Go on; tell me what else papa said.'

'He explained what he meant afterwards,' continued Rachel. 'He said that when people are benevolent they dislike to see others suffer, and can't bear to give pain. It is not any good in them exactly, they can't help it. And, Miss Campbell'—Rachel's colour rose, and she rather hesitated—'I think perhaps he may be right; for it does make me so exceedingly uncomfortable to see other persons so. He told me then that I was to act upon the feeling whenever I possibly could, and that it would help me to keep myself what he called practical. And so I have tried to do it; but sometimes it is very difficult; only I think it is easier than it was. You know it is a good thing to be told what one ought to encourage most in one's self.'

'And did not papa tell you that benevolent people are very often in danger of becoming weak?' said Bertha, following out her own ideas, without considering what effect they might have upon her little companion.

Rachel looked distressed. 'He did not tell me so : but is it true? must I be weak?'

'I don't say you must, but I know that a great many persons who set up for being benevolent are very weak.'

'Perhaps they are nothing else except benevolent,' observed Rachel, after a moment's thought. 'Papa declares that virtues, when they stand alone, become vices.'

'Yes.' Bertha considered a little. 'That may be.'

'It was rather difficult to understand it all, that day he talked,' continued Rachel ; 'but I think he said, that perfection—God's perfection'—and her voice changed into awe—'is because all His great attributes (that is what I ought to say, isn't it?) are equal—equally balanced, papa called it ; that He is not more just than He is merciful, and not more merciful than He is just ; and therefore we ought to try to be the same ; and when we pride ourselves upon any one virtue above others, we may be quite sure we are likely to go wrong. It made me rather unhappy to hear him say so, because he spoke as if the very best people must be so imperfect.'

'Yes, indeed they are,' said Bertha.

'I suppose they must be. But, dear Miss Campbell, it does not seem so to me.'

'You are so young, Rachel. But certainly you must take care not to pride yourself upon benevolence.'

'Else I shall become weak ; but you know there is my love of standing still and thinking to check it. O Miss Campbell! doesn't it seem very hard sometimes, to think that we must go on always in that way, first at one thing and then at the other?'

'Trying to make the scale equal,' said Bertha.

'Yes. Do you know, papa says that when we have learned to keep our faults under, our next work is to keep our virtues even. And he told me that he had known some good persons do such wrong things because they did not attend to this. One very generous person would give away sums of money, and never cared in the least for his own comfort ; but he did not check himself properly, and at last he had nothing left to pay his debts, and so was dreadfully unjust ; and another very just, particular person was so careful not to owe anything, and so determined to provide for everything which might be a claim upon him, that at last he would not give away at all. That was the difference, papa told me, also, between large and narrow minds. I didn't know what was meant by them before. He said that if persons try to keep their virtues evenly balanced, they have large minds ; but if they allow one to weigh down the rest, then they have narrow minds.'

A large subject, and one which opened a wide field of thought to Bertha Campbell. Rachel was unable to read her friend's countenance ; she even doubted whether she had listened ; she could not feel that she was interested. Reserve was creeping over them. But the hall bell rang, and Mr Lester and Edward Vivian entered the room.

Rachel's greeting hid Bertha's start of surprise. She ran up to Mr Vivian with the simple affection natural to her, and exclaimed : ' Oh ! is it you, sir ? and are you hurt ?'

' Not hurt, my child ; how should I be ? I was in no danger ; but '— and he turned to Bertha, and his manner became very stiff and awkward—' I hope Ella—Miss Vivian ' he did not seem to know what inquiry to make, and sat down in the nearest chair, turning his head away from Bertha.

' Rachel, my love, your bed is waiting for you,' said Mr Lester.

Rachel knew quite well what that meant. Business was going on which she was not to hear. But curiosity had been checked in her from infancy ; and the instinct of refined feelings made her at once ready to go without asking, as she might have done at another time, to be allowed to learn more of the accident.

' Good night, dear Miss Campbell.'

Bertha's kiss was icy, so also was the touch of her fingers ; it did not appear that she was quite conscious of Rachel's presence.

' Good night, little one,' said Mr Vivian. He laid his hands upon her shoulders, and gazed at her intently.

' I am so glad you were not hurt,' whispered Rachel ; and she went up to her father, always under all circumstances the claimant of her last words and thoughts.

' God bless you, my precious child ?'

' Good night, darling papa ! You will come and see me the last thing ;' and Rachel ran away, happy in the consciousness, that even if she should be asleep, a fond kiss and an earnest prayer were in store for her again before the night should pass.

The door closed. Mr Lester placed himself between Bertha and Mr Vivian. There was a painful, awkward silence. Then Mr Lester asked a few questions about Ella. Bertha answered in a tone of nervous confusion. After a few moments she said that she must go.

'Not just yet.' Mr Lester touched the arm of the chair to prevent her from rising. 'Mrs Campbell will spare you a little longer. There is,—we have '—— he broke off suddenly, and glanced appealingly at Mr Vivian.

Bertha turned very pale ; her eyes moved uneasily from one to the other. Mr Lester seemed about to speak again ; his lips even framed the words ; yet he hesitated.

Bertha broke the spell ; and, gently pushing aside Mr Lester's hand, rose, and approaching Mr Vivian, said, in a firm, calm voice, ' Edward, you cannot deceive me.' The struggle was over, and she sat down and burst into tears.

'Leave her to me, Lester.' Mr Vivian knelt on one knee by Bertha's chair, and holding her hand in his, said, ' Bertha, you are not grieved to see me? My Flora's sister; the adopted mother of my children ! you don't think it wrong in me to be here ?'

Bertha's voice was choked, but she returned the kindly pressure of his hand. He went on—' You must not say I have deceived you, Bertha. I have deceived no one. I acted upon an impulse : the opportunity offered ;—I was unable to resist it. I will be true ; I did not try to do so ; I was so wretched. Lester did not know it ; no one knew it. I meant to have gone to London. I could have hid myself there ; but it was accident —Providence—which brought me here ; and I am going ;— don't be frightened at what may seem my recklessness ; I am not reckless now, I have learned prudence ; and I am going ;— but I could not leave you in ignorance.'

'Going again !' repeated Bertha, in a tone of bewilderment, whilst her eyes were still fixed upon him, as if she scarcely believed in the reality of his appearance.

' He is going, because it is best and wisest that he should, for a time at least,' observed Mr Lester. ' But, dear Miss Campbell, you must hear him tell his own tale. I will leave you, unless you think it might be better to delay what must be said until to-morrow.'

'If you would tell me what it all means,' said Bertha, her

manner recovering itself, and returning to something of its former composed self-restraint. 'Edward, have you really done wisely ?' Her tone was a little severe.

He answered quickly,—'Not wisely in Lester's eyes, nor perhaps in yours; but wisely in my own. Bertha, you were a child when we parted, yet I should have thought that events had taught you to feel for me.'

Her lip quivered. 'Our love lies buried in the same grave. Your children are as my children; your interests as my interests.'

'Then your feelings must be my feelings,' he exclaimed, with impetuosity; 'and from you at least I shall meet with sympathy. Ten mournful years of solitude, Bertha, may and must be my excuse.'

'Yes; but if all is marred in consequence.'

'It shall not be. I put myself into your hands. I trust you as'— his voice faltered—'as my Flora's sister deserves to be trusted. You and Lester shall decide for me. To-morrow I leave this place; I will hide myself in London, and appear again only when I am summoned. Let me but have the blessing of feeling that I am within reach of my children; that I may, though at a distance, watch over my boy. O Bertha! is he also to bring care upon us?'

Bertha hesitated.

'Tell me truly. I would know the worst. Are my children to bear the curse of their father's sins!'

'It is early to judge,' replied Bertha. 'Clement requires a father's authority.'

'And he cannot have it; he might have had it if his father had not been the fool—the madman—he was. To be deceived, entrapped, by that man!' He paced the room angrily.

'You could not have been prepared for treachery,' replied Bertha.

'I ought never to have given him power over me,' was the reply. 'Yes; I can trace it all now; I have gone over the steps again and again. It has been the occupation of my leisure for years,' he added, with a bitter smile. 'When first I went abroad, Bertha, I was innocent, innocent as the child who has just left us—at least of every grave offence; my heart, my thoughts, were all given to one object,—an earthly object,—and God took it from me;' and his voice trembled: 'but I shrank from gambling; I abhorred low company; my impulses were noble. I might have been—O weakness! weakness! surely it is more fatal than sin.'

'The weakness which is conquered may become doubly strength,' observed Mr Lester, gently.

'Yes, when it is; but is it ever conquered? I feel it still in myself. I struggle with it; but too often I yield. I tremble to think that it may be so with my boy.'

'Vivian, you must deal with yourself justly,' replied Mr Lester. 'You have laboured and suffered patiently; you have risen from ruin which might have been the death of every better feeling. Eighteen years of probation have made you, if not a good and wise man, in your own eyes, at least one whom the world may respect, and friends love, and whom—from my heart I believe it—God will approve. It is vain, therefore, to look back upon the past with self-reproach, which is unavailing. Rather rouse your spirit for the future; hope, and if you cannot hope, trust. The God who has not deserted you will not forsake your children.'

'But to have brought evil upon them! to have injured them! O Lester! the long lingering train of sorrow which the fiery comet of sin drags after it!'

'Even so, for us all,' replied Mr Lester. 'Yet there can be no cause for despair, especially as regards Clement.'

'But is there the power in him to improve? that is what I doubt, and dread.'

'Power lies with God, not with us,' replied Mr Lester.

'Clement has great faults,' began Bertha.

'But he has very noble qualities,' interrupted Mr Lester.

Bertha looked annoyed. 'It is quite true,' she said, 'that Clement has many points which would, in themselves, form a fine character; but he has one great foible,—I think his father was always free from it,—he is vain.'

Mr Vivian showed by his face that he shrank from the suggestion. 'Vanity!' he muttered, 'in a man!—it must lower him.'

'It must, and does lower every one; does it not?' inquired Bertha.

'But Clement has sense and conscientiousness,' observed Mr Lester. 'He is a gentleman, too, with the refined feelings of a gentleman, and a keen sense of the ridiculous. All these things will be, humanly speaking, aids.'

'And I suppose we may believe,' continued Bertha, 'that his

position, as comparatively poor and unknown, may have been
better for him than if he had been brought up as the heir of
Cleve. He at least has not been petted and spoiled by the flattery
of servants.'

'Thank you; you are very good, very kind. And Ella, too, is
she vain?' The question was asked with some bitterness.

'Not exactly. Not at all, I think; at least'—— Bertha looked
at Mr Lester for assistance.

'We will talk over the children's faults to-morrow,' he said.
Miss Campbell will come to us in the morning.'

Bertha rose; she seemed conscious that something of uncomfortable restraint had crept over them; and remarked that it was
growing late, and they had talked of nothing definite.'

'Because there is little to be said as yet,' replied Mr Lester.
'Vivian leaves us to-morrow for London. That, at least, you
will consider a safe step.'

'Safe, if it is always so to act against inclination, as moralists
contend,' observed Mr Vivian, with an attempt at ease. 'Lester
has fears for me, Bertha, which I can't share.'

'Miss Campbell will understand them, I am sure,' observed
Mr Lester. 'She has as little faith in John Vivian as I have.'

'Less,' replied Bertha; 'for I have known him longer and
better; but, Edward, you won't content yourself with remaining
in London.'

'He will content himself with doing whatever we think best
for him, at the present,' said Mr Lester. 'In the meantime, Miss
Campbell, we must trust to you to find out, as soon as possible,
whether Ronald suspects our secret; and if he does, to caution
him as to keeping it.'

'Ronald! impossible!'

'Scarcely impossible, when a man betrays his own counsel.
Perhaps it was not to be expected that Vivian should be master
of himself at the moment he saved Ella.'

Bertha looked at her brother-in-law for explanation.

'It is very true,' he said; 'I was thrown off my guard, and
forgot the young fellow was near. Whether he heard or not,
I can't say. He looked unconscious; but I would not trust
him.'

'Not trust Ronald!' exclaimed Bertha, quickly. 'Noble,
true-hearted, unselfish, he would sacrifice his life before he
would betray you.'

'Mr Vivian glanced at her in astonishment. Her manner

was singularly unlike what it had been when she spoke of his own children.

Mr Lester read what was passing in his mind. 'Miss Campbell has reason to trust Ronald,' he said; 'she has known him from infancy.'

'Oh!' But the explanation did not seem thoroughly satisfactory; and Mr Vivian's manner was cold, as he added,— 'Bertha must forgive me for distrusting the son of my greatest enemy.'

'I know that every one must distrust him,' said Bertha.

'Every one but myself,' observed Mr Lester. 'I had used almost the same words as yourself, when speaking of him to Vivian, a short time since. All that we have to fear is, that he may incautiously reveal the truth before he knows that it may do mischief. That is, always supposing he heard Vivian's exclamation. You, perhaps, will find that out more easily than any one.'

'We are safe either way,' replied Bertha, still with the same cold reserve of manner. 'Ronald knows enough of his father's proceedings to be on his guard. If you have nothing else to fear, Edward, I congratulate you.'

Mr Vivian's countenance was moody, and he made no reply.

Bertha gathered her shawl around her. 'My mother will be surprised at my being out so late. What time shall I see you, to-morrow, Edward?'

Mr Lester answered,—'He will be here to breakfast. My study will be at his service, and at yours, all the morning. In the afternoon I will myself drive him into Cleve, and see him fairly on his journey. Starting so late, he will not reach London till the next day; but that will be better than any very rapid movement, which might excite observation.'

'Thank you. Then to-morrow, Edward,'—she offered him her hand, and he took it mechanically, but turned to Mr Lester—

'Must I be denied the sight of my children? May I not say one word to Clement?'

'You can answer your own question, my dear Vivian. Do you think it safe?'

'Clement could not possibly be trusted to keep your counsel,' observed Bertha.

Mr Vivian dropped her hand coldly, but something seemed to reproach him for it, and he spoke kindly: 'Good night, Bertha, and a father's blessing for your care of his children.'

M

Bertha was touched and softened. 'Good night, Edward. If I don't think your children perfect, it is not from any want of love for them.'

She hurried from the room. Mr Lester followed her. 'I must walk with you across the garden, Miss Campbell;' and he offered his arm, which she took silently. Mr Lester felt that she trembled. 'This has been a most trying, exciting day,' he said. 'I would, if I could, have spared you the discovery of to-night; but I doubted what to-morrow might bring, and feared that Vivian might be obliged to go without seeing you.'

'It was no discovery,' replied Bertha. 'I was certain before, —that is, nearly. O Mr Lester! it seems such a dream!'

'Yes.' He seemed considering what to add.

'He is not altered,' continued Bertha; then, in a lower tone, she added: 'I had hoped he might be.'

'He is altered, I trust,' observed Mr Lester. 'He looks at things very differently from what he did.'

'He cannot bear truth,' said Bertha.

'Not under some forms.'

'Not under any form, I fear,' continued Bertha: 'at least when it is unpleasant. In that, Clement is so like him.'

They had reached the gate between the two gardens; Bertha was going to cross the little bridge, but Mr Lester stopped her. 'May I give you one warning?'

'As many as you will; I am always grateful for them from you.'

'It can never be right to say what we don't think; but is it always necessary to say what we do?'

'You mean about the children?'

'Yes, I fear you have pained him, and he is already suffering greatly.'

'I am very sorry; I meant no harm. He must know it in time.'

'In time, yes; but not at this time; or at least not without some softening words.'

The change in Bertha's voice showed her vexation. 'I am always doing wrong,' she said; 'how can I help it?'

'Perhaps, if you had put yourself in his place, you might have understood.'

Silence followed till they reached the door of the Lodge. Then as Bertha rang the bell, and wished Mr Lester good night, she said: 'You may be right, but I cannot speak in a way which I don't feel.'

CHAPTER XXII.

MR LESTER returned to find his study empty. Mr Vivian was gone. That impulsive, irritable nature which had led him into so much evil in earlier years, was, as Bertha had said, in some measure, unchanged. Still, if thwarted, he was, for a season, moody; if forced to listen to unpleasing truths, he was disheartened. The child was father of the man, and the faults which had grown up unchecked till he was four-and-twenty, would yet too often be his tyrant at two-and-forty. He wandered forth now, desolate and dispirited to a degree greater than even his situation might occasion. He had gone to the Parsonage, excited, sanguine, longing and hoping for sympathy; but he had been disappointed. He felt as if he had been repelled, and by one to whom he ought to have been especially dear. The sister of her for whose sake he had sacrificed home, fortune, all that could render life precious. If Bertha had educated his children to be what she was herself, there could be but little union between them; and he might now be wearing away his life in a distant land with as much prospect of happiness as he could hope for in a restoration to his own country.

Very unreasonable, perhaps, such thoughts might seem at such a time; but whatever may be the romance, or poetry, or even danger of our position, we are still, except at the very moment of excitement, subject to the everyday impressions, which, for the most part, make up our existence.

The prejudiced, unbalanced tone of Bertha's mind, which stopped the current of her natural sympathies, had thrown her brother-in-law from her at the very moment when it was most necessary that he should be drawn towards her.

And Edward Vivian could not be what Mr Lester was—impartial. He knew little of Bertha's character, except from letters; and those had been generally kind, but formal. He did not doubt her right principle, but he did her spirit of self-devotion; and with the impatience natural to him, which made him chafe against every impediment to his wishes, he fancied that he was about to place himself in the power of one who looked coldly upon his interests, cared little for his children, and would allow him to linger week after week in exile, whilst waiting for the opportunities which a hearty determination would at once have found.

It was a grievous injustice to Bertha, whose chief thought was to see him restored to his inheritance, and her one object that his children should be educated to be an honour and comfort to him. But the thought and the object were the results of duty rather than affection, and with this Mr Vivian's susceptible feelings could not be satisfied.

He lingered on his way, for motion was soothing to his chafed spirit ; and a thousand busy thoughts were passing through his brain. Why should he have returned to England ? Why strive for that which, ever as he drew near, receded from his grasp ? The hope of restoration, how bright and dazzling had it seemed when viewed across the distance of the far ocean ? Now, in his native village, within sight of his father's Hall, within reach of his sister's voice, and the influence of his friend's counsel, it was dwindling, fading, till nothing seemed left but solitude, comfortless and dreary ; with coldness where he had expected warmth, prudence where he had looked for energy.

It might have been an unreasonable, an unthankful feeling, that rose up in the heart of the weary exile, for, alas ! sorrow tends to exaggerate our faults, as well as to strengthen our virtues ; but it was Bertha's work—Bertha the unselfish, the pure-minded, the devoted—her work, because she had never yet learned to heal the wounds of truth by the oil of sympathy.

It was a beautiful starlight evening, and the moon, though not full, gleamed clear in the cloudless heavens, and brought out every near object distinctly. The path through the village was the nearest to the farm, and Mr Vivian pursued it without thought, or rather with that engrossing thought which blinds us to the external world. He did not see the figure of a man standing below the porch of the first cottage which he passed; neither did he hear the footsteps which slowly and cautiously followed his. He went on, with his usual rapid, irregular pace, every now and then pausing, as some fresh idea struck him, and occasionally raising his arm high in the air, following out in action the feelings either of hope or despair which were at the moment paramount in his breast. The figure which followed him kept at a certain distance, stopped when he stopped, advanced when he advanced, still keeping in the shade, or, when obliged to emerge into the light, hurrying on, and then delaying, evidently with the wish not to approach too near.

The upper and open part of the village was passed, and they entered the ravine. The shadows there were deeper, the light glanced through the foliage of the trees more stealthily. Occasionally the barking of a dog broke the stillness, but, for the most part, all was silent save the quick, dashing murmur of the brook, tossing its way over rocks and pebbles to the ocean.

Mr Vivian quickened his pace; he seemed to feel the chilliness of the evening air, and presently he stopped to button his coat more closely around him. He was opposite to a cottage, standing high upon the bank, the only one in which a light still gleamed below. The door was open, and a man was standing on the threshold, his form clearly defined by the brightness of the light behind him. As Mr Vivian passed, a sharp, shrill, and very peculiar whistle was heard. It must have been an instinct, certainly it was not fear, which induced Mr Vivian to quicken his step, keeping close against the garden-wall, so that he might not be perceived. The figure behind also crept back farther into the shade. Mr Vivian was out of sight; the whistle was heard again, and answered; and Goff, the fisherman, stealing out of his cottage, met Ronald Vivian at the foot of the rough flight of steps which gave admittance to the garden from the road.

' I saw you, youngster. Why didn't you answer? I thought you had given me the slip !' was the insolent greeting ; to which Ronald replied by striding over the little stile, and leading the way up to the cottage door, where he placed himself so as to intercept the view of the road.

Goff followed impatiently. ' Twenty steps where one would do !' he muttered to himself, and then added aloud, ' You 've no need to go so far to learn your duty.'

' My father bade me come to hear the result of your inquiry,' said Ronald, haughtily. ' He spoke mysteries, so do you ; but I am used to them. Only let me hear what you would say quickly.'

' The Captain 's been out all day, I suppose ?'

' Yes, at Cleve. He has only just returned. If the inquiry was not satisfactory, I was to say that he expected you to-night at the Grange.'

'' High and mighty ! but he 'll learn differently some day. You passed no one on the road—eh, Ronald ?'

' I came by the back lane till I was in the village, and there I saw a pedlar man at the door of a public-house. Is that part of your mystery ?'

' The parson went home an hour since,' said Goff, carelessly, 'and the man at the farm—Bruce they call him—with him. He'd be back about this time. I've a notion he's friends with the Preventives; so we'd best not meet him.'

'Perhaps so; what message am I to take to my father?'

Instead of answering, Goff went again down the flight of steps, and looked up and down the road, 'I thought I heard a tramp; and it's time to be on our watch for those Preventive fellows.'

'My father is gone to the Point, and he bade me follow him; what message am I to take him?' repeated Ronald.

'Tell him I've an inkling I was right as to the cargo, but the craft was too far off to be searched. I may know more before to-morrow. Your father is at the Point, you say?'

'He expects his vessel in,' replied Ronald.

'I doubt whether they'll try the landing to-night; the tide doesn't serve.'

'He will be back at the Grange soon, then,' said Ronald; 'and is he to see you there?'

'Umph! that's as may be. Say I've business at home, both for him and for me. If he doesn't hear to-night, he will in the morning. And now, my young scamp, you may depart.'

He went down some of the steps, beckoning to Ronald to follow. But one bound, as it seemed, had brought Ronald to the stile. He vaulted across it, hallooed a hasty 'Good night' to Goff, and ran with his full speed, taking short cuts and by-paths, in the direction which Mr Vivian had pursued, whilst Goff seated himself on the garden-wall, and occupied himself with a pipe.

The end of the ravine was reached; Mr Vivian was about to emerge from it into the open space in front of the farm. The night was so calm, the effect of his walk so soothing, that he was doubtful whether to stop or proceed farther, and his step lingered as he gazed upon the old building, standing gray and ghost-like in the moonshine, and revolved in his mind the changes and sorrows associated with it.

'If Mr Vivian is wise, he will rest when others rest,' was uttered in a low, deep voice by some one at his side. He started, scarcely conscious at the first moment that he had been addressed by his true name; yet his hand grasped his stick with the quick perception of possible danger, and he turned sharply round with an indignant ejaculation.

'Those who betray their own secrets have no right to be angry when they are reminded of it,' continued Ronald.

'Ronald Vivian! Speak plainly, young fellow. Let me hear your object.'

'That you should know I know you,' said Ronald, boldly. 'We meet, then, upon equal ground.'

'John Vivian's son can never stand upon equal ground with me,' was the reply. 'You have aided me in danger, and I thank you for it, heartily. Name your recompense; you shall have it. For my secret, do with it as you will; I am indifferent to it.' Yet as he spoke, Mr Vivian's eye glanced quickly round, fearing apparently that the boy's approach was to be followed by that of others, whom he might have more cause to dread.

'Thanks! Recompense! Mr Vivian, let me tell you '—— and Ronald drew nearer, and his voice was harsh and hesitating. But suddenly it changed, as he muttered, 'Fool that I am! to think he would understand!'

'Say to your father if he has sent you '—— began Mr Vivian.

Ronald interrupted him. 'I do not come from my father. I have that to say which may be for your good; but first we must understand each other. Your thanks I do not desire them; your reward I would not accept it, if it were the wealth of the Indies you could offer me. Now, then, will you hear me?'

'Yes, say what you will, but shortly.'

'And not here,' said Ronald. He threw back the wicket-gate, entered the farm court, and tried the door into the garden, which was bolted.

Mr Vivian touched his arm. 'If we are to speak upon private matters, there is no place so secure as my own apartment.'

'I am used to the free air,' replied Ronald. 'I can speak better in it.' He drew back the bolt. 'Now, then, we are safe,' and carefully refastening the door again, on the inside, he turned into the broad turf-walk which divided the garden into two equal parts.

'Your father has doubtless learned that I am here,' said Mr Vivian.

'I came on my own account; my father'—— Ronald paused, and then went on impetuously. 'You don't trust me. I am used to that. God help me to bear it. Mr Vivian, you are my father's enemy.'

'Rather, your father is mine,' was the answer, uttered more gently.

'An enemy makes an enemy. You hate him; justly, perhaps;

yes, justly it must be. You think, too, that you have cause to
hate me also.'

'Hate you, Ronald! I owe my own life to you, and to-day
you have aided in saving my child.'

'The new favour will not wipe out the old grudge,' replied
Ronald. 'Young though I am, I have seen too much of the world
to believe that. Safety, both for yourself and your daughter,
would have been more precious if purchased by any other
means. Nay, let me speak,' he added, seeing that Mr Vivian
was about to interrupt him. 'I have nothing to say upon that
subject. It is gone—forgotten. It is of yourself, Mr Vivian,
that I would have you think. You are my father's enemy, and
your secret is in my hands. Upon what terms think you it is to
be kept!'

'Upstart! insolent!' exclaimed Mr Vivian. 'Do you think
I fear your father?'

'You have cause to do so,' was Ronald's calm reply.

'Cause! Yes, cause indeed!' And the tone was bitter in its
remorse. 'I do fear him, but not as you think; not for the injury he may have done me in former years, not for the evil he
may yet bring upon me in this world. I fear him as I fear the
spirit of evil ; the demon that tempts man to his eternal destruction. There is no bargain to be made with such fear.'

A look of agony passed over Ronald's face at the last words.
He pressed his hands tightly together, and when he spoke, his
tone was hollow, in the effort to repress his feelings: 'Yet the
question is unanswered. Upon what terms is the secret to be
kept?'

'Upon no terms, sir ; let the whole world know it, and come
what may, I will abide it.'

'That may be a hasty word long to be repented,' replied
Ronald.

'Never to be repented. There must be war ; ay, for ever
between John Vivian and myself ; between his children and my
children. Young fellow, you have your answer.'

'I have not my answer,' replied Ronald. 'Mr Vivian, you
think you are speaking to a boy, and you are right. A boy I am
in years, but they have been years in which a man's experience
has been condensed. You cannot and shall not turn from me in
this way. You shall listen as to a man, your equal, and you shall
grant me my demands as to one who holds your fate in his hands,
and will never be tempted to swerve from his resolve either by

threat of punishment, or hope of reward. Once more, upon what terms shall your secret be kept?'

He folded his arms, and leaned his back against a tree, and the pale gleaming of the moon showed a face, anxious, haggard, yet immovable. Mr Vivian was touched by its expression, whilst his spirit revolted from the proud words which he had just heard. 'You are a strange fellow, Ronald,' he said, more lightly. 'Do you think that a man who has reached my age, and has the happiness of so many depending upon him, would have placed himself in a situation, which a hasty word of his own, and the wilfulness of a boy like yourself, might render really perilous? You delude yourself. It has been my will, for purposes of my own, to remain for a time concealed; but the truth must, before long, come forth. Your betrayal of it, or that of your father, can have but little effect upon my fortunes.'

'Trust to that hope if you will,' replied Ronald; 'believe that the man whom you injured in the point nearest to his heart will suffer his revenge to die; trust that he will allow you to return, and rake up the ashes of past deeds, and search out the offences which, it may be, are hidden amongst them; but, remember, it is at your own peril, against the warning of one who knows that life and death are at this moment trembling in the balance of your decision.'

Mr Vivian started. 'Ha! Are you come to threaten me? I might have known the spirit of John Vivian hidden under the form of his son.' And he laughed scornfully.

'I bear with your injustice—with your suspicions, Mr Vivian. God knows, I feel too truly how they have been deserved. Doubt me if you will, yet still listen to me. One word from me, and the thought which is now but a slumbering ember will be kindled into a flame, and the most hidden recesses of English ground will not insure your safety.'

'You want money, young man; you shall have it, so far as my poverty will admit; but not to purchase secrecy and safety. There is a God above, and He will protect me.'

'Money!' Ronald's deep voice sounded as the burst of thunder on the clear air. But the check followed in a moment, and the tones of a child could not have been more gentle than his, as he added: 'Mr Vivian, I want not money, but pardon.' He covered his face with his hands, and a bitter groan burst from him. Then, resuming his former attitude, and speaking almost coldly, he continued: 'But for my aid you might have perished

in the storm, your child might have been dashed from the heights
of the Croome. But for my secrecy now, danger, near and pressing, little though you may believe it, must haunt your steps. Is
it too much to ask forgiveness in return for life?'

'Forgiveness, Ronald! you speak riddles; you have never
offended me.'

'My father has. He has injured you. His injuries may, they
must, some day come to light : yes, and by my instrumentality;'
and again he hid his face and shuddered. 'Mr Vivian, when
that day shall come, will you not remember that Ronald was your
friend in the hour of peril ?—that for your sake he risked the
hastening of that fearful account which we are told we are all to
give before God?'

'Remember!' Mr Vivian grasped his hand. 'Ronald, so
surely will I remember your good deeds as I pray that God in
His mercy may forget my evil ones. But even yet I cannot see
your purpose.'

'It may be a sad history, yet I will beg you to listen to it,'
replied Ronald. 'Mr Vivian, I have not now for the first time
learned that I was the son of a man whom the world terms re-
probate. I discovered it in my childhood, when I said my prayers
at my mother's knee, stealthily, because my father would interrupt them ; I saw it in my mother's tears, when he left her to join
in riot and intemperance. I heard it from her own lips as she lay
on her death-bed, and charged me never to follow his evil courses,
and yet, if possible, never to forsake him. It was the one burning thought which made me what I have been,—reckless and
desperate. I was too young then to profit by counsel ; perhaps
even if I had been older, I should have been too weak, and I did
follow my father into scenes and society which I have since
learned to shrink from with horror. There I might have been
at this moment ;—God only knows why I am not there : but
through it all, even in my worst moments, the warnings of one
friend have recalled me to better things, reminding me of days
of innocence, carrying me back to my mother's death-bed. If
the past can ever be redeemed, it will be through the teaching of
my mother's only friend, Miss Campbell. I owe everything to
her, and I will repay the debt, cost what it may.'

'And Miss Campbell, then, has told you our family history?'

'In part. She has put the possibility of benefiting you within
my reach, at the expense of my father's honour, and perhaps
safety.' He spoke with an accent of bitterness, and Mr Vivian

said, hastily, 'Bertha Campbell has been inconsiderate; she never could expect such a sacrifice.'

'Miss Campbell did not know what she exacted,' replied Ronald. 'I did not know what I promised, until I thought over my promise; but if I had known I could not have drawn back. Gratitude and honour must make me labour to discover the truth; justice would require me to make it known. I do not for a moment blame Miss Campbell; neither do I repent for myself. I ask only that the good deed which I may be enabled to do for you, may not be turned into the agony of remorse, by bringing destruction upon my father.'

'It could never be,' exclaimed Mr Vivian. 'I would rather die myself, and see my children beggars, than I would urge you to act against your father.'

'When I was told the history, the deed was done,' replied Ronald, mournfully. 'I needed no urging then. I can never rest till restitution has been made.'

'Leave it, leave it,' replied Mr Vivian, hastily; 'forget that you have been asked. A son to turn against his father!—impossible!'

'And a family to be sacrificed, when one word might restore to them a lost inheritance!—equally impossible!' replied Ronald.

'Bertha Campbell has unintentionally deceived you, Ronald,' said Mr Vivian. 'She has an idea that something which your father said or did was the cause of my exile; but she is mistaken. The offences were my own; they may have been exaggerated; my father's anger may have been increased by misrepresentation; but the main facts must have been true, and for them I only am answerable. Are you not satisfied by my assurance?' he added, as Ronald continued silent.

Still there was a pause. Mr Vivian repeated the question.

Ronald seized his hand. 'Mr Vivian, you are a man of honour; ask me no more questions. Only, if you value the life which through my means was restored to you, promise me here, as in the presence of God, that whatever may hereafter be discovered and revealed by me, shall only so far be used as I shall permit, and never be made known by you to any other person except by my permission.'

'I promise; solemnly, faithfully.'

Ronald shook his hand eagerly. 'Honour for life! Mr Vivian, there is now no obligation; I thank you from my heart.' His tone was quite changed, it was almost hopeful.

Mr Vivian turned to go into the house. 'If you are satisfied, we must part now,' he said.

'I am satisfied about myself, not about you. Mr Vivian, this place is not safe for you?'

'I am going to leave it.'

'When? Another day's delay may be of infinite importance.'

'I go to-morrow to '——

'Do not tell me where. Let me know nothing of you that I can avoid. Whatever must be known, Miss Campbell will tell me.'

'I do not see the need of so much mystery,' exclaimed Mr Vivian, rather haughtily. 'I fear no man.'

'Yet there may not be, therefore, the less cause for fear. You would be safe from my father ; you are not safe from the fellow Goff.'

'Rascal !—he is too contemptible to dread.'

'Mr Lester will give you his opinion upon that point,' replied Ronald. 'I cannot expect you to take mine. But you are going, and that is all I ask.'

They walked a few paces together, without speaking ; but when they reached the garden-door, Mr Vivian grasped Ronald's hand, and said, in a voice hoarse with suppressed feeling, 'Ronald, you are a noble fellow. Let my own boy be but like you, and I shall be contented.'

He was detained.

'Never ! never ! O God ! save him from it ! Innocence ! Mr Vivian, the riches of the universe would I give for innocence !'

CHAPTER XXIII.

A BRIGHT fire was blazing on the hearth in Mildred Vivian's apartment, an old-fashioned Christmas fire, though it was only the beginning of December,—logs of wood kindling and inspiriting the coals ; and Mildred's sofa was drawn near it, and her little work-table was placed by her side ; and, reclining in a low and very luxurious chair on the other side, Ella was reading to her aloud. 'They looked very comfortable, all the more so because snow was falling, and the sky heavy with gray masses of clouds, which threatened to prevent anything like going out all day.

'Grandpapa has not been in this morning,' said Ella, as she laid down the first volume of the book, and looked round the room for the second.

'He is busy with the bailiff, I think,' said Mildred. 'There are parish matters and magistrate's business to attend to. He never leads an idle life?'

'No,' replied Ella; 'it is strange, Aunt Mildred, isn't it, what people find to interest them in life?'

'Parish matters and magistrate's business being very uninteresting to you, I suppose,' said Mildred, laughing.

'They are so low,' replied Ella.

'I don't know what the world would do without them, though,' said Mildred. 'And I really don't see why they are to be called low.'

'Oh, because they don't serve any purpose; they don't exalt one's mind. You know, Aunt Mildred, parish matters are always about gruel and blankets; and magistrate's matters about poaching.'

'All very necessary, Ella.'

'Oh yes, necessary, but I hate necessities; now don't you.'

'I can't say exactly that I do. I am afraid such a good-for-nothing person as I am in the way of health, must always think a good deal of them. But I do know what you mean, Ella, and I feel with you in a certain way. One wouldn't like to live upon necessaries.'

'No;' Ella's face brightened at being understood,—'and that is what some people do; and what I dread doing, and, Aunt Mildred, it is what I am sure I shall do, if I live at Encombe much longer.'

'Six months' trial is a very short one.'

'Enough for me,' said Ella, yawning. 'If it weren't for coming here, sometimes, I shouldn't have an idea left. But you do let one rhapsodise a little.'

Mildred's face was rather grave.

'Now, Aunt Mildred, that is an expression I don't like,' continued Ella; 'it always seems as if there was something hidden behind it, and I choose to know all. Now confess, what were you thinking of?' she added, playfully.

'Merely whether rhapsodising, as you call it, was a good, or a bad thing.'

'Oh, good : infinitely good ! It encourages enthusiasm, and enthusiasm leads to heroism, and heroism to—why, all the noble things which have been done in the world are owing to heroism.'

'Most true ; you had better write a book upon it some day.'

'You are laughing at me ; but I don't see why you should,' and Ella, rather petulantly, took up some work.

'Not at all laughing, dear Ella ; quite the reverse.'

'Then crying ; I would rather you should do that than laugh. I hate ridicule ; it chills me.'

'Dear Ella, you know I never ridicule any one—intentionally, that is. My words may certainly be twisted to a wrong meaning.'

Then why did you say I had better write a book upon heroism? Of course that means, I had better not.'

'Of course it does. Perhaps I said it because I thought persons' never write well upon subjects which they don't understand, and that no one can understand heroism who doesn't practise it.'

'There is little enough opportunity for practising it at Encombe,' observed Ella.

'One might think so at first sight, but you have had occasions more frequently than most people.'

'I don't quite see when. There have been no adventures, only the wreck, which I had nothing to do with, and the Croome ; yes, that was terrible :' and Ella became much graver in manner ; 'but the heroism belonged to Ronald and Mr Bruce.'

'I think you were something of a heroine, Ella. If you had lost your presence of mind there would have been no hope.'

'One is inspired, I suppose, at such times,' said Ella. 'I could never have supposed it possible to bear up as I did. But to be a heroine for one day is nothing. What I wish is to be one all my life, and in these times there is nothing to give one the opportunity. Oh for the days of chivalry and the Crusaders !'

'When ladies lived shut up within walls, and occupied themselves in working tapestry with their maids, every now and then relieving their tediousness by taking a stroll upon the battlements, to see if their lords were coming.'

'You are so absurd, Aunt Mildred. Whoever thinks of beautiful ladies in the olden times taking a stroll ?'

'But they did stroll, Ella, unless, as I suppose sometimes happened, they felt it good for their health to have a good, quick, constitutional walk.'

'I can't talk to you,' said Ella; 'you always laugh about knights and chivalry.'

'Quite the reverse, dear Ella ; I have the greatest possible admiration for them. All I ever regret is, that people should spend their time in grasping at the shadow, and so lose the substance.'

'I don't know what you mean by that,' said Ella. 'I never could discover any knightly substance, as you call it, in these days.'

'I should scarcely imagine you could,' replied Mildred, quietly.

Ella looked up, a little piqued, and answered, 'But if there is any, I don't see why I am to be more blind than the rest of the world.'

'You are not more blind than most people,' replied Mildred. 'Half the persons you meet would tell you that they can discover nothing but matter-of-factness in the nineteenth century.'

'Please, Aunt Mildred, don't talk mysteries ; you can't think how they tease me.'

'The meaning of my mysteries may not suit you, Ella,' said Mildred, gravely.

'Perhaps so, but I should like to know it.'

'I think that what we are accustomed to call chivalry was an earthly adaptation of the Christian spirit, suited to rude times and men of half-cultivation,' said Mildred ; 'that, in fact, it was a type of real chivalry.'

'Then, what do you call real chivalry ?' asked Ella.

'The spirit of self-devotion, self-denial, courage, endurance, perseverance, not for the praise of men but the praise of God.'

Ella was silent.

'That does not quite approve itself to your ideas, does it ?' said Mildred.

'It is all very good,' replied Ella, 'but I don't see any chivalry in it.'

'No ; and you never will in your present state of mind. You are a knight going unwillingly to the wars, and always sighing for the repose of his own halls and the gentle glance of his ladye love.'

'That would never have been my case !' exclaimed Ella. 'I could have fought, I know I could, like a lion.'

'O Ella ! I wish you could do so now.' Mildred's voice was sad.

'Dear Aunt Mildred, don't speak so; I would think as you do if I could.'

'You can, Ella, if you will; all of us can. The thoughts would come if you would only act.'

'Action ; that is the difficulty ;' and Ella sighed.

'A knight to sigh and say action is the difficulty ! '

Ella blushed. 'Aunt Mildred, I am not a knight.'

'No, Ella ! A Christian knight you can't be, because—is it very hard to say it ?—you live only for yourself.'

Ella's countenance betrayed a momentary annoyance, but she recovered herself quickly, though her tone was still a little con-strained, as she replied, 'You are rather severe in your con-demnation, Aunt Mildred.'

'More severe than is merited, am I? But, will you set me right then, and tell me whom you do live for,—Grandmamma ? Aunt Bertha? Clement ?'

'Oh ! for no one in particular ; who does ? I am very·fond of everybody, but I don't know what you mean by living for them.'

'But Ella, that will not do for chivalry. The knights of old could never have fought as they did if they had not had some special object.'

'But you say I am not a knight.'

'We come round to the point from which we set off. I don't think you have the spirit of a knight in you. I am sure, indeed, you have not. No one who is self-indulgent can have,' added Mildred.

'You don't like my sitting in easy-chairs,' said Ella, half raising herself.

'I don't like it, because it puts your mind into an easy-chair too,' replied Mildred.

'No ; indeed I assure you I can think twenty times as well when I am comfortable.'

'There is a difference between being comfortable and not being uncomfortable,' said Mildred. 'People can't think when they have the toothache, but there is a wide neutral ground between that and positive luxury.'

'One's imagination works so much better in the pleasant, dreamy state, which sofas and arm-chairs put one into,' said Ella, throwing herself back and laughing. 'I do so wonder,. Aunt Mildred, that you who are so fond of poetry can't under-stand that.'

'Perhaps I can and do understand it too well,' answered Mildred, thoughtfully. 'But one thing, Ella, I am quite certain of, that imagination and every other faculty will infallibly degenerate if it is not kept alive by practice. If you can write good poetry when you sit and dream all day in your arm-chair, you will write much better if you rouse yourself and do a kind act for a person in need. I believe myself, that one chief reason why we so often see persons of great powers of imagination degenerating and writing things quite unworthy of their first efforts, is that they think mental work everything, and so neglect to recruit their poor minds by bracing practical duties. Even in an intellectual point of view, Ella, you see, I object to the arm-chair.'

'Oh, dear! so comfortable;' and Ella sighed, and drew her chair nearer to the fire.

'It seems very unfitting for me to say it, I am afraid,' continued Mildred, 'when I lie on a sofa all day. But then, Ella, against that perhaps I may put the pain which God has sent me. I am never quite free from it. And in other ways I do try to practise what I preach; at least I hope so.'

'Yes, Aunt Mildred, who could think you self-indulgent?'

'I was inclined to be so once,' she replied. 'When my dear sister was living, she took so much from me in the way of duty, that I often felt there was no occasion for exertion, and then I gave way. But it has been different of late years, and I have taught myself to open the windows of my mind, and let in the fresh breezes from without, even though now and then they are a little chilling.'

Ella considered a little, still reclining at her ease. 'Then, Aunt Mildred, what would you have me do?'

'What would I not have you do? You like plain speaking, you say. Nothing that you have done since you came here, at least not in the same spirit.'

'I can't alter the spirit,—it is that which I am in always,' said Ella, rather moodily.

'Yet it was to have been different after your fright upon the Croome.'

'I thought so for a time, but it went off; that is always the case with me,—I can't help changing.'

'Simply because you think and don't act,' replied Mildred. 'The notes which you sent me the week after your adventure were full of good resolutions.'

N

'Oh yes ; good resolutions ; but what are they worth ? I am tired of them.'

'So am I,' was Mildred's grave remark.

Ella rose from her seat, and as she knelt by Mildred's side, said, ' Please not, Aunt Mildred : any tone but that.'

' Do you deserve any other, Ella ?'

' No. I deserve nothing, I am very unhappy,' and Ella burst into tears.   יסע

' You were to have taught the children regularly,' continued Mildred, ' and you have neglected them just as you did before. You were to have been thoughtful for your grandmamma, and obedient to your Aunt Bertha, and there have been nothing but complaints.   I asked you to come here, and told you what I wished you to do, and you promised what you have not in the smallest degree attempted properly to perform.   You are late at breakfast always, although your grandpapa particularly wishes you to be in time ; when he asks you to walk with him, you move reluctantly ; when he desires you to play, you make excuses ; when he recommends you books to read, you waste your time over poetry and novels.   And all the while sighing for heroism, and the days of chivalry.   O Ella ! you would have made but a poor knight.'

' Aunt Mildred, yes ; if those days had been like these.   But they were different.'

' No, Ella, they were the same,—formed for and by human beings like ourselves, with the same foibles, the same passions and temptations ; and what we are now that we should have been then.'

' Then I am a poor knight,' said Ella, faintly attempting to smile, ' doomed to be always defeated.'

' And yet entrusted with the highest possible gifts ; talents far above the average, a quiet home, leisure, friends '——

' No, Aunt Mildred ; begging your pardon, that is just what I have not ; a quiet home, and leisure, and friends.   I am continually interrupted, and there is no one that I can talk to as I like.'

' Ella, Ella ; if you have the smallest value for goodness or happiness, be honest with yourself.   You allow the interruptions, and shut yourself up from your friends, and then turn your own faults into excuses.'

' Indeed ; it is true.   I never can talk to Aunt Bertha.   She is very good, I know ; but — I must say it, if it is ever so wrong, —she is intensely disagreeable.'

'So I suppose am I,' observed Mildred, gently.

'Oh no ; you know I love you dearly, and I would do any-thing in the world for you.'

'Except the trifles, I ask. You disobey me just as you do Aunt Bertha.'

'If you would ask me great things, I could do them. I would cut off my hand to serve you.'

'But you would not use it to copy a piece of music yester-day.'

'O Aunt Mildred ! I forgot.'

'Dear Ella, if I could only once hear you say,—not I forgot, —but I was wrong.'

'I do say it very often,' replied Ella.

'Yes, when the accusations are general, but never when they are particular. This is the test of humility and sincerity, not to say merely I have a bad temper, or I am indolent ; but I was very passionate on such an occasion, and sat still when I ought to have exerted myself on another. I fear, Ella, your repentance is as vague as your resolution ; and we can only cure our faults by knowing their details, and having rules by which to correct them.'

'Then mine will never be cured,' replied Ella ; 'for I hate rules, they are so narrow-minded. Aunt Mildred, you must allow that.'

'They may be narrow-minded. I don't see that they are so necessarily,' replied Mildred.

'Well ! but—don't be angry with me,—Aunt Bertha is full of rules. I am sure she never allows herself to eat, or drink, or sleep, except by rule.'

'Dearest Ella ; always alluding to Aunt Bertha, never think-ing of yourself !'

'I am a heathen compared with her, I know that, but I can't help believing—I really don't mean to be conceited, and I would not say it to any one but you,—I can't help fancying that I am more agreeable.'

'And you think the rules are the cause.'

'I am sure of it. If one tries to throw one's self into her ways, it is like being in a prison, and one is always running up against the bars. You know you have scarcely seen her, so you can't at all tell what she is like.'

'She is coming to see me soon,' replied Mildred, thoughtfully.

'I hope you will understand her better than I do ; but I don't think you will ; you are so unlike her. How she makes me hate duty!'

'Well, then,'—Mildred's voice became graver,—'what do you say to love ?'

'Love of you ? It would make me work for ever.'

'Only you can't copy music for me. Ah, Ella, you see you have been tried and failed. No, it is not *my* love which will help you.'

'I am not fit for any higher love,' said Ella, gravely.

'Only that you cannot escape it,' said Mildred, earnestly ; 'the love which upheld you when you stood on the brink of death, which inspired you with presence of mind, which sent you succour at the very moment of need. O Ella! for the sake of *that* dear love, will you not try to be really good?'

'Aunt Mildred, it is so terrible to say it : but I don't feel it.'

'But, Ella, dearest, it is not a question of feeling ; you are the child of God's love even when you turn away and forget Him. And now He has recalled you to Himself; and has bestowed upon you a great mercy, and only requires you to show your thankfulness by attention to little duties. Can you have the spirit of a Christian knight if you refuse?'

Ella looked distressed.

'Please don't remind me of that,' she said. 'I know I never could be a knight or anything else that is good for much.'

'But, indeed, I must remind you of it, because, though you think I laugh at you, I do really and truly feel that the longings which you have so often, those poetical dreams of bygone days, are really the indications of what you ought to be, and may be if you will.'

'Not if I will.'

'Yes, most certainly if you will. It is only the will which you want.'

'But I can't make myself will.'

'But you can pray ; that is the beginning of willing, and without it will is nothing.'

'I have no perseverance ; I do everything by fits and starts,' said Ella ; 'and when the mood is upon me I can't resist.'

'All which shows that you have certainly, as regards goodness, a weak will. But against this you must put enthusiasm, taste, quick perception of all that is beautiful and noble ; the advantages ought to balance the defects.'

'I must be what I was made,' replied Ella.

'No, dear Ella, never, never!' exclaimed Mildred, eagerly. 'God gives us all the materials for the formation of character. He leaves it to ourselves to decide into what form it shall be moulded; only He tells us that if we come to Him and ask His aid, He will teach us how to form it to the greatest perfection.'

'I am sure I don't know what my materials are,' said Ella.

'Then, my dear child, it is high time you should know. It is the root of all education whether of ourselves or others. Look at yourself closely; it will do you no harm. Search out all your good points; bring out all your natural advantages; inquire at the same time into your faults. When you have done this, you will be able to understand what ought to be your course of self-education.'

'It is a fearful task,' said Ella, wearily. 'Aunt Mildred, I think you had much better do it for me.'

'No one can do it thoroughly but yourself, Ella. It is very well to be educated by others when we are children; and it is very necessary for those who wish to educate properly, to study the characters which they have to form; but when we have passed the age of early childhood, no persons but ourselves can really do much for us.'

'I am sure no one ever studied me or understood me,' said Ella.

'So much the more reason that you should understand yourself. Only one caution I would give you. It is not wise to attempt or wish to be anything but what God has marked out for us. It is useless for a very imaginative person to endeavour to become matter-of-fact; and useless in the same way for a very matter-of-fact person to try and be imaginative.'

'Then you will leave me my imagination, and not call it a sin, like Aunt Bertha?' said Ella.

'Leave it, and encourage it to the very utmost,' replied Mildred; 'only I would make it what it was intended to be,—a help and not a hindrance. Our strongest characteristic, whatever it may be (I am speaking of course only of that which is good), is the grappling-iron by which we are first to seize on heaven. O Ella! if you long for beauty and perfection, and sigh because there is no one to love with all your heart, why do you not turn to the Source of all beauty,—the love which can never change?'

'Because I can't,' replied Ella, candidly. 'Aunt Mildred, I have had the same thing said to me again and again. Mr Lester has talked to me. I have read it in sermons. I know it is all true and good, but I can't feel it. I can't make myself love.'

'Dearest Ella, no. Love is a gift,—the highest gift of all, But action will, through God's mercy, bring you to it.'

'And tiresome, troublesome rules, make me feel as if I never could love,' said Ella. 'They make me dread religion.'

'I should be sorry to deceive you, Ella. Religion, to a person of your self-indulgent, imaginative temperament, must always, at the beginning, be irksome. But the very excitability of your disposition may be your help. You say you cannot feel love, but that is not true at all times. You did feel it the other day when you were saved from that horrible danger.'

'Yes, I couldn't help it;' and Ella's face showed a quick, inward self-recollection, and self-reproach.

'And you feel it when you read beautiful poetry, or hear of noble deeds,—of heroism, chivalry, for instance.'

'Yes, but that is only feeling.'

'Yet clench the feeling at once, whenever it comes, by some action, however slight, and you will, unknown to yourself, have made a step in advance towards rendering love permanent.'

'Rules,' murmured Ella, 'I hate rules.'

'And don't fetter yourself with rules,' replied Mildred. 'They are not religion, only aids to it. They clog some minds, whilst they strengthen others.'

'But Aunt Bertha says people are worth nothing unless they live according to rule,' said Ella.

'She is right, no doubt, to a certain extent. You know I did not say, don't attend to rules, but only don't fetter yourself with them. A few rules, simple, easy, and capable of being stretched if necessary, are quite sufficient, especially for you. For, Ella, you will never be happy yourself, or assist in making others so, until your rules are the result of your feeling of love, and not merely of your sense of duty.'

'But, Aunt Mildred,'—and Ella started up in astonishment, —'at home they are always preaching to me about duty.'

'So would I preach, too, Ella, if I thought it would make you do your duty. But, as I said before, we have certain materials given us by God, out of which our religious character is to be formed. With many minds, when the temperament is calm, and there is an instinctive love of order and method, the idea of duty is infinitely powerful. It will never, indeed, by itself, produce a very earnest, religious feeling ; but it will put us in the way which leads to it. But it is not so with all. There are those to whom the very name of duty sounds cold and repulsive. Those are the minds which take the highest flight and sink to the lowest depth. Ella, will yours be amongst them?'

Tears glistened in Ella's eyes. 'Aunt Mildred, if you would only tell me what to do? Even now I don't see.'

'Pray, dear Ella, first ; without that, nothing can succeed.'

'Yes, I know ; but in other ways.'

'You would not be obliged to inquire, if you could remember that your life has a second time been given you ; and that He who restored it, asks for your love in return.'

'Aunt Mildred, I do wish to please Him.' Ella's tone was humble and more gentle.

'And the wish is not lost, dear Ella. Every wish, the very least, is remembered by Him. If it is followed by an action, it is accepted.'

Ella stood up, and pushed the easy-chair aside. 'Aunt Mildred, I will copy the music for you at once.'

Mildred smiled. 'And, Ella, may I suggest one little rule ?— that the easy-chair should never be used till evening, and not then unless you are really tired.'

It was a very trifling ending to a long conversation ; yet Ella was neither moody nor indolent for the remainder of that day.

CHAPTER XXIV.

MR VIVIAN had taken up his abode in an obscure lodging, in one of the tall, decayed, mournful streets of departed grandeur, to be found in the north-west region of London. His shabbily-furnished apartment was large, and had once been handsome, and still retained indications of ornament in the outline of a heavy cornice, and the stuccoed richness of an old-fashioned ceiling. A few books were on the table, with a writing-desk and papers ; and a fire blazed in the huge grate, shadowed by a high mantelpiece, which was supported by Medusa heads. There was an attempt at comfort in the room —but only an attempt ; it wanted a lady's hand to arrange the furniture, and the niceties of a lady's taste to give it in the least an air of home ; and Mr Vivian, used though he had been to years of solitude, sighed, perhaps, with the recollection of the days when even an humble dwelling had been rendered cheerful and inviting, by the affectionate care which had adorned it.

Neither was the scene without more cheering; a yellow London fog, streets covered with mud, black chimneys, smoke-stained brick walls; no wonder that Mr Vivian turned with disgust from the window, and sitting down to his desk, endeavoured to while away the weary hours by writing.

His letter was the outpouring of a burdened and not entirely chastened mind. He was an altered man, humble-minded, heartily religious, but he was himself still; and often, as his pen was moving rapidly, he paused to consider, whether the impulse which urged him was one to which it was safe to yield, or whether it was but the indulgence of that craving for sympathy which had often in other days led to weakness.

'My dear Lester,—I wrote to you three days ago, and why, you will say, should I write again? Because I am lonely and dispirited, and have nothing else to do. A sufficient answer for my conscience, though not perhaps for your patience. London is very dreary, my life here most wearisome. I try to bear it, as you say I ought, and I fail. Moreover, I cannot see the reason for delay. Hope grows less. The children, you tell me, are scarcely ever with their grandfather; nothing, then, can be done through their means. You and Bertha may want to open my way more clearly, but you have undertaken a task beyond your powers. John Vivian is far too experienced a rogue to betray himself. Let me go to my father, cast all upon the die, and, if rejection is my answer, I will submit; leave England, take my children with me, if not to Jamaica, to some other home, and forget that I ever indulged the vain hope which has already brought me so much sorrow.

'Any certainty is better than this killing suspense. I am not strong enough to bear it—morally strong—I feel it does me injury. I am becoming captious and impatient. Your letters are the only things I can bear. Bertha's try me beyond endurance. She is always telling me of my children's faults,—that Ella is wilful, and Clement desultory,—and dinning it into my ears, that it is the uncertainty of their present life which is so bad for them.

'I know it as she knows it; and better, ten thousand times better. It has been the remorseful lesson of my life, that I have injured them. Why does she add bitterness to a saddened spirit?

'But I am unjust to her, I feel. She has done for my children more than I could have asked; she loves them, I fully believe, sincerely, if not tenderly. I have no right to require more; and yet when her letters come they dishearten me to such a degree, that again the impulse seizes me to throw off disguise, once more appear at Encombe, and take the decision of my cause into my own hands.

'Preach to me, my dear Lester; I need it sadly; my mind is terribly undisciplined, and I can so little bear with myself. You told me to accept my life as my punishment. It is the only way in which I could endure it. But there are times—they come more frequently now in solitude and leisure—when the spirit of submission seems to forsake me, and when the thought of having brought the suffering upon myself, by my own wilfulness, my own folly—worse than folly—my sin, is almost maddening.

'Men talk of repentance as if the past might be wiped out by tears, and no scar left to mark where the evil has been. Lester, I have shed tears of agony. My first thought in the morning has been sorrow, my last consciousness at night has been of penitence, and in the silence of midnight I have risen to pray that God would think upon me in His Mercy, and "remember not the sins and offences of my youth." And I believe that I am forgiven. I can look forward to death with an humble hope of acceptance, through undeserved Goodness, and the Atonement once made for all; and yet the stain is there—indelible to my own eyes—though it may be unseen by man, and in mercy forgotten by God.

'Repentance does not place us, in this world, in the position in which we should have been if we had never sinned. The mark once set upon us, it is ineffaceable. The wound once given, and it must and will at times reopen. Oh! if I could make Clement feel it! —now, whilst he is comparatively innocent, whilst his offences are the opening faults of a boy, not the full-grown wickedness of a man. And yet many would scoff at me for saying this; they would tell me that my mind is morbid; that whatever my youth may have been, I have redeemed it by the years which followed. Alas! my early life lingered far longer under the dominion of evil than those who have only watched its outward course would imagine. When I left England to work in a foreign land, I was

not penitent, but exasperated.   Irritation and repining darkened
not only my own existence, but that of her who had sacrificed all
for me.   The thought is as a dagger to me.   Not till she was
taken from me, and the past, as regarded her, had become irremediable, did I fully see what my course had been.   And then—
I have heard it said that the knowledge of evil is necessary, that
it is experience, and consequently, power—O Lester! how little
can such persons imagine the agony of those moments when
first the heart is awakened to the knowledge of its guilt ; the
sickening glance cast upon the past, the despairing darkness of
the future, and the longing, the intense longing, to hide one's self
deep from all eyes, even, were it possible, from the Eye of God.
Those feelings are not strength, but weakness ; they make the
eye dim, and the hand weak.   Even when the offer of mercy
comes to sooth us, their remembrance still haunts us ; and when
we should be pressing forward to the brightness of heaven, they
bid us turn back to gaze again upon the blackness of our own
hearts, and once more seek to wipe out our offences with our
tears.

'I need not say this to you.   You know it all ; not by your
own experience.   God be thanked, your career has been very
different from mine ; but by the griefs of others.   Yet it is a
relief to me.   There is comfort in working out in my own mind
why, though I have attained to peace, I have never yet reached
forward to joy.   It may come—you will perhaps tell me that it
must come—with the increasing sense of God's infinite love ;
but I doubt it.   The more deeply we love, the more keen must
be the grief for having offended.   Joy is for those who have from
the beginning held on their course unwaveringly.   Peace and
hope are, I believe, the highest boon granted in this world to
those who have sinned grievously and repented truly.   But no
more of this—it is but another form of self-indulgence.   I must
learn to live to myself and by myself, not disturbing the happiness of those who have never wandered by the cloud which it
seems, now, must for ever rest upon my own spirit.   For my
children's sake, I would especially strive to do so :—the open
brow, and the glad smile, must be for them and for the world ;
the sackcloth, and ashes, and the tears of humiliation for the Eye
of God.   Yet to you I would say that even when I am most apparently repining at the punishment which I have brought upon
myself,—I could accept my grief, ay, were it a hundred times
greater, and from the bottom of my heart thank God for it, if by

It I were enabled successfully to warn Clement against the fatal yielding to small temptations, which ruined my own character as a boy, and then sent me, stamped with the disheartening brand of weakness, to encounter the temptation of a man. Victory at fourteen would have been victory at four-and-twenty. Victory at four-and-twenty would, through God's mercy, have been safety for life and for eternity. Tell it him, Lester, as you love me, as you would save yourself, in the Great Day of account, from the reproach of having failed to warn when the opportunity was placed within your reach.

'And now, farewell! I began my letter with impatient complaints, I end it with the confessions of repentance. A true epitome of my whole life ; yet so far what I said at first was not mere impatience, that I do not see we are progressing, and time is passing on, and if I cannot remain in England I must prepare for establishing a home elsewhere. Bertha's complaints of Ella make me uneasy, and Clement too cannot be left to his present course of life. Something must be done for both. I feel repugnant to allowing Clement to accept as a favour from my father, what even now I cannot help feeling ought to be his as a right. Even if I am cut off for my offences, there would seem to be but little justice in punishing my child.

'I sometimes think that a situation in a merchant's office— and I have interest enough to procure him that—might be more honourable for him, and, in a worldly point of view, more advantageous than the University. At any rate I must have him under my own eye. The little I saw and heard at Encombe made me feel that direct authority is imperatively necessary for him.

' Some things about him I can so well understand; they are so sadly like what I was at his age! Write to me soon, and give me some definite views, or I shall relapse into despair.

'Always most affectionately
'and gratefully yours,
'G. B. V.

'Don't think I am expecting to hear of success as regards John Vivian and his plots. I scarcely think about them. They are so vague, and so far in the past. I feel that whatever they were they have done me all the harm they could, and that the discovery of them could not profit me.'

Mr Lester's answer was received in the course of the same week.

'MY DEAR VIVIAN,—You write me volumes. I hope you don't expect volumes in answer. Yet I shall have a good deal to say before I have done. First to business. You can do nothing better than preach patience to yourself, and by the time the lesson is learned we may look forward to a little hope. I think I see some already. Ella is at the Hall,—the first opening that is for awakening interest ; and whatever may be the end of our researches into John Vivian's doings, we shall have good cause for bright anticipations if we can once induce the General to look favourably upon the children. Mrs Campbell's step in bringing them to Encombe was dangerous, but she has plenty of worldly wisdom. I don't think Clement as yet likely to win his way to his grandfather's heart. With a great deal of good about him, he is too careless and self-sufficient ; but I have some hope of Ella under Mildred's influence. So still patience, my dear Vivian—patience with me if you can, and patience with your sister-in-law, even if you cannot. I assure you she deserves it much more than you would think. A peep into the home at the Lodge would convince you of this ; and you must remember that she has been trained up in a school which gives her a quick eye for defects and a slow one for virtues.

'There are two theories of education—one which checks faults, the other which encourages virtues. I lean to the latter ; but then I am a man, and don't pretend to know much about the education of any of womankind, except my little Rachel.

'All my hopes rest upon Mildred. When I speak of her I am raising up the whole question, Why may you not tell her where you are? The answer is soon given—she knows it. Don't quarrel with me for acting upon my own responsibility. Your last letter made me unhappy. I felt that she could comfort you much better than I could, and, moreover, I was certain that you would not bear the concealment much longer. Miss Campbell and I took counsel together, and yesterday evening I told her.

'Perhaps I ought to say, too, that I found myself getting into a difficulty. Mildred had been complaining of your only writing short notes through me. As a proof that I am not given to plots and deceptions, it never struck me till the other day that we could not go on very long keeping up this kind of mock correspondence.

'Of course she was considerably startled, and for a few moments I was rather frightened at the effect the news had upon her; but she soon recovered herself. I think too, that, at first, she was much annoyed at not having been told before. But she is always most good and reasonable, and I made her see how impossible it was for you to meet, and, therefore, that it was much better she should know nothing about it. She feels with me that we must not hurry matters; but she will write and give you her own ideas. The fact of your being in England is an immense relief to her in one way—it makes it possible to see you; but, as is natural enough, she is full of anxieties. The necessity of keeping up before the General will be very trying to her; but Ella may be a great help by diverting her attention.

'I am inclined to be vexed that we did not tell her before, now I see how well she bears it; but I was afraid of the surprise for her, and certainly we have spared her a good deal in that way.

'This, I trust, will be one great load off your mind. For the rest I would say—remember that you came unsummoned, and have, therefore, no right to complain that we are not ready for you. By your own acknowledgment you have still, humanly speaking, some months before you. Give us time, and if at last we can do nothing for you, you can but come forward yourself, and, whatever may be the result, at least you will not have to say that you have again marred your own fortunes by impatience.

'John Vivian is going on much as usual. He looks askance at me, knowing I am your friend and have an interest in Ronald; so we seldom exchange more than a few words. It makes me often unhappy; but I feel that a day must, in all probability, come when he will be forced to hear me. Ronald is at home still. Miss Campbell and I had planned getting him into the merchant service, but it made the father so outrageous that we did not dare press the point. All I can do now is to urge him to educate himself as well as he can, in preparation for whatever may open. He has taken my suggestion, and works at Latin and mathematics as heartily, though perhaps not as willingly, as he shoots, fishes, climbs the hills, or manages a boat in a storm. A most noble fellow he is! but there is a cloud over him, and sometimes I am afraid of its effect. I can't help feeling sorry that Bertha ever told him his father's history. He feels now, I can see, that he is the born enemy of all your family, and shrinks from receiving kindness. That is part of his mother's sensitive nature, which he inherits strongly. He is scarcely at all with Clement now. When he once knew that we disapproved of the intimacy, he was the first to break it off. I suspect he has suffered a good deal in consequence. Miss Campbell, who manages to know more of him than any one else, tells me that he often hints at a state of affairs with his father which must be terrific. John Vivian is a madman when aroused.

'As regards Clement (I believe I am a moral coward, for I have kept the most difficult subject to the last), I confess I am not thoroughly comfortable. Encombe is not the right place for him, but where else to send him is a problem I can't quite solve. I don't at all like the notion of a merchant's office; his fastidious pride would revolt from it, and I suspect it would render him very bitter. The University would do well, if we could make him work, and turn him into a barrister; but I don't see, at present, any inclination for exertion of that kind. He makes me at times very anxious. I hoped, when withdrawn from the temptation of Ronald's companionship, that he would make himself happy at home; but this is not the case. In some way or other, there has sprung up a kind of rivalry with Ronald, whose energy and independence, and even recklessness, are just now the objects of Clement's envy and imitation. He hears them exaggerated and admired by the villagers and fishermen, and so he must needs endeavour to copy them; not seeing that his advantages are of a totally different character. I keep as strict a watch over him as possible, but I can't neglect my parish, and I must leave him some degree of freedom, or I should drive him into deceit. In a certain way he gives me his confidence, but it is principally confined to generalities, and I see vanity creeping out even in his fits of good intention. Then his disobediences, which are the chief topics of complaint on my side, are but small; and to be always harping upon what seems to him trifling faults frets his temper, and sometimes, I fancy, makes him worse, instead of better. I should care less, but that I feel there may be some hidden mischief at work. John Vivian and Goff are continually putting themselves in his way, and tempting him to be with them. I have, of course, strictly forbidden the intercourse; but the law I have laid down is perpetually broken upon slight pretences, and, in some instances, the fault can scarcely be said to lie with Clement. They haunt and persecute him till it would require a firmness much beyond what we can expect in him to resist; and then, as I said before, comes the spirit of rivalry and envy of Ronald to aid the temptation,—and so he falls.

'This must not continue, or it will be his ruin, and the destruction of all our hopes. The General already believes that Clement has a taste for low company, because he has seen him talking to Captain Vivian and Goff, and heard him use slang expressions. Nothing can be more false than such an impression. Place Clement in his right position at Cleve, and give him companions of his own age, who would raise his tone, instead of lowering it, and his natural cultivation of mind and honourable feeling would, at least, prevent him from sinking, till he had attained that higher principle which alone will give him stability.

'Certainly, the analogy of life teaches one more and more the infinite wisdom of God's providence in giving us our position as Christians, and bidding us keep it, instead of leaving us in our natural state of degradation, and then telling us to work, even with His aid, to raise ourselves. Clement's mind is just one of those which can retain, but cannot reach forward; and the uncertainty of his position is his stumbling-block. An additional reason, my dear Vivian, for hastening the moment of decision. Trust me, it shall not be delayed a moment longer than is absolutely necessary. I have dark suspicions sometimes of John Vivian's falsity; but the more dark the less to be brought forward without substantial proof.

'I have talked to your friend the sexton lately, and led him to repeat to me again all which passed on that eventful day of your cousin's visit to the Hall. He dwelt more than ever upon the strangeness of Goff's manner, and his certainty that some villany was pending. Could it have been forgery? I believe either, or both of them, capable of any amount of iniquity. John Vivian left England immediately afterwards. He has only returned to Encombe within the last five years, and that not till Goff had pioneered the way for him. I could never understand what became of them both in the interim.

'I have pondered much, lately, upon the consequences of opening the inquiry with the General. A year ago I should have hesitated less, but he has broken very much latterly, and I tremble to think what excitement would do. Then there must be a trial,—public exposure,—all the old griefs brought up. No one can say how I dread it.

'If you can think of anything which will remove Clement from Encombe, please let me know. A private tutor at a distance might be the right thing, but then—the money! You must not let your pride stand in the way of your boy's good. I should not myself at all mind sounding the General on the subject.

'Good-bye, my dear Vivian! from my heart I feel for you. You must require this assurance when I write so calmly upon questions in which all the happiness of your life is at stake ; still more when I take so little notice of the burden of your letter. But I have said before all that can be said, at least by me, on that point. Repentance, as you say, cannot place a man in this world in the position in which he would have been, if he had never erred ; but it may deepen his love, and quicken his gratitude ; and I don't think that feeling can ever be sound which would make us so mourn over the past, as to render us insensible to the blessings of the present and the hopes of the future.

'This, I think, is the tendency of your mind. May there not also be something of repining in the spirit which, instead of being thankful for peace, is inclined to despair because it cannot attain to joy ? I am lecturing myself at the same time that I seem to be warning you. He is indeed happy, who has not some sin upon his conscience, which, though it may not have brought disgrace upon him in the sight of men, has lowered him in his own eyes, and still haunts his memory,—as the one black spot which, in moments of weak faith, it would seem could never be effaced.

'God give us strength to bear the sight of our own hearts, and still to trust in His mercy.

'You shall hear from me again soon.

'Always most affectionately yours,

'ROBERT LESTER.'

CHAPTER XXV.

MR LESTER was at the Hall the day after the preceding letter had been sent. The day was bright, for snow had fallen in the night, and Clement, taking advantage of an exhilarating frost, had called to take Ella for a long walk. Mr Lester, therefore, found Mildred alone, busy as usual, and very cheerful ; yet with the worn lines of thought particularly marked. She received him nervously, as if expecting he must bring fresh tidings to startle her, but she tried to be calm, and her first remark was a slight reproach that he had not seen her father the previous day. 'He heard you were here the evening before,' she said, 'and he declares that you will never come to him, but that all your visits are to me.'

'I hoped General Vivian was getting better,' was Mr Lester's reply; 'they told me he was down-stairs again, and had been out in the garden.'

'He is better; yes, I think so,' said Mildred, with an air of consideration, 'but he is more feeble than he was, and his spirits are not good.'

'Is it illness, only, do you think?'

'I don't know; it is very difficult to tell anything about him. O Mr Lester! why are some natures so unapproachable?'

'To teach others patience and submission, we may suppose. But, Mildred, this state of things can't go on much longer.'

'No,' exclaimed Mildred, 'for every one's sake. I have written as you said I might. I have told Edward he must be patient, but my heart grows sick with fear. The intense, at times agonising, longing to see him, seems even worse now he is so near. And my father, too, makes me unhappy. He will never confess it, but his spirit is broken. I am sure he feels very desolate.'

'His own act, an act which one word might revoke.'

'Yes, if he could think it right to revoke it; but the weaker his physical powers, the stronger becomes his will. Yet I try not to despair.'

'Despair is for those who have said in their hearts "There is no God,"' replied Mr Lester.

'Thank you; I remind myself of that very often; and I feel that things are better now, and have more hope for the future, than at one time I could have expected. I am thankful to have Ella here.'

'Does the General take much notice of her?'

'A good deal, in a curious way; never by praise, but as though he were always weighing what she said or did.'

'That must be anxious work with such a person as Ella.'

'Yes, and she is so incautious, so entirely wanting in self-restraint. There must have been something sadly wanting in her education.'

'Not something, but many things. Chiefly, though, the spirit of love. But I trust to you to do wonders for her.'

'Please not to do that,' said Mildred, eagerly. 'I have seen so little of girls of her age, I don't feel as if I at all knew what to do with her.'

O

'You have educated yourself, which is the chief and best guide in our education of others.'

'God has educated me,' said Mildred, reverently. 'Many times when I have been inclined to murmur at the trials of my life, I have subdued and comforted myself by the thought. But what I feel about Ella is, that she has not an eye to see the meaning of her troubles. Self-indulgence blinds her. O Mr Lester! there are times when she is so sadly like my poor brother.'

'You must not call him poor now. He at least has learned the meaning of his trials.'

'They have come to him in the form of punishment,' said Mildred. 'I would strive to save Ella from that. Punishment and discipline are very different.'

'I trust that Vivian's future life may be only discipline,' replied Mr Lester. 'I shall have great hope if we can once open the way with the General. Does he never allude to the past?'

'Never, except in that stern fashion of self-congratulation which is so terrible to me.'

'He wraps his heart in his principle of justice, as a man does his body in a waterproof cloak,' said Mr Lester, 'and it shuts out all other claims, and makes him feel so warm and comfortable, that he does not know they exist.'

'Yet it is dreadfully oppressive to him,' said Mildred. 'He feels he has had such a disappointed life.'

'Perhaps, because he has been trying to fit the world to himself, instead of fitting himself to the world. But a man with only one moral principle of action must be disappointed. It absorbs all others into itself, and becomes darkness. Whereas the love of God, the only perfect motive, is formed of the many rainbow hues of heavenly perfection, melting into one, and producing light.'

Mildred smiled, rather sadly. 'We must not hope to make him understand that,' she said.

'No. I have learned at last to think that, after a certain period of life, true, and I hope not wrong, worldly wisdom, consists less in trying perpetually to alter the persons we have to deal with, than in taking their characters as they are, and framing our own actions accordingly. When the outline of the character has once become rigid, nothing but the special interposition of God's grace can soften it. But we will hope for that, Mildred, and pray for it.'

'That is my father's footstep,' said Mildred, listening. She turned very pale.

'He walks firmly,' observed Mr Lester.

The door opened, and General Vivian entered the apartment.

It was strange the power which his presence exercised. Mildred's cheek was still colourless, but in one instant she was composed and seemingly indifferent in manner ; and Mr Lester, too, turned to address the stern old man in the quiet tone of affectionate respect, which seemed to have no thought except for the usual civilities of life.

'You are a stranger, Mr Lester,' and General Vivian held out his hand with an air of stately cordiality.

'Not willingly, sir. I have had more to do than usual in the parish. There is a good deal of sickness about. I heard better reports of you, though, and I hope they are true ; you are looking tolerably well.'

'As well as an old man of seventy-five can expect to look. Mildred, Hardman says that the poachers were about in the woods again last night.'

General Vivian sat down, and clenched his stick with both hands in thoughtful deliberation. 'I wish, Mr Lester, you could preach a better spirit into your people.'

'I wish I could, sir, most heartily. But Hardman doesn't suspect any in particular, does he ?'

'He tells me the leaders are from Cleve. It seems that Encombe and Cleve divide the honours of villany between them. Encombe patronises smuggling, and Cleve poaching.'

'An evil choice,' observed Mr Lester.

'Evil, indeed ; but at any rate we can claim pre-eminence it, example. The Cleve poachers are not likely to have so distinguished a leader as the Encombe smugglers. We may expect the name of Captain Vivian to head the list of indictments at the next sessions.'

'He has not been taken? There is nothing found against him, is there ?' inquired Mr Lester, hastily, and Mildred also raised her pale face to her father's, with a look of quick interest.

'If he has not been taken, the more shame to the coastguard,' exclaimed the General. 'It is the talk of the neighbourhood that the trader lying off the shore belongs to John Vivian, and is a smuggler, and yet they are for ever laying hands upon some poor wretch, whose only fault is that he is too weak to stand out against those whom he knows he ought to respect. But it will come at last. The name will figure bravely in the annals of the county gaol. Ay, and I would be the first to put it there.'

'Are they on the look-out for him, then?' inquired Mildred.

'Why, child!' he turned to her suddenly, with a scrutinising gaze : 'You are ill this morning, Mildred.'

'Only a little tired, dear sir. Did you say they were on the look-out for Captain Vivian?'

'Pshaw! wretch! leave him. Mildred, my darling, you mustn't look so.' He went up to her couch and stood beside it, and his manner became as tender as before it had been severe.

'My dearest father,' and she took his hand affectionately, 'there is nothing really the matter.'

'You talk too much ;' he looked at Mr Lester distrustfully.

'Mr Lester has only been here a few minutes,' said Mildred, smiling.

'One minute is quite enough for mischief, Mildred. I give Mr Lester credit though, for not doing intentional harm.'

'Not any harm at all, I hope,' said Mildred ; 'his visits always do me good.'

'Yet I must take him from you, my child. Mr Lester, have you a few minutes to spare for my study?'

'As many, sir, as you desire ;' and the General's impatient glance caused Mr Lester to rise at the same instant.

They passed through the hall, and went up-stairs. General Vivian's private room was on the same floor as his bedroom. Mr Lester remarked that the steps were a difficulty to him, otherwise he might have been a man of fifty-five rather than seventy-five. Some ordinary parish business, no doubt, was to be discussed, yet the General's manner, when he closed the door, and sat down in his great arm-chair, motioning to Mr Lester to place himself opposite, betokened something more than ordinary. For a few seconds he said nothing, but opening the drawer of his library table, searched in it for some paper which it seemed he wanted. It was soon found. General Vivian's papers were in such order that he used often to boast that he could place his hand upon any one in the dark. His old military precision, indeed, was to be seen in all his arrangements, and joined with it there might possibly have been discovered traces of the carefulness which some had even ventured to term, though most unjustly, penuriousness. The furniture of this, his private room, was homely. A dark, common carpet, in parts completely faded. covered the floor ; a large,

square library table, old-fashioned, with innumerable drawers
and long projecting legs, filled the centre of the apartment;
around it were shelves, not filled merely with books, but with
small boxes, packets of parchments, and papers; whilst a few
good prints hung on the wall, and near the mantelpiece, close to
the chair which the General usually occupied, was a small, graceful miniature of a very lovely woman.

Mr Lester took up a book to while away the spare minutes.
The General glanced at him keenly. 'In a hurry, I am afraid,
Mr Lester? Pardon me, I won't keep you long.'

'No hurry, sir, for myself; only for others.'

'Still I may ask for a few minutes. An old man's claims will
not be many or long.'

'Yours will be first always with me, sir, if possible. Pray don't
hurry yourself.'

'I could not, if I would, Mr Lester; the time for haste is past.'
He placed a packet of papers before him, and slowly drew the
arm-chair nearer to the table. Mr Lester saw that the exertion
was too much for him, and yet he could not help him. The offer
would have been considered an insult.

'I have been looking over my papers, Mr Lester; a work for
all to do at stated times, especially a man of my age.'

'Certainly, sir. I wish your example were more generally
followed. It would save a great deal of trouble.'

'And worse than trouble; evil of all kinds. If my father and
my grandfather—but never mind that,—you are in a hurry—only
I will take the opportunity of saying one thing. You are likely
to be on the spot when I die, and Mildred will look to you. Poor
child! she has no one else.' A pause, and a clearing of the
throat, but the voice which continued was unchanged. 'I should
be sorry to have any confusion. I have tried to prevent it. All
that will be necessary for—whoever comes after me, will find all
papers relating to the estate in the escritoire,' and he pointed to
an ebony cabinet which stood by the side of the fire-place; 'all
personal papers in the desk above it; all parish and public papers
in the large drawers of this table. I did not mean to take up
your time with these details, only lest I should forget, I mention
them. Now to business. Time goes on, Mr Lester; what do you
intend to do with Clement?'

Mr Lester might have been startled by the abruptness of the
question, but he did not show it. 'Mrs Campbell wishes him to
go to College, sir.'

'And she has the means of providing for him there. That settles the point. I trust the boy will do well.'

'I trust so too,' replied Mr Lester, 'but Mrs Campbell has not the means of fully providing for him ; and that is our difficulty.'

'Then what do you intend to do with him ? I understood from what you said that it was settled.'

'Settled, if wishes could settle anything,' replied Mr Lester. 'But we thought that you would not be angry, sir, if we were to ask you for assistance ; and I meant, when the fitting time arrived, to make application to you.'

The General bit his lip. 'Mrs Campbell has taken every step hitherto without consulting me, and I don't see why she should look for help now. But I am not going to dispute the matter, Mr Lester ; the boy shall go to College. It shall never be said that I neglected my grandson. He shall have an allowance from me. His debts I leave to others.'

'We may hope, sir, that they may not be incurred.'

No reply for some seconds. The General looked carefully over the paper of memoranda which he held in his hand. Then he continued :—'He will have a hundred and fifty pounds a year paid to him by me, from the time he enters College till he is one-and-twenty. If I die before, he will receive it—out of the estate.' His keen eye glanced at Mr Lester ; apparently what he read there was not perfectly satisfactory. 'I wish to put him in the way of providing for himself, Mr Lester ; I wish to give him a chance. Am I not right ?'

'He deserves more than a chance, sir,' was the bold reply.

The General's eyes flashed. 'His deserts must be left to my judgment. It is my intention, besides, to leave in your hands, as trustee, the sum of five thousand pounds, to be applied by you as shall seem most likely to further his prospects.'

Mr Lester sat immovable ; it might almost have seemed that he had not heard.

'I look to you as Clement's guardian,' continued the General. 'I believe that you have done, and will do, all that can be done to serve him. His ruin will never be attributed by me to you.'

'I suppose I ought to thank you, General Vivian,' replied Mr Lester, somewhat proudly. 'You have shown a confidence in me which I hope I sufficiently value. I should be glad to be able to carry out your wishes ; but I can scarcely think they will long continue to be yours.'

'And why not ?'

'Because I trust,—forgive me for the liberty I am taking,—that consideration may show you sufficient cause to alter them,' replied Mr Lester.

The General bent forward in his chair and frowned. 'Mr Lester, I asked assistance in furthering my views ; not advice as to how they should be formed.'

'I am aware of it, sir. I have no right to intrude advice; but when I am called upon to be a party in any act, I am bound to consider whether it be equitable.'

'Equitable ! Mr Lester'—and the General's foot moved up and down rapidly—'You are a clergyman, and the friend of years. You had not dared else to insinuate such a reproof.'

'I would not insinuate, sir. I hate insinuations. I would say openly,—your grandson deserves more at your hands.' The words were free, yet Mr Lester's manner betokened deep respect ; and the self-controlled spirit of General Vivian received the check which was intended.

'We won't discuss that point. I ask again, are you willing to accept the office of trustee for Clement, and for his sisters ? I propose to leave them that which will secure for each a hundred a year.'

Mr Lester was silent.

'Then I will turn to some other friend. Good morning, Mr Lester ; I regret that I have intruded upon your time?' and the General rose, though with difficulty, and stood with his tall figure drawn up haughtily, though, at the same moment, he supported himself by resting one hand upon the table.

Mr Lester rose also, but not proudly. His eyes were bent upon the ground in deep thought. When he spoke, his words came with some degree of hesitation :—'General Vivian,' he said, 'you have always been a most kind friend to me,—more than a friend. In hours of sorrow I have looked to you as to an elder brother, and I could, yes, from my heart, I could, obey you reverently ; but I have another office, which compels me to speak freely; in consideration of it I am sure you will hear me. May I entreat you not to decide on this matter hastily? It involves many interests, and great principles of right and justice.'

'It does ; right and justice to my people; my tenants, and the poor.'

'Can an unjust act at the beginning work justice in the end?' inquired Mr Lester.

The General's eye sparkled with indignation. 'Who ventures to say that it is unjust?' he exclaimed ; his tone deepening with the effort at self-restraint. 'My property is my own ; I may do with it as I will.'

'We are stewards,' replied Mr Lester ; 'not owners.'

'Let it be so ; as steward, I do that which is for the good of those entrusted to me.'

'When we devise means and instruments of our own, and put aside those which God has marked out for us, we cannot be sure that we are working for good,' was the reply.

'I don't understand your philosophy, Mr Lester ; neither do I wish to hear more of it. Justice, not philosophy, is my object.'

'Justice without mercy will cease to be justice,' replied Mr Lester ; 'for it is not the justice of God.'

'Again I say, sir, I don't understand you. I seek the good of my people. I will not undo the work of a life at its last moment.'

'I should be the last person to wish you to do so,' replied Mr Lester ; 'but I fear we err when we take the ordering of the future into our own hands. You are afraid to trust your grandson,—you think it right to choose another heir? Who is to guarantee that he shall be irreproachable? Or, if he should be, who can answer for his children?'

The General took out his watch. 'Excuse me, Mr Lester, I have gone over the ground often : my resolution is unalterable. Time presses. I have an engagement at three o'clock. If you decline accepting the office I propose, I will make other arrangements.'

Again Mr Lester deliberated. 'I hope,' he said, at length, 'to send a written answer ; if not to-morrow, yet in the course of a few days. I trust that may satisfy you.'

The General bent his head coldly. Mr Lester continued : 'And I will ask now to be allowed a few more words upon another point. Clement would be safer removed from Encombe.'

'Unquestionably :' there was an accent of scorn in the word.

'If he is to go to the University he should first have a private tutor.'

'I should suppose so.'

'Then may we look to you for assistance in that case, as well as for supporting him at College?'

The General's countenance changed. He slowly walked up to the ebony cabinet, removed the desk which stood upon it, and placed it upon the table. 'Mr Lester, pray sit down for a few moments longer; I won't detain you more.' He unlocked the desk. 'My private accounts,' he murmured, in a tone of apology.

'I am sorrow to give you so much trouble, sir. I did not in the least mean to press the question as to details—merely to know generally whether we might look to you for help.'

'A certain sum has been set aside. I don't know how much of it remains.' The General took out several packets of paper and laid them on the table.

'I am giving you a great deal of trouble, sir, and there is really no hurry.'

'No time like the present.' The desk was drawn nearer the edge of the table, and the General sat down.

Some one knocked at the door; he turned round quickly. accidentally pushed the desk, and it fell: the papers were scattered on the ground.

Mr Lester stooped to pick them up. 'Come in,' said the General, and a servant entered.

'Farmer Brown wishes to speak to you, sir.

'Let him wait.'

'I told him you were engaged, sir, and he has waited a quarter of an hour. He says he must go now.'

General Vivian never sent business away; it was one of his most rigid principles.

'Well! show him into the ante-room. Mr Lester, I will return immediately. I am afraid you have a tiresome task.'

'The papers are all disarranged, sir. Can't I help you in replacing them?'

'No, thank you, no;' and the General's manner was almost nervous. 'Pray, only lay them on the table; nothing more.' He stopped as he was leaving the room, and looked back, apparently about to give some other direction; but he altered his mind, and left the room, saying that he should return directly.

Mr Lester gathered up the papers. They were for the most part letters, all carefully placed together in separate packets and endorsed. Mr Lester's eye unintentionally caught the superscription of two. One was Edith Vivian, with the date of her birth and death. The other only bore the initials E. B. V., and consisted apparently not of letters only, but of loose papers and bills. It was larger than any of the rest, and arranged with less attention to order. It seemed as if it had been put together in some moment of confusion, and fastened hastily, for the string round it was loose, and when Mr Lester put it down a few of the papers slipped out. He had only just gathered them together, and taken up the string to secure it more firmly, when the General returned. Mr Lester laid the letters down again. The General cast a hasty glance upon the table. ' Never mind, Mr Lester, that will do, thank you,' and he laid his hand nervously upon the packet. ' Old letters, as you see. It mayn't be worth while to keep them, but one never knows of what use such things may be.' There was an attempt at unconcern in his tone and manner, but it did not deceive Mr Lester ; and his hand trembled so much that he was unable to collect the papers, and, instead 'of placing them in order, scattered them again. He tried to stoop. Mr Lester picked them up for him, and as he restored them, the General seized and looked at them carefully.

' That will do, Mr Lester, thank you. There are no more ; only your handkerchief which you have just dropped.'

Mr Lester took up his handkerchief, and with it, unknown to himself, a paper which was lying under it. Both were put into his pocket.

The General allowed the rest of the papers to remain on the table. His manner was confused. ' I don't know what we were talking of,' he began. ' Oh yes ! I remember, my private accounts.' He opened a book which had been taken from the desk. ' I look upon Clement, Mr Lester, as the son,'—he hesitated :—' the inheritance of the child of a younger son is all he has any right—absurd ! there is no right—it is all that, on any principle, could be demanded of me. Let me see,' and he unclasped the book. ' A private tutor, you say. He will not have that under two hundred a year.

' No, sir, certainly not. Travelling, dress, pocket-money, we may reckon as fifty more.'

' And well if he keep within it ! ' The General sat down, and began to calculate with a pencil and paper. ' Seventy pounds per annum, Mr Lester, is the sum I can afford.'

Mr Lester tried not to look disappointed.

' You expected more ? '

' I had hoped that half the expense of the tutor might have been taken by you, sir. The additional thirty pounds is a large item '—— He did not seem to know how to finish the sentence.

'It is a large item in the affairs of any person who wishes to be exact. My income is appropriated ; I can't alter it.'

The tone admitted of no further reply. Mr Lester only said, ' I must thank you, sir, in Clement's name.'

' No thanks are required. I desire to do justice—justice'— the word was repeated emphatically,—' by every one.'

Silence followed. The General occupied himself in restoring the papers to their place in the desk. Mr Lester looked round for his hat, yet in a way which showed that he was unwilling to go. The General closed the desk and took out his watch.

' May I put the desk back for you, sir ? ' asked Mr Lester.

' Thank you, no.' General Vivian carried it himself, and then returned to the fire-place.

' If I have said anything to offend you, sir,' said Mr Lester, ' I trust you will forgive me ; it was very far from my intention.'

' There is no offence, Mr Lester. You act upon a principle of duty ; I try to do the same myself.'

' And I should have hoped, therefore, sir, we might have been likely to agree.'

' I have not found that a natural consequence in life. Few persons have agreed with me in my notions of duty.' The shadow of a smile crossed Mr Lester's face, but General Vivian, without perceiving it, went on, rather in an exculpatory tone. ' I find the moral code of many men lax, Mr Lester. They, on the contrary, think mine strict. I have no wish to quarrel with them ; but when a principle has been adopted from conviction of its truth, I can never think it right to sacrifice it to expediency.'

' To expediency ! No, sir, never ! ' exclaimed Mr Lester.

' The reasons which I have heard brought forward in opposition to my own views have always been those of expediency,' continued the General.

' Expediency is a word bearing many interpretations,' observed Mr Lester.

' Only one in my ideas. It is the sacrifice of duty to individual feelings or individual interests.'

' It would be my own definition,' continued Mr Lester ; ' but duty must always be compounded of two virtues balancing each other. It can scarcely be considered expediency to endeavour to keep the balance equal.'

' You are metaphysical, Mr Lester. My idea of duty is of a law. I don't understand the principle of two laws.'

' Yet both the moral and the natural world are governed by

opposing laws,' said Mr Lester. 'Love and fear, justice and
mercy, cause the beings of the spiritual creation to move har-
moniously round the one Centre of their worship, as the two
counteracting forces cause the planets to move round the sun.'
He was almost sorrow when he had said it, the General looked
so impatient. They parted rather coldly, but when Mr Lester
was gone, General Vivian leaned back in his chair, and thought.

CHAPTER XXVI.

ENCOMBE GRANGE was a large, lonely, white house, standing beyond the village, and fronting the open common
terminated by the cliffs. It was a very dreary-looking place.
Originally it might have been picturesque, for the building was
low and irregular, with a singular high turret at one corner, which
had been added as a kind of observatory by one of its former
possessors; but now all beauty was lost in the appearance of decay.
Nearly all the trees which once surrounded it had been cut down.
Two or three indeed remained near the turret, but these shut out
the view over the sea which at one time had been an attraction,
whilst others more exposed to the south-west winds were not only
stunted in their growth, but had that feeble, oppressed look which
always belongs to trees bent in one direction. There was some
attempt at a flower-garden and plantation near the house, but all
was in a neglected state ; the branches of the shrubs spreading at
their will, and covering the narrow gravel walks, which were dark
and green with grass and weeds ; the flower-beds completely over-
run, and poultry, dogs, cats, and occasionally a horse or a cow,
straying at their pleasure over the unmown lawn. Within, the
scene was equally desolate. A great portion of the house was shut
up, and in the rooms which were used the walls were hidden by
the scraps of papers of different generations; the paint was worn
from the wainscoting ; and near the kitchen and the servants'
apartments even the floors were unsafe. One parlour there was
comparatively comfortable, with a carpet, and a horsehair sofa,
and a great arm-chair, and some convenient corner cupboards ;
and this was Captain Vivian's dwelling-room, and here he lived
contentedly; for as long as he could sit by a blazing fire if he was

cold, and eat when he was hungry, and rest when he was weary, and form his plans of adventure or speculation without interruption, he cared nothing for the elegancies of life, and little for what many would have considered ordinary comfort. He was a man sunk below anything approaching to refinement of taste ; and amongst the many secondary supports which keep us from utter ruin in this world, perhaps none are more powerful, or more deeply to be lamented when lost, than taste. Yet it was not because he cared for money in itself, that he strove to gain it by evil means, and lived without the advantages which he had the means of obtaining. He had run through a large fortune, and still was carelessly extravagant as regarded personal self-indulgence ; but a consciousness of degradation from guilt had led him to seek forgetfulness in low company and low habits, till the claims of his position as a gentleman by birth, and in some degree by education, had been totally put aside.

It would be long, and perhaps tedious, to tell how it was that he reached this point. There was the traditional tone of his branch of the family to begin with ; and reputation has more to do with the first formation of character than we may be inclined at the first glance to imagine. Then there was evil example, bringing opportunity for evil, and followed by the loss of personal self-respect ; and when this is gone, moral descent is very rapid. Yet there had been occasions when the past might have been redeemed. Even the most hardened villain can probably look back to some period of his life when, like the angel arresting the steps of the prophet, repentance has met him in the way; and perhaps had the secrets of Captain Vivian's heart been made known, it would have been found that, even with him, there was one period from the recollection of which he turned in hasty anguish, with the feeling that the example of his wife had opened to him the gates of heaven, but that he had wilfully refused to enter in.

. Possibly the influence of a different mind might have had more power over him. Mrs Vivian was extremely gentle, implicitly obedient, except where religious duty was concerned; but she had been made religious by the means of sorrow,—disappointment in him ; and this had given a mournful tone to her character, and at times irritated him. It was the excuse which he made to himself, when at the time of her death remorse had for a few weeks been busy with him. Now he made no excuses; he showed his feelings about her only by refusing to hear her name mentioned. It was the one especially painful barrier, amongst the many which existed, between him and Ronald.

For Ronald lived upon his mother's memory; not to the knowledge of the world, scarcely even to that of Mr Lester and Bertha Campbell; the rare occasions when he did give a momentary vent to his feelings were as the sudden rush of the tempest, which passes, and all is calm as before. But in a remote part of the dreary old house there was a small chamber which he had fitted up with the few articles belonging to his mother that had escaped the wreck caused by his father's extravagance; and there, with her picture before him, her few books arranged in a small Indian cabinet, her work-box, and writing-case, and a few special ornaments placed on the little table which had stood beside her dying bed, Ronald had formed for himself a sanctuary which her spirit seemed still to inhabit, and from which a softening, chastening influence had been permitted to reach him, even in his most reckless moments.

It might have been sentimentalism with many ; but Ronald, in his loneliness, and the heaviness of his self-reproach, had no room for sentimentality, even if the feeling had not been totally foreign to his nature. He never showed his little room to any one ; he never even spoke of it ; he scarcely ever realised to himself why he reverenced it. The feeling had grown up unconsciously from the time when on their first arrival at the Grange, and when the grief for her loss was still fresh, the few things which belonged to her had been placed in it. Captain Vivian avoided it ; the servants did not trouble themselves to enter it ; and Ronald himself never thought of inhabiting it. Only at times when his heart was most oppressed, he would pause before the door, and it would seem as if he still could hear her voice within ; and occasionally,—very rarely, for Ronald's fits of devotion had, till lately, been as uncertain and varying as the winds,—he would venture in gently, reverently, as if intruding upon the presence of the dead, and kneeling down confess, in the simple words which she herself had taught him, the guilt which burdened his conscience, and the fears which lay heavy upon his heart.

These were his calmest and best moments. In his hours of desperate remorse—and they were far more frequent—he would no more have intruded himself into that quiet chamber than he would have thrust himself unbidden and unprepared as a partaker in the holiest rites of the Church. But even then, the remembrance

was not without its influence. It was as if there was still a resting-place within his reach—a haven which he might hope to
attain when the storm was past; and when Ronald spoke of, or
thought of home, in the sense which renders it so dear to all,
his imagination recurred not to the empty chambers of the
almost deserted house, nor to the parlour where his father was
wearing away life in coarse self-indulgence,—not even to the
little room in the turret, with its rude uncurtained bed and rough
furniture, where he had piled in heaps the heterogeneous articles
which served him for use or for amusement,—but to the small
closet—it could scarcely be called more—in which his mother's
spirit seemed yet lingering.

Yes, that thought had saved him in many an hour of temptation. For Ronald's life had been far less guilty than in his
despairing self-accusation he represented it.

He had seen evil often, in its worst and most debasing forms,
and to a certain extent he had himself mingled with it; but
Captain Vivian, hardened though he might be, would not force
his son to become what he himself was; and Ronald had many
times escaped the actual contamination of wickedness, which
yet had been so present with him that he could not realise to
himself that he had been saved from it. To separate himself
from his father seemed impossible; and when Captain Vivian
sank, Ronald felt that he himself had sunk likewise. Perhaps
but for the recollection of his mother he would have done so.

His life had in a degree been happier during the last few
weeks. Before that time, his refusal to tempt Clement to disobedience had caused bursts of passion which were often terrific; but now he was left more to himself and his own pursuits.
A change had taken place, apparently, in Captain Vivian's
schemes. He confided them more to Goff; perhaps he felt that
he had to deal with a will as unbending as his own, and therefore did not endeavour to alter it; perhaps—there is some
redeeming point even in the very worst—the one humanising
feeling yet left, his affection for his boy, made him shrink from
implicating him in the guilty plans which yet he would not
relinquish. Be that as it may, since the abandonment of the
idea of the merchant service, Ronald had been suffered to carry
out his own wishes for the employment of his time for the most
part undisturbed. He was studying now not for pleasure; it
was a great effort to him, and the escape from his books into the
free air, with a gun or a fishing-rod in his hand, was eager

delight. But the energetic spirit, once turned in the direction of self-discipline, could not be checked. Bertha had given him the impulse of good, Mr Lester had suggested a few rules for its direction, and with the same intensity of purpose with which, if commanded, he would have endeavoured to expiate his faults by bodily penances, did he now attempt to follow up that far more difficult penance, the subjugation of the mind.

He was happier,—yet not for that reason at rest. Mr Lester had said truly that there was a cloud over him. How, indeed, should it be otherwise? The farther he advanced on the right path himself, the more sensible he must necessarily become that his father was moving on the wrong one. This alone would have been enough to sadden him, but Ronald could never forget that worse might be behind ;—that fallen as his father was now, there might be darker evil hidden in the past, and that to him the task of discovering and revealing it had in a certain way been entrusted. Therefore it was that he would sit alone in his own chamber, or pursue his solitary wanderings over the wild hills and by the lonely shore,—shrinking from companionship, dreading conversation,—and though forced to live with his father, and at times to mingle with his associates, yet keeping watch over his hidden grief, whilst anxiously guarding every avenue to the temptations which might lead him back into the vices of which he had repented.

The idea which thus oppressed him had first been suggested by Bertha, but it was in no way followed up by her. After that one conversation which had made him acquainted with his father's history, the subject had never again been mentioned between them. Probably Bertha repented what in her eagerness she had done, perceiving the effect of the disclosure upon a spirit sensitive as a woman's, and impetuous as a man's. At any rate, whenever they met, which was but seldom, it was only to exchange the confessions of sorrow and penitence on the one side, and of affectionate interest on the other ; whilst Mr Lester never by word or look allowed it to be supposed that he considered Ronald in the slightest degree involved in the cause which he had so much at heart.

It was late in the same day on which Mr Lester had been with General Vivian. Ronald had been out upon the hills shooting ; Captain Vivian on the shore and at the Point, for purposes best known to himself. They had returned about the same time, and Ronald, wearied and yet excited by his day's sport, was dreading less than usual the dinner with his father; for on such occasions they had common subjects of interest without touching upon those on which they would have been likely to jar.

Captain Vivian's countenance also wore a satisfied expression, and he greeted his son without the uncomfortable reproaches which were generally his vent for any disappointment. Ronald asked no questions. The success or defeat of his father's projects brought him almost equal pain. He was only thankful to be allowed to eat his dinner in peace, and to narrate the progress of the day's sport without interruption. When dinner was over, he was preparing, as usual, to go to his own room, when Captain Vivian stopped him. ' Off! my boy ? Where to ? '

' To read or to rest,' replied Ronald; 'I've had desperately hard work.'

' Read ? Pshaw ! What are you talking of ? I thought you never troubled yourself about reading. Why can't you stay here ? '

' I can if you wish it,' was Ronald's cold reply.

' Oh ! if you 're tired, it 's another matter. Be off.'

' I am not so tired,—at least, I shouldn't be going to bed for the next three hours,' said Ronald.

' Only brooding over books. Why, Ronald, you're worth something more than that.'

' I don't know what I am worth, father,' replied Ronald; ' I have never been tried yet.'

' At the old story ? Wanting to do something ? Perchance I may put you in the way of it before long.'

' Thank you,' replied Ronald, in the same unmoved tone ; and he walked a few paces towards the door.

' A game at backgammon would be better for you than books after a day's work,' said Captain Vivian.

' I had rather read, thank you, father, unless we play without betting.'

A cloud of displeasure crossed Captain Vivian's face ; but he only said, ' Well, bring out the board. If Goff comes in, we may have a turn.'

Ronald placed the backgammon-board by his father's side, and went to fetch his books. He brought them back with his writing-desk, but he looked very little inclined for study. His father laughed at him as he threw the books upon the table, whilst a tired sigh escaped him.

P

'Why, you foolish fellow, one would think you were going to turn clergyman. What d'ye think, now, is the good of all that rubbish?'

'I suppose it may turn to good some day,' replied Ronald. 'At any rate it's better to do that than nothing.'

'Books don't make a man's fortune, trust me for that, Ronald. Why, there are secrets—and to be had for the purchase, too—which give a man, in one hour, what books wouldn't give him in a whole life.'

'And to be lost as quickly as gained,' replied Ronald; 'that's not in my way, father.'

'But it used to be. Time was when you were as daring a fellow as any in Christendom, and would have got at anything that could be had at a leap. 'That's the good of consorting with women and clergymen,—they would eat the spirit out of a lion.' Captain Vivian's colour rose, and he muttered to himself, 'But it won't last, though.' Then, speaking aloud, he added, 'I say, Ronald, it's time you should be off.'

'Where, father?'

'Anywhere; if you mean to seek your fortune for yourself.'

'It is what I wish,' was the answer.

'Ay! wish in your own way, but never in mine.'

'I wish to obey you, father, in all things in which I may,' replied Ronald, speaking very quietly, though his clenched hands showed the effort which it cost him.

'Well, then, I take you at your word. Our little vessel at the Point goes off again next week; try your hand at command. The fellows will be glad enough to have you on board.'

Ronald's flashing eye showed how much his own inclination accorded with the suggestion, yet he hesitated.

'It's an offer that I should have jumped to clutch at your age,' continued Captain Vivian. 'But boys now aren't what boys were, nor men neither.'

'Regular service is more to my taste.'—Ronald began the sentence boldly, but the change in his father's countenance made even his spirit quail.

Captain Vivian burst forth in a storm of passion. 'It was his will,' he said. 'He had waited long enough, keeping Ronald tied at home to be a burden to him; and now the time was come for action, and act he must and should.' And Ronald acquiesced in the determination; but again, and with less hesitation, insisted upon the desirableness of the merchant service.

Just then there was a loud knock at the outer door ; but the fierce words still raged, whilst Ronald, bending down, with his head averted, looked steadfastly into the fire. As the knock was repeated the second time, however, he rose, and was about to close the parlour door, when he was stopped by the entrance of Goff, and, to his consternation, Clement Vivian.

Captain Vivian's wrath subsided in a moment ; perhaps that was the reason why Ronald felt his to be rising. He advanced before his father to meet Clement, and they shook hands ; but Clement's manner was coldly nervous, and he glanced reproach-fully at Goff, as if he had been betrayed into society which he had not expected.

Goff came into the room with the manner of a person quite at his ease, and sat himself down by the fire, motioning to Clement to seat himself also. 'You didn't expect company to-night, eh, Captain ?'

'Not quite so many. But, Clement, my boy,'—and Captain Vivian put his hand across the table, and shook Clement's heartily, — 'you 're welcome anyhow. What's the business, Goff ?'

'No hurry ; it's a cold night, and the fire's comfortable ;' and he drew his chair in.

'What brings you out to-night, Clement ?' asked Ronald, in a careless tone.

Goff answered for him,—'A bold spirit, to be sure, Ronald, that's ashamed to sit over the fire like a girl.'

Ronald turned round upon him rather roughly,—'You'll be careful what you say, if you please ; let us hear your own tale, Clement.'

'Ask him how he escaped from his master,' said Goff, sneer-ingly.

'I will ask him if Mr Lester knows he is here?' replied Ronald.

Captain Vivian broke in upon the conversation,—'What sig-nifies? He's here, and he's going to stay. Here's a health to you, my lad ! and we won't ask what brings you here, only we are glad to see you.'

All this time Clement had been sitting, shyly at a little distance from the table, casting furtive glances round the room. Now, as Ronald fixed his keen eye upon him, he answered with ap-parent indifference,—'I was at the Hall with a message, and Goff and I met coming back, so we bore each other company.'

'It's not the nearest way from the Hall to the village,' said Ronald, quickly.

The colour rose in Clement's cheek, but Goff helped him. ' If it isn't quite as near it's twice as good ; and it's better going two than one on a winter's evening, and so Master Clement and I must needs trudge it together.'

'And take a resting-place on your way,' observed Captain Vivian ; 'and a very good notion too. It's the first time, but we hope it won't be the last.'

Ronald stood moodily by the fire, and there was a momentary silence. Goff took up the dice from the backgammon table, and tossed them. Captain Vivian called out the numbers and laughed as they came down right. 'Now, Clement, try your luck ; ' and Clement did the same, watching with some eagerness to see the result.

' Bravo ! you 'll do, I see. Now, once more ; ten to one you are right.'

Clement was again partly successful.

'Luck's with him,' said Goff. ' It's born with some people.'

'Just opposite to what it is with him,' said Captain Vivian, pointing to Ronald ; 'he never made more than one good hit in his life.'

' Try, Ronald,' said Clement, rather eagerly.

' Thank you, no.'

' He's afraid,' said Goff : 'he hates losing.'

' Oh ! nonsense, Ronald,' exclaimed Clement. ' There's no betting ; what does it signify ? '

' Some folks are too proud to be beaten in anything, betting or no betting,' said Goff.

' I see no fun in it,' said Ronald ; 'and if I did, I wouldn't do it now.'

' Wouldn't ! why not ? ' Captain Vivian turned to him angrily.

Ronald hesitated for a second, then he said, 'Because I wouldn't be the one to lead Clement to that which may be his ruin. There's a warning for you, Clement ; ' and he walked out of the room.

Captain Vivian's anger evaporated, so at least it might have seemed, in a laugh, whilst Goff threw up the dice again, and made Captain Vivian guess, without any reference to Clement, who sat by uneasily.

The clock struck eight and he started up. ' I ought to be at home ; they expected me back at seven.'

'And you keep your word, do you?' said Goff. 'That's more than you do with me.'

'Clement will be out of leading-strings before long, I'll venture to say,' observed Captain Vivian, lightly. 'I wish I could hope as much of my boy. He's turned quite tame, and won't even take a cruise for a few days.'

'Won't Ronald take a cruise?' inquired Clement, with some eagerness.

'Not he; though I offered to put him in command of a vessel. But the very life's gone out of him; he'll do nothing but sit at home over his books. Old ocean was but a fancy with him, after all.'

'As it is with a good many youngsters,' continued Goff. 'Well enough on a fine day, with a sea which a baby might sleep on; but come a storm, and they're nothing but pale-faced cowards. I'll bet you anything you like, though, that I bring Ronald round.'

'Volunteers, not pressed men, for my money,' was the reply.

'Ay; volunteers if they are to be had.' Goff glanced at Clement. 'I say, Master Clement, if I don't go with you, can you find your way home?'

'I should hope so. I have been over the fields often enough,' said Clement, proudly.

'And been in time for roll call,' said Captain Vivian, laughing. 'Why, Clement, what will you say for yourself?'

'The truth, if I am asked,' replied Clement.

'The truth, to be sure. Who ever heard of a Vivian not speaking the truth?'

'Only it's a bit awkward, sometimes,' muttered Goff. 'We shan't see you here again, I suppose, Master Clement, when the truth's out?'

'I don't see that. I go where I choose, and return when I please.'

'They'd think you had been at some dire mischief here,' said Captain Vivian, carelessly, as he threw the dice into the air.

'That was a curious calculation you were making with those things the other night, Captain,' said Goff. 'I'm not up to figures. What did Ronald say to it?'

'Ronald has no head for figures neither; he always hated them.'

'Very curious it was,' repeated Goff, in a musing tone.

'What was curious? A calculation? I can calculate pretty well,' said Clement, eagerly.

Goff looked at him with pretended amusement. 'Of course, you can do everything.'

'I have calculated very difficult questions,' continued Clement. 'I believe'—and he touched his forehead—'I have a mathematical head.'

'Possibly! But you mightn't be able to do this. Besides, there isn't time, and you are wanted at home.'

'Nonsense, to send him away!' observed Captain Vivian. 'Why shouldn't he stay, if he likes it?'

'I'll try the calculation for you at home, if you choose to give it me,' said Clement. He spoke eagerly, longing to show his superiority to Ronald.

'Thank you; but I can't give it you just in a minute. You will be coming by this way another time, I dare say, and then I'll show it you. But your master would be after you, if you were to take it home.'

The word master always touched Clement on a tender point. He instantly began a lengthened explanation of his true position with Mr Lester; that he was his father's friend, and was kind enough to teach him some things; but that he had no authority over him beyond the hours of study; whilst Captain Vivian and Goff listened with an incredulous air, which only irritated him the more to assert his independence. When he had ended, Goff's exclamation was, 'Deeds, not words, Master Clement. Show us you are your own master, and we'll believe you; but don't waste such a quantity of breath about it. Why, you are afraid now to go home for fear of the rod!' And he laughed heartily.

Captain Vivian took Clement's part, and found fault with Goff for ridiculing him, saying, 'that it was very natural that such a young fellow should be kept under. It wasn't every boy that could be what Ronald was at sixteen—though he had gone back sadly of late.'

This told more keenly upon Clement than all Goff's coarser ridicule, especially when it was followed by some characteristic anecdotes of Ronald's dauntless bravery, which goaded his envy, whilst they excited to the utmost his admiration. A pause came at last, and Clement summoned resolution to go, without any more last words of boasting. Captain Vivian went with him to the door. His tone was much softened, and there even appeared to be some interest in it. 'We shall see you again,' he said ; 'and if you could look in and help Ronald and me about that calculation, we should both thank you. I've no head for it ; neither has he. But don't come, if you think you will get into disgrace. Good night !' They shook hands cordially, and Clement, though shrinking from the word disgrace, walked away, saying to himself, that Captain Vivian had certainly been condemned unfairly. He had still the spirit of a gentleman in him, when he chose to exert it.

CHAPTER XXVII.

CAPTAIN VIVIAN returned to the parlour, carefully locked the door, tried another which led through some passages to a distant wing of the house, and then going up to Goff, who was bending down over the fire, with his hands spread out to warm them, exclaimed, 'He's caught !'

'Ay! thanks to me !' was Goff's rather surly reply; and without looking up, he added, abruptly, 'and high time ; the game will be up soon !'

Captain Vivian moved so as to confront him. 'Up? What d'ye mean?' His tone was hollow, though the words were uttered calmly.

'We were fools,' continued Goff, 'mad fools ! He has escaped us !'

'Edward Vivian! Ha !' And a strong hand clutched the shoulder of the rough fisherman, till it must have been actual pain. 'No need for fierceness, Captain,' continued Goff, disengaging himself. 'It was luck that might have befallen any one. When you put me upon the track, I followed it; and if I'd met him that night, we should soon enough have come to an issue. But who was to make me guess his sneaking ways? You, yourself, said that we might rest content, for that if it was he, he would be back again at Encombe before a week had passed over our heads. He's in London now : never mind how I found it out, but 'tis true.'

A long pause followed. Captain Vivian's face was pale with fear and anger.

'It may go hard with us, if the old General and he make one again,' he said, at length, in a low, deep voice.

Goff took up his words. 'Hard with us? Put them once together, and the sooner old ocean roars between us and this part of the world the better.'

'He must be kept at bay.'

'Easier said than done. It's one thing keeping a man at bay, when of his own accord he takes to the Indies; and another, when he thinks fit to show his face in England. I warn you, Captain, the time's at hand when Encombe Grange may be too hot to hold you.'

'You are in for it yourself, too,' was the sharp rejoinder.

'Not as principal; that makes all the difference.'

'You swore to the handwriting,' said Captain Vivian.

'And got five hundred pounds for my pains, and little enough for the jeopardy. But it's you, Captain, that's to be troubled for. There's none of them will have an eye to me.'

Captain Vivian leaned his head upon his hand in deep thought, whilst Goff threw himself back in the arm-chair, with the attitude of a man who feels that he has the upper hand in the affair under discussion.

'It's best always to look matters full in the face,' he continued, composedly. 'The game is one of chances. First of all, the paper may have been destroyed.'

Captain Vivian started up. 'May? A hundred to one that it is. The old General was too mad with anger to keep it. It told against his honour.'

'Then the forgery's safe.'

'If I hadn't thought so, do you think I would have set foot in Encombe again?'

'Yes,' replied Goff. 'When more than a dozen years had gone by, and Edward Vivian was in Jamaica, and at daggers drawn with his father; why shouldn't you? If there was danger, why there was safety too. You were at hand to watch, and might start at a moment's notice. You'd have lost a capital opening for trade if you had let fear come in the way of settling here. No, no; all that's been done is well enough; but things are altered now; and since we are reckoning chances, we mustn't forget there's a risk on the other side. The paper may be forthcoming.'

Captain Vivian's knees trembled, and he sat down.

'Let Edward Vivian and his father meet,' continued Goff, 'and it's an even chance that you are done for.'

'If the paper's gone, there's no legal proof,' said Captain Vivian.

'And so no mischief!' exclaimed Goff. 'Why, man, you're an idiot. Think of Edward Vivian at the Hall, lord and master, with the grudge rankling in his breast. If he can't have revenge in one way, trust him to have it in another. The story will be blazoned over the country; even your own people will take it up; there'll be a hundred eyes spying at you, and Edward Vivian himself set to ruin you, to say nothing of the General. How's the trade to go on then? and what kind of life, think you, we shall lead? Do as you will, Captain, yourself, you'll not find me sitting down quietly with a foe at my very door. Let him set one foot in the Hall, and I'm off.'

'It might be the best plan, anyhow,' said Captain Vivian, thoughtfully. His assent was evidently unacceptable to Goff, who answered with a look of cool contempt. 'And will you please to tell me, then, why you ever came here, since you're to be off at the first fright?'

'I came because it would be a good speculation, and we might make the thing answer. I didn't reckon that Edward Vivian would be back like a ghost from the grave.'

'Well! and hasn't it answered? Aren't we carrying on as pretty a business as a man might wish for; plenty of hands to help us; and the place just fitted for it? I tell you, Captain, if you cut the cable, you'll be swamped.'

'Possibly.'

'Certainly; as sure as I stand here. There's no hope but to stick by Encombe to the last.'

'With a view of Botany Bay beyond.'

'Shame on you, Captain. There isn't a fellow belonging to us who wouldn't cry craven if he heard you.'

'I am only doing what you yourself advised,' was the reply, 'looking the matter fully in the face.'

'And what's the end of that? You look your enemy in the face one minute, to knock him down the next.'

Captain Vivian started. 'I've enough on my hands already,' he said, quickly. 'I'll have no more.'

Goff's laugh was one of cold, fierce sarcasm. 'Chicken-hearted! are ye, Captain? Yet, I've known you calculate even to a penny the chance of a man's ruin. But don't be afraid. I'll keep your neck safe enough from a halter, though maybe it will be a more difficult matter to keep your hands from fetters.'

Then, as he saw Captain Vivian wince at the suggestion, he added in an undertone, 'A pistol shot would settle it quick enough between me and my enemy any day; but if you arn't up to that, you'll surely be thinking of something else.—The boy might help us, but for your marplot Ronald.'

'We must be rid of him.' Captain Vivian spoke coldly and sternly.   •

'I told you that long ago. When the Lodge folks came to Encombe, said I, it isn't a fit place for Ronald. Have you warned him, that if you fall he falls too?'

'Warned him! Ronald?' Captain Vivian's eyes flashed with indignation, and then a sudden paleness overspread his face, and rising, he paced the room in great agitation.

Goff went on without noticing him. 'It's not so much the ill will against the son as against the grandson, which will work our way. There's prejudice enough against Edward Vivian already, and if Clement is thought to be running the same course, why, the thing's done; and the Hall door shut against them both, let who will say, open. It's what you and I have said hundreds of times, and acted upon too.'

'And what's to be done now, then?' inquired Captain Vivian, moodily; 'we can't do more than we have to keep up the old prejudice.'

'It must be more than a prejudice for our purpose,' replied Goff.

'You are too deep for me, man;' but Captain Vivian sat down again as if prepared to listen.

'Why, look ye. Suppose we get Clement into the net,' and Goff laughed mockingly;—'not a difficult task with the boasting young sparrow, he's close upon it now;—suppose, I say, we make him one of us, set him on a sail to the coast yonder, and to return with our men. A hint to the preventives will put them on the look-out, and not much harm done to us—only the loss of a keg or two if we manage properly. But the skirmish will do our work with the General. He'll take a vow as deep as when he thought that his son had paid away his money before ever he got into possession of it, and never a step will Clement Vivian, or his father, set in Cleve Hall from that hour.'

Captain Vivian was thoughtful. 'The plan may do,' he said, 'to cut short Clement's prospects, but not to stop Edward Vivian's return, and the possibility of our discovery.'

'Why, the one goes with the other!' exclaimed Goff; 'or if it doesn't, still we have the game in our own hands. Trust me, and I'll bring the youngster into such a plight, that his father would buy his safety with five times the sum you took from him; and he should too, if I had to deal with him.'

'You mean the boy no harm?'

'Harm! I'll make him worth twenty-fold what he is now! I'll show him what work is ; put a little spirit into him! Why, his father might thank me, if 'twere only for making a man of him. But let there be harm ; you might just think to yourself that you're only squaring matters. If you get Clement on your side, it's clear as a pike-staff to me, that they are getting Ronald on theirs.'

The insinuation stung Captain Vivian to the quick, and he burst out in a torrent of vehement indignation. Goff allowed his anger to have free scope, every now and then adding fuel to the flame, by recalling circumstances connected with the old enmity between him and Mr Vivian.

He had his own purposes to gain in stirring up the rankling spirit of revenge. Years before, he had left Mr Vivian's service on a charge of dishonesty, which, being proved, though not · brought forward in a court of justice, had entirely destroyed his character. The feeling of enmity was the first tie between him and Captain Vivian. They had carried out their schemes together, and hitherto successfully. For some years Goff had remained with Captain Vivian as his confidential servant, or rather adviser ; afterwards, circumstances had led him again to Encombe, where he entered upon his smuggling life, and at last persuaded Captain Vivian to join him. The speculation was more profitable to him than to Captain Vivian ; it suited his daring temperament ; and putting aside any personal feeling of ill will, he would have hazarded very much rather than relinquish it. As it was, with the possibility of being discovered as an accomplice in an act of forgery, and the certainty that, if Mr Vivian were once restored to his father's favour, there would be an enemy at his door, keeping a constant spy upon his proceedings, it was no wonder that Goff's fierce nature should be roused to projects from which the more calculating spirit of Captain Vivian would have naturally turned, as involving risk that might only end in greater ruin. Yet the feeling of revenge for the wrongs of former years was excited without difficulty; and though Goff, if left to himself, would doubtless have provided, if necessary, for his own safety by shorter and more desperate means ; he was apparently contented now, when he found Captain Vivian willing to take part in the project he had proposed, and to discuss the steps by which it was to be accomplished.

On one point, however, there was no discussion. Ronald was, as soon as possible, to be removed from the scene of action ; and it was determined again to tempt him by the expedition in which he had already refused to join, and which might be so arranged as to give him occupation for some time on the opposite coast. In his absence, Clement would, as it was supposed, be led without difficulty into the snares laid for him. By careful arrangement, the means of making terms with Mr Vivian, if he should reappear at Encombe, would then be in their own power; and, at the worst, if every plan should fail, and a reconciliation with the General lead to an inquiry into the past, the possibility of escape was always within their reach.

CHAPTER XXVIII.

CLEMENT VIVIAN did not hurry on his way home, although quite conscious that he was late, and that if questions were asked, the answers required might be awkward. He delayed for that very reason ; once in a difficulty, and he seldom had moral courage sufficient to meet it face to face. He had been sent to the Hall, as he had stated, on a message to Ella, and had been met by Goff on his return, and induced, partly by ridicule, partly by the love of adventure, which the smuggler's conversation always aroused, to go considerably out of his way, through by-paths and copses, till coming suddenly upon the Grange, he was taken unawares, and lured into the house, under pretence of waiting only for a moment with Ronald, whilst Goff said a few words in private to Captain Vivian.

There was not very much to shock a conscience like Clement's in all this. He had done nothing—so he said to himself—which could lead him into mischief; and he had accustomed himself too much, of late, to slight disobediences of a similar kind to be very scrupulous on that point. And yet he was uneasy. There was no exact claim upon him to confess, for no strict law had been laid down, only general advice given ; and if there was harm in Goff's companionship, he could say, honestly, that he had not sought it. Yet something within whispered, that Mr Lester's displeasure would be greater than it had ever been before, if it was known that he had actually gone into the Grange. Hitherto the intercourse between him and Captain Vivian had been confined to occasional chance meetings, for it had been a matter of policy not to tempt him to any glaring act of disobedience. Even at the time when he had been most friendly with Ronald, they had always parted company at the shrubbery-gate. Now, the deed was done. He had entered within the charmed walls, and what had he seen ? Nothing, indeed, to tempt him to repeat his visit ; yet nothing which, to his ideas, would be a reason for not doing so.

Captain Vivian amused himself with dice : but he did not bet, or ask Clement to bet ; on the contrary, from the little that had passed, it seemed as if he rather occupied himself in questions of calculation than of profit : certainly he had upheld Clement in obedience, instead of tempting him to the contrary. A reaction began to spring up in Clement's mind ; a sense of injustice, such as before had made him cling to Ronald. Captain Vivian, he fancied, had been unfairly dealt with ; Mr Lester knew little about him ; his Aunt Bertha was prejudiced. They could not see, as he saw, that Captain Vivian, being Ronald's father, was certain to have some of Ronald's redeeming qualities. All this, and much more, passed through Clement's mind, with some show of reason. Only one thing might have suggested itself as a reason for doubting the correctness of his conclusions—he could not resolve to mention his visit at home, still less to Mr Lester. Many were the excuses he made ; that it would be causing a fuss about nothing ; exciting groundless suspicion ; that it was no fault, being only the result of accidental circumstances ; these, and other equally sophistical arguments, such as are always at hand to tempt us to follow the course we like : yet, ever as Clement repeated them to himself, his own natural honesty of heart reproached him for untruth, and caused him to linger on his way, repeating again the reasoning which the moment before he had imagined was quite conclusive.

His thoughts were engaged in this manner as he slowly wended his way over the fields, which lay between the Grange and the village, when he perceived in the twilight a figure which he had little difficulty in recognising as that of Ronald Vivian, advancing to meet him from a cross-path. He stopped, and Ronald came up with him quite out of breath.

'Well, Ronald, what's the matter now? what do you want?' was Clement's first inquiry, spoken rather impatiently, for his spirit was still rebelling against the warning which had, unasked, been given him.

'You are going home, aren't you?' replied Ronald, recovering himself. 'I suppose, if I am travelling the same road, we may as well go together?'

'To-night? What is your business? Is there anything going on?'

'Nothing that you'd care to hear about. I'm not going far. But you had the start of me, Clement; I had no notion you were off.'

'I stayed longer than I intended as it was,' replied Clement; 'but you are wonderfully anxious for my company to take the trouble to lose your breath at such a rate. Just now I thought you had made up your mind not to remain in the same room with me; you were out of it as soon as I came in.'

'I should have made mischief if I had stayed,' replied Ronald.

'Mischief? how? what?'

'I've a tongue in my head, and nine times out of ten it runs away with me; so I decamped.'

'I don't see what there was to make it run away then,' replied Clement. 'No one was going to quarrel that I saw; I am sure I wasn't.'

'I wish you had been. Clement, you'd best stand at arm's length with my father. There,—I say it, that would sooner die than have cause to say it, but I must.'

'There is never any other way of standing with him,' replied Clement. 'It's little enough that I see of him, and, as you know, this is the first time I ever set my foot within the Grange.'

'Then let it be the last time.'

'It may be, and it may not be; I don't choose to tie myself down: but I am obliged to you, Ronald, for your hospitality, at least.'

'I care nothing for your obligation, one way or the other,' exclaimed Ronald, impetuously; 'but once for all, Clement, if you wouldn't rue the day that ever you came to Encombe, you'll keep as far from the Grange as you would from'—and his voice sank—'the pit of destruction.'

The eager tone of his deep voice struck forcibly, and even awfully, upon Clement's ear, and grasping Ronald by the arm, he said, earnestly: 'Ronald, you didn't talk in that way when first I came here.'

'I did not know then that there was any cause. But don't trouble me, Clement, don't ask questions. You are to be off soon, aren't you?'

He tried to speak lightly, but the effort was unsuccessful, and Clement, passing by the question, returned to the former topic.

'It is the way they all talk to me,' he said. 'They are full of mysteries, and I don't choose to put up with them. I am old enough surely to have some judgment of my own. I can tell right from wrong as well as they can; and if I don't see that things are wrong, why am I to be forced to give them up? As for your father, he might as well be at Nova Scotia for anything I get from him, whether good or bad; and if a man doesn't do me any harm, I don't think I have any reason to think he means to do it.'

'You'll argue differently one of these days,' was the reply.

'Preaching are you?' and Clement laughed. 'I didn't know that was one of your gifts. I suppose Aunt Bertha has put you up to it; come, tell me now,' and he laid his hand playfully on Ronald's shoulder, 'hasn't she been setting you to jaw me in this fashion?'

Ronald drew back. 'When you want to know what Miss Campbell says to me, you had better go and ask her. I have said my say.'

Clement stopped him as he was turning away. 'Answer me one question, Ronald. If you were in my place, shouldn't you do as I do?'

Ronald considered for a moment, and answered firmly, 'No.'

'Then, what should you do?' Clement's tone betrayed considerable pique.

'I hope I should act the part of a brave man, not of a coward.'

'Coward!'

'Coward,' repeated Ronald, quietly. 'I would have my head cut off, before I would be trusted and betray my trust.'

'I am not trusted. It is the very thing I complain of; they do not trust me.'

'If you weren't trusted, you would be locked up.'

'You are mocking. Lock me up? As if any one had power to do that!'

'Mr Lester has power at any time.'

'Physical power. Folly! who thinks of that in these days?'

'Honour is instead of power, then,' said Ronald; 'and honour would keep me from deceiving him.'

'Ronald, you would madden a saint!' exclaimed Clement. 'I tell you I don't deceive him.'

'Then he knows everything you do. He will hear of your having been at the Grange to-night?'

'Hear! if he asks. I wouldn't tell a lie.'

'And I wouldn't act one.'

'I don't understand; you make me angry; I won't stand it!' exclaimed Clement, in a fretful tone of wounded pride and irritation. 'I.vow, if it weren't for old days, I should think you had come just to insult me and give me the opportunity of knocking you down.'

'Try, if you will,' replied Ronald, quietly, and perhaps a little contemptuously; 'I shall not return it.' But he added more quietly, 'Don't let us make fools of ourselves, Clement, by sparring for nothing. You know I don't mean to insult you, as you call it.'

'Then, what do you mean?'

'Simply to make you get up pluck enough to be honest; and when you are out upon *parole*, not to break it; and when you do break it, to own it.'

The question seemed to strike Clement in a new light. 'I never thought about that sort of thing,' he said. 'I was at school before I came here, and the boys there thought that pluck was to risk getting your own way without being caught.'

'I suppose they did. I don't know about school-boys; I never was at school.'

'Then who told you what pluck, and honour, and such things meant?'

'My own heart, and '—— Ronald added in an undertone— 'things I was taught when I was a child.'

'It's all very fine, Ronald!' exclaimed Clement, after a moment's thought; 'but twenty to one you've done more wild things in one day than I have done in all my life.'

Perhaps it was well for Clement that the dim light hid from him the change which passed over Ronald's countenance as the words were said. He might have reproached himself too bitterly.

Yet even without seeing, there was something deeply touching in the changed, humbled, faltering tone of the reply. 'Yes; oh, yes. Clement, you must never be like me.'

Clement seized his hand kindly. 'Cheer up, old fellow! I'm sure I didn't mean reproach. If you did twenty bad things, I dare say I should have done a hundred. I wasn't thinking a bit of boasting; I'm far enough off from that, really.'

'And I was not told; I never betrayed trust,' continued Ronald, with something of his former energy.

'No, of course you didn't. You are true to the backbone. But I shouldn't like you to think I could do so either.'

'You mightn't mean it, but you might do it; and you will if'——

'If what? out with it.'

'If you don't tell Mr Lester that you have been at the Grange to-night.'

'I don't see that. I shall tell if I'm asked.'

'Honour is in telling without being asked.'

'Going to confession,' said Clement, with something of a sarcastic laugh.

'If it's necessary.'

'Yes, if it is; that's the point. But I'll think about it.'

They stopped, as if by mutual consent. Ronald made one more effort. 'Clement, you told me once that you wished we had been brothers; is the feeling all gone?'

'Gone! no;' and Clement shook his hand affectionately. 'I would wish nothing better than to have you for my brother; if only you wouldn't be on one day and off another in the way you are. I can't understand that.'

'Then, if we are as brothers, give me a brother's confidence, and promise, even if you don't see the necessity, that you will tell Mr Lester where you have been to-night.'

Clement hesitated,—began to speak,—was silent again,—and at length, after grasping Ronald's hand violently, ran off, exclaiming—'I hate promises; but I'll see about it.'

CHAPTER XXIX.

CLEMENT reached home just as tea was being made, after a delay of three quarters of an hour, which had been very trying to the whole party; and particularly so, as the two children had, for once, been allowed to sit up for the late tea. His excuse was hasty and incoherent,—that he was kept longer than he had expected at the Hall, and had walked back rather slowly; both statements being true in the letter, though false in the spirit. Fanny, who was the make-peace of the party, found a place for him at the table, and provided him with a plate, but every one else treated him as if he was in disgrace; and Bertha, especially, not quite understanding how to show her annoyance with one individual, except by making all suffer, sat perfectly silent, except when every now and then she asked in a tone which had a peculiarly melancholy intonation, whether any one wished for more tea.

Louisa occasionally attempted a little conversation. Quick observation was teaching her tact; and, besides, there was a love of power innate in her, which made her feel pleasure in the consciousness of taking the lead in any matter however small.

'How was Ella, Clement?'

'Oh! pretty well;' and Clement cut for himself a large slice of bread.

'Had she been out to-day?'

'I don't know; I didn't ask her.'

'When is she coming home?' asked Mrs Campbell. 'I can't let her stay away much longer.'

'She doesn't want to come home yet, she says, grandmamma.'

'It must be very pleasant to sit by the fire all day, and read,' observed Fanny, who partook largely of her sister's indolence.

'Aunt Mildred won't let her do that, I'm sure,' said Louisa. 'It's very bad for Ella not to go out; she always gets ill if she doesn't take exercise.'

'Louisa, my dear, you had better not trouble yourself about what is good, or bad, for Ella,' said Bertha. 'Give me Grandmamma's cup for some more tea?'

'Just half a cup, my dear; not so much sugar, and a little more milk,' said Mrs Campbell.

That was the first attempt at conversation. Bertha poured out the tea; then put too much sugar, and too little milk; then too much milk, and too little water; then too much water, and too little tea ; and was rewarded by hearing the beverage she had provided pronounced totally undrinkable. A martyr could not have been more touching in her resignation. Louisa was aware of the fact; and, when Aunt Bertha began the concoction a second time, she attempted once more to arouse the dormant energies of the party by a fresh observation.

'What a heap of letters went to the post to-day! Do you know, Betsey said there was as many as Anne, at the Rectory, could carry.'

'I don't know who could have written them,' observed Mrs Campbell, with rather a sharp glance at Bertha. 'Writing letters is a great waste of time, unless people have real business to write about.'

'There were three of Aunt Bertha's,' said Fanny, who had a remarkable talent for *mal-à-propos* observations.

Bertha coloured, and looked annoyed. Lousia came to her rescue :—'They weren't all ours, though. You know there were Mr Lester's letters, too. I don't know how many there weren't of his ; and Rachel had been writing besides.'

'Rachel is a great deal too young to write so many letters,' said Mrs Campbell. 'It is a very bad thing for children ; it teaches them to scribble. I wonder Mr Lester allows it.'

'My hand is not spoiled, at any rate, by the number of letters I write,' observed Clement. 'I'm sure I don't get through half-a-dozen in a twelvemonth.'

'And when you do write, you don't waste many words, or much paper,' said Louisa.

'No ; why should I? It's an awful bore anyhow.'

'Mr Lester's hand must quite ache,' said Louisa. 'He writes so small, and crowds in ,such a quantity. I am sure one of the letters to-day looked quite like a book.'

'Louisa, how could you know?' and Bertha turned to her hurriedly ; whilst even Mrs Campbell gave a glance of sur-prise.

But Louisa was unabashed. 'I couldn't help knowing,' she said; 'Anne came with us down the lane, when we were running after you, Aunt Bertha, and she let them fall, and Fanny and I helped to pick them up.'

'I think it was seeing Goff coming round the corner suddenly, that frightened her,' said Fanny. 'She can't bear him.'

'He was very civil, though,' observed Louisa. 'He made us

such a funny bow, and asked if he should carry the letters for us, because he was going in to Encombe, and he thought he wanted to go to the shore.'

'And Anne was very glad he should,' continued Fanny; 'because she had so much to do, and it saved her the walk,'

'But it wasn't quite right, Aunt Bertha, was it?' inquired Louisa. 'When she was told to go, she ought to have gone. I said so, and I made her quite angry.'

'And we said that we would ask you to let us go through the village, and put the letters in the post,' continued Fanny, perceiving, by the change in her aunt's countenance, that some one had done wrong.

'It was very wrong. Anne ought to have known better,' began Bertha; when Mrs Campbell interrupted her in a fretful tone: ˙

'What is it all about? I don't understand. What did you do about the letters, my dears?'

'Nothing at all, grandmamma.'

'Then, Bertha, why do you find fault with them? You are always hard upon them. You ought to inquire before you blame.'

'I am not aware that I did blame them,' replied Bertha. 'Louisa, did Goff take the letters?' She spoke rather anxiously.

'I think he did, Aunt Bertha, but I am not sure. Fanny and I ran on before it was settled.'

'No great harm if he did, that I can see,' observed Clement, moodily; 'Goff's not likely to lose the letters.'

'And I shouldn't think he could read them,' said Fanny. 'Such a rough, odd man he is.'

'For that matter, Fanny,' answered Clement, 'he can read as well as you or I. He told me all about the loss of that ship, off the Irish coast, word for word, nearly as it was in the newspaper. He had read it all.'

'That was in to-day's paper,' said Louisa; 'Aunt Bertha read it to us. How could he hear about it before?'

A curious look of confused discomfiture crossed Clement's face; he answered abruptly, 'I didn't say that he had read it before to-day.'

Bertha appeared to be engaged it putting away the sugar, and locking up the tea-caddy; but she heard all that passed.

'You have seen Goff to-day, then, Clement?' her sharp, inquiring look abashed, whilst it made him angry.

'Yes; I have seen him.' And he played with his tea-spoon, whilst his features assumed an air of impenetrable determination, which Bertha had no difficulty in interpreting.

'You saw him this evening, I suppose?'

'Yes.'

'And I imagine that was the reason you were at home so late.'

Whatever might have been Bertha's object in her questions, it was manifestly unwise to put them before Mrs Campbell and the children. Clement's countenance became only the more dark, whilst Mrs Campbell, as usual, taking her grandson's part, and forgetting that she had been kept waiting, insisted that it was folly to tease him about where he had been, when he came in in time; and breaking in upon the subject, told Fanny to ring the bell and have the tea-things taken away.

Bertha went out of the room, and Clement took a book, and sat by the fire; but his reading was merely a pretence. He was in reality thinking of the difficulty into which he had been brought, and wondering how much of his proceedings he should be obliged to tell. Not more than he could avoid, that was undoubtedly his conclusion, in spite of Ronald's warning. Something he supposed he must say, but he would be guided by circumstances; a most convenient salve to the conscience, when there is not sufficient moral strength in the character to act upon principle. What he really intended to do might have been clear to him by the manner in which he reverted, in his own mind, to the folly of having mentioned Goff.

'Louisa, where is your aunt?' inquired Mrs Campbell, as Bertha failed to return at the usual reading time.

'I don't know, grandmamma; I will go and see.'

Louisa left the room, not so much from obedience as to satisfy her curiosity. She came back almost immediately. 'Betsey says, grandmamma, that Aunt Bertha put on her bonnet and cloth cloak, and she thinks she has gone up to the Rectory.'

'Very strange!' was Mrs Campbell's observation. 'I suppose, then, there will be no reading to-night!'

'I will read, grandmamma,' said Clement. He was too uncomfortable to do anything else; and even when he began to read, betrayed the wandering of his mind by the mistakes which he made.'

Mrs Campbell was accustomed to Bertha's independent modes of action, and was not likely to disturb herself as to her absence, so long, at least, as she was amused; and Clement's voice, after a short time, lulled her into her usual quiet evening doze ; and then Louisa and Fanny went to bed, and Clement prepared some lessons for Mr Lester.

CHAPTER XXX.

THE evening at the Rectory had been more pleasant than at the Lodge. The hour for tea was earlier, at least, nominally, though Mr Lester's engagements did not always admit of his being punctual. This evening he happened to be very fairly at leisure, and had given Rachel more of his time than he was often able to do. They were very precious hours for Rachel, which were thus snatched from other duties. They tended more to enlarge and form her mind than any which were devoted to regular study. Mr Lester's character was peculiarly simple, notwithstanding the depth of his intellect. He never dogmatised or patronised, even when talking to a child. There was no effort to obtain influence or produce an effect, and so conversation with him, even when touching upon the most abstruse subjects, flowed easily, because no one could feel shy, or be afraid of betraying ignorance, before one who never seemed to lose the consciousness that he himself was but a learner.

It was this characteristic which had so tended to develop Rachel's intellect. It had been nurtured in a genial atmosphere, free from the blight of coldness, or the stunting influence of condescension, or the weakness caused by the cultivation of any faculty merely for the purpose of display. She was not quick in acquiring mere knowledge, and had therefore never been considered clever ; and this, perhaps, was rather an advantage, since it served to make her like her father, simple-minded and free from self-consciousness. But she had great powers of comprehension, and could grasp a vast idea almost as it seemed by intuition, even when she was unable to follow out the detailed evidence by which it was supported. If Mr Lester's mind had been controversial, this alone would not have satisfied him ; if he had found pleasure in reasoning for the sake of controversy, or delighted in argument from the love of victory, he would have required a companion who could at times throw

down the gauntlet against him, and give interest to his researches by opposition. But truth alone was his object; and
if all the world could see and recognise truth, he was only so
much the better pleased. And it was very pleasant to find a
willing listener always ready at his fireside, and to listen to
Rachel's remark, and set her difficulties at rest. Intelligent
ignorance is most valuable when we are endeavouring to reason
correctly. It makes us view our theories from many different
points; and those, peculiarly, which our own preconceived ideas
would have been likely to hide from us; and Mr Lester often
learned more from Rachel's humble question, How can that be,
papa? than he would have done from hours of study.

The danger was lest this kind of abstract speculation should
be too absorbing for·both. With a less amount of conscientiousness, it might have rendered them unreal. But Mr Lester's
own training had taught him, as a moral caution, the lesson
which is sometimes learned to our cost, in another sense, by the
bitter experience of life. ' Save me from my friends, I can save
myself from my enemies,' would have been translated by him,
though in a secondary sense, ' Save me from my virtues, I can
save myself from my vices.' His warnings to Rachel were but
the expression of those which he gave to himself; and fearful
of the enticing nature of such intercourse, he continually
checked and limited it, never allowing it to interfere with the
slightest practical duty, even when a plausible reason for the
indulgence could be brought forward, and always, if possible,
deducing, even from the most abtruse theories, some definite
conclusion which might operate upon the daily course of life.

A conversation of this kind had been carried on by the
flickering, cheerful firelight; Mr Lester leaning forward with
his arm round Rachel's neck, and Rachel on her low stool,
resting her head against his knees. He had been explaining to
her the kind of argument used in Bishop Butler's 'Analogy,'—
trying to make her comprehend the true strength and goodness
which are to be found in being contented with the faith of probability, rather than the certainty of demonstration; or rather
not so much endeavouring to make her understand, as pouring
forth his own ideas,—showing her how the argument had worked
upon his own mind. And Rachel was drinking in his words,
finding in them, not indeed an answer to the difficulties which
her working, thoughtful mind often suggested; but that calm,
trusting, enduring principle, based upon the consciousness of

our own infinite ignorance and God's Almighty Wisdom, which,
if we think at all, can alone support us through the mysterious
scenes of this mortal existence.

It was not quite agreeable to be recalled from these favourite
subjects, and the enjoyment of the hour so rarely free from interruption, yet Mr Lester did not even look annoyed when
Bertha's knock was heard at the door, and Rachel only said, 'It
is over now, papa, thank you so very much,' and kissed him, and
moved away before the door opened, that Miss Campbell—for
she guessed it could be no one else—might not think she had
disturbed them.

Bertha entered the room slowly, and, after saying that she was
afraid she had interrupted them, sat down by the fire. Rachel
begged her to take off her bonnet and shawl, but she declined,
still in the same unmoved voice which gave no indication as to
why she had come, or how long she intended to stay. Mr Lester
was used to her, however, and went at once to the point. 'Do
you wish to see me for anything particular?'

'Thank you, I should like to say a few words to you, alone.'

'Then, Rachel, run and see if the fire is burning in my study;
perhaps, we had better go in there.'

'I won't keep you long,' said Bertha.

'The study is the best place for business, whether it be long
or short,' said Mr Lester; and to the study they went.

Rachel asked for the lamp, and began her evening work for
the poor; her thoughts occupied with all her father had been
saying, whilst her fingers moved nimbly.

'Clement has been with Goff again to-night,' began Bertha at
once. She was abrupt upon principle, when business was concerned, from an idea that abruptness was a species of honesty.

'Has he? when, and how long?' Mr Lester always treated
her in her own way, and never offered consolation or sympathy
till everything relating to the matter before them had been
said.

'My mother sent him to the Hall on a message. I did not
think it desirable, but she was determined. Clement met Goff
coming home, and stayed with him nearly three quarters of an
hour beyond his time. At least—no—I can't be sure that he
stayed with him all the time, but he was certainly three quarters
of an hour behind time.'

'And what excuse does he make for himself?'

'None; I did not give him the opportunity. Another thing I

wanted to say. Your servant took the letters to the post to-day,
and met Goff, and allowed him to carry them for her. I don't
think that is safe.'

Mr Lester's countenance changed. 'Took them, do you say?
Did she let him have them?'

'Yes, so the children told me.'

Mr Lester rang the bell. It was answered by the delinquent
Anne.

Bertha turned round upon her sharply ; but Mr Lester spoke
very gently, much more gently than when he was addressing
Bertha ; 'Anne, you took the letters to the post to-day?'

'Yes, sir.'

'Did you put them in yourself?'

A blush and a hesitation. 'I gave them, sir—that is, I took
care that they should be put in.'

'That is not the point. Did you put them in yourself?'

'No, sir ; but'—— Anne looked round for help, but there was
none to be obtained from Bertha.

'Don't be frightened, there is no good in excuses. Who did
put them in?'

Anne's voice trembled, and her tears began to flow, as if sentence against her had been already passed. 'I met Goff, sir,
and he was very civil ; and I was so busy ; and I didn't know
you would mind.'

'And you gave them to him? Did you ever do so before?'

'Yes, sir ; I think so.'

'Recollect you must be quite sure. You have given them to
him before?'

'I can't tell, I don't remember. Please, sir, don't send me
away, I will never do so again.'

'Foolish girl! You will be certain of being sent away if you
deceive me. Let me know at once how long you have been in
the habit of allowing this man to take the letters for you.'

Mr Lester doubtless intended to be gentle still, but his uneasiness and anxiety gave a sternness to his voice, and an impatience
to his manner, which effectually frightened poor Anne, and without any further attempt at excuse, she poured forth a confession
which, though comparatively slight in its evil as regarded herself, was the cause of the most painful misgivings as to the
affairs in which Mr Lester was interested.

It seemed that Goff had for a long period been endeavouring
to make friends with Anne, always putting himself in her way,

talking to her, and from her obtaining a good deal of information as to the proceedings at the Parsonage and the Lodge. Anne had given her information in the simplicity of her heart, not in the least intending to do harm, not knowing that what she was saying could be of the slightest consequence, but only at first yielding to the love of gossip, and perhaps a little intimidated by the questions of her interrogator, which were generally put in such a way as to give her little choice as to her answers. By degrees, however, he had drawn her into a confidence which she herself saw to be wrong and dangerous, but it was then out of her power, or at least so she thought it, to recede. Whenever she went out, Goff met her, persecuting her with questions, and threatening her mysteriously if she refused to answer them. However she might try to avoid him he was sure to cross her path ; most especially he put himself in her way, as had happened on the present occasion, when she was entrusted with the letters for the post, sometimes making her show him the directions, and more than once inducing her to give them up to him. Anne's excuse was that she could see no harm ; it did not seem to her that it signified much whether one person or another took them ; and it saved her a walk which she was very glad of, as she had so much to do. Yet she was forced to acknowledge that she never came back without a fear of being scolded, if she was found out, and for that reason had carefully avoided letting her fellow-servant know what she had done.

It was one of those many instances in which a fault has been committed much greater than has been intended or understood, but for which there is little excuse, since the warning of conscience ought to have been a sufficient safeguard. Anne was dismissed with a severe reprimand, and cried bitterly when she was told that her master had lost his confidence in her ; but Mr Lester's thoughts were at the moment too painfully occupied to permit him to dwell long upon her share of the offence ; and as the door closed behind her, he sat down, and, forgetting Bertha's presence, gave way to a train of perplexing considerations.

Bertha remained by him unmoved. She would have waited for an hour without interrupting him, but her patience was not quite so sorely tried. Mr Lester looked up at length, and said, ' We have been utterly outwitted by him.'

' I hope not,' was Bertha's quiet answer.

' What hope do you see ? ' inquired Mr Lester, quickly.

' If he had discovered anything, we should have known it before this. At the utmost, he can but suspect.'

' I would not trust. He might know everything, and still keep quiet till the last moment. This affair of the letters, you see, has been going on for some time.'

' Yes.'   Bertha looked more anxiously grave.   ' I will take them myself for the future.'

' Or I will; we can trust no one but ourselves. But I think less of that.' He paused; then added suddenly, ' What do you say to the time being arrived for the decisive step?'

The colour rushed to Bertha's cheek in a quick glow, and faded away as suddenly.   ' O Mr Lester! do you at last say that?'

' I see no other alternative. The moment the fact of Vivian's being in England is absolutely known, or even very probably suspected, we are exposed to schemes against which it is impossible for us to be on our guard. Goff may have opened our letters or he may not; at any rate, it is clear he has found out that ,Mr Bruce is not Mr Bruce, or he would have had no curiosity in the matter.'

' And you would have Edward go openly to his father?' inquired Bertha.

' I see nothing else that is to be done.'

' But, dear Mr Lester, you speak so despondingly.'

He hesitated for an instant; then he said, ' I have seen General Vivian to-day.'

' And you have sounded him? Why didn't you tell me before?'

' I sounded him as much as I dared, with regard to Clement; but he has entrenched himself within a wall of false principles, and there is no reaching him.'

' And you don't think that Edward's appearance in person will have any effect? A father! it must soften him.'

' And it may harden him; he may, I think he will, call it a fresh act of disobedience.'

Bertha looked discouraged.   ' There is no time to work upon him,' she said, ' as we had hoped, through the children.'

' No; and if there were, I am afraid I should not be very sanguine as to the result.'

' General Vivian is too keen-sighted not to see Ella's faults, even if they were less hidden than they are,' replied Bertha.

' Yes; and there is the old prejudice.'

'She is a Campbell,' said Bertha, bitterly. 'Little enough the Campbells would have to do with the Vivians, if they could help it.'

Mr Lester laid his hand kindly upon hers ; yet there was reproof in his tone, as he said, 'I hoped that old feeling had been buried.'

Bertha coloured. 'General Vivian takes pains to revive it,' she said.

'It must be buried, if there is to be any hope of success with us. We must trust almost everything to you and Mildred, and you must therefore be friends.'

Bertha was silent.

'You will find her anxious to prove herself a friend,' continued Mr Lester, gravely.

'She has made no advances,' was the reply.

'Is that quite a fair judgment ?' replied Mr Lester, 'consider-ing how little she is her own mistress. And surely she has sent you kind messages.'

Bertha's habitual candour conquered her momentary pique. 'I dare say Miss Vivian has done all that I ought to expect,' she said : 'but it is very difficult to forget that if it had not been for the old family feud, poor Flora must have been received by them, and all that happened afterwards would have been spared. There was no fault in her.'

'Miss Vivian feels this as much as you do,' replied Mr Lester ; 'and you on your part must consider that, but for what, no doubt, there was cause to consider an unfortunate attachment to your sister, her only brother might never have been an exile from his home. I don't say this to pain you,' he continued, observing Bertha's face of distress ; 'I only wish to make you view the question from both sides. It may be most essential that there should be no misunderstanding between you and Mildred. You have both something to forget and to forgive, as regards your family histories.'

'I will try not to be prejudiced,' said Bertha ; but the tone implied a mental reservation.

'And you will succeed,' replied Mr Lester, 'if you don't attempt too much. These vague feelings of family dislike are scarcely to be combated like actual faults. We can only accept them, and deal with them as we do with individual character-istics—negatively, that is, rather than positively.'

'I don't quite understand,' replied Bertha.

'What I mean to say is, that we can't actually make ourselves all at once forget them, or feel as if they did not exist, any more than we can suddenly become insensible to certain peculiarities of manner or expression which may offend us ; but we can prevent ourselves from allowing them to weigh with us unduly ; and it is always in our power to put them aside in action.'

'I have never seen Miss Vivian yet,' replied Bertha ; 'so there have been few opportunities for action.'

'She would like to see you as soon as you can make it convenient to go to her; the sooner now, I think, the better. She is one with us, and has, I think, quite forgotten the concealment of Mr Bruce's identity.'

Bertha seemed undetermined ; and said she could not perceive what good was likely to accrue from the meeting.

'Essential good, if our hopes should fail,' replied Mr Lester. 'In that case you will be the only person to keep up any satisfactory communication between Mildred and the children. Poor Vivian will be more cut off than ever.'

'I am so unfortunate and awkward,' said Bertha. 'I feel that I mar everything I come in contact with. I don't mean it, I am sure,' she added, as tears rose to her eyes.

Mr Lester answered eagerly : 'No, I am sure you don't. Perhaps,—don't think I am taking a liberty in saying so,—perhaps contact with another mind may throw more light upon your own. Only, I will just remind you,—you mustn't think it necessary to fall in love with Mildred.'

Bertha smiled in spite of herself. 'Not much fear of that,' she said.

'I am not so sure. I really believe that conscientious people have great difficulty in accepting antipathies, and so they make violent efforts to overcome them, which have just the contrary effect from that desired.'

'The antipathies are wrong, of course,' replied Bertha.

'Their indulgence is wrong, but the feeling may be the result of circumstances beyond our own control, and we are much more likely to be just to persons when we acknowledge to ourselves we have a prejudice against them, than when we try to conceal the fact and persuade ourselves that we are fond of them. But we must leave all that now. I am sure you will try to understand Miss Vivian, and I hope when I come back from London I shall hear that you have met.'

'Are you going to London ?' inquired Bertha, quickly.

'I think I must see Vivian ; but I shall only be absent two or three days.'

ı 'And he will come down at once, then ?'

'He will wish to do so, I suspect ; any risk will seem better than the monotonous life he has been leading. But even without this fresh call I think I must have gone to talk to him about what is to be done with Clement. The General offers to assist in placing him with a private tutor.'

Bertha's countenance brightened. 'Oh ! then, he does acknowledge it a duty.'

'Partly ; I don't mean to be perverse, but I honestly would rather he did not. Persons are so difficult to deal with who go half-way with a duty, and then say good-bye to it. He promised —let me see—I made a memorandum as to the conversation when I came away.'

Mr Lester felt for his pocket-book, and in doing so took out his handkerchief, and with it the paper which he had, without knowing it, brought away from the Hall. It fell upon the table, and Bertha took it up. ' ' Is this it ?' she said.

'Thank you, no: I wrote it on a blank leaf.' Without looking at the paper, and supposing it to be a bill, Mr Lester placed it in the pocket of his little book, and then proceeded to read to Bertha the heads of his morning conversation.

'You see,' he said, when he had ended, 'there is little if any hope : the feeling is as strong—stronger perhaps than ever ; and each day that goes by strengthens it, by enlisting pride in support of what seems justice. No, we have now only one alternative, to make a last appeal to the General's feelings, and possibly in doing that we may find the clue to John Vivian's rascality, and so at least place Vivian's conduct in its true light, even if we can do nothing else.'

'And if all should fail, Edward must return to Jamaica,' said Bertha.

'I trust not that ; he would never stand it : we must make a home for him somewhere ; and with you and Mildred to feel with him we may hope that it may be fairly happy. But that is running on very far ahead, and we must not forget Goff and the present moment.'

'I don't see what is to be done about him,' said Bertha.

'Nothing just now but to watch. O Clement ! Clement ! the despair it is not to be able to trust him.'

'And he piques himself so upon being honourable, and having the feelings of a gentleman,' said Bertha.

'Yes, not at all perceiving that the very essence of honour is never to abuse confidence.'

'Don't you think it might be as well to see him, and inquire what he has been doing with himself this evening?' asked Bertha. Mr Lester considered a little. 'I hate being suspicious, and the very fact of inquiring so minutely very often suggests deceit. Yet perhaps it may be as well : I will walk with you across the garden, and then I will bring him back.'

'There is no occasion for that,' answered Bertha, in reply. 'The moon is just up, and it is quite light. Besides, I must stop for one moment at Duff's cottage, to ask for his child. I will send Clement to you ; that will be the best way.'

Mr Lester demurred, but Bertha was positive, and just in that way which made him feel that he should annoy her if he insisted upon carrying his point. So they said good-bye ; and Bertha walked across the little garden, and Mr Lester returned to his study to wait for Clement.

One thing could not but strike him, as he recurred to what had passed : the very matter-of-fact way in which all had been said and arranged, not in the least as if great interests were at stake, or there were grounds for unusual uneasiness. Throughout the whole of the conversation Bertha's rather monotonous voice had scarcely been raised above its usual low pitch ; she had seldom laid any peculiar emphasis on her words, or, in fact, in any way betrayed that the topics discussed were of importance to her.

Accustomed though he was to her, Mr Lester marvelled. Perhaps in his heart he felt pained. It was very difficult to work with such a person, to give or receive the sympathy necessary for support in doubt and difficulty. And then with Mr Vivian and the children ! What was to be the end? Could they possibly live together? Would Bertha ever really obtain a right influence in her own family ?—Yet the uncomfortable misgiving partially vanished when he remembered how she had given him her hand at parting, and said, very timidly: 'I don't know how to say, thank you, as I ought.' There was something so humble, simple, child-like, and true in her ; such a consciousness of her own deficiencies !

That unfortunate early education,—nipping, blighting, as it had been ; what a noble nature it had marred !

CHAPTER XXXI

'MR LESTER wants to see you, Clement.' The words broke most uncomfortably upon Clement's slumber, as, having finished his writing, he established himself in an arm-chair, opposite to his grandmother.

'Wants to see me, does he?' and he rubbed his eyes. 'It's awfully late and cold.'

'It won't take you two minutes to run across the garden, and you must not keep him.'

Clement delayed, and Bertha was obliged to repeat the message.

'Mr Lester will be very much annoyed, Clement, if you don't make haste.'

'Going, Aunt Bertha, going.' . He went out into the passage, but came back again. 'Where on earth can that girl have put my greatcoat?'

'Your greatcoat, Clement, nonsense. It is not a hundred yards to the Rectory.'

'Enough to feel the cold, Aunt Bertha; I must have my coat.' He rang the bell; Bertha left the room, called out to the servant not to answer the bell, and went herself to the closet where she knew that the missing coat was to be found.

Clement looked ashamed. With all his faults he had the feeling of a gentleman. 'I beg your pardon, Aunt Bertha; I really didn't mean to give you the trouble, but that girl is so intolerably careless.'

'And a boy ought to be ashamed to be dependent upon her. She has enough to do without waiting upon you, Clement.'

'Then I wish she wouldn't meddle with my things at all,' muttered Clement, determined to have the last word. He drew on his coat very slowly. Bertha looked at him with that evident self-control which shows that impatience is on the point of bursting forth. Clement, however, did not see this. He buttoned his coat up to the chin, preparing, as it might have seemed, for a walk of ten miles; and set forth as leisurely as if he had felt quite at his ease.

He was shown at first into the room where Rachel was sitting at work. A poor man had just come up from the village, having business with Mr Lester; and a message was therefore sent, begging him to wait.

Clement's heart sank. 'What are you doing there, Rachel?'

he said, drawing nearer to Rachel's chair, and watching her busy fingers. He said it merely tó distract his thoughts. Anything was better than that wretched standing by the fire, waiting fo the door to open again.

'Making a warm coat for Barney Wood,' replied Rachel. 'Won't it be comfortable?' and she held it up for him to see.

Clement looked at it carelessly, and Rachel, a little disappointed at receiving no admiration of her performance, returned to her work in silence.

Clement still finding his own meditations uncomfortable, spoke again—'I thought Barney Wood was worse.'

'Yes, so he is, a great deal; that is the reason he wants something specially to keep him warm. Who do you think is going to give the coat?' she added, her face brightening with pleasure.

'You are, I suppose,' he replied.

'Oh no; I haven't half money enough. I am making it for Ronald to give. It was so kind of him to think of it.'

'So odd, you mean,' replied Clement.

'Odd! why?' She turned round quickly, and looked at him with wonder.

'It's a queer thing for a fellow like him to think about a child's coat. That's a woman's business.'

'Not to think about it, is it?' said Rachel. 'It's a woman's business to make it, and that is why I am working for him. But Ronald is odd, I suppose,' she added, thoughtfully.

'Have you found that out for the first time to-day, eh, Rachel?' and Clement laughed a little satirically.

'I don't think I ever should find it out myself,' replied Rachel. 'People say Ronald is odd, and so I suppose he is, but he never seems so to me.'

'Much experience you must have had of him, little woman,' said Clement, patronisingly, as he patted her on the shoulder.

Rachel drew back with an air of annoyance. She could not endure familiarity, and answered, rather coldly, that she certainly did not see Ronald often; but when she did she liked him very much, and thought him very good.

Clement laughed. 'A doughty champion Ronald will have,' he said, 'when it comes to a fight for his character. But, Rachel, you will have no one else on your side. I don't think Ronald's goodness is what the world admires him for.'

'He is good, though,' said Rachel, resolutely.

'Then he must make you his confidante, and tell you all his virtues,' said Clement. 'You wouldn't discover them your-self.'

'I think I should,' said Rachel; 'I do, indeed, for he never praises himself. That is one thing I like him for.'

'Virtue the first; and what next?'

'He doesn't think about himself,' continued Rachel; 'I mean he will take any trouble for any one, and he is always civil; and, —I can't tell exactly everything,—but I am sure he is to be trusted.'

'Trusted! yes, I suppose he wouldn't steal.'

Rachel's eyes kindled. 'I should think not, indeed,' she ex-claimed, laying down her work, and turning to Clement, with a flushed cheek; 'But it wasn't'that I meant; being trusted doesn't mean money, but honour. He wouldn't tell a story, or deceive; or pretend anything that wasn't true; and he keeps his word. When you look at him you feel that he is to be trusted.'

Clement bit his lip, and answered coolly—'No great praise, after all. Most persons speak truth.'

'Yes, but it is not speaking truth,' replied Rachel, her musical voice becoming deeply earnest; 'it is feeling truth. Clement, don't you know what I mean?'

'Perhaps I do, only you express yourself so oddly; you always do.'

'Do I? I didn't know it;' and in a moment she was the humble child receiving a reproof, as she added, 'I will try and be clear, but I don't quite know how.'

Perhaps Clement had no wish for her definition of truth, for he gave her no encouragement to continue. Yet, in her simpli-city, Rachel did not perceive this, and thinking that he was waiting for her to explain herself, she went on, with a blush on her cheek, and a little hesitation in her voice,—'I mean that Ronald never seems to be two persons, or to mean two things. When he promises anything, he does it, and when he says he likes anybody, you always see that he really does. Sometimes I have heard him say he dislikes what papa thinks he ought not to dislike, parts of books and such things; but that doesn't pre-vent his being true. Papa says'—she continued, and she glanced at Clement doubtfully, in the fear that she might be relapsing into odd expressions—'that truth is formed of two halves, fitting into each other, and making one whole. I am sure Ronald's words and his actions always fit; and I dare say his heart and

his words fit too, only I can't tell so much about that, and it is
so much more difficult to make them fit.'

'You are desperately given to metaphysics, Rachel,' said
Clement.

'Am I? I only say what papa says. But, Clement, I am sure
you know what I mean about Ronald.'

'He's a very good-hearted, honest fellow,' replied Clement ;
'but I can't tell how you seem to know so much about him,
Rachel.'

'He comes to talk to papa about his Latin,' said Rachel, 'and
about Barney Wood, too; and sometimes we have met him when
we have been to see Barney. I don't know much about him,
really, though.'

'And so he means to pay for that wonderful coat you are
making ?'

'Yes ; he asked Miss Campbell and me to get it; and we went
to Cleve, the other day, and chose it.'

'Barney Wood is fortunate in having so many persons to look
after him,' said Clement, carelessly.

'He won't want care very long,' replied Rachel; 'so it is right
to make him as comfortable as we can whilst he is here. I can't
think how he comes to be such a nice child, when he is Goff's
grandchild.'

'Oh ! you hate Goff, like the rest of the world, do you ?' said
Clement.

'I don't hate—I don't hate any one ; but I don't like him ;
and I know papa thinks he does a great deal of mischief, and I
am sure he is afraid that Barney's father is going to be like him.'

'And Ronald, too, then,' said Clement, 'as they are always
together.'

He said it merely to tease her; but she could not see this, and
fancying him in earnest, she threw down her work, and starting
up, exclaimed, 'O Clement ! you don't know anything about
Ronald ; you are very unkind to him ; and I used to think you
were fond of him,' she added, more gently, but still very reproachfully.

'Perhaps I am just as fond of him as you are, Rachel ; only I
see more of him, and know more of his ways.'

'You don't know more than papa does,' continued Rachel,
taking up her work, and evidently trying not to speak as if she
was annoyed ; 'and he thinks that if Ronald has good persons
about him, he will be a very good man.'

'Possibly. I wouldn't for the world dispute it; only I don't see where the people are to come from who are to make him good. His father won't do much in that way.'

'I don't know anything scarcely about Captain Vivian,' replied Rachel; 'but I am afraid of him.'

'He's a good sort of fellow enough,' was Clement's off-hand reply; 'only not very pretty company for girls.'

'Then I shouldn't think he could be good for boys,' observed Rachel, with a quick glance at Clement, which made him a little angry.

'I should be glad, Rachel, if you would decide for yourself, not for me,' he said. 'You can't possibly be a judge.'

Rachel looked distressed. 'Did I vex you, Clement? I didn't mean to do it. I only thought that papa is so sorry when you have been with Captain Vivian.'

'I can't help being with him sometimes.'

'Can't you really? Then I suppose it won't do you any harm.'

The remark was made with such apparent childish simplicity, that Clement began to laugh.

'Was it anything very odd that I said?' continued Rachel. 'I thought nothing could do us harm which we couldn't help.'

'What an absurd child you are!' exclaimed Clement. 'You take up one's words as if you were weighing them. Can't help, doesn't really mean, can't help.'

'Papa won't let me say I can't help a thing,' replied Rachel, 'unless I really can't. He says that people teach themselves self-deceit by their words. And you know, Clement, nothing can be wrong which we really can't help.'

'Then I am quite sure I am the most virtuous being in existence,' exclaimed Clement; 'for I can't help half—no, not three quarters—of the wrong things I do.'

'But if we ought to say, I don't try to help it,' persisted Rachel, 'that would be a great mistake.'

'I don't read learned books, and study metaphysics, as you do, Rachel,' said Clement, sarcastically. 'And, happily for me! My head would get addled in a month. You are enough to perplex a saint with your quibbles.'

'It is no quibble; and I don't learn it from books, nor from anything,' exclaimed Rachel, her naturally quick temper being roused by the taunt; 'I learn it from my own heart. When I say I can't help a thing, and I really can help it, it is something inside that tells me it is untrue. But'—— she paused, her tone changed, and she added humbly, 'I ought not to speak out so, Clement ; please forgive me.'

Clement murmured something in reply, which was scarcely audible. He glanced at the door, feeling, he did not know why, that the interview with Mr Lester would have been more endur- able than this conversation with the open-hearted, true-minded child, whose every word was a reproach to him.

Rachel fancied she had deeply offended him, and again begged for forgiveness. She knew, she said, that it was her way to speak out, and she did try to keep her temper under ; only not so much as she ought. 'You will forgive me, won't you, Clement ?' she added, in her most pleading voice.

It must have been a very hard heart that could refuse ; and Clement was naturally good-tempered, and really liked Rachel, only he took pleasure in shocking what he called her matter-of- factness. He pretended to hold out a little, for the purpose of hearing her again beg for pardon in that very sweet, humble tone ; and then suddenly changing and startling her by a laugh, he exclaimed, 'Why, Rachel, you are more silly than I took you to be ! I never said I was angry, did I ?'

'I didn't know. I very often do speak out when I ought not,' was the answer ; and there was rather an awkward silence, which perhaps neither of them were sorry to have broken by the entrance of the servant, who summoned Clement to Mr Lester's study.

CHAPTER XXXII.

I T is a marvellous and fearful subject, that of unconscious influence. It might almost paralyse us with its enormous responsibility, if it were not for the fact, which becomes obvious to any person who studies the formation of character, that the weight of indirect good always in the end preponderates over indirect evil. We advise, and warn, and reprove, and—either from some defect of manner, some deficient mode of expression, or perhaps some latent vanity or temper—we neutralise our own words ; and the person whom we are attempting to lead in the right way, leaves us to follow the wrong ; but, if we are not called upon to give counsel, and yet are in a position to act, each deed of self-denial, self-control, thoughtful kindness,—each word or tone which may tend to reveal our secret motives, comes un-marred from Him who has enabled us to serve Him, and brings with it a power which is, in its very nature, necessarily victorious over evil. A child brought up by two persons—neither attempt-ing to direct in words, but the one practically earnest and good, and the other practically careless and indifferent, will cling to the former and reject the latter. But a child receiving excellent advice from one person, and very bad advice from another, will, in nine cases out of ten, listen to the bad, and reject the good. Who has not felt the indirect influence of a child's goodness? Who would not have felt, as Clement did when he left Rachel Lester, that those few unconscious warnings, the result of her own honest, simple, high-minded spirit of truth and obedience, had a power which even impressive eloquence might have failed to exercise? Clement was in a different frame of mind, when he appeared before Mr Lester, from that in which he had left the Lodge; then he had quietly made up his mind to say nothing; now, on the contrary, he was inclined towards candour and sincerity; and when Mr Lester addressed him with his usual kindness, and told him he was sorry to have kept him wait-ing, it seemed as if he could at once have acknowledged his offence, and make reparation by promises for the future. But he was still trusting to himself, unaware of the weakness of his own resolution.

Mr Lester began the conversation cautiously. 'You went to the Hall this evening, Clement?'

'Yes, sir.'

'And you returned late, and met Goff?'

'Yes, sir.'

Mr Lester paused, hoping for something besides the mono-syllable; but Clement's courage was not equal to the confession, without help.

'Were you with him long?'

'I don't know the exact time, sir.'

'Did he force himself upon you?'

'He came and walked by my side, sir.' A keen pang of con-science, and a recollection of Rachel, and Clement added:—'He said he was going my way, and so we went together.'

Mr Lester's countenance brightened. There was a tone of candour in this which was cheering. He thought that Clement had told all. 'I suppose you came straight home?' he said.

'No, sir; we went round by—the fields.' Another pang of conscience, worse than the first. He had almost corrected himself as before, and added,—by the Grange. But he waited for another question.

'Oh, by the fields. I suppose, then, that was what made you so late.'

Alas for Clement! the almost right was changed, as so often happens, into quite wrong; and seizing on the suggested excuse, he replied,—'It was a good way round—farther than I thought.'

Something in his countenance and tone struck Mr Lester painfully. 'Clement,' he said, 'you are above suspicion,—I cannot possibly doubt your word; but if there is anything in this which I ought to know, beyond the fact of your having been with Goff, I trust to your honour to tell me.'

A minute before Clement would have responded to the appeal, by at once acknowledging his visit; but the first equivocation, contrary to the voice of conscience, had done its work. He had not spoken out at first,—he was ashamed to confess his evasion,—and so he covered it by another, still intending to say the whole presently.

'I don't think anything Goff said could have done me much harm, sir. He talked about the loss of the steamer off the Irish coast, most of the time.'

'What he talked about, Clement, is not the question. If he had been giving you the most excellent advice all the time, I should still have objected to your being with him.'

That was an unfortunate speech for Clement's courage. If Mr Lester so strongly objected even to a walk and an innocent conversation, what would he say to the visit to the Grange! The old excuses suggested themselves again, but the pang of conscience was intensely keen. Rachel's voice and words were ringing in his ears. To resist now would be a more wilful sin.

Mr Lester seemed considering deeply. Clement stood before him in an agony of weak intention. He delayed; and there are cases—many and most common—in which delay is all that the tempter requires for his victory.

Presently Mr Lester said, with a slight nervousness of manner, —'You must know, Clement, some of the reasons which make us all so anxious to prevent your having any intercourse with that man Goff.'

'I know people say he is a smuggler,' replied Clement.

Another pause. Mr Lester's tone was still more uneasy, as he replied—'There may be deeper reasons than that,—family reasons ; you have heard of them.'

'Family affairs are a mystery to me,' said Clement, shortly.

'That is not the exact truth, Clement. You do know something.'

'I know that my father has been very ill used,' replied Clement ; 'and that we ought all to be much better off than we are.'

'Possibly,' answered Mr Lester, drily. 'But, Clement'— his voice became deeply earnest and serious—'your father has been suffering for years from the consequences of that same spirit of wilful independence which will infallibly be your ruin if you yield to it. He was warned against companionship—against Captain Vivian's companionship ; he saw no necessity for the warning, and he would not take it. The result was the loss of home, friends, and fortune—exile for himself, poverty for his children.'

'My grandfather was unjust !' exclaimed Clement, indignantly.

'Let it be so. Your father erred, and has grievously repented his error.'

'If he was disinherited unjustly, I don't see what there was to repent of,' replied Clement.

'What we suffer, Clement, has nothing to do with the extent of our offence. And there is one truth which I would most earnestly strive to impress upon you. It seems to be one of the marked rules of God's providential government, that seemingly trifling offences should, if committed wilfully and against warning, bring upon us irremediable punishment. One thought of evil admitted into our hearts, by our own choice, will do us more harm than all we are taught by experience, without our choice, as we pass through life. The word or suggestion of sin which Goff or Captain Vivian may bring before you, when you are wilfully seeking their society, or, what is the same thing, wilfully refusing to avoid it, will haunt you to your dying day ; and one weak yielding to a slight temptation to disobedience may be, with you, as it was with your father, ruin for life. It is the first time I have spoken in this way,' continued Mr Lester. 'It is intensely painful to me to bring up the remembrance of faults which have been expiated, as far as sorrow and amendment can expiate any guilt ; but your father would be the first to bid me warn you by his example and his sufferings. In his name,

Clement, I bid you remember that it is not the amount of our offence, but the wilfulness with which it is committed, which is our sin in the sight of God, and which brings upon us His just vengeance.'

Clement's heart beat very fast ; the words, ' I have done very wrong, sir,' escaped him. He might have added more, but Mr Lester, seizing upon the acknowledgment,—almost the first which he had made without any attempt at excuse,—interrupted him by saying in a lighter tone :—' It is all I wish, Clement, that you should see that these little disobediences are very wrong. I dare say you have excuses for them. I dare say Goff thrusts himself upon you. Very often you may have a difficulty in ridding yourself of him. But that ought only to give you the more spirit in resisting. Where would be—I will not say the merit— one ought not perhaps to use the word—but the satisfaction, of victory, if there were no struggle ? '

The expression was rather an unfortunate one, for Clement's vanity was piqued. He answered hastily,—' There is not much struggle, sir, I am sure, in getting rid of a fellow like that ; I am not so desperately fond of his company, after all ; only he thrusts himself upon me, and I can't shake him off.'

' Not can't, Clement ; you can if you will.'

' He wouldn't go to-night, sir ; I tried several times to take short cuts.'

Quite true this was, as before, in the letter ; but the excuse had led Clement a long way from the spirit of truth. If he were to say now that he had gone into the Grange, it would seem as if he had spoken an untruth, or at least something approaching to it. Mr Lester looked at his watch, being anxious to close the conversation. ' Well, Clement, I can only say, what I have often said before, that I trust to your honour. I cannot possibly tell how much or how little you put yourself in the way of these men, or whether they only pursue you for their own bad purposes. They have some, you may be sure ; and if they could lead you into serious mischief, their end would be gained ; but in this, as in everything else, your only safety is openness. If you have been betrayed into disobedience, say it. Don't wait till you have been tempted to great sins, but acknowledge the small ones. Of course I believe to-night that Goff thrust himself upon you ; that you only walked with him through the fields ; and that he said nothing which I should object to your hearing. I very much disapprove of anything of the kind ; and most unquestionably you were wrong in not taking the shortest path. If the thing should happen again, some stricter precautions must be taken, as it would be evident that you are not fit to be trusted.'

Clement's heart was very full. He was upon the point—all but upon the point of being candid ; but he hesitated still ; a knock at the door was heard—and he was silent.

So it is : we will not take the right step at the right moment ; when we wish to take it, the opportunity is past. Surely not in vain is it written, ' To everything there is a season, and a time to every purpose under the heavens.'

Clement went home weak and miserable.

CHAPTER XXXIII.

' HERE is a note from grandmamma, Aunt Mildred,' said Ella, entering Miss Vivian's morning-room with a countenance expressive of anything but satisfaction.

' No bad news in it, I hope ;' and then Mildred, catching the meaning of Ella's face, added, ' She does not want you back again ? '

' She says Aunt Bertha is coming to talk to you about it to-day.'

It was Mildred's turn to look a little uncomfortable then. This visit of Bertha's had been hanging over her like a nightmare ever since Ella had been with her. Yet she answered cheerfully, ' We must make the room look pretty and comfortable if Aunt Bertha is coming. I should like her to have a pleasant impression of the Hall.'

' I am sure she will have one if she is like me,' said Ella, drawing her chair nearer to her aunt's sofa. ' But then she is not at all like me, that is the misfortune ;' and she sighed.

' Or you are not like her, Ella, and that is the misfortune ;' and Mildred looked at Ella, and laughed.

' Now you wouldn't wish me to be ? Aunt Mildred, you must say it ; you wouldn't be pleased if I were like Aunt Bertha.'

Mildred considered. ' I should be pleased, Ella, I am sure, if you were like her in some things.'

' Some, yes; of course she is not a monster, she has some good points.'

' A very great many, if report says truth.'

' Report and Mr Lester,' replied Ella. ' He lauds her to the skies.'

' Then she must deserve to be lauded. I don't know any one more unprejudiced than Mr Lester.'

' But what is being unprejudiced, Aunt Mildred? It is one of the words I hear so often, and I never can in the least tell what it means.'

' Derivations help one very much in the meaning of words,' replied Mildred. ' Prejudice is prejudgment, judging beforehand; unprejudiced persons, therefore, don't form their judgment before they are acquainted with facts.'

' That scarcely applies to Mr Lester and Aunt Bertha,' observed Ella. ' Of course Mr Lester judges according to what he sees ; and so would every one.'

' I beg your pardon, Ella. One of the rarest qualities to be met with in this trying world is that of judging according to what a person sees.'

' Is it ? ' and Ella looked extremely surprised.

' I will tell you how people generally form their judgments,' continued Mildred. ' They have their own preconceived notions of right and wrong, possibly correct, possibly incorrect; but, either way, these notions are their standard, to which they think all ought to submit. When they become acquainted with any individual, they try him by them. If they are religious, they find out whether he holds certain doctrines; if they are politicians, they test him by his opinions upon some of the questions of the day. They don't look upon his whole character, but without having had time to become acquainted with him thoroughly, they form their judgment, and like or dislike him.'

' I am sure that is natural enough,' said Ella. ' I can always tell after I have seen persons twice whether I like them.'

' No doubt you can: but the mischief is that prejudiced persons allow their private feelings to blind them to facts. I will give you an instance of what I mean. Suppose you were reading a book written by a person you disliked; if you were prejudiced you would begin with a conviction that the writer held certain opinions, and instead of taking his words in their natural meaning, you would twist them to suit your own preconceived ideas of what he thought. So again, if it were a book which you could not help admiring because it showed great talent, you would leave the beauty and dwell upon some small defects. This is especially common in the case of sermons. If a clergyman does not hold precisely the opinions approved by those who hear him, they will put aside all that is really true and right in what he says, and harp upon what may be defective, till at last one is apt to forget that he really has told one anything from which one might profit. Now all this kind of narrow-mindedness Mr Lester is totally free from. He would give a candid and impartial judgment of his greatest enemy.'

'Does that mean Aunt Bertha?' asked Ella, mischievously.

Mildred laughed. 'Not quite. He admires Aunt Bertha extremely.'

'He hasn't to live with her every day,' said Ella.   .

'That does make a difference, certainly. He sees enough of her, though, to know what she is really like; and he is quite aware of her defect of manner; but it would never make him form a false judgment of her.'

'Then you think I am prejudiced, Aunt Mildred?'

'Yes, very.'

'Thank you for being honest,' and Ella blushed, and tried to smile, but almost cried.

'Prejudice is a most common fault with young people,' continued Mildred; 'one may almost say it is natural to them. But there is hope for you, Ella, for that very reason. The prejudiced persons whom one really grieves over are the well-meaning people who shut themselves up in their own fancies, and mix only with those who agree with them, and so never give themselves the opportunity of being cured.'

'Oh, Aunt Mildred an advocate for dissipation!' exclaimed Ella.

'I hope not. Worldly people are just as likely to be prejudiced in their way as religious persons are in theirs. But certainly it does vex one heartily to see the mischief that is done in these days by the prejudices of really kind-hearted people, who yet can see nothing good beyond their own narrow circle. The moment an unhappy individual differs from them on certain points, he may be as earnest, and honest, and self-denying as a saint, but his words and actions are distorted until one begins to think that truth has left the earth. There, Ella,' and Mildred laughed, 'I have delivered my testimony, as Mause in "Old Mortality" would say. You didn't think I could get so excited, but if there is one thing in the world I dread more than another, it is prejudice. Perhaps,' and her manner became graver, 'it is because I know that I have a tendency to it.'

'If I am prejudiced, I don't know how to find it out,' said Ella.

'One can easily test one's self,' replied Mildred. 'You are fond of me, you are not fond of Aunt Bertha. Suppose each of us had done something very noble, or written something very clever, which should you admire the most?'

The reply was a hearty kiss.

'Thank you for the kiss, dear child, but not thank you for the prejudice.'

'Seeing a fault is not curing it, though,' said Ella.

'It is the first step towards it. I found out my own prejudice before Mr Lester came, when we had a clergyman whose manner I disliked extremely, but who really was a very good man, and preached excellent sermons. In those days I was not quite such a cripple as I am now ; at least, I was able to go to church oftener. I discovered that, instead of thinking of what the clergyman was saying in church, I was always criticising his unpleasant manner, or some particular expression which I disliked. One day he preached a sermon which my father admired very much, and as usual I cried it down, and seized upon certain sentences which I disliked. The next week I was reading a new volume of sermons by a person whom I especially reverenced, and I actually found this very same sermon amongst them. I really was shocked at myself, and from that day I set to work to cure myself of prejudice.'

'I dare say you did it at once,' observed Ella; 'you could never have had any difficulty in conquering your faults, Aunt Mildred.'

'I beg your pardon, Ella ; it has been the work of years. You know I scarcely see any persons except the few living near Cleve and Encombe ; and that kind of life certainly tends to encourage prejudice. However I do try to guard against it.'

'But how?' inquired Ella.

'When I am going to meet a person whom I think I shall dislike, I try to give up any preconceived idea I may have formed of his character, and to judge him only by what actually comes before me.'

'That is so difficult,' said Ella.

'Yes ; and for that very reason a rule I have made for myself is never, if I can avoid it, to express an unfavourable opinion of anything said or done by a person whom I don't like, until I have thought the question over twice.   If it is impossible to praise I try to be silent.'

'But, Aunt Mildred, I do dearly love hearty likes and dislikes. That constant caution is so tame.'

'I go with you entirely, Ella.   Like or dislike actions or principles as much as you choose, and I will join with you to your heart's content.   But there is no real, honest approval or disapproval in prejudice.   It is a mere petty, narrow-minded, uncharitable giving way to personal feeling, the only thing about it which is not exclusive being that it is common to all sides and all parties.'

'Good people as well as bad ; then one need not be so ashamed of it,' said Ella.   .

'Prejudice again, Ella.   A fault is a fault, whoever is guilty of it.   I can't help thinking myself, indeed, that it is all the worse when it is found amongst the good, and I am sure it does more mischief.   Truth requires no support from prejudice ; it needs only the faith of those who profess to fight for it.'

'Dear Aunt Mildred, you are so tired,' said Ella ; and she looked at her aunt anxiously.

Mildred smiled.   'That is because I have been talking so much, Ella ; but you don't know what a rare thing it is for me to find any one to whom I can speak out freely, except perhaps, Mɪ Lester, and I see him so seldom.   I lie on my sofa and read in the newspapers what is going on in the world ; all the prejudice, and bitterness, and party-feeling ; till at last I become so interested and excited that I feel as if I really could bear my solitude no longer ; and sometimes I write it all out, and sometimes I talk it out, and that is what I have done to-day.   But it is not wise.'

'When I am gone from you, you will be in solitude again,' observed Ella.

'Yes, but you must come and see me often ; I feel as if I had learned to know you now.'

'To know how bad I am,' replied Ella.

'To know how good you may be, rather.   Ella, dear, you have done wonders lately.'

'Because I have had you to help me and keep me up.   I have had sympathy : Aunt Mildred, that is what I require.'

'What you would like, you mean,' replied Mildred. 'We require only what we have.'

'It does not seem so at home,' said Ella, sorrowfully.

'Is any one of your duties too much for you?' inquired Mildred.

'Not any one exactly, but all together are.'

'That can scarcely be. Duties are not like soldiers. We don't confront them in masses, but singly. When two come together, one is forced to yield.'

'But it is possible to be wearied with fighting singly,' said Ella.

'Ah! there I grant you is the difficulty, especially with persons who are a little inclined to be lazy;' and Mildred looked at Ella and smiled. 'But, Ella, there is a remedy for that too. To use another simile, indolent people, who have not strength to swallow their disagreeable duties at one dose, should learn to sip them by degrees.'

'I don't understand what you mean by sipping,' replied Ella.

'Each day's duty is a drop, and we are never required to take more at a time. However indolent we may be, we can rouse ourselves to swallow the drop; and if we do this every day, we shall have the victory in the end quite as surely as if we had endeavoured to take the whole at once.'

'But persons never can take the whole at once,' replied Ella. 'They can't tell what will be required of them.'

'They can rouse themselves to the effort of resolution,' replied Mildred; 'and if you inquire, you will find that in many cases this is done. When a duty is put before a very energetic, persevering person, it is generally seized and determined upon at once. I mean in this way :—Take the case of a bad temper. Energy generally goes with it. An energetic person making a humble resolution to strive against ill temper will not always succeed; yet the resolution once taken, its impetus is sufficient, through God's grace, to carry him on for years. Of course, constant watchfulness, and self-recollection, and, above all, fervent prayer, are necessary;—but once let it be determined that the evil shall be subdued, and, humanly speaking, it is subdued. The resolution made cannot be shaken. So it is with bad habits, evil company; one earnest exertion of the will, in dependence upon God's help, and the victory is gained for life. This I call being able to swallow the duties of a life at once; and a great advantage it is : only, when we are inclined to envy

it, we must remember that special dangers go with special
blessings. There is a risk of self-reliance in this strength of
purpose. It requires great watchfulness not to be led to rest on
ourselves, when we find that what we resolve to do we can do.'

'It must make it much more easy to be good, though,' said
Ella.

'Perhaps so, in some ways; but indolence is not so very difficult to cure if it is properly dealt with. What I meant in your
case by sipping your duties was, that you should not try to make
the strong resolution I have named to subdue a fault at once.
Resolve for one or two days, or for a week, and learn to leave the
rest to God. Don't ever allow yourself to think of what it will
be to continue striving for your whole life. Our Lord's warning
about earthly anxieties is equally applicable to spiritual ones—
"Sufficient unto the day is the evil thereof." You must remember that to discipline ourselves properly, it is necessary to accept
our characters as they are, not to deal with them as if they were
what they are not. A very indolent and changeable person
cannot possibly make the strong resolution which will carry him
through life ; but a continuous determination will do the same
work as a strong one. And it is a great point, Ella, to keep ourselves from being disheartened. Half our task would be done, if
we were sure of success.'

Tears gathered in Ella's eyes, and, resting her arm upon
Mildred's pillow, she said, 'I have more cause to be disheartened than any one, for I have made so many resolutions,
and strong ones too.'

'Excitable resolutions, you mean, dear Ella,' replied Mildred.
'There is a vast difference between strength and excitement.'

'I don't feel the difference.'

'Strength is quietness, calmness ; the power to foresee difficulties without shrinking from them. It is the effect of reason
rather than of feeling ; and where it exists, it is accompanied by
a certain consciousness of power granted by God, which is, in
the warfare of the soul, what the courage of the soldier is who
has never been known to retreat in battle.'

'Oh ! if I did but possess it !' exclaimed Ella.

'It is nature, not grace,' replied Mildred ; 'and grace can
make up for all the deficiencies of nature. Only we must remember that grace will not destroy nature,—it will but guide it.
Once more, dear Ella, I would entreat you to deal with yourself
wisely ; and whatever resolutions you may make, let them be for

a day, a week, or at the very utmost a month, and then renewed. So, through God's mercy, we may trust that you will have that prestige of victory which carries us half-way towards our next success.'

'And I must go home to-day and begin,' said Ella, mournfully.

'I hope not. My father would like to keep you here; and I think your grandmamma will wish to please him.'

'It is not grandmamma, it is Aunt Bertha,' said Ella; and then, seeing Mildred look a little grave, she added, 'Aunt Bertha thinks I am only a trouble here; but it is not quite that, is it?'

'Not since you have taken to reading out to grandpapa at night, certainly,' said Mildred, kindly.

'And he let me walk with him yesterday,' continued Ella; 'and we got on beautifully till he fancied, I am sure, that he saw Captain Vivian talking to Clement, and then he turned away, and scarcely spoke again. I found afterwards that it was not Captain Vivian, but I didn't venture to tell him so; was I right?'

'Perhaps so. I can scarcely tell. It depends so much upon the mood he is in.'

Ella looked thoughtful. 'Aunt Mildred, there are some questions I should like very much to ask you, only I am afraid you wouldn't like them.'

'Then don't ask them,' replied Mildred, a little quickly, but checking herself, directly, she added, 'Doubtful questions are always better avoided, unless there is some good to be obtained by them.'

Ella was evidently rather disappointed.

'You shall have them all answered some day, dear Ella, but I doubt if this is the time.'

'There would be no opportunity, if it was the time,' said Ella, as she went to the door. 'I am sure I heard the hall-bell. It must be Aunt Bertha.'

She went a few steps into the passage without remarking how very pale Mildred looked, or in the least guessing her feelings. For herself, there was some excitement in the idea of doing the honours of the Hall, in spite of the little pleasure she had in seeing her aunt.

Ella was right; it was Bertha, and she ran up to her quickly. Bertha's manner was kind, but extremely nervous; and her first question was, whether General Vivian was at home?

S

'No; it is his hour for going into the park; he won't be in for another half-hour or more. How are they all at home, Aunt Bertha?'

'Pretty well; tolerable. You are quite sure General Vivian is gone out?'

'Oh yes; grandpapa is in the park, isn't he, Greaves?' and Ella turned to the gray-headed butler, who was the General's confidential servant.

'The General went out about ten minutes since, ma'am. He will return to luncheon at one.'

'And you will stay to luncheon, Aunt Bertha? I don't think you have ever seen the dining-room, have you? It is such a beautiful room.'

Twenty years before, Bertha had once been in that room, on the occasion of a public meeting, the first at which she had ever been present. It was a dream of awful grandeur to her,—one of the most impressive of her youthful recollections; and she could recall the stately courtesy of the General,—the polished civility of his manner, giving that undefinable impression of dislike which can neither be reasoned against nor overcome; and Edward Vivian,—young, handsome, full of hope and energy, distinguishing himself by a speech of considerable talent,—and Flora listening with her head bent down, but with a rapt attention, which had been the first thing that awakened in Bertha's mind the perception of her attachment. Yes, they were memorable associations connected with the great dining-room at Cleve Hall. Bertha had no wish to disturb them by the sight of the stern old man,—the martyr to his own principle,—sitting alone in his proud consciousness of rectitude, amidst the ruins of happiness which himself had caused; and she hurried on with her eyes dizzy, her memory full of shadowy images, and scarcely conscious whether she was walking in dream or in reality, until she found herself at the door of Mildred's apartment.

Ella threw it open eagerly. She was amused and excited, and her eyes were bright with animation,—a strange contrast to the cold and self-restrained, yet somewhat furtive glance which Bertha cast around her, as, for the first time, since the events which had shed a gloom over both their lives, she stood face to face with Mildred Vivian.

'Ella, dear, draw the easy-chair near for your aunt. I am such a cripple, Miss Campbell, that it is difficult to move; but I can give a welcome still;' and Mildred held out her hand,

and the rebellious tears which rose to dim her eyes were kept back by a strong effort, as she added, with a winning smile, ' I think I ought to quarrel with you for not having come to see me before.'

'I fancied you seldom received visitors,' was Bertha's reply, uttered with a quietness and precision which even Mildred's quick perception could not have discovered to be a cloak for painful feelings.

'Not very often ; we have so few neighbours ; but,'—Mildred was a little confused by Bertha's composed gaze, and rather hesitated, as she added, ' I hoped that Ella's being here might have proved an inducement ; but it is rather a long walk.'

'I am a very good walker,' replied Bertha, not accepting the excuse. 'It is scarcely more than a mile and three quarters by the cliff.'

'Oh, you came that way, did you ?' Mildred's voice showed her relief at having reached an easy topic : 'the wind must have been rather high.'

'Rather ; but it was deliciously fresh. Ella, shall you mind returning that way ? '

'Return, must I ? O Aunt Bertha ! '

'Grandmamma thinks you have had rather a long holiday,' continued Bertha.

'But I have not been at all idle, have I, Aunt Mildred? especially the last week. I have worked much more regularly than at home.'

'If Mrs Campbell could spare her a little longer, I think my father would be pleased,' said Mildred. 'She reads to him in the evening, and I think he will miss her.'

Bertha's face lighted up in an instant. 'Of course,' she said, ' if General Vivian wishes her to remain, it would cause a difference.'

'And she has been walking with him, lately,' continued Mildred ; 'making herself much more useful than I can. I am only afraid,' she added, with an air of interest, 'that her absence will throw a burden upon you with the little ones. I wish I was near enough to help you.'

With any other person the wish might have seemed only matter of civility ; but there was an innate truth in Mildred's manner which made it impossible to take what she said for mere words. Bertha's ' Thank you,' was cordial.

'Ella tells me that you give her a great deal of assistance always with the children,' continued Mildred. 'That must be rather troublesome, when Mrs Campbell is such an invalid.'

'Aunt Mildred tells me I am not to let you help me any more.' said Ella, bluntly. 'And if I were to go home now, perhaps I should be good and do it all myself quite properly. I have made a number of resolutions.'

Bertha's face was graver than the speech required, and Mildred, fearing a lecture, said lightly, 'Aunt Bertha will think with me, perhaps, Ella, that good deeds are worth more than good resolutions ; however, I give you credit for both here.'

'I have had experience of Ella's good resolutions,' said Bertha, coldly ; 'but I am glad she has improved in any way.'

Nothing, perhaps, tests humility more than being told one is improved. Ella had not yet reached the degree of lowliness which would permit her to hear it with patience, and she said angrily, 'I know, Aunt Bertha, you are not likely to give me a character for improvement.'

A very gentle sigh escaped Mildred ; Ella heard it and went up to her : 'You are vexed with me, Aunt Mildred. I ought not to speak out so ; but Aunt Bertha never gives me much credit for anything.'

'I dare say she gives you as much as you deserve, and perhaps a great deal more,' said Mildred, smiling. 'But suppose you take your books up-stairs now, if you really are not going home, and leave Aunt Bertha and myself to talk a little together, we shall find a good many things to say which will not exactly concern you.'

The bright, loving face was very inviting for a kiss, and Ella gave one, and said, in a half whisper, that she did not think she left her character in very good hands, and then departed ; whilst Bertha sat in silent astonishment at the ready obedience to a request which, if she had made it herself, would have been followed by the moodiness of hours.

CHAPTER XXXIV.

WHEN Ella was gone, Bertha's manner was much changed. It was as though she felt more at ease with herself, and had lost the unpleasant consciousness that her acts were watched and commented upon. Mildred, on the contrary, was more awkward. It might have seemed that she had topics to bring forward which she was studying how to introduce. She made an observation upon Ella's unusual height, and then paused for an answer, which was given her by Bertha's walking up to the sofa, and placing a note before her saying, 'Mr Lester begged me to give you this : he is gone to London.' Mildred's speaking countenance in a moment betrayed her feelings whilst she read the note ; her face was of an ashy paleness ; when it was ended, she laid it down gently, and said, raising her eyes steadily to Bertha's, 'Then the hour is come for action ?'

'Mr Lester thinks so,' was Bertha's reply.

Mildred said in a low voice, 'Thank God !' and there was a pause.

'Suspicion is the worst of all evils,' observed Bertha.

Mildred appeared scarcely to hear her, and only answered, 'Mr Lester tells me you will give me details.'

Bertha drew her chair nearer ; it was an involuntary movement of sympathy. Mildred noticed it. 'We have one feeling,' she said.

'Yes, I hope so. O Miss Vivian ! how will it end ?'

'Not Miss Vivian—Mildred, if you will—we have so many interests in common.' She took Bertha's hand affectionately.

That little movement !—Bertha could never have made it herself,—but it touched the secret chord of cherished and hidden feelings ; she forgot that Mildred was a Vivian as she answered, 'I always hear you called Mildred, but few call me Bertha.'

'May I be one of the few ? It would seem most natural, for Edward calls you so.'

'It is strange that he should,—your brother.'

'Why strange ! where would his comfort, his hope, his children have been without you ? I have so often longed to thank you.'

'I have only done my duty,' replied Bertha.

'But none can do more. He must thank you himself. He does deeply, heartily ; but perhaps he has never found words to say it rightly.'

'He has other things to think of than gratitude now,' replied Bertha.

'He ought not to have. Yet perhaps we must forgive him if he is engrossed. Is this determination his own ?'

'No ; Mr Lester's. He thinks that concealment is no longer

safe. Goff has been making friends with one of the servants at the Rectory : taking the letters to the post; and we suspect prying into them. We can't tell how much he knows, but something, we are nearly sure, he has discovered.'

Mildred was silent ; but her hand shook tremulously.

Bertha went on. 'We only found this out yesterday. Mr Lester had no time to write, except those few lines. He left me to tell you all. He has no settled plan yet ; he says he can't form any till he has seen Edward ; then he means to write to you, and'——

'And what ?' Mildred regarded her anxiously.

'He must trust to you to prepare General Vivian's mind for the knowledge that Edward is in England, unless——it struck me whether it might be better that they should meet without preparation.'

'No, never !' Mildred started up. 'I beg your pardon ; I did not mean to be so hasty ; but it might be his death.'

Bertha's colour rose, and she looked much distressed.

'I know it has been Mr Lester's notion,' continued Mildred ; 'and it might have answered last year, but my father appears very much shaken within the last few months. We might ruin all by such incautiousness. No one knows him,' she added, her voice sinking. 'Mr Lester thinks him hard ; he is hard externally ; hard in his own eyes ; but he is a father still.'

'But there must be no delay,' said Bertha, with something of her former coldness and determination.

Mildred shrank a little from her manner ; but the feeling was scarcely perceptible in her tone, as she replied, 'No, indeed ; if there is danger for Edward, how could there be delay ?' Yet she spoke doubtfully, perhaps unwilling to comprehend the possibility of danger.

'Mr Lester thinks that both Captain Vivian and Goff have reasons for being your brother's deadly enemies,' continued Bertha.

'I know it. There is a mystery ; but my father has never allowed me to approach the subject. He has never mentioned Edward's name since—since that fatal day.'

'If they are his enemies, there must be danger,' continued Bertha ; 'they are both desperate men.'

Mildred clasped her hands in silent prayer. 'The God who has protected him hitherto will protect him still,' she said. 'But I wish I could have seen Mr Lester himself.'

'He felt it better not to wait,' replied Bertha. 'It was only yesterday we discovered what Goff had been doing. Of course there was a motive for his interference. Perhaps it was unwise to send our letters as we did, but we had not calculated on any risk. It seemed only natural that Mr Lester should write to Mr Bruce, and your letters and mine were always enclosed in his. Mr Lester said it was best to go to London immediately, for he could not trust to any more letters.'

Mildred remained silent for some seconds, as if forming some inward resolution ; then she looked up at Bertha, and said, 'You will think of me, and pray for me : none can tell the effort it will be to speak to my father.'

Bertha's softer feelings were touched; and she answered gently and kindly, ' God's help is always with those who live for the happiness of others.'

' I hope so ; if one does live for that purpose. Yet I have never been able to make my father happy.'

'General Vivian does not give me the idea of an unhappy man,' said Bertha, with a bluntness which was somewhat painful.

'Possibly not. I have heard it said before ; but, Bertha'— the name was spoken in a tone of apology—'must one not live with persons daily before one can venture to judge of that deep question of happiness ? '

'Yes, indeed,' Bertha spoke eagerly ; ' I know none can judge.'

'Not the nearest and dearest, at times,' continued Mildred ; 'still less those who only see others as the world has seen my father—in public meetings and formal society. It has been his pride to appear happy, and he has succeeded with all but me.'

'And Mr Lester and Mrs Robinson,' observed Bertha. 'They have always said that he was a crushed and broken-hearted man.'

' The wound which God makes, God will and can heal,' said Mildred. 'There is no healing for that which we open for ourselves.' She dashed away a tear from her eyes, as she added, in a low voice, ' My poor father l his sorrow is greater than Edward's.'

' It would scarcely seem so to those who look upon them,' observed Bertha.

'Ah l I forgot,' and Mildred's face became suddenly animated ; 'you have seen Edward. Is he changed ? Does he look very old—older than I do ?' and she smiled, and then, in a sadder tone, added, 'Perhaps we may not recognise each other.'

' He does not look like General Vivian's son,' replied Bertha.

' Then he is changed,—he was so like ! See !' she unclasped her locket ; ' should you have known it ? '

' I should have remembered it,' replied Bertha, regarding the miniature closely. The allusion was painful,—for an instant it carried both back to the days when they had met as strangers, having a mutual antipathy : and when the first thought of a near connection had been the death-knell of their happiness.

Bertha was the first to speak again. 'Ella is like it,' she said.

'Yes, very ; much more so than Clement, though they are twins.'

' There is such talent in it,' said Bertha, still looking at the miniature.

' Yes, but Ella will surpass both her father and her brother in that. She is wonderfully clever.'

' Talent thrown away,' said Bertha, shortly.

Her tone was like the opening of a closed door to Mildred, it revealed such intricacies of feeling. ' Is it thrown away ?' she asked, with some hesitation.

' It may not be yet, but it will be. It produces no fruits.'

' It wants culture,' observed Mildred.

' A great deal has been given her, but it is useless.'

' She seems young to say so.'

' Yes, if she were not so clever.'

' But disproportionate talent becomes awkwardness,' continued Mildred.

' That didn't strike me before. I don't know now that I can tell what it means.'

Mildred waited for a moment. An effort was needed for the reply, which at the moment she could scarcely make. Yet she conquered her reluctance, and turning from the subject of all-engrossing interest, answered in a tone as unconcerned as Bertha's : 'Moral powers and mental powers take different times for growth, I imagine. Mental powers appear to spring up rapidly, whilst moral powers require a lifetime to come to anything like maturity. So one is continually struck with a sense of disproportion between talent and goodness, and then comes disappointment.'

' Certainly, I don't know a more disappointing person than Ella,' observed Bertha, in the same cold tone.

'I think she is very disappointing till one begins to understand her.'

'Understanding doesn't help me,' observed Bertha.

'Doesn't it? I should have thought it would have kept you
from expecting too much.'

'But how can you help expecting a great deal from a person
who can talk and reason like a woman of thirty when she is only
sixteen, and can acquire more knowledge in a day than others
can in months or years?'

'According to my theory, this is only intellectual growth,'
said Mildred, 'and therefore must not be depended upon for
action.'

'But it ought to be power,' said Bertha.

'Scarcely,—I should say indeed that it tends rather to weakness, like any other want of proportion.'

Bertha looked doubtful, and again Mildred was obliged to
urge herself to continue the conversation by remembering that
it might be long before a like opportunity would recur.

'I confess to having a theory about proportion, very vague,
and perhaps very unfounded,—but one must think of something
when one is obliged to spend hours alone upon a sofa;—an idea,
it is, that the principles of all beauty, both physical and moral,
are to be found in proportion,—that perfect beauty is nothing
more than perfect proportion,—and that perfect goodness is the
same. But all that is very dreamy, and not much to the purpose; only I think one can see as one goes on in life, that the
characters which leave the most lasting impress upon the world
are those in which the mental and moral powers are the most
equally balanced. So I fancy, if I had the management of a
child, that is what I should the most strive to attain.'

'And if you had the management of Ella, what should you do?'

'I can scarcely tell till I have seen what she is at home.'

'But you can form some idea; what is it you think she
wants?'

'Sunshine,' said Mildred, smiling; and seeing that Bertha
looked a little annoyed at not receiving a clearer answer, she
continued, 'Ella's intellectual growth seems to have been so
rapid as to cast a shade over her moral growth, if one may so
speak. Perhaps, therefore, she wants hope, encouragement,
cheerful sympathy, and patience, to expand and foster her better
feelings. She is morbid now, and wayward, and has a great
tendency to unreality.'

'She is very unreal,' observed Bertha.

'Would she be if she understood herself?' inquired Mildred. 'She deceives herself now because she fancies that talking of goodness, which is an effort of the mind, is the same thing as carrying it out in practice, which is the work of the heart. But I think she is beginning to open her eyes to the vast difference; when she sees it clearly, the danger I should fear would be despair.'

'She does have fits of despondency now,' observed Bertha.

'And I suppose then the right thing would be to give her encouragement,' said Mildred.

'It is so difficult, when she is continually vexing and disappointing one,' replied Bertha.

'Still, without encouragement—without sunshine,—how can there be any growth?' asked Mildred, gently.

'Yes, I suppose you are right. I dare say I manage her very badly.'

'She must be exceedingly trying,—especially to a person who has fixed principles of right, and always acts upon them.'

'Not always,' said Bertha, quickly; 'very seldom.'

Mildred smiled. 'Perhaps others can judge for us better than we can of ourselves on such points.'

'I know we ought to give sympathy,' said Bertha.

'Yes, because one receives it; and what should one be without it?'

A shade of sorrowful thought crossed Bertha's face. She said abruptly, 'Can people acquire sympathy?'

'I think—I hope so. Most of us have very little of it by nature.'

'I have none.'

'Oh! indeed, indeed!' Mildred raised herself up eagerly; 'If you had not sympathy, how could you have done what you have! And Mr Lester tells me of others who are indebted to you. Ronald Vivian, for instance.'

'That is from circumstances,' replied Bertha, her changing voice showing the quickness of her feelings.

'But if we have sympathy in any one case, it proves that we have the power within us, only we may not know how to exercise it.'

'Then it is useless.'

'Yes, till we teach ourselves better.'

'That is the question. I don't think we can teach ourselves; it is a feeling.'

'But we make ourselves feel by action.'

'I don't know that. I can't act well without feeling at all.'

'Perhaps you don't understand yourself,' said Mildred. 'I am sure you feel a great deal more than you know.'

'Whatever sympathy I may have, it is not enough for the children,' said Bertha.

'It may be their fault in a great degree; and they must be so different from you.'

'Yes, Ella and Fanny are, and Clement too. I can understand Louisa better.'

'But I suppose it may be possible to practise putting one's self in the place of the children,' said Mildred, 'trying as a matter of reason to see with their eyes and feel with their feelings.'

'But reason won't be of any use,' persisted Bertha.

'I should have thought it might be. I should have imagined that it was one of the chief instruments which God has given us to help us to guide others; one of the great causes of the superiority of a mature mind over a young one.'

'I don't understand,' said Bertha, as shortly as before, but with a greater show of interest.

Mildred felt that she must follow the leading of her strange companion, who seemed to have no perception that this was not the moment for carrying on abstract inquiries upon education, so she continued—

'I suppose this kind of reasoning, and trying to place one's self in the position of another, is the best way of learning sympathy; and children we see can't avail themselves of it thoroughly, for they don't know what a grown-up person feels. But we have passed through childhood and youth, and have only to make an effort of memory to recall our own difficulties, and by that means understand their troubles.'

'But all children are not alike,' persisted Bertha. 'How is it possible to reason upon feelings which we have never had?'

'Imagination, I suppose, may help us,' said Mildred, 'and books—fiction, which many grave people laugh at. Whatever displays human nature truly, is an assistance to the lesson of sympathy. And then, too, the least sympathy invites confidence, and confidence is experience, and experience enables us to give greater sympathy. You see there is a continued reaction if we can only make up our minds to begin.'

'And how would you show Ella sympathy?' inquired Bertha,

her mind turning at once from general theories to a direct object.'

'I know how I should act myself,' replied Mildred. 'I could not venture to say what any other person should do.'

'But what would you do yourself?'

'I think I should try always to bear in mind her constitutional indolence, and so, as a beginning, not expect her to be energetic; and whenever she did exert herself, I should praise her, even for a very slight amount of energy. Then, as to her pride and self-will, I should endeavour to make allowance for them, by judging her not according to what, strictly speaking, she ought to be, but according to the effort which she would need to be humble and obedient. I should remember too that her very talents are her temptation, causing her to be carried away by feeling and excitement, and I should try to throw myself into her pursuits, for the very purpose of being a balance to her mind. Perhaps by this kind of watchfulness I might avoid irritating her, or being irritated myself, which I am sure I should be otherwise.'

'Yes,' replied Bertha, speaking more freely when she found that Mildred could share, or at least comprehend her difficulties, 'that is the great trouble after all; she is provoking and I am angry, and then I dare say I speak out quickly.'

'She has made me speak out quickly several times since she has been here,' replied Mildred. 'I am just beginning to learn to think twice before I find fault.'

'But don't you find that spoils her?' inquired Bertha. 'I am sure people require to be stirred by a quick word now and then.'

'Quick words are sometimes very good for quick natures,' replied Mildred, 'but I doubt if they are good with slow ones.'

'Ella, slow! oh no; she is immensely quick.'

'Intellectually, not morally. I think quick words repel her, and make her creep like a snail into its shell. Besides, I fancy they only do if one is generally very affectionate in manner; that in a degree neutralises the quickness.'

'And I am not affectionate, I know,' said Bertha, candidly. 'I dare say Ella has complained of me.'

'She thinks you are more fond of the little ones,' was Mildred's evasive answer; and Bertha, not satisfied, put the question again more directly.

'I can scarcely call it complaint,' replied Mildred. 'She thinks you don't understand her, but she is quite aware that a great deal is her own fault.'

'And do you understand her?' inquired Bertha, quickly.

'I am not sure that I do, but I see some things in her very like my brother. I don't encourage her, though, in that notion of not being understood; it is an excuse for a great deal of sentimentality, and even selfishness of feeling, in young people. I always tell her that you and every one else would understand her if she would only try to act up to her principles, and be humble and considerate; but it is such an age for moods, and fancies, and pet griefs, one must be merciful to it.'

Bertha had not been at all merciful to Mildred, who was nearly tired out, but there had been a painful fascination in this conversation with a person whom hitherto she had regarded with a kind of respectful antipathy, which carried her beyond what she had in any way intended. It was a pleasure to be drawn on, even though in a certain degree against her will. She did not see that on Mildred's side there was a continual effort : she only felt that even if they differed, they were not antagonistic. Mildred had said nothing hard of Ella, quite the contrary; yet she could see and acknowledge her faults : and neither had she been flattering to herself; she had suggested, indeed, several possible blunders in education, but it was always as though she herself was the person liable to make them. The effect of the conversation was unquestionably soothing, and when at length Bertha was recalled from it by the striking of the clock, which warned her that it was time to return home, she rose with evident regret.

The feeling was not shared by Mildred,—solitude, leisure for thought, was her one longing desire. Yet even then she could throw herself into Bertha's character; and she asked again, as a special favour, that Ella might be allowed to remain.

It was a well-timed and well-turned request. Bertha liked deference. She was a little sensitive as to her position with the children, and had an undefined dread of Mildred's influence and interference. Two aunts on different sides might very well have found matter for disagreement; but Mildred was thoroughly unselfish, and had no love of power. Bertha's answer was very cordial. She was quite sure that her mother would consent; there could not be any objection, if General Vivian liked it.

The point settled, Ella was summoned.

The look of delight which followed the announcement of the permission was a little painful to Bertha ; but she had learned something, much indeed, in that half-hour's interview with Mildred, and, instead of thinking of her own chilled feelings, she threw herself into Ella's pleasure. 'Shall you want any books sent you, Ella ? The Cleve carrier will call to-morrow morning.'

'Aunt Bertha, thank you ! yes ;' and Ella's eyes sparkled at this unlooked-for instance of consideration. She ran out of the room to make out a list.

Bertha drew near to Mildred. Now, for the first time, she perceived that the conversation had been carried on too long. Yet Mildred smiled, and said she should be quite well after luncheoh.

'Strong people forget what weak ones feel,' said Bertha, in a tone of self-reproach.

'And weak ones are a great trouble and burden to strong ones; but I am most grateful to you for having come.'

' I hope I shan't forget what you have said,' observed Bertha, bluntly.

Mildred smiled. ' I dare say I make many mistakes. It is all theory,—I have had no practical experience.'

' But you must have thought a good deal.'

'About my own faults; that teaches more than any-thing.'

' May I come and see you again sometimes ?'

A very awkward question. General Vivian might not at all like to see Miss Campbell frequently at his house.

Mildred could only answer it honestly. 'Will you let me write and ask you to come? It may be the best plan.'

Bertha understood, and coloured deeply.

' It is not my will, nor my doing, you will believe, I am sure,' said Mildred, timidly.

Bertha felt very contradictory, but she was too good to give way to the feeling. ' I suppose it may be the best plan,' she answered, in a tone tolerably free from restraint.

'Thank you very much for understanding ; but I shall hear from you.'

' Yes ; if there is anything to communicate. I scarcely see what there can be.'

'One lives always in fear and expectation,' said Mildred. She sighed, and the sigh revealed to Bertha that the sister's anxiety was far keener than her own could be.

She reproached herself, and said, 'I have been troubling you about Ella, and asking your advice,—I ought not to have done it now.'

'It has done me good, by distracting my thoughts. I shall try not to think till the time comes. Mr Lester, you suppose, will write to-morrow?'

'I imagine so. He was going direct to your brother, and I know he is anxious that no time should be lost.'

'Then God help us all!' said Mildred; and Bertha silently echoed the prayer.

Ella came back again with the list of books, and asked a good many questions about home, to which Bertha answered fully and kindly; but Mildred did not speak again until just at the last moment, when, as Bertha was wishing her a final good-bye, she said, in a voice so low as to be inaudible to Ella, 'If Mr Lester is away, keep Clement at home.'

'Yes, if I can; but he is so wilful.'

Bertha departed; and Mildred, too tired to talk more to Ella, or even to listen to reading, lay quite still, thinking upon the practical experience which life had given her of all that is involved in that common word—wilful.

CHAPTER XXXV.

'HAS the postman been yet, Louisa?' It was Mrs Campbell's question when she came down to breakfast on the second day after Bertha's visit to the Hall, and it was addressed to Louisa as a matter of course, for no one else was so certain to be on the watch—at least so Mrs Campbell thought. She was not aware that Bertha, in her anxiety, had stationed herself at the shrubbery gate to intercept the letters before they were delivered at the house. Louisa's answer was in the negative; but almost immediately afterwards Bertha entered, laid the letters on the table, and left the room. Louisa saw that Bertha had secured her own; Mrs Campbell saw nothing but that there was a long epistle from an old friend, and this she began to read.

Bertha came back to read prayers and make breakfast; again,

no one but Louisa noticed that she was less quiet and indifferent than usual, and certainly no one else would have had the quickness to suspect the cause, or the overweening curiosity to inquire into it. But Louisa had no mercy when the indulgence of her besetting propensity was in question, and as soon as they were seated at the breakfast-table she began the attack. 'Aunt Bertha, when is Mr Lester coming back?'

'I don't know, my dear.'

'But he is only gone for a few days, is he?'

'I can't say, my dear.'

'Rachel said she hoped he would return soon.'

'Very possibly, my dear.'

A pause, and a little diversion of Louisa's thoughts, from the fact that Betsey came in with a message from a poor woman, which, of course, she fully attended to. But she began again. 'Mr Lester is gone to London, isn't he, Aunt Bertha?'

'I believe so.'

'Rachel said she thought you would hear if he were coming back to-day or to-morrow, because he told her that perhaps he might be obliged to send her a message through you instead of writing himself.'

'Perhaps so.'

'But can't I give the message for you? I am going up to the Rectory after breakfast.'

'Thank you, Louisa,'—Bertha's tone was chilling and reproachful,—'but I can take care of my own messages.'

'Oh! I beg your pardon, Aunt Bertha; I only meant to save you the trouble.' Louisa was satisfied then. She had learned what she wished to know, that Mr Lester had written. She went on: 'Then if Mr Lester doesn't come back, Rachel may come and stay here, mayn't she?'

'We will see about it.'

Here Mrs Campbell interposed: 'I can't have Rachel staying here. She can come to drink tea as she did last night; but I don't want her this week; the servants are busy.'

'Mr Lester must be coming back by Saturday,' persisted Louisa, in a disappointed tone.

'Very likely, my dear; but I can't have Rachel staying here; I won't allow it.'

Louisa looked extremely disconcerted, and repeated that Mr Lester would be at home on Saturday, and then they should not have Rachel for weeks.

'Louisa, that is very perverse,' said Bertha. 'You know that Mr Lester never objects to Rachel's coming here, except when she has some special engagement at home.'

'I don't understand. What is all this fuss about Rachel and Mr Lester?' inquired Mrs Campbell.

Bertha's quick reply was, 'Oh! nothing of any consequence;' which did not satisfy Mrs Campbell.

'But where is Mr Lester? When did you say he was coming home?'

'Some time this week he hopes it may be,' replied Bertha.

'When he does come he can bring down that packet of tea for us,' observed Mrs Campbell. 'Remember you ask him, Bertha.'

'I don't know the exact day when he is coming,' replied Bertha.'

'He must be back by Sunday,' persisted Louisa.

'Or he must have some one to take his duty,' observed Fanny, delighted at the idea of novelty.

'He will be sure to be back by Saturday,' said Clement, in a very moody tone. 'I never knew him stay away yet.'

'What is to keep him, Bertha; do you know? Have you heard from him?'

Louisa's eyes sparkled with amusement. Her grandmamma had asked precisely the question she was longing to put.

Bertha could not avoid a direct answer. 'I had a few lines from him this morning,' she said. 'He does not mention when he shall be at home.'

'But is it business he has gone for, or what? It was quite a sudden notion.'

'Rachel said she thought he was gone to see a friend,' observed Louisa.

'My dear Louisa, I didn't ask you. Pray don't answer unless you are spoken to. Your aunt will tell me. Is it any friend we know, Bertha?'

Louisa whispered loudly to Fanny that she was sure it was Mr Bruce, because she happened to see the direction of a parcel Mr Lester took with him, and it was the same as that on Mr Bruce's letters; and Fanny communicated the fact to Clement; whilst Bertha, blushing and hesitating, answered, evasively, that she never inquired into Mr Lester's private affairs.

'That is no answer, my dear Bertha; what is all this mystery? I can't bear mysteries. Why shouldn't you say to me that he is

T

gone to see Mr Bruce, if he is gone?' Mrs Campbell spoke very fretfully, and Louisa glanced at Clement in triumph.

Bertha felt she must speak out at once. 'Mr Lester talked of seeing Mr Bruce,' she replied; 'and he says to-day that he is kept in London, because Mr Bruce is not very well. He doesn't mention the day of his return, and he thinks it may be necessary to provide for his Sunday duty. He writes, besides, about some little parish matters.'

'Well! but let me see the letter; can't you show it me?'

'There are one or two things private in it,' said Bertha; 'I am afraid he wouldn't like it.'

That was sufficient to annoy Mrs Campbell for the whole day. If Louisa had wished to render every one about her uncomfortable, she had most certainly succeeded; and she had punished herself too, for she was very quick in discovering the impression she had made, and could see plainly that it was not likely to be a smooth day with Aunt Bertha.

She said very little during the remainder of the breakfast, and when it was over went up to Clement.

'Clement, what is the matter about Mr Lester and Mr Bruce? and why does Aunt Bertha make such a mystery about it all?'

'I don't know; how should I?' was Clement's blunt reply.

'But you do know something, I am sure.'

'Not I. How you do tease, Louisa!'

'And how cross you are, Clement! and you were cross all yesterday; it was that reckoning made you cross. Who gave it to you to do? Did Mr Lester?'

'Nonsense, nobody. What on earth do you pry into my concerns for!' Clement spoke very impatiently, and made his escape as soon as he could; Louisa looking after him, and thinking that something strange must be going on, when every one was so easily put out. And what was Clement calculating? She would find out that, if she did nothing else.

Bertha had a better excuse for being put out than any one else. The last thing she would have desired was that the children or her mother should believe there was at this time a mystery connected with Mr Lester's movements. There was enough to make her anxious, without the dread of incaution and idle curiosity in those with whom she lived.

Mr Lester's letter was short, and by no means satisfactory.

'MY DEAR MISS CAMPBELL.—I arrived yesterday, about five

o'clock, and found my friend very far from well. He has had an attack of influenza, which confines him to his bed. He is improving, but I don't think it would quite do to let him travel to-morrow. It is possible that I shall be obliged to make arrangements for having my Sunday duty taken ; the week days are provided for. I have not been able to say anything about business. I will write again as soon as I can. I shall send a few lines to Miss Vivian. Will you please to give the enclosed note to Rachel. I trust her quite to your care.

'In haste, most sincerely yours,

'ROBERT LESTER.'

In the postscript were a few directions about some poor people, whom Bertha was taking charge of ; and the last words were, 'I need scarcely urge upon you caution and great watchfulness, especially as regards occupying Clement, and keeping him out of mischief. You may be certain I shall return the very earliest day possible.'

Perhaps Bertha could scarcely have expected, in reason, anything more decisive in this, Mr Lester's first letter; but suspense was intensely trying to her, and now it was aggravated by the knowledge of Edward Vivian's illness, which might protract it considerably. She felt sadly faithless, and conscience painfully reproached her for it ; but it seemed as if, for the first time, the magnitude of the interests at stake were revealed to her.

It was as though she had gone on in a dream of hope for years before, never really hoping or expecting anything ; talking of the changes which might some day come, without really anticipating them. Only within the last few days, since Mr Lester himself had acknowledged that the moment for action was arrived had she dared to realise to herself the possibilities of success or of failure.

It required all Bertha's conscientiousness to bring her mind to the contemplation of her ordinary work. But she was a person who could never waste time in useless regrets or fears ; each hour in the day had its occupation marked, and she was almost scrupulously exact in keeping to it. A few minutes of leisure were, however, always to be found directly after breakfast, whilst the children were preparing their lessons ; and, taking advantage of them, she pleased herself by carrying Rachel's note to the Rectory instead of sending it. There was something in the gay smile and the affectionate glance that would meet her there, which was soothing even when she could not open her mind and tell all her anxieties ; and perhaps one of Bertha's few self-deceptions might have been discovered in the excuses which she made, when anything particularly vexatious had occurred at the Lodge, to go to the Rectory, and spend a quarter of an hour with Rachel.

Rachel was met in the porch, with her bonnet and shawl on. She had expected a letter, and not receiving one, was going to the Lodge to make inquiries. She ran up to Bertha eagerly ; ' Dear Miss Campbell, how kind of you ! and you have a note !' She seized it eagerly, and then recollecting herself, added : ' May I read it ? you won't think it rude ? But you must come in and sit down by the fire ; it is very cold this morning.'

Even in her anxiety for news from her father, she could not forget consideration for one present with her ; and Bertha was taken into the study, and the fire was stirred, and she was made to unfasten her cloak, and then Rachel turned away to the window to peruse her precious note. It was read through twice, and a kiss given to the name at the bottom ; but still Rachel stood looking out of the window with a watery mist dimming her eyes. Bertha, seated by the fire, waited patiently. She knew well the struggle that was going on in the poor child's mind. Rachel had never calculated upon the possibility of her father's being away more than two days. But it was a calm voice which spoke at last, only rather lower and more restrained in its accent than was wont ; and if tears were gathering in Rachel's eyes, they were not allowed to go further, as she stood again by Bertha's side, and said, ' He doesn't know when he shall come back.'

' Not exactly the day, dear Rachel ; but it can't be long.'

' Can't it ? but he promised, he thought he should be back to-morrow.' A rush of sorrow rose up in Rachel's throat, but she swallowed it with a strong effort. ' I don't mean to be wrong, Miss Campbell, I wan't to bear it,—I will',—and there was another effort at self-command.

' Yes, because small trials come to us from the same Hand as great ones.'

' Thank you ;' and Rachel put her arm fondly round Bertha ; ' that is just what papa would say. It does me more good than telling me the time will soon pass,' she added, as an April smile brightened her face. ' But you think he will come ?'

'Certainly, the very first day he can. He must, you know, for the sake of his parish.'

'And for mine; what should I do without him? It is so lonely.'

That was a little unmeant reproach to Bertha. It seemed very hard that she could not at once take Rachel to the Lodge, but she knew it would not do to propose it. Her mind was set at rest, however, by Rachel's saying: 'Papa tells me that if I don't hear from him about his coming home to-morrow, he shall ask Aunt Mildred to let me go to the Hall. I shall enjoy that excessively, but it won't be like having papa.'

'You will have Ella, too, as a companion,' said Bertha.

'Shall I? How very nice! Yet I thought she was coming back.'

'Miss Vivian wants her to stay. She thinks her grandpapa will like it.'

'Will he really?' Rachel seemed about to add something very energetic; but she stopped, and concluded by saying, 'Did you see Aunt Mildred yesterday?'

'Yes, for an hour nearly. We had a long talk.'

'And you think—yes, I am sure you think as I do—that she is very—I don't know what to say—not at all like any one else.'

'No, very unlike.'

'And Ella is so fond of her!' continued Rachel. 'She sent me a little note the other day, and told me that she was beginning to love her just as I said she would. It will be very nice going there; only if papa could be there too '—— and she heaved a sigh.

'We can't have all we wish,' said Bertha.

It was a truism; yet Rachel's simple humility took it as it was intended, and she replied, 'No, I ought to remember that; I ought to be thankful. And the Hall will be very pleasant, and ' —— she stopped, for tears would come in spite of her efforts.

'Doesn't papa say anything else in his note?' inquired Bertha, wishing to distract her thoughts.

'Yes, one thing—I forgot.' Rachel read it through again. ' He has left his pocket-book behind him ; he wants me to look in it, and send him a receipted bill that is in it. He says if I am in any doubt, you will tell which it is. It is a school bill, which he paid in Cleve the other day.'

'Perhaps we had better find the pocket-book at once,' said

Bertha, looking at her watch. 'I have just ten minutes to spare. Then we can settle which is the bill.'

'I saw it yesterday, I remember,' said Rachel, searching about the room. 'I thought why he had left it. Oh! here it is.' She gave it to Bertha.

'You had better open it,' said Bertha, returning it.

'There are such loads of papers!' Rachel took them out, one after the other. 'This—no, it is a note; and this is a list of school children; and these are letters.—I don't think the bill is here.'

'Perhaps that may be it,' said Bertha, pointing to a folded paper which had a name written on the back.

'I don't know; it may be.' Rachel opened and looked at it. 'I don't think—it isn't a receipt—what does it mean?' She put the paper into Bertha's hands.

Bertha read :—

'Three months after the death of my father, I promise to pay John Vivian, Esq., or order, the sum of five thousand pounds. Value received.

'EDWARD BRUCE VIVIAN.'

'Dear Miss Campbell, aren't you well?' Bertha's colourless cheek, her fixed gaze, might well warrant the question.

She started. 'What did you say? Yes, I am very well, thank you. It is not the bill, I think. Hadn't you better ask the servants if they have seen it?'

'Perhaps I had.' Rachel was frightened by Bertha's manner. She hardly knew what she was to ask the servants; but she ran away, glad to be out of the room.

Bertha was alone—the strange paper in her hand; but she could scarcely read it again—the letters swam before her eyes. Yet her thoughts, her powers of reasoning, were singularly clear. It must mean, it could not mean anything but that Edward Vivian had deceived them; that he had really been involved to an extent five times as great as he had ever ackowledged; that he had extricated himself by means calculated to exasperate any father, most especially a man with General Vivian's jealous sense of justice, his keen, family pride and personal dignity, reckoning upon that as already his own, to which his only claim lay in his father's will. She recalled Mr Lester's manner during his last conversation, and fancied now that his tone of despondency was greater than she had ever known it. Perhaps he had only lately, in his interview with General Vivian, been made aware of the extent of Edward's offence ; perhaps he had not liked to give her his true reason for going to London, and had seized upon Goff's interference with the letters as an excuse ; perhaps, when he said that the hour for the decisive step was arrived, it was from the conviction that Edward had sinned beyond the hope of pardon, except by a final despairing appeal to mercy.

Bertha's fears gave strength to her convictions ; yet even in this there was much to perplex her. A paper so important left to chance, placed in a pocket-book with trifling memoranda, and, as it seemed, forgotten,—very unlike that was to Mr Lester, so careful and particular as he was in all matters of business. And how did it come into his possession ? How long had he kept it from her ? These were questions not to be solved. She heard Rachel returning, and her impulse was to restore the paper to its place ; but a second thought made her hesitate. It might be unsafe. Mr Lester might have forgotten it. It seemed better to take care of it, and then tell him what she had done. Happily, Bertha's conscience was so free from any double motive, that she had no cause to mistrust her own intentions, and safe in the certainty of Mr Lester's kind interpretation of her actions, she took possession of the mysterious document ; whilst Rachel came back with a forlorn face, having heard no tidings of the receipted bill.

Bertha was too anxious to be willing to wait till further search had been made, and, even in the excitement of her feelings and the perplexity of her thoughts, was conscious that the ten minutes she had given herself were expired ; and Rachel, knowing her strict punctuality, would not ask her to stay a moment beyond the appointed time, but insisted upon looking through the pocket-book papers again herself, and promised to bring the bill to the Lodge to be inspected if it were found. Just at the last minute Bertha thought whether it would be wise to tell Rachel that she had taken the paper ; but she felt a little shy of confessing what might appear a liberty, and was afraid of exciting remark. She fancied, besides, that Rachel was not likely to miss it, as she had scarcely looked at it, and certainly did not understand what it meant.

Bertha, therefore, went home to teach the children, give directions to the servants, wait upon her mother, and, in the midst of all, to ponder upon the painful light which had thus suddenly been cast upon the family affairs. Rachel remained in the study, and went through the papers carefully again ; this time, perhaps, because she was not flurried by Bertha's occasional glances at the timepiece, she found the bill without any difficulty ; and then, having a vague recollection that she had missed something which ought to be there, took another survey in search of the old dirty-looking paper which she had put into Bertha's hands, and which at the time she remembered to have thought very unlike all the rest.

Most provoking it was, just as she was going to sit down to read, to be hindered in this way ; but now the old paper was gone. Twice she went through the letters and notes as they were folded in the pocket-book ; then she unfolded and examined them, looked under the table, under the chairs, under books and sofa cushions, in every place where such a paper was most un-likely to be found, and at last went again to the kitchen to con-fide her troubles to Anne.

And Anne was standing in the back-yard, and a door which led from it into the Rectory lane was open, and near this door was Goff, haunting the premises still, and trying to make friends with Anne at home, as he had not met her the day before in the village. Rachel came out, full of her annoyance, with an idea that, by means of a sweeping-brush, Anne would be able to penetrate into the secret recesses of any hiding-place in which the tiresome paper should have secreted itself. And she gave a full description of it, to the best of her ability ; said that it was old and discoloured, and was written in a scrawly hand, with a great name signed at the bottom which she thought was Edward Vivian ; and that she remembered what it was like especially, because Miss Campbell turned so pale just when the paper was given her that she fancied there must be something written on it which frightened her. Of course it was not that, because it was only an old kind of bill, and there was nothing really the matter with Miss Campbell. To all which details Anne gave very little heed, though promising to use her best endeavours to assist Rachel's wishes, and to pick up every piece of paper she might see on the ground in the hope of discovering the truant.

Anne did not heed, but Goff did ; and when Anne, at Rachel's request, went back with her to the study, Goff, cool, reckless, desperate in danger as in the carrying out of schemes of guilt, hurried to the Grange to communicate to Captain Vivian what

he had heard, and discuss the plans which it might be necessary to adopt in the probability that the missing paper was the
evidence of their guilt and the cause of Mr Lester's sudden
departure.

CHAPTER XXXVI.

NO news from Mr Lester the following morning. Bertha
had looked forward to the post with intense anxiety ; and
when the blank 'no letters to-day' was heard from Louisa, as
the postman passed the gate, her heart sickened with disappointment. She had waited hoping to hear of his return, and
intending to delay any inquiry as to the paper in her possession
until she could see him. Since the discovery of Goff's interference she had a superstitious dread of trusting anything
which might be of consequence to the post ; and the more she
considered the subject in calm moments, examining carefully
the signature, and going over in her own mind all that she had
ever heard as connected with Edward Vivian's affairs, the more
her first feelings were altered, whilst a strong conviction forced
itself upon her that the document of which in so singular a
manner she had become possessed was false. The writing unquestionably strikingly resembled Mr Vivian's, but it was stiff and
careful ; not such as his would have been under any pressure of
anxiety. There were slight differences in the letters also, but these
could not be so much depended upon, because years tend very
much to alter handwriting, and she could not well recollect what
her brother-in-law's had been so long ago. But that which most
weighed with Bertha was the full belief, impressed upon her
mind by family troubles, that his debts had never amounted to
more than one-fifth of the sum named in the paper. Mr Lester
doubtless must, like herself, have had suspicions upon the subject, and the paper must be connected, she felt sure, with his
London journey ; perhaps he did not say so for fear of exciting
false hopes ; perhaps—but that was all a mystery, not to be
dwelt upon if she wished to keep her mind quiet ; only Bertha
felt that whether her conjectures were true or false, the discovery of the paper threw light upon General Vivian's feelings,
and gave him a claim to sympathy fully as much as to censure.

Nothing of this anxiety was shown outwardly. The quietness

of Bertha's ordinary manner was an assistance to her in keeping up the necessary self-restraint. She was so grave usually, that no one noticed a shade more or less, except it might be Louisa, and even she was often baffled by her aunt's composure. Yet it was a serious effort during the day to keep her wandering thoughts in order, and go through the routine of lessons; and the preoccupation of her mind, added to a natural want of observation and quick penetration into character, prevented her from watching Clement, or discovering in him anything which might have led her to think that his heart was ill at ease.

That first deception had led him on much further than he intended. When Captain Vivian met him the day succeeding his visit, and proposed to him to repeat it, asking, as a favour, that, besides giving him help for amusement, he would assist him in a case which was a question of business, Clement had nothing to fall back upon to support his weak will, and, of course, yielded ; and a second visit involved a third, still apparently innocent, but making him, after the excitement was over, very uneasy, and enabling Captain Vivian to discover in the course of conversation all he required to know as to Mr Lester's movements, where he was likely to be in London, and the probability of his return ; Clement telling everything with perfect simplicity, and never for one moment suspecting a meaning in this apparent interest.

And he flattered himself, too, that he was gaining something by the intercourse. Captain Vivian talked to him of the sea and his fancy for it, and gave him some useful advice not unmixed with flattery, promising, any day that he could manage it, to take him for a short sail, merely that he might have a few practical lessons, which were better, he said, than any talking. If it had only not been against Clement's conscience, he would quite have enjoyed going to the Grange, especially as he found that by some means he was free from Ronald's warning voice. Both days he had been there Ronald had been absent, sent by his father on some business to Cleve, or over the hills; and Captain Vivian had cautioned Clement playfully against mentioning his visit, saying, that when they had made out their puzzling questions, he meant to surprise him with his cleverness, for Ronald never fancied he had a head for reckoning.

There had been a proposal that they should meet again on this day, still with the excuse of what Captain Vivian called business ; and Clement had given an evasive answer, which left it at his option to go or not, as he might choose. So his conscience was tolerably easy for the present, though the past weighed upon him most uncomfortably.

It was not likely that Bertha should suspect any of this evil. Clement had kept regularly to hours, and walked once with his sisters, and was attentive to his studies. This afternoon, also, after some demur, he agreed to go with them over the hills to Greystone Gorge, to see Barney Wood ; and although Bertha was not at all fond of being left in any way in charge of Clement, feeling that her control was not sufficient for him, she was satisfied that he seemed more disposed than usual to be obedient. Perhaps it was the consciousness of his unacknowledged fault which made him particularly grave and quiet.

It was a long walk, and the days were now so short that it was necessary to leave home early. Without Clement, indeed, Bertha might have hesitated about undertaking the expedition ; for it was unpleasant to return over the hills alone, or only with the children, when it was growing dark, and Barney Wood's cottage had not the best possible reputation. His mother, who was dead, had been Goff's daughter ; and report said, that the crafty smuggler made use of his son-in-law's house as a resort for himself and his comrades, in case of necessity. It was certainly very much out of the way of inspection, although within an easy distance of Dark Head Point, and not very far from the Grange,—all advantages to persons engaged in the contraband traffic carried on to such an extent upon that part of the coast. Dark Head Point was well known to be the general rendezvous of the smugglers. It was the highest headland in the neighbourhood, and from it they could keep a strict watch over the country for miles ; and though called inaccessible from the shore, it was said that the practised foot of the smuggler could find a footing upon narrow ledges, which scarcely a goat could venture to tread ; and that the tubs, when landed, were often hidden in recesses of the cliffs, which the preventive men, with all their hardihood, could not reach. But all this was but hearsay. Smugglers have a code of honour peculiarly their own, and no one of the Encombe band had ever yet been known to betray the secrets of his comrades ; whilst the villagers would have believed it an act of the grossest treachery to reveal aught, either by word or look, concerning the traffic in which so many of those nearest and dearest to them were deeply engaged.

It was a difficult task entrusted to Mr Lester, that of guiding these lawless people : to himself they were uniformly civil, and, for the most part, there was little more to find fault with amongst them, than amongst the generality of their class. Drunkenness was the prevailing vice, but there were few petty thefts; the children were sent regularly to school; the wives worked diligently at home ; the attendance at church on the Sunday was as regular as it commonly is in a seafaring place ; on the week-days, few men would have been found, in any village of the size, able to leave their daily work. Only now and then, some affray with the preventive men roused the fiercer passions of the people, and revealed the depth of the mischief which, at other times, was doing its work secretly, but surely. And it was not easy to find occasions for warning, where the offence was so carefully concealed. The men called themselves fishermen ; their boats were ostensibly fishing-boats, and, indeed, often used for that purpose ; they were connected, too, with other smuggling bands along the coast, and it was customary to shift the offence from one to the other, till it became almost impossible to attach it to any individual. But, worse than all, they were unquestionably supported and encouraged by powerful example ; and whilst Captain Vivian remained in the village, Mr Lester felt bitterly that all hope of really improving his people, or teaching them the actual culpability of their conduct, was vain. Yet with him there was even greater difficulty in fixing the offence, than with the lower classes. The vessel kept off the coast, and known to belong to him, and to be engaged in smuggling expeditions, was owned nominally by another person, and was ostensibly a trading vessel, which went backwards and forwards for apparently innocent purposes of business. It had even been searched, but nothing had been found. Yet there was no more real doubt of its being used for smuggling purposes, than that the man chiefly connected with it was a lawless villain ; all that was needed was proof, and proof was never at hand.

It seemed hard to visit the sins of the guilty upon the innocent ; harder still, when it was known that temptation and threats were used in the village to no slight extent ; and that those who would not join the smugglers from interest, were compelled to do so from fear. This had been the case, in some degree, with Mark Wood, the father of little Barney. He had been a quiet, respectable man, till he married Goff's daughter. Even then he seemed anxious to keep himself aloof from the evil practices prevalent around him ; but once nearly connected with a man of bad principle, and he could not again set himself free. Mr Lester had been a friend to Mark and to his wife ; he had attended her through a long illness, and been with her at the moment of death ; and at that time it seemed that the unhappy husband's heart was open to good impressions, and Mr Lester, anxious to follow them up, had taken especial notice of his sickly boy, left without a mother's care. With the assistance of Rachel and Bertha Campbell he had provided Barney with comforts, and even luxuries, in the wish to keep up his influence with the father by the means of his child. But the case was not as hopeful now as it had been. Goff was more frequently at the cottage ; his son-in-law was with him oftener in other places. It had even been reported that Mark Wood was to be seen, late at night, watching on Dark Head Point ; but this was only report, and Mr Lester could not leave the sick boy to suffer, because his father was yielding to evil example. He still allowed Bertha and Rachel to visit him, and aided them in any little plans for the child's comfort, often making an excuse to visit the boy himself, with the desire of meeting the father, and gaining an insight into his habits. But, once a smuggler, and Mark Wood's sense of honour and truth was as perverted as that of his companions. He would treat Mr Lester with civility, listen to his advice, and show himself grateful for his kindness ; but there was no more confidence between them. Mark had given himself to a service which would admit of no compromise ; and if a lie could serve the purpose of concealment, he would not scruple to use it for smuggling purposes, though he would have scorned to avail himself of it for any other.

The visits to Barney Wood were very satisfactory to Bertha, for they were almost her only opportunities of seeing Ronald alone. His care of the child was watchful and unceasing. It seemed as if the little fellow was a safety-valve for the softer feelings which could find no other vent. For Ronald Vivian could not live without some one to love. The strong feelings which at times carried him beyond his own control in anger, or exhausted themselves in the better impulses of fiery resolve and strong determination, took also, occasionally, other forms of intense longings for affection, eager and passionate desires to find some work which would draw him away from himself, and give him personal love in return for devoted self-denial ; and then he seized upon the first object which presented itself, and gave

himself up to it unremittingly, and with the same spirit of intense
reverence with which he had watched his mother, during her
lingering illness, whilst receiving the impressions that had so
often been his safeguard during his most perilous life.

We cannot forget purity when once we have been brought in
contact with it. The memory of evil may die when the soul has
long dwelt in the presence of goodness, but the vision of holiness
is immortal, even as He from whom it proceeds. Ronald
Vivian had learned from his mother what a woman can be in
meekness, self-devotion, endurance, and faith ; and not all those
terrible scenes into which he had since been plunged, had suf-
ficed to eradicate the impression. Still the best resolutions of
the present, and the strongest wishes for the future, were formed
from the images of the past. In Bertha Campbell, and Ella, and
Rachel, he saw, or fancied he saw, his mother's virtues reflected;
and when he tended the sick boy on his suffering bed, he acted
over again in imagination the scenes so deeply imprinted on his
memory when his mother had in like manner watched over
him.

It was a marvellous power which could thus keep before him
a standard of goodness so infinitely beyond anything actually
present to his eyes. Bertha was wanting in his mother's grace
and tact ; and Ella, he could sometimes discover, was wayward;
and Rachel was too young and seen too seldom to exercise any
very direct influence ; but to Ronald they were beings of a
superior order. They had the refinement and delicacy—the soft
voices and the gentle consideration of manner—with which all
his better feelings were associated ; and when disgusted by the
coarseness and freedom of the rough men with whom he was so
often brought in contact, his thoughts reverted to them with a
feeling almost superstitious in its reverence,—as if they, and such
as they, alone prevented this earth from sinking to the horrors
of Pandemonium.

And thus it was, from the longing to escape from the scenes he
loathed into a purer atmosphere, that the care of little Barney had
become Ronald's solace, as offering a vent for his pent-up yearnings,
—a duty which would associate him with those who were as his
better angels, pointing him the way to heaven. When he found
that Bertha and Rachel Lester were interested in the sick child,
his work became ennobled: when he could act with them, or for
them, in any plan which they might have for Barney's gratification, it was as though he had been raised above his natural

sphere, and higher, purer pleasures and hopes were being placed
before him ; and in this spirit he had begun, and for a time
carried on, his visits to the child. But a still deeper blessing,
though yet an earthly one, was in time granted him. Love he
must in some form, either in remembrance, or reality, or hope.
Whilst he lived alone with his coarse-minded father he had
loved the memory of his mother, and it was long before he could
persuade himself that any other affection could be vouchsafed
him. But the possibility dawned upon him as a star rising
upon the darkness of night, whilst he watched by the sick-bed
of Barney Wood. His father might be harsh and repelling ;
Bertha might be too far above him for everyday sympathy ;
Ella and Rachel had interests quite removed from his ; but
there was one face which always brightened when he drew near ;
one little voice which never failed to entreat in longing accents
for his return ; one eye which had learned to know when he was
sorrowful, to look lovingly and anxiously for his smile ; and the
pent-up fountain of Ronald's heart was touched by the loving
hand of a child's sympathy, and the affection which had hitherto
exhausted itself in regret, or been dried up by the scorching
furnace of sin, gushed forth pure and free to revive the droop-
ing spirit of the boy, and be in turn refreshed and strengthened
itself.

It was now very nearly Christmas, and Greystone Gorge, inviting though it might seem in its wild loneliness beneath the
beauty of a summer sky, looked mournfully dreary under the
dark atmosphere of a December afternoon. There was not even
the excitement of frost and snow ; the sky was a cold, hard
gray, and though the sun tried to break through it at intervals,
it had but little power ; the thin coating of turf had become
brown ; the fern leaves were dry and withered ; the straggling
bushes seemed only fit to burn ; all was faded, and the cottage
itself had a mournful, neglected appearance. Barney had long
ceased to enjoy being laid upon a mattress out-of-doors, though
he was generally drawn every day over the few paces of level
ground in his little carriage. Bertha and Rachel had provided
him with a thick wrapping-shawl, and Ronald had brought him
a sailor's coat to put over him, so that he could be kept tolerably
warm ; but since the winter had set in he had taken up a position on a small couch by the wide open hearth, and when he did
go out, could bear the fatigue only for a few minutes. He was
left very much to himself. An old woman who lived in a cottage

lower down the Gorge was hired to take daily care of Mark's household, but it was very little attention which the suffering child obtained from her. She dressed him roughly, then laid him on his couch, and proceeded to her household work ; scolding Barney if he interrupted her, and now and then reproaching him with having so many friends that he wanted for nothing.

A grown-up person understands such a trial, and suffers from it ; a child happily scarcely does, and Barney was quite contented when he was left with his picture-book, and his scissors and paper, whether Mother Brewer, as the old woman was called, attended to him or not. He would occupy himself for hours together with them, whilst his brothers and sisters were at school ; and when they returned, though it was fretting to be disturbed, there was excitement and interest in hearing all they had done ; and they were not at all rough with him, and his father was especially tender ; altogether Barney was not an unhappy child, and his little, wizen face, though thin and sharp from illness, could brighten up with a smile which often became a hearty laugh, when Ronald told droll stories or the children amused him with their games.

He was looking out for Ronald this afternoon, fancying it a long time since he had seen him ; and he had persuaded the old woman to move his couch to the opposite side of the hearth, and to leave the door partly open, that he might hear the first sound of footsteps. So he sat half upright, cutting pieces of paper into strange figures which he called men and women, and making a game of them for his own amusement, all the time fully on the alert for what might be approaching.

'Such a litter ! there's no end to the work,' grumbled Mother Brewer, as she picked up the shreds of paper which, in a sudden move, Barney had scattered upon the floor. 'Why can't you keep quiet, child, eh ?'

'He's not coming yet,' was Barney's reply,—giving vent to his own thoughts, without noticing the angry tones to which he was so well accustomed. He laid down his scissors, and listened again.

'Well ! and what's the use of an imp like you fussing ? He'll come if he can, and if he can't he can't. I won't have you lie there with the door open much longer.'

Barney strained his neck to try and look round the door.

The old woman gave him a tap on the shoulder, sufficient to

startle, not to frighten him. 'Lie quiet, can't you? Don't you know the doctor says you must?'

''Tis Captain John, and father, and grandfather, 'tisn't Ronald,' said Barney. His face changed its expression; he would have cried if he had not been ashamed.

'What sharp ears the child has! I don't hear any one.' The old woman went to the door. 'O yes! there they be; we must move you, my master;' and she drew the child's couch back to the wall, placing him in a position where, even if the door were open, he could see nothing. 'No crying; don't let's have any fuss; father will beat you if you cry.' The threat was disregarded, for Barney had never experienced a beating; but he was very quiet, and self-controlled, and shrank up into a corner of his little couch, and turned his face away, as though he longed to escape notice.

The three men came into the room together; Captain Vivian first, Goff following him with the air of an equal. Mark Wood lingered behind; and when he did enter, went up at once to his child's couch, and patted his head.

'We don't want you, mother,' was Goff's uncivil greeting to the old woman, who instantly left the cottage; 'and we don't want him neither, eh, Mark?' he pointed to the child.

Mark looked at his boy for a moment. 'No fear for him; here Barney, child, cut the Captain out a wolf; and he tossed him a scrap of paper. ''Tis a fuss to move him; it gives him pain, and besides we've no time to lose.'

'No, that's for certain; your young fellow will be upon us before long, Captain; so now to work.'

They withdrew to a distant corner, and carried on the conversation in an undertone. Goff began: 'You're in for it, Mark, remember.'

Mark gave rather a sullen assent.

'And in for a good fifty pounds,' said Captain Vivian, jocosely. 'Why Mark, my man, you'll be off to America upon it.'

Mark replied as gravely as before: 'I should like to understand the work, though, better, Captain. I see no good in a man's undertaking a job till he sees where it will lead him to.'

'Folly!' interrupted Goff. 'Haven't I told you 'twill lead nowhere? The young gentleman's up to a frolic, and we are going to help him to it, that's all. But we'll have none of this nonsense. Do you mean to keep your word, that's the question?'

Mark hesitated.

U

'It's my own relation, my own flesh and blood, as you may say,' observed Captain Vivian, more gently. 'I'm not likely to go in any way against one of my own kin. He and I are the best friends possible. It's only a boy's lark.'

'And the fifty pounds has nothing to do with it,' continued Goff, observing Mark's perplexed countenance; 'that's for the other work, you know. Land your cargo safe, and then come and hold out your hand for the money. The boy's affair has nothing to do with that.'

'And it's not against the young gentleman's will?'

'Not a whit, not a whit, man. And if the parson's up in arms, why we know how to laugh at him.'

The allusion was an unfortunate one. Mark Wood might neglect Mr Lester's advice, but he respected him extremely. 'I've no fancy to go against the parson,' he replied. 'He's been a kind friend to me and mine; and if I've sometimes gone contrary to him, more shame to me.'

'Of course, of course. But the boy's not going to be a parson; so where's the use of keeping him tied up as they do. Besides, Mark, my man'—and Captain Vivian, resting his hands upon his two knees, bent forward and fixed upon Mark a gaze of stern penetration and defiance—'once ours, always ours. Who is it the preventives would give their right hand to catch? and who may we give up to them in a moment, eh?'

Mark's countenance changed. The threat implied would, he knew, be executed without remorse if the occasion offered. Once suspected by his comrades, he would on the first opportunity be left to the vigilance of the coastguard, even if no deeper revenge were taken.

'It's not I that am wishing to draw back, Captain,' he said, in a more yielding tone. 'I've gone far enough with you, as you know—too far, it may be,' he added, in a lower voice; 'but no matter for that. Sink or swim together is a needs be, when men have done what we have in company. But I've no will to drag others in, specially a youngster who is only just beginning to know his right hand from his left.'

'Trust him for that!' exclaimed Goff, bursting into a loud laugh. 'He's as cunning a bird as any in England. But put aside all that rubbish, Mark, and tell us plainly, once for all—will or nill? that's the question. Down on the beach with a quick, firm oar, to-night at half-past seven, or'—his voice sank ominously—'wandering like a skulking wretch, afraid to meet his bold comrades? Come, man, I thought better of you.'

'And his life is safe, you are sure !' said Mark.

'Life ! safe ! Why man, you are enough to drive a saint frantic, let alone Richard Goff. I tell you it's a question of fun. He'll be taken out safe, and brought back safe ; and then, won't we turn round and have a laugh at the parson?'

''Twill be the third night I shall have been away from him,' said Mark, pointing with one finger to his child.

'Oh! he! nonsense ! the old woman will take care of him, and thankful he's not in your way.'

'And we are to be away, how long?'

'How can I tell? It's according to what time you'll want. Just take your work, man, as it's given you, and don't trouble about anything else. You're not in command yet; when you are, you'll know more about it.'

Captain Vivian rose and went to the door. 'I don't see my boy, yet,' he said ; 'but he'll surely be here soon. We must have no more trifling.'

'There's no disobeying you, Captain,' replied Mark, surlily.

'To be sure not,' said Goff, in a cajoling tone. 'What would you be without the Captain, I should like to know?'

'Very different from what I am,' muttered Mark to himself ; and then he added, more loudly, 'I must understand what's to be done clearly. To-night, at half-past seven?'

'Ay, down on the beach, in the West Cove, by the Point,' replied Goff.

'And the vessel waiting outside,' added Captain Vivian.

'Then, when we and the young one come down,' continued Goff, 'we shall put him on board ; and you are to haul off to the bark. When you are there, your business will be done as to orders, and you'll have nothing to think of but your old concerns.'

'And he is to go with us, then, across seas?'

'Yes, just for the sail. He'll be back with you.'

'And we to show him all our sport? That seems folly enough,' said Mark. 'Why, he'll turn sharp upon us when he gets back.'

'Never you trouble your head with that matter,' said Goff. 'We are not going to let him see an inch beyond his nose if we don't choose ; and one way you may make special use of him,— if the sharks are after you, put him first, and see if good doesn't come of it.'

Mark gave a start of horror. 'Put him first! into danger?—why, Goff, you are a scoundrel.'

'Thanks for your good opinion,' said Goff, carelessly; 'I'm not more a scoundrel than my neighbours, only I speak out and they keep in. But I'm not saying the boy's to be put in danger, —only put first. Let the sharks know who he is, and there's feeling enough for the old General, to keep them from doing him harm. And if they catch him, 'tis but an hour or two's rough handling for him. He's not such a tender chicken for that to hurt him. Come, trust me, Mark,' he continued, seeing his companion's changing and undecided expression. 'You've never got into mischief yet by trusting me.'

'Pshaw! what signifies urging?' exclaimed Captain Vivian, impatiently. 'If he won't do it, there are a dozen others who will. ' And we shall know where to look for our friends for the future.'

'And we shall have the boy with us at all hazards,' continued Goff. 'We are not going to be baulked of our plans by a down-hearted fool, who hasn't a spark of fun in him.'

The observation seemed to strike Mark in a new light. 'You are bent upon it, then?' he said.

'Ay, to be sure. Who ever knew Richard Goff take a plan into his head, and give it up?' And Goff laughed loudly and harshly.

Mark considered.

'A loss of fifty pounds,' muttered Captain Vivian.

Mark glanced at his child, who was sitting up on his couch, his large black eyes sparkling with eagerness as he fixed them upon his father. Probably he feared to attract notice to the boy, for the look was but momentary; and then he said, more boldly, 'Fifty pounds paid down?'

'Sterling gold, if you will,' said Goff.

'Fifty pounds, which will go a pretty long way towards paying the old General the rent of the cottage and the land,' said Captain Vivian.

'And which if you don't have, you must needs go forth to wander where you can,' pursued Goff.

A second quick glance at the child:—perhaps imagination pictured the little fellow's grief in having to give up the only home he had ever known,—perhaps there were images of bygone days and past happiness rising up before Mark Wood. It would be a terrible trial to leave the cottage in the Gorge; but so it must be, unless the rent of the house and the land could be paid before another month was over. His faltering resolution was betrayed by the question, again repeated,—'You are sure the boy's life is safe?' to which Goff replied by shaking his hand violently, and exclaiming, 'As safe as yours or mine, man! and what would you want more?' He laughed again, so did Captain Vivian. Mark Wood only replied, sullenly,—'Then the matter's settled, and we'll say no more.'

He took up his hat, intending to leave the cottage. Goff followed him to the door, looked out, and dragged him back. 'Hist! I say; not a word to the youngster; he's coming. Captain, it's time for us to be off. Where's your back outlet, Mark?' He tried a little door near Barney's couch. Mark went up slowly and opened it.

'Not a word, remember,' said Captain Vivian, in a low, hurried voice,—he slipped half-a-crown into Mark's hand;—'I am glad we caught you at home; but remember, not a word.'

They passed through the little door, whilst Mark sat down on a chair by the deal table, and resting his elbows upon it, buried his face in his hands.

CHAPTER XXXVII

'ARE they gone, father?' Barney's voice broke suddenly upon Mark Wood's meditations.

'Ay, I suppose so. What do you want, child?'

'Grandfather speaks out so, and Captain John's wicked; I wish they wouldn't come here.'

'That's a bad boy to say so. We'll have Mother Brewer back;' and Mark stood up.

'Ronald's coming; I don't want Mother Brewer,' said Barney.

'Ronald won't come; nobody won't come, if you talk like a bad boy. There, go to your cutting and clipping again.' Mark tossed him a piece of paper from a quantity which Rachel had provided for his amusement.

Barney scarcely noticed the gift; but as his father still stood moodily by the window, he continued, 'Mother Brewer says Captain John makes folks wicked.'

'Idiot! what does she know?' Mark turned angrily upon his little boy; and the child, frightened at the expression of his eyes, began to cry. The father's heart softened. 'There, leave off; don't fuss, Barney, boy; don't whimper; take to your cutting, and we won't have Mother Brewer back. And here's Ronald; you'll be glad to see Ronald.' He placed the child more comfortably on his couch, gave an uneasy glance round the room, wishing to be certain that no traces of his recent visitors were left, and went to the door just as Ronald came up.

'Good day to you, Mark; how's Barney?' Ronald's open face, and manly, good-humoured voice, were a great contrast to Mark's clouded brow and sullen tone of half welcome.

'The boy's nigh the same, thank you, Master Ronald. You'll be going in, I suppose?' and Mark moved aside to let Ronald pass.

'There's no one in, is there?' asked Ronald, stopping. 'I thought I saw one moving about in the back yard.'

'Mother Brewer's been here, but she's gone home for a bit,' was the evasive answer.

'I thought Goff might have been here, or my father; they were before me some way on the hills. But I suppose they turned off to the Point.'

'I suppose so. Will you please to walk in? The child will be glad enough to see you.' Then recollecting himself, and remembering that Barney would be sure to mention the visit he had just had, he added,—'The Captain and Goff were here for a bit; but they're off now; I don't know where.'

Ronald had early been taught the watchfulness engendered by guilt and suspicion; even these few words of Mark's, showing an unwillingness to mention Captain Vivian's visit, gave him the clue to something not satisfactory. He would have asked some questions, but Mark was evidently unwilling to stay and talk. He muttered a few words about business and waste of time, and again begging Ronald to go in, for Barney would be mighty glad to see him, he walked away with a lounging, idling step.

Ronald went up to Barney's couch, and the child threw his arms round him, and kissed him, but without speaking.

'That's enough! Why, Barney, my man, I shall be stifled!' Ronald laughed, and tried to disengage himself, but the child still clung to him.

'I like you to come. I don't like Captain John; and Mother

Brewer says he's wicked; but father won't let me say it.' He stopped suddenly, catching the expression of Ronald's face:—'Is it naughty in me to say it?'

'Captain John is my father, Barney,' said Ronald.

'He ain't a bit like you; and father is like me,' continued Barney.

'All fathers and sons aren't alike, Barney; but what made you think of Captain John?'

''Cause he's been here ever so long, and grandfather, and father; they've been talking.'

'What, this morning? A long time?'

'Ever since Mother Brewer moved me up in the corner. Captain John doesn't speak out like grandfather.'

'And they let you stay here?'

'Father said it was a trouble to move, and they hadn't time; and he gave me this'—Barney held up his paper—'to cut out a wolf for Captain John; but I didn't cut—I listened!' His brilliant eyes were fixed with keen intelligence upon Ronald.

'But, Barney, they didn't mean you to listen; that was wrong.'

'They talked out, sometimes,' said Barney, quickly. 'Grandfather made most noise.'

'And they went away just before I came, I suppose?' said Ronald.

'Just a bit before. Father was cross then.'

'Barney, Barney, what does Mr Lester tell you?'

'I ain't to say father's cross. I won't say it, but he is.'

'But you do say it; and that's naughty. You must try to be dutiful. I've told you so often.'

'Captain John's cross to you sometimes, ain't he?' said Barney.

A perplexing question! Ronald replied to it, indirectly, 'He tells me when I don't please him.'

'Then ain't you dutiful?'

Ronald's countenance changed, and Barney's quick eye noticed it. 'When father's cross, I don't like him,' he said; 'that's naughty of me; but you always like Captain John, don't you?'

'We mustn't talk about liking our parents; we must like them, anyhow,' said Ronald.

Barney seemed perplexed; but presently he went on—'Mr Lester says that God likes good people; must we like wicked ones?'

Ronald made no answer; his head was turned aside, and a large tear was rolling down his cheek.

Barney caught his hand, and forced him to look at him. 'Why do you cry? I didn't mean to make you cry!' he said. 'Is it 'cause Captain John's wicked?'

'Because I am wicked myself, too, Barney;' and Ronald brushed his hand across his eyes, and tried to smile.

'Miss Campbell and Miss Rachel think you very good,' said Barney. 'They say if I go to heaven, that you'll go, too. I asked them one day, for I shouldn't like to go alone.'

'Miss Campbell and Miss Rachel may wish me to go to heaven, but they can't tell that I shall,' said Ronald; 'and we must be very good, indeed, you know, Barney, to go there.'

'That's why I shan't go, then,' said Barney, quickly; ''cause I don't like father when he's cross.'

'But you know you must say your prayers, and ask God to forgive you, Barney, when you've been so naughty; and then, perhaps, He will let you go to heaven still.'

'Is that what you do?' asked the child, with a strangely inquisitive expression in his worn face.

Ronald hesitated; but Barney was determined upon obtaining his answer. 'Do you say prayers when you are naughty? Is it "Our Father," you say?' He would not let Ronald move, but kept his hand closely clasped between his own small, long fingers.

'Yes, sometimes. People don't always say the same prayer, you know, Barney,' was Ronald's answer.

'I like "Our Father" best,' continued the child, 'because Miss Campbell says it's God's prayer; but I don't say it when I am naughty. I say, "Pray, God, forgive me, and make me a good boy, for Jesus Christ's sake." Is that what you say?'

'Something like it, sometimes;'—Ronald still hesitated.

'I'm glad you say it. I like you to say the same things as me. But then you aren't naughty when Captain John's cross. What makes you naughty ever?'

'A great, great many things, I am afraid,' said Ronald.

'But tell me what; I want to know.'

'I couldn't tell you; you wouldn't understand.'

'Shouldn't I?' A look of thought came over his face. 'When I'm a man, then, I shall understand; but I don't want to be a man.'

'Don't you, Barney? why not?'

'Men are wicked,' said Barney. 'Wicked's worse than naughty.'

'O Barney, Barney! who taught you anything about wickedness?'

'Father taught me some, and Mother Brewer. She hopes I shan't be like father, nor grandfather, nor Captain John, nor any of them; and so I say in my prayers,—"Please God take me out of this wicked world." Do you say that, too?'

Something seemed to rise up in Ronald's throat, to choke his utterance.

Barney kept his eyes fixed upon him intently, and, obtaining no answer, said, half reproachfully,—'You wouldn't like to go.'

'Shouldn't I? O Barney! if I were but sure?' The words escaped apparently without intention; for, the moment afterwards, Ronald added,—'Never mind me, though; you are sure.'

'I ain't,' said the child, quickly. 'Miss Campbell tells me to say, "through Jesus Christ," to make sure; and you can say it too.'

Ronald half smiled. 'Yes, I can say it, certainly; but saying's not everything. You'll know that, fast enough, Barney, when you're a man.'

'I shan't never be a man; but I know about that now,' was the grave answer.

'What do you know?' Ronald sat down by the couch, and leaned over the child fondly.

'I know He got us the place, and made it all ready for us; and if we say our prayers properly, and try not to cry and be cross, He'll give it us.'

'But if we don't say our prayers properly, and are cross, what then, Barney?' and the sorrowful tone struck upon the child's ear, though he could not comprehend its meaning.

'Somebody else will take our place,' he said, with a scrutinising look, which seemed to inquire whether Ronald could possibly be alluding to himself.

'And we shall be punished,' said Ronald.

'You won't be,' said Barney, 'because you say your prayers when you are naughty.'

'Ah! but, Barney, that isn't everything. If we don't do right, we deserve to be punished.'

'Parson Lester says He was punished for us,' said Barney,

quickly. Ronald made no answer, and Barney continued :—
'Parson Lester told me that one day after I'd had a dream; and
I thought God was going to put me down into a deep, dark place,
'cause I'd called father cross. He said that if I'd say my prayers,
and try to be a better boy, God wouldn't punish me, because
Jesus Christ had been punished for me. It was very kind of Him
to be punished, wasn't it?'

'Yes, very kind; but still, if we don't try to be good, we shall
be punished,' said Ronald.

Barney looked up rather impatiently : 'But I don't like to
think about being punished—I like to think about being good;
and Jesus Christ loves me, and so He won't punish me.'

'Oh yes, indeed, Barney, He will; if you are naughty.'

'But He won't if I try not to be naughty. Mother Brewer was
scolding me last time Miss Campbell was here, and she said she
wasn't to scold me, 'cause I was trying; and so, if I try, God
won't scold me. And I do try,' he added, looking earnestly at
Ronald's face; 'I didn't cry once all day yesterday.'

'There's a good little man; I'm glad to hear that;' and
Ronald stroked the child's head.

'And He loves me then, don't you think so? Miss Campbell
says He does, and Miss Rachel said He loved me better than
you do. Does He?'

'Ah! Barney, yes, I know He must; but I love you very
much.'

'And I love you with all my heart;' and Barney raised himself suddenly, and tried to reach Ronald's head, that he might
bend it down to kiss him. 'I love you now, and I mean to love
you when I get to heaven; and then by and by you'll come
there. I'm sure there's the place ready, with your name
upon it.'

Ronald looked away, and busied himself with replacing the
child's cushions. When he spoke again, it was to make some
trifling observation.

Barney was perplexed; presently he said, in a low, almost
frightened voice, as if conscious that he was venturing upon forbidden ground, 'I should like to know whose name's there,
besides. Do you think Captain John's is?'

Ronald could bear it no longer; and, careless of the child's
presence, he leaned his forehead upon the arm of the couch, and
groaned.

'Don't take on; what's the matter? Please don't take on,'

said Barney. 'I dare say he'll be there,' he added, seizing upon the point the most likely to have caused such distress. 'Don't take on,' he continued, trying to draw away Ronald's hand, and force him to raise his head. But Ronald did not look up for many moments. His countenance was so haggard, when he did, that the poor child gazed on him with alarmed amazement.

'If Captain John says his prayers he'll have his place there, too,' he said, timidly. 'And we'll ask God to teach him his prayers, shall we? I'll ask it every day, if you will.'

Ronald bent down and kissed him with a woman's tenderness. 'Barney, will you? I shall like that.'

'Shall you? I like to do what you like. I can say it when I pray God to bless father, and grandfather, and brothers, and sisters, and Ronald.' He paused, then added—'I never forget that. One day I asked if you might have the place next mine, so I dare say you will; and 'twill be so happy.'

It was a strange, thrilling feeling which those few words created in Ronald's breast; he could scarcely call it hope, and yet it was hope: even when he felt that they were but the expression of a child's affection, touching upon subjects immeasurably beyond its comprehension. They were so vivid, so undoubting; the faith was scarcely to be called faith, it was reality; and it is this which our dim-seeing, earthly minds require to give them strength.

A smile reassured Barney, and made him feel that the cloud had passed away; and suddenly, with a child's quick forgetfulness of the serious questions which had been occupying his mind, he insisted upon Ronald's sitting down by him to show him how to cut out some curious figures which he had promised him. All his thoughts were turned into that channel, except at intervals, when any sudden noise made him look up timidly. He was evidently afraid of the usual visitors at the cottage, and at last he begged Ronald to go to the back yard and see if Captain John was there. 'I shouldn't like him to be out there,' he said; 'perhaps he'd stay there all night.'

'O Barney, how silly! People don't stay out-of-doors all night; and if he did, he wouldn't do you any harm.'

'People do stay out all night,' replied Barney, quickly. 'Father's going to be out to-night.'

'To-night? What for? What do you mean?'

'Mother Brewer's coming here; grandfather said she'd do for me.'

'I don't understand. Do for you?'

'Father's going away,' continued Barney ; 'but he doesn't like it.'

Ronald's interest was excited ; but he said, without expressing the least surprise, 'Was that what father, and grandfather, and Captain John were talking about?'

'They made a great hushing and whispering up in the corner ; I couldn't hear.'

'But you heard something?' Ronald's voice was tremulously eager.

'I heard grandfather say Mother Brewer should come when father was gone in the boat. They didn't stand here ; they were out by the door.'

'The boat? oh!' And Ronald's interest sank, for he thought it was only some smuggling scheme which had been planned.

'Is it anything wicked, do you think?' continued Barney ; ''cause father doesn't want to go.'

'I can't tell. Was that all you heard?'

The question was too direct. The boy had been trained to silence, though he often forgot his lesson ; and now recollecting himself he said, 'I mustn't tell any more ; father won't let me ; he 'll beat me, he says, if I do ever tell what I hear.'

'But Barney, if I want to hear,—if it is of great consequence that I should,—you would tell me then?' Ronald's conscience reproached him as the words were uttered. He corrected himself quickly, and added, 'But never mind, never mind. When is Mother Brewer coming back?'

'I don't know. You aren't going?'

'Perhaps so ; I think I must. Which way did Captain John go, Barney?'

'Out at the back yard. D'ye think he's there now?' The old frightened look returned.

'No, no, lie quiet. There's nobody.'

'There is somebody ; I hear him. O Ronald, won't you look?'

'Barney, that's naughty, I tell you there's no one ; only'— he stepped to the window—'Yes, can't you see? I 'll move you ;— now, look out at the door, across the Gorge ; who's that coming? Some one you 'll be glad to see, I 'll answer for it.'

The child stretched his neck forward, so as to catch a glimpse of the pathway up the Gorge. His eyes sparkled with delight,

'Miss Campbell and Miss Rachel!' he exclaimed, 'and the young gentleman, too, and the little ladies !'

'What, Clement?' Ronald hurried to the door. The party were drawing near. Ronald returned again to the child :—'You are sure, Barney, that grandfather and Captain John are gone.'

' They went out at the back, you can see.' Barney paid but little attention to the question ; his interest was given to the new arrivals.

Ronald quietly opened the back door, and went into the scullery, and from thence into what was called the yard. It was shut in by the hills, which rose immediately behind the cottage, but there was no regular enclosure. Nothing was to be seen from it, but the precipitous banks which formed the head of the Gorge ; bare, and desolate, and scattered over with large, loose stones and rocks. Upon one of these rocks Ronald mounted, and gazed around with the quick sight of one who, from infancy, had been tutored to vigilance. At some distance was the track which led from the secluded Gorge to the open common between Cleve and Encombe, and from thence to the headland of Dark Head Point. Along this path one figure was to be seen ; it looked like Mark Wood ; but no one else was near, except the party just arrived from Encombe. He heard their voices ; the children and Clement were running races,—Bertha trying to keep them quiet, lest they should come too suddenly upon Barney. They seemed all in high spirits. Rachel was with them ; and her laugh especially, with its sweet ringing tone, came distinctly to the ear. Ronald watched, and listened ; and the feeling, painfully morbid, which so often checked him in his happiest moments, riveted him to the spot. What was he, that he should attempt to mingle with those so much beyond him ; —whose innocence and ignorance of sin he could never hope to attain ? He left the rock, and walked a few paces away from the house, to a smooth bit of turf, almost the only level spot near. His inclination was to go away without being seen, but there were other restraining feelings, one especially, which he could not account for ; a dread,—a thought that he must remain near as a guard, though why, or for what purpose, he could not reasonably tell. He waited till they had entered the cottage, and then sat himself down on the further side of the rock upon which he had been standing, till he could quiet the tumult of his feelings and summon courage to meet them.

There was an intense stillness immediately around him. The

sea-gull, the only living creature to be seen, was winging his
flight towards the ocean noiselessly, and not even the tinkling of
a sheep-bell broke upon the wintry quietness. And yet Ronald
listened ; and as he listened he heard the closing of a wicket-
gate, which gave admission to the small plot of ground near the
cottage, cultivated as a garden. It startled him, and his impulse
was to stand up and look round ; but he did not stand, he only
moved so as to see without being seen. Two men passed from
the back yard into the garden, one was Captain Vivian, the
other was Goff. They stood and spoke together for a few
moments ; then Captain Vivian went down the Gorge ; and
Goff—Ronald did not see what became of him, but when he
looked again he was gone.

There was no shyness nor morbid fancifulness in Ronald's
mind now ; his thoughts were distracted from himself ; they
were set upon suspicion—very incoherent, but still enough to
quicken his perceptions. Yet his only definite idea was, that
Goff was lingering about in the hope of meeting Clement, and
that, by watching, he could be a safeguard. This idea made
him go at once to the cottage, walk round it, ascend the hills
a few steps to look about, and then go through the yard and
the scullery, glancing quickly and carefully around. He could
not see any one ; but the door of the scullery (which Ronald
remembered to have shut behind him, fearing the draught for
Barney) was open,—an indication that some one had gone out
since himself. As far as he could tell, no one was there when
he went through, yet he could not feel quite sure. The scullery
was large, for so small a cottage, crowded with things which
did not all belong to Mark Wood,—several casks, and boxes,
and an old mahogany chest, which were Goff's property ; and
it was dark, lighted only by one little window, and that dimmed
by the hill rising behind the cottage ; a person might easily
have been overlooked, standing in the farthest corner. Perhaps that might have been the case before ; but there was no
one there now, Ronald made quite sure of that ; and then he
fastened the door in the inside, and entered the outer apartment.

Bertha had taken Barney in her lap, and was showing him a
book of prints, which she had brought with her, whilst Rachel,
kneeling by her side, watched with eager interest the expression
of the child's face. Clement was playing with Mark Wood's dog,
in front of the cottage ; and Louisa and Fanny were running up
and down the banks.

Barney recognised Ronald's footstep the moment he entered, and called out to him, without any introduction—'Here's a beauty, Ronald! isn't he? And ain't she kind?' he added, lowering his voice to an aside, as Ronald came close to him.

'Very pretty indeed, Barney. What a house for you to live in!' And Ronald drew his attention to the brilliant white edifice with yellow and green trees standing behind it, which formed the frontispiece. He was glad of anything to cover his shyness, for he was always particularly shy with Bertha Campbell; she knew so much more of him than any one else did.

'Barney told me you were gone, Ronald,' said Bertha, giving him her hand with a cordial smile, which said more than any words.

'And I said I was sure you were not; that you had only run away to hide yourself,' said Rachel, laughing. 'Do you know, Barney, that Ronald very often tries to hide himself when he sees us, only he is so tall that his head will peep out, wherever he is.'

'I don't like hiding,' said Barney, quickly and bluntly. 'Father and Captain John hide. Ronald went to see after them.'

'They are not here, are they?' Bertha inquired of Ronald.

'I think not; I believe not.' But Ronald's manner was a little hesitating.

Bertha looked uncomfortable. 'I felt sure,' she said, 'that we should meet no one here, unless it might be you, Ronald; you told me your father was always on the shore, at this time of the day.'

'My father is not here, now,' replied Ronald. 'I saw him go down the Gorge. Goff, too, I think, is gone; but he has been here.'

Bertha turned pale. 'He won't be coming back, you think?'

'I hope not; I don't know what he should come for;' but as he said this, Ronald glanced uneasily at the door.

'Look! Here's a cow and two sheep, and a big dog like father's Rover! Look! you must look.' Barney drew Ronald towards him impatiently.

But Ronald did not look, his thoughts were wandering.

'Show them to me, Barney,' said Rachel, whose quick tact made her see that both Bertha and Ronald were full of anxious thoughts. She came close to the child and turned over the leaves of the book for him, and began, in her simple way to describe the pictures.

'Can't you come out with me for a few minutes?' said Bertha, addressing Ronald.

He followed her to the door without speaking; then, as he caught sight of Clement, he went up to him and shook him heartily by the hand.

'I did not expect to see you here, old fellow,' said Clement, good-humouredly. 'I thought you were buried in your books. What a rage you have for them now.'

'I came over to see the child. I come most days when I can. Have you seen any one go by here just these last few minutes?'

'Not a soul. Whom did you expect?'

'I fancied Goff was here, he was just now; but I suppose he's gone,' said Ronald, carelessly. 'When does Mr Lester come back, Clement?'

'I don't know. Aunt Bertha is the person to ask.'

'He doesn't say when he will come; he may be here any day,' replied Bertha.

'But not to-day?' said Ronald, quickly.

'No, not to-day, certainly. A friend of his is ill; that detains him.'

Ronald raised his eyes to hers, and read in her face that Mr Lester's absence was a source of anxiety. There was an awkward pause. Clement began to play with the dog again, and ran off, scrambling up the bank, and trying to make the animal follow.

Ronald called him back. 'Holloa! Clement, won't you do something for me?'

Clement could scarcely refuse, but he came back unwillingly.

'I've got a word to say to Miss Campbell, but I meant, if I could, just to have drawn Barney once or twice up and down the green. He mustn't stay out more than a few minutes. Would you mind taking him out for me? Rachel will wrap him up.'

'It won't do to trust her,' said Bertha; 'let me go;' but Ronald prevented her. 'Please not: I am sure he will let Rachel put his coat on. Be off, Clement;' and Clement, naturally good-natured, and flattered at being trusted, went into the cottage.

Bertha followed him with her eyes, so did Ronald, till he was

out of hearing ; then he turned anxiously to Bertha, and said—
'I wanted him gone ; isn't Mr Lester coming back soon ?'
'Soon, but not directly ; at least, I can't be sure, Ronald ; why
do you ask?'
'I can scarcely tell. I wish he was here, or that Clement was
away.'.
'You must have a reason ; why don't you tell me it at once?'
said Bertha, with slight impatience in her tone.
'Because it is not a reason—only suspicion—and it may all
be wrong.'
'But tell me—tell me—this is mere tormenting;' and Bertha
looked and spoke great annoyance.
Ronald was pained, and his answer was cold—'The last thing
I should desire is to torment any one, still less Miss Campbell.
My father and Goff keep their plans secret, but that they have
them I don't doubt. It can scarcely have been for nothing that
Goff brought Clement to the Grange the other night.'
'To the Grange?—what?—where?'
'Surely you know. He was there three nights ago.' Then
seeing Bertha's countenance change, he went on—'There is
nothing to alarm you ; he only came with Goff, on his way back
from the Hall, and rested there for about a quarter of an hour.
Clement may not have thought it worth while to mention it,' he
continued, in a tone of exculpation ; 'he does not know what
I do.'
'Unjustifiable!—disgraceful!' began Bertha; and she looked
towards the cottage door, as though she would at once have gone
to reproach him.
Ronald interrupted her—'I will ask, for my own sake, that
the matter may pass now. He will feel that I have betrayed
him, and he won't understand my motive.'
'So mean! so deceitful!' exclaimed Bertha ; and, with a sigh,
she added—'These are the things which make one feel that one
is working for nothing.'
Ronald made no reply to the remark. His attention was still
directed to the cottage.
Bertha considered a little. 'I shall write to Mr Lester, and
tell him that he must return without delay.'
'Yes, that will be the best plan—much the best;' and Ronald
spoke eagerly and earnestly. 'Till he comes'—— he paused,
not wishing to exaggerate her fears—'I will do my utmost to
keep Clement from the Grange; so, doubtless, will you.'

X

'Yes, of course. Would he were to be trusted ! But, Ronald, I may trust you for him.'

'I would entreat you to keep him with you,' replied Ronald, gravely. 'It may be quite out of my power to help him.'

Bertha's fears were again awakened; and she said, 'You have a motive for speaking in this way, and you are afraid to tell it me.'

'No, indeed ; I could not fear to tell you anything—everything. I have a motive—Clement's safety.'

Bertha looked round her anxiously, and said, 'We had better go home at once.'

'Yes. Not that there is cause for fear now ; so far, at least, as I know. I dread more Clement's renewed visits to the Grange ;' and Ronald sighed deeply.

Bertha saw the expression of his face, and read his thoughts. 'Ronald,' she said, 'I need scarcely tell you how I thank you.'

He stopped her. 'Miss Campbell, that can never be required.'

Bertha, without heeding him, continued—'You will believe, I trust, that, even if forced hereafter, from circumstances, to estrange ourselves apparently, neither Mr Lester, Edward Vivian, nor myself, can ever really forget your noble conduct. We feel that Clement is as safe with you as with us.'

'I have a debt to pay,' he replied, gloomily. 'It is not yet discharged.'

'The debt is not yours,' replied Bertha. 'I was unwise to lay the obligation upon you. Mr Lester has made me see this. Let me entreat you to forget it.'

'Forget it !' he exclaimed. 'Forget that the name I bear can never be uttered without a thought of reproach—that even now I may be reaping the fruits of dishonour ! Miss Campbell, tell me rather to forget my own existence ; to bury it, as full often I fain would, in the grave !'

'Ronald, this is wild and wrong. Your position is the ordering of God's providence ; and the grave, when we seek it for ourselves, is not the death of dishonour, but its birth for eternity.'

'Yes, I know it, I know it. But, Miss Campbell, there are feelings to which you, a woman—nurtured in innocence, your name untainted,—must be a stranger. You have never known that goading feeling for which even Heaven's mercy has no cure —disgrace !' The word, as it escaped his lips, was almost inaudible.

'I may not have known it, Ronald, but I can imagine it, and feel for it.'

'Impossible! I also once thought I knew it by imagination,' and he laughed bitterly. Then in a half scornful, half sorrowful tone, he went on, speaking rapidly:—'There is a tale—my father read it to me once, when I was a child—he little thought then that I should find its likeness in my own history;—it tells of the living man bound to the dead, and left to perish in the lonely wilderness. Miss Campbell,'—and his eyes flashed for a moment, and became dim again with struggling anguish,— 'that is disgrace—the dead sin that clings to the memory—inseparable!'

'But, Ronald, it is not your own disgrace; and, as yet, it is not disgrace in the eyes of the world.'

He smiled grimly. 'Who can separate the father and the son? When the living man sank beside his dead burden in the wilderness, there were none to see; but did he, therefore, feel its horror the less? The eye of heaven is upon him who is disgraced; and were it possible for that eye to be hidden from creation—were he alone, the one, solitary, living being, in the vast universe— there would be the eye of his own heart, from which there can be no escape! Miss Campbell, do not try to comfort me; tell me only how I may serve you.'

'I will not try to comfort you, Ronald,' replied Bertha; 'in your present mood you could not receive comfort. You have brooded over your position till its evils have assumed a giant magnitude. Years, and experience, and God's blessing upon your sincerity, will prove to you that even when disgrace is irretrievable in the eye of man, it is never so in the sight of God; that before Him we are all dishonoured, the best even as the worst; and that repentance, which has restored the one, can also give the place of honour to the other. It is but human pride which looks upon any disgrace as indelible before God, for it is only that which rejects the Atonement that can make 'the sins which are as scarlet to be even as white as wool.'

'It may be so; the time may come when I may feel it.'

'It will come; I do not doubt it,' replied Bertha. 'And, in the meanwhile, Ronald, there may be means'—— she stopped, afraid of being carried away beyond the limits of prudence.

Ronald waited respectfully, but, finding that the sentence was not concluded, he said, 'What means? For what purpose? There are none which Miss Campbell could suggest that I should not be too glad to use.'

Still Bertha's face expressed doubtfulness; but, after a few seconds, she replied, 'Means of averting public disgrace, I was going to speak of; but I ought not to name them to you, except that they may be your father's safety.'

'I am willing to hear them,' he replied.

'It is but repeating what I have said before,' continued Bertha.

'You will, I am sure, understand that, if any influence of yours could induce your father to own the wrong we have every reason to believe he has done, Mr Vivian is the last person who would · press a charge against him. If it were only for your sake, he would overlook everything; he owes his life to you, and the obligation can never be forgotten. All that we desire is that any false impression should be removed from General Vivian's mind. Perhaps there would be less difficulty in bringing him to this point, if he knew that we may be soon in a position to compel what now we only request.'

A cloud of haughty feelings darkened Ronald's countenance, and he turned away. But the feeling was momentary. He came back again, and said, with stern self-control, 'It is not an easy task to require a son to bring his father to confession.'

Bertha looked distressed. 'I fear I have done wrong,' she said; 'yet I have spoken in the hope of averting greater evil. One thing is most certain, that your father's danger will be as nothing if he himself will come forward and acknowledge the truth.'

'And if he does not?'

'It may be, I must not say it is, imminent. O Ronald!'—and Bertha's voice suddenly changed into earnestness most unlike her usual placidity,—'think, I beseech you, of what I say; think of what you may avoid,—for your own sake, for your mother's sake.' He stood by with a face pale as death, but made no answer. She read the working of his mind:—'Forgive me, forgive me, that I have so grieved you. At first, when I told you all, I scarcely knew what I was doing; I longed only to have a friend on our side. I thought you might do more for us than any other person.'

'I will do more. As there is truth in heaven, I promise it; but not against my father's safety.'

'Not against it, but for it. Time presses, and events are hastening on. A few weeks, a few days even, may see Edward Vivian openly arrayed against your father; they may place a barrier, Ronald, between us for ever. I am not speaking from fear or fancy, indeed I am not. If you ever believed my word, count upon it now, if possible.'

He wrung her hand in silence, and, as with one consent, they both moved towards the cottage.

CHAPTER XXXVIII.

THE twilight shades were gathering round the woods of Cleve; the heavy trunks and leafless branches were becoming one dark, indistinct mass, above which lurid clouds were gathering together in the wintry sky, piled into fantastic shapes of mountains gilded at their crests, and traversed by lines of fiery light; and islands floating in seas of liquid gold, appearing for a moment, and then passing into other forms, and sinking swiftly, yet almost imperceptibly, into darkness. And in the library at Cleve, in a heavy arm-chair, covered with crimson leather, drawn close to the wide hearth, sat General Vivian; on a low stool at his feet was Ella; whilst, resting on the sofa opposite, lay Mildred. The room was dark; yet the dancing light from the blazing logs flickered along the walls, and seemed to mingle mysteriously with the departing rays afar in the western sky, which glimmered faintly through the narrow diamond panes of a window deeply embayed.

It was an hour for kindly thoughts,—the expression of those inward feelings which never come forth so freely as when twilight or darkness veil the changes of the countenance, and we speak, as it were, to ourselves, not willing to recognise the shadowy, ghostly forms of the friends who are scarcely visible in the dimness.

A change had come over General Vivian's home since Ella had become its inhabitant. Months before, he would have spent that sobering hour in reveries—severe, if not gloomy; and Mildred, fearing to intrude upon him unsummoned, would have used the lingering moments of day in thoughts of quiet meditation,— blessed indeed, and most soothing, yet solitary, as regarded aught of communion on earth.

Now they were together, talking little, thinking much,—and probably very differently,—yet with a certain feeling of common interest, of added cheerfulness and hope. Ella was scarcely to be thanked for this; at first, indeed, her presence had been a restraint; it had fretted the General's conscience, though he would not acknowledge it; and he had seized upon all the weak points in her character, which were many, and dwelt upon, and exaggerated them. Yet still she was an interest to him. The lonely, stern mind, which had, for years, lived to itself, brooding over its own plans, and building up a tower of self-confidence, was now, in a degree, diverted into another channel. · Even when he found fault with her, he liked to watch her; and when he did watch her, his strong sense of justice assisted him against his prejudices. Ella was improved, under Mildred's guidance; she had made resolutions, few and simple, but they had been kept; and this had given her confidence; and, of her own accord, she had then ventured to do more. The General perceived this. Ella was more punctual at breakfast and dinner, and that pleased him; she read steadily, and when he questioned her, the answers brought out her talent; and, as Mildred had hoped, he began to feel proud of her. When it was proposed that she should go home, he felt that he should miss her. Not that he would acknowledge it to himself; the excuse which he made was, that she was a comfort to Mildred. Yet once it had flashed across his mind whether it would be possible to keep her with them always,—he did not say to adopt her,—that would have brought up the old question of justice; but without minutely considering the arrangement, he fancied that she might just as well live at one place as the other. And Ella, on her part, was not without some degree of romantic reverence for her grandfather. His very faults inspired the feeling. She could see into, and through, most minds; she never seemed to reach beyond the surface of his. It was a painful fascination at first, and had sometimes rendered her perverse. She amused herself by appearing wayward, and expressing strange, wild opinions before him, and watching their effect upon him. It was a kind of play, in which she was the heroine; but she was baffled by him. His notice was too slight to be exciting; often she could not tell whether he even heard what she was saying; and when, with an absurd self-consciousness, she became more extravagant, and more wilful, she was put down by a sharp rebuke, which yet was not felt to be irritating; for it was the reproof of a strong, powerful character, given without petulance; and there is more pleasure than pain in this kind of subjection, especially to those whose strength is mental rather than moral.

She became in consequence more gentle and submissive ; and the very difficulty of discovering whether her grandfather was pleased, or the contrary, gave an interest to her efforts. There was a little quiet excitement always going on at the Hall, which afforded a stimulus to her indolence, and so satisfied her conscience, and put her in better humour ; and at length, as the consciousness dawned upon her that he was beginning to like her, came the pleasure of power,—power over one whom every one else dreaded ; and Ella loved power dearly, in spite of her indolence. She felt that she could amuse her grandfather,—that he was interested in her conversation ; she had that sense of being appreciated, which especially tends to bring out talent, and this made her exert herself the more. All these motives were, of course, very mixed,—they could not, in any way, be depended upon for the steady improvement of character ; but Ella's faults were not those which the labour of days or weeks, or even of months, could cure ; they were insidious evils,— pride, wilfulness, indolence,—requiring patience and self-examination, and constant watchfulness ; and Ella was only just beginning to understand her defects,—how then could she be expected, all at once, properly to apply the remedies ? Mildred was often obliged to say this to herself, for Ella was continually disappointing her,—and even her good deeds were not seldom alloyed by some taint of the old leaven. Most especially it was difficult to make her see the effect which her faults had upon others. Indolence had rendered her selfish, and selfishness prevented her from putting herself in the position of those with whom she lived, and understanding their feelings. Besides, without being conceited, she had the consciousness of talent, which is inseparable from its possession ; and knowing that she could make herself very agreeable, it was not easy to believe that she was often just the contrary.

Then, too, her offences, though very tiresome and irritating, were not the result of wilful malice, if the expression may be used. She was always wishing to be much better than she was, and fancied that every one must see this, and understand it ; and so, when she had done wrong, the fault was blotted from her own memory quickly, because there was no depth of bad intention in it, and she forgot that, without a confession or an apology, it could not be forgotten by those who witnessed it. She would be most provokingly disregardful of Mildred's wishes, and would even speak to her proudly and disrespectfully, and then go about

her usual occupation as if nothing had happened, and return to
Mildred in perfect good-humour, without, perhaps, the thought
once crossing her mind that her aunt had reason to be annoyed.

Every day made Mildred see more plainly how much Bertha
must have had to bear with in a character so unlike her own.

Yet there was an improvement, an obvious one, and Mildred
was by nature patient and hopeful, and Ella was very young,
and had, it was to be trusted, a long life before her for the task
of self-discipline, and so it was not difficult to give her encouragement; and this made Ella's life much happier than it
was at home, and rendered even the silence of the old Hall more
cheerful to her than the mirth of the Lodge.

She was cheerful now as she sat with her grandfather and aunt
in the twilight, ruminating upon her own fancies, and from time
to time venturing to give them forth, and Mildred had a pleasure
in listening to her, even though occasionally she saw cause to
check her.

'Grandpapa, do you and Aunt Mildred never go to London?'
was the question, after a silence rather longer than usual.

'What should we do in London, child? We can neither of us
move about.'

'But it would be the world ; Encombe and Cleve are not the
world.'

'They form our world,' observed Mildred, 'and that satisfies
us.'

'But they are not *the* world,—the real world. It is like being
in a dream living here.'

'And you don't like the dream, Ella?' The General did not
mind asking the question ; he knew he was quite safe as to the
answer.

'Oh yes, grandpapa, I do. Sometimes I think it is a dream
I should like never to waken from.'

The General patted her head, and Ella drew nearer to him.
'But, grandpapa, don't you know what I mean ? There is a
difference between dreaming and living.'

'A wide difference,' said Mildred, laughing, 'but I should have
thought, Ella, that dreaminess was quite in your way ; you don't
like active exertion.'

'But I like to see it in others,' said Ella, 'and that is why I
should like to live in London.'

'You would soon grow weary of it,' remarked the General,
shortly.

'Did you, grandpapa?' The question was an experiment. Ella often tried to make him talk of his young days. Occasionally he would, but he was very uncertain.

'Yes, too soon for my own good, or for others' pleasure,' was the reply. 'They would have had me live in London, Mildred,' he added, less gloomily. 'What would you have said to that?'

'Not part with Cleve, grandpapa!' exclaimed Ella, interrupting the answer.

'Ay, child, part with it, every acre ; sell it, divide it, scatter it to the winds ; the property which had come down from generation to generation for the last four hundred years.'

It was strange the impulse which made the General revert to such a subject ; perhaps his conscience was never thoroughly satisfied as to the course he had taken in life, and so he tried to talk himself into the conviction that it had been in all respects a right one. He went on : 'We should have led a different life, Mildred, if we had lived in London. I might have been a gay cavalier ; a courtier ; who knows? But it was a weary life, the little that I saw of it.'

'But you never went much into society, did you, sir?' asked Mildred, encouraging the conversation, since he seemed to enter into it.

'I had not the means,' was the quick reply. 'Ella,' and the General turned to his granddaughter, and spoke with sudden harshness, 'remember that ; whatever you do, never live beyond your means.'

'I have no means, grandpapa.' She said it simply, without any purpose, but it had one unconsciously.

The General moved his hand, which had been resting on her shoulder, and relapsed into silence.

Ella was not aware what she had done. It was too common an occurrence for a conversation to break off abruptly, to cause any surprise. She looked into the fire, and made imaginary hills, and rocks, and roads, out of the red coals, and was quite happy.

Not so Mildred. The spirit of the old times was creeping over her ; she waited anxiously for the General's next words.

'We had better have candles, Mildred.' Very little there was in the words, but very much in the tone.

'Oh, please not yet, grandpapa,' exclaimed Ella. 'I was just in the midst of such a charming story.'

'A fireside story, I suppose,' said Mildred, relieved by Ella's having given a turn to her thoughts.

'Yes, a fascinating one. I wish I could make you see it. There is the pass over the mountains, and the travellers have just got to the top, and now they are going down the other side, into such a lovely country. Do, grandpapa, let us have the firelight a little longer.'

'Waste of time, child;' but the General delayed to ring the bell.

'Is it? But why were such fancies given if they are not to be indulged.'

'They are very well for children,' replied the General.

'Then, grandpapa, please, I am a child.'

'There is no doubt of that,' said Mildred, laughing. 'You are much worse than either Louisa or Fanny, I suspect, in your love of stories.'

'They won't help you on in the world, Ella,' observed the General. 'Trust my word for that.'

'But, grandpapa, have you ever tried? Did you like stories when you were young?'

'Real stories; not such as you fancy.'

'Stories of things which have really happened,' said Ella, in a musing tone. 'Perhaps every one's life is a story, if one could but read it.'

'Yes, Ella,'—General Vivian spoke with mournful earnestness,—'a story only understood when it is too late to rectify its blunders; so I would have you consider it carefully before it begins.'

'Mine is begun, grandpapa.'

'Not begun so that it can't be altered, though,' observed Mildred, with something of tremulousness in her voice.

'No person's life is such that it can't be altered,' said Ella.

'Not exactly, but there is a very different feeling about it as one grows older. It becomes, as it were, fixed; circumstances and relations are formed; it seems as if one could better foresee the future. Now your future, Ella, may be'——

'Anything,' exclaimed Ella, quickly. 'I like to think of it sometimes, it is so exciting; only frightening, too.'

The General had been sitting in a musing posture, apparently only half hearing the last words of the conversation. He broke in upon it, however, here. 'Why should it be frightening, Ella?'

She hesitated, and the General repeated his question more peremptorily.

'Because,—I don't quite exactly know why, grandpapa; but we have led a wandering life, and strange things have happened; and '—— a pause, and a glance at Mildred. 'You know we can't always live with grandmamma.'

Mildred raised herself, and stretched out her hand to ring the bell.

'Not yet, Mildred; we won't have candles yet. You can't live with your grandmamma, you say, Ella. What change do you expect?'

'I don't know, grandpapa. Aunt Mildred,' and Ella looked round for help; 'do you think we shall always live with grandmamma?'

'Perhaps not, my love; we had better leave the future.'

'Yes, much better,—a great deal better.' The General spoke very gravely. 'Ella, it won't do to make dreams of the future.'

'Aunt Bertha tells me enough to frighten me about it,' replied Ella; 'she says, when she is angry, that I may have to work for my bread.'

'O Ella!' the words escaped Mildred involuntarily, and a sudden movement made it seem that, but for her helplessness, she would have sprung from the sofa to stop Ella.

'Let her go on, Mildred; what else does your Aunt Bertha say to you, Ella?'

'Nothing,—not much else.' Ella felt she was getting into a difficulty.

'She thinks you will have to work for your bread, does she? Are you prepared for that?'

'I don't know.'

'Should you like it?'

'Grandpapa! No. Does any one like it?'

'Persons with energy don't mind it,' said Mildred, rather sternly.

'Stop, Mildred, don't interrupt her. Should you like it, Ella?'

'No, grandpapa, I don't think I should.' Ella looked up at him, perplexed by the question.

He stirred the fire and spoke at the same time, turning his head away from her. The accent was low and trembling; it came from a weary heart: 'Would you live here, Ella, with me, then; and I would provide for you?'

A strange, unbroken silence. Mildred could hear the beating of her own heart, running its rapid race with the ticking of the quaint old clock in the corner of the room. The General pushed back his chair as though he would rise. Ella felt the movement, and laid her hand on his knee. 'Grandpapa,—Aunt Mildred,— what must I say?'

'What you feel, dear Ella,' said Mildred.

'The truth,' said the General.

'Grandpapa, I should like it, but—oh! Aunt Mildred, help me;' and Ella rose and went to Mildred's sofa, and knelt down by her.

'What is it, Ella? Speak, dear child, without fear,' she whispered.

'I can't. I could tell you alone.'

Mildred glanced at her father. A clear flame from the fire cast a bright, yet ominous light upon his features; it seemed to alter them,—to make them look more worn; the haggard face was set as in a framework of darkness.

'Go to him and tell him what you mean,' whispered Mildred to Ella. And Ella looked round at her grandfather, and shrank from the cold severity of the fixed gaze directed to the fire. 'Ella, he will be angry if you don't,' repeated Mildred.

Ella went up to him. 'Dear grandpapa, it is very, very kind of you;' she kissed his forehead. 'I should like to stay here; I am very happy here; only'—her hesitation was almost suffocating—'would it be right if papa were kept away?'

A groan was heard, but the tall figure sat erect, cold, immovable; it might have been a lifeless statue rather than a living being into whose ear the words were spoken.

'Ella, my crutches! Help me, will you!' said Mildred. Ella gave them to her. 'Now, leave us; I will send for you when you may come back.' And Mildred moved slowly across the room, and seated herself in a chair which Ella placed for her by the General's side.

The door was closed, and Ella gone. The General heard the sound, and slowly turned his head. 'Mildred!'—She laid her hand in his; her eyes were raised to his face; she saw tears streaming down his cheeks.—'My child! clinging to me through all!' he murmured.

'To whom else should I cling, my dear, dear father?'

'Whom else, indeed. We are alone in this world; even Ella cannot sacrifice herself to live with us.' He said it bitterly.

'Hers is a strange nature,' replied Mildred.' 'I should not have expected such thought.'

'It has been her teaching,' said the General.

'Or the teaching of nature. Would you like her as well if she did not feel it?'

'She has no cause for it,' he replied, abruptly.

'If it were my case, you would expect me to feel it.'

'I have not brought disgrace upon you, Mildred.' The General averted his head, and withdrew his hand.

Mildred's heart seemed to rise up in her throat as she said, 'Ella does not see her father's disgrace, dear sir. Neither, perhaps, do others.'

They were bold words. Month after month, and year after year, since the first outburst of anger, had the father and daughter dwelt beneath the same roof with that one mutual sorrow, yet never approaching it, except by distant allusions.

The General replied calmly, his tone and manner so unshaken that it struck Mildred as something fearful. 'The world does think him disgraced, Mildred; though his relations may not.'

'He did very wrong, sir; his marriage was most unfortunate; indeed, we see it all.'

'Only it is not disgrace,' he replied, with cold sarcasm.

'Not his marriage certainly.'

'And not his gambling? — his friendship with that rascal, John Vivian? Mildred, Mildred!'—he put his face close to hers and lowered his voice—'I know, if you do not; he dishonoured my name once; and I would have it blotted for ever from the earth rather than trust him to dishonour it again.'

Still Mildred's voice was gentle, though earnest. 'I am aware I don't understand it all, sir.'

'No, you don't understand; no one does, nor can. And I have borne all;—Mr Lester's strictures, your sorrow, my friends' judgments—all—all I have endured rather than tell,'—his voice changed suddenly, it became fiercely eager—'but would you know it, Mildred? Shall I show you what your brother was? what he could do? He stood up, pushed aside his chair, and turned to the ebony escritoire which was close to it. Mildred gave him a taper: he lighted it, and, with an unsteady hand tried the lock. The taper went out; he relighted it, opened the cabinet, drew out some small drawers, searched in them, then put his hand to his head, trying to recollect, and searched again.

'Your private papers are in the upper box, sir,' Mildred ventured to say.

'Yes, yes.' He was impatient at the suggestion, but he took down the box. The light of the taper was faint, and he could scarcely see by it, but Mildred did not venture to propose ringing for a lamp.

The General, however, did so himself, and till it was brought, sat silent in the arm-chair.

'Put the little table near me, Greaves, and that box upon it.' He watched the butler's movements with an irritable eye. Then, when the man was gone, he began to look through the papers.

The search was perplexing, though Mildred thought at first that it was only painful. He muttered to himself, 'It was here, —in this packet. I can't have mislaid it,' and again he searched through the packet, whilst his features assumed a most distressed look of doubt, and effort at recollection.

Mildred said at length : 'If you would not trouble yourself, my dear father, but tell me, if you don't mind. I would rather hear than see.'

He took no notice, but went on as before. Mildred watched him anxiously, for she fancied he did not quite know what he was doing.

'I would look, dear sir,' she said, 'if you would tell me what to find.'

'I can't ; it was here ; somebody—Mildred, who has touched my box ?' he addressed her angrily.

'No one, sir. No one could ; it is always in your room.'

A sudden dawning of recollection crossed the General's mind. He muttered Mr Lester's name.

'You were looking at papers the other day, sir, with Mr Lester,' said Mildred.

His face became more troubled, but he put aside the box, and leaned back in his chair.

'Mr Lester may be able to assist you in finding it,' said Mildred ; 'but you could tell me if you would what it was ; it makes me very anxious.' And the tone certainly gave full effect to her words.

He raised his head, and gazed upon her as one in a dream ; his voice, too, had something in it of a wavering, faltering tone.

'I don't know why I should tell it ; he is gone from us, Mildred, —well that he is ; he would have squandered all.'

'He was extravagant, but he might have learned wisdom,' observed Mildred, timidly.

'Extravagant! yes.' The General tried to raise the lid of the box, which he had unintentionally closed. Mildred stopped him.

'Do you wish to show me a list of his bills, dear sir? I think I know them.'

'Bills, did you say, Mildred? Little cared he for bills when he could give checks, and promise away what was to be his after my death. His! his!' he repeated, and his scornful laugh struck an icy chill to Mildred's heart. 'But it was reckoning a little too much without his host; don't you think so, Mildred? A man can't build upon his own, when life stands in the way of possession. My life! his father's! But that was easily set aside. His wish was father to his thoughts, eh, Mildred? He didn't think I should have been such an old man. But I have outwitted him—stopped him when he least expected it; he has no inheritance now to play ducks and drake with.'

'I don't understand you, dear sir,' said Mildred, indescribably alarmed at his manner.

'No, how should you? What do women know of such matters? I would have shown it you, but I can't. He tried again to open the box, but his hand trembled so violently that Mildred took the key from him, yet without placing it in the lock.

'Do you mean,' she said, 'that he drew upon you for more money, sir, than he had a right to?'

'Drew upon me, Mildred? Promised it, I say;—pledged it; would have given my lands to the Jews,—to worse than Jews,—to that scoundrel, John Vivian. Pshaw, why can't I show you the proof.'

'It is impossible! Edward could never have done it,' exclaimed Mildred, in a voice of agony.

The General shrank from the sound of the name, but almost immediately recovered himself. 'I will find it, and you shall see it; not now,—to-morrow, by daylight I can find it. I have it here,' he added, with a tone of sad triumph; 'in his own hand-writing; the promise given to John Vivian, Esq., that after my death,—after my death, remember,—the sum of five thousand pounds should be paid to redeem his debts of honour; his own writing, his own signature.'

'There must have been a mistake; it could not be; it is impossible,' exclaimed Mildred again.

'Doubtless! a mistake! impossible! John Vivian must have

been deluded ; the evidence of my own eyes must have deceived me ; the evidence of one who saw the promise signed must have been at fault. Why, Mildred, child, did I not say the same myself? Say it, almost believed it, when the actual proof was before my eyes. And did not John Vivian stand by, with his bold defiance, and urge upon me to call up the man,—the poor wretch who had been the plotter of that miserable marriage,— the confidant of both ; he who had seen the actual words written ? Talk not to me of mistake, Mildred ; there are deeds in which there can be no mistake.'

'Edward had no opportunity given him of explanation,' said Mildred.

'What ! child, when I wrote to him, and my letter was unanswered? He had no explanation to give. He had been befooled himself. He gave his worthless bond to John Vivian, little thinking that it would be brought to me ; and when it was brought, he was sunk in my eyes, and in his own, for ever.'

'But you paid the money, and so owned the justice of the claim, sir,' said Mildred.

'Justice to myself, to my own honour, for the last time. My son's debts were a claim upon the name which he bore, and I acknowledged them even to the utmost farthing. But from that hour he ceased to be my son ; and now let him go and pray the winds to hear him ; they will listen as soon as I.'

Mildred's heart failed her. A few minutes before, she had fancied that the time might be near for telling him that Edward was in England. Now, she only said, ' He has severely suffered for his offences.'

No reply. She went on further, her words being uttered with extreme precision :—' He is very penitent, whatever he may have done.'   •

' So are we all, when punishment falls upon us,' was the stern answer.

' Years have given him experience,' she continued.

' So have they given to me,' replied the General.

'And you would not trust him, then ?' She spoke in a tone of doubtful timidity.

'Trust him ? Yes, I would trust every man whose hands are chained, and whose feet are fettered. He is doing well, you say. Let him thank God for it, as I do.'

' But if he has suffered, and is penitent, my dear father, would there be no hope for him ever ?'

'Mildred, you speak ignorantly. It may seem that you are addressing a cold, harsh old man,—nay, don't stop me;—I am not blind to what is passing around me, though often it is thought I am. The world thinks me such, so do you, so does Mr Lester. Cold, strict prejudice, that is my character;—a true one, in a certain sense. Do you know who made me so? My father— my grandfather—his father before him; for the sins of my ancestors have been my conscious inheritance from my boyhood. Listen, Mildred. As a little child I was generous, open-hearted, unsuspicious. I flung my money away to the right hand and to the left. I gave when I was asked; I promised when I could not give. I was a true Vivian. That was my disposition; it continued mine till I was twelve years old. Then came a change; how or when it dawned upon me I cannot say; but there is an atmosphere in every home, which we breathe insensibly; the atmosphere of mine was care—carking, harassing, lowering care. It crept into my heart, and dulled my spirits; it made me fearful and doubtful towards those with whom I ought to have been open as the day. It pressed upon me heavily and more heavily; and it pressed upon others also. I saw it in the countenances of the old servants; I heard it in the murmurs of my father's tenants; I read it written on the broken-down fences, and the walls falling to decay. We were a family on the verge of ruin; and in striving to keep ourselves from degradation, we brought hardship and exaction upon those of whom we ought to have been the·protectors. The name of Vivian, once honoured, was now execrated. I was but a boy, Mildred, when first I realised to myself the true position in which I stood; and it may seem strange that I should have allowed the fact to weigh with me; it may appear more natural that I should have cast it away with a boy's thoughtlessness. But it did influence me; it tinged my visions for the future; it shaped my plans; and at last it gave me a definite object for which to work. I stood, one day, at the head of my class at school, and the murmur went on around me, among the masters, that I was capable of a great work; that whatever I set my heart upon I must attain. They spoke, I knew, of worldly distinctions; but I read their words differently. Distinction was mine by right of inheritance, for the Vivians, even before they came to Cleve, had been the lords and the leaders of others for centuries; but it would never be mine in possession, unless I retrieved the follies of the last generation. My heart swelled within me, and in secret I vowed that, from that hour, I would

Y

toil without complaining, and suffer without repining, until once
more I could face the world, a Vivian of the olden times, with
my honour untainted, free to devote myself to the people amongst
whom I lived, and regarded by them, not as an oppressive landlord, exacting to the last penny, but as a master and a father,
living only for their happiness.   There is no need now, Mildred,
to tell you how my vow was accomplished.   A mission was
given me, and I fulfilled it ; let those who know me best say
how.   But do you think that, after the labour of those many
years,—the self-denial of a life,—I am now to be persuaded to
throw myself and my people into hands which will, which must,
undo my work.   Is the man who could act as—as your brother
acted—fit to be entrusted with the happiness of others.   Is his
boy, is Clement, likely to be such a successor as I should desire
for the accomplishment of the work for which I have lived ?
Put aside inclination, Mildred, put aside prejudice, and answer
me fairly : my honour and the happiness of my people are at
stake ;—can I be justified in sacrificing them to the weak instinct
of affection ? '

'My dear, dear father, don't ask me.   I cannot put aside
prejudice, if it be prejudice ; it is impossible.'   Her arm was
flung around his neck, and she rested her head on his
shoulder.   'Let him be as he is—disinherited—yet let him return.'

'Madness ! Mildred, madness !'   He almost shook her from
him, as he sat more upright, and every limb seemed to become
stiff with the effort at self-restraint.

'My father, not madness—but mercy ; ' and she clung to him
so that he could not release himself.

'Leave me, Mildred; let me go.'   With a great effort he
withdrew himself from her, and rose, and stood with his back to
the fireplace, looking fixedly at her ; but Mildred saw him not,
for her head was buried upon the arm of the chair, and her sobs
came fast and bitterly.

He spoke again, seeking to excuse himself :—'Your fancy is a
woman's weakness, Mildred.   Were it good for me, it would be
misery for him.'

Something in the tone struck her as relenting, and she raised
her head, and dashed away the tears from her eyes.   'Misery !
oh, never ! it is his one last hope.'

General Vivian crossed his arms on his breast and made no
answer.

Mildred's voice was heard again, clear, and slow :—' Mercy for him, father, even as you would find mercy yourself.'

' It cannot be. To live with me as my son, and not my heir —Mildred, you don't know what you are asking.'

' Perhaps not to live with you, but to see you, if but for once only, to hear that he is forgiven. It is for you and me, and the sight of his home he yearns.'

' Lost through his own fault.' And silence fell again upon the darkened chamber ; and the flickering gleam of the dying fire showed the General standing in his place, immovable, and Mildred's slight figure rigid as if carved in stone.

Yet once more she spoke, and the tone was that hollow whisper which speaks the agony of a broken heart :—' Father, pardon him, and see him, he is now in England.'

A strange, gurgling, convulsive sound struck upon the ear ! General Vivian staggered to a chair, and sank back senseless.

CHAPTER XXXIX.

'BERTHA, how late you are, and where have you left Clement?' Mrs Campbell, having enjoyed her afternoon's siesta, and then worked whilst there was light remaining, had begun to feel impatient for the return of the party, who had been wandering over the hills.

' I can't say exactly,' was Bertha's reply. ' He was with us just as we came off the hills ; but he will be here presently, I dare say.'

' He stayed behind with me first,' said Louisa ; ' and then he clambered up the bank to get a stone, which I thought was a fossil. He was so long finding it, that I didn't like to wait for him.'

' If he doesn't come in time we can't have tea kept for him,' observed Mrs Campbell. ' I have no notion of every one's being put out for a boy of his age.'

' It is not tea-time yet,' said Bertha. ' Louisa and Fanny, you have your history to read for to-morrow ; you had better fetch it.'

' Poor little dears ! after their long walk ; I am sure they can't possibly read history. You must let them off, Bertha. Take off

your things, my dears, and then come down and warm your-
selves, and tell me all you have been doing.'

'There is not much to tell,' observed Bertha, in an uncomfortable tone, which was the only safety-valve she allowed
herself, when interfered with ; 'we only went to Barney Wood's
cottage.'

'But you took him his coat, didn't you? You always take
him something.'

'The coat wasn't quite finished,' said Bertha. 'Rachel had
been busy writing to her father.'

'Oh, Mr Lester is not coming home, then. Betsey told me
that, and she heard it from Anne.'

'They are both great gossips,' observed Bertha, quickly.
'I don't think anything is settled as to Mr Lester's return.
Rachel only wrote in case he might not come.'

Her manner fretted Mrs Campbell, and, being inclined to
complain, she returned to Clement :—' Where do you say you
left him, Bertha? You ought not to have left him ; there are a
great many bad people about ; no one knows what mischief he
may be led into.'

'A boy of his age must learn to keep himself out of mischief,'
said Bertha, rather proudly. But though she spoke with seeming unconcern, she looked out of the window to see if he was
coming.

'I am glad he has given up being with Ronald,' observed Mrs
Campbell, 'now that we know what a mess Captain Vivian is
likely to get into.'

'Is there anything new about Captain Vivian? anything
particular?' asked Bertha, with quick interest.

'Betsey tells me that the preventive officers are not going to
be outwitted any longer ; and they vow they will search the
Grange from the garret to the cellar,' said Mrs Campbell.

'And very much they will find there!' said Bertha. 'If they
mean to do anything, they should not let Betsey know it.'

'She can't help knowing it ; it's talked of everywhere,' continued Mrs Campbell ; 'and what's more, Betsey has a brother
somehow mixed up with them.'

'Poor girl! that is trouble enough,' said Bertha, thoughtfully.

'She asked me to let her go out and see him,' continued Mrs
Campbell ; 'and I said she might, if she was in in time ; so she
went about four o'clock.'

Bertha was too much occupied with painful thoughts of her own, to take any particular notice of this piece of information ; and Mrs Campbell continued—

'Betsey thinks there's something going on now. Mark Wood had come for her brother, and had taken him out with him, so that she couldn't see him. She takes it to heart a good deal. I think, Bertha, you might just as well see her presently, and find out what she is afraid of.'

'Perhaps the less we know about such matters the better,' replied Bertha, looking again out of the window. 'If Mark Wood has been in Encombe,' she added, with an air of consideration, 'it must have been after we saw him going down the Gorge.'

'He and Stephen Hale had left Betsey's cottage just ten minutes before she got there,' continued Mrs Campbell, evidently pleased at having something to talk about, which seemed to draw Bertha's attention. 'Betsey was told they went off towards the Point ; it is the place they all go to. There is a cave, or some such place, I believe, where they meet.'

'Not a very convenient rendezvous,' replied Bertha ; 'it must be so difficult to reach. But it must be all talk about anything particular going on now ; if there were, they would never let it out in that way.'

'I don't know, I am sure,' replied Mrs Campbell; 'at anyrate, it is high time that something should be done. The village is getting into a sad state. Betsey says her brother is quite a different person since he mixed himself up with the smuggling. I can't think, for my part, what Mr Lester can be doing, to let things go on as they do. He calls himself a good parish priest; I know his parish is the worst in the county.'

Any suggestion to Mr Lester's disadvantage was felt as a personal incivility by Bertha, and she immediately began saying, that no one could be better aware than Mr Lester himself of the bad state of his people, or do more to remedy the evil ; but whilst things were carried with such a high hand by those who ought to set a good example, there was little hope of amendment. Whilst Captain Vivian remained at Encombe, it must and would be a disreputable place.

'Well, then, he will be taken from it soon, we may hope,' replied Mrs Campbell, rather triumphantly. 'Betsey has a cousin in the preventive service, so she hears both sides ; and she tells me that they vow they will have the smugglers in their power

before the new year begins ; that is what makes her so afraid for
her brother.'

' They must be quick about it, then,' said Bertha. ' It wants
but a very short time to the new year.'

' We shall see something before it comes,' said Mrs Campbell,
oracularly; and Bertha echoed the words in her own mind,
though with a different meaning. Mrs Campbell relapsing into
silence, she took the opportunity of leaving the room, and going,
not up-stairs to take off her things, but into the garden and lane,
to look for Clement.

Bertha went a little way down the lane without meeting any
one; then, hearing some persons approaching, talking noisily, she
turned into a by-path, by a cottage garden, and stood there till
they had passed. The voices, which she recognised made her
very glad that she had avoided the meeting. Mark Wood,
Stephen Hale, and Goff, were together, apparently disputing.
Bertha watched them till they were nearly out of sight,—if sight
that could be called which was only the indistinct perception of
twilight,—and, even when they were gone, felt unwilling to move
from her hiding-place, lest they should return. Not that she had
any cause to fear,—it was unlikely that they would notice, still
less speak to her; but the rough voices, and the very distant
possibility of being brought in contact with them, made her
shrink into herself. She waited what seemed a long time,—
though, in fact, it was only a few minutes,—then, scolding herself for folly, ventured back into the lane, and had gone some
little distance, when, once more, as she had dreaded, the voices
were heard, and very near. The men had taken a short cut, and
were returning. Bertha did not like to run back, that would
attract notice ; still less did she wish to proceed. For a
moment she stood irresolute ; but the sound of a footstep
behind gave her confidence, especially when, on looking round,
she recognised Ronald. His finger was raised to his lips, as a
sign for silence, and without noticing her, he turned shortly,
strode down the lane at a rapid pace, and entered the path which
Bertha had just left.

Bertha was surprised, yet her momentary feeling of fear was
over. She felt that a protector was near ; and went on boldly,
smiling at her own weakness, as the men lowered their voices
when she passed, Mark Wood and Stephen Hale even touching
their hats.

Five minutes afterwards, as she stood at the Lodge gate, Ronald joined her; his voice was agitated, and he began without apology or explanation. 'Clement is with you, Miss Campbell, of course.'

'No, not yet! I expect him.'

'Not with you? When did you leave him?'

'He left us just as we entered the village; he stayed behind.'

'Behind! Alone?'

'Yes; that is, Louisa was with him; but she came back to us. What is the matter, Ronald?'

'Nothing. Have you been long returned?'

'Not very; we were all late. For pity's sake, Ronald, tell me what this means?'

'I thought Clement might be with Goff. I knew he was loitering about the cottage, and I watched after you were gone, but could not see him at first; I did afterwards. He followed the path you took, and I followed, too, some distance. Then'——

'Well! what then?'

'I met my father; he sent me back to the cottage on a message; and I lost sight of you all. Good night,'—he broke off abruptly; 'I will look for Clement;' and he hurried away.

His course was rapid and intricate. He knew all the by-lanes and short cuts of the village, and every cottage garden was open to him as to a friend; and so, with almost a direct course, he made his way to the Grange, noticed only by a few stragglers returning late from work, who, recognising his step, greeted him with a laugh, and 'How are ye, Master Ronald?' but not troubling themselves as to his wandering movements, and scarcely even making a remark upon his evident haste.

The shrubbery gate of the Grange was wide open, and the large, lonely house was silent and dreary in the glimmering twilight, neither fire nor candle to be seen through the uncurtained windows of the deserted apartments; and when Ronald entered, his footstep sent a hollow echo through the long stone passages. He went first to the parlour, which was empty; but the cloth was laid for dinner, and the shutters were closed. A rough club stick lay on the table, and a glove was on the floor. Ronald, without any particular thought, picked up the glove and laid it down carelessly, whilst he stood for a few moments thinking whether to remain for his father or return to the Lodge to satisfy his mind about Clement. An uncomfortable misgiving was still haunting him. Barney's imperfect hints of a mystery returned to him, and with it came the impulse to go at once to the Point, and watch whether anything more than usual was going on there. But the evening was growing darker and darker, and the moon would not be risen for another hour; he could see nothing, even if he were to go; and, in the meantime, if any mischief were afloat, it would most probably be something which would bring Clement to the Grange. Just at that moment Ronald's eye fell upon the glove, a rough winter glove—too small, surely, for Captain Vivian's hand. He tried to put it on; it was too small for himself; it must be Clement's, left there probably the previous night he had been there. But no; Ronald recollected now that he had seen Clement wearing it that very day, and had thought at the time that he would try and procure a pair of the same kind for Barney.

He rushed out of the room; but still, habitually cautious, controlled his eager step as he passed through the hall and back passages, and softened his voice when he encountered the solitary domestic, of whom he inquired whether his father had returned to the Grange within the last hour.

It might or it mightn't be an hour, the woman couldn't say, but the Captain had been in and put off dinner;—and she walked away, sulky from the additional trouble.

'Stop, Madge! can't you! Was my father alone?'

'Who's to say, Master Ronald? not I. D'ye think I showed my nose in the parlour?'

'But you may have heard. Was he speaking to any one? Did he seem as if he was alone?'

'Seem? Why, he was alone when I saw him. What should you keep me here talking such daft folly for?'—and Madge retired within the precincts of her own domain, and closed the kitchen door violently, as a hint to Ronald that he was on no account to follow.

Ronald opened the hall door, and went out into the gravel sweep, and listened; and he heard the distant trampling of a horse's hoofs, and the cry of a sick child, in a cottage occupied by one of the farm labourers. But the wailing wind drowned all other sounds, save that which mingled with and deepened it—the hoarse rush of the waves beating against the precipitous cliffs.

For several minutes he stood there, his face turned towards Dark Head Point. A rising mist had now obstructed even the faint gleam of lingering day; but twice Ronald fancied he saw a light gleaming in that direction, though so far off that he knew it must be from a vessel at sea; and then, again, there seemed another moving, and higher up, upon the cliff; but the mist gathered over again more thickly, and all was obscure.

Some one clapped him on the shoulder with a heavy hand. ' What, Ronald, my lad, watching? what's that for?'

' For you, father; I wondered where you were.'

' No cause for wonder, I should think; I'm out often enough many hours later than this. But, come, let's in to dinner.'

Captain Vivian hurried on; and when Ronald would have lingered to watch the light on the cliff, he called to him impatiently, saying that they had both waited long enough, and he was ravenous. Yet Ronald did linger for some seconds, and when his father had entered the house, he stood for several moments on the step of the door with a longing, which he could scarcely resist, to brave Captain Vivian's displeasure, and run back to the Lodge to gain some tidings of Clement.

' Ronald, where are you? Come in, I say. I won't have that wind through the house; shut the door, and come in.'

And Ronald obeyed mechanically.

They sat down to dinner. Captain Vivian talked more than was his wont. Ronald gave but short answers. He was considering in his own mind, whether it would be wise to mention Clement's name, and ask how his glove had been found there. Nothing in any way, however, led to the subject. Captain Vivian's conversation was confined to discussions upon the superiority of the little smuggling vessel over the regular traders upon the coast, and anecdotes of the wonderfully short voyages she had lately made. Once Ronald mentioned Barney Wood, and made a remark upon Mr Lester and Miss Campbell's kindness; but it was badly received, Captain Vivian turned it off with a sneer, and went on as before, somewhat incoherently and unconnectedly—his words uttered very fast, his tone half jocular, half hasty. Ronald could not think, he could only listen and reply.

A loud peal at the hall bell! Captain Vivian went himself to answer it; Ronald also followed a few paces behind. A message from the Lodge was brought by Mr Lester's gardener. ' Mrs Campbell's compliments, and she would be glad to know if Master Clement was at the Grange.'

Captain Vivian burst into a loud laugh, and almost shut the door in the man's face. ' Master Clement here? What folly will be asked next? My compliments to Mrs Campbell, and Master Clement doesn't trouble me much with his company. She must look for him elsewhere. What, Ronald!' he grasped his son's shoulder, as Ronald was going to reopen the door; 'rushing after? what for? Do you think the tender chicken's lost?'

'He has been here. I know it; I have a proof.' Ronald tossed Clement's glove upon the floor.

Captain Vivian kicked it from him; his face was livid, either with anger or fear :—'Clement was here. He is gone home, or he ought to be. Now, back to dinner, and no more of this folly.'

He led the way to the parlour; Ronald followed moodily. Both sat down to the table, but only Captain Vivian talked. He had apparently repented his hasty show of authority, and tried to bring Ronald round, pressing him to eat, urging him to take wine, joking him about his books; but Ronald still sat with his abstracted gaze, listening for distant sounds, and giving only such short answers as were absolutely necessary. Irritated by his total absence of interest, Captain Vivian began in another strain :—' So, Ronald, you mean to show yourself a pleasant companion, to leave the conversation in my hands; I thank you for it; it is all, of course, I have a right to expect from my only child. Yet I might have thought that so much woman's teaching might have given you a touch of good manners. Bertha Campbell sets up for a lady, but it's little enough of a gentleman that you have shown yourself since she - set foot in Encombe. Don't think I am surprised, though; it's the old grudge, malice carried on for a dozen years—cunningly, too, setting my son against me.'

Ronald had given his full attention to this last speech, but he could not answer it. Had not Bertha Campbell, though unintentionally, been the means of embittering the feelings which, even before, were but too acutely conscious of his father's faults?

Captain Vivian went on more painfully, because with less of sarcasm :—'I am not what many fathers are, I know that. I'm not the man to set up for a squire, and make a fuss about my boy, and put him in the way of fine people. It never was my way, and it never will be. I was brought up roughly myself, and I've led a rough life, and it's too late now to mend it; and what I am my son must be. But I should never have thought that for that reason he was to be made to turn against me, to plot with my enemies.'

'Plot with them ? O father ! how little you know.'

'Aye! plot with them,' continued Captain Vivian. 'You don't think, do you, that I 'm so blind as not to have an eye for what 's going on close at my door ? '

' I don't know what you refer to, father,' replied Ronald.

' Probably not ! You would be the last person to own, if you did.'

Captain Vivian's manner was proud and coldly determined. It might have been the manner of his early days, never entirely forgotten ; and it struck a chill, and something of a feeling of awe, into Ronald's heart. It was as if, after all, there was something better left than that low recklessness, which had of late been his chief characteristic.

Ronald answered more quietly, and even respectfully : ' If you are suspicious of me, father, and will tell me your suspicions, I will try to remove them.'

' What ! how ? ' Captain Vivian started up and went to the door looking out into the hall : ' Folly; it 's only the old woman's tramp.'

He came back again, and stood with his back to the fire ; ' Suspicions you were talking of, Ronald : what would you give to hear them ? '

' A great deal, father, if I could make you believe they are unfounded.'

' Well then ! '—a pause—a second commencement, and a second pause—at last the words came with thundering emphasis : ' Suspicions that I have a traitor in my camp, who would desert me at the last gasp ! '

Ronald pushed aside his plate, and rising, paced the room in a tumult of excitement.

Captain Vivian went on coldly : ' What is the care for this miserable boy, Clement Vivian ? What is the devotion to Bertha Campbell, and the obedience to Mr Lester ?—treachery, treachery from the beginning to the end.'

' Are they your enemies, father ? ' Ronald's voice was husky with agitation, for his promise to Bertha was present to his mind, and even now it seemed he might be called to fulfil it.

' Circumstances made them my enemies,' was the reply ; ' that 's enough for you to know.'

' Then Clement is your enemy for his father's sake ? '

Captain Vivian answered cautiously: 'Such a boy as that my enemy! he is beneath me.'

'Yet'—Ronald hesitated—'through him you might work harm to his father.'

'Who tells you that?' and Captain Vivian turned upon him fiercely.

'My own reason partly,' replied Ronald; and summoning more courage, he added: 'I know through Miss Campbell that you have, as you yourself say, cause for mutual enmity.'

'Ha! the family secrets! And pray what may Miss Campbell have thought proper to confide to you?'

'She has given me warnings rather than confidence—warnings, father, which I would fain give to you.'

'I am obliged to her.' Captain Vivian's face showed a change of colour. 'Threats, I presume; a notice that I shall be taken up for a smuggler, as they call me.'

'They were very vague, indirect threats,' replied Ronald, in an unmoved tone, though his heart beat painfully; 'yet they made me feel that danger might be at hand.'

'Danger at hand, and you not tell me of it—ungrateful boy!'

Bitter reproaches followed, which Ronald, leaning against the wall, heard, yet without hearing, for still his thoughts reverted to Clement; and the words fell upon his ear, as they had often done before, almost as sounds without meaning.

Captain Vivian stopped at length, and then in a calmer voice insisted upon knowing everything which Miss Campbell had dared to say. Ronald was hesitating for a reply, when another and more violent ring at the hall door a second time interrupted the conversation.

This time Captain Vivian did not go out himself, but stood in the open doorway; and both he and Ronald, as by mutual consent, paused to hearken.

It was a man's voice speaking, and angrily. Mrs Campbell had sent another message: 'Master Clement had been seen with Captain Vivian, going to the Grange. Mrs Campbell desired to know when he had left it, and what direction he had taken.'

Ronald turned upon his father a look of keen distrust.

Captain Vivian's countenance did not alter. He went directly to the door, and said: 'My compliments to Mrs Campbell. Master Clement was here for two minutes, and I walked with him a little way down Long Lane, but he turned off at the end. Is she uneasy about him?'

'He hasn't been home yet, and it's past eight,' said the man, gruffly. 'Mrs Campbell said she was sure the people at the Grange knew something about him.'

'Who is looking for him?' inquired Ronald, anxiously.

'One or two people have been asked; but we have been expecting him in every moment, when we were told that he wasn't here.'

'We will go to the cliff,' said Ronald, and he took up his hat, and stepped into the porch. To his surprise his father made no attempt to stop him.

'We thought he might have been with Goff, and some of his men. He's fond of getting about with them,' continued the gardener, more cordially; 'but Goff's at home, and doesn't know anything about him.'

Captain Vivian came out, and stood with Ronald in the porch: 'You may tell Mrs Campbell, that my son and I will go down to the shore, and make inquiries,' he said.

'Yes, tell her we will go in every direction,' added Ronald, eagerly; 'we will not return till we have had tidings of him. You may trust me, man,' he continued, laying his hand on the arm of the gardener, as he lingered with an evident feeling of hesitation.

The light from a little oil lamp in the hall fell upon Ronald's face; it bore an expression which could not be doubted. Captain Vivian's was hidden in the shade of the porch. Ronald repeated again—'You may trust me,' and the words were received with a hearty 'To be sure, Master Ronald; every one trusts you.'

The man departed; and Ronald would have set off instantly for Dark Head Point, but a strong hand detained him: 'You don't escape me, my lad, in this way. Every word that Bertha Campbell has uttered about my affairs before you stir.'

'I have told all,' replied Ronald; 'and yet—no, I have not told all. She has said, father, that whatever wrong there might be between Mr Vivian and yourself, he would be the last to press it against you, if only you would acknowledge it, and clear him in the General's eyes.'

A mocking laugh interrupted him: 'A woman's folly! And you believed it? Was that everything? At your peril deceive me.'

Ronald paused,—in the tumult of his mind, he could scarcely tell whether he was at liberty to betray more of what had passed; he added, with hesitation, ' She warned me also that it might soon be in their power to enforce what now is only a request.'

Not a word escaped in reply, but the dim thread of light from the little lamp showed a face ghastly with conflicting passions; and Captain Vivian, seizing Ronald by the arm, strode forth into the darkness.

CHAPTER XL.

MORN rose gorgeously over the sea; an atmosphere of orange light seeming to penetrate and mingle with the long line of gray clouds, which stood as a wall against the horizon, and here and there breaking through it in a crimson line, until at length the full burst of radiance flooded the eastern sky, and shed its myriads of golden sparkles upon the waters; not resting upon them with the long and lingering gaze which sunset gives to the world its brilliancy has gladdened, but lightly playing upon the surface of the rippling ocean, and tracing upon it, in a pale yet far-spread glory, the joyous smile of the opening day.

Ronald Vivian wandered alone upon the sandy beach. Behind him were the red cliffs, and the dark headland worn by the fretting of the sea, hollowed into caves, cut into projections, and in parts clothed with scanty lichens; before him spread the interminable expanse of ocean, without a sail to mark its distance. Ronald's eyes were fixed upon the beach. He would have appeared deep in meditation, for the water plashed gently against the rocks, and rippled close to his feet, and still he seemed unconscious of the tide; whilst, with folded arms and a slow and weary step, he walked towards the jutting point forming the western extremity of Encombe Bay. Occasionally, however, it might have been seen that he was not so abstracted. As the passing breeze brought to his ear what might have been the echo of a schoolboy's shout, or the morning greeting of the labourers passing to their work, he would pause for a moment and listen, and then glance quickly round, and perhaps stoop to examine some dark object at his feet—a stone, or a knotted mass of sea-weed ; he was looking, and watching, and searching still, but it was not the search of hope.

Three hours of that night had Ronald spent in fruitless, and, in a great degree, irritating inquiries. His father had been with him, allowing him no freedom, stopping every question which might possibly have led to the discovery of Clement's movements, whilst pretending the warmest interest in the result. Ronald had at times been tempted to break from him, and insist upon carrying out his own views in his own way ; but it was difficult to resist a parent's authority, and Captain Vivian had always some plausible reason at hand to silence his remonstrances.

Yet he was kind in his manner,—much kinder than Ronald had supposed possible, when they left the house together, after Ronald had communicated Bertha's warning. A moody silence had followed for some little time, and then all seemed passed away and forgotten, except that the softness which succeeded, carried with it at times a tone of mockery more galling than reproaches.

One thing, however, was quite clear to Ronald—whatever might be concealed under Bertha's hints, they had worked upon his father to a degree which gave cause to think that they were well founded. The defiant, self-reliant manner which had been Captain Vivian's characteristic was gone. He was fitful, abstracted,— often lost in thought, only fully conscious, as it seemed, of one fact, that he must not lose sight of Ronald ; and when, after their long search, they had returned for a few hours' rest to the Grange, it was with a promise that they should go again, at daybreak, to the shore, to renew their inquiries together.

This was now Ronald's purpose. He had risen very early, disturbed by anxiety and foreboding. But his father was gone before him, and had left a peremptory message in writing that he was to join him directly at the cave under Dark Head Point ; the reason given for the order being, that Captain Vivian was himself going to the shore, as the most likely place to hear what they wished. Ronald felt bound to obey, yet his step unconsciously lingered as he drew near the place appointed for the meeting. Sleep had raised a barrier of years between his present feelings and the excitement of the past night. He looked back upon it, in a degree, as men look upon the turmoil of youth from the dreary waste of middle life. His spirit had been roused to anger then—now he was only saddened. His thoughts had been full of eager excitement for Clement then ; now he was tempted to consider his absence as possibly a boyish freak. Doubt and delay were wearing his spirits, whilst exhausting his energy. More than all,—then, in the bitterness of his heart, and the rush of his fiery temper, he had felt able to cope even with is father, and dare and suffer peril or misery, if only he might save Clement, and redeem the evil which had been wrought ; now, in the glad light of morning, with the sights and sounds of daily life and daily toil around him, spirit, and heroism, and self-devotion had vanished, and all that he could feel was the consciousness of his father's degradation, and the stain of disgrace, which had not even the strength of passionate feeling and impulse to enable it to be endured.

The test of our true selves is to be found in the morning resolution and the morning feeling ; and Ronald had yet to acquire the temper of mind which can be as resolute to begin work, without previous excitement, as to pursue it, when circumstances, both moral and physical, have aroused the imagination, and given force to the nervous energies.

Yet that quiet walk along the sea-shore was soothing to him, and in its measure supporting. The ocean is always great, and it was the feeling of greatness which Ronald needed. The hard beach, furrowed with ridges, spread for about half a mile before him, crossed at times by little streams, tinged with deep yellow from the iron-ore of the rocks. The water in some places was deep above his ankles ; yet he turned neither to the right nor left, but went on, directing his course by a dark spot visible at the height of about one-third of the cliff. This, on a nearer approach, was seen to be a hollow, perhaps the opening of a cave, perhaps only a cavity formed by the mouldering away of the rocks. There were many such along the coast, and report said they were often used by the smugglers for the concealment of contraband goods.

The cliff at this point projected far into the sea, and at high tide could only be passed with difficulty, by scrambling over the huge broken rocks which, having fallen from above, were heaped around its base. Ronald, however, made his way over them with the ease which showed that every stone was a familiar resting-place, and paused only upon the summit of one of the highest rocks, when a glance along the beach showed that no one was in view ; then stepping upon the nearest point of the cliff, a few bounds brought him, slightly out of breath, but in no other way exhausted, to a level with the opening, which was now seen to be not so much a cave as a passage, formed partly by nature, partly by the hand of man.

It was carried for a distance of about twenty feet inwards, and where the cliff had fallen away, it had been built up by stones ; then it terminated in a more regular cave, remarkable only for being a clear, hollow space, capable of containing perhaps a dozen men. The walls were smoothed artificially, but one large stone had been left at the further end, probably to serve as a seat. The place was evidently used for the purposes of rest or concealment. Some burnt sticks showed that a fire was occasionally lighted in it, the smoke escaping through vent-holes at the side ; a hammer and hatchet lay in the corner, and a rough, wooden bench, and small deal table, gave it some appearance of a human habitation.

It was empty, however, now ; and Ronald, throwing himself upon the ground, rested his back against the wall of sandy rock, and bending his head forward, so as to catch the glimpse of sea discoverable at the extremity of the passage, awaited in gloomy meditation his father's arrival.

The delay was not long. Five minutes had scarcely passed, when a long, shrill whistle from below gave notice of an approach. Ronald answered it, but without moving from his resting-place ; and not till his father appeared in sight, ascending the cliff by what was something of a regular pathway, did he remove his gaze from the fixed point in the far horizon, upon which his attention seemed to have been concentrated.

Then he rose slowly, and went forward a few steps. The greeting was abrupt on both sides ; yet Captain Vivian expressed himself well satisfied with Ronald's punctuality. 'I should have been here myself before,' he said, in a tone of indifference, as he sat down upon the bench ; 'but there were more searchers being sent out for this young scamp. A pretty game he has played us !'

He raised his eyes stealthily to Ronald's face, as he spoke, seeking, probably, to read there the difference between his evening and his morning mind.

Ronald replied, that if searching was still going on, he was willing to take his part as before.

'That's as may be. I don't see why we are to put ourselves out of our way any more for those who, if the opportunity came,

z

would do us an ill turn as soon as not. The boy's off, and let those look after him who have driven him off.'

' Driven him ! ' repeated Ronald.

' What else has done it, but the being shut up with books, and tied to his aunt's apron-strings ? What boy of any spirit would bear it ? Not you, Ronald, I am sure.'

' If I were in Clement's place, and did not bear it, I should be to blame,' answered Ronald.

' Eh ! what ? But it's folly even to name you two in the same breath ; even Bertha Campbell would own that. You have seen her, I suppose, this morning ? '

It was a conciliatory question, but Ronald's answer was cold. ' No ; I came here direct, as you had appointed.'

' Good !—obedience for ever, say I. It's Mr Lester's lesson, isn't it, Ronald ? '

' Mr Lester tells me I am bound to obey you in all things in which I lawfully may,' replied Ronald.

' Good again ! ' repeated Captain Vivian. He rested his elbows upon his knees, and leaned his forehead upon his hands. Presently he looked up, and said, ' Lawfully—what does he mean by that, Ronald ? '

' I understand, though I mayn't be able to explain,' replied Ronald.

' You understand ; that won't do for me. What I understand is the question. It's my belief that Mr Lester and I have different views upon that same point of obedience. Before long it may be we shall test them.'

' I am willing, I hope, father,' replied Ronald, ' to show you all the obedience you have a right to require ; but '—he paused for a second, the flash of his father's eye startled him—' I should be sorry to have the trial carried too far. Perhaps, though, you will tell me without delay what you wish, for you do wish something.'

His frankness seemed to take Captain Vivian by surprise. He hesitated, stammered, uttered a few broken words, and at length laughed ; but it was a dreary, skeleton laugh—the body without the soul ; and the wind bore it through the arched passage, and its echo died away in the faint wailing of the breeze which murmured over the sea.

Ronald spoke again : ' I thought we were to plan another search ; if you have nothing to say, we ought to lose no time,' He moved, as though he would have gone out.

'Sit down ;' Captain Vivian touched Ronald's shoulder with his stick. 'You are a brave boy, Ronald ; I trust you.'

'I hope so, father. I don't know what I have done to cause distrust.'

'Yes, I trust you. You wouldn't go against your father, Ronald.'

'Never, father, never !' But Ronald's voice was faint, for his heart beat quickly.

'I thought not—I knew not ; I told Goff you couldn't.'

'Goff ! father, do you consult him about me ?'

'I didn't consult, we talked it over. He doesn't do you justice, Ronald.'

'A matter of very little consequence,' was Ronald's answer.

'To you, perhaps—not so to me. Ronald, if I didn't trust you '—he paused.

'Well, father; if you didn't trust me ?'—Ronald looked at Captain Vivian steadily, and the gaze which he encountered sank.

'If I didn't trust you, I couldn't ask you to help me out of a difficulty.'

A pang of doubt shot through Ronald's heart, yet still he answered quietly: 'You know that you may reckon upon me in all things in which there is no breach of the laws of God and man.'

'Umph !' the limitation was unsatisfactory. Captain Vivian considered a little. 'Are you ready for a long story, Ronald ?'

So steadily was the question uttered that even Ronald could not perceive the trace of any inward agitation.

'I will listen,' was all he could say. He rested against the rock, and turned his face from his father ; but the changed voice, which spoke in accents low and deep, made him look round again.

'A promise, an oath never to betray, that must be given first.'

'A son may be trusted without an oath,' replied Ronald.

'Not so ; he may be led away.'

'Never to betray his father to ruin.'

'A quibble ! an unworthy quibble !' exclaimed Captain Vivian.

'Yet all which I will give,' replied Ronald.

A look of fierce anger crossed Captain Vivian's face : yet there was less real indignation in the softer tone in which he said, 'Then my son will not promise, but forsakes me,'

'Your son will promise to do nothing, and to reveal nothing, to his father's injury.'

'A play upon words; but'—Captain Vivian took out his watch—'there is no time to argue the point.'

'No arguments would alter me. If I am worthy to receive confidence at all, I am worthy to receive it freely. Father, if this is all you have to say, I will leave you.'

'Proud boy! wilful from your childhood. But you must— you shall hear. Betray me, and a father's curse will be yours, and it lights surely and heavily.'

Ronald shuddered, but he was silent.

Captain Vivian went on: 'I take your promise, I hold it to be binding. You have heard Bertha Campbell's threats; you know what she is always hinting at, aiming at. She talks of my standing between the General and Edward Vivian;—did she ever explain herself more clearly?'

Ronald felt his father's eye upon him as he answered, 'She told me Mr Vivian's early history and yours.'

'She told it, did she? In her own way, doubtless. She said nothing, of course, of deception, treachery,—how I was led on to believe myself secure—encouraged, flattered, befooled, triumphed over; as they thought,' he added, in an undertone, 'but I had my revenge.'

'She told me that you were led away by false hopes,' replied Ronald.

'False! yes, false with a woman's falseness! What that is, let those tell who have experienced it. Flora Campbell deceived not me only, Ronald; she deceived her father and her mother. Again and again they told me that I was safe, that she had no other attachment, and her honeyed words and her treacherous smile said the same. I loved her—Heaven knows how—I can't talk of it; and she might have made me what she would.' He paused, and Ronald, touched by a confidence so unlike what he had expected, said in a tone of sympathy, 'It must have been a hard trial.'

He received no answer for some seconds. Then the momentary softness seemed to have passed away, and Captain Vivian spoke again: 'Mean spirits sink under hard trials, as they are called. That was not my way: I lived for revenge, Ronald; you would do the same.'

'It would be my temptation,' he replied.

'Temptation! pshaw! What a man is made, that he must

be. Neither you nor I could ever live to be trampled on. Yet
revenge must be taken according to circumstances ; and if it falls
in with profit, where's the blame ? What I did might not suit
all. Some would have called Edward Vivian out and shot him ;
but I had no fancy for that game.'

The mocking laugh which followed the words curdled the
blood in Ronald's veins ; and, without lifting up his eyes, he said,
in a hollow voice, ' You ruined him.'

There was the hesitation of a moment, but the assertion was
a relief, and Captain Vivian continued, hurriedly, ' Well ! let it
be said, I ruined him. He was a fool, Ronald ; it was not fit to
deal with him as with a man of spirit, and he threw the game into
my hands. For months he had let himself be led blindfold. He
told me all his follies ; I even wrote his letters for him. He had not
the sense to see I was his rival : not, at least, till the very last.
Then he turned round and reproached me with plotting against
his happiness—he who, at the very moment, was plucking from
my grasp the prize I valued above all on earth. Surely, when
he had succeeded, I had a right to take the advantage he had
put into my hands. I knew his debts and his difficulties ; he
had placed me in possession of all before his miserable marriage,
and had arranged that I was to go to England, and see the old
General, and get from him all I could, whether in fair words or
good deeds. That, again, was his folly—for the General hated
me—but his fate blinded him. " *Quem Deus vult perdere prius
dementat,*' as they used to teach me at school. How I laughed in
my heart as he played into my hands. It so happened, too, that
just at that time I had another ally,—Goff, who was his servant.
Long before I had bought the fellow over to my side, and a good
deal I learned through him ; nearly enough to have stopped the
marriage, only, as ill luck would have it, they had a desperate
quarrel about a week before it came off, and Goff was turned
away at an hour's notice, and came straight to me. When the
deed was done, and the marriage could not be prevented, he was
my right hand in my plans, for he knew all the ins and outs of
Edward Vivian's life, and was as much his enemy as I was ; why
—he didn't tell me then, but I found out afterwards. There was
some question of honesty pending. Goff was never very scrupulous, and there were threats of inquiry into his doings. But all
that was nothing to me. I had got the man I needed, and he
had got the master who suited him. We understood each other,
and he was willing to back me, and so we started for England

directly upon the news of the marriage, I taking care not to betray my disappointment, but still writing to Edward to trust me, and I would put all straight with the General.'

A groan was uttered by Ronald.

Captain Vivian laughed faintly. 'Tut! lad, cheer up. You don't understand such matters. Well for you! perhaps. But a man who means to carry out a scheme mustn't be scrupulous ; and you know it's all gone by now. I was young then, and hot-headed, and what I'd set my heart to do I would do. 'Twouldn't be the same now. Cheer up,' he repeated, as Ronald still hid his face from him.

'Go on,' was all he said ; and his father went on, yet less carelessly than before. He was approaching that part of his story where even his hardened spirit shrank from the confession of its guilt.

'We came to England, and saw the General ; and there was a long talk about the marriage and the money affairs. He was primed to take offence, and, of course, I didn't let matters appear too smooth. I had full credentials given me some weeks before, so there was no question that I was an accredited agent. To do the old man justice, he was so straightforward he would have run his head against a stone wall, if it had been built up right before him. He took my word for truth, and if there was a doubt, Goff was at hand as a witness. So we told him some pretty gambling histories,—a little embellished, perhaps, as was fair—and the marriage history as a conclusion ; and he was willing to consider me as his son's friend, and talk over arrangements for settling the debts. But that wasn't quite my notion. He was stiff and hard, but there was a twinkle in his eye which told of yielding and forgiving ; and if it had come to that, good-bye to all hope of revenge. No ; I wasn't to be baulked in that way !' Captain Vivian uttered the last words as though addressing himself, for something seemed to check him when he would have pronounced Ronald's name ; and he rose up, and walked once or twice up and down the cave, and went to the extremity of the passage to look out upon the sea. Then he came back again, and said, in a tone of icy unconcern, 'That was the tug of war between us, but I gained the day. When nothing else would answer, I handed him a paper which did for Vivian: a promissory note for five thousand pounds.'

Ronald started up. 'A forgery, father ! Say it was not a forgery ! O God ! have mercy !'

Miserable he was, but not so miserable as the wretched man, from whose face every tint of colour had faded, and who stood, haggard, yet defiant, convicted by the confession of his own mouth.

A long, long silence—whilst the waves plashed softly upon the smooth-sanded beach, and the cry of the sea-gull was faintly heard amongst the rocky cliffs.

Captain Vivian was the first to recover himself. ' The deed's done, Ronald, and the day's gone by ; and if you wish for sorrow, I've had sorrow enough. But, good or bad, it 's not for a son to go counter to his father, or refuse to lend a helping hand when the time is come to save him from ruin.'

Ronald did not answer, and he continued—'It's what I have always looked to. When it has crossed my mind that things might take an awkward turn, I felt I had a friend at home. Your mother said it.'

' My mother ! Thank God, she did not live to see this day !' and Ronald, roused for a moment, sank again into his former attitude.

A trace of emotion was visible in Captain Vivian's face. ' Thank God, too !' he said ; 'but she would have helped me.'

'Father, what would you have me do?' Ronald looked up steadily, with a glazed eye, and a countenance which in those few moments seemed to have been stamped with the suffering of years.

' Edward Vivian is in England,' was the reply.

' Yes ; I know it.'

' He has been at Encombe ; he is coming again. When he does come, it will be to reclaim his inheritance.'

Ronald only bent his head in assent.

'His success will be my ruin,' continued Captain Vivian, ' unless——. There is a paper, Ronald—that which did the mischief ; it is in Bertha Campbell's hands. How she got it passes my comprehension, but it is there. It would be proof certain, and your father would end his days as a convicted felon. That paper must be in my possession before another day has passed over our heads.' He paused, and in a lower tone, added, ' You must contrive to lay hold of it.'

Captain Vivian's penetrating glance rested upon his son, and a secret, yet irresistible, influence seemed to compel Ronald to confront his gaze. Their eyes met, but neither of them spoke for some seconds.

' Well ! ' burst at length from Captain Vivian's lips.

'You must find another to execute your purpose,' was the answer.

' Traitor ! ' exclaimed Captain Vivian.

Ronald continued, in a tone cold and hard, as if every feeling were petrified. ' Mr Vivian's claim is just ; to destroy the proof of his innocence would be unjust.'

The rocky walls of the cavern rang with a fearful imprecation, and, standing before his son, Captain Vivian poured forth a torrent of reproaches, which yet only served to deepen the immovable expression of Ronald's face. When his father's violence had in a degree exhausted itself, he said—' Ask me what you will that may be granted without sin, and, were it to give up my life, it should be done.'

Captain Vivian laughed scornfully. ' Sin !—to save a father, by the destruction of a paltry paper ! The boy is mad.'

'Then God grant that the madness may last !' replied Ronald. Changing his tone, he continued, in a voice of pleading earnestness, which might have been the whisper of that womanly tenderness inherited from his mother—' Father, you have asked a favour of me, and I have refused to grant it. I have no right, therefore, to seek kindness from you ; yet I do—I must. Miss Campbell's warnings are clear to me now, so also are her promises. Trust her—trust Mr Vivian—and, by all that is sacred, I do affirm my conviction that you are safe.'

Captain Vivian looked at him wildly.

' Yes,' repeated Ronald, 'safe by their own promises, by all the obligations of gratitude. Once I have saved Mr Vivian's life —once I assisted in saving his daughter. He acknowledges the claim ; I have heard it from his own lips—no matter how or when—but, for my sake, he will dread to injure you. As surely, father, as there is truth in man, he will be true to you, if only you will trust him.'   ·

He was interrupted mockingly. ' And give myself up to the nearest magistrate ? Ronald, you are a desperate fool ! ' and Captain Vivian paced the floor of the cave with short and hurried steps.

After a few seconds he stopped. ' You have seen Edward Vivian ; I guessed as much. Let me know the how and the when.'

' I saw him the last evening that he was here ; we had met upon the Croome, and he had betrayed himself. I knew then that there was enmity between you. I did not know for what cause.'

'Mean, wretched boy! Plotting against your father, deceiving him for months! And Edward Vivian—an idiot still, preaching of promises and trust, when wealth or ruin was at stake! The experience of centuries would not be enough for such a man.'

'It was I, father, who extracted the promise. I who spoke of trust. I who do, and will, trust.'

'And you who sold yourself to his purpose, and promised to aid him for your father's destruction.'

'O God! pardon me! Have pity upon me! I am very miserable.' Ronald's spirit gave way, and he cast himself upon the floor in an agony of grief.

Captain Vivian stood by him silently. Whatever might be his feelings of indignation against his son for having kept from him his communication with Mr Vivian, it was not then the moment to show it. Too much depended upon Ronald's consenting to be a partner in his schemes, to admit of any expression which would be likely to repel and irritate him; and during those first few moments of suffering there was sufficient time for self-recollection to convince him that if his object was to be obtained, it must be by very different means than threats or violence.

When Ronald, somewhat calmed by the outburst to which he had given way, at length rose and moved towards the entrance of the cave, willing, apparently, to put an end to the conference, he was stopped by a voice which sounded rather like the entreaty of a brother, than the command of a parent :—'And you leave me, then, Ronald, to ruin?'

'I leave you, father, because I cannot help you as you would be helped; but I will wait your orders at home.'

'Home! I have none. I am a wanderer, sent forth by my own child. Is it so that you keep your mother's last wish?'

Ronald put his hands before his eyes. 'My brain is dizzy— I can't think; give me but an hour's rest.'

'When we are in safety,—not before. Your father's shame will be yours also.'

'I know it; oh yes, I know it too well!'

'And if it is so that Edward Vivian is under such deep obligation, he can never find fault with you for taking from him what, according to your own story, he would never consent to make use of as proof.'

'I don't know, father; I can't understand. My head is burning.' Ronald leaned against the wall for support.

Captain Vivian went on slowly. 'He says that he is willing to hush the case. It may be so, but I won't put my head into the lion's mouth; or, if I do, I will first draw his teeth. Granted that he takes no measures against me, who is to answer for the General? I have not lived fifty years in the world to be duped by promises. The paper must be mine; if not by fair means, then by foul. But with you, Ronald, it would be an easy matter. Bertha Campbell puts faith in you, even to folly.'

'Impossible! I have no excuse. I could make no pretence.'

'Pshaw!' Captain Vivian's tone relapsed into coarse good-humour, as he fancied himself gaining the ascendant. 'You don't think I have learned what I have without forming my plans accordingly. The thing is easy enough. Mr Lester had the paper; it must have been given him by the General. In my folly I fancied that the old man, in his stiff, family pride, would destroy it, that it might never tell the tale of his son's misdeeds. Doubtless Edward Vivian and his friend are, at this moment, planning to make use of it. But while there's life there's hope. It is not in their possession now. Bertha Campbell has it,—she keeps it about her in her pocket-book. I learned that by ways which you would never guess. You must go to her with news of the boy—of Clement; the story is easily concocted. He shall be suspected to have gone off on a lark, with some strange friend of Goff's,—a smuggling friend, if you will,' and Captain Vivian tried to laugh. 'You may guess that they'll be back some particular day, and have a fuss about the date; anything to induce her to bring out the book. Then let Goff or me be near, with some sudden message which shall make her lay it down at the right moment, and leave you with it, and good luck to your cleverness in taking advantage of the opportunity. A good scheme, eh? Don't you think so?' and he pryed keenly into Ronald's pale and stony face. Obtaining no answer, he added — 'What's an easy job for you, would be desperately difficult for me. She's on her guard the moment she sees me. Ten to one that I should ever get admittance to the house; and twenty to one that, if I did, I should make her forget herself enough to leave the book with me. And there's no time for failure; what's done must be done to-night, or good-bye to Encombe, and hurrah for Botany Bay!'

Ronald neither moved nor spoke.

'Well, are you agreed?' was his father's next impatient query. He shook his head, but he could not utter a word.

'Senseless boy! this is no time for jesting. Say, shall we be off?'

'Impossible!' The word seemed to come from the depths of his heart.

Captain Vivian caught its accent of resolution. 'Impossible! Let Heaven be witness, it shall not be impossible. Yet stay; it may be as well to hear the wise reasons which you can produce for bringing your father's gray hairs to the grave in shame.'

'It is false and unjust; and I have pledged myself to repair injustice,' was Ronald's answer.

'Pledged yourself against me!'

'Not against you,' replied Ronald, 'but to restore Mr Vivian to his right. Father, your son would sacrifice life for you, but he cannot sacrifice honour. And if your plan were carried out,' he continued, more calmly, 'it could but partially save you; all feeling of obligation as regards myself would be cancelled. Mr Vivian would be your open enemy, and mine also, and every motive of self-justification would induce him to sift the matter to the bottom. What the event would be, who can say? Disgrace; yes, at least, disgrace!' he repeated, shuddering at the word.

'A noble, cautious boy! Most sagely prudent! And what then would be your wise advice?'

'A wrong has been done,' replied Ronald; 'therefore let the wrong be repaired. I do not ask, father, that you shall put yourself into danger, or trust even Mr Vivian as I would trust him. If you will, let us leave the country, and place ourselves in safety, and then let the confession be made by writing. So far all will be done that could be to replace Mr Vivian in his right position with the General. As regards the debt, let me work. Father, you do not know how I can work,—how I can endure. Give me but this object, and death only shall hinder me from obtaining it. And when we have restored to General Vivian, or to his family, the sum unlawfully taken from them, even though we may never return to England, we yet may live honoured and free.' A gleam of bright hope shot across Ronald's face as he stood up proudly; and the expression of his young and noble features told how earnestly, how unwaveringly, the plan he had proposed would be carried to its conclusion.

But the unhappy man to whom he addressed himself was too

far entangled in his own snares to be willing to adopt it. He
did not indeed ridicule it; perhaps even a softened look of admiration might have been traced in his countenance; but he put
the idea aside, as he would the dream of a simple child, and
merely replying, 'Good enough, perhaps, for some people, if it
were only possible,' again inquired whether Ronald would consent to yield obedience to his will.

And Ronald answered, 'On this point, never!' And both
were silent.

Then Captain Vivian spoke once more abruptly—'So the
boy's doom is fixed.'

Ronald caught his arm. 'The boy? Clement? Father, you
know where he is.'

Captain Vivian withdrew himself, and strode to the entrance
of the cave, muttering as he went.

'Father, in mercy—in pity tell me! Let me save him.'

'You may, but you will not,' was the answer.

'Cruel, cruel!' exclaimed Ronald, and he covered his face
with his hands.

'Do my bidding, and he is safe,' continued Captain Vivian.
'Refuse, and this very day I leave England, and give him up to
his fate.'

'His fate! what fate? O father! where is he? Let me
only know that I may judge.' There was yielding in Ronald's
tone, and in his words.

Captain Vivian returned again into the cave, and sat down.
'Where he is, I can't say just now. Where he may be, I can
guess. In a desperate scrape,—in prison, probably, before the
night is over our heads.'

Ronald looked at him in wild terror. 'In prison? Then he
has been tempted,—led away.'

His father interrupted him. 'Led away! The boy's of an
age to judge for himself.'

'Help me,—help me!—what can I do for him?' And Ronald
clasped his hands together in the anguish of his entreaty.

'I have told you. I am not going to trust more to a son who
won't stretch out his hand to save his father from public disgrace.
Clement's fate is in your hands.'

'I can't tell,—I can't think.' Ronald threw himself upon
his knees, and words of earnest but incoherent prayer burst
from him.

His father turned away,—he could not mock him.

The long, shrill, well-known whistle ! Ronald started up.
' 'Tis he ! Goff !' exclaimed Captain Vivian. ' He comes to
know your determination.'

Ronald's face had recovered its expression of calm resolution.
' Tell him that I will not do evil that good may come. Father,
God grant you repentance and pardon.'

He would have rushed away, but a powerful grasp arrested
his movements. ' We will talk of this again, in another place ;
you go with me now to the Grange.'

Ronald had no means of escape. They were met at the foot
of the cliff by Goff. A hasty glance and murmured words told
that the interview had been fruitless, and Ronald had no will to
enter into explanation with his father's base accomplice.

They reached the Grange. Captain Vivian led the way into
the house. He had not uttered a word on the way. Now he
said, moodily, ' We have much to talk of still. Ten minutes
hence I will call you, and you shall hear more of my plans ; in
the meantime, you will wait in your room.' Ronald hurried to
his chamber unspeakably thankful for the few moments of rest
and solitude. He did not know that he was watched, he did not
see that his steps were followed ; but as once more he knelt by
the side of his rough bed, seeking relief in prayer, he heard the
heavy lock of his door turned on the outside, and realised that
he was a prisoner.

CHAPTER XLI.

THE same glorious sunrise which Ronald had beheld as he
walked along the beach, was watched also by Bertha
Campbell, whilst she stood at her bedroom window. Yet to
her, as to him, it brought but little perception of beauty.

She had stood there very late on the preceding night, and she
had stationed herself there again long before dawn ; and now
she was lingering still with that heavy load of wearing suspense
and responsibility which deadens both heart and intellect to
every sense but that of wretchedness.

Bertha had but a woman's power, and even that had never
been fully exercised. She did not know what she could do, and
she was not confident what she ought to do. That last night had

been a terrible trial. Mrs Campbell's nervous, angry uneasiness, the children's fears, and her own infinitely worse forebodings, were all to be borne; and they were borne with Bertha's characteristic composure, but the trial did not work the less inwardly. Messages were sent, and men despatched in all directions, and every necessary inquiry was made; and at length, about half-past eleven o'clock, Captain Vivian and Ronald made their appearance at the Lodge, to announce that they had traced Clement to the shore, where he had been seen in company with some strange men, supposed to be a party from Cleve, but beyond this, no tidings had been heard. Mrs Campbell found comfort in this. It proved, she said that he had not fallen over the cliffs, or been drowned. She thought it might be a boy's freak,—perhaps planned for the very purpose of frightening them, and she confidently anticipated his return the next day; but Bertha's mind had, from the beginning, been more harassed by the idea of his being led into evil company than by the dread of an accident; and the information only confirmed her worst forebodings, except that it seemed to exonerate Captain Vivian and Goff from any share in misleading him. She had parted from Ronald with the earnest assurance, on his part, that he would, with the earliest dawn of light, prosecute his inquiries, and would not rest till they were satisfied; and then she had gone to rest but not to sleep. Conscience, stimulated by anxiety, was busy with reproaches, and, perhaps, not all unfounded. She felt that she had not watched over Clement rightly; she had lived apart from him, allowing herself to be engrossed with interests peculiar to herself, and not realising that, having been placed towards him in the position of a mother—or, at least, of an elder sister—she was called upon for sympathy which should draw him out, and make his home happy. Mr Lester had often warned her that irritation and coldness might drive him to seek amusement from home; and yet she had not always—she had very seldom, indeed—been able to command herself. So she had thrown him entirely upon Ella's companionship; and this—wayward, indolent, proud, and self-indulgent — had tended to strengthen his faults, and made him fall a more easy victim to slight temptations.

Doubtless Bertha exaggerated her own shortcomings, and ascribed to them worse consequences than could properly be said to fall to their share. We are all responsible for our misdoings, whatever may be the defects of those set over us; and Clement had received instruction and warning sufficient to keep him from evil, if he had been inclined to attend to them. But it is nevertheless true, and it is one of the great mysteries of our present state of being, that the influence which we exercise without thought, daily and hourly, is working, either for good or ill, upon the moral character, and consequently upon the eternal condition of those with whom we dwell.

We go on, it may be, sinning and repenting,—making faint resolutions, and breaking them, fancying we are in the right way, and that if we offend, our offences are those of human infirmity, upon which God will look mercifully ; and so, searching only into our own hearts, we are, upon the whole, satisfied.

But there is another reckoning,—it will be seen at the Judgment Day,—which tells the effect of every hasty word, every proud, cold look or tone, upon the hearts of those who dwell with us. God have mercy upon us when that revelation is made !

Even now its bitterness is, at times, forestalled. Petulance, coldness, selfishness, proud reserve, an overweening love of power, labour silently, day by day, in raising up barriers in our homes ; and at length some unlooked-for circumstance shows us that the work is done,—that we have estranged affection ; and lost respect ; it may be that we have saved ourselves, but ruined the souls intrusted to us.

Not that all which has been said could be applicable to the case of Bertha Campbell. With her the evil was but in its infancy, and she was beginning to open her eyes to it, before Clement's unlooked-for disappearance had called forth her self-reproach so bitterly. But it was quite true that Clement had often been induced to linger with Ronald, or to idle his time upon the shore, because Bertha's cold words, and constant habit of finding fault, made home distasteful to him. It was quite true that his indolence and wilfulness had been fostered, because Bertha, by never taking any interest in his pursuits, had thrown him entirely upon Ella for sympathy ; and now, when foreseeing the fatal consequences which might arise from such apparently trivial circumstances, it was not to be supposed that she could exactly discriminate what her own share in the evil had been.

They were very mournful moments which she passed standing by the window, watching, as she thought, but in reality lost in reverie ; and the sun, as it rose higher in the eastern sky, brought to her mind only a burdensome sense of chill and darkness in her own heart, rendered more evident by the contrast of external brightness. She was physically weary also ; her rest had been broken, and the atmosphere of a December morning, though the season was unusually mild, made even the fur cloak in which she had wrapped herself, a very insufficient covering. Yet it required an effort to dress and prepare for the business of the day. All order seemed broken up : she did not know what to do,—what to think of ; and this to a mind usually regulated like clock-work was a considerable addition to every other trouble.

The post was late, and Mrs Campbell's excitement much increased in consequence. The point to which every one looked was Mr Lester's return, and this, Mrs Campbell now asserted, was impossible. There were no letters, and, if he did not write, it was certain he would not come. It was in vain that Bertha pointed to the clock, and showed that the postman was only five minutes behind his time, which was a common occurrence, and therefore there was no need to despair. Mrs Campbell's fears were as quickly excited as her hopes, and her anxiety showed itself by incessant suggestions and orders, mingled with complaints of Bertha's quietness, which she called indifference, and reproaches against Mr Lester for being absent ; whilst every now and then she wandered into murmurs against General Vivian, and reminiscences of things said and done in bygone years, which had doubtless, in her own mind, some connection with the present uneasiness, yet which it was not very easy to follow.

Bertha bore all quietly, not attempting to reason, but listening to what was said, with her head turned towards the window. At last she observed, in a very calm voice, ' I think that is Rachel coming up the garden.'

Louisa was at the front door with lightning speed. ' A letter, Rachel !—have you heard ? '

' Yes, he comes to-night,' was Rachel's answer, but her face was only partially brightened ; yet she followed Louisa quickly to the parlour, and meeting Bertha at the threshold, repeated the fact instantly.

' Thank God ! ' was Bertha's whispered ejaculation, and she kissed Rachel heartily ; but it seemed as though she had no power to say more.

' Come here, my dear—sit down by me ; tell me what message your papa sends,' said Mrs Campbell, beckoning Rachel to her.

Rachel sat down and unfolded her letter, with a slight feeling of pride at being the bearer of an important communication.

Bertha sat opposite, her breath coming quick and faint.

'He says,' began Rachel, reading aloud,—' " My friend seems better, and I think it possible I may bring him down with me for a little change ; we may be at home to-morrow night. Don't depend upon us, but don't be surprised if you see us."—'That is very nice, isn't it ?' she added, looking up doubtfully in Mrs Campbell's face, as if nothing could be very nice just then to any one.

'Yes, my dear ; but I wish,—oh, dear ! Bertha, what time does the coach come in ? '

'There are two coaches,' replied Bertha. 'Mr Lester doesn't say which he shall come by.'

Rachel turned immediately to Mrs Campbell to answer the question : 'Papa comes by the five o'clock coach generally,— when he does go away, that is. Dear Miss Campbell,' and she addressed herself to Bertha, with an accent of gentle sympathy, ' won't it be a comfort to you to have him back ? '

'Yes, great ; but the letter with the receipted bill may go astray.'

Even at that moment of anxiety, Bertha's mind would fix it- self upon anything which happened to be irregular.

'Oh ! it won't signify. Everything will be right when papa comes.' Rachel paused, for she was thinking of Clement, yet could not bring herself to mention his name. She repeated again : ' Everything will be right when papa comes.'

'Do you think Clement will come with him ?' asked the blundering Fanny, who had only paid a half attention to what was being said.

Louisa caught up her words ; 'Fanny, how silly! You always do say such silly things. What bill was it, Rachel ? '

'Never mind, my dear ; it is not your concern,' said Bertha, alive directly to her duty as monitor.

Louisa still persisted ; ' But I thought, Aunt Bertha, that you didn't send the bill ; it was in your pocket-book.'

'What bill, Louisa ? You astonish me. What do you mean by prying into every person's concerns in this way ? '

' I didn't pry, Aunt Bertha '—and the angry flush rushed to Louisa's cheeks ; ' but if you remember, when I told you yester- day that Anne at the Rectory was still fussing about a lost paper, you said, "Oh ! she needn't trouble herself ; Rachel knows all about it ; I took it, and put it in my pocket-book." I remember quite well that was what you said, and I told it to Anne when I saw her, as we came back from our walk.'

2 A

'I wish you to have no gossip with Anne of any kind,' observed Bertha, quickly ; 'I won't have you speak to her.'

'I don't think Anne gossips more than other people,' muttered Louisa.

'She does, though,' exclaimed Fanny, anxious to put in her opinion upon the state of passing affairs. 'She was talking a long, long time to Goff last evening, after we came home—I saw her from my window ; and he looked so ugly and fierce, I wonder she wasn't frightened at him.'

'I want to hear no more of either of them,' observed Bertha. She turned to her mother, and added—'I am thinking of going to the Hall. Miss Vivian will be anxious to know what we have heard and done.'

'I don't know what there is to tell,' replied Mrs Campbell ; 'I can't understand myself what any one is doing.'

'The gardener is gone off to Cleve, trying to trace the men who were on the shore last night,' answered Bertha, without endeavouring to excuse herself ; 'and there is another man sent to give notice to the police ; and Job Horner is over the hills by Barney Wood's cottage ; and Ronald said he and his father would search along the cliffs, and keep a watch upon the beach. I don't think we can do anything more till Mr Lester comes,—only wait ;' and she sighed deeply.

'I wish you could cheer one up, Bertha ; you always take the black side. Poor boy! I am sure he will be back soon. But those dreadful men must have led him into it for a freak. I am sure he will be back this evening. Where did you say you were going?'

'To the Hall,' replied Bertha. 'I think some one ought to see Miss Vivian. Rachel, will you go with me? Fanny and Louisa have colds.'

Mrs Campbell, not choosing her consent to be taken for granted, began to make objections. She disliked, she said, to be left ; if persons came in, she shouldn't be able to see them, and Bertha ought to stay at home and give orders ; and Bertha acquiesced, and began to prepare for the children's lessons. And then Mrs Campbell changed her mind, and was surprised that Bertha could be so indifferent, and thought that all kinds of stories might reach the Hall if some one did not go and explain matters. She was in that irritable, nervous state in which nothing can please, and when to see others quiet is only an aggravation of suffering. But Bertha felt that she must do something, if it were only for the sake of the children. No good could accrue to them by sitting down in idle lamentations, or walking continually from one room to the other, and looking out of every window; so a compromise with Mrs Campbell's conflicting wishes was made at last; and it was settled that Bertha should wait till after the early dinner, set the children to their lessons, and hear all that might be heard of the result of the different inquiries, and in the afternoon walk with Rachel to the Hall; whilst Louisa and Fanny were left with their grandmamma.

This was the best arrangement Bertha could think of, but it did not thoroughly satisfy her. She disliked leaving the children at home, for with Louisa's curiosity there was always the dread of gossip with the servants, and though Betsey at the Lodge was very discreet, the same could not be said of Anne at the Rectory. In spite of her promises of amendment, Bertha had reason to believe that she was by no means thoroughly to be trusted; and the little hint which Fanny had thrown out respecting the last evening's conversation with Goff, rested in her mind with a very uneasy feeling. Anne had nothing to tell, so far as Bertha knew, which all the world might not hear; but Goff's constant communications made it evident that he must have some object in keeping up the acquaintance. Bertha resolved that Mr Lester should be put thoroughly upon his guard, and Anne's place was already, in her own mind, vacant. That was not, however, to be thought of at present; Mr Lester was to return in the evening; and then all this trouble, anxiety, and responsibility would be lessened, even if before that Clement did not make his appearance.

CHAPTER XLII.

BERTHA and Rachel had a very quiet walk. They were both too thoughtful to talk—at least, at first. Rachel often looked round, fancying she might hear or see something of Clement. Bertha went on, apparently noticing nothing, but in reality with eye and ear thoroughly open, whilst the mind was dwelling upon the most painful and, as it might have been supposed, absorbing topics. And absorbing they were, only all connected with the one idea of Clement's absence. She thought of what he might have been led to do ; of his father's horror ; Mr Lester's pain ; General Vivian's indignation ; the downfall of that fabric of hope which for the last few months they had been building. And then her own share in it ! That came back again and again, and always with the despairing feeling that she did not know how to amend, that she gave offence without mean- ing it, and had no power of expressing her feelings, and was thoroughly misunderstood—even by Edward Vivian, for whom the best years of her life had been sacrificed. At length the lonely feeling could be borne no longer, and it came out to Rachel, in answer to a passing observation of delight at the pro- spect of her father's return. 'Yes, it will be very nice for you. It must be very delightful to have some one to whom you can say everything.'

'So pleasant !' exclaimed Rachel ; and then, checking herself as though it were wrong to think of anything pleasant just then, she said, 'But it won't be pleasant to-night,—unless we have news, that is.'

Bertha avoided the painful allusion, and answered the first part of the speech : 'Very few people have that happiness, Rachel ; you should learn to make the most of it.'

'I do try, I hope ; but I suppose grown-up people don't want it as much as children.'

'Yes, they do—quite as much,' said Bertha, abruptly.

'But they don't want human beings to tell things to, I sup- pose,' replied Rachel, reverently, yet timidly.

'They want them, but they don't find them,' continued Bertha, 'and that is why they are unhappy.'

'I shall tell everything to papa as long as I have him,' said Rachel ; 'but if he were not with me, I don't think I could go and talk in the same way to any one else.'

'Then you would miss it dreadfully,' replied Bertha.

'Yes, dreadfully ; I know that. It used to make me unhappy to think about it, till papa said that love for him was like a step- ping-stone, that it was meant to teach me how I was to love God ; and since that, I have tried sometimes, when he has been away, to think that I had God to go to ; and now and then—not always, only now and then—it seems as if that would make up for everything.'

'Ah, yes ! Rachel—now and then ; but what one wants is to feel it always,' said Bertha.

'It would be wonderfully pleasant, wouldn't it ?' replied

Rachel. ' How it would help one in the world ! But, dear Miss Campbell, persons who are as good as you are must always feel it.'

'Oh no, Rachel ; what a mistake !' and Bertha stopped suddenly.

Rachel was thoughtful and silent. Presently she said, without any attempt at a preface, ' One day I was going up the hills, feeling very tired, and trying so to get on, and then being quite out of breath ; and at last papa came, and put his hand at my back, and it made such a difference—I went on almost without feeling it. And afterwards papa reminded me of it, and said it was like the different ways in which I could go through life ; trying to overcome difficulties by myself, and thinking I had a point to reach, and then God would love me, and be pleased with me—that, he said, was acting from duty alone ; or else, feeling that God was really with me now, helping me on at every step ; and loving me, not because I had done the things, but because I was trying to do them—and that, he said, would be acting from love. And, do you know, Miss Campbell—it is so odd—I have had it in my mind ever since ; and when I feel cross and lazy— and I do very often—then I think that God is quite close to me. And I have a kind of fancy—I hope it does not sound irreverent —that He is really putting His hand at the back of my heart, and telling me, that if I will move, He will keep it there, and make the tiresome things easy. Is there any harm in such thoughts ?'

'No harm, dear Rachel'—and a melancholy smile crossed Bertha's face—'if you can really keep such notions in your head.'

'And it is true, isn't it ?' continued Rachel, earnestly. 'Not, of course, quite as I say—that is only my way of fancying it ; but you know God does love us now, and help us on, and make things easy.'

'Yes, of course '—but Bertha's answer was not quite as hearty as Rachel had expected ; yet she went on, as was her wont, with her own thoughts.

'It makes such a difference to me now I think of these things. When I only try to do what is right, it all seems hard, and I get cross with myself because I don't do all I want to do—it is just like a cold, sharp March wind blowing over one ; but when I have the other feeling, it is like sunshine, and I go on so happily. It is quite a pleasure to do disagreeable things, because, you

know, the Hand is there to help me ; and when they are done,
I can turn round and, see that God is pleased. I wish I
could make you understand ; it is almost like seeing, it is so
real.'

' Yes, very real, undoubtedly.'

The full, implicit, childlike belief lit up Rachel's thoughtful
eyes with a brilliancy that was even startling—and the flush of
excitement was on her cheek ; and in her eagerness she paused
in her walk, and resting her hand on her companion's arm,
looked at her with a gaze which thrilled through Bertha's heart,
for it might have been the expression of an angel's love.

Strange ! the power which touches one heart by the influence
of another. That look did its work. Not then—Bertha's
thoughts were too occupied, her heart was too full of home cares
to understand it—but it lingered by her till other days, haunting
her with its only half-understood meaning ; it did more than Mr
Lester's instruction, more than Mildred Vivian's suggestions—
for it was the soul speaking to the soul ; and He who made the
soul, gave its language a power beyond words. It was Bertha's
first vivid perception of the softening influence of the motive of
love.

The short conversation ended there as suddenly as it had
begun. Bertha felt, though she did not quite know why, that
she could not continue it ; and Rachel had said what was in her
mind, and relapsed into silence. They walked for a short distance ; Bertha pondering upon Rachel's simplicity, wishing that
Ella was like her, and thinking that she might have been if she
had been brought up in the same way.

That, however, was a mistake ; the two characters were essen-
tially unlike, and what was extremely good for one would have
been very bad for the other.

Mildred Vivian's personal rules and suggestions as to strict
self-scrutiny were absolutely necessary for Ella, because she never
took the trouble to think about herself at all. They would have
been injurious to Rachel, by engendering self-consciousness, and
irritating a naturally sensitive conscience into a state of constant
scruple and morbid search into the state of her own feelings.
Ella required to be taught to live in herself—Rachel out of herself. But Bertha was not quick in perceiving such distinctions,
and the medicine which was good for one, she would have considered good for all.

Her meditations were not left long uninterrupted ; a man's

quick tread was heard behind her, whilst at the same moment a rough voice called out, 'Why, Miss Campbell, you walk so fast, one would think you were running for a wager.'

Bertha stopped, telling Rachel to go on, and let her speak to Captain Vivian alone. He had probably, she thought, something to communicate to her about Clement ; and since his kindness in the search of the preceding evening, she felt a strange mixture of suspicion and cordiality towards him.

Captain Vivian came up and held out his hand : 'Good day to you, Miss Campbell. I was thinking of coming up to the Lodge, but I was afraid it would be no good.'

'Then you have heard nothing ?' said Bertha, in a tone of keen disappointment.

He shook his head : 'Two of my men have been out, round by Cleve, trying to hear something of the fellows we traced last night; and Ronald's off somewhere. We must have some tidings before night.'

'I trust so ;' but Bertha's tone was not hopeful.

'Come, cheer up; it's no use to be cast down,' continued Captain Vivian, rather good-naturedly. ''Tis but a boy's freak, after all. I'd have done the same at his age. But where may you be going now?'

'To the Hall. Miss Vivian and the General will be anxious.'

'You have heard, of course, that the old General is ill,' said Captain Vivian.

'Yes, we had a message. He had an attack of faintness last night, but he is better this morning.'

'He does not leave his room though, and at his age attacks of faintness are serious matters.'

'Yes, but Miss Vivian doesn't seem alarmed. Is there anything else you think we can do ?'

'Nothing, unless —— when do you expect Mr Lester home ?'

Notwithstanding Bertha's newly-awakened friendliness, she had an instinct of caution, and answered ambiguously, that it was not quite certain.

'It ought to be. Haven't you sent a message to him ?'

'No.' Bertha was caught in a snare then, and felt herself obliged to add, 'He may be at home this evening.'

'Ah ! very good. The sooner he comes the better. And his friend comes with him, doesn't he ?'

'I can't say.' Bertha looked up in surprise.

Captain Vivian laughed : 'You 'll think I have a wonderful knowledge of what goes on ; but it so happened that one of my men was at the Rectory just now, about this business, and heard say that Mr Lester was expected, and perhaps a friend with him ; so you see I 'm no magician after all.'

' No.' Yet Bertha felt uncomfortable.

' They 'll be here by the five o'clock coach, I suppose ?'

' Probably, if they come at all.'

Captain Vivian considered a moment ; then his eye glanced at Rachel, who was standing a few paces of, just sufficient to be beyond reach of hearing: 'You have a little companion with you, I see. Is she going to the Hall, too ?'

'Yes ; we are rather in a hurry. I must wish you good-bye, if you really have nothing more to say.'

'Nothing more just now ; but I may have. What time shall you be coming back from the Hall ?'

'I can't quite tell ; it depends on how long I may be kept there.'

'But you 'll not come home in the dark, I suppose ?'

'I shall have a servant with me, if I do,' replied Bertha, rather surprised at his thoughtfulness.

'Oh !' Not a very well satisfied 'Oh !' and Captain Vivian's face bore a gloomy and troubled expression, though he tried to laugh, and said, ' I would offer myself as an escort, only I know you would not accept me.'

Bertha showed involuntarily how she shrank from the suggestion, and she began a hurried excuse. He laughed again, ' Of course, I don't offer myself ; only perchance you 'll be anxious to know what we 've been doing, and as it will be rather out of my way to come to the Lodge, perhaps we might manage to meet again half way. What do you say? Shall it be the turning into Encombe Lane, just as you get out of Cleve Wood ?'

'I can't say ; I don't know.' Bertha did not at all like to promise a second interview. Even this, short though it was, made her nervous and impatient.

'Ronald promised to let me know everything,' she added, after a moment's thought. ' Perhaps you could be kind enough to send him to the Lodge, even if you can't come yourself. I don't at all know what time I shall be returning from the Hall myself, or whether it will be before dusk or after ;—the days close in so soon.'

'I can't say for Ronald; he's off somewhere. He mightn't be back before midnight; anyhow, I dare say you'll hear news before long.'

He turned from her without even wishing her good-bye.

Bertha fancied she had made him angry, and feared she might be throwing away a hope for Clement. But in another minute he returned : 'I say, do you chance to have an almanac in your pocket? I wanted to make a reckoning about some sea matters I happen to be acquainted with, which might help us to a glimpse of Clement.'

Bertha took out her pocket-book, and asked what he wanted to know.

'I can't explain exactly. Perhaps you'd just let me look one minute,' and he held out his hand for it.

Villain though he was, the moment was too anxious for him to be quite calm. The faltering tone of his voice struck Bertha, and she instinctively hesitated.

'Oh! I beg pardon ; I didn't mean to pry into secrets.'

'There are no secrets,' said Bertha, slightly blushing ; and not knowing what excuse to make, she was on the point of giving it to him. At that instant Rachel ran up to her : 'O Miss Campbell! some one so like Clement—so very like! He has just gone down the lane to the common : do come!' And Bertha forgot everything else, hurriedly replaced the book in her pocket, and ran after Rachel.

It was happy for her that Captain Vivian's muttered exclamation was lost upon her. Standing upon a bank overlooking the Common, he satisfied himself, by his small telescope, that Rachel was quite mistaken, and then walked away across the fields to the village.

He went on, looking neither to the right nor left—gloom on his brow, passion and fierce disappointment in his heart. Could he but have possessed himself of the paper, so close within his grasp, all might have been well. But the opportunity was gone, and now what remained?

The question could only be solved by an interview with Goff, and to his cottage Captain Vivian repaired. His own mind was bent upon escape. Perhaps he was weary of the load which for eighteen years had burdened his breast, reminding him day and night that the hour of discovery and retribution might be at hand ; perhaps, too, the morning's conversation with Ronald had touched some latent feeling of remorse, which made him long to flee not only from danger, but from the scenes associated with the pangs of a guilty conscience.

But the influence of the comrade with whom he had connected himself was more powerful than the weak impulse of a heart softened only because it despaired of success. When told of the failure in the attempt to obtain the paper from Bertha, Goff only scoffed at Captain Vivian's cowardice, and insisted that if the undertaking were entrusted to him, he would even now gain possession of it before the evening closed in.

They had succeeded, he said, hitherto; Clement was in their power, a hostage. Through him any terms which they chose to impose were certain to be accepted by Mr Vivian. Why was all to be given up without one more effort? Even if they failed as regarded the paper, he would, if it depended upon himself, brave the question, and by threatening Clement's life, force Mr Vivian to destroy it. It was not even certain, indeed, that the paper was that which they imagined—notwithstanding all they had learned from Mr Lester's servant, they were acting only upon suspicion; and if it were not, nothing could be more senseless than to flee and leave the game in their enemy's hand.

His arguments were plausible, and aided by one which he had always found sufficient to stimulate the sinking spirit of his companion. To bind Mr Vivian to secrecy would be to complete the revenge already taken, by shutting him out for ever from the hope of restoration to the General's favour; whilst by driving him from Encombe, and probably from England, they would be left free to carry on their schemes as before. Goff dwelt upon these points cunningly and successfully; yet it was long before any fixed agreement could be attained between minds so differently bent, and each with a deeply-rooted selfishness of purpose —Goff, desperately bold, and willing to run all hazards for the furtherance of his own schemes, and the opportunity of pursuing his profitable trade at Encombe; Captain Vivian shrinking from the prospect of meeting the man whom he had injured, dreading the evils which his misdeeds had brought upon him, and brooding in bitterness of heart over Ronald's alienation and his own degrading position.

A compromise between the two was at length effected. It was arranged that Captain Vivian should linger upon the shore or amongst the cliffs till dusk, taking care to conceal himself carefully from observation; whilst Goff should be on the watch for the return of Bertha from the Hall, when he was to make another attempt to obtain possession of the precious paper. In the event of success, immediate notice was to be given to Captain Vivian, who might then put in practice the scheme which he had so long planned—meet Mr Vivian, threaten him with Clement's perilous position, as certain to be engaged in a smuggling affray, and induce him, in the hope of saving his boy from danger and public disgrace, to agree to any terms of silence with regard to the past which his cousin might demand.

If, on the contrary, the important document on which so much depended could not be secured, Captain Vivian still insisted upon escaping without delay. A boat was therefore to be in readiness which would carry him off to his vessel. In that case, Clement was to be left to his fate. Ronald, the only person likely to help him was a prisoner, and to remain so till night ; there would, consequently, be no one to interfere with the iniquitous scheme, so cruelly laid, to ruin him in his grandfather's eyes, and raise, if possible, a still more formidable barrier than that which now existed between Mr Vivian and the General. All minor arrangements as to Ronald's release and future movements were left till the main points were settled. Goff agreed apparently to the plans proposed ; but he had his own views for the future, and his own plans as to their furtherance. They were such as could not be communicated ; yet in the secrecy of his heart there lay a desperate and fixed resolution that, come what might, the stake for which he had already dared so much should not be yielded without a struggle, even, if it were necessary, to death.

CHAPTER XLIII.

GLOOM and silence brooded over the oak-panelled apartments, the deserted lobbies, and mazy corridors of Cleve Hall. Stealthily passed the measured footsteps of the old servants ; and when, occasionally, a lighter or a quicker tread ventured to break upon the stillness, it seemed a profanation of the solemn grandeur of the stately mansion. General Vivian would not leave his dressing-room ; Greaves waited upon him, Mildred sat with him, Ella occasionally went in and out with messages. He was not ill, it was said, and he would not consent to see a doctor. That was not surprising ; he hated doctors, and professed to have no faith in them ; and he was never known to be nervous about himself. He often talked of death, but never seemed to realise in himself the possibility of dying ; and he was not going to die now, as far as any one could judge. The attack of the preceding evening had passed and left no very marked effects. Yet he would neither leave his room nor enter into conversation, nor do anything except attend to what he called necessary business. That he appeared to be engrossed in, only Mildred saw that his eye was often fixed as in inward thought when it seemed to be resting on the papers or book before him ; whilst his hearing, lately rather impaired, had suddenly acquired a singular keenness—the distant opening or shutting of a door, the roll of a waggon, even the shouts of children in the distance were all observed. No, whatever there might be of mental suffering, there was nothing of death in the quick flash of his eye and the instantaneous turn of his head ; but rather life,—vivid, active, most keenly sensitive, yet crusted over by an exterior so petrified that only those who watched him narrowly, and understood him by the experience of years, could have traced the current that flowed underneath it.

Mildred seldom sat with him in the morning ; he said, generally, that it was an interruption to him, but now he could scarcely bear her out of his sight. Yet he spoke to her seldom, and then never upon the subject so paramount in its importance to both. It had come, and it was gone. Who could tell what he thought of it, or how it would influence him ?

Mildred was brave by nature—the gift of moral courage had been hers from infancy—yet she could not venture to break in upon this ominous silence. Her father's character was still an unknown and unexplored region. Though they had lived together, one in interest and in love, for years, she could rarely venture to speculate upon the way in which events, or words, or actions would be taken by him. She could not say but that by attempting to turn the stream into one channel, it would, in resistance, be diverted into the opposite course. All with him was artificial ;—not untrue or put on for show ; but his was a heart which had been drilled into obedience to self-imposed laws, and the free instincts of nature had been curbed till it might have seemed that they had ceased to act.

Long and weary were the hours that morning ; memory lingering upon the past, fear busy with the future, and a sharp, present anxiety goading the natural despondency incident to such a position into suffering which it was almost impossible to conceal.

Clement's disappearance had been known at the Hall on the preceding evening, yet not so as to occasion any peculiar uneasiness. But in the morning, soon after Mildred and Ella had finished their breakfast together, another message brought the intelligence that he had not been at home all night, that a search had been instituted, ponds dragged, messengers sent out,—but hitherto all in vain, except that there was a report of his having been seen in company with some desperate-looking men on the road to Cleve.

Mildred's head turned sick and faint with fear. Almost her first thought was of her father, and strict orders were instantly given that the General was not to be alarmed,—it might do him injury. Greaves, who was the only person that ever waited upon him, promised to be careful. Yet Mildred could not be satisfied unless she sat in his room ; and it was a source of infinite thankfulness that, on this most trying morning, he was not only willing but even desirous of having her with him. Still, every time the door opened she fancied that some one was about to enter with painful tidings ; and Ella's careworn face was sufficient in itself to have excited the General's remark, if his thoughts had not been otherwise and so intently preoccupied.

'You had better sit down quietly and read ; you disturb me, coming in and out so often,' said the General, impatiently, as Ella entered for about the sixth time, to glance at Mildred, and tell her by mute signs that nothing new had been heard.

'Thank you, grandpapa, but I have my music to practise,' and Ella went out again.

The General did not like a will contrary to his own, however small the matter in question might be, and Mildred seeing it, ventured upon an apology : 'Ella won't come in again, sir ; she was only anxious to see whether I was comfortable.'

'She might have trusted that to me. You are not uncomfortable, are you ?'

'Oh no ! not at all, but '—— Mildred fancied she heard distant voices, and stopped to listen ; then remembered she had better not do anything to attract attention, and murmured something unintelligible, whilst the General looked at her a moment in surprise, and continued his writing.

A long silence followed—in the room, at least ; below there certainly were loud voices. Mildred was in an agony to stop them, but the General took no notice until two persons were heard talking in the lobby leading to his room : ' Ring the bell, will you, Mildred? I think it is within your reach. I won't have that noise in the house.'

Mildred rang, and the General laid down his pen, preparatory to a reprimand.

Greaves entered, turning the handle of the door noiselessly.

' Who is that talking in the passage, Greaves ? '

' Mrs Robinson, sir '—and Greaves looked at Mildred, doubting how much more he was at liberty to say.

' Mrs Robinson ! What has she come for ? '

' To speak to Miss Vivian, I believe, sir, upon business. I was just coming to say so.'

' Let her come in. There are no secrets, I suppose, Mildred ? '

Mildred turned very pale ; but the General was busied with himself rather than with her. He was working himself up into stern coldness. Of all persons he would least have desired to show weakness, either in feeling or in action, before Mrs Robinson.

It was a curious meeting. She came in as stiff and rigid as himself, and made her respectful yet rather proud curtsey, and sat down at a little distance from the table—all without speaking. And the General bent his head, and hoped she was well, with the stiff civility of a gentleman of the old school ; but the merest stranger might have perceived that they did not like each other.

Mildred broke the silence : she asked whether Mrs Robinson had come about parish business.

' Not exactly, ma'am. Mr Lester, they say, is to be home this evening, so I could go to him if I wanted anything.'

The observation was made quite unconcernedly, yet Mildred read in the tone that it was intended for her comfort.

' My lodger comes back to Encombe with Mr Lester, I believe, ma'am,' continued Mrs Robinson ; and Mildred involuntary made an eager gesture, which the General perceived, though his eyes never moved apparently from his letter.

' You have had a lodger, have you, Mrs Robinson ? ' he said, inquiringly.

' Yes, sir, a little while ago.'

' A little while ? but how long ? '

' I can't say exactly how long, sir ; it might have been three months or more.'

'Oh !' the General's pen moved with greater decision.

'Does he come with Mr Lester did you say?' asked Mildred ;
and in spite of herself her voice trembled.

'I believe so, ma'am, but I don't know whether he is going to
stay at the farm again.'

The General laid down his pen and listened.

Mrs Robinson went on quite unmoved : 'I was going to send
down to the Rectory to learn for certain, but our farm people
are all engaged. They have been all day, and I don't know
when they will be at leisure ; and as I was coming up here, I
thought I would ask, ma'am, whether you had heard anything
about Mr Lester's plans. But, perhaps, you haven't, so I won't
disturb you ;' and Mrs Robinson rose from her seat, and was
about to retire, when the General spoke again ; 'You don't take
in lodgers, Mrs Robinson, do you, generally?'

'Only sometimes, sir, in the summer. This was a very civil-
spoken gentleman.'

'And he is coming again, you say ?'

'There is a talk of it, sir.'

'I thought you said he was to be here with Mr Lester.'

A scrutinising glance accompanied the words, which might
have perplexed any one but Mrs Robinson. She, however, was
perfectly imperturbable, and answered, 'He may come with Mr
Lester, sir, but I can't be certain. I thought Miss Mildred
might have heard. I won't disturb you any more, sir, now. I
wish you good morning.' A respectful curtsey! and Mrs
Robinson addressed Mildred, as though merely completing her
sentence : 'If you were coming into your bedroom, ma'am, I
might show you the patterns of print for the school children ; I
got them at Cleve yesterday. Mayn't I help you?' Without
waiting for an answer, she handed to Mildred the crutches
which were her support in walking, and offered her arm.

Mildred turned to the General : 'My dear father, I shall be
back again directly; you don't want anything before I go, do
you ?'

'Nothing.' The General looked as if he would have said
more, but Mrs Robinson did not give him the opportunity. She
fidgeted with Mildred's shawl, and talked about the cold, and
hurried her to the door. The General called out, 'Mildred, you
must be back directly ; I want you to copy a letter for me.'

Mrs Robinson answered for her with another curtsey: 'I
won't keep Miss Mildred five minutes, sir ;' and the General,

having no other excuse for detaining them, suffered them to go.

'The General looks ill this morning, ma'am,' was Mrs Robinson's first remark, after the door closed behind them.

'He fainted last night,' said Mildred.

'I heard so, ma'am; perhaps there wasn't so much harm in that. He has kept clear of Master Clement.'

Mildred stopped, and leaned against the door of her own chamber, which she had just reached : 'You are come to tell me something about him, Granny ?'

'Just come in, my dear, and lie down for a moment. I 'll go presently and tell Greaves to take the General's lunch up, and then he won't fuss so at your staying.'

She led Mildred into the room, placed her on the sofa, and continued, without requiring any questions to be asked : 'He 's off with the smugglers, Miss Mildred—certain; and the Captain 's in some way at the bottom of it.'

Mildred caught her hand : 'Quick, quick; how do you know ?'

But Mrs Robinson was not to be turned aside from her own course : 'One of our farm boys was coming over the hills last night, behind Miss Campbell and the children. He saw Master Clement stay behind, as they were near the village ; the Captain was close by—he 'd been following them. He went up to Master Clement, and they talked a little,—the boy saw him go off with the Captain to the Grange, for his road lay the same way.'

'We heard something of that last night,' interrupted Mildred.

'The Captain says he went home afterwards,' continued Mrs Robinson ; 'but the boy declares that, as he was going across the common an hour later, he heard voices off towards the Point, and one he was sure was Master Clement's. He had a message to carry to Rock Farm, out by Cleve, and he went ; and coming back, there was a light upon the Point, as if men were moving about with a lantern, when all of a sudden it disappeared. Joe was going along the path near the edge of the cliff then. He didn't like much, he says, to go and put himself in the way of meeting them, for he knew they must be folks that wouldn't fancy being interfered with ; and so he kept quiet amongst the bushes and the furze for some little time ; and he declares that he quite plainly heard a party of them scramble down. Master Clement was one, he 's pretty certain, but he thinks that he didn't much wish to go. The boy didn't wait to see what became of them; only he knows all the boats along the beach, and he says that Mark Wood's was there in the morning, and it's not there now. And Mark himself isn't at home ; and the child Barney's been questioned, and they've got out of him that his father had settled beforehand to be away all night. Putting things together, its pretty clear, ma'am, what the young gentleman's been after.'

No voice came. Mildred's hands were folded together, and her countenance expressed the most intense dejection.

'I shall go and tell Greaves to take up the General's luncheon ; and you'll have yours brought in here, my dear,' continued Mrs Robinson. 'It was best for you to know the worst at once.' Not waiting for Mildred's assent, she departed to give her orders.

Poor Mildred ; she did indeed feel crushed. Edward—Mr Lester—Bertha ; none could help her now. Far better than others did she know the fixed prejudice, the stern laws which governed her father's conduct. Far more truly could she read that martyr spirit of self-torture, which had shown itself for years in General Vivian's every word and action. If there had been a glimmering of hope before, it had faded since the preceding evening, and now it was utterly quenched. An offence deadly in the rigid judgment of General Vivian, even if capable of extenuation in the eyes of the world, had been laid to her brother's charge ; and when her last hope was in the acknowledgment of his faults, and a final appeal to mercy, on the plea that its punishment had been borne unmurmuringly for eighteen years, a further excuse for severity was to be found in the fact, that the sins of the father had descended as an heirloom to the son—that Clement was what his father had been, when he brought sorrow and desolation to Cleve.

Mrs Robinson returned. Greaves was gone up to the General with his luncheon, and would take care that Miss Mildred should not be wanted again just yet ; only she remarked that it would not do to stay away very long—people might come upon business to see the General, and talk ; and the story was getting about fast.

'He must know it before long,' replied Mildred, in a low voice.

'It mayn't be till to-morrow, ma'am ; and before that Mr Lester and Master Edward will be here, and it will be better broken to him.'

2 B

'And that unhappy boy! What will become of him?' said Mildred.

'My husband and two of the men will be down upon the shore to-night waiting, if they should land again,' replied Mrs Robinson. 'But it's scarcely to be thought they'll be back so soon. It's the spirit of a Campbell that's in him,' she muttered to herself.

Mildred looked at her sadly and reproachfully; 'A Vivian, rather, Granny; Edward might have done the same.'

'Master Edward would never have taken to such a low set,' exclaimed Mrs Robinson, with sudden animation. 'When he consorted with the Captain, he was not at all the man he is now. No, no, Miss Mildred; my dear, it's the Campbell blood; and when once it's in, there's no rooting it out.'

Mildred would not argue the point for Mrs Robinson, like the General, was strong in her prejudices. She could only murmur, 'What tidings for Edward and Mr Lester!'

'I've been thinking of going on to Cleve to meet them,' continued Mrs Robinson. 'It would be better for Master Edward to hear it from some one who is up to things, and can help him to keep his own counsel. He was never to be trusted when things took him by surprise.'

Mildred took her hand affectionately. 'Always kind and thoughtful,' she said. 'Yes, it would be better; but, dear Granny, it is giving yourself a great deal of trouble.'

Mrs Robinson drew back her hand rather proudly. 'I was not one of the family for eight-and-twenty years for nothing,' she said. 'Who should I take trouble for but those who are like my own kin? Master Edward will be wishing to put himself foremost in the search; but he mustn't.'

'No, indeed. But, Granny, my father must know of his being here before many days are over. He has been told now that he is in England.'

'Know it? does he?' Almost for the first time Mrs Robinson's face changed colour, and she spoke anxiously: 'Ah! Miss Mildred, my dear, who had the courage to tell him?'

'I had, Granny; there was no one else.'

Mrs Robinson shook her head sorrowfully. 'Ah! no one. It has all come upon you. Strange that it hasn't carried you to your grave. But he's softened; surely he's softened?'

'I fear not. You saw him just now. He has been like that ever since—sharp in manner; and when he has spoken, saying only a few words.'

'Conscience troubles him,' was Mrs Robinson's comment. 'I knew he had a meaning in his questions.'

'Yes, I knew it too. He is full of suspicion. He thinks we are all plotting. What will it be when he hears about Clement?' 'He will say, as I do, that it is the Campbell blood, and there's no hope for it. O Master Edward!—the marriage was the worst thing of all. But you mustn't stay here, my dear. The General will be asking questions, and it will never do to let him know what's going on till Mr Lester comes. Let me help you back to him, and then I'll set off for Cleve.'

Mildred could scarcely summon resolution sufficient to move; and said she dreaded encountering the General's questions, and felt she had a thousand other things to say to Mrs Robinson.

'It won't do to wait, my dear, or—hark! There's a visitor, I heard the bell.' She left Mildred, and went to the head of the stairs to listen.

Her face was discomposed when she returned : 'Miss Campbell and Miss Rachel. Miss Campbell wants to see you. We mustn't let the General know she is here. He is not in a mood for that. Hadn't I better send Miss Ella to talk to him ? and perhaps he will let her copy his letter.'

Mildred smiled gratefully—'So like you, and the old times, Granny ; managing for every one. Perhaps it will be best ; and Miss Campbell can come and see me here. And Rachel,'—she considered a moment,—' Rachel must wait in the morning-room. Thank you so much for arranging it,' she added, as she pressed Mrs Robinson's hand affectionately.

'No thanks, my dear ; but God help you and all of us.'

The prayer was needed, for Mildred's complexion was of a livid paleness ; and even that one day of anxiety seemed to have made her cheeks thinner, and shrunk her slight frame.

CHAPTER XLIV.

BERTHA and Mildred met as old friends. The one common fear had melted away whatever remains of bygone antipathy might have been lingering in their minds. Bertha entered, tired with her walk, and worn with suspense and watchfulness ; but Mildred's hearty 'Thank you for coming ; I have been hoping

you would,' cheered and encouraged her ; and when she unfastened her bonnet, and sat down by the fire, they might have
appeared to be even sisters in cordiality.

Mildred began the conversation, for she had the most to tell.
Mrs Robinson's intelligence had given a definite form to her
fears, and so, after the first startling announcement had in a
measure relieved her. She believed, she said, that Clement's
absence was a boyish freak,—the love of adventure,—that he had
gone for a sail and would return. She thought they might
expect him at any moment ; and her mind did not rest upon the
thought of him with overwhelming uneasiness, except so far as
his conduct might ultimately influence his father's fortunes.

And Bertha sat still and listened, taking in what was said, yet
not able to receive comfort from the removal of suspense. Clement was more, personally, to her than his father could be ; and
Mrs Robinson's intelligence confirmed the worst suspicions which
she had entertained. Mildred had lived in retirement, hearing
only of evil, never being brought in contact with it. Bertha had,
from circumstances, learned the real facts and roughnesses of
life ; and the dangers which to the one were a dream of imagination, were to the other a vivid and terrible reality. When
Mildred at length paused, Bertha sat for some time in deep
thought. She was pondering in her own mind a question which
had suggested itself whilst Mildred had been speaking—the paper
in her possession, should it be shown to her ?—or would it be a
breach of confidence ? She could not decide, and the doubt
made her reply in an abstracted tone to Mildred's inquiry,
whether she could think of anything necessary to be done on
Clement's account before Mr Lester's return.

' You are not satisfied with what Mrs Robinson says ?' continued Mildred, anxiously.

' Not quite. Did you tell me,—did you say. that the farm
people would be on the shore watching for him ?'

' Yes ; it seemed all that could be done. And Mrs Robinson
herself is gone to Cleve to meet Mr Lester. He will be here, if
he comes at all, soon after five.'

' There must be no if,' murmured Bertha to herself. She rose
and looked out of the window ; it commanded a distant view of
the sea.

Mildred followed her with her eye ; ' You don't see anything ?'

' Not close. There are several vessels far out in the horizon.

How the days close in!'—Bertha took out her watch: 'five-and-twenty minutes to four.'

Mildred started—'And I have been away from my father all this time; yet there seems a great deal to say still.'

A quick step was heard along the passage, and Ella ran into the room.

'Aunt Mildred, grandpapa wants you this minute—this very minute; let me help you?' she gave Mildred her arm. 'Aunt Bertha, I will be back with you in a minute; please wait for me.'

'And bring Rachel up,' said Mildred; 'she must be tired of being alone. I am afraid I shall not come back; but you will rest here without me,' she added, addressing Bertha.

'Shan't you come back?' said Bertha. 'I wished'——

'Grandpapa is in such a hurry,' whispered Ella.

Yet Mildred lingered: 'I don't think there is anything to settle, or that we can do.'

'Grandpapa wants you to help him to find a paper,' continued Ella—'one he has lost out of the box in his study. He has had the box up, and has been looking for it.'

Mildred turned pale, and sat down. 'I don't feel very well, Ella dear. Tell grandpapa I will come to him as soon as I possibly can.' Ella left the room.

Bertha gave Mildred some water. 'Thank you. I ought not to be so silly; but it brought back last night to me. I thought I would not say anything till I had seen Mr Lester; but I had better tell you now. There is no real hope for Edward. He drew a bill for five thousand pounds, payable after—after my father's death. That was his offence—you understand now. But no, you can't—no one can understand my father who has not lived with him.'

Bertha put down the glass upon the table, and said, very quietly, 'I had heard of this.'

'And I had not!' exclaimed Mildred. 'Does Mr Lester know it?'

'I don't know; I think he must. I think General Vivian must have given him the paper.'

'He said it was mislaid. Last night he looked for it,' said Mildred, hurriedly. 'Once'—and she sighed deeply—'I fancied it was a mistake, and that his mind was wandering. He didn't mention it again this morning; but then he was not up till late, and he has had business ever since he was dressed.'

'Is this it?' Bertha produced the paper from her pocket-book, unfolded it, and gave it into Mildred's hands.

Tears, bitter, scalding tears of anguish coursed each other down Mildred's worn face; less, perhaps, for the offence which had been so deeply repented, than for the agonising remembrance of the direful evils which had followed in the train of that one act—death, desolation, exile; and she laid her head upon Bertha's shoulder, and murmured, 'Edith! my sister! if he had told her the truth, she would not have died.'

She held the paper in her trembling hands, and tried to read it.

Bertha bent her head down to examine it: 'That is not like Edward's signature now,' and she pointed to a peculiar turn in the letter V.

Mildred assented mechanically.

'It is a very careful signature, not such as a man would write in a fit of desperation,' continued Bertha.

Mildred looked at it now more closely: 'Yes, it is very careful;' but it did not seem to strike her that it was in any other way peculiar.

Bertha's heart sank. It would be too cruel to suggest the possibility of forgery, if after all the idea were but the coinage of her own imagination; and concealing her disappointment, she said, 'I should scarcely have thought it an offence so unpardonable, after eighteen years of suffering and repentance.'

'It might not have been with any one but my father; but— I can't talk of it—may I have it to take to him?'

Bertha hesitated, and said she had no right to give it up; it was found in Mr Lester's pocket-book, and she must return it to him.

Mildred looked annoyed: 'It is my father's,' she observed; 'he is inquiring for it.'

'He must have given it himself to Mr Lester,' replied Bertha.

'I don't know—at any rate it is his.'

Just then Ella came back: 'Aunt Mildred! Aunt Mildred! indeed you must come! You can't think what a state grandpapa is getting into.'

Mildred turned to Bertha: 'Trust me with it; I will keep it for Mr Lester if I can. My father may have forgotten that he gave it, and it would work upon his mind terribly to think he had lost it.'

'You are at liberty to say where it was found,' replied Bertha, rather proudly, 'and to assure General Vivian that immediately on Mr Lester's return I will speak to him about it. I can't possibly do more.' She replaced the paper in the pocket-book ; but seeing Mildred's face of vexation, she added, 'You must forgive me ; but it is against my conscience.'

Mildred scarcely trusted herself with a reply. She merely said, 'I hope you are right ; I cannot tell,' and left the room.

Bertha waited about ten minutes at the Hall after seeing Mildred. Ella came back to her, and they went down-stairs and talked with Rachel. Ella was uneasy about Clement, yet not so much so as Bertha expected, now that she knew what had become of him. Hers was not an anxious nature ; and besides, she had often heard Clement boast of what he would do some day, when he was his own master, and so it seemed less strange to her that he should take the opportunity of Mr Lester's absence to indulge himself in an adventure ; and she decided that he must be back either that evening or the next morning. She seemed unable to understand the possibility of danger, and her sense of duty and obedience was not yet sufficiently strong to make her regard the offence in the same light as Rachel.

It was very trying to Bertha to hear the kind of discussion which went on, and to listen whilst Ella talked confidently of things of which she knew nothing, and excused faults which were likely to be of the utmost importance to so many in their consequences. It was an exaggerated form of the trial which all must bear who are in earnest in education, insisting upon duties and habits which children will think trifles, because they have not the understanding to see whither they are tending. Often she was tempted to break in upon the conversation, and remind Ella that, whatever might happen, she must be answerable for many of Clement's misdeeds, since it was from her he had first imbibed the spirit of disobedience. But Bertha's conscience was busy with herself also ; and besides, she was learning to leave Ella for awhile to the nurture of God's providence—the clouds, and rain, and sunshine of life—which, when the weeds have been taken from the soil, and the heart is in consequence open to good impressions, will do far more for its improvement than any direct culture.

Ella was unwilling to let them go. She prized their society more now that she had so little of it ; and since Mildred had been so occupied with General Vivian, the hours had seemed long and lonely. Bertha also waited in the vain expectation that Mildred would return, and that she should hear the result of the interview with the General. She was not thoroughly satis- fied with her own pertinacity—there had been some pride in it ; yet strict right was on her side, feeling on Mildred's. She thought that, if Mildred came back, they would discuss the point again ; but the clock in the hall striking a quarter to four, and reminding her that if she lingered longer it would be dark before they arrived at home, she set off with Rachel, after giving a promise to Ella that the very earliest tidings of Clement should be sent to the Hall.

There were two ways by which they might reach the Lodge : one through the Cleve Woods and the village ; the other across the Common and the cliffs. Bertha chose the latter ; she could then look over the sea, and watch for the vessels which might be coming in. There were several in the distance, and she was tempted to linger and observe them. They walked near the edge of the cliff, and looked down upon the shore. Rachel re- marked that there were fewer boats than usual on the beach. But there was one near the Point which she thought looked like Mark Wood's. That seemed rather to contradict the report brought by Mrs Robinson ; and Bertha, uncomfortable at any- thing which disturbed what was now her settled impression as regarded Clement, said they would go nearer, and make certain of the fact.

' There are two men out there,' said Rachel, pointing to a spot where the Cleve plantations joined the open Common ; ' perhaps they can tell us.'

' I don't see them,' replied Bertha. ' Oh yes, there they are, keeping close by the edge. I wonder whether they belong to the Grange.'

' If they do, they are smuggling people,' said Rachel. ' And they will be sure to be civil to us ; they always are to ladies and children.'

' But not if we ask questions about their boats,' replied Ber- tha ; ' they will think that interference.'

' Will they ?' and Rachel went nearer to the edge of the cliff, and looked over it again. ' Do come where I am, dear Miss Campbell. Now that it is low tide, one can tell so well how they get up to the cave. Don't you see the kind of steps up the cliff ?'

' Yes ;' but Bertha cared more for the boat than for the cave just then.

Rachel went on in rather an excited tone, keeping close to
Bertha as she spoke : 'Shouldn't you like to go into the cave?
Anne told me a long time ago it was such an odd place, and
that the preventive men never can find the smugglers when they
get in there ; they always escape. But I don't talk to Anne
now about such things,' she added, seeing that Bertha's countenance was grave. 'I have never done it since papa told me
not.'

Bertha was not grave on account of anything which Rachel
said, she was watching the men who had left the path by the
plantations, and were coming towards them, across the Common.

'Isn't that Goff, Rachel?'

'Oh no ; it's too tall.' But Rachel looked a second time, and
changed her mind : 'Yes, though, I think it must be ; he walks
like him.'

'Never mind the boat,' said Bertha, turning quickly homewards. 'It is too late to wait.'

'They are not coming this way, they are going towards the
Point,' observed Rachel.

They went on a few paces further. Rachel looked back :
'How very strange ! He's gone,—one of them—all of a sudden.
There were two, Miss Campbell, weren't there ?'

'Never mind, my dear ; come on. You can't see because of
the brushwood.'

'Yes, I can indeed ;' and Rachel could not resist another
stealthy glance. 'The brushwood couldn't possibly hide him.
Dear Miss Campbell, do you know, that is where Clement says
the smugglers get down in some way to the shore. We never
could find out how ; but he says they do. It has something to
do with the cave.'

'Never mind, my dear, now ; it doesn't concern us.'

'I think the short man is coming behind us,' said Rachel.
'Shall I look ?'

'No, don't look ; come on.'

'Are you frightened, dear Miss Campbell, you walk so fast ?'
Bertha slackened her pace.

'The Common seems so long always,' said Rachel, in a timid
voice.

'We should have done better to go by the village,' observed
Bertha ; but then she reproached herself for alarming Rachel
without cause, and added : 'It is only that I dislike meeting that

man Goff, if it is he; but we shall be near the Cliff Cottages soon.'

'No, indeed—not for a long time; the nearest is half a mile off. But there is the gamekeeper's cottage behind us. The man won't do us any harm, will he ?'

'Oh no, of course not! What harm can he do us?' Yet Bertha's trembling heart belied her brave words.

'If we could go across to the plantation, we should be near the gamekeeper's; and Hardman would walk home with us,' said Rachel.

Bertha thought for an instant. 'Perhaps it might be better. We can get in at the little gate, and you can run on and ask Hardman.'

'And leave you ?'

'Yes—you will be back again directly; and he won't follow us into the plantation.'

Again Rachel glanced round. 'He is coming, but he is not very near. We had better go this way;' and she went on in the most direct course, finding her path through the furze, without considering the prickles, and not stopping until, nearly out of breath, they reached the plantation gate. It was locked.

'Get over it, and run on to the cottage,' said Bertha.

'And you will come too?'

'Yes, after you ; only you will be quicker than I shall.'

Rachel clambered over the gate, and wished to wait and assist Bertha ; but her help was refused, and she hurried on through the plantation, and was soon out of sight.

Bertha put her foot on the first bar, but the gate was an awkward one to mount, and she slipped back, and nearly fell. Looking back, she saw the man coming towards her. She tried a second time—a bramble caught her dress and entangled it. He was so close now that she could hear his footsteps—nearer and nearer. She tore away her dress—made a third attempt—reached the second bar, and was upon the point of jumping over, when a hand grasped her shoulder, whilst another covered her mouth, and a harsh voice said, 'Silence ! as you value your life.'

She turned. It was Goff.

Fear was gone then. She confronted him without shrinking: 'Your business with me ?'

'You have a paper signed by Edward Vivian ; give it me.'

'If I have, I will keep it ; you have no right to it.'

'Power is right. I must have it!' and he touched the trigger of a pistol concealed under his coat, adding: 'Take care; this is no child's play.'

'Let that come which God may appoint. I will not give it,' replied Bertha.

He again put his hand upon her mouth. 'Attempt to scream and you are a dead woman. Now, let me see everything you have in your possession.'

Bertha threw her keys and handkerchief upon the ground.

'That's not all—the pocket-book;' and, seeing she hesitated, he thrust his hand himself into her pocket, and drew it out.

The first paper which presented itself was the old, discoloured bill. Holding her very firmly with one hand, Goff unfolded it with the other; and then, putting his face close to hers, muttered: 'The first word that whispers to man or woman what has passed, your life is not worth an hour's purchase.' Still keeping the paper, he relaxed his grasp; and Bertha, with a speed which only extreme fear could have given, climbed the gate, and ran towards the gamekeeper's cottage.

Goff carefully tore the paper to atoms, and scattered it to the winds; and making his way across the Common to the headland, disappeared almost instantaneously amongst the brushwood.

CHAPTER XLV.

THE path which Rachel had taken towards the gamekeeper's cottage was not very well known to her. It was seldom that she had occasion to go through that part of the plantation; but it seemed direct enough, and she ran on without fear till she came to a point where it branched off in two opposite directions —one leading to the right, into the wood; the other to the left, keeping near the outer fence. She paused for an instant, and then chose the latter, under the impression that Hardman's cottage was near the Common. On she went till she was out of breath; but the cottage did not appear; and at length she became fully alive to the fact of having missed her way. But she was not frightened for herself, only worried for Bertha. She was safe within the plantation, and the cottage certainly could not be very far off, and there must be some cross paths leading to it. It would be a very long way back; and wishing to take a short cut, she proceeded still a little further, and then saw to her great satisfaction, a chimney rising from amongst the trees to the right. The sight gave her renewed vigour, and she ran forward hopefully, until turning an angle in the path, she discovered that the cottage just seen was not in the plantation, but on the outskirts of the Common, and immediately in front of the Grange.

The dreary old house, which was full in her view as she leaned for an instant over the fence, showed her how far she had gone out of her way; but the sight of the cottage was a comfort. It was inhabited by a man and his wife, very civil, respectable people, who would be as willing to render her any assistance as the gamekeeper; and now that she had made such a stupid blunder, it seemed wise to take advantage of their help. And Rachel, trained to decision from infancy, lost no time in thinking what she would or would not do, but mounted the fence, tearing her dress and hurting her hand in the act, and in another minute was at John Price's door.

A knock, but no answer—a second knock, equally unsuccessful. The door was locked; and when Rachel peeped in at the latticed window, she could see no symptoms of fire. John Price and his wife had evidently gone out together. Exceedingly vexatious that was; and something like fear did then creep over Rachel's heart, for the light was growing faint, and the Common looked interminably dreary; and she had a notion, that if she were once to find herself again in the plantation alone, she would never be able to make her way out.

And what was that coming across the Common, looking like a speck, but certainly moving? Could it be Goff? Rachel hid herself on the other side of the cottage, and did not venture to peep round the corner for several seconds; when she did the black speck was gone. But she was still fearful it might be Goff; and how could she cross that piece of the Common again to get into the plantation, if he were lurking near?

A thought struck her—but not a very bright one—should she go on to the Grange? Perhaps Ronald would be there, and he would be sure to help her. But no, it must not be; her papa would not like it. Yet she looked with longing eyes at the rough road, worn into ruts, which conducted to the farm premises and the back of the house. Just then a man, whom Rachel felt nearly sure was John Price, came from a paddock behind the cottage, and turned into the road as if going up to the house. Rachel ran after him and called, but he did not hear. The road terminated by a gate opening into the farm-yard, which was heavy for her to open, and this trouble delayed her a little ; and by the time she had managed to get through, she had lost sight of the man. This could not well have happened unless he was gone to the back of the house, for Rachel must have seen him—at least, so she thought—if he were crossing the yard ; and she passed through the gate which separated the farm premises from the shrubbery, and found herself in a small overgrown flower garden, completely screened from the rest of the grounds and from the farm-yard by tall trees rising up immediately in front of the high turret built at one angle of the house. It was difficult to know what to do next. She dared not go round to the front of the house and ring at the bell, and run the chance of meeting Captain Vivian—and she did not like the thought of skulking about at the side ; still less could she make up her mind to go all the way back alone ; and at last she ventured to call 'John ! John Price, is that you ?'

An answer !—but not as Rachel had expected. A voice came from above, from a window high up in the turret : 'Rachel here! What is the matter?'

It was Ronald's voice, and Rachel actually screamed with delight.

'Hush ! hush ! don't speak loud. What is the matter?'

Rachel told her tale. She had been with Miss Campbell, and they were late and frightened ; and Goff had come in their way, and they wanted some one to go home with them. She had left Miss Campbell waiting at the plantation gate. 'Please come, Ronald ; be quick,' was the end.

He spoke again, in a voice so low that she could scarcely catch his words : 'Come near, Rachel—under the window, as close as you can. I can't come to you, I am kept here as a prisoner. They have fastened my door. I can't get away, unless you will help me.'

'Help you, oh yes ; I will go round directly.'

He stopped her with a voice agonising in its eagerness : 'Stay, Rachel : be silent and listen. Don't be frightened, no one will hurt you ; they may hurt me. Have you seen any one here?'

Rachel's excitement was perfectly subdued now ; she answered, 'No one, except one man ; I think it was John Price.'

'Where is he now?'

'I can't tell. I think he went round at the back.'

'Go to the corner of the house, and look if he is there still : don't show yourself.'

Rachel did as she was desired, and came back : 'I can't see any one.'

'You are certain it was not Goff?'

'Quite, it was a taller man ; and Goff is out upon the Common.'

'It was not—my father?' he uttered the name reluctantly.

'I don't think it could have been ; it was not like him.'

A pause. Rachel thought of Bertha, and said, 'Can you come with me, Ronald?'

'If you will—Rachel, will you do as I bid you?'

'Yes—that is, if I can ;' and Rachel's voice trembled a little.

'You must go round to the back door ; don't be frightened. If you meet any one, say what you said to me about wanting help, but don't mention my name. In that case you must go home, for you won't be able to do anything for me. But tell Miss Campbell from me that I am a prisoner here ; that Clement is in great danger ; that if I could be set free I might aid him ; but that, anyhow, there must be a watch kept upon the shore, for Clement is with the smugglers, and there will be a landing to-night, and a skirmish with the coastguard. Do you understand ?'

'Yes, quite.'

'That is what you are to do if you do meet any one ; but I don't think you will.' He paused, as if hesitating whether it would be right to say more : 'What I am going to ask you to do, Rachel, I would not ask, only it may be a question of Clement's safety, and of other things—more than I can tell now. Will you do it ?'

'If papa would not mind—if there is nothing wrong.'

'There can be no wrong, and—but you will be frightened.'

'No, indeed, Ronald ; God will keep me from being frightened.'

'I would ask you to get me a ladder, but you couldn't bring it ; and you might be seen by the farm people. I could fasten the sheets and blankets of my bed together, and let myself down, but the window is too high. I want more; if you could go into the house, you could give them to me.'

'Yes,—how ?' Rachel's heart a little failed her.

'There is an attic over mine—you see the window ;—if you

were in that attic, you could let them down to me, and I could catch them.'

'Yes, I see; but I don't know the way—and I shall be heard.'

Ronald's heart smote him. It seemed putting the poor child in such danger. And yet not really so; if she were discovered, the punishment would fall upon him. But her fear—no, it was cowardly to let her suffer for him; and he looked again out of the window, and calculated the possibility of reaching the ground without more help. A broken leg, if not a broken neck, seemed the best he could expect. And in the meantime what might not be plotting against Clement! Not without a purpose, surely had he been detained a prisoner, threatened with unknown danger if he attempted to obtain help, kept hour after hour in expectation of Captain Vivian's return; and now, just when he was growing desperate with anxiety and indignation, escape was within reach, yet in a form in which he could not make up his mind to avail himself of it. It was a moment of cruel uncertainty, ended by Rachel.

'Ronald, I have prayed to God to help me, and I will do whatever you wish.'

Still Ronald hesitated: 'Are you sure you won't be frightened.'

'I will try not to be; please tell me what I must do?'

'Dear Rachel, I can never thank you enough.'

'Let me do it, Ronald; thank me afterwards. Must I go into the house.'

'Yes, at the back door; it is almost always open. A long passage leads from it straight into the hall; the kitchen is away at the right. Old Mrs Morris and the girl are not likely to be in the passage. When you get into the hall, you will see the staircase; and you must go up. There is a lobby at the top. The farthest door on the right opens into a passage by the back staircase. Then you must go up the stairs, up to the very top; and just before you will be the door of the attic above me.'

'Stay, let me say that over again,' said Rachel, speaking firmly, though she trembled from head to foot. She repeated the direction correctly, and added: 'What then?'

'You must open the window, and let down the sheets; I will catch them. After that you had better come back, and wait for me here.'

'Yes; is there anything else?'

'Nothing—except, if you meet any one in the passage, give your message about wanting some one to go home with you. If you meet any one on the stairs, or in the bédroom, say it was I who sent you ; and no harm will come to you, whatever may to me.'

Rachel moved away a few steps, but returned : 'Are you sure I shan't meet Captain Vivian ?'

'Very nearly ; I can't be quite sure. Dear Rachel, don't go if you are frightened.'

'I won't be frightened. This way, isn't it ?'

'Yes, to the right—round the corner.'

'Good-bye,' and Rachel was gone.

The back door was soon reached. Rachel would not give herself time for thought, and entered. The passage was very long and dark, and she heard voices talking in the kitchen, quite close, so it seemed, but no one came out. A heavy swing door closed the passage ; she pushed it open, feeling almost sure that she should meet some one on the other side ; but there was no one, and her light footsteps sounded ominously loud on the uneven stone floor of the large hall. On one side of the hall were the doors opening to the other parts of the house ; on the other the wide, shallow staircase. Rachel touched the first step, and it creaked. She stood still, and thought she heard a door slam— her heart beat so that she could scarcely move ; but on she went, and creak, creak, went the stairs, so loudly that it made her bold. She reached the lobby in safety. Then her recollection became confused. Was she to go straight forward or turn to the right ? Straight forward she thought, and she pushed open a door. A pair of man's boots caught her eye, and she almost screamed,— happily not quite, and recovering herself, went back again, seeing that she was wrong. The back staircase was before her ; as she opened the right-hand door, a girl was singing below in the kitchen—that was a great comfort. She almost ran up the stairs, but they were steep and worn,—they grew worse and worse as she went on ; and when she stood, as she thought, at the top, there were others still above. Again she paused to take breath. A door did slam then,—there was no doubt of it,—a door below ; and there was a footstep on the stairs, slow and heavy. Rachel's knees tottered. She hurried on : the slow step came behind, and stopped at the foot of the last flight. Was it coming higher ? No ; to Rachel's inexpressible relief, old Mrs Morris, the housekeeper, slept in one of the lower rooms : and she could hear her muttering to herself whilst wandering about her chamber, and then descend again with the same ponderous tread as before.

Rachel was now in the attic—a large, comfortless apartment, with two beds, which seemed half buried under the sloping roof. The window was high, and she had to climb a chair to unfasten it; and the chair was heavy, so that she could not lift it, but was obliged to drag it along the floor.

A fearful noise that was ! But Mrs Morris was by that time in the kitchen again, and Rachel was grown desperate in her boldness ; and at length, after considerable difficulty, the window was unfastened, a sheet dragged from the bed and let down, and in a moment caught by Ronald from below.

' Any more ?—do you want any more ? ' she ventured to say.

' Yes, one more. Stay ; not till I put out my hand ;' and Rachel, stationed at the attic window, looked down, and saw the man whom she had fancied to be John Price, but whom she recognised now as one of Goff's constant companions, pass through the farm-yard.

When he was out of sight, Ronald waved his hand from the window : ' Now, then.'

The second sheet was let down.

' Is that all ? '

' Yes ; come down quickly.'

Rachel left the window open, and went to the head of the staircase. Her impulse was to rush. And she did rush, not heeding the creaking of stairs, or listening for the sounds of doors, or voices, but going on blindly, desperately—by the worn steps, across the lobby flitting like a gust of wind down the broad staircase, and across the hall, till she had passed through the dark passage, and was again in the open air, and under Ronald's window.

Ronald looked out : ' Rachel, are you there ? '

' Yes, safe. Are you coming ? '

' Directly. I am tying them together. Keep close under the wall,—away to the left.'

She waited, it seemed, an interminable time : she did not understand what he meant to do.

The rope of sheets was fastened at the top, and was let down.

' Now, Rachel, keep away ; don't be afraid, it will hold me.'

She hid her face, and prayed.

When she looked up, he was standing by her side : ' O Ronald ! I am so thankful ! ' Her voice was faint and trembling.

He pressed her hand earnestly; ' Thank God first, Rachel ;— you afterwards ; ' and they went on together in silence.

2 C

Their steps were directed towards the gamekeeper's cottage. There Ronald proposed, in case Bertha was gone, to give Rachel in charge to some person who might accompany her home, whilst he went in search of Mr Lester or Mr Vivian. It was the only plan he could form on the spur of the moment ; but as he went on it occasioned considerable misgiving. He was not able at first to think. Every dark object, every gate-post or trunk of a tree, suggested the idea of some one tracking his footsteps, or stopping him on the way ; but when they had crossed the Common, and were again within the shelter of the plantation, he ventured to pause for a moment, to consider whether the course he had determined upon would be the best he could adopt.

So little knowledge had he of his father's movements, that he was unable to tell to what degree the danger which he supposed menaced Clement, might or might not implicate Captain Vivian ; and the doubt upon this point, so intensely painful, pressed upon him overwhelmingly, at the very moment when it was most necessary to act with decision.

True, Mr Vivian had promised to take no advantage, to his father's injury, of any communication which he might make. But this was not now the point. Whatever might be his duty hereafter, as regarded the terrible secret which had that day been confided to him, there was no time now to ponder upon it,— Clement was his object. But in saving Clement he might be brought into personal opposition with his father. If Captain Vivian should, himself, join the smuggling party ; by aiding Mr Vivian, Ronald might be forced to act against him. The thought was horrible. But how could he leave Clement, knowing that machinations were going on, having promised again and again that he would watch over him ? It seemed equally impossible ; the sense of honour and gratitude, which lay as a burden upon his conscience, forbade it. He stood for a few moments irresolute, gazing upon the flag-staff on the headland, as is was seen through an opening in the trees.

Rachel drew near : ' Look Ronald ; there is a light on the Point. Is it any one moving ? '

' It is a fire, not a lantern.'

' A fire there ! What for ? '

' Never mind, there are often fires on the Point.'

Rachel continued : ' Some one said one day that they were always lighted by smugglers; will it have anything to do with Clement ? '

He made no reply.

'May we come on, Ronald? Miss Campbell will be so tired and frightened.'

'Yes ; I had forgotten ;' and he went on quickly, still, however, looking towards the Point.

' Are you very much afraid for Clement, Ronald ? '

' I don't know ; I hope not. See, Rachel, there is the cottage. Should you mind going to the door alone?'

' I would rather not, if you don't care ;' and she drew nearer to him. ' If Hardman should be out, or Miss Campbell shouldn't be there, what should I do ?'

'But I would wait for you here ; I would be within sight.'

' Hark ! there is a voice—papa's voice ; and there he is at the door, and Miss Campbell with him. He must have come by the Cleve coach. Mrs Robinson went to tell him about Clement.'

'Mrs Robinson ! Did she know?'

' Yes, about his having gone with the smugglers. I don't know how she heard it. Please let me go;' and she would have sprung foward, but Ronald kept her back.

' Listen, Rachel. I can't see Mr Lester. Tell him what I said. He must watch for Clement on the beach. Say to him that I will watch too. Say to Miss Campbell that I remember my promise, and '—his voice failed him—' good-bye, Rachel. I shall never forget this evening.'

' Good-bye, and thank you so very, very much, Ronald.'

She ran to the cottage, and Ronald turned into a narrow track in the wood.

CHAPTER XLVI.

THE day closed ominously, though the upper part of the sky was clear, for thick masses of vapour were collecting in the horizon, and gusts of wind rushed threateningly over the chafed waves.

Captain Vivian, wrapped in a rough seaman's coat, watched the failing light from the shelter of the rocks gathered around Dark Head Point. Immovable as he stood for a long time, he could scarcely have been distinguished from them ; yet as the glimmer became fainter and more faint, he might have been seen slowly ascending the rough path cut in the cliffs, till he stood before the passage entrance to the cave, in which he and Ronald had met that morning. The light yet lingered within, forcing its way through apertures in the rock ; and flinging himself upon the ground, so as to command the entrance, Captain Vivian placed a pistol by his side, lighted his cigar, and waited, as it appeared, with tolerable tranquillity the course of coming events.

His watchfulness, however, was not chiefly directed to the entrance of the cave ; more frequently he turned his head towards the large stone near the rough hearth, and several times he took his cigar from his mouth and listened. He grew impatient at length, and rose and paced the cave ; and once he touched the stone, as if to move it ; but then something checked him, and he sat down again near, still listening.

The long, low whistle so familiar to him was heard at last, very faint, coming, as it seemed, from within the rock. Captain Vivian answered it, and immediately pushed aside the stone, rolling it from him with the strength of a giant. Behind it only the side of the cave was discovered ; but the surface was uneven, and pieces of the rock had been detached one from the other, and heaped together against it. Some of these Captain Vivian removed carefully, and a small opening was seen behind it. He put his head close to it : ' Goff ! '

' Ay, Captain ! '

It was but the work of a minute to remove a few more of the stones, and an opening was made large enough to admit the body of a man ; and through this opening crept Goff.

' Better close our door, only not too close,' said Captain Vivian. He pushed the stone against the opening, but without building it up as before.

Goff sat down on the wooden bench without speaking.

' Successful,' said Captain Vivian.

He nodded his head.

' What ! in earnest ? ' and a gleam of wild exultation shot across Captain Vivian's face.

' What else should a man be but in earnest ! They may search to the poles now for the bits of their precious paper.'

Captain Vivian drew a deep breath : ' One of ten thousand ! Did she give it ? '

' Give it ! she'd have fought single-handed first ; but it's quick work with a woman.'

' You have done her no harm ! ' exclaimed Captain Vivian, quickly.

Goff laughed : 'Frightened her little wits out of her, no more. You might have done the same if you 'd had but a grain more of pluck in you. But now to business.'

Captain Vivian sat silent ; and Goff spoke again : ' The work 's not done,—remember that, Captain.'

He started. The mood of thought had passed away, and the first success stimulated his longing for greater. ' I 'm ready,' he said ; 'the time draws near. Mr Lester and Edward Vivian are returned.'

' You have seen them ? '

' I watched amongst the brushwood, after we parted, till they were in sight. They came by the Cleve road, and went straight to Hardman's cottage. I came off to the shore then. If they had an inkling of the state of affairs, their object must have been to get help.'

' Then they will be here soon,' said Goff.

' I care not,' was the reply. ' Edward Vivian is in my power now. I will meet him, and make him yield to any terms of silence as to the past.'

' When and where ? '

' Here on the shore. I will watch for him. You have sent abroad the report of the landing ? '

' It 's over the village by this time,' replied Goff. 'A hint I gave to the boy Styles has set it going. The preventives are on the look-out ; and the woman at the farm has been spreading the tale at the Hall. I heard Bertha Campbell and Rachel Lester talking of it as I followed them when they first came out of the Hall grounds. They little thought I was so near.'

' We light the beacon then, and the vessel makes to shore.'

' Yes. When the first fire burns, she tacks in ; at the second, she sends off the boat with Clement on board. Between the two, therefore, is the time for Edward Vivian, if you still keep your purpose.'

' Keep to it ! It will be my triumph or my revenge.'

' There might be a surer one,' muttered Goff, handling his pistol. ' But as you will—safe 's safe, all the world over. But how if Edward Vivian refuses to give in ? '

' Then let they boy meet his fate ; and for ourselves—there 's the boat and escape to the vessel, and a run on the coast opposite till we see the turn things take. There 's no fear.'

' Fear ? ' and Goff laughed scornfully. ' If I had feared I should never have ventured myself into the deep waters with

you, Captain : you are the last to lend a helping hand to get
one out. But it's settled then.'

'Yes, settled—certain. We keep near the boat, and can be
off at a moment's warning if necessary. It's waiting by the
East bay ; I took care it should be in readiness before I joined
you just now on the Common.'

'The beacon must be lighted,' said Goff, surlily.

Captain Vivian was silent.

'Do you repent, Captain? Will you leave it to me to settle?'

'Repent! when we have triumphed!' There was scorn but
no triumph in Captain Vivian's tone ; perhaps he thought of
Ronald.

Goff spoke more lightly : 'Stop a minute then, whilst I light
the beacon which will bring the little craft to her duty; and we'll
go along the beach towards the boat. We shall have a watch
over Edward Vivian at the same time, for he'll be down before
another half hour is over.'

Goff left the cave as he had entered it, and in a few minutes
returned again. 'It burns bravely,' he said. 'We'll leave the
passage open—with only the door shut, I mean. It may be useful.' He pushed the stone again into its place. 'Now for the
boat.'

They went down the cliff together; as they reached the bottom,
Captain Vivian approached his companion, and drew him within
the shadow of the rocks : 'Hist! hist! d'ye see?'

Three men were walking at a little distance along the shore.
They exactly intercepted the course which must be taken to
reach the boat.

'Preventives!' whispered Captain Vivian. 'They'll not
disturb us yet.'

'I'm not sure ; the middle one has something like Edward
Vivian's stalk.'

The men drew nearer, then turned again : they were evidently
keeping watch.

'Risk it, and go by,' muttered Captain Vivian.

'Not safe. We don't know what he may be up to ; and we
must catch him alone for your purpose—and for mine too,' was
added in an undertone.

They stood still deliberating. Goff looked up at the cliff, considering whether it were possible to scale it. It was rugged, but
not by any means inaccessible ; yet he seemed unwilling to
attempt it. 'It's safest where we are,' he said : 'keep down

amongst the rocks, and bide your time. He must pass this way; if not, I 'll give him a hint that will send him. Leave me to look after the boat : when needed, it shall be in the inner bay. Yet stay ; — how is the second blaze to be cared for? I said it should be lighted at the East Point.'

' If Edward Vivian comes I will take him there. The boat will then be below us, ready.'

' Good! Then you set the second light yourself.'

' Ay, and Edward Vivian's obstinacy shall kindle it; and when it blazes it shall destroy his hopes for his boy for ever.'

An hour and a half later the moon had risen ; but her light was obscured by passing clouds, and the wind was still moaning sadly and occasionally rising into shrill, prolonged howls. But it was a land wind, and the sea was as yet sufficiently calm to enable a boat to approach the shore.

The little smuggling vessel was riding at anchor at a considerable distance to the west of the headland. The sands were covered, for it was recently high tide; and heavy weaves crashed upon the stones of the beach, and tossed themselves against the sea-weed-covered rocks.

There were no signs of any one upon the beach ; but once, as the moon glided forth from the clouds, her light touched a figure moving high up along the face of the cliff, to the east of the headland ; and then, in a sudden lull of the wind, came the rush of loose stones detached from their position.

The flash of a dark lantern was seen from behind the rocks below the Smugglers' cave ; and two men in the dress of the coastguard advanced and looked up towards the cliff.

' They've not given us the slip, surely?'

' Not they ; and if they have, there are enough waiting for them. 'Twas but a fall after the rains.'

The man who had spoken first stepped cautiously over the rocks to a little distance, and then returned.

' They've help waiting for them, Ryan,' he said : ' I heard a call above there, behind us.'

' A call !—for us, perhaps.'

' No, no ; I saw them away to the right. Now look, they are moving.'

A very keen sight might perceive the objects pointed out, but they were now stationary again. Ryan seemed certain that they belonged to the coastguard, though he kept his attention directed towards them.

'Why, Dennis, man,' he said, 'the landing was to be made to the west, so their friends would be away beyond the Point!'

'I don't hold all that for gospel,' replied Dennis. 'Ten to one but the hint we had was putting out a false light ; I thought so at the time. Now, don't you see? They're creeping along again.'

Four persons could now clearly be distinguished near the edge of the cliff, but the dim light was not at all sufficient to determine their dress; and a rather eager discussion began in an undertone between Ryan and Dennis,—the latter insisting that they should move to the east side of the Point, and keep guard upon the movements of the suspicious individuals above ; Ryan as firmly holding to his determination to remain where he had been placed, according to a hint given through a boy in the village, known to be connected with the smugglers, that the landing would be made, if possible, west of the headland.

'A few steps up the cliff would settle the matter quietly,' said Dennis, tired at length of endeavouring to persuade his comrade of a fact of which he himself was firmly convinced. 'Keep your stand here, man, if you will ; I shall be with you in half a second, if there's need.'

Without waiting for an assent, he climbed up several feet, and threw himself with a spring upon a square projecting rock, standing forth like a table, from which his eye could reach any objects moving either to the right or left along the cliffs, besides commanding an extensive reach of the coast.

Voices sounded above, but they were not distinguishable. The cliff was in this place tolerably easy of ascent, for it was worn into ledges ; and the preventive man, accustomed to scale it under all circumstances, found no difficulty in approaching still nearer, so as at length to be very near the summit, yet not himself within view.

Mr Lester's voice was the first recognised : 'The coast-guard fellows are away beyond the Point ; that ought to be our direction.'

Hardman, the gamekeeper, answered : 'They are all along, sir. Three of them have been upon the shore, near the boat-house, for the last hour, so John Price here says. He saw them as he came back, after taking Miss Campbell and Miss Rachel home. We might ask them what they are after.'

'No, no,' interposed another voice, stopped suddenly by Mr Lester.

'Impossible to ask them, Hardman. They have their duty to perform, without respect of persons. It must be our own work.'

A slide of stones, as Dennis retreated down the cliff to give the information he had gained to his companion, startled the little party into silence.

Mr Lester drew Mr Vivian aside : 'Once more, Vivian, think : this can be no work for you.'

'If it is not mine, it is no one's. I am resolved. And I can defend myself now : I am armed.'

'No protection from a pistol bullet ; but you are wilful ;' and Mr Lester turned to Hardman. 'We had better separate ; the cliffs for you, the shore for us. If the landing is made safely, and Clement is of the party, you have but to meet him and force him to return with you ; if there should be an affray, twenty pounds reward to each, if you succeed in saving him from being engaged in it.'

'Twenty pounds ! Forty ! fifty ! a hundred !' exclaimed Mr Vivian ; then seeing the men's start of surprise, he checked himself, and added, 'What sum can be too great to save General Vivian's grandson from public disgrace ?'

The men touched their hats in silence, and moved on along the cliffs. Mr Vivian and Mr Lester took a more difficult path downwards.

The descent was about half made when Mr Vivian stopped : 'I know a better road than the shore, Lester. The tide is high, and we shall have hard work to get on. There is a ledge along the cliff—or there used to be in the old days.'

'It passes the cave ; I know it.'

'Above or below, as we will. It will carry us round the Point if needful, and if your head is firm ; and we shall command the shore.'

'My head will carry me wherever your heart carries you, Vivian.'

They moved on slowly for some distance. The ledge was narrow and uneven—in some places the cliff sank perpendicularly below them to the depth of a hundred and fifty feet ; in others it was more a path over fallen rocks and projections.

'Look ! Lester,'—Mr Vivian delayed for an instant—'one of the preventive men in his hiding-place.' He pointed to some large rocks, brought out into strong relief by the passing of the moon from amongst the clouds. It was just possible to distinguish a man crouching behind them.

'Yes; that seems as if the landing would be on this side. The figure below stood up in a listening attitude. 'We had better not make ourselves remarked,' whispered Mr Lester, and they drew back from the edge; but Mr Vivian seemed inclined to pause.

'I might get something out of him,' he said, 'if I were down on the beach alone. None of them know me; and a few chance questions might help us a good deal as to the point at which these fellows will land. Wait here, and I will see what I can do.'

Mr Lester demurred to the separation; but Mr Vivian's eager-ness would not stand opposition, and he immediately began the descent. It was much more difficult in this spot than he had ex-pected; and, in trying to find a safe footing, he was led away from the place where he had, as he thought, seen the preventive man hiding; and when at length he stood upon the beach, the rocks appeared heaped one upon another in such confusion that, without instituting a regular search, it would have been impos-sible to discover him.

Feeling provoked with himself for his useless trouble, Mr Vivian walked along the shore to the East Point, under the idea that he should probably meet the other preventive men of whom Hardman had spoken. His thoughts were painfully busy, and his attention in a measure withdrawn from the purpose before him. That rolling, tossing sea was as the image of a remorseless fate; its dark-green glassy hollows were types of the dangers which had opened in his own path, and seemed now about to engulf his boy. And on it came,—pitiless, irresistible, foaming in its mocking brightness, tossing itself in the pride of its tremendous power. Could there be the hope of success in struggling against it? Mr Vivian's heart failed him for the moment, for in the keenness of his fears for his boy, he forgot that to the tide of life's dangers, as to the flow of the great ocean, the decree has been pronounced, 'Hitherto shalt thou go, and no farther.' He wandered on to the East Point. A boat was lying close under the cliff, upon a point of sand left by the tide, which had just begun to ebb, but there were no signs of the preventive men; and it seemed better to make his way back to Mr Lester. He turned; but suddenly found himself confronted by a square-built man, wearing a slouched hat very much drawn over his face, and a shaggy sailor's coat. They stopped as by mutual consent.

'Rather a rough evening,' remarked Mr Vivian.

'Rough now, and likely to be rougher before nightfall,' was the reply. The words were uttered in a tone of careless boldness, and they struck Mr Vivian's ears with a painful shock of recollection; yet he was not certain, and he dreaded to betray himself. The man placed himself directly in his way, and continued, 'Are you going farther?'

'I thought of reaching Dark Head Point yonder. There is no way of ascent here.'

'An easier one than you think for;' and the man struck his foot upon a little step cut in the cliff. 'These steps will carry you to the top direct, and from thence it's plain sailing to the Point.'

'Thank you, but I prefer the shore.' Mr Vivian would have passed on.

'We don't part quite so quickly'—the slouched hat was pushed back, and the speaker stood forth in the moonlight: 'Edward Vivian, there is no disguise from me; I know you, and I would have a word with you.'

'John!—at last!' and Mr Vivian instinctively looked round to see if they were alone.

'At last met, and well met!'

'Well met—never! There is that between us which it were wise the ocean should bury.'

'Perhaps so; yet old ocean herself cannot always keep her secrets.'

'I have business on my hands which cannot wait,' said Mr Vivian. 'Since you know me, you will know also that I am likely to give you many more opportunities of explanation.'

'Were it the business of the united world, it must wait my pleasure; and for once'—and Captain Vivian laughed bitterly—'our interests are the same. I would speak to you of Clement.'

'Clement!—my boy!' Mr Vivian started forward, and his voice was lowered with intense eagerness: 'John! you have done many a deadly deed to me and mine, but help me to save him, and'—— he paused.

That very evening, when he had met Bertha at the cottage, he had heard, in hurried words, interrupted by anxiety for Clement, the suspicions, almost the certainty, of his cousin's deep treachery. He dared not promise to forgive.

'And what!—what offer of good will Edward Vivian make to

the man whom he basely deceived—whom he robbed of all that
his heart desired !'

'Deceived !—robbed !—but you have the strong hand over
me, John.   Say what you will, we will seek another occasion for
that tale.'

'This night's meeting is our first and last.   Do you suppose
that I intend to wait tamely and witness my enemy's triumph ?
I must be a different man now from what I was eighteen years
ago for that to be !'

'The questions between yourself and me are too complicated,
and lie too far back, to be reached at a time like this,' replied
Mr Vivian.   'They concern not my present need ; and be the
consequences what they may, I will not enter upon them.'   He
would have passed on.

'The questions between yourself and me do indeed lie far
back,' replied Captain Vivian, placing himself again in his way,
and setting his teeth firmly together ; 'but if they are not remedied now they will never be ; and, what is more, the hour will
come—yes, even before this night has passed over your head—
when you will wish that the sea had sunk you in its depths rather
than you had refused to listen to me.'

'If your words apply to my unhappy boy,' replied Mr Vivian,
'I say again, you have the strong hand over me.   Speak your
will.'

'Not here ; we may be interrupted.   The preventive men are
on the look-out, and will be coming by.'

'Here, or nowhere.   From this point I keep watch over the
shore, and may aid my boy when he may not be able to aid
himself.'

'Pshaw ! the boy's fate is in my hands.   Till I lift my finger
not a shadow of harm can happen to him.'

'You !'   Mr Vivian drew back from him, and murmured,
'Can revenge be carried so far ?'

'So far ! ay, and much farther !   Will you come ?   He placed
one foot upon the cliff.

Mr Vivian hesitated.

'Trust me, or we part instantly, and Clement's fate is fixed.'

'I follow you ;' but Mr Vivian laid his hand upon his pis-
tols.

Captain Vivian saw the movement, and laughed : 'Coward !'
he exclaimed ; 'if I had willed you mischief, could I not carry
out my purpose now, even here as we stand ?   But even in the

days when you did me the deepest wrong, your life was safe in my hands.'

'You are right!' was Mr Vivian's bitter reply; 'the life of the body was always safe; it was the life of the heart at which you aimed! But go on, we are at least equal in power;' and silently and hastily he followed Captain Vivian up the rugged steps.

They stood together on the top of a cliff which had a lower elevation than Dark Head Point, yet, like it, commanded a wide view over the sea. The little smuggling vessel was still at anchor to the west of the Point. There were no lights on board, nor any signs of movement. On the summit of the headland several figures were indistinctly seen, and two were pacing up and down at some distance from the East Point. Captain Vivian cast a hasty glance around him, and then drew near a pile of dried fern, furze, and brushwood, collected as it might have appeared accidentally, or perhaps with the intention of being carried away for fuel.

'We are safe from interruption here,' he said. 'The preventives have gathered together after their prey yonder,'—and he pointed to the headland. 'They may wait to-night, and to-morrow night, and the next, if I will it,—or, rather, if you will it.'

'Let us have few words, John; for what purpose have you brought me here?'

'To give you the opportunity of saving your boy from disgrace and deadly peril. He is on board that vessel yonder : when I raise my signal he will come on shore. Would you know who are after him! Three men on the headland—three on the shore—others waiting within call. But the smugglers are not men to give up their prize without a struggle. They will put your boy first, thinking it for their safety, and that the preventives will deal gently with him. Trust to that, if you will. His life is in danger ; and should he escape, his deeds will be blazoned over the country, as a disgrace to the proud name he bears.'

'Serpent !' exclaimed Mr Vivian ; 'and it is your doing.'

'That matters not. If it has been mine, it will be yours. Say but the word, and the smuggler lies quietly at her anchorage ; the preventives are outwitted ; and a boat brings your boy on shore, with nothing against him but the rumour of his frolic.'

'Your price ?—name it !' The tone was agony but ill-concealed by a cold haughtiness.

' 'I might take you at your word and ruin you, but you are poor enough already'—and Captain Vivian laughed mockingly. 'I have no wish to injure you ; I require only that, whatever your purpose may be in returning to Encombe, there shall be no raking up of the grievances of past days—a small favour to demand for saving your son from disgrace, and it may be death.'

'A small favour, indeed ; too small if it had not a hidden meaning. John'—and all the bitterness of long-smothered enmity broke out in the words—'from my heart I distrust you.'

'From my heart I hate you, might have been better,' was the sarcastic reply.

'No; I may have had cause enough, but God knows I have forgiven,—I would forgive, if I dared. You have played a desperate game against me. I see it now, for my eyes have been opened. It was you who ruined me with my father.'

'And you who ruined me with the woman who should have been my wife.' Then, with a taunting sneer, which perhaps concealed the pang of some painful memories, Captain Vivian continued : 'Let bygones be bygones ; it is all I ask.'

'And if it is only by recalling bygones that I can explain myself to my father, then to promise is my destruction.'

'And not to promise is your boy's.'

Mr Vivian turned away to control the agony of his feelings, 'We will endeavour to understand each other,' he continued, after a moment's pause. 'It is useless to endeavour to persuade me that the stipulation you demand is of no consequence. It is, and it must be, of the very utmost consequence to me ; yet, do not think to deceive me, too well I know that it is far more so to you.'

'Prove it! prove it!' exclaimed Captain Vivian, scornfully. He clenched his hand and muttered between his closed teeth, 'Would I have put myself in your power if you could prove it?'

'I care not for legal proof ; but were the deed hidden in the depths of the earth, it should come forth to clear me with my father, and to be an eternal dishonour to you. I make no stipulations with a forger.'

'As you will.' Captain Vivian slowly took a match-box from his pocket, and held it as if about to strike the light : 'The first blaze, and the boat makes for the shore.'

' 'Stay! stay!' exclaimed Mr Vivian. 'There may be a compromise.'

' 'No compromise! Silence for ever with the General and with the world upon all points—sworn for yourself, your sister, Mr Lester, and Bertha Campbell.'

' 'My oath must be for myself; I cannot bind others.'

'It must be given by them also,—and to-night, before two more hours have passed.'

' 'My father is generous; he will never raise a word against you when he finds that I am under a promise of secrecy.'

'General Vivian's generosity! Ask me rather to trust to the mercy of the winds and of the waves. Silence or disgrace: make your choice between them.'

He struck the light. Mr Vivian caught him by the arm, and the movement brought the burning match in contact with the light, dry brushwood. The flame sprang into the air, and fast and wide spread the rushing blaze, hissing and crackling among the withered leaves and the broken twigs,—and far away across the sea gleamed the cold light of the moon,—darkened by one black speck, as the smuggling-boat made its way over the surging waters to the shore.

CHAPTER XLVII.

THE shore was safe, for it was deserted before the boat had landed. The four men who rowed, had loaded themselves with the tubs, and were making their way towards the cliff. A fifth lingered behind, and with him came Clement Vivian. He walked slowly and doubtfully,—not with the eager energy of a boy in the height of his adventurous spirits. His step was unequal; his head turned quickly from one side to the other. Perhaps he was planning an escape, but his companion kept close by his side and urged him on.

They reached the foot of the cliffs, and the men paused and gathered together. Mark Wood was foremost. They looked up at the cliff, then took a survey of the shore.

'Safe! now for it; along the ledge to the cave! Come, youngster!' and the man who seemed to have charge of Clement stood back to put him first: 'It's plain sailing.'

Clement delayed: 'I have had my frolic; I will go no farther.'

'What! that's new talking!—up I say.' He would have pushed Clement forward, but the boy drew back indignantly: 'Touch me again, if you dare.'

'On, young Master—on, for your life;' and Mark Wood drew near, and pointed to a projecting angle of the cliff above them, where a dark, immovable spot was to be seen.

The men, as with one consent, began to scale the cliff, not by the path, but by ledges, corners, shelving rocks, often with a footing which a goat could scarcely have held; and not in the direction of the cave, but away beyond the headland, to a point which all seemed to know as by instinct. They reached a smooth ledge, wide enough for them to stand together. The cliff rose perpendicularly behind them; before them a huge rock, which seemed about to precipitate itself into the sea, threw a dark shadow on their resting-place. They waited to take breath. Clement, who had followed them with difficulty, approached Mark: 'Is there danger? Are the preventives abroad?'

'Above and around, that black head was on the look-out,—now on.'

Before Clement could ask another question, Mark was leading the way again, but now in a different direction, towards the cave. He stopped after he had gone some paces, and muttered a few words to Clement's first guide. The man evidently differed from · him, and Mark spoke angrily, and went on by himself. The four who were left kept close to Clement. A sound like a call, · which might, however, have been nothing more than the wind, fell on the ear, and it was answered by Clement's guide. The others interchanged a few words : 'The cave's free for us !'

'Was that the cry?'

· 'Yes; didn't you hear?'

'All right !' and they went on.

They were drawing near the cave. From the west side it was difficult of approach—the ledge was narrow, and the angle by which it was entered sharp. The men settled their tubs on their shoulders, and seemed prepared for a false step. Mark Wood, who had been considerably in advance, came back. Clement heard him say : 'I've a doubt that we're in for it, Hale; let him go.'

'Go, and peach,' was Hale's answer. 'You are a fool; on

with you.' He thrust Mark forward, and then looked back to Clement: 'Keep close, youngster. If I throw you the tub, you'll know how to carry it;' and they moved forward again, one by one, with slow and cautious steps, clinging to the cliff, and once or twice sliding where the footing was too unsteady for support.

Mark turned the corner first; Clement and Hale followed. They were then before the entrance of the cave.

'Now, youngster! I must be left free.' Hale took the tub from his shoulder.

'Best not,' whispered Mark, drawing him within the passage: 'look below.'

A body of the coastguard were at the foot of the cliff; a little behind lingered Mr Vivian.

'In with you, man,—in: clear the way; and Hale forced Mark into the cave, and tossed the tub upon the ground. The others followed his example.

A shout rose from below, and the preventive men hurried up the cliff, followed by Mr Vivian.

'Stand to it boldly! for your life.' The smugglers placed themselves before the cave, and Clement stood with them,—his spirit excited by the danger.

'Clement! Master Clement! this way,' shouted Mark from within; but Clement did not or would not hear. The preventive men were nearly on a level with the cave—Dennis and Ryan foremost.

'A step nearer, and we fire!' shouted the smugglers, and the preventive men drew back.

There was a mutual pause. Whilst the two parties confronted each other, Mr Vivian, unperceived, scrambling, clinging to the side of the cliff, advanced to the smugglers' rear, and seized Hale's arm. The preventive men rushed forward. Hale strove violently to extricate himself, and his companions came to his rescue. A desperate, deadly struggle began.

'Clement! Clement!' called out a voice of thunder, in the tumult, 'up the cliff,—to the left; for the sake of Heaven—for your father's sake!' and the boy, terrified, yet excited, looked round him with the impulse to obey.

'Not to the cliffs—through the cave; Mark Wood waits you there.'

It was Ronald Vivian, who standing before the cave, spoke hurriedly, yet in tones low, and deep, and clear.

2 D

Clement paused for one moment in indecision, and the grasp of Dennis, the preventive man, was laid upon his collar.

' A prisoner ! a prisoner !' he exclaimed ; but a sudden blow from Ronald felled him to the ground. He rose again instantly, and they grappled together.

' Into the cave,' shouted Ronald, turning his head for a second; and Clement waited no longer.

' Ronald Vivian to be dealt with at last !' burst from the lips of Dennis, maddened at recognising the boy from whose hands the blow had been received.

Mr Vivian heard the call : ' Save him !—do him no injury ; I will bear you free ;' but his call was in vain.

The contest with Hale and his comrades had ended in Hale's capture. The other smugglers had escaped, but not without pursuit from the preventive men. Ryan, however, remained be·hind, and came to the assistance of Dennis.

' Yield, or we fire !' was the cry.

But Ronald fought desperately, for danger to him was safety to Clement.

' Yield ! Ronald, yield ;' called Mr Vivian, and he placed himself by his side.

A dark face, not till that moment seen, peered from behind a rock, and a pistol was levelled at Mr Vivian's head.

' Ha ! Goff ! the scoundrel !' shouted Ryan, catching the out·line of the well-known features. He moved aside, and a bullet aimed at Mr Vivian, whizzed past, and Ronald, struck by it in the shoulder, fell to the ground.

' Murder !' The cry echoed wildly amongst the rocks, as the men, catching a momentary glimpse of Goff, followed him down the cliff and along the shore. It was a frantic chase, over the loose shingles, and rough stones, with masses of broken cliff im·peding them. Goff kept close by the cliff, the path most difficult of pursuit. On, with the speed of a maniac,—for safety or for ruin ; on, to the East Point. Behind it, in a little cove, lies a small boat ; and there waits Captain Vivian, ready, eager to carry him to the vessel which will be his harbour of safety.

He was close upon the Point; the path was difficult—the moon had become darkened; he stumbled, and the delay brought his pursuers near. Their voices were heard high above the booming of the waves and the increasing roar of the wind. Con·cealment ! no, it was impossible ; the spot which he had reached was bare of the sheltering rocks. Escape by the cliffs ! impossible also ; they rose frowning above him,—no longer easy of access. He turned towards the edge of the shore, and shouted long and loud ; and a little boat manned by one person rounded the Point. It was lifted high by the waves, then again it sank,—for a moment it might have been thought engulfed,—it could not near the beach.

'Rascal ! scoundrel !' shouted the preventive men. They were rushing from the cliff; their feet were crashing the pebbles. He almost felt their grasp ;—one plunge, and he was breasting the waves towards the boat. The foaming water rose high, and he was hidden ; it broke upon the shore, and his black, shaggy head was seen rising as a spot in the moonlight.

Fierce and strong are the angry billows,—they are bearing him away from the boat. He sees it, and one hand is uplifted, and a howl of terror comes across the watery waste. He is struggling,—his head is tossed as a plaything by the crested waves. The boat is drawing near : he will be saved,—yes, he must be ;—his hand is actually touching the boat.

And the grasp is faint, and the waves are strong, and—the wretched, guilty head moves with one agonising effort, and sinks, to be lost to sight for ever.

CHAPTER XLVIII.

R ONALD lay upon the ground, the blood oozing fast from his shoulder ; by him knelt Mr Vivian, vainly endeavouring to stanch the wound. The shouts of the men, and the cries of pursuit, reached them as distant echoes. Mr Vivian thought that Ronald had fainted, but he was still sensible, only growing weaker and weaker—his sight becoming dim, his lips refusing to utter a sound. Mr Vivian made him rest against his knee, and spoke to him. There was a feeble smile upon the cold, white lips ; and Mr Vivian took off his coat, and making it into a pillow, laid Ronald's head gently upon it, and leaving him for an instant, went a few steps forward and called, but received no answer. The spot a few minutes before so dizzy with tumult was now utterly deserted.

He came back again, and groped his way into the cave. It was quite dark ; but something soft lay on the ground,—a coat, and he took it up and felt in the pocket. It contained a small flask. Mr Vivian brought this out into the light, and moistened Ronald's lips with the brandy which was in it, and covered him with the coat. He was a little revived then, and it seemed possible to move him within the shelter of the rock; but the start when he was touched showed that the attempt would be agony.

In despair Mr Vivian called again; and this time a voice answered him, but from within the cave; and the rattle of stones, accompanied by a few hasty ejaculations, was followed by the appearance of Mark Wood.

He came forward with stealthy steps, glancing doubtfully at Mr Vivian; but the sight of Ronald's ghastly features seemed to give him courage to draw near. 'You called,' he said.

'Yes, I called.' Mr Vivian pointed to Ronald. 'He has been wounded in the skirmish, and we must move him.'

'The sharks! Cowardly villains! Are they gone?' Mark went a few steps down the cliff.

Mr Vivian called him back: 'Gone now, but they may return. It was not they who did it.'

'All safe now,' muttered Mark. He put his arm under Ronald tenderly.

'We must have more help,' said Mr Vivian.

'By and by; we'll take him inside first. Stay!'—he lighted a match and set fire to a brand, which he thrust into a crevice of the rock,—'that will do to show the way. Now then;' and with Mr Vivian's assistance he raised Ronald, and disregarding the moaning which showed the suffering he caused, bore him into the cave.

Some straw and dried fern leaves lay in a heap in one corner, and over this Mr Vivian stretched the coat with which Ronald had been covered. He was then laid upon it; and Mark proceeded to collect together some dried sticks, which he lighted.

Mr Vivian looked at him with some surprise. 'Is he safe?' he said. 'The preventive men may be back.'

'Safe enough just now. We've left a couple of kegs in their way at the foot of the cliff, which they'll seize, and then, ten to one, be off. They've caught Hale, and are after the others.'

'But if they look for him?' and Mr Vivian glanced at Ronald.

'He's as safe here as elsewhere. If we tried to get him home, we should meet them on the cliffs. An hour hence it will all be right enough. Now, give him another taste of the brandy-flask, and see if he 'll come-to more.'

The warmth of the fire, and the cordial, had the effect desired for a few moments, but Ronald soon sank back again into his former state ; and Mr Vivian, greatly alarmed, insisted upon the necessity of summoning more aid. Mr Lester, he said, was certainly within reach.

'The parson ! He's off home with the young gentleman. 'Twas he who met me, and bade me come back. I shouldn't have ventured myself so soon again within reach of the sharks, if it hadn't been for him.'

Ronald slowly opened his eyes, and by the lurid light of the fire Mr Vivian saw that his lips moved. He bent down, and heard the word 'Clement.'

'Safe, thank God !'

Ronald smiled, and his head fell back.

They waited for nearly a quarter of an hour longer in silence —Mark keeping up the fire, and occasionally watching at the entrance of the cave ; whilst Mr Vivian, supporting Ronald, stanching his wound, and from time to time forcing him to sip the flask of brandy, succeeded at length in restoring him to some degree of strength.

His sufferings, however, became greater as his power increased. A suppressed groan followed every attempt to move him, and a clearer consciousness brought a look of anguish to his face, which Mr Vivian vainly endeavoured to read.

'If we had another hand we might move him now,' said Mark, returning to Ronald's couch, after another survey of the cliff.

Ronald raised his hand, as a sign against it.

Mr Vivian replied to the gesture : 'You must not remain here, Ronald ; it will kill you. Mr Lester will come, and we will carry you very gently.'

He looked impatient, and beckoned to Mark. Mr Vivian moved aside.

'Sad work, Master Ronald,' said Mark, compassionately. 'What made you mix yourself up with us ?'

'My father,' murmured Ronald, taking no notice of the question,—'where is he ?'

Mark glanced at Mr Vivian, who was, however, too far off to hear the answer.

'Gone on board by this time. He was to be off to the vessel, so we were told, as soon as the second light flamed up.'

'On board,—away!' A look of convulsive agony crossed Ronald's face.

'Not away yet. She's off there still, I take it; and pretty close she was five minutes ago.'

'I must see him.'

'To be sure; he'll be back, if not to-night, to-morrow.'

'No, no; to-night,—now.'

'Not so easy that—the Captain's not to be sent for in a moment; and he's gone for a purpose.'

'It must be,—it must. Mark, who knows? I may be dying.'

'Not so bad as that, Master Ronald. You've had a good knock, however it happened; but you'll come round. Let me just go and get a helping hand, and we'll have you at the Grange before half an hour's over our heads.'

The mention of the Grange renewed Ronald's excitement, and he exclaimed vehemently, 'Not there.'

His accent caused Mr Vivian to draw nearer. Ronald raised his glassy eyes to his with a glance of mingled confidence and despair; and as Mr Vivian stooped to be nearer to him, he took hold of his hand, and held it within his own, and tried to speak, and then the words seemed to fail, and he muttered something unintelligible.

'You have a wish—let me hear it; it shall be granted.'

'Let my father come, now—safe.'

'He shall come, and be safe, if it is in my power to bring him; we will take you home, and you shall see him.'

'Here! here :—not home.'

Mark interposed, and drew Mr Vivian aside. 'It would never do,' he said, 'to take Master Ronald at his fancy; it might be easy enough to get hold of the Captain, who was sure to be on board the vessel, and within call ;—but to leave him there on the ground—he would be shot himself sooner.'

'It frets him to insist upon moving him,' replied Mr Vivian; 'and it will really make but little difference. Let Captain Vivian come, if you know where to find him; and when he comes, let me go into the village for further help. I will bring back a surgeon with me. There will be less delay then, and'——

A faint call from Ronald summoned Mr Vivian again to his side. His face was bright with thankfulness: 'Let Mark tell him quickly. To-morrow'—and the light of his eye became darkened, and his voice grew fainter—'I may not need him.'

Mr Vivian pressed his hand affectionately, and repeated the order.

Yet Mark still lingered. "'Twas a mad errand,' he said, as he once more appealed to Mr Vivian ; 'and likely to be the boy's death—waiting there instead of being tended. And if the Captain came, it might be sore work for them ; no one knew what he would be like when things went contrary. If they might have taken Ronald to the Grange '—— He stopped suddenly, for a moan escaped from Ronald, drawn from him by excessive pain. Yet even then he waved his hand for Mark to leave him ; and Mr Vivian seconding the entreaty, the man departed.

The time of Mark's absence seemed hours to Mr Vivian. It would have been unendurable but for the thought of Clement's safety—that was comfort through everything , and Ronald's wan face was a sufficient reproach, when impatience was about to master him. Yet as the moments passed on, many doubts as to the prudence of agreeing to his wish suggested themselves : danger from the preventive men ; the possibility that Mark would not be able to manage his boat ; the difficulty of landing again :—obstacles which Mark had not appeared to contemplate, but which seemed aggravated, as Ronald's suffering evidently increased, and the necessity for surgical aid became more and more urgent.

He scarcely thought of himself, his own fears and hopes and plans for the future. He could but look at the pale countenance of the noble boy, so suddenly struck down in the pride of his strength, and think of the short, stormy life, with its strong impulses, its earnest resolve, and unflinching will—and ponder upon the deep mystery that one so formed for good should have been placed under the dominion of evil. It was a thought only to be borne by the remembrance of that inscrutable Wisdom which ' searcheth the heart,' and ' knoweth what is in man,' and will require only what has been given. And bitterly in contrast rose up before Mr Vivian's memory the recollections of his own boyhood—with virtuous examples, the rules of strict rectitude, the support of an honourable name, the prospect of a fair inheritance to lure him to good ; yet all deserted, and bringing upon him only a severer condemnation. What we might have been ! It is a terrible thought to realise ?

' Mr Vivian,'—Ronald stretched out his hand and touched him ; ' are they coming ?'

' I don't know ; I think not ; but I will see.' He went out to look, and returned : 'The boat has left the vessel ; I can't tell who is in it.'

'My father will be here—you must go.'

. 'Not till he comes.'

'Yes, before—now ; raise me.' · And Mr Vivian lifted him up, and made him support himself against the wall. He spoke more easily then, and seemed relieved by the change of position : 'Now go, please ; quickly.' Yet as Mr Vivian looked towards the entrance of the cave, he held him back ; 'One word. I have done what I could ; are you satisfied ?'

'Fully—entirely—thankfully ; more than tongue can tell.'

'But I have not done all. I will try.'

'But not now. O Ronald, is it for my sake you would see your father ?'

'I told Miss Campbell I would do the utmost ; if I am to die, I must do it.'

'You have done everything that could be required ; and more, a thousand times. It is for Clement's sake that you are here now.'

'The utmost,' repeated Ronald ; 'it was my promise. Tell her I kept it. And you will pardon him if the offence were '— he stopped suddenly.

'I know what it was.'

Ronald let Mr Vivian's hand drop, and turned his face to the wall.

Mr Vivian continued, quietly, 'I will not tell you now, Ronald, how it was discovered. But one thing may satisfy you, —there is no legal proof ; I could not bring it home to him, if I would.'

Ronald turned slowly round and fixed his ghastly eyes upon him : 'Then the evil to you is done.'

'Yes.'

'And without remedy ?'

'Without remedy from him, except by his own confession : that might indeed help me with my father.'

'You shall have it. When it is in your hands, and I am gone, Mr Vivian, you will save his name from disgrace.'

Mr Vivian seized his hand : 'Disgrace cannot attach to the name you bear, Ronald : whatever your father may have done to tarnish it, you have nobly redeemed it.'

He did not smile nor answer, but a tear rolled down his cheek, and his lip quivered with anguish. He recovered himself again quickly, and pointing towards the entrance, said : ' Look out ; when they are at the foot of the cliff, you must go.   Hark !'.

' God bless you, and help you, Ronald ; ' and Mr Vivian held Ronald's hand with lingering affection.

' Go! go !'

Ronald's face grew troubled and eager ; yet as Mr Vivian left the cave, his eye rested upon him with an expression that would fain have asked him to return.

CHAPTER XLIX.

' E H ! Ronald ! my lad ! in a scrape and calling for me to help you out !   That comes of not keeping to quarters. How on earth you got loose passes me.'   Captain Vivian entered the cave blusteringly.   He would not listen to Mark's request to tread with caution, and in the dim light of the dying embers scarcely distinguished where his son lay stretched upon his rough bed.

' No one here,' said Mark, groping around, and collecting some more sticks.   ' You 'll see, Captain, that it's as I said ; he 's mortal bad '—and he held a lighted brand so as to cast a gleam upon Ronald's face, and then walked away to the entrance.

Captain Vivian snatched the brand from him, drew near, looked,—then throwing the torch aside, staggered back against the wall.

' Father ! ' Ronald's voice was hollow as a call from the grave.

Captain Vivian threw himself on the ground beside him.

' Shot ! my boy, my poor boy !   The rascals !   But we 'll be revenged.   We'll get you on board, and look after you, and you 'll do well ; there 's no doubt of that.   Many's the ugly touch I 've had myself.   Here ! Mark.'

' Stay, father.   I must not go ; listen.'

' Listen ! to be sure.   The rascals !   I 'll be revenged.'

' It was not they.   It matters not who it was ; I would forget revenge.'

' Forget it : you may ; but I tell you, Ronald, the reckoning shall be kept till the last hour of my life—ay, and paid too.'

' Then your reckoning must be with Goff.   He raised the pistol ; I saw him.   It was levelled at Mr Vivian.'

No answer came, only a quick gasp of breathless horror.

' It is for Mr Vivian to revenge,' continued Ronald. ' Father !
can you hear me ? can you listen to me ?' for Captain Vivian
was kneeling upright,—his form rigid, his eyes fixed.

' Revenge ! let him seek it down in the green ocean—down,
down ; he will not find it. Let him look for it,—it is gone.'

' Father ! speak to me,—oh, horrible !' and Ronald raised himself for a moment, and sank back shuddering and exhausted.

' He's gone, my boy ; don't think of him, Ronald. Rouse up
—we'll forget. Where's Mark ?'

Mark came, and Ronald's lips were moistened with brandy,
and he found strength to utter, ' Is he killed ?'

' Drowned, Master Ronald,' said Mark, coolly. ' I heard it
said as I came across the Common ; but I don't understand the
rights of it all.'

' Drowned, Ronald, my boy ;' and Captain Vivian stood up,
and drew near to Mark with an air of restored confidence.
' But we won't talk of him now. Mark and I will put you into
the boat, and be off to the vessel, and see to you to-night ; and
to-morrow, if it's needed, we'll get more help—but I'm a clever
surgeon myself.'

Ronald motioned Mark away : ' Raise me, father. Drowned,
lost in the deep waters !' He hid his face with his trembling
hand. ' O God ! have mercy ! it is Thy judgment.'

' Cheer up, my boy ; don't think.'

' He is gone, father. I may be going too. Where?—where?'
he repeated, and he caught his father's hand, and held it with all
the little strength he retained.

' We can't think ; we don't know till the time comes. Why
trouble yourself, my poor lad ?'

' Oh ! it is time now ; there is no other time. Father, think,
repent. God will hear now.'

' Too late for me !' and Captain Vivian's voice slightly
trembled. ' Well enough for you.'

' His body lies beneath the waves, his soul is before God,'
murmured Ronald, shuddering ; ' and he had so many crimes to
burden it.'

' May be so ; but none can tell what excuses may be at hand
for him or for any one. There's no need to talk of him.'

' Father ; yes,—let me but speak now. If only one sin could
be lightened, death would be less terrible. Is it not so ? tell
me ; answer.'

'If it could be, but past is past.'

'No, no, it is present ; it never dies ; it will come full again. But it may be repented of, then it cannot harm.'

'My poor lad ! He's wandering.' Captain Vivian bent down anxiously.

'Father, I speak truth ; I know what I say. Oh ! by the thought of that fearful death—that awful judgment, do not turn from me.'

'If sorrow's necessary, I'm sorry enough,' was the moody answer ; 'but I didn't come here to talk of it.'

'Yes, indeed,' and Ronald almost sat upright in his eagerness. 'It was for that I sent for you. I may be dying ; God knows. I could not carry the load to my grave. Father, our name has been pledged to dishonour,—disgrace ; it has caused Mr Vivian's ruin.'

'Not caused it : it was his own doing. None could have touched him if he hadn't dealt the first blow himself.'

'But the work he began—it was completed by you.'

'Then it's done, and it can't be undone.'

'It may be. Oh ! indeed it may. It may be acknowledged, and, to the utmost extent of your means, the sum may be restored.'

'Acknowledge ! Restore ! Why, he knows all ; he would pursue me to the last gasp to be revenged on me. He would take from me every penny I possess, and leave me to beggary if it were possible.'

'He has promised to forgive, and his word is honour. If it were not, when we have injured others, God will never forgive us, without confession and reparation.'

'I don't know where you learned your teaching ; it's not my doing.'

'I learned it from my mother, when I said my prayers to her. She talked of it when she was dying. She would repeat it now. Father, your confession may replace Mr Vivian at once in his home.'

'And balk me of the last hope of carrying out the revenge for which alone I did the deed. Was it the paltry money, boy, for which I hazarded ruin ? Would the miserable thousands have tempted me ? If they had been multiplied ten, twenty, a hundred, a thousandfold, I would have scorned them all rather than lose my revenge.'

'God also can revenge,' replied Ronald, faintly. 'And you are safe ; he says himself there is no legal proof.'

' If there had been, would I have ventured myself within his grasp? No; he has chosen his course, let him follow it out.'

'To-night will go against him,' said Ronald.

' Of course ; I know it. I should never have troubled myself with the boy if I had not known it. He may thank his stars that it is no worse,—that the young scapegrace is not now in the hands of the magistrates. Let him make his way with the General as he can, with only his bare words to fortify him, and Clement's folly to stand against him.'

' Mercy! father! His life has been most miserable.'

' He had no mercy on me,' was the bitter reply.

Captain Vivian was about to rise, and again summon Mark, but Ronald's feeble hand rested on his arm.

'Father! if the gurgling waters were closing round you, as they closed over that wretched man, would you not wish that you had done it ?'

' I could never wish that I had disgraced myself.'

' The disgrace was when the deed was done. God help us to bear it.'

' We will not bear it,' exclaimed Captain Vivian. 'We will be off. We will set up our fortunes in another place.'

' The future is with God,' said Ronald. ' May it please Him to spare me that sorrow.'

' What! would you forsake me ?'

' I would die, if it be God's will, for life without honour is very terrible.'

' Mad boy! yet you wish me to disgrace myself.'

' Because what you call disgrace is to me the only road to honour. Father, grant my request, and if God should spare me, I will follow you, labour with you, slave with you, die with you, —so that the path you take is one in which there is no sin. Refuse me, and there is another duty before me. The debt to General Vivian shall be repaid, and by my hands. I will travel the world over, but I will work ; I will toil, if necessary, with the poorest ; I will live the life of an anchorite, and die the death of an outcast; rather than he shall be defrauded of one penny of that which is his just due. We part to-night for ever!'

The words might have seemed prophetic, for Ronald sank back exhausted with his own energy, and pale and motionless as in death.

' Ronald, my boy, speak to me, only one word.' Captain

Vivian bent over him in agony. He opened his eyes, and at that moment Mark re-entered the cave.

'Quick, Captain, one way or t'other. They are coming from the cliff. The strange gentleman, and the surgeon, and Mr Lester. If you've any reason for wishing to be off, you'd best be quick.'

Captain Vivian looked at Ronald. 'We'll take him with us.'

'Can't be. He's too far gone. We may come for him to-morrow. They'll take care of him to-night; but you must be quick,' and mark went out again to watch.

'Father!' Ronald held Captain Vivian's hand; his glassy eyes rested on him long and steadily.

The hand was withdrawn, and with the other Captain Vivian roughly dashed away a tear.

'If I die, still think of me.'

'Think of you! Ronald, Ronald! forgive what I have done to you.'

'Not mine, God's forgiveness. Oh! if the truth were told. It might be written, even now, before you go. Then I should be at peace.'

'There is no forgiveness for such as I, Ronald.'

'Yes, father, yes; one act; it may be the entrance on the right way. God grant us to meet at the end.' He spoke very feebly.

Captain Vivian pondered. 'If it is done, I go disgraced by my own word, never to be heard of again in England.'

Ronald raised his hand to his head: 'My eyes are dizzy; I can't see you. Will you do it? Will you write?'

Captain Vivian took a card from his pocket, wrote a few words upon the back, and put it into Ronald's hands. 'It is done,' he said; 'your father is a lost man.'

'Saved! saved!' exclaimed Ronald, and he fell back and fainted.

CHAPTER L.

THAT had been a long and intensely trying day to Mildred Vivian. When Bertha left her she had spent several hours with her father, vainly endeavouring to persuade him to dismiss the thought of the lost paper, until Mr Lester could appear himself to account for it. But General Vivian was not easily to be persuaded in any matter, least of all in the control of his own mind, when he was touched upon one of the tenderest points of honour.

His keen sense of justice was connected with the strong feeling of personal claim to his property, and this had aggravated his indignation, when his son's supposed misdeed was first brought before him. But the offence had been punished, as he said to himself, rightfully, and then he felt at liberty to bury it from all knowledge but his own.

That Mr Lester, Mildred, above all, Bertha, should be acquainted with it, wounded him almost beyond endurance, and the mind which had so long allowed itself to be warped by a one-sided justice, was no longer proof against the prejudice which in any other case he would have despised.

He spoke to Mildred of plots and conspiracies; he questioned her as to the stranger whom Mrs Robinson had received at the farm, and whom she imagined might return. He would allow of no evasion, and drew from her at length the confession that Edward was expected—that he might be at Encombe that very night. He was satisfied then so far that he asked no more questions; but it was evident that his mind had taken a wrong turn, and that the step his son had made in coming back to England, unsummoned, was likely to prove a stumbling-block, rather than an assistance, in the way of his restoration to favour.

Mildred was very gentle and patient, but she could not help being sad, and this irritated the General. It was a reproach to him. He said at last that he would be left alone, and when Ella offered to read to him as usual, he refused; and then Mildred went back to her own room, to bear, as best she might, the burden which had fallen upon her.

Night drew on, and still the General did not send for her. She tried to work, and made Ella read aloud, but it was impossible to attend. She was thinking of her brother, and longing for news of Clement. Greaves was on the watch, and came in every now and then to tell her anything he had heard, but it was all unsatisfactory. The smugglers were certain to land; they had a traitor amongst them, supposed to be Mrs Robinson's farm-boy, Joe Styles, and he, it was said, had given warning to the preventive men who were on the watch. No doubt if they did land there would be a desperate struggle.

Then came a report from the gamekeepers. Mr Lester and his friend had arrived ; they had walked over the cliffs from Cleve to Encombe, and had gone straight to Hardman's, and from thence to the shore. Somebody declared that Miss Campbell and Miss Lester had been very much frightened by a smuggler on their way home, but it was thought that it could not be true, because the smugglers were proverbially civil to ladies.

Eight o'clock came, and tea was brought. Mildred sent a message to know if they might have it with the General, in his room ; but the answer was brought—No, the General would drink tea alone ; Miss Ella might go to him afterwards. That was a little comfort, and when Ella was gone, Mildred lay quietly on the sofa, feeling it a relief to be as anxious as she pleased, without the fear of dispiriting Ella.

Nine o'clock ! Ella came down and said grandpapa was tired. Greaves was to go to him in a quarter of an hour. He would not have Mildred see him again, because it was such a trouble to her, but he sent his love, and begged she would take care he had his sleeping-draught.

' Ring the bell, Ella, and I will ask about it,' said Mildred. The bell was rung, but not answered directly.

' Ring again, my love, I can't think what the servants are doing.'

They waited still some time.

' Just open the door a little, Ella ; I am sure I hear a good deal of talking.'

Greaves was trying to silence some one who was speaking, and he came himself to answer the bell.

' The General will want you, Greaves, in a quarter of an hour; he is going to bed. I rang to remind you of the sleeping-draught.'

' Yes, ma'am.' Greaves looked at Ella, doubtfully.

' Go again to grandpapa, Ella ; tell him Greaves will bring him his draught directly. I send him my very best love, and trust he will have a good night. Greaves,' and Mildred turned to the butler almost before Ella was out of the room,—' you have news.'

' Not much, ma'am ; that is,—pray don't be frightened, Miss Mildred ; it's better than could have been thought. Master Clement is safe.'

' Thank God ! but he must have been with the smugglers.'

'He was with them, and landed with them,' replied Greaves, rather sternly; 'and the preventives were down upon them, and there was a skirmish, more than an hour ago that was. But Master Clement got away, I am told. Some say Mr Bruce, that came with Mr Lester, this evening, helped him; others, that it was the Captain's son; but anyhow, he got free, and Mr Lester went home with him. One of the smugglers was taken, and '——

'Well? what?'

'It's an ugly story, the rest, ma'am. I can't say how much is true. But that wretched fellow, Goff, is put out of the way.'.

'Killed? By the preventive men? How horrible!' and Mildred turned very pale.

'Worse than that, if the tale's true. Hardman, who was watching about the cliffs with Mr Lester, says that he had kept himself hid when the skirmish began, and just at the end fired deliberately at Mr Bruce.'

Mildred uttered a scream of horror.

Greaves paused for a moment. 'The General's waiting, ma'am, I must not be long.'

'But Mr Bruce—Mr Bruce!' faintly ejaculated Mildred.

'He escaped, ma'am; which was all very well; though, being a stranger in these parts, one doesn't seem to care so much about him. But the poor young gentleman at the Grange has been mortally wounded, and there's many a sad heart for him. The preventives were after Goff in a moment, and, trying to escape, he was drowned.'

Even in his haste to go to the General, Greaves watched Mildred's countenance narrowly; but she exercised immense self-control, and uttering inwardly her thankfulness for her brother's safety, only said aloud: 'O Greaves, how terrible! so desperate —so unprepared. And the poor boy, what have they done with him?'

'Carried him off to Mark Wood's cottage in the Gorge; so I'm told, ma'am; though I can scarce believe it, with the Grange so near at hand. But they say, too, that he insisted upon it, and that the Captain is off somewhere. People think there must be something more in it all than a mere smuggling fray; and why that fellow Goff should have had a spite against Mr Bruce, no one can say.'

'Yes, very strange; very strange, indeed!' but Mildred spoke wanderingly. 'Was that the hall bell? She raised herself up and listened.

Greaves listened too. ' I think so, ma'am ; I will see,' and he left the room.

Mildred's heart beat with painful rapidity ; everything seemed to swim before her ; her eyes were dim, and her knees trembled. She tried to hearken, but could catch no sound. The rush of roaring waves, the noise of tumultuous voices, the phantom sounds of an excited imagination, were filling her ears with their ghostly echoes ; and the undertone of voices approaching, with the tread of footsteps across the stone hall and along the corridor, mingled with her fancies, so that she could scarcely distinguish their reality.

Yet the door opened, and two persons entered, Mr Lester first, and Mildred's exclamation of pleasure was changed into a sharp cry of almost terrified delight, as the next moment her brother knelt by her side.

She flung her arms round his neck ; her tears fell fast and long. When she did speak it was to say, ' I have prayed for this, and God has heard me ! '

Mr Lester looked round and closed the door. ' I sent Greaves away, but he may come back. Remember, you are still to be careful.'

' Not after to-morrow,' exclaimed Mr Vivian. 'All must be decided then.'

' So soon !—My father must be prepared. O Edward ! you little know what you have to contend with. And it seems—if I could but keep you here with me as you are,'—and again she clung to him, as though fearing he would escape from her grasp.

' It is useless to delay,' replied Mr Lester ; ' and we have arguments, Mildred, which may work a great change in General Vivian's feelings. You are ignorant of the charge brought against your brother, and therefore you cannot hope, as we do, that it may be refuted.'

' I do know it,' said Mildred ; and turning to Mr Vivian, with a look of sad, yet tender reproach, she added : ' When I learned the truth, I judged my father more reverently and charitably. He was wounded in the point on which his feelings are the most sensitive.'

' Not by me !' and Mr Vivian started to his feet. ' As there is truth in heaven, Mildred, it was a forgery ; a base, miserable forgery !'

' The paper !—the handwriting ! Is it possible ?'

' It was not mine. I would have died rather than do such a

2 E

deed. John Vivian is responsible for it. I have heard the acknowledgment from his own lips.'

' O Edward ! God indeed be thanked !' She sat silent for
some seconds, then turned to Mr Lester : 'I can't understand
The paper—did my father know about it ?—did he give it to
you ? He says that he has forgotten it.'

'There is a mystery about that,' replied Mr Lester. ' Miss
Campbell says it was found in my pocket-book. I had not the
most remote idea that it was in my possession. Yet I can so far
account for it, that on the day when I was here, talking with
General Vivian about Clement, a box of papers was upset, and
several were scattered. I picked up all, and restored them, as I
thought ; but this I must have carried off accidentally. Miss
Campbell says she recollects seeing it drop out with my handkerchief, when she was conversing with me the same evening, and
that I took it up, without looking at it, and put it in my pocket-
book. Of course she did not know then what it was.'

'And you have it, and will return it, and it will all be
proved.'

' Ah ! Mildred, no,' exclaimed Mr Vivian ; 'that is a sore
point ; it is gone. Almost the last act of that wretched man
Goff, who has to-night been summoned to his dread account,
was to take it from Miss Campbell by force, and to destroy it.'

Mildred sank back on the sofa.

' I have nothing but my word to support me,' continued Mr
Vivian,—' that, and Bertha Campbell's evidence that the paper
was taken from her. Yet what need is there of more ?' And
he drew himself up proudly.

' He does not know my father.' Mildred spoke despondingly
to Mr Lester.

' I hope he does. I can't imagine General Vivian's doubting
him.'

' Doubt me !' Mr Vivian withdrew the hand which had
been clasped in Mildred's, and strode up and down the apartment
rapidly : ' Let him breathe but the thought, and I will go back
to Jamaica—to India—I care not where ? Doubt me ?—doubt
his son ?—a Vivian ! '

' Edward ! dearest, he is old ; his mind has lost its elasticity,
and it has been warped by sorrow.'

' Yes, through me,—my faults. O Mildred, Mildred I help
me to be patient ! '

' God will help us all,' replied Mildred ; ' only let us trust

Him. My father may believe, yet he may insist upon proof. Is there no other to be brought forward ?'

'None, at least forthcoming at present. John Vivian is beyond our reach; if he were not, I scarcely see how we could substantiate our charge.'

'And Clement's conduct will work against you,' continued Mildred. 'He must, perhaps he ought, to hear of it.'

'To condemn me for my boy's follies ! Mildred, is that justice ?'

'It may be his justice,' replied Mildred ; and a long pause followed.

Mr Vivian broke it : 'It matters not, Mildred ; delay cannot help us. If it would, I could not bear it. Even now, the suspense of my position is often almost maddening. Let my father reject,—let him even doubt my word; if he will ; the honour of a Vivian rests not on words, but on the consciousness of the inmost heart. One thing at least he cannot take from me,—the comfort of having cleared myself in your dear eyes ; of having seen you,—talked with you,—looked again upon the old, familiar walls. Home ! my childhood's home !' and his eye wandered round the well-known apartment. 'Does my father know what home is ?'

'Too well ! dearest Edward. If he had cared for it less, he might have been less severe in his endeavour to uphold it.'

'Rejected again ! Dishonoured! doubted !' murmured Mr Vivian. 'Yet I have loved and reverenced him, oh ! so deeply. Mildred, he must see me ; he must give me his blessing. I cannot die in peace without it.'

'Hope, Edward. I have lived upon it for many years. It may seem impossible,' she added, speaking to Mr Lester, 'to reject such evidence ; yet no one can calculate upon the turn his feelings may take.'

'He will not reject it,' replied Mr Lester. 'I have no fear upon that point ; it would be an insult to his feelings as a gentleman. I have but one misgiving, that the old prejudice may still linger so as to bias his mind, and that the absence of proof will, without his being aware of it, rankle in his breast. I believe he will grant John Vivian's offence, and yet I do not say that he will forgive your brother, so as to restore him to his inheritance.'

'Then be it so !' exclaimed Mr Vivian. 'Let the paltry acres go ; it was not for them that I grieved when he disinherited me,

and it is not for them that I have sought him now. Let him ac‑
knowledge that I am not the base wretch he thought me, and
admit me to intercourse with my home, and I will be content.
The labour of my own intellect shall, through God's aid, support
me for the future, as it has supported me during the past, and
when I die I shall have the satisfaction of knowing that not even
to my father was I indebted for my own prosperity, or that of
my children.'

'Proud, dearest Edward, still,' said Mildred, gently.

'O Mildred! does not this unjust world make one so?'

'Yes,' and Mildred sighed; 'it is one's struggle.'

'To bear punishment and own it to be punishment, Mildred,
that is what I find so hard. Yet I have had many years in
which to learn the lesson.'

'And many things to teach it you. I must hear all before
long.'

'Not till you have told me all. One question I must ask
now.' His voice became tremulous and sank, and Mr Lester
withdrew himself, and walked to the other end of the apartment.
'Mildred, did Edith think of me as my father did?'

'Not as he did. He would not tell her what he thought the
truth.'

'But she suspected me?'

'She feared, and the fear'——

'Killed her; I knew it. God forgive and aid me!'

'She had been ill and anxious before,' continued Mildred;
'the shock was very great, but it might only have aggravated,
not caused the evil. She had a brain fever at the time, but she
rallied from it, and lived many months afterwards.'

. 'And did she speak of me? Did you talk together?'

'Alas! no, that was my grief; but it was all pent up; it
worked inwardly. It was very strange, she who had been so un‑
reserved before.'

'John Vivian's doing,' he murmured. 'Can it be possible to
forgive? And all that time she considered me a wretch, Mil‑
dred; lost—sunk.'

'Forget it now, Edward. If the dead know the secrets of the
living, she has long since learned that you were innocent. If
not, the day will come when she must know it. It was God who
appointed her trial and ours.'

'She thought me guilty,' he continued; 'and I was so, though
not as she believed. O Mildred, the indescribable wretched‑

ncss of that time !—but for my wife, I must have been over-whelmed by it.'

'And the years of misery that have followed!' continued Mildred : 'when my father thinks of them he must yield.'

'Yet remember, Mildred, it must be to justice, not compassion. He did me wrong unknowingly ; when he is convinced of his error, he must do me right freely. I can accept nothing but pardon for the offence I did commit—restitution for the suffer-ings borne for those which I did not commit.'

'You are like him,' said Mildred, smiling sadly.

'Then there is the more hope that we may understand each other. For my own reputation's sake,—my character in the sight of the world,—I must demand a full acknowledgment that I have been wronged.'

'And for his own reputation's sake,—his character in the sight of the world,—he will demand a full proof that he has wronged you.'

Mr Vivian was silent, and very thoughtful.

The remembrance of Bertha's refusal to deliver up the paper crossed Mildred's mind, but she would not speak of it ; her brother's countenance showed feelings which needed no aggra-vation.

Mr Lester came up to them : 'We must go now, Vivian ; re-member we have business on our hands, and explanations to be made to the preventive men,—possibly to the magistrates also, if we wish to prevent inquiry as to Clement's share and Ronald's, and your own, in this unhappy affair ; and to-morrow early I have promised to be at the Gorge.'

' To see Ronald?' inquired Mildred. 'Is it not a miserable place for him?'

'Not miserable, but very uncomfortable. He insisted upon being taken there, as well as he could insist upon anything, so utterly exhausted as he was. He dreaded the Grange evi-dently.'

'He will have no one to take care of him or nurse him.'

'I said so. I urged Mark to carry him to the Rectory, but his agony of distress at the idea was so great that we were forced to give way. The old woman who has the charge of Barney is a tolerable nurse, and Mark has given him up his own bed, and is off himself to get out of the way of observation. Vivian and I went with Ronald, and saw that he was in no want of anything for the present ; and so we must leave it.

To-morrow he may rally,—and then we may bring him to reason.'

'You don't speak very anxiously,' said Mildred.

'The medical opinion is favourable. A good deal of the exhaustion we found proceeded from his having eaten nothing for many hours. But I don't venture to say he will recover.'

Mr Vivian had been standing by them in silence. He bent over his sister and kissed her : ' My doing ! Mildred ; the curse falls on all connected with me.'

'Dearest Edward !—the curse is taken away when there is repentance.'

'Not in this world, as regards temporal suffering,' he replied.

'Save that the suffering may be converted into blessing,' observed Mr Lester. 'And for Ronald, sorrow would be idle : should·he live, he will live to redeem his name ; should he die, who can doubt that mercy is in store for him ?'

CHAPTER LI.

'THE General has had another attack of faintness, sir ; Miss Vivian is with him.'

That was the information which greeted Mr Lester when he appeared at the Hall the following morning. Greaves looked uneasy, and spoke anxiously, but said that Dr Lawes assured them there was nothing to be alarmed at.

The intelligence was seconded by a note from Mildred, written in pencil : 'We must be patient. It is worry of mind. Nothing can be said to him yet.'

Patience was comparatively easy now—at least, for Mr Vivian. He had taken up his abode at the farm in preference to the Rectory ; and thither Ella was sent, to make what might be called her first acquaintance with her father. Louisa and Fanny also were with him ; whilst Bertha was preparing Mrs Campbell's mind for his return. Only Clement was absent.

Mr Vivian's was one of those easily depressed, easily excited minds, which seem never entirely to lose their elasticity ; and now that personal danger was at an end, and he was restored to the free companionship of his family, he would scarcely allow the happiness of the present moment to be disturbed by any fears for the future. He was charmed with Ella's talents, Louisa's sense, and little Fanny's beauty, and turned from any remembrance of Clement's misconduct, till it was forced upon him at last, when Mr Lester came, and it was necessary to make inquiry into all that had taken place.

Clement's story was short, but full of warning. He had not offended to the full extent intentionally—that was his excuse ; and yet every word he spoke showed that most fatal of all intentions, the determination to follow a weak self-will.

To do him justice, he did not for a moment endeavour to evade blame by equivocation. The first most marked and wilful wandering from the right path had been the concealment of his visit to the Grange. 'Had it been confessed, Mr Lester's strict injunctions would have supported his weakness, and probably enabled him to withstand further temptations. But once on the downward path, and the impetus of evil carried him easily forward. His vanity had been excited by the praises bestowed upon his quickness in figures ; and, under the pretence of being further useful to Captain Vivian, he had for the fourth time been enticed by him to the Grange, as he was returning from the hills. Clement knew he was doing wrong—he quite confessed it ; but Captain Vivian, he said, was pressing. In the course of conversation it was suggested to him that Captain Vivian's vessel was at Encombe, and upon the point of making a short sail of about an hour round by Cleve ; if he would only go on board, he was to have a good lesson in seamanship, and might return almost before he was missed.

The offer, accompanied by flattering prophecies that he would make a first-rate sailor, was too tempting to be refused. And Clement went with Captain Vivian to the cliff ; and then finding it growing dusk, wished to return. But he was laughed at, as being inclined to sneak out of an adventure, and told that the moon would be up directly ; and so having, as he fancied, no good excuse, he went. Captain Vivian, he thought, meant to accompany him, but at the last moment he put him in charge of Mark Wood.

From that time Clement's existence had been one almost of terror. The vessel sailed in the direction of the opposite coast ; and he found himself in the hands of men who would neither listen to him nor explain their intentions. They treated him civilly, but were deaf to his remonstrances, except that Mark

Wood assured him, from time to time, that no personal injury was intended him.

If he had erred greatly, the agony of mind of that one night had been a punishment in which seemed condensed the lesson of a life. Of what went on in the vessel, Clement was very ignorant. They had met and spoken with another vessel, and he imagined had received contraband goods on board ; but he was kept close in the cabin, and indeed, was too ill a great part of the time to enter into anything but his own sufferings.

Mark Wood waited upon him, and told him when they were about to return ; but, as they neared the shore, Mark left him, and another man, Hale, took charge of him. He felt himself then a prisoner, and, from the casual observations which were dropped before him, understood the nature of the expedition in which the men were engaged, and resolved, at all hazards, to leave them as soon as they touched the land. But this he soon found to be impossible. Hale kept close to him, and had even threatened to shoot him if he attempted to escape. The result Mr Lester and his father already knew.

It was all told concisely and abruptly, drawn from him in a great measure by questions ; and when, at last, the history was ended, Clement stood humbled and silent, not even venturing to ask for forgiveness. His father pitied him ; perhaps there were too many and too keen recollections of his own follies to condemn him. Mr Lester pitied him also, yet his manner was coldly stern. One comment only he made upon the facts he had heard : ' Absence of intention, Clement, will not save us from the consequences of our faults. There is a straight and narrow path to heaven ; no one who leaves it intends to go to hell.'

' I have had a lesson for life, sir ; I don't mean to forget it,' replied Clement.

' A lesson for eternity, it ought to be, Clement. If small disobediences will produce such terrible consequences on earth, we may be quite certain that they will, without repentance, produce a thousandfold more terrible consequences hereafter. I would say it to you, and to Ella also. Neither of you have, as yet, learned what strict duty means ; and if you do not learn it now, it will be taught you by the bitter experience of life.'

Clement turned to his father. From him it seemed that he expected greater palliation of his faults ; but Mr Vivian sat with his forehead resting on his hands. Only once he looked up for a moment, and said that he should like Ella to be sent for.

She came, bright, excited, full of hope and happiness, having only just begun to realise that the quiet, strange Mr Bruce could possibly be her own father. The sight of Clement, and the grave countenances which she saw, awed and subdued her. She sat down by her father, and he put his arm round her, and looked at her tenderly, but his eyes were dimmed with tears, and he did not speak.

' You have forgiven him, dear papa,' whispered Ella.

' Mr Lester says he is not the only person to require forgiveness,' replied her father, evasively.

Ella looked up inquiringly.

' Am I very strict, Ella,' observed Mr Lester, ' in saying that, if your influence had always been exerted on the side of obedience, last night's sufferings might have been spared us ?'

Ella's colour rose. She could bear her Aunt Mildred's gentle and sympathising reproof, but Mr Lester's cold, severe tone touched her pride.

She was not aware, she said, that any influence of hers had induced Clement to join the smugglers.

' I didn't join them, Ella,' exclaimed Clement ; ' I wouldn't for the world have been mixed up with such a low set. I was taken off against my will. But I was very wrong,' he added, more gently.

Ella glanced at him in surprise.

' You will think me hard, I know, Ella,' continued Mr Lester ; ' but I can easily make you see that I have reason on my side. Who encouraged Clement to spend the time that should have been devoted to study upon the shore, and so gave him desultory habits ?'

Ella blushed, and was silent.

' Who set him the example of disrespect, disobedience, wilfulness, in small everyday matters ; and so led him into the same in greater ones? Who never would allow that punctuality to hours was a duty; and so made him think it of little consequence whether he stayed with those men or not ? Who used to excite him by talking of chivalry, and adventure, and daring—and forgot that the noblest daring is that which shall conquer self?'

No reply ; but Ella leaned her head on her father's shoulder, and burst into tears.

Clement was much distressed. ' If you wouldn't be angry with her, sir. Indeed it was my own doing. I ought to have known better ; and I did, too.'

'Ella won't be angry with me by and by,' said Mr Lester; 'she would rather hear the truth.'

'I am not angry, now,'—and Ella looked up, and half smiled through her tears ;—'Aunt Mildred has told me all before.'

'And Aunt Mildred has taught you to be a very different person from what you were, Ella,' replied Mr Lester, kindly ; 'and if there had not been something of a sense of justice in my mind, which made me feel that you could scarcely be exonerated from a share in Clement's faults, I doubt if I should have spoken to you as I have ; certainly I should not have chosen to do so the first day of your father's being with you.'

'Mr Lester has lectured me, too, very often,' said Mr Vivian, kissing her fondly. 'You know he was my tutor, so he was accustomed to it years ago. God grant they may profit by it better than I did,' he added, in a lower voice.

Clement came forward boldly ; 'I am willing to bear any punishment, sir, which my father or you may think right. And I would rather.'

'You have had your punishment, Clement, from God ; if that should fail, nothing else will have any effect.'

'And you won't trust me, sir, again.'

'Yes, you will ; it is impossible not to trust him,' exclaimed Ella.

'I trust him entirely, implicitly—as a general trusts a prisoner on his parole,' said Mr Vivian, quickly.

Mr Lester was silent.

Clement looked disheartened ; Ella inclined to be angry.

'Shall I tell you, Clement, why I scarcely dare to say I trust you ?' replied Mr Lester. 'Not only because of that one in-stance of deception, most grievous though it was, for I believe you are heartily ashamed of it; but because your besetting sin— almost more fatal to a man than to a woman—is vanity.'

Clement winced under the accusation.

'It is very painful, I know, to hear it. It is such a weakness so entirely opposed to a manly spirit, that we are apt to give it any name rather than its true one. You think that you like adventure—deeds of enterprise ; what you really like is admira-tion of any kind. Let it come from your father, from me, from the fishermen on the shore—it matters not who or what may be the source—if you are admired, you are satisfied. There, Clement, is your snare.'

'Yes, sir, I know it.'

Mr Lester's countenance brightened a little, and he laid his hand affectionately on Clement's shoulder; 'Remember it as well as know it, and I shall be satisfied. Own that you are vain; repeat it to yourself; think of it; watch against it; pray most earnestly that you may be saved from it, and you will, through God's mercy, be all that we most earnestly desire; for a man who is fighting against vanity posts a sentinel upon eye, and ear, and tongue, and every imagination of the heart: yield, and there is no surer way to mar success in this world, or to destroy your hopes for another.'

Clement stood silent; and Ella, longing to withdraw attention from him, said, rather lightly; 'You won't tell me my great fault, Mr Lester.'

'Perhaps I don't know you as well as I do Clement,' he replied, coldly; 'besides, I have said enough for one morning.'

'But I should like to know; please tell me.'

'Really?—can you bear it?'

'Clement can bear it, and so can I, I hope,' replied Ella, drawing herself up.

'I could see one great fault peeping out in the way you spoke just then,' replied Mr Lester—'pride!'

'Yes, I know I am proud,' said Ella.

'But you are not ashamed of it.'

'It is very wrong, I am quite aware of that.'

'But it does not lower you, you think, in the eyes of others. You wouldn't shrink from being called a proud person?'

'Not very much'—and Ella coloured, though she almost smiled.

'No; and there is the great danger of pride;—persons are not ashamed of it. I have known many who rather pride themselves upon it. But, Ella, that is not according to God's judgment; and it will be no satisfaction to us, when heaven is lost, to know that it was through a sin which we fancied was a noble one.'

'I don't know that I thought it noble exactly,' observed Ella, 'only not so silly as some others.'

'But even in that you are mistaken,' replied Mr Lester. 'Proud persons don't think they are ridiculous, but they are so; and many times, when they imagine they have only been upholding their dignity, they have actually made themselves absurd.'

Ella looked grave and uncomfortable, and said that it was very difficult to know when she was proud.

'Of course it is,' replied Mr Lester. ' You think that pride is a family failing, and you admire it for its antiquity. I can trace it back farther than you do, Ella; it was Satan's sin when he rebelled against God.'

Ella looked towards her father, to hide from Mr Lester the blush which crimsoned her cheek.

'Pride and indolence,' whispered Mr Vivian—'these, I have always been told, were my child's great faults.'

' Yes, papa, indolence, I know; but I never thought so much about pride, and '—'—

' And what?'

'It seems hard upon me.'

' It is just what I used to say, Ella; he was so very unsparing when he told me my faults.'

' But I would rather know them ; I would rather he should tell me of them. I don't want any one to think better of me than I am; only it always seemed that indolence was much worse than pride.'

' There is not much to choose between them, I am afraid,' said Mr Vivian.

'But pride !—people would be nothing without pride,' exclaimed Ella, and she sat up, and turned to Mr Lester for an answer.

'Nothing without self-respect,' replied Mr Lester ; 'and that must be founded upon truth, and those who see themselves truly can never be proud.'

' I don't know what you mean by self-respect.'

' A respect for ourselves as being God's creatures, redeemed and sanctified by Him ; made the dwelling-place of His Spirit, and destined to live with Him hereafter. That respect will make us fear to do, or say, or think anything which may lower us in His eyes ; but, when we have done so, it will force us at once to acknowledge our fault, because it is only by that acknowledgment that we can be restored to His favour.'

' That scarcely meets Ella's notions,' said Mr Vivian, as he watched his child's face ; ' she is thinking of this world.'

' Well, then, as regards this world ; self-respect, Ella, is but a phase of that foundation of all things—truth. Proud people place themselves in false positions ; persons with self-respect see exactly what they have a claim to. No one calls a prince proud because he requires to be honoured as a prince; self-respect teaches him to claim such attention. But when he forgets that other persons have their stations requiring honour also, then pride begins, and self-respect ceases. In this point of view, however, self-respect is only a natural virtue, and may be possessed where there is no real religion. The genuine feeling is that which I spoke of before, and which must always go hand in hand with humility. But we have had enough lecturing upon faults this morning,' added Mr Lester, suddenly stopping, and changing his tone. 'I must go and see after my other parishioners, and talk a little to Rachel. I only saw her for a minute last night, and she had a wonderful story to tell me of her adventures yesterday.'

He held out his hand to Ella; she took it shyly but cordially, and said, 'Thank you.' Her heart was quite full.

'Don't consider me very severe, dear child, if you can help it; I only want you to be perfect now papa is come.'

He went up to Clement, who was standing in the background. 'It may be all forgotten,' said Mr Vivian, 'may it not?'

'Yes, indeed, as far as I am concerned. And one thing, Clement, I say from my heart—I trust you now more than I have ever done before. I am sure you are heartily sorry.'

Clement's eyes sparkled through tears. 'You shall have cause, sir; indeed, I don't mean to forget.'

'God bless you, my dear boy, and give you strength to keep your resolution.'

Mr Lester departed, and Clement threw himself into his father's arms, and sobbed.

CHAPTER LII.

WEARY and anxious were the hours spent by Mildred Vivian in her father's sick-chamber. She was told there was nothing to fear; she scarcely thought there was; and yet the suspense and watching, the sense of personal helplessness, the boding care for her brother, the longing to search into the depths of her father's thoughts, aggravated every symptom in her eyes. One fear after another presented itself. He lay still and silent, and she thought that some sudden weakness had paralysed his powers. He was restless, and she fancied that fever was coming on. He looked flushed, and she thought there was a rush of blood to the head. But the fear which most haunted her was that of paralysis. Such an attack, coming at his age, might weaken his mental powers, and render futile all endeavours to explain her brother's conduct. She was with him constantly, but he said very little to her. He did not sleep, but his mind seemed absorbed with thoughts which he would not communicate, but which seemed working and goading him almost beyond endurance.

As he neither questioned her concerning Mr Lester's return, nor referred to the missing paper, Mildred feared to agitate him by bringing the subject before him. Yet it was evident that such a state of things could not long continue. The feelings preying upon him would inevitably work their way fatally, if some stop were not put to them; and on the fourth day after the beginning of this miserable suspense, Mildred ventured to mention Mr Lester's name, and ask whether her father would be willing to see him.

'If he will, he may come;' that was all the answer; but it was sufficient for Mildred, and she despatched a messenger to the Rectory, with the request that Mr Lester would, if possible, be at the Hall in the course of the afternoon.

The General insisted upon dressing and sitting up, then, though he had been told that to rise might bring back the giddiness and faintness. He was very weak, but he would scarcely allow Greaves to wait upon him, and when he went into his dressing-room, he ordered his books and papers to be brought, and endeavoured to write a letter, but his hand shook so much, that he was obliged to give up the attempt. Mildred was sitting with him at the time, and offered to write for him. He refused. 'It was no matter of consequence,' he said, 'and would do just as well another day. His hand was a little shaky from lying in bed so long.' It was evident that he did not choose to be thought ill.

Luncheon came, and he made an effort to eat, but nothing suited his taste. He was full of complaints, and at last took only a little wine and water and a biscuit; even that he only pretended to eat, and soon put it aside, and sent for the newspaper.

Greaves brought the *Times*.

'Not that; the county paper. Where is it?'

Greaves looked at Mildred.

'I thought you wouldn't care to read that, sir, and I took it to my room,' replied Mildred.

'Bring it,' and Greaves went unwillingly.

He came back. 'I am very sorry, ma'am, I have looked everywhere in the morning-room, and can't find it.'

Mildred regarded him scrutinisingly: 'Are you sure it is not there, Greaves?'

'Very nearly, ma'am. I will look again if you wish it.'

'Ask Miss Ella; she may have it,' said Mildred; but Greaves showed no alacrity to obey.

'Ella! what has she to do with newspapers?' inquired the General. 'You don't let her read them, do you?'

'Not often, sir; only'——

The General interrupted her: 'Go and ask Miss Ella for the paper, Greaves. Tell her to bring it herself if she has it.'

He sat bending over the fire, and did not even look at Mildred.

Ella came, the newspaper in her hand: 'Do you want me, grandpapa? Shall I read to you?'

'What is there in the paper worth reading? Anything particular?'

Ella became as pale as death,—then the blood crimsoned her very temples.

The General repeated the question: 'You have been reading it yourself, child. What was there in it?'

'Aunt Mildred let me see the account of the smuggling fray,' replied Ella.

'What smuggling fray? At Encombe? Let me see it?' He adjusted his spectacles, turned to the light, but could not read, and gave the paper back to Ella. 'It tires me, my dear. Lying in bed so long makes one's eyes weak. Read it out.'

Ella would fain have handed the paper to Mildred. The General observed it.

'Read it yourself, my dear; don't trouble your aunt.'

And Ella read a long, prolix account of the landing of the smugglers, and the watchfulness of the coastguard, with some uncomfortable particulars of the struggle between them, and the detail of Goff's death. Then she stopped.

'Is that all, my dear?'

'Nearly all, grandpapa.'

'Well, make haste, finish it. Mr Lester will be here.'

'It isn't exactly about the smugglers, grandpapa; it is only'——

'Read it,—read it, child.'

Ella's voice shook so that her words were scarcely intelligible: 'We regret to say, that a rumour is abroad implicating a young gentleman of honourable birth in this disgraceful affair. The circumstances are very mysterious, but are said to be connected with a train of unfortunate events by which the succession to one of the finest estates in the county has been alienated.'

'What?' General Vivian caught the paper from her hand and looked at it, though it was clear he could scarcely distinguish the words. 'Carry it to your aunt, Ella.'

'I have read it, sir, thank you. Ella, you may go.'

The storm was about to burst when Ella closed the door. Mildred said timidly, 'I did not like to worry you, sir, when you were so unwell.'

'Nothing worries me. When did it happen?'

'Four nights ago, sir: the evening you were taken ill the second time.'

'Where is the boy?'

'At home, sir, with Mrs Campbell. But indeed the papers are hard upon him.'

'Of course, when they say disagreeable things. Does he mean to take up smuggling as a profession?'

'My dear father! indeed, indeed, you are cruel upon him. He did not join them,—at least not willingly ; he was led away.'

'No doubt : all persons are who go wrong.'

'I think, sir, if you could hear him,—if you could see him, you would judge him more gently. He is so entirely penitent for his folly.'

'All persons are when they are suffering from the consequences.'

'But he is so young,' continued Mildred,—'such a mere boy; and he did not in the least intend to go with the smugglers,—he was entrapped. It was Captain Vivian's doing.'

'Doubtless the same game which he played years ago.'

'Mr Lester will say more for poor Clement than I can,' continued Mildred ; 'he has heard all the particulars, and he is thoroughly convinced that Clement is deeply grieved for what has happened, and is resolved to amend.'

'I never said that Clement was not grieved. But since Mr Lester knows everything,'—and there was a peculiar stress upon the words,—'no doubt he can explain more of the mysterious circumstances alluded to.'

Mildred looked thoroughly disheartened ; 'I would rather Mr Lester should talk to you, my dear father. I know all so indistinctly,—by hearsay.'

' Hearsay troubles itself with things which very little concern it,' observed the General, 'when it remarks upon the disposition which it may please me to make of my property. Whoever wishes, however, to know my final and irrevocable decision upon the subject, is perfectly welcome to do so. The old lands of the Vivians shall never, with my consent, descend to the hands of base swindlers, or be wasted by the companion of smugglers.'

'Edward a swindler ! My dear, dear father, how little you know !'

'What else is it but swindling,' continued the General, 'to promise that which you have no power to pay ; to give away that which is not your own ; to mortgage an inheritance which a single word may alienate ? Like father, like son. Let them go. And for you, Mildred, and Mr Lester,'—he paused—his words came thickly—' you may plot too deeply for your own honour and for mine.'

'Father, you mistake me ; you do me wrong.' Mildred's voice was eager, and her cheek flushed with all the inherent pride of her race ; but in one moment it was checked. 'I am sorry,—forgive me—I will not speak of myself ; but, indeed, you are unjust to Mr Lester. And for Edward, oh believe me ! there is indeed a mystery, but he never did the deed for which you disinherited him. The paper brought before you was a base forgery.'

General Vivian's eye was stony and fixed, his face was rigid. Mildred drew near, and sat down beside him. 'My dearest father ! You hear it ; it is truth. Edward himself says it. May he not—will you not let him come to you and tell you so ?'

He regarded her almost vacantly, yet he repeated the word, ' Forgery ?'

'Yes, indeed,' she continued ; 'you can't doubt him. It was revenge,—Captain Vivian's revenge. It is certain.'

'Let me see the paper.' The General passed his hand across his forehead.

'Dearest father ! will you listen to me? Shall we wait ? Mr Lester is coming, and will explain.'

'I must see it,—it was his handwriting—his own. Give it me,—in the box ; but it is gone, Mr Lester took it. O Mildred !

2 F

my child ! plots, plots, everywhere !' and he turned his head away from her, and rested it in utter feebleness and exhaustion against the back of his chair.

Mildred allowed him to remain thus without interruption for some seconds ; then she again said, very gently : ' Mr Lester's coming will make all clear to you, sir. He will be here almost directly.'

He kept her hand clasped in his, clutching it at times convulsively. She thought he did not hear when the hall-door bell rang ; but he raised himself with a sudden effort, pushed her aside, and tried to draw the table near to him, then sank back again powerless.

Mildred watched him with anxiety. ' If it is Mr Lester, dear sir, will you see him ?'

He bent his head in assent, and again tried to sit up. Mildred put a cushion behind him, and made him rest his feet on a footstool. Even at that moment, it struck her how old and worn he looked—much older than his age. ' Shall I stay for Mr Lester, or will you see him alone ?' she asked.

' Stay: put a chair ; tell Greaves to bring me my draught first.'

That caused a little delay, which Mildred did not regret, earnestly though she longed for the interview to be over. It was a breathing time ; it gave her a moment for prayer. Greaves bustled about in the room longer than seemed necessary ; but he did good ; he distracted the General's attention and roused him. He said, at last, ' That will do, go.' And the irritable tone was a comfort to Mildred.

One glance interchanged between Mildred and Mr Lester told little to either of aught except suspense. Mr Lester went up to the General : ' I am afraid I find you ill, sir.'

' Better, thank you ; I am sitting up.'

' Yes : he has kept his bed the last four days,' observed Mildred. ' I don't exactly know what has been the matter.'

' Gout hanging about. You have been to London, Mr Lester.'

' For a day or two, sir. I returned just before you were taken ill, and should have called to see you if I had been allowed, but they said you ought to be kept quiet.'

' I have business with you.'

' Have you, sir ? Might it not be as well to delay it till you are rather stronger ?'

' I am obliged to you, but I am the judge of my own strength. You have a paper of mine. I gave it ' ——. He stopped, and looked distressed, and turned with an appealing glance to Mildred.

'No, dear sir; if you recollect, you did not give it. It was that which worried you. But Mr Lester will tell you about it. He was telling me last night.'

That acknowledgment was repented of as soon as made, for a frown rested on the General's face.

'It must have been taken up by me accidentally,' observed Mr Lester, 'the day I was with you, sir, looking over your papers. That is the only way I can account for its having come into my possession. Certainly I was not aware that I had it, until Miss Campbell told me she had found it in my pocket-book.'

'Campbell! Campbell!' muttered the General to himself. 'Is she in it?' The mention of the name had evidently awakened some old prejudice and dislike. He spoke more distinctly, 'I must have it back; it is important. Mildred says' ——.

'What is quite true, sir,—that it is a forgery.'

'I would look at it,—fetch it for me, Mildred. I beg your pardon, Mr Lester, I don't know who has it,—it has been taken from me—I must see it.' The tone became more and more excited.

Mildred and Mr Lester glanced at each other in alarm.

'What makes you look so? Why don't you speak out? If it's a forgery, why isn't it proved? It shall be proved; I will have it tried. The last penny I have shall be spent to try it.'

'If you will see your son, sir,' said Mr Lester, mildly, 'he will convince you. Had you not better see him? He is at Encombe, longing to be admitted to you.'

General Vivian turned round upon him sharply: 'Is that your object, Mr Lester?'

'My object is to see justice done, sir.'

'And mine,—mine too. I don't doubt you, Mr Lester. You are a gentleman. Where is the paper?'

'Destroyed, sir;'—there was no escape from a direct answer; —'by a most unhappy mischance. The villain Goff, Captain Vivian's witness, and the sharer, I presume, in the profits of his crime, took it by force from Miss Campbell, as she was returning the other evening from the Hall, and tore it to atoms. How he obtained the information that she had it I cannot tell.'

The General was quite silent.

'I need not say, sir, that Miss Campbell's word is above suspicion.'

'You saw the paper, Mr Lester?'

'No, sir; I knew nothing about it until my return from London.'

'I saw it,' exclaimed Mildred.

'Then you can tell; yes, you must be the best judge of all. Was it your brother's handwriting?' and the General's eye rested upon her with its cold, clear, scrutinising glance.

Mildred felt herself defeated by her own words. She could only say that certainly it was very like it, but that of course it would be, to be a successful forgery. She had not examined it minutely.

'And Miss Campbell obtained possession of it,' murmured the General to himself.

'Accidentally, sir. She found it by mistake in my pocket-book.'

'Where it should have been left, Mr Lester. It was not Miss Campbell's business to pry into the concerns of another family.'

'She meant no harm, my dear father. It was very natural; she felt the paper to be of importance.'

'Of the greatest importance. So much so, Mildred, that without it'—he stopped—'Mr Lester, I don't doubt you.'

'Then, sir, you will see your son.'

'My son,—tell him from me that I forgive him.'

'My father! My dear, dear father, have pity upon him! His heart yearns to see you,' exclaimed Mildred.

'I have pity, I forgive him. Justice forbids me to do more without proof. Mr Lester, bid him look after his boy, or there will yet be a further disgrace awaiting us. Mildred, ring for Greaves. I would go to my room.'

Mildred delayed, with her hand on the bell, and looked entreatingly at Mr Lester, then doubtfully on her father.

The General read their countenances.

'You think me hard. If you could stand in my place, you would judge me better.' He tried to rise himself from his chair, but he was too weak. And as he sat down again, and leaned his head upon his hands, Mildred saw tears trickle through them.

She kissed his forehead, and he did not repel her, though he would not notice her.

She whispered to him: 'Is there not comfort in the thought of his innocence?' And then he dashed away the hand which lay upon his, and told her to leave him.

Mr Lester made one more effort. 'General Vivian ! You speak of justice. It is unjust to refuse to see your son, and to hear what he can say in his own defence.'

' Proof,' murmured the General; 'let him bring proof.'

' But if he cannot, my dearest father ; if you insist upon that which it is impossible to obtain?'

The General shook his head, his clearness of intellect seemed failing again.

' We must not urge it,' whispered Mr Lester to Mildred.

She rang the bell, and when Greaves came, Mr Lester left the room, the General taking no notice of his departure.

CHAPTER LIII.

RONALD VIVIAN sat in a large arm-chair, by the side of the low, open hearth in Mark Wood's cottage. Barney's couch was opposite : the child was much attenuated, and his face expressed more constant pain. In a distant corner, Mother Brewer was busied in knitting a pair of small woollen socks. The traces of what might have been years of sickness and sorrow were visible in Ronald's worn countenance ; yet still more visibly was stamped upon it the energy which might still struggle and conquer, grounded upon the endurance which might suffer but would never yield.

His wound was not deep, though it was very painful. He spoke of it himself now as something light, scarcely worthy of a thought. Yet it distressed him so much to move, that it was clear that great care would be needful before it could be expected to heal. Barney was trying to amuse himself with cutting out figures, but it was an effort to him to hold the scissors. From time to time he looked up wistfully at Ronald, whose eyes were closed.

' He's asleep, isn't he ?' said the old woman, laying down her knitting.

' Not asleep, thank you, mother ;' and Ronald opened his his eyes, and smiled.

' Why do you shut up your eyes if you ain't sleepy ?' asked Barney, rather sharply.

' Because it rests them. When one's ill one's eyes ache '

'I'm ill, but my eyes don't ache. Is it 'cause they shot you, that your eyes are bad?'

'I suppose it is; but I dare say they won't ache long. You know I'm getting well.'

'Sooner talked of than done,—that,' muttered Mother Brewer from her corner ; and Barney turned round and looked at her, but did not trouble himself to ask what she said.

'I don't want you to get well, Ronald. I like you best to be ill ; only you can't play so easy.'

'I don't know that it's very kind of you, Barney, to wish that I should always be ill ; but I suppose you mean it so.'

'You'll be going off if you get well,' said Barney ; 'and father said one day that if you didn't you'd go to heaven with me, and that's what I should like.'

'But, Barney, you know we may travel the same way, and meet at the end, though we don't go quite together. I've got a good deal to do before I get to heaven.'

'I dare say you'd be let off, if you asked,' said Barney ; 'and you'd like best to go.'

Ronald was silent.

'You would like it, sure,' continued the child ; 'everybody likes to go to heaven, 'cause it's so beautiful. I want to see the golden streets : Mother Brewer thinks that they shine as bright as Miss Rachel's picture-frame yonder, when the sun's on it. Shouldn't you like to see them?'

Ronald still delaying his answer, the question was repeated again, rather querulously. 'Yes, by and by ; very much indeed,' was the reply. But Ronald spoke as if his thoughts were scarcely in his words.

'It's wicked of you if you don't wish it,' continued Barney. 'Parson Lester says, nobody ever speaks cross there, or says bad words.'

'No indeed, they don't,' said Ronald, sadly.

'And there are beautiful angels all dressed in white, and singing wonderful,' continued Barney ; 'and a river so clear, you can see quite through, and fine trees, and fruits. Don't you want to go?'

'If God is pleased to take me, I hope I shall be quite glad to go,' replied Ronald. 'But, Barney, I don't think God does wish me to go yet ; and so I would rather stay and do His work here.'

'Work! what work? Captain John don't work.'

'But I must.'

'Fishing?' asked Barney.

A smile came over Ronald's face; but Barney looked at him quite steadily and earnestly.

'Not that kind of work, but trying to make myself good; and others too,' he added, in a lower voice.

'That's not work,' said Barney; 'that's praying.'

'But praying is a kind of work, because sometimes it is a trouble to say one's prayers.'

'I don't like it, sometimes; but that's 'cause I'm not good. When I get to heaven I shan't say my prayers to Mother Brewer; and then I shall attend.'

'Ah! but, Barney, we must learn to attend before we get to heaven: and we must do a great many other things besides, which are hard to us, and we must try to set a good example.'

'What's 'sample?' asked Barney.

'Behaving well before others,' replied Ronald, 'and so showing them how to do the same.'

'Well, then, if you and I go to heaven, we can set a good 'sample there.'

'But people don't want to have any examples set them in heaven, because they live with God and Jesus Christ, and so they have the best example before them, and never do wrong.'

Barney was thoughtful. Presently he said: 'Father don't set me a good 'sample; he says bad words, and speaks out. And Captain John don't set you one, does he?'

'He speaks out sometimes,' replied Ronald, evasively.

'Then do you mean to set him a good 'sample instead?'

'If I can.'

'And that's why you want to stay,' said Barney, still looking as if he were pondering deeply. In another moment he turned his head aside and sobbed as if his little heart would break.

'Barney! my poor child!'—Ronald was going to move from his chair, but was stopped by the old woman, who put down her knitting and went up to the couch.

'What's the matter now? what's a crying for? Come, stop; be a good boy, leave off,' said Mother Brewer, alternating between anger and coaxing.

'I want to be put next Ronald, in my chair,' sobbed Barney.

'You shall be put next me if you leave off crying; but I can't let you come till you do,' said Ronald.

The child exercised singular self-command. His tears were

swallowed almost instantaneously; but his neck still heaved convulsively.

The old woman placed him in a high chair, propped him up with pillows, and carried him to the opposite side of the hearth.

He put his hand in Ronald's, but did not speak till Mother Brewer had retired again to her corner ; then he hid his face on Ronald's shoulder and whispered in a voice interrupted by sobs: ' I don't want to stay and set father a 'sample. Must I ?'

Ronald passed his arm lovingly, for support, round the poor, little skeleton frame, and answered : ' I don't think God wants you to stay, Barney ; He only wants you to be good whilst you are here.'

' I 'll be very good,—I won't cry once, and I won't look about when I say my prayers, and I 'll say all my hymns through ; only I don't want it to be long ; it pains me so ;' and again he began to cry, but more gently, from weakness and over excitement.

Ronald let him rest quietly, and hoped he might go to sleep ; and he did close his eyes for a few moments, but opened them again to say in a dreamy voice, ' You 'll come too, Ronald ?'

And Ronald answered, cheerfully, ' Yes, soon ; by and by ;' and that seemed to satisfy him. At length he fell asleep, and Ronald, motioning to the old woman, he was taken back to his couch, and laid upon it.

Mr Lester came whilst Barney was still asleep. He saw Ronald regularly ; and his visits were comforting, yet not to himself quite satisfactory. Ronald was very reserved, and seemed unwilling to say what was on his mind ; and though Mr Lester knew what had passed between him and Mr Vivian, and that he was fully acquainted with his father's conduct, he dared not bring forward a subject so full of pain. Yet there were many allusions to it. Ronald's chief interest was for Mr Vivian, and the probability of his being admitted to an interview with the General, and obtaining his pardon. Almost the first question he asked when he saw Mr Lester the day after the smuggling skirmish, had reference to this point; and he was now frequently referring to it. It was indeed an engrossing subject of thought ; for on the failure of the meeting depended the necessity, so intensely painful, of coming forward with his father's written confession. Mr Lester once proposed that Mr Vivian should come and see him, but Ronald seemed to dislike the idea. He had not even as yet begged to see Miss Campbell, though he always sent a message to her. A spirit of torpor seemed, for the most part, to have succeeded his natural daring excitement of temperament; and he was willing to sit for hours brooding over the fire, now and then apparently asleep, but in reality alive to everything which might take place around him.

He was more like himself this day, for Barney had done him good by making him anxious, and when the old woman had left him alone with Mr Lester, there was a topic to enter upon at once, without the preliminary questions as to his own health, which were always irksome to him.

' He is looking worse to-day,' was his remark, made in a low voice, as he pointed to the child.

Mr Lester went up to the couch, and stood for a few moments, watching Barney's irregular breathing and the burning spot on his little, thin cheek.

'Yes, he does look a good deal worse,' he said, coming back to Ronald's chair, and drawing his own near the fire. ' Has the doctor seen him ?'

' He is coming by and by ; but no doctor will help him now ;' and Ronald brushed his hand across his eyes.

' One can't wish it ; it would be no good to him to keep him.'

' And it won't matter to me,' said Ronald. 'Anyhow, I shouldn't be here to see him ; and I would rather think of him as safe.'

' And look forward to joining him,' replied Mr Lester. ' That may be before very long for any of us ; though it may seem long to you, Ronald, with life before you.'

' I mustn't think of that yet,' replied Ronald. Changing the subject, he said quickly : ' Is Mr Vivian still at the farm ?'

' Yes.' Mr Lester seemed doubtful what further to add.

' And the General is not better, then ?'

' Yes, he is better, in a way ; though he looks ill.'

' Then you have seen him, sir ?' and Ronald waited for an answer, with evident anxiety.

' For a little while, just before I came here. He is a singular man, Ronald. The wall of prejudice and warped principle is too strong for us.'

Ronald leaned forward eagerly. ' It mustn't be. O Mr Lester !' and his voice sank, ' if he has dealt hardly unintentionally, surely, surely he will make amends.'

Mr Lester's reply was delayed for a few seconds. Presently he said, not looking at Ronald, ' He knows all, but I can't say what impression it has made upon him; he demands proof.'

Ronald's face, before very pale, became quite colourless. 'Then he would have vengeance,' he said.

'He would call it justice, not vengeance.'

'And it would be justice,' murmured Ronald.

'But he cannot have it; there can be no legal proof; your father is safe. My poor boy!' and Mr Lester laid his hand upon Ronald's, 'you mustn't think of that.'

'I do; I think of it always, and I try to feel the comfort.'

'You will do so by and by. You are weak now; you can scarcely realise it.'

'But I do realise it. I know that some might say I should be content. They would feel the outward, not the inward wound.'

'Even that God can comfort, Ronald, and He will as years go on.'

'He is very merciful; I pray to Him to help me; but to begin life with disgrace!' And he shuddered. The next moment he turned from the thought, and asked, 'Has the General seen Mr Vivian?'

'Not yet. There is an immense amount of hidden excitement preying upon him, and I dread the consequences. It is the strong-indulged will, and the warped spirit of manhood, working upon the enfeebled body of age, and becoming its torture. No one has, and no one, I believe, ever will, influence him.'

A long silence followed. Mr Lester again went to Barney's couch, and looked at him attentively. When he came back, Ronald was seated more upright, his face and attitude expressive of some strong self-control.

He returned to the subject without any preface, and said: 'Then there is no hope?'

'I don't allow myself to think so; it is too hard and unnatural. I must, to-morrow, speak to him myself, alone—as only a minister of God can speak. He has no right to demand proof against his son's word.'

'He shall have proof, to-morrow,' repeated Ronald, quietly.

Mr Lester looked at him, doubting whether his ears had rightly caught the words.

'He shall have it, to-morrow,' repeated Ronald. 'If Mr Vivian will meet me at the Hall, we will see the General together.'

Mr Lester felt uneasy. Ronald's voice was so changed and hollow, and his eye had a fixed glare. 'You could not go with him, my dear boy, even if you wished it,' he said, gently, 're- member how weak you are.'

'Mark Wood will help me. To-morrow, at three.'

'My dear Ronald, this will not do ; you are dreaming of what it is impossible you should perform. And your notions are wrong. You can't think that you are bound to come forward in this sad business. It is a feverish fancy.'

Ronald touched his pulse. 'Feel it, sir; I am quite calm. Say to Mr Vivian that I rely upon the promise solemnly made, when I had aided in saving his child's life. Now, will you read to me ? It will do me good.'

Mr Lester paused, but there was that in Ronald's countenance which made him shrink from pursuing the subject or attempting to gainsay his will, at least without consultation with Mr Vivian. He read to him and prayed, and Ronald thanked him gratefully and affectionately ; but he made no more reference to his deter- mination, except by repeating when they parted, 'To-morrow at three.'

The remainder of that afternoon Ronald spent in sitting by Barney's couch, holding the child's hand, smoothing his pillow, repeating verses of hymns,—trying, in every way that he could think of, to soothe his pain. And from time to time the little fellow dozed for a few moments, and then woke again to ask that Ronald would please to say the prayer for God to make him patient, for he was very tired of the ache. The other children returned from school, and were taken into the back room by Mother Brewer, and kept quiet with playthings ; and about six o'clock Mark Wood, who, finding that he was likely to escape detection, had ventured back to his cottage, came in and had tea with them ; but Barney was in a great deal of pain just then, and Ronald had no heart to join them, though he was very weary.

The old woman put the little ones to bed early ; and Mark said he would go into Cleve to get something from the doctor to make his boy sleep ; but Mother Brewer muttered that there was no need for that ; he'd sleep sound enough before many hours were over ; and Mark gave up his intention, and sat down moodily by the fire.

So they went on till about eight o'clock ; about that time the pain ceased entirely, but Barney was almost too exhausted to speak. He asked Ronald once to move, that father might kiss him, and bade Mother Brewer say 'Good-night' to little brothers and sisters, and tell them to be good; and after that he went to sleep, and they thought he would wake refreshed, as he had often done before after similar attacks. He was quiet for more than two hours; then he roused himself, and Mark gave him a little water. The child looked at him intently for an instant, and said, 'Thank you, father. Please say prayers.' And Mark knelt by the side of the little bed, and buried his face in the coverlet.

Barney felt feebly for Ronald's hand; 'You'll set the 'sample, Ronald, and then you'll come.' And the light grasp relaxed, and Barney fell asleep, to wake to the sight of the golden streets, and the river of pure water, and the fruits of the trees of everlasting life.

CHAPTER LIV.

BRIGHT were the gleams of the December sun, although it had already passed its low meridian height, as Edward Vivian and Mr Lester walked slowly through the Cleve Woods on their way to the Hall. They spoke of many things; the past perhaps more than the present or the future. It was a natural feeling, which would fain linger over the recollections connected with those scenes of happier days now, before the sentence might again be spoken which was to be the decree of separation from them for ever.

Mr Vivian was greatly depressed, yet a tone of only partially subdued indignation occasionally escaped him. He felt bitterly the doubt which had been cast upon his word, and would with difficulty listen to Mr Lester's explanation. It was useless, he said, to tell him that he was not doubted. If it were so, why was he not received, and the wrong acknowledged? There could be no alternative in such a case. Even duty to his father seemed scarcely to call upon him to enter into more detailed explanations.

'Years ago it might have been so,' was Mr Lester's reply. 'But you are fighting against a feeling first fostered as a duty, and encouraged the more since it has been against natural in-

clination. General Vivian fears himself. He has rested upon
his sense of justice, and made an idol of it ; and now, conscious
of his own weakness—such, at least, he would call it,—he dreads
being betrayed into an offence against it. He thinks himself
bound to treat you as he would a stranger. There is prejudice
in this, the rankling of former grievances, but he does not see it.
His is the spirit of the old Roman, who would sit in judgment
upon his children, and condemn them.'

'I don't understand it,' exclaimed Mr Vivian, hastily. 'We
are Christians, not heathens.'

'Even so. But General Vivian's principles are—I say the
word in all reverence, and, of course, with great limitation—
heathen. I mean that he has formed his own standard of right,
without looking at that given in the Bible. If justice were the
one virtue alone to be upheld, where should we all be ?'

Mr Vivian stopped suddenly. 'It goads me,' he said ; 'it
makes me feel that I would give up everything and go. If it
were not for my children I think I could.'

'My dear Vivian, that would be an action which you would
repent for ever. You have no right to act upon pride. Remember—forgive me for saying it—that your own conduct was the
first cause of offence. If it has since been exaggerated and mis-
construed, yet the original evil lies at your own door.'

'Your are right, Lester. I must bear all. And if I could see
him—oh! were he ever so stern—ever so cruel—all angry
feelings would go. I could throw myself at his feet and ask for
pardon, as in my childish days. But he will not see me ; there
is no hope of it.'

Mr Lester, without answering, opened the little gate which
led into Mildred's flower-garden. From thence a private door
admitted them into the morning-room. It was empty. Mildred
was with the General ; but her work-basket and books were
lying about ; she had been there only lately.

'Eighteen years !' murmured Mr Vivian. 'It seems but
yesterday.' He went to the lower end of the room, and drew
aside the curtain from the picture hanging there ; looked at it
for several minutes, then covered it again, and sat down without
making any comment.

'If Ronald should come, as he said, he must wait here,' observed Mr Lester.

'Yes.' But Mr Vivian would take no comfort from the
thought of Ronald's promise. 'My father wants proof ; and

words are no proofs to him,' he said, indignantly. 'And the boy will not speak to his father's prejudice. Who could ask it of him? I would not accept restoration on such terms.'

'He was bent upon being here,' observed Mr Lester.

'He was feverish and excited yesterday, no doubt. If he had anything that would really help us, he would have come forward before.'

'He was not in a state to do so,' remarked Mr Lester.

'I can't hope, Lester. I would rather fear the worst.'

And Mr Lester was silent, and rang the bell.

'Will the General see me, Greaves?'

Greaves, now fully aware of the interests at stake in the family, looked important, and was doubtful. The General had slept badly, and was, he thought, inclined to doze; but he would see.

Ella and Rachel appeared at the window, and drew back, startled at seeing gentlemen; but they soon came forward again, laughing. Rachel's bright eyes were raised lovingly to her father, as she exclaimed, 'We didn't know you were here, papa. Ella had been at the farm, and was coming back, and I said I would walk with her. Mrs Robinson was coming too, and said she would go back with me. There wasn't any harm, was there?'

'None at all, my child; but you mustn't disturb us now.'

'Let them come in,' said Mr Vivian. He seemed glad of anything which would distract his thoughts; and Ella and Rachel were admitted.

'We saw Mark Wood, papa, as we were coming,' said Rachel; 'he looked so very sad; he was driving Hardman's little cart, and said he was going to take Ronald out. I didn't like to ask if Barney was worse.'

'He died last night, Rachel. I was going to tell you.'

Rachel walked away to the window. Her father followed her, 'We mustn't grieve for him, Rachel.'

'No, papa, only—I will try not; and she struggled against her tears, and smiled, and then gave way again, and cried bitterly. 'I don't want him back, but I loved him so.'

Ella looked very grave and sorrowful, yet she could not quite feel with Rachel. She began telling her father about Barney, and Mr Vivian was interested, and made her repeat to him what Ronald had done for the child; and when Greaves returned and said that the General was ready, and would see Mr Lester, if he would walk up-stairs, though he turned pale for the instant, yet he went on talking to Ella, whilst Rachel sat down on a stool in the recess of the window, gazing at the pale sunlight which still flickered upon the lawn.

Mr Lester passed through the dressing-room, and found Mildred there. The door into the bedroom was open, so that he could only press her hand kindly, and ask a few ordinary questions. The General's hearing was wonderfully quick for his age, and he dared not stay to talk with her.

'You will find him very weak,' she said, in an undertone, when he asked what she thought of her father; 'but he has referred to nothing; only he has been trying to write this morning, sitting up in bed. Now he is dressed, and in his armchair.'

The General looked at least eighty, but that might have been his position, supported by pillows, and with only a partial light falling upon him through the half-closed curtains. He spoke with tolerable firmness, and thanked Mr Lester for coming, and accepted his offer of reading to him.

'Mildred is not strong enough to read much to me,' he said; 'and Ella has been out, they say, this morning. I should like to hear the morning lessons for the day.' He spoke decidedly as if he did not choose any other subject to be discussed.

Mr Lester turned over the pages of his Bible slowly, and remarked that in another week it would be Christmas Day.

'Yes; I forgot it was so near, till Mildred reminded me. She will receive your lists of the poor as usual.'

'You are very kind, sir. The poor people are extremely grateful.'

'It is no kindness, Mr Lester; it is their right. I am their steward.'

'I wish all persons with property would think the same, sir; but it is in many cases a difficult lesson to teach.'

'I learned it in my childhood, from warning. When I came into possession of my property, I vowed that the poor should never be defrauded.'

'It is a happy thought for old age, General, that the vow has been kept; and yet '——

'Well, sir, have you any fault to find with it?' and the General turned his keen eyes upon Mr Lester.

'I was thinking of the completeness of God's demands upon us,' replied Mr Lester; 'that one good deed will not stand in the stead of another.'

The General was silent, but there was an uncomfortable, nervous twitching about his mouth.

Mr Lester again turned to the Bible, and opened it, not at the lesson for the day, but at the Epistle of St James ; ' Whosoever shall keep the whole law, and yet offend in one point, he is guilty of all.' 'That has always struck me as one of the most fearful texts in the Bible,' he said. 'It strikes at the root of such a common error. May I say to you, dear sir, that it has been upon my mind very much since our parting yesterday ? '

It was an immense effort to him, and he watched the General's countenance with an anxiety which made his voice tremble.

' You mean rightly, Mr Lester ; go on.'

' You are most kind, most thoughtful, and considerate for your poor neighbours, sir. It seems strange to beg that you will be equally so toward your son.'

' My conscience is clear upon that point,' replied the General, ' and my judgment, Mr Lester, lies with God. If I have wronged my son, I will repair the wrong.'

' And see him, sir ; hear his confession ; restore him to your love ; that is what he asks ? '

The General tried to take up a paper which lay upon the table, but his hand trembled too much. 'I have tried to write it,' he murmured to himself.

Mr Lester interrupted him. ' But will you not tell me, dear sir ? Speaking is better than writing ; there is more truth in it.

' No, sir, no ; I can't. Mr Lester, you mustn't urge it. I am old—God knows I have been tried—you must leave me.'

' I would speak to you, sir, because you are old. Life may be very short, I would not have you go unforgiving to your grave.'

' I do forgive—all. I did him wrong, perchance. He mayn't have done what I thought. He says it ; Miss Campbell says it. Let it be tried and proved ; but let me rest, let me rest, for my days are few.'

' There will be rest in mercy,' replied Mr Lester, solemnly ; ' for so only can we hope for mercy. General Vivian, at whatever risk, I must speak to you as God's minister. Whilst you thought your son had dishonoured your name, there was doubtless an excuse for the severity with which he was treated. Whether it was right to cast off his children also, need not now be discussed. But you have at length the proof that you suspected him wrongly. Not the proof which would stand, it may be, in a court of justice, but the word of an honourable man, and the cor-

responding testimony of a lady, who, whatever may be your prejudice against her family, lays claim to universal respect. If you
still persist in your suspicions, if "judgment without mercy" is
still to be your motto, think what will be your condition when
you are summoned to that awful account, at which our only
hope must be in the "mercy that rejoiceth against judgment."'

The General's countenance underwent many changes during
this speech,—surprise, anger,—then a more chastened, solemnised
feeling; but it would have seemed that the indomitable will remained unshaken. 'Mr Lester, I asked you to read to me,' he
said, his voice sounding hollow and tremulous.

And Mr Lester read, and when he had finished reading, he
knelt in prayer; and the General's voice was heard in the confession, that he was a miserable sinner, that he had erred and
strayed from God's ways like a lost sheep. At the close Mr
Lester paused, remained for a few moments in silent petition,
and rose.

The General turned to him hastily: 'Your prayers are short,
sir,' he said.

'I leave it to yourself, General, to pray: "Forgive us our tres-
passes as we forgive them that trespass against us."'

The old man turned away his head, and wept.

A knock was heard at the door; it was Mildred. She came
in, and stood by the General's chair.

He gave her his hand without looking up: 'Mildred, child,
your father is very weak.'

'You have been tried, dear sir, very much. It is no wonder.'

'Mr Lester would have me see him, Mildred. I would do it,
if it were right,—if it were good; but it mustn't be,—there is
no proof. My people would be sacrificed; and the Campbells,
—they are not to be depended on. Years ago they defrauded
and ruined us. He married a Campbell, and they uphold him.
The boy, too,—it would all be ruin.' He spoke with difficulty;
his eyes were dulled, and his voice was weak. Old feelings of
dislike and prejudice were working together, with more newly-
excited mistrust, to cloud a mind already, in a degree, enfeebled
by illness.

'Don't think of the future, my dearest father; let it be as you
will. See him, that is all we ask,—all he would ask either.'

'But, Mildred, if I see him,—help me,—I said I wouldn't,—I
must keep my vow. I mustn't yield.'

3 G

'You said it when you thought him guilty of a grievous offence, dearest father; he comes now to prove his innocence.'

'Proof! proof!' The General repeated the words to himself again and again. Then he said suddenly, 'Is he changed?'

'Not as much as I expected; he looks older, of course. But he is changed in mind wonderfully.'

The General shook his head, and motioned her from him: 'You tempt me,—go.' His complexion became of a livid paleness.

Mr Lester gave him some water, and he recovered a little, and murmured, 'To-morrow.'

Poor Mildred looked at Mr Lester in despair: 'And Ronald Vivian is here,' she said, 'on business.'

The General caught at the word as a relief: 'Business! let me hear it. I am well enough now.'

'Impossible!' whispered Mildred to Mr Lester.

To her surprise, Mr Lester answered quietly also, 'I will go to him; perhaps it may be as well.'

He left the room. The General leaned back in his chair, perfectly still. Mildred sat down by him. The minutes were very long. She dared not speak to him again. Steps were heard along the corridor,—in the dressing-room. The General moved, and pushed away the footstool, and placed his writing-case before him.

'May we come in?' Mr Lester entered, Ronald with him: another shadow darkened the doorway.

The General bent his head stiffly, with all his former precision of manner. Ronald scarcely returned the greeting. His eye took a rapid survey of the room, and rested on Mildred. She moved to go.

'If it is private business, Mildred, you can leave us,' said the General. 'Young gentleman, you look ill; you had better sit down.'

'Miss Vivian, pray stay.' Ronald drew near the table, and rested one hand upon it; his countenance, naturally pale from illness, was ghastly in its expression, but his eye was calm and cold. 'I have intruded upon you, General Vivian,' he began.

'No intrusion, young gentleman. I have had a slight illness, but I am recovering. Can I, in any way, help you?'

'I have no claim upon you, sir. I am the son of—Captain Vivian.'

Mildred's eye glanced uneasily at her father ; the nervous motion of his mouth was visible again.

' Captain Vivian may have done my family injury; yet I would not visit the injury upon his son. What do you ask of me ?'

Ronald paused.

' I beg you to explain yourself, quickly,' repeated the General, rather sternly. ' What do you need ?'

Ronald approached nearer. His figure was erect, whilst pride was giving its impress to his countenance.

' Speak, sir,' exclaimed the General.

And the tall form bent as though crushed by a mighty load, and the agony of humiliation convulsed every feature, as, laying a paper upon the table, Ronald said, ' You require proof of your son's innocence, General Vivian ; you have it.'

Mr Lester pushed a chair towards him, but he still stood.

' Read it, Mildred,' said the General ; and Mildred read tremblingly :—

' I forged the bill. They can take all I have to repay themselves.

' JOHN VIVIAN.'

The General caught the paper from her hand, and there was a long, death-like silence. He looked at the words fearfully,—doubtfully.

The shadow passed from the doorway, and Edward Vivian knelt by his side. ' Father, forgive,—forgive me ! '

The General sat as one paralysed ; but his hand rested with a tremulous touch, on his son's head.

' Pardon me, father ! Speak to me ! '

The white lips moved, and the glassy eyes became dim ; and, leaning forward, the old man threw his arm round his son's neck and kissed him.

He looked up again, and his eye wandered for an instant round the room, as if in search of Ronald ; but even in that moment he had left the apartment, unnoticed by all save Mr Lester ; and the General, worn and exhausted, could only say, ' I was so wrong Edward, so wrong. God forgive me ! I was so wrong.'

The bells rang merrily from the tower of Encombe Church, on Christmas morning; cheerful were the greetings, hearty the good-wishes which met at the entrance of the old Norman porch ; and fervently went up thanksgivings to Heaven, whilst the notes of the Angels' Hymn rose, and echoed, and died away amidst the arches. Eighteen years before, Mr Vivian had knelt in that church, proud in his self-reliance, a young man ; with the hopes, the fears, the follies, the offences of youth upon him. He knelt there now, humbled, chastened, penitent, yet unutterably thankful, with one prayer, earnest above all others, that his children might never learn the same lesson at the same price of sin and suffering.

That day was the first of Christmas days spent as in the olden time at Cleve Hall, since sorrow and death had laid their chill grasp upon it, and rendered it desolate.

The General, infirm and shaken though he was, sat at the head of his table, and told of his plans for the poor, and discussed alterations in his farm, and seemed to forget that the lapse of years could be a difficulty in the way of his son's understanding anything which he wished him to undertake ; and Mildred, smiling as she had never smiled before since her sister's death, talked with Ella of what must be done to make the old home happy in its new character, and devised schemes by which they might do all she needed in the village ; and read with her, and have lessons, and be constantly with her ; helping her, as she said, to grow old without feeling it.

Mr Vivian's feelings were mixed. Moments there were when he paused in the midst of his children's merriment, to think anxiously of Clement's future course, and watch the impression which he made upon his grandfather ; or to recur to the memories of the past, and dwell upon the joys which could never come again. But the sadness was transient, the brightness lasting ; and when the recollections of those bygone days most oppressed him, he could think upon the mercy vouchsafed to the repentant upon earth, as the type of the free and perfect pardon of Heaven.

It was a glad day of hope, a second spring in winter, the beginning of the sunshine which was to gild the old General's pathway, for the few remaining years of his earthly existence.

Mrs Robinson, when she came in the evening to drink Master Edward's health, in the dining-room, was heard to say, as she went back to the servants' hall, that it did one's heart good to see the General taking, as it were, a new lease of life ; and Greaves as partial to the old master as Mrs Robinson was to the young one, insisted that it was trouble which had furrowed the General's cheek, and made him feeble before his time ; and now that trouble was gone, who was to say that the best landlord, and the kindest master in England, was not to outlive the halest and heartiest among them?

And there was gladness at the Rectory, quieter, yet perhaps, with Mr Lester and Rachel, even fuller. Mrs Campbell and Bertha were with them, and although missing the children's mirth, it was impossible to feel otherwise than grateful and happy at the load of anxiety and responsibility which had been removed. The object desired for years had been attained, and if, as is the case in the attainment of all human wishes, success was accompanied by alloy, it seemed unthankful to allow the mind to rest upon it. Bertha's energy already made her turn to the thought of being useful to Rachel, and finding employment amongst the poor, more congenial than that training of the mind which she had yet to practise successfully for herself; and but for one thought, she could have called it the happiest Christmas Day that had been granted her for many a year.

There was an evening service ; the church was full. Bertha sat near the east end with Rachel, and was amongst the last to depart. Mr Lester was detained in the vestry, and they waited for him, until all the lights were extinguished, except those in the chancel.

They walked to the lower end of the church, and looked back. ' Passing from darkness to light, like it will be from earth to Heaven,' whispered Rachel.

A sigh answered her, but it did not come from Bertha. Some one passed her quickly, from the side aisle, and went out into the porch.

A minute afterwards Mr Lester joined them, and they left the church. The moon was shining on the tombstones, and a long line of pale light was traced upon the distant sea.

' Papa,' said Rachel, ' should you mind? I should like to see where Barney is buried.' Mr Lester took her hand, and they went on together. Bertha lingered behind.

' Miss Campbell ! ' She started ; though the voice was well known, it was very changed.

' Ronald ! here ! That ought not to be ; it is very imprudent.'

He tried to laugh. ' Mrs Robinson allowed me. I am at the farm now, and well.'

' Yes, I heard that. Mr Lester told me ; I had hoped to see you, to thank you.'

He would not hear her gratitude. ' I go to-morrow,' he said ; 'you will still think of and pray for me.'

' Go ? Where ? So soon ? Surely General Vivian, Mr Lester '——

He interrupted her : 'They have done all, and more than all, I could have dared to expect. They would do far more than I could allow.'

' That may be pride, Ronald.'

' Pride ! Miss Campbell !' he repeated the word bitterly ; 'pride for me ! yet it may be so. If it is, I pray God to make me humble. But I do not feel that it is. They would provide for me. I would accept their help, but only to provide for myself. My father's property is heavily mortgaged. When the debt to General Vivian is paid, if anything should remain of the little that I might once have expected to inherit, it must of course be appropriated for my father's comfort. I go to make my own way in the world.'

' Alone ?'

' Where my father is, there is my duty, and there will be my home.'

' O Ronald, what a sacrifice !'

' You would not wish it to be otherwise ; you, who first taught me the claims of duty ?'

' No, I cannot, and yet the example may be terrible.'

' I do not fear it,' he said, meekly : ' God, who saved me from it, before I sought Him, will strengthen me to withstand it when I have learned to seek Him.'

Bertha gave him her hand,—but her voice failed her.

' From darkness to light, from earth to heaven,' said Ronald, thoughtfully. ' I shall not forget it.' He looked towards the little, new-made grave, beside which Rachel and Mr Lester were standing.

They drew near it. Rachel was the first to see Ronald. She ran up to him directly. ' I didn't know it was you, Ronald ; but you don't mind our coming, do you ? I asked papa if I might.'

She felt instinctively that the little grave was his charge.

' Who could mind, Rachel ? No one has more claim to be here than you who made him happy.'

' He doesn't suffer now,' said Rachel. ' I think of that.'

' I try to think of it too,' said Ronald. ' I shall more by and by. When I am gone, Rachel, perhaps Mr Lester will let you plant some flowers here. I should like that.'

'Yes, of course; indeed, I will,' but Rachel was perplexed; she could not understand what he meant by going, and was too shy to ask. She turned to her father, who had been talking with Bertha.

'You must go home, my child,' said Mr Lester, 'it is too cold for you,—and for Miss Campbell,—and, Ronald, for you, too,' and he kindly touched Ronald's shoulder.'

'Good night, Ronald. · Did you understand? I promise, if papa doesn't mind,' said Rachel.

'Good-bye, Rachel.' He kept her hand for a moment, then let it fall suddenly; 'your word needs no promise.'

He watched her, so did Mr Lester, as she walked with Bertha through the churchyard, till the gate closed behind them.

Then Mr Lester said: 'You go to-morrow, Ronald.'

'To-morrow, sir. The vessel is even now ready, and my father waits for me. When my way for the future is clear, I will write.'

'May God guard you, Ronald, hitherto, as He has guarded you before. You have no wishes that I can fulfil?'

'I had one, sir, but it has been told to Rachel. I have no other, but—that my name may be forgotten.'

Mr Lester's voice faltered: 'That should not be the wish at your age. Life is before you to redeem it.'

'In another country, in another home; but never here,' replied Ronald.

Mr Lester was silent.

'I am not desponding,' continued Ronald; 'the load is taken from me; I can breathe freely. Mr Lester, I would not have you think of me as weak.'

'Weak! oh no, Ronald—most strong. I only pray you may feel that there is hope always on earth.'

'I have a work to do,' replied Ronald, 'therefore I must have hope.'

'And it will be accomplished,' replied Mr Lester. 'The prayers and the labours of such a son will surely be answered. God bless you!' He wrung Ronald's hand and left him. And Ronald, kneeling by Barney's grave, prayed fervently; and rose strengthened and comforted, whilst still the little voice seemed sounding in his ear, 'You'll set the 'sample, Ronald, and then you'll come.'

Cleve Hall yet stands, gray and stern as him who was once its

master ; the sea washes the sandy beach round the dark headland ; the Encombe Hills frown over the deep ravine. And,
whilst changes of joy and sorrow, of life and death, have passed
over the human hearts which sought their resting-place amidst
those scenes of beauty, the name of Vivian lives associated with
them, as in bygone years ; the heirloom descending from generation to generation.

Its echo has been heard even in distant lands. There is a tale
told of one—an exile, lonely, unaided, exposed to many and
dread temptations—who entered upon life with the inheritance
of a stained name and a ruined fortune, and looked back upon
it with a conscience which angels might approve, and a reputation which princes might have envied. It is said that he
laboured,—and successfully,—for one object ; the restoration of
a father who had sunk, it might have seemed, beyond hope ; and
that, in the progress of that work,—spent for the most part in the
drudgery of a merchant's office—he gathered round him, by the
force of an intense earnestness, young and old, the cultivated
and the ignorant,—warning, guiding, aiding them on their path
to heaven.

They tell of him, that he dwelt apart, mingling little with the
gaieties of life ; a man of quiet exterior, gentle and reserved, and
with the deep traces of early suffering stamped upon his brow.
The happiness of a loving home was never his, the voices of
childhood never gladdened his hearth,—it may be that he dreaded
to transmit the stain which he himself had felt so deeply. But
the widow and the orphan were his family ; the desolate, the
poor, the tempted were his friends ; and when the honoured
Vivians of Cleve Hall recount the histories of their race, the
name of the exiled Ronald stands first in the list of those who
have been prized on earth because they sought their inheritance
in heaven.

THE END.